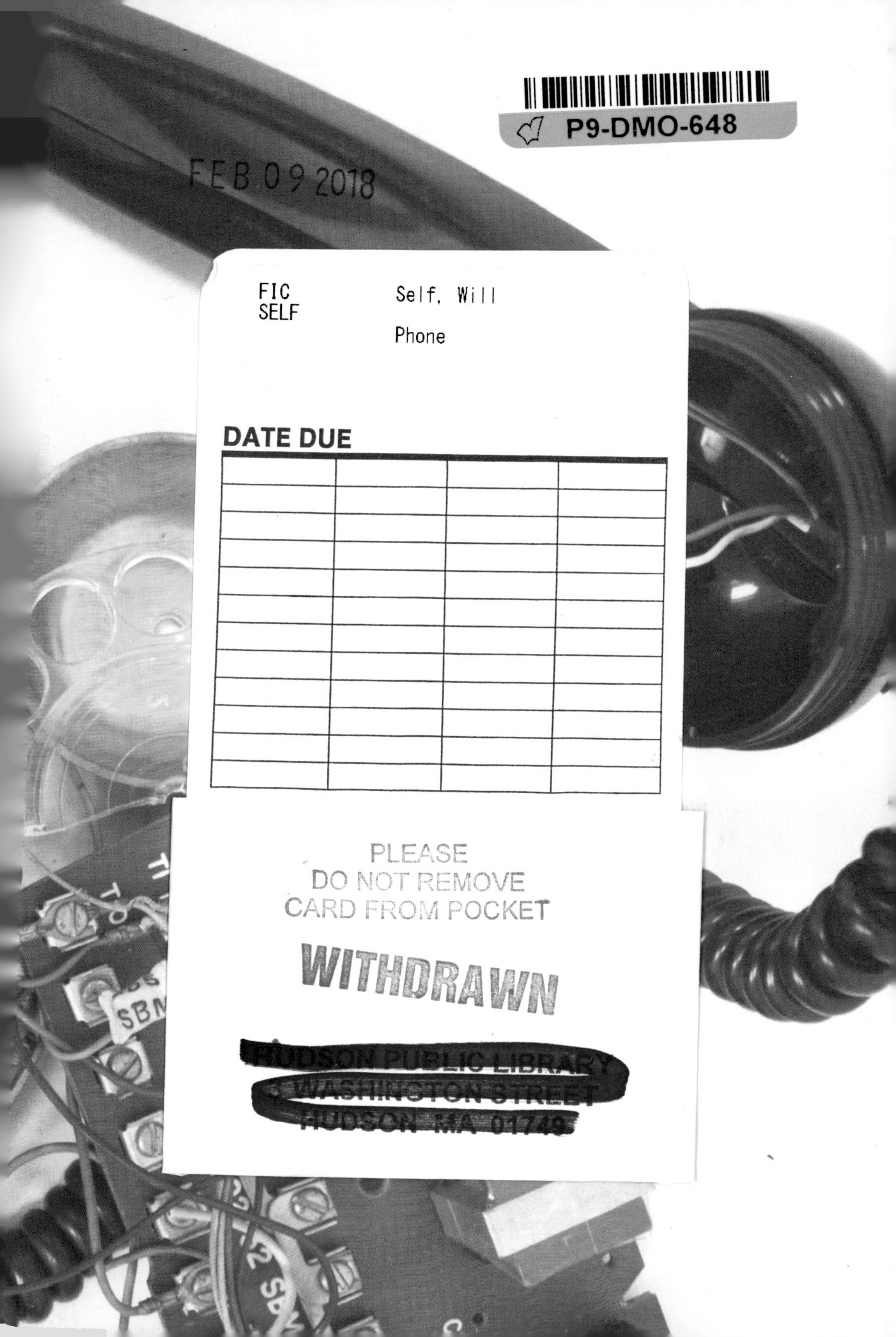

DATE DUE

Phone

Phone

WILL SELF

Grove Press

New York

First published in Great Britain in 2017 by Penguin Random House UK

Published simultaneously in Canada
Printed in the United States of America

First Grove Atlantic hardcover edition: January 2018

Library of Congress Cataloging-in-Publication data available for this title.

ISBN 978-0-8021-2537-8
eISBN 978-0-8021-8939-4

Grove Press
an imprint of Grove Atlantic
154 West 14th Street
New York, NY 10011

Distributed by Publishers Group West

groveatlantic.com

18 19 20 21   10 9 8 7 6 5 4 3 2 1

For Nelly

These arabesques that mysteriously embody mathematical truths only glimpsed by a very few – how beautiful, how exquisite – no matter that they were the threshing and thrashing of a drowning man.

– R. D. Laing, *The Politics of Experience*

. . . .! and again . . . .! two groups of four . . . .!
on it goes . . . .! insistently persistently . . . .! not that
one hears it quite so much nowadays . . . .! If one does it's a
fake – a recording of an old phone . . . .! done with a lot
of echo . . . .! so's to suggest it's ringing in a largish, darkish
hall . . . .! poorly lit by tall, narrow windows . . . .!
many little stained panes . . . .! altogether depicting a square-
jawed medieval knight and his equally mannish lady . . . .!
sword and spear . . . .! spindle and distaff . . . .! two
groups of four . . . .! on it goes . . . .! relentlessly . . . .
. . . .! Can we make anything mysto-mathematico-significant out
of this? No, probably . . . .! not – if it were . . . . . and
then . . . .! possibly, for the converse would be the six-five special
coming down the line . . . . and here he comes . . . .!
right on time – but what time? Mid fifties, I s'pose . . . .! the
mid fifties at Redington Road . . . .! Somewhere on a
catwalk Sabrina's forty-two-inch bust is being riveted into her
brassiere . . . .! Somewhere in a giant hangar the nacelles
of Vulcan Bombers are being embroidered with . . . .!
rivets . . . .! Wasp-waisted she was – this skyscraper as well
. . . .! nipped in the middle — the people with the luxury flats
on the upper storeys . . . .! tits, every man-jack of 'em . . . .
. . . .! Self-satisfied arse I chatted to in the changing room
yesterday evening, blithering on about his terrific views and
high-achieving children . . . .! From the thirty-fifth floor he
can see all the way to London . . . .! see them balancing their
bloody chequebooks . . . .! He turns away from the picture

window …. ….! turns away from his own self-satisfied face …. ….! turns towards his glass-topped coffee table …. ….! his black leatherette sectional sofa …. ….! his stainless-steel hatstand …. ….! Stainless-steel hatstand! – always ahead of the pack, Maurice …. ….! Remember him coming back from Heal's with one like that during …. ….! the Malayan Emergency …. ….! Here he comes now, rounding the metallic Horn at a steady clip …. ….! He's heeling …. ….! his tailored sails flapping in the draught — never dealt with the draughts …. ….! it was a draughty house until the day he died …. ….! Just as well …. ….! Evacuated Missus Mac's Harpic reek and all our cabbage-water farts …. ….! Then came the wind of change that changed the winds …. ….! Poor Maurice …. ….! didn't get it – hats were being flung fast out of fashion …. ….! No God, see – no need to cover up your third eye …. ….! he can't see inside your mind – he isn't up there …. ….! That one's up there …. ….! very flat and shiny …. ….! Spreadable tan and paper-white shirt folded in a Swiss papeterie – I know his name: Eamonn Holmes …. ….! I hate that – that I know his name …. ….! Eamonn Holmes …. ….! And again: …. ….! thick as a chicken – still talking 'though his head's chopped off …. ….! No-no-no …. ….! you must never do a tango with a …. ….! Native American? Inuit …? No-no-no – doesn't sound right at all. Loved her, though …. ….! …. ….! Amelia what's-her-face, 'specially the little helium-squeaky bounce in …. ….! …. ….! Esss-ki-mo — He's turning, Maurice – turning back. He's turning back – one highly polished toe flips up the corner of the old Persian rug . . . pashas in profile. . . birds embroidered into cages . . . traced their outlines with my finger for . . . .! ages – tracing 'em still. He cries: Turn it down, old chap! Before pressing on towards the teak console table . . . .! Oh, no-no-no! Trace the leaf-and-blade pattern of the Sanderson's wallpaper as well – slip my fingernail in the crack between the sheets . . . .! another world in back of it – hung on the front of it . . . that map. Old framed map. Curious mixture of the surveyed and the imagined. Real settle-ments – mythical beasts. Little pictograms of villages . . . .! each one with a steepled church . . . .! sitting on a titty tumulus, shaded in with cross-hatching. The place names written in cursive script and full of lifping effs . . . Fussex . . . Suffex – that sorta thing . . . .! . . . .! Here he comes – spry he was . . . as well as . . . dapper. Spry. Dapper. Another thing that's gone – those words. Maybe gone 'cause he's . . . gone – gone with him, placed in his tomb to ensure he'll be spry and dapper for all . . . .! eternity – except that he was cremated . . . .! . . . .! at Golders Green. Whole family burned there – ashes scattered on the Heath, mingling promiscuously with those of hundreds of other North London Jews who've died of . . . .! cancer. Here he comes – right hand down . . . right hand down hard . . . swerving and skidding and skittering right out of fashion . . . But he was what then? . . . .! In his early fifties p'raps – easily young enough to be . . . my . . . son. Here he comes and snatches up the black give-a-dog-a . . . . – Hello, Hampstead four-five-oh-six, how may I help you? Then a pause – actually,

3

more than a pause: a hiatus . . . Because it was odd, certainly – and never stopped being so: that abrupt transition from being in the room . . . being in the very particularity of the hall at Redington Road, with the day's newspapers laid out on the dark, mirror-shiny wood next to the telephone . . . the post fanned out beside them – lots of envelopes, since he worked from home as much as from his office in Long Acre . . . .! . . . .! Mostly manila ones with little glassine windows on to a world of . . . .! . . . .! numbers – a world in which Rab Butler solemnly announces, We can double the size of the national cake . . . No doubt a proper big cake such as Missus Fitz used to bake, using a full tin of Golden Syrup once it came off the ration . . . .! . . . .! real strength from genuine sweetness – none of your asparta– . . . asp– . . . arse-spurting? None of that stuff anyway – those things . . . Muff-things . . . stupid little muff-things – pull off the waxed paper and half the thing comes with it. Bingo! You've halved the size of the national cake . . . .! . . . .! Bitten lips and bruised eyes. Creased collar – painted-on hair . . . That's jolly serious, the Chancellor of the Exchequer announces from behind an ornate silver ink stand: the builders have been freed, so the number of new houses will rise year on year . . . .! . . . .! the national cake will double in size, and everyone can have an extra slice – Uncle Maurice was never a chap for an extra slice . . . Spry and dapper, neat and quick – his hair lustrous in the multi-coloured spangles of light tumbling down from the narrow, tall stained-glass windows . . . .! . . . .! What was that stuff he put on his hair . . .? I twitted him . . . unmercifully. Ponged as well – not unpleasantly, but a definite aroma, suggestive of barbers' shops: singed-hair-shushing-shortie-grey-nylon-coat-hot-crotch-pressed-against-hard-shoulder . . . . ! . . . . ! something stiffening in there . . . . ! . . . . ! Will that be all, sir? . . . . ! . . . . ! Something for the weekend? . . . . ! . . . . ! No need for any of that carry-on now – stand up in the church, say it out loud. Out loud and proud – that's what they are now: Do you, Maurice Busner, take this hairdresser, Henry Tonks, to be your lawful wedded husband? All jizzed-up to lift the burlap veil – kiss the cowboy's chapped lips . . . . ! . . . . ! when some fascist in a black leather overcoat stands up at the back of the church, whips out a gun and let's all the cotton-pickin' faggots have it . . . . ! . . . . ! Times ten tubes at two-and-six . . . under plain wrapper . . . Extra one-and-eleven on the postal order to cover postage . . . and . . . packing. Nuctol! That was it – Nuctol! Can't remember my own bloody room number – but I have that: Nuctol! A Must for Immaculate Men Who Care for Their Hair! The dressing that nourishes and controls the hair! Your hair will double in size, along with the national cake . . . . ! . . . . ! In two-and-six tubes and three-and-six jars . . . Total swizz – prob'ly made up from a job-lot of wholesale hair cream . . . portioned out in a Billericay bike shed or a Grays Thurrock garage . . . . ! . . . . ! Utter, utter, swizz: but he swore by it – Remember him dying on the medical ward at Heath . . . Very brave – I shan't be . . . . ! . . . . ! easy way out – here and happy, then there and . . . nothing. Not poor old Fred – not that. Very brave – bore everything without a murmur so long as he'd his Nuctol ....! ....! Will you be a dear chap and fetch me my Nuctol from that cabinet-thingie . . .? Last thing I did for him – my father . . . Who was he, my father? Always wondered that – worried at it: Grrr . . . Grrr . . . Grrr . . . side to side . . . up and down . . . Grrr . . . Grrr . . . Grrr . . . bit of meat – bit of gristle . . . .! . . . .! The gristly truth – caught there, between my teeth and swollen gums: Maurice – Maurice was my father – not biologically but in every other way – and my father was one of the Immaculate Men Who Care for Their Hair ....! ....! Had to be a euphemism – or, more properly, a sign. Later on . . . seventies, I s'pose . . . it was other things: a pierced ear, or a spotty handkerchief in your back pocket. But back then it was all just that little bit . . . subtler – you'd to reach out through the postwar fog ....! ....! feel tentatively for the touch of another Immaculate Man . . . Spies they were – agents from Ganymede. All part of the same frigid conflict – until they touched and it caught fire ....! ....! One second you were reading the carefully worded advertisement in Reynold's News, the next you were in a bedsitting room in Hainault, naked on a cold and quilted bedspread . . . One sec' you were in the hall at Redington Road ....! ....! the next you were in a velvety void with a stranger's lips nibbling at your ear – while your tongue tasted wax as it wriggled around the alien whorls ....! ....! No-no-no, oh dear, no – if you do you'll get a breeze-up, and you'll end up with a freeze-up! The bewilderingly intimate oddity of a call on a private line in an era when it was still Mister Busner and Missus Mac – even

after she'd been mopping up after him for a decade ....!
....! Suddenly, here he is: in the fuzzy darkness ... and
I'm in there with him. On the radio the other day some disembodied voice said, Virtual reality is where you go to when you
make a phone call ....! ....! Where you go to
now, p'raps – but then? There was nothing either virtual or actual
about it at all – only invisible mouths and immaterial ears tangoing
together in a numb clinch, no-no-no ....! ....!
Hampstead four-five-oh-six, he says again – and that being the
way of things then, and the necessary being right to hand, he gets
out a cigarette from the split-bamboo box and lights it with one of
the job lot of Dunhill gold lighters he bought from Bramlow's in
Camden Town when it went under ... fifty-two, was it, or possibly
fifty-one? ....! ....! And whoever was on the other
end of the line prob'ly lit up, too – way of it then ....!
....! Old Kay-sixes still about – interior surfaces were
Bakelite-faced plywood ... there was an ashtray-cum-pipe-rack,
and a prominent hook at groin-level for your um-ber-ella ...
Umbrellas! Umbrellas for men ... Men's umbrella, lady ... Mend
by hand, lady ... Umbrellas to mend ... Toodle-uma, luma-luma
... Toodle-uma, luma-luma ... Toodle aye-ay ... Any umbrellas –
any umbrellas to mend today ....! ....! People,
I recall, used to pride themselves on all the phone numbers they
could remember – not any more, no need for that carry-on. Used
to say, Ooh, I can remember the phone number of every house
I've ever lived in ....! ....! a mnemonic exercise
that, finger-in-dial, connected them to the world. Still, it was

7

understandable, given telephone directories steadily grew fatter by the year ....! ....! The ones at Redington Road were kept shelved in the console table, behind glass – big fat paperback books that made for dull reading ....! ....! plot-wise – although if you sat and scanned the columns of minute print they could be really rather frightening ....! ....! All those people – all those Busners. Despite being orphaned, Henry and I soon came to realise we were part of a wider Busner community spread throughout Greater London ....! ....! most of 'em immediate relatives, but some – those bedevilling Ponders End Busners, for example – were quite unknown to us ....! ....! Then there was that junior registrar at Saint Mungo's – O'Shaughnessy? Said his name was far less common than my own – and they were Lords of Tara, or some other hazy Celtic Twilight nonsense. Got a bit aerated – drink had, I believe, been taken ....! ....! Fiver said it weren't so and we ended up with the relevant directories open on our knees, running fingers down lists of kikes and taigs – and he was right: there were more of us than them ....! ....! Moreover, I've increased the imbalance – single-prickedly, so to speak. Not that there's any way of establishing the scores now – haven't seen a phone book in ages ....! ....! Don't have one of my own any more – everything in this thing, this slick and slippery ... thing. Turn it over, feel the smoothness of the bevelled-glass screen – turn it over again ....! ....! Annagain. Run your finger round the precise concavity of the home button – sorta tummy-button, really: touch it

8

againannagain ... stay in touch ....! ....! Feelies – that's what we called them back in the day: small objects which sit in the palm of the hand – nice feeling to hold and touch them. I tried to make the Riddle tiles a bit like that ....! ....! carried one or two round in my pocket for years – only connect: connect with the world, connect with other people ....! ....! But it's damnably hard – getting harder all the time: I say something – anything – but they don't seem to hear me ....! ....! What does Ben call it when his screen doesn't reload fast enough? Lagging – that's it. Annoying little spinning widget appears as well: lagging – yeah, lagging – that's it, I'm lagging ....! ....! I'm lagging and there's a sorta circlet – or corona, more properly – spinning in the very dead-centre of my visual field ....! ....! Spinning and spinning and stimming and spinning and ... stimming some more – a corona of precisely ruled lines, radiating round into and out of existence ....! ....! Rota tu volubilis – status malus ... Just goes to show, whatever they may say, there's not much wrong with my memory – it's only that I have to ... sort of ... download things ....! ....! while in the meantime there's all this other ... data – such a lot of it, it pours in, more and more – and the more there is, the more it reminds you ....! ....! you're alone in here – while out there it's a Snowden aviary of a dining area, full of trilling laughter and cheeping chatter, out of which emerges this pleasing Scouse whine: Don't wanna jib youse, but shall we cummere fer oor tea t'night? ....! ....! Above them not Lennon's only sky but only fire-resistant tiles – always a lot of fire-resistant tiles in hotels, even expensive ones ....! ....! But why – why does that old codger have a sweatshirt with Jack Jones written on it? Is it part of a series – an entire fashion line featuring seventies union leaders? If so, where're Vic Feather and Clive Sinclair? ....! ....! This is where their winter of discontent ended: in a summer city-break, complete with Hilton Honors points. There they are: queuing up in front of a wooden bench piled high with croissants and those muff-things, while their seriously overweight wives saw at the greasy meat on their plates with serrated knives – a mortuary sound ....! ....! Hang on to the phone – that's the thing to do. It's all in the phone: my itinerary, my train times, my medical information – the whole lot. Hang on to the phone – feel the smoothness of its bevelled screen ....! ....! place your thumb in the soft depression of its belly-button – turn it over and over ... a five-hundred-quid worry bead – and all I worry about is losing the bloody thing ....! ....! Sign on the toilet seat in the train yesterday afternoon: PLEASE DON'T FLUSH NAPPIES, TAMPONS, CHEWING GUM OR OLD LOVE LETTERS DOWN THIS TOILET – and a whole list of other stuff besides – whimsical things such as hopes and dreams, but also old phones ....! ....! Why old phones, why not new ones? Have to think about that – assemble a brains trust is what Maurice would've said: We'll have to assemble a brains trust ....! ....! There would be Cyril, leaning back in his chair, pipe at a preposterous angle, pouchy, puckish, bearded face – carping, querulous, strangulated voice ....!

. . . .! Eeeoooh, an old phone preeohsupposes a neeohw one –
and surely, what we neeohd to ask ourselves is what sort of society
we're living in when anyone at all takes it upon themselves to discard
an expensive piece of GeePeeOh equipment quite so casually
. . . .! . . . .! When did he quit the stage . . .? Before
fifty-five, I'd wager – and he wasn't that old, prob'ly, though
he looked like Methuselah so far as I was concerned . . . .!
. . . .! On it goes – and if Maurice were to answer it?
Hampstead four-oh-five-six he'd say – then he'd repeat it twice,
before beginning to panic: Push Button A! he'd yelp, at once
convinced there was some Mitteleuropean Busner on the end of
the line, fresh off the boat train, the dirt of the shtetl trapped
in his turn-ups, and wholly unversed in the ins and outs of
British public telephones . . . .! . . . .! Push Button A!
Maurice'd cry again, becoming increasingly agitated – he was
still doing it twenty-five years later: long after Button A had
gone . . . he lingered on. I'd call from a pay phone, and, as I fed
the ten-pee piece in, I'd hear, soaring above the instrument's
mechanical digestion, his anguished confusion: Push Button A!
Push Button A! . . . .! . . . .! And what – what exactly
would happen? B, I s'pose – B would happen – you'd have to push
Button B! . . . .! What did Button B do . . .? Not that Maurice
was restating the fundamentals of causation – oh, no, because the
exact same thing happened when answer-phones came in . . . .
. . . .! . . . .! He kept on applying the old rubric of communication to this new means – could never get the hang of leaving
a pithy message . . . .! . . . .! Not really known for his

pith, Maurice – any more than I am. He'd ramble on, speaking as if he were dictating a letter: Dear Zachary, it's Maurice here, I do hope you, Miriam and the boys are all well. Barbara and I went to see the Pirates of Penzance at the Savoy Theatre last evening. It wasn't a terribly impressive production, I'm afraid – several of the chorus were woefully out of tune . . . While as for the very model of a modern major-general – why, he was nothing credibly of the sort at all . . . .! . . . .! And so on . . . .! . . . .! again annagain – really, I should've obtained the services of a scribe to copy down these messages – which often ran to hundreds of words – then sat and read them over breakfast . . . .! . . . .! Bless him – we're all like him now, smoothing our remaining Nuctol-enriched hair, putting a record on the gramophone . . . attempting to make our way across this new wasteland using the same old ways . . . .! . . . .! The old Bakelite phone . . . its twelve-eyed minstrel face still goggling at me from the screen of the smart one Ben gave me . . . .! . . . .! hearken to its persistent insistence . . . .! . . . .! reverberating on the telephone table, a specialised item of furniture, the walnut-burled compartment of which seems to've been purpose-designed to amplify its . . . .! . . . .! carping self-importance: Answer me . . . .! Answer me . . . .! And we did – by golly we did. Didn't matter what you were doing – eating dinner, making love, making war . . . sitting on the lavatory . . . .! . . . .! The reverence accorded the malevolent little household god was so great – you'd no sooner dream of not answering it than you would of not standing for the

National-bloody-Anthem …. ….! …. ….! Hunchbacked across the parquet, trousers and pants bunched around your ankles, turd halfway out – a waggling Devil's tail … Hello! Hello! Yes … Hampstead four-five-oh-six …. ….! …. ….! Annagain: Hampstead four-five-oh-six – Push Button A! Push Button A! Push Butt–. It stops: the thrumma-dum-dum, the insistent trilling. It stops – and is slowly succeeded by: Scritch-itch-itch … scritch-itch-itch … scritch-itch-itch … When I've done what? Scritch-itch-itch … scritch-itch-itchright away! What if he won't come quietly? Scritch-itch-fuckitNormanyou'vegotta-mantherewithhiscritch-scritch-itch … A very small trapped bird or possibly an insect, Busner thinks – sealed in plastic, not Bakelite any more, but it still sounds the *scritch-itch* same. Everyone … he persists … has either done it or thought of doing it: smashing the handset against the telephone table … *againannagain 'til it disintegrates* – leaving a rice-paper disc *macarooned* there now the voice it once contained has … *busted out of this wiry prison* and *straight into my head!* — A world is shimmering into being, Busner thinks, bodying-forth from the handset the Manager of the Podium Restaurant holds clamped against his head – visible waves of materiality ripple into the human spectral range, bearing this flotsam on their crests: Eamonn Holmes slapped across a wall-mounted flat-screen telly, a news thread ever unzipping his comfortable belly … A whole melon poised on a mound of crushed ice, its flesh elaborately tooled into tight, leafy tessellations so it resembles … *a monstrous artichoke!* Beyond this are more shape-shifting legumes: a forest of miniature carrot-trees surrounded by swirls of cucumber and tomato roundels – a steel tripod bearing a jungly mess of salad leaves and multicoloured peppers. Further away, through the misty atmosphere, Busner spots an entire Continental section: frills of ham and cooked meats, cheese slices fanned out around an entire Gouda on a wooden trencher. And there are people – *guests* – shuffling alongside the counter, tonging black bread, dill pickles, mini-muff-things and full-sized croissants on to their already high-piled plates, or spooning porridge into deep white bowls, or thrusting specialist scoops into Tupperware tubs full of organic muesli, honey-nut cornflakes and Rice Krispies . . . *blebs*. All Busner can see, as his own head waggles furtively, first to the right . . . then to the left . . . are other heads, hanging in the air, eerily illuminated by the spotlights above the counter, disembodied by the steam rising from it. They are, he thinks, each and every one a world entire, around which all . . . this . . . orbits – all the coconuts and the curries and the Castlefield Canal . . . *All conditioned phenomena are a dream, an illusion . . . a bubble . . . a shadow . . . like dew or a flash of lightning . . . thus shall we perceive them . . .* He holds this thought, while thinking that it, too, is a conditioned phenomena – then all at once is puffed up with giddy spiritual pride: P'raps this is it? he exalts. I've slipped into enlightenment, as a lesser man might . . . *a ditch!* – But then, he considers: That's exactly the sort of pride which can lead novices into the most awful . . . *glistening, glutinous, sickly smelling* . . . swamp. Busner's gaze wanders from the serving dish heaped with baked beans into . . . *a charnel house*: glinting, calcified slices of black pudding . . . *oozing grease* – still greasier sausages, and a great *Rattenkönig* of bacon, smeared with globs of white fat, its rinds woven into a . . . *gristly plait.* This is where desire, that most conditioned phenomena of all, ends – he acknowledges wearily – in the abattoir, where the poor beast is first poleaxed, then . . . *flayed.* The MANAGER (it says as much on the badge he wears on his lapel) has freed his ear from the wall-mounted phone behind the breakfast buffet and shimmered into a dark green suit with lighter green silken lapel-facings, pocket flaps and . . . *reveres.* I've Maurice to thank for that: Never spare money on tailoring, Zachary, see the flaps on these pockets . . . lovely bit of stitching – *the clothes maketh the man . . . the clothes maketh the man . . .* Down to Dave Wax on Hammersmith Broadway – soft touch on the inside leg: *Nice bit of shmatte, that . . .* Never afraid of a cliché – Jews or Englishmen, as for English Jews: *It's a fair cop, guv'nor – you've got me bang to rights for saying, Nice bit of shmatte, that . . .* What was the final result of all those fittings? In Maurice's case a wholly irrational belief that he . . . *passed*, that he could have himself sewn into the . . . *very model of a modern major-general* – not that he was fool enough to try passing for a military man, but he wore tailored English suits and shirts, handmade English shoes, Saint Michael's not-so-hairy vests, pants and socks – gold cufflinks from Asprey's, gold fountain pens from Parker, leather wallets, pocketbooks and card cases from Smythson's . . . That he sported Italian and French silk ties only confirmed him in his opinion of his own essential Englishness: if the Angels of Death were to come swooping down over Whitestone Pond on swept-up Stuka wings – if they were to dive, deploying some sort of Semitic-blood-seeking equipment – then they wouldn't locate

Maurice, who'd remain in the drawing room at Redington Road, sipping tea, listening to the Light Programme . . . *You can do it with a Latin from Manila to Manhattan, You can do it with a gaucho in Brazil . . .* The ready-to-wear others would be selected, transported, forced to remove their own inferior clothing, gassed, then flayed – *The clothes maketh the man . . . and the meat puppet . . .* Would you come with me pl– . The MANAGER's opening salvo is sung over by the smartphone in Busner's pocket, which bursts into life, throbbing in a hand that had forgotten it was holding it: *This old man, he played one, he played knick-knack on my thumb!* ringing tones that lance between Busner and the MANAGER, then pierce the wavering heads further along the buffet, looping them into: *With a knick-knack paddy-whack, give a dog a bone!* The MANAGER, Busner's amused to see, cannot proceed: he is held in check by the . . . *singing ringing thing I hold . . . this old man came rolling HOME!* Busner withdraws the smartphone from his pocket and together *this old man . . .* and the MANAGER stare at its screen, while the rondo continues: *This old man, he played two, he played knick-knack on my shoe!* NO CALLER ID. The semantics of this simple statement bother Busner: how should this be interpreted? Is it that the caller is devoid of an identity due to some psychological or physical trauma? Or is it the smartphone which is unable to establish the identity of the person making the call? The latter would seem more logical, and to be consistent with Busner's – albeit hazy – telecommunications knowledge – although to support the former comes this *paddy-whacky* notion: surely only a sentient machine could establish that the entity contacting it is devoid of self-consciousness? That the smartphone's self-aware seems indisputable, since it continues to cry out, *Give a dog a bone!* and launches into the next verse . . . *This old man he played three!* with positively gay abandon – while the MANAGER and the disembodied heads are unable either to look away or to intervene. Busner can remember well enough when Ben downloaded the ringtone: Choose something catchy that you'll definitely remember, Gramps, he'd said, 'cause you can have just about anything you want as a ringtone, and when you're in public it's confusing if you hear a phone ringing and don't know if it's yours . . . *and don't know if it's yours . . .* Yes, it was confusing – ever since his grandson had alerted him to the phenomenon Busner has heard them: the old Bakelite phones resonating in new suit pockets and shiny patent-leather handbags – the young people doing some sort of Schuhplattler: slapping their thighs and hips as they hopped from one foot to the other. – You don't gotta have an abstract sorta noise-thingy, Gramps – you can download a tune, or even someone singing an old pop song . . . *or even someone singing an old pop song . . .* He'd scrolled down the options, clicking on one after another, but Gramps hadn't wanted to twist and shout, do the locomotion or rise up on a dizzying theremin fugue. He'd tapped the screen: That one – play me that one . . . although he'd no idea why. Doo-doo dooby-doo doo-a-doo-a-doo! *Knick-knack paddy-whack, give-a-dog-a-bone* . . . the synthesised tootling summoned up the old nursery rhyme's words so effectively he'd heard the voices of . . . *scores of marching Chinese orphans* – but why? And why were they singing an English nursery rhyme? It hardly mattered – the important thing was, being the possessor of a smartphone with a distinctive ringtone made him able to . . . *hold the manager at bay*, because with *thumbs* and *knees* and *shoes* and *doors* the ringtone assembles . . . *a little booth* around Busner: a sequestration within which . . . *I can press Button A* . . . while the MANAGER remains impotently outside, unable to enter this very public, private space. Instead they stand and stare, and Busner wonders if the MANAGER is also preoccupied by possible meanings of NO CALLER ID, until . . . *on my hi–* it stops. The MANAGER gently grasps Busner's elbow, and, speaking very slowly and distinctly, says, Come along now, I hope you aren't gonna make any trouble. Slipping the smartphone into his jacket pocket, Busner replies: Trouble, why would I make any trouble – 'sides . . . why'd'you want me to go anywhere? Come along now, sir, the MANAGER says, tightening his grip, this is hardly the appropriate place to be . . . to stand about in . . . Oh, bloody hell, man, you're naked. – It's true: Busner has forgotten he's in . . . *some dishabille* . . . Or, rather: since coming to consciousness standing at the breakfast buffet in the Podium Restaurant, he hasn't until now considered the matter of . . . *my attire.* But with his invisible booth demolished, Busner's eyes are compelled to follow the MANAGER's hand, which rises, describing a severe arc that takes in: Eamonn Holmes, the Jack Jones man, tables decorated with single orchids in skinny vases, some bizarre giant optics full of breakfast cereals, and, beyond these, in between shoulder-high white pots housing . . . *giant bonsai trees – how can that be?* . . . the sunny tumult of a summer morning in central Manchester, before falling to point out the deeply familiar . . . *alien* in its *segmented, skin spacesuit* that lies on the counter's mosaic-tiled edge, seemingly questing towards the glistening piles of pork with a . . . *Cyclopean eye.* Busner is indignant: I'm not naked! bursts from him, even as he hunches over, partially hiding his penis with his roomy tweed jacket's shadowing skirts, I'm half naked at best! – Mister and Missus Jack Jones are probably reconsidering their dinner options, Busner thinks, since the poor MANAGER has succeeded in creating the very scene he was determined to avoid — and now, *slowly-sandily-trickling* . . . minute flecks of recollection pitter-patter into his mind: Walking down the long, low, carpeted treads of the stairs from the lobby area . . . encountering a dumpy East European waitress with thick ankles, who asked for his room number, pointed out a table to him, took his order for a pot of tea, then watched, stunned, as Zack worked his way between the other tables, his big fat old naked pitted pitifully-bald buttocks . . . *swinging,* before heading over to the wall-mounted phone behind the counter and calling in this . . . *public morality strike.* Crowding him, the MANAGER goes on: There're the other guests to consider, sir, and you're in danger of doing yourself a m-mischief. Their eyes fall . . . *Does anyone ever closely examine a penis besides a clinician?* and he stammers on: It m-m-might get b-burned. I'll come quietly, Busner says, I've no wish to make problems for you . . . In fact – he picks up one of the oiled and wooden-looking sausages and lays it on the tiles beside his penis, their grid of grout providing *an instant means of comparison* – I've no desire at all to speak of – not any more. I've attained Sannyasa, y'see – the life-stage of renunciation. But the MANAGER sees nothing besides . . . *my shvantz,* and so Busner further informs

19

him: Even if I were still potent, it wouldn't be much of an issue – I've always been a grower, not a shower, frankly, I'd've liked something a little more impressive than this chipo- . . . chipo- . . . chip-o-thing to bandy about in the changing room. He looks up, sensing a change in the atmosphere: the unionists, their wives and grandchildren have all retreated behind the chest-high partition separating the dining area from the buffet, and are lined up there goggling at . . . *the floor show.* As he watches he sees a child's madly inquisitive face being pushed down out of sight by an adult hand . . . *another intolerant beheading* . . . which somehow summons up the cold comfort of camping with the Eighth Golders Green: a fat boy called Weiss who wore shorts . . . *lederhosen-tight*, despite which his *ging-gang-goolie-wash-washes* . . . were always . . . *winkling their way out!* Lissen, chummy, 'less you can prove you're a guest at this hotel, I'm going to escort you off the premises. Are you, chummy? Can you show me your key card? *Key card, card key . . . carkey . . . Karpov . . . massive intimidation – staring the poor little Short down, a million calculations going on behind hooded Russian eyes . . . drinking and drinking and drinking glassafterglass of water, a thick and corded stream powers the irrigation wheel . . . out there on the Deccan Plateau . . . Keccan Cocteau . . . Ke-ca-nate . . . Ke-carnate . . . Key card, car key –* Come along now, chummy, you clearly ain't got it . . . Oof! They've collided . . . *we've collided* . . . with a pair of security guards, whose squawking walkie-talkies and general jobsworthiness surround Busner and the MANAGER, so it's as an *awkward squad* that they negotiate the tables and gain the ramp up to the lobby. This is a bit of a mither, says the younger security man, who has *nibbled* cauliflower ears, where've his bloody keks got to? The MANAGER is indignant: How should I know – I just got an eyeful of his bits dangling down on the sausages . . . Called Marshalsea – 'e said get the old loony to his office and he'll look after it from there . . . Busner supposes he should be offended by being referred to as the old loony, but he isn't – his eye shoots from its socket, rolls up the ramp and across the lobby, then *bagatelles* around the spiral staircase up to the mezzanine . . . *Fitness Centre* – and now he remembers yesterday evening: swimming in the hotel's pool, a hot trough of sweat and chlorine he'd swilled about in for half an hour, quite enjoying the odd sensation of being at once semi-naked and floating over the workmen erecting a scaffold in the shadowy alleyway below. Less enjoyable had been the braggart in the changing room afterwards, going on about his luxury apartment thirty floors up . . . With his bins he could see walkers on the High Peak . . . With his telescope he could see his over-achieving children down in London . . . *coining it*. With his t'riffic financial acumen he could see the shape of capital to come . . . *his way*. The man, recently retired, had rubbed his towel gently between his wobbling breasts, revolved it over his bulging belly. Zack had shuddered then – Busner shudders now . . . *clap-clap* his feet applaud the cool lobby tiles . . . *flip-flop* his scrotum flaps from thigh to thigh . . . *click-click* his nails are in *a shocking state* . . . Busner's buggered old knees near-buckle as the odd trio limp on across the lobby area of the Hilton Deansgate, the MANAGER holding one of his arms, the security guard the other. There are burly young men in well-pressed T-shirts leaning against mighty pillars, making phone calls – there are screens behind the concierge's desk displaying the departure times of flights from Manchester Airport. There are clocks designed to resemble the binnacles of ocean liners in the Blue Riband era. All places, Busner hypothesises, now exhibit the characteristics of hotel lobbies: at once somewhere, nowhere and everywhere – simultaneously then, now and . . . *whenever the zoetrope of style stops spinning.* While all people feel like paying guests, checking in, checking out, never truly . . . *at home in this world . . . I've got a home on high* . . . Shalluz gi' t'dibble a bell, Pete? says the security guard – and the MANAGER is terse: Think we'll leave that up to Mister Marshalsea, shall we . . . Yes! Zack remembers his room number now: Five Hundred and Twenty – revisits *knick-knack* the hellish chamber's sprayed-on soullessness . . . Recalls how he'd sat on the edge of the bed, staring down at his *Melba toasty* old toes, crusted with calluses and corns, and thought, Those need clipping . . . toenails go on growing after you're dead . . . therefore . . . I must be dead. He'd carried on examining his feet . . . *which is the first thing any remotely competent doctor should do for an elderly patient* . . . both little toes had been farcically broken at different times: the left catching-then-snapping on the leg of a coffee table when, naked, he was actually fleeing an irate husband – the right, decades later, as he'd been hobbling from a podiatrist, verruca just excised, and tripped over a kerb. So it was they'd ended up ironising their fellow "*toes*", which, blobby and misshapen, hardly seem fit for purpose . . . *any more* – Bunyan, Busner thinks, he was a walker . . . striding from village to village, preaching from the hip. They were all t'riffic walkers, those Protestant proselytisers . . . the

Sannyasins of their day, stepping out gaily towards the next world
. . . certain as . . . as . . . nail clippers – their anodised legs levering
together . . . closer and closer . . . marrying with a loud . . . *snick!*
It occurs to him: Once upon a time I was married . . . *three fairytales,*
actually . . . and when he'd been in this estate he'd had lots of possessions . . . *a set of autographed Jack Nicklaus championship golf*
clubs . . . *why?* along with flats and houses to hold them – but that
was all over now: the varicose veins bunch so heavily on his calves
he can feel them . . . *squidging* as he hauls one leg in front of the
other . . . *will they carry me?* Yesterday evening, when he'd arrived at
the Hilton Deansgate, the Duty Receptionist was waiting for him,
behind the L-shaped desk in this same vast lobby – there'd been
a conga of young people queuing for the express lift to the cocktail
bar on the twenty-third floor, the men honking of aftershave and
with short sleeves exposing their pumped-up biceps, the women
in the miniest of skirts, their unhosed thighs mottled with fake
tan. The Receptionist had been . . . *a fairy* in the same dark green
suit as the Podium Restaurant's MANAGER: *six-button cuffs and*
a butterfly collar . . . who rubbed Zack up with the high polish of
his indifference, then shined it still more . . . *with his bounteous-*
bloody-hair. To either side guests had been checking in: curt queries
were being punctuated by monosyllabic replies – while for him it'd
proved a lot more testing: Can you provide me with a credit card,
please, Doctor Bisner? Laboriously, he'd worked his way through all
twelve pockets in all three pieces of his yellowish tweed suit looking
for the smartphone Ben had given him, and his reading glasses . . .
must get some bifocals! How very maddening it is to have to interpose

a glass surface so's to see . . . *a glass surface* . . . As he'd rummaged, his grandson's breathy monotones returned to him: *It's got touch eyedee, all you gotta do, Gramps, is place your thumb here* . . . and returned to him again: *All you gotta do, Gramps, is place your thumb here* . . . because however great the progress Ben had made in coping with his disability, he remained . . . *profoundly palilaliac*. Retrieving the enigmatic little slab from his right-hand trouser pocket, Zack did indeed do as he'd been told and . . . *I've set it up so the very first thing you'll see on the screen will be your schedule . . . and if you scroll down like this . . . a further top-up tutorial on how to use the phone's other functions . . . on how to use the phone's other functions . . .* There it'd all been: his itinerary – his train and ferry times, his accommodations and their locations, a list of the pills he needed to take, how many and when . . . *And all the host of heaven shall be dissolved, and the heavens shall be rolled together as a . . . scroll . . .* Under the mocking eyes of the Receptionist, he'd scrolled through his own immediate future, still marvelling – as he had ever since Ben had introduced him to the wonders of capacitive touch – at the way his fingers intuited how to prink, palp, pinch and wipe . . . *the Gorilla Glass – it's just one old silverback stroking another . . . I'm an ape-man, I'm an ape-ape-man . . .* There, right beside the Hilton's name and address, had been this stentorian slogan: YOUR ROOM AND BREAKFAST HAVE BEEN PAID FOR IN ADVANCE, so he'd relayed this to the Receptionist, while thinking, Just as well – since I am Bhikku, one who lives by alms alone . . . Then he'd been asked to sign . . . *here, here* and initial *there* . . . before the Receptionist enquired if he'd be needing any assistance with his luggage. Zack hadn't been able to suppress the little warm thrill of . . . *pride – yes, pride*: Oh no! he'd cried, since I am Sannyasa I carry only these . . . He'd held aloft his walking stick and begging bowl, but the Receptionist carried on . . . *reading from his training scroll*: Will you be needing any assistance with them, sir? Which was no good at all – not even palilaliacally. No doubt, as soon as the Receptionist had handed over the key card in its little card folder, he forgot all about the funny old codger in his eccentric get-up – When Ben found the material online Camilla had guffawed, Don't be bloody ridiculous! Granted that's tweed, Gramps, but it's not stuff for clothes – it's for covering furniture and that sorta stuff . . . Zack loathed the way they both called him Gramps – loathed equally Camilla's hippy-dippy bullshit and her syntactic mangling, which reminded him of a broadcaster called upon to extemporise . . . *the situation for David Cameron is difficult, although not as difficult as difficulties he's had to cope with in the past* . . . By contrast her son's sentences were always well formed and cogent – he simply repeated them word for word, sotto voce. Still slapping across the wipeable white floor of the lobby with his burly escorts, Busner ponders the matter further: Was it her constant proximity to Ben that had done it to Camilla? Having to communicate with an autist – even a high-functioning one – was always an oddly alienating experience, some would argue more like transmitting than truly communicating. Did she p'raps experience their life together, sequestrated in a flat off the Kilburn High Road, as a broadcast that had run . . . *decades over time?* He knew her well enough – knew she often teetered on the edge of delusion, sometimes stepping over its threshold into outright fantasy. He knew also this was why he'd taken to her in the first place – long ago, long before he'd swung on to the Via Negativa and embraced . . . *the logic of not*, he'd had a professional interest in such borderline mental states: *I was a sigh-kaya-tryst* . . . the syllables are strange to him now – it was a line of work he'd fallen into . . . *for want of any great impulse towards anything else*, but which in hindsight had turned out to be . . . *a haven for me*. Back to Redington Road, where the seventeen-year-old Zack had spent the summer holidays of nineteen fifty-five – his last before embarking for medical training at Heriot-Watt – trying to talk Ben's great-uncle down from his dizzying psychotic spirals . . . *he believed himself to be a kite, spinning at the end of its string high over West Heath* . . . and it was Zack who'd held the other end . . . *my words came to him in pulses as I jerked on its fraying end*. It had been a tragic situation . . . *although not as tragic as tragedies I had to cope with in the future*. A future now long in the past . . . *he played knick-knack on my thumb* . . . When he'd eventually reached Room Five-Twenty the hotel's general manager had been there to welcome him personally . . . *from the television screen*. And once he'd shot this apparition with the remote, it'd immediately been replaced by the Prime Minister . . . *and his difficulties*. Busner knows David Cameron is Prime Minister because his own geepee, the ridiculously enthusiastic Doctor Faaris Zarq– . . . Zarq– . . . Zarq-something-or-other, asked him every time *Zack-me* went in to the surgery to have his postural hypotension checked: And who's the lodger at Number Ten nowadays, Doctor Busner? Really, Cameron's greasy pole has been . . . *my gnomon*: he thinks back to the man's elevation in two thousand and ten. — That May, Zack had been mouldering away in a grotty rented flat on Fortess Road in Kentish Town. He'd already quit the family home to make it available to whichever of his children . . . *and my children's children . . .* wished to reside there, and was seriously considering *going the whole hog . . .* by gifting the property to them in its entirety. For tax purposes, certainly, because . . . *I was fixing to die.* He'd sat there, in Room Five-Twenty, staring down at . . . *the platters that don't matter any more* and been overwhelmed by shame – *yes, shame.* Who had he thought he'd been fooling? Had he imagined he was some heterodox devotee of Saiva Tantra, for whom popping the little Krishna-blue pill was . . . *all part of the liberation process?* Athena Dukakis, who Zack had encountered at the so-called luxury gated community which she and her father had made out of what had once been Friern Mental Hospital . . . *did to me what I'd once done to the post-encephalitic patients.* Or, at any rate, she awoke a part of him – Athena had a thing about conversions as well as erections, and, being a property developer, she'd worked on him for over a year – stripping him down, sanding him . . . *before applying a sensual undercoat.* It was disconcerting to summon up desire at will rather than having it incontinently thrust upon you – but Zack was amused, at least, by the way a hundred milligrams of sildenafil confirmed some feminists' biological reductionism . . . *including that of most of my . . . wives.* After all, give a boy a loaded gun and he'd always feel duty-bound to use it – it was quite possibly this Maurice had been groping towards in his dotage, with his Push Button A! Although the poor old sod would've had to've lived another twenty years for effective treatment of erectile dysfunctions to give him . . .

a tumescent B. After the detumescent end to their first date, Athena had said jollily: It's up to you, Zack – you can let Old Father Time chop your cock off, or you can pop the little blue pill like everybody-bloody-else. He'd stayed the night at Princess Park, demurring – and his demurral continued the next morning, all the way to the Health Centre in Kentish Town. She'd parked outside in her sporty little red coupé, then sat in the waiting area, reading a leaflet about essteedees and the over-sixties, while doctors Zack and Zarq consulted. Back at her chilly penthouse – which featured an octagonal bedroom in one of the old hospital's looming towers – Athena had disrobed, peeling off stretchy black Lycra to reveal the generous billows of her soft white flesh. Zack had been aroused – but that was the drug, *wasn't it?* While the idea of sticking *this* in *that* had remained both anatomically and emotionally *preposterous!* Behind the sunken spotlights – beneath the fitted carpets and quarry tiles, hidden by the floor-length drapes . . . *they clustered*: the post-encephalitic patients he'd awakened forty years before. And not just those psychonauts who'd speeded into the star-studded seventies with their reactivated brains only to . . . *splashdown once more*, but his brother, Henry, was there as well – Henry, whose kite's life had been spent fluttering about in institutions for half a century until . . . *he got all tangled up in his own string.* Sitting on the bed in Room Five-Twenty, staring down at his own "toes", Zack had seen only this: the thin red line of the ligature cutting through the engorged dewlap which had once been his brother's neck . . . *toenails keep on growing after you die.* Had Henry's – had they curled ironically from the cremulator at Golders Green Crematorium even

28

as the rest of him went up in smoke? Had they spiralled out over North London, snagging in phone lines, scratching past chimney-pots, growing and spiralling, until there was enough primordial keratin from which to fashion . . . *a brand-new schizophrenic*. Pulling down Athena Dukakis's stretchy-black panties, kissing her wiry pubic hair, feeling the davit of his own engorged penis . . . *swinging below my belly*, Zack had thought of . . . *its payload*: Henry's nephew, his own eldest son, Mark. *Mark this . . . Mark that . . . bad Marks . . . black Marks . . .* He remembered him as a boy, all overbite and blondish fringe. Remembered his adolescence, obsessed by minutiae and their categorisation – remembered how, as Mark neared twenty, these data-sets hardened into durable worlds apart. And, finally, fought to repress the memory of Mark's twenty-first birthday: the marquee on the back lawn at Redington Road, the lights revolving, the beat thumping, Mark's young friends happily gyrating back on earth, while their host was orbiting a strange new planet. Zack had found him at last, sitting on the compost heap at the bottom of the garden, and saying over and over, *I'm rotten to the core . . . I'm rotten to the core . . .* It had hardly been ethical – Zack thought at the time . . . thought for many subsequent nights . . . thought last night as well, and Busner still thinks as he *knick-knack*-slaps across the lobby – to have his son admitted to his own acute ward at Heath Hospital. He looks back down the long, white-tiled corridor of his professional life and sees himself . . . *disgustingly* inserting his child's case history into a data-set of his own devising, and pleased – *Yes, pleased!* – by the neatness with which it fit: *There's only so much sanity to go around in any given people-grouping, and that applies to families as well – who knew? I bloody-well knew . . .* Knew most of all, p'raps, because, in the Busner Family, *I kept it all for myself.* It was true: Zack had continued staring unflinchingly into the abyss for all these years, while the others stumbled about on the blasted heath. Henry may've been long dead, but poor Mark was . . . *still stumbling.* And now, as he's hustled towards an uncertain fate by these heavy, Mancunian men, Busner wonders whether Alzheimer's itself may be a form of good mental health – after all, what could be saner in a world in which every last particle of trivia is retained on some computer or other than to . . . *forget everything.* If only he could . . . *if only I could!* – It'd been the *Euston Road School* time of year – when stark black twigs whipped the cold white sky and the west wind scratched cat's claws on *oil-skinned* puddles. Heading north from it, Zack had considered London's struggle against abstraction – the distortions of its most fundamental geometry. The tower blocks subtended by the Hampstead Road were wonky in the fog, while the entire city aspired to the condition of . . . *Harrington Square: a dirty and discarded nappy.* En route and on foot, he'd been heading back from a lunch with Athena at a trattoria on Southampton Row – *that's the slap-slap, my soles smacking the paving stones, I turned my overcoat collar up, ahhh . . . never better.* The lunch had been carefully scheduled, and had a single item on the agenda: processing their relationship . . . *what is my penis – a pea?* He'd enjoyed making love to Athena that first time – at least he had once the ghosts of his patients and relatives had been stuffed under her tapestry-covered tuffets. Enjoyed making love to her several more times as well – he'd been deeply grateful to this methodical and concupiscent woman for not rearing back in disgust once he raised the curtain on the . . . *freak show my body's become.* As they'd made love, he'd felt her fingers bring back into cultivation those remote parts which, for want of anyone troubling to survey them, had relapsed into sterile wilderness . . . *I became fertile again.* Yes! he had – and remained so, even when the sildenafil was no longer coursing through his system – a state of affairs he found almost as unnatural as Athena's attraction to his hairless shanks and apron of slack belly-flesh. Although not as outlandish as her fervent desire – after a few months had elapsed – that her new-old boy-friend should . . . *meet her mother!* It was what did for them – because, despite Missus Dukakis being a good decade younger than Zack, under his new, eroticised dispensation she was far too old . . . *to be fanciable.* And fancying was what he'd been doing – Athena reanimated the lover in him – but this charming man came chained to a repeat offender: Zack-the-adulterer, who wandered around town, his eyeballs rolling up the thighs of the rushing girls. He even played the odd game of . . . *pocket billiards*, hefting the cue in his underpants, feeling its turbid pulse as he'd wondered *what's up there nowadays?* Not the anatomical obvious – although he'd heard tell they shaved themselves bare, which was, when you considered the current paedophilia panic . . . *disturbing* – but what shrouded it . . . *this old man came rolling home!* — Aren'cha gonna answer the bloody thing? – I'm sorry? – I said, aren'cha gonna answer the bloody PHONE! Gingerly, Busner removes the warm pulsing object from his jacket pocket, and is relieved to discover it isn't his own penis but the smartphone . . . *It's the one Ben gave me, isn't it?* He peers down at the screen, which bears the flashing legend BEN CALLING. The MANAGER and the security guards peer down at it as well. They all listen, dutifully, to the nursery-rhyme ring-tone, which rolls tinnily on through its ordinal verses . . . *he played three, he played knick-knack –.* Who's Ben, then? asks the MANAGER. Aren'cha gonna answer it? the security guard with the cauliflower ears reiterates. There's a button on the screen labelled REJECT, and, although it pains him to do so, Busner touches the red spot . . . *and Ben's gone*, falling away, end over end, into the humming void. It was my grandson, he says, I'll call him back later. Well, the security guard remarks as they move on, aren't you the daft 'appeth, your grandson'd probably be able to help you get out of this mess . . . That I doubt, Busner murmurs, that I doubt . . . He roundhouses his heavy, old legs, feeling the *knick-knack* of his ball sack as it *paddy-whacks* from thigh to thigh, but Zack isn't in the lobby any more – he's travelling back down the rabbit hole of memory, travelling back . . . *way back* to a cluttered little bedsitting room off the Corstorphine Road. He's sitting there on a candle-wick bedspread, holding a doll sporting kilt, sporran and tam in one hand, and he's marvelling at all the careful planning it's taken *our escape-from-respectability committee* to place him on Isobel McKechnie's bed, under the glassy, gold-flecked brown eyes of her teddy bear, Fergus . . . *Look your best – feel your best . . . Travel the Kayser Bondor nylon way!* Her inner thighs hold his right hand in a slick, damp vice of hosiery . . . *Travel Light! Travel Gay!* Yet it makes no difference how lightly or gaily he caresses her – there's only so far she'll allow his fingers to travel. So far – and no further.

It's taken months to reach the land of inner-thigh – and at this rate it'll be another year at least before he can confirm his suspicion that Isobel is indeed the proud if prudish possessor of a pair of . . . *gay and saucy briefs from the Pompadour range.* Which would be strange, so little correspondence is there between this upright daughter of the manse and the celebrated . . . *grande horizontale.* And so it'd gone on – her starched rectitude quite as much as her easy-to-care-for nylon lingerie having both been . . . *expressly tailored with You in mind.* On that Euston Road School afternoon, Zack had taken the tube from Mornington Crescent to Hampstead, then walked along Church Row, down Frognal and up Redington Road. All the solid Edwardian villas and Victorian terraced houses he passed had been *defanged* . . . Dying Christmas trees lay in their front gardens, or were propped up against railings and hedges. He'd been thinking – and he recalls this quite distinctly – about how disproportionate it had all been: the affair with Athena had lasted less than a year, yet there they'd been, still . . . *processing it three years later!* Proof – if any further were needed – that while love is mostly ephemeral . . . *neurosis is never-ending.* When he'd reached Number Forty-Seven they were waiting for him: *the ghosts of Christmas present* . . . his middle-aged sons, Daniel and Oscar, together with their partners, Pat and Vigo – his daughters, Charlotte and Frankie, and the latter's partner, *Dave?* Thankfully, his youngest children weren't there – Alex and Cressida, the annoyingly non-identical twins his third wife, Charlie, had borne him, were holidaying with their mother in Mantua . . . *or possibly Mustique.* Charlotte and Frankie's mother, Lalage, was very much in evidence as well: cross-legged on a Moroccan leather pouffe, wearing a mad dress – wide at the hem, high in the neck, multicoloured and woolly all over – which made her appear to be some stoned Asiatic potentate. As Zack came through the front door, she was taking a deep toke on a fat joint of her home-grown marijuana – a toke she exhaled in a long and noisome smoke-streamer. It was, he thought, a bit rich – especially given she and the rest of them were evidently gathered for some sort of . . . *intervention*. It had all seemed horribly fitting: the large, open-plan living area - which had eaten up the old, echoing hall, Maurice's study and the chilly nook which was always referred to as the Boot Room . . . *as if we rode to hounds* – had been very much Lalage's own creation, along with a lot of other drastic remodelling she'd insisted on when they'd been married in the mid seventies. *If Maurice were to be resurrected, he wouldn't know what'd hit him* . . . mismatched armchairs and sofas, slews of cushions, piles of floor ones – thickets of standard lamps, tussocks of table ones. All this *clutter* . . . A job-lot ill-lit by the spotlights Daniel had implanted in the high ceiling . . . *a dismal, disordered scene*, not cosy or home-like at all – more akin to the aftermath of some traumatic and forced departure . . . *the chattels the Nazis put on sale . . . piled up . . . those wheelie-bags over there – they'd be selling Asians' clobber as well nowadays* — The parties to this latest intervention have reached a door inset in the wood-cladded wall at the foot of the spiral staircase. The Podium Restaurant's MANAGER knocks – but any reply from within is rendered inaudible by yet more knick-knacking, as the smartphone bursts once more into life. For heaven's sake, man, why don't you turn the bloody thing off! Cauliflower Ears says, although he makes no move to take it away from Busner, only stands – as they all do – staring down at the trilling thing, which pulses back at them: NO CALLER ID . . . NO CALLER ID . . . NO CALLER ID — Lalage's pot smoke had spurted from her horse-lips*sssshhhhfffft!* Zack's daughter, Lottie, a rangily overgrown girl with . . . *virtuosic ambition but little real ability* had sprung from a floor cushion and launched into what was clearly a prepared speech – *onanon* she'd gone: her father was living a disorderly life . . . His liaison with a woman thirty years his junior had been embarrassing enough – most of all to himself. But that was in the past – now he was was neglecting that self mentally as well as phys-ically – and then there were his companions . . . Zack's mind had wandered . . . *doesn't it always*, taking him with it to the upstairs rooms of suburban pubs . . . *where men known as Tel* introduce the acts and encourage you to leave your business card in a goldfish bowl on the bar, in the hope of . . . *winning a hamper – Poor Lottie!* grinding out smooth ballads from her permanently sore throat, wig-gling her wide hips – every time she paused for breath her supportive father heard the grating after-tone . . . *send in the clooownssshhrrghhh.* The intervention had been, perhaps, her finest ever performance: standing there, for once with an audience at least close to double figures, and proving how much more mature she could be than her spaced-out mother and senile father. Poor Lottie! The least objection – the slightest check to one of her outbursts – was, Zack knew only too well, the way to really enrage her . . . *such a temper – such anger.* Yet on this occasion . . . *I threw caution to the winds.* Why? There was the reopened wound of his split from Athena . . . *it's the* *last, not the bloody first, that's the deepest,* and so he'd shouted her down: That's enough! You've no right to browbeat me in this way – not you, Lottie, or any of you other ungrateful whelps . . . *or words to that effect.* Oscar, who has his mother's neat, dark features . . . *and permanently shaded top lip,* had looked up from his phone-fiddling and guffawed: You're seventy-eight years old, Zack Busner – you're seventy-eight years old! Who was he, this pseudo-intellectual, pseudo-biker in all his pretentiousness, to berate the father who . . . *wiped his fucking bum!* It'd been Daniel, one of life's conciliators, who'd eventually calmed them all down. Busner felt a great affinity with his second son, who . . . *like me,* has always had a . . . *mutating mental thunderhead* between him and the sunlight: a profoundly disturbed elder brother. It'd made of him a coper as well as a conciliator – a coper and a tosher and a mender and a marrier of one two-by-four to the next. Daniel had been the first of Zack's children to move back into the Redington Road house with the stated intention of . . . *keeping a bit of an eye on Dad* – the Fortess Road flat had gone the way of all rental properties, and, although he'd been saying for a while that when the lease ended he'd . . . *take to the open road,* winter was coming – so he'd scuttled back up to Hampstead . . . *my shitty-little tail between my bemerded legs.* Zack couldn't help feeling a little cynical about Daniel and Pat's eye-keeping: the doctoring wasn't . . . *that lucrative,* while his partner, the earthy and mostly indolent Patricia . . . *hadn't stopped pushing 'em out until she was nigh-on perimenopausal.* They'd had a house of their own, once . . . *Palmers Green, wasn't it?* But, as the years passed, so the shortfall between their earnings and the mortgage payments grew. Unlike

36

the thrifty Oscar, who'd scrimped and saved and bought-to-let, they'd been compelled to *sell-to-borrow* . . . moving further and further out, sending their vast brood of kids to wilder and wilder schools, until they were marooned out in the Essex flatlands. There were rooms aplenty at Redington Road for these whelps' whelps – of whom there were so many their grandfather couldn't remember their names . . . *if I even knew them to begin with*. He'd encounter one or other of them on the stairs, or emerging from a bathroom, and reel back, shocked by this particular expression . . . *of my own phenotype*: faces of a greater or less . . . *frogginess*, but all with standard, Busner-issue receding chins, wide mouths and prominent yet flat-bridged noses – all of them with mild blue eyes, mostly goggling behind thick lenses. And their grandfather would gaze at them dumbstruck, thinking . . . *Who are they, my descendants?* Who indeed. – Nonetheless, on the afternoon of the Big Intervention, it was Daniel who'd . . . *mended fences*, just as he'd mended the guttering, put the wildly overgrown garden in order and installed the inset ceiling spotlights . . . *possibly with a view to this interrogation*. Dad, he'd said, we're quite simply worried about you . . . *or words to that effect*, and we wonder whether you might be more, um, comfortable somewhere where people can keep an eye on you consistently . . . It was sort of okay when it was just Pat, me and the kids here – but now so many of the others have pitched up as well . . . and I've taken this Southwark job . . . Well . . . we rather sort of . . . feel . . . you're getting sort of . . . lost between the . . . cracks. Surely . . . some sort of . . . assisted . . . living . . . ? He had tailed off as his courage *sort of* deserted him – it was left to his half-sister to do the . . . *soothsaying*: You're getting forgetful, Dad – you don't take your medication . . . You have, um . . . these accidents – what if you fall? And left it to her younger sister in turn to deliver the . . . *coup de grâce*: It's Simon, really, Dad, he's a complete fucking loony and none of us can stand him . . . There'd been, Busner thinks now, still standing before the *groovy* wooden door, waiting for admission to this . . . *chamber of secrets – what're they gonna do to me? What possible sanction can there be for putting your meat-and-two-veg' on a buffet counter?* a spring-loaded catch in the collective throat of the family . . . *and Frankie released It . . .* Clever Frankie – direct Frankie. Smart and efficient Frankie – fully-medically-qualified Frankie, who works as a locum only because she wants her time free to pursue . . . *other projects.* Smart, neat, almost . . . *reet-petite* Frankie, who's got all her sister's share of their mother's ethereal good looks, yet . . . *makes very little of them . . .* The expressions on the other Busneresque faces had shifted – they all became animated, sat up, stopped mucking about with their mobile phones, and so had begun . . . *a clamour of complaint*: Simon had burned the carpet and the sheets in the attic bedroom, he'd blocked the downstairs toilet with excessive amounts of toilet paper, he'd woken the entire house at three in the morning playing Carmina Burana . . . *vita de-tes-ta-bi-lis . . . nunc obdurat . . . et tunc curat . . . ludo men-tis ac-i-em . . . Sors sa-lu-tis!! Et vir-tu-tis!! Michi nunc con-traaaria!! Est affectusss! Et de-fectussss! Semper in an-garia . . .!!* Because he'd been enslaved by the same bloody thing that forever enslaves all of us: having gone out to some dreadful-bloody-dive in Kilburn, where he succeeded in picking up someone *at least biologically female* – as Pat-the-Prude put it. Someone who – it transpired the following morning when she refused to leave the house – was even crazier than Simon! Zack gagged trying to *drink in* all this poisonous resentment – he'd spluttered, I-I d-don't rightly know where to begin when it comes to rebutting this dreadful calumny . . . Whereupon his third son . . . *dangerous to know* piped up again: You are seventy-eight years old! You are seventy-eight years old! His leathery, bearded face creasing, his hands shining his leathery knees, You are seventy-eight years old! You are seventy-eight years old! Basking in Oscar's fury, his father had considered . . . *yet again* the stereotypic character of younger siblings' resentments: *He thinks Simon crazy . . . therefore Simon is Mark, so he's plunged into insecurity . . .* And it might've been at that precise point . . . *or possibly sometime later,* that the malefactor had himself appeared, slinking into the big Busner-filled room and squatting down beside the mirrored cocktail cabinet – another relic of the Maurice Years . . . *You'll have a cocktail, won't you, Zachary-dear? Gin-and-it? Kill a few brain cells while we tune in to the Brains Trust?* This – *this!* Then – *now!* This much he knew – *I know:* he has reached the final Ashrama, the life-stage of renunciation, so then – *as now* – he'd sat tight-lipped behind his mask of akrodha . . . *the state attainable by sustained practice wherein the Sannyasin maintains his equanimity despite being roundly abused by his own sickeningly ungrateful grown-up children,* venturing only this feeble riposte: He's more sinned against than sinning . . . Right away Oscar was up on his hind-legs . . . *like his wet-nosed name-sake . . . long dead – Miriam took him to the vet, should've liked to say goodbye* . . . and the venom had spurted out: You may be seventy-eight years old – you may even be a bit confused – but that doesn't disqualify you from hearing hard truths . . . hard stuff – yeah. Yeah! All of our childhoods, yeah – all of 'em buggered up by you with this bullshit: your great healing empathy – your magical healing touch, which you insisted on bestowing on all-and-fucking-sundry all the fucking time! *All-and-fucking-sundry!* To've conceived a child at all was miraculous – to've watched him weaned and grown to manhood a series of amazing revelations . . . *thousands each day – if you troubled to look*, yet there he'd been, a Pecksniff pointing the way towards responsibilities . . . *he'll never ever experience – all-and-fucking-sundry, indeed!* Zack had remained implanted in the shoddy upholstery beside Pat-the-Prude – and last night, in Room Five-Twenty, he'd stared balefully down at his parenthetic toes . . . *they say toenails grow when you're dead – therefore I must be* . . . And right now, still standing in front of the groovy wooden door in the Hilton's lobby, his son's execrations return . . . *to soil me again.* Y'know, to be honest, Dad – because honesty is what you value above all else, isn't it . . . Well, to be fucking honest, Dad, I think I'd've been better off without a father at all, instead of one who picks saddo charity cases up off the streets and drags them into the bosom of his own bloody family 'cause he's got some fucking messiah-complex! Such hateful words . . . *he took his mother to the hospice – I should've liked to say goodbye* . . . poor Miriam! Her beautiful, youthful curves planed flat by age . . . her lovely smooth skin foxed by liver spots and melanomas . . . then varnished by the chemo' . . . Her limbs stiffened by rigor mortis – then assembled into a coffin so she could be burned in the blown-out shell of her younger self . . . How horrible! Best not touch her . . . might be nailed to her – *thrust atop the same flaming grill . . .* And Simon? Poor, benighted, homeless and helpless Simon – Simon whose mind is a bloody battlefield all day, every day, what did he do? He laughed! He roared with laughter! He rocked and rolled with merriment so much the cocktail cabinet he was leaning against rocked and rolled as well – Lottie had simply roared: He swore at me! Told me to fuck right off out of it in my own bloody home! While her sensible sister quietly added: He can be a lot more abusive than that if you get in his way – there're ample grounds for a section . . . And Simon had roared some more, his spotty-and-stubbly Adam's apple *bouncy-bouncy* as he . . . *volleyed their selfishness back in their faces*: Fair enough . . . fair enough – you're Fair-enough-Frankie, innit . . . bin it . . . S'me – s'him . . . Sick as a pig-in-shit, me – true enough, but where's all your money and your edyucashun and your sickotherapy got you lot? What I see – what I see's Guardian-reading fucking ingrates squatting in the strictly-I'm-a-celebrity-Big-Busner-house . . . That's what I see – and the lot of you got the squabbly-wobblies over money-can't-buy-you – that's what I hear . . . Zack, attuned as ever to the ultrasonic whine of psychosis, heard the extreme neediness lurking behind Simon's words – heard it, and registered also the impossibility of anyone . . . *or ones'* ever being able to fulfil it and make good the neglect of parents, teachers, officers and, of course, psychiatrists. It's this incommensurability – between his own capacity to care for Simon . . . *for Henry, Mark and all the others as well,* and the caring such

distress so plainly demands – that Busner experiences as . . . *love –
I confess it: I love Simon, just as I loved Henry, love Mark . . . all the
others as well* . . . At any event, he'd always been more partial to
psychotics than these . . . *neotenous neurotics*, and, while conceding
his behaviour could be pretty . . . *primal at times – I'm an ape-man,
I'm an ape-ape-man*, theirs was simply . . . *brutish.* He'd encountered
the woman Simon had picked up one morning at the breakfast
table – Zack had been huffing and puffing into his porridge, while
Simon, proud of his conquest, introduced them thus: Ann, this
is Doctor Zebadius Obadius Anthraxobadus. He is a great healer,
scientist and alchemical worker – he can see the future . . . all of
our futures . . . This is his castle on the hill, dearie, and we're his
guests . . . Ann, who looked to be in her early thirties, had an
electro-shock of ginger hair on her narrow head, peeling lips . . .
rubber cement and the warily defiant, yet terrified eyes of the
psychotic. All she'd said was, And? Which Zack accepted as . . . *the
mot juste* – not only in that context, but in all others as well. For
did not *And?* perfectly convey that nothing . . . *nichts, nada, rien du
tout* is discrete – everything is conjoined: one moment to the next,
space to time, cause to effect . . . *at least in our own minds.* And
so Simon had . . . *carried on conjoining*: explaining to Ann how
Doctor Zebadius Obadius Anthraxobadus had met him when he
was lying on a flattened cardboard box next to the steps descending
into Tottenham Court Road tube station – lying there pinioned by
the eyes of Freddie Mercury's giant effigy, which stared down from
on top of the Dominion's portico. I want to break free, Simon had
croaked – but there was scant chance of that: Zack, hurrying to

Foyle's, in search of a book on Ch'an, had heard this – and at the
same time been struck by the beggar's Buddhistic posture: cross-
legged in a child's flower-patterned sleeping bag, his black hair
hacked into a disturbing divot, his face a bashed-about conker:
wind-browned and gaunt, his mien *innocently guilty*. In his mitty
hands he'd been holding a flap torn off a cardboard box on which
he'd lettered: EX-ARMY SOLDIER ON THE RD WAS 25138694
I HAVE PTSD CAN YOU HELP ME TO FIND A BED FOOD SHELTER
THANK YOU'S SO MUCH COMPLEX SIMON. It'd been the complex
that really hooked Zack – and, after giving him a pound, he'd
asked the ex-squaddie if he'd mind being photographed. It'd been
the very first snap he'd bagged with the smartphone given him by
his grandson, and in the weeks which followed, whenever Simon
grew distressed . . . *They're taking me into the dark chamber – don't let
'em PUT THAT THING ON ME!* Zack faffed about until this
pitiful vision was once more before them, and he'd say, Look at
this and tell me things haven't got better . . . He'd installed Simon
at Redington Road – while he went to Camilla's in Kilburn to sleep
– saying to Daniel and the others when they bridled: C'mon, don't
be a sickening bunch of Missus Jellybys – this man is as worthy
of your compassion – all of your compassion – as anyone else . . .
Don't bother with covenanting Oxfam, or filling out a tax-payer
declaration for Amnesty – that's not charity, it's accessorising
your own bleeding hearts . . . Go to any high street in any of our
marvellous towns and cities and you can find men and women
simply lying on the ground suffering – all of them are as deserving
of this house as you lot – as deserving of your cars, your clothes,

43

your Sardinian cultural tours and your mobile-bloody-phones as well – you all know this. You MUST know this – I've been teaching it to you your entire-bloody-lives. At least, that's what I remember, *not the catalogue of crimes you accuse me of . . . Toenails grow when you're dead – therefore I must be . . . rolling home* — Last night, in Room Five-Twenty, Zack had arisen from the bed and stared into the sallow and labial petals of the sub-Georgia O'Keeffe daub planted in the alcove behind. What was it Ann had added to Simon's description of their beneficent host? Ah, yes – she'd said that besides being a wise and charitable man Doctor Anthraxobadus was the Great White Spirit who lived in the fifth dimension – an unreal estate, from which he nonetheless managed to control everything that happened in the world . . . *with wires – WIRES!* So charmingly recherché, this, in an era when psychotics – modish, as they always are – were incorporating the new digital technologies into their delusions . . . *faster than Silicon Valley can innovate.* Busner's younger colleagues – protégés who'd troubled to stay in touch since his retirement – kept him abreast of such developments: the minute calibrations of the delusional, who, with transceivers implanted in their brains, were remotely controlled by the American military's global-positioning satellite network, driven this way a few milli-metres, then that, *a couple of microns . . .* In Room Five-Twenty, tottering on tender feet, he'd taken it all in: the bottle of Hildon Mineral Water standing on a circular glass table with a sign round its neck reading *I cost four quid – don't drink me!* and beyond this the wall-sized window with its patterning of grey dots – dots which, when joined together, formed a picture of a contemporary

North British inner-city: a gallimaufry of huge Victorian *bricky things*: arched viaducts, humped warehouses, scooped canals – the places in between them poured full of off-white concrete and roofed by steel-cantilevered glass. Gazing down to where lousy commuters scuttled in and out of a Continental-looking tram, Zack had thought then – and Busner thinks again, now: It might be Marseilles . . . or Mainz . . . or Manchester . . . Might be – could be, but then again . . . *All conditioned phenomena are a dream, an illusion . . . a bubble . . . a shadow . . . like dew or a flash of lightning . . .* You can always count on the Diamond Sutra, he ruminates, to get straight to the heart of the matter . . . *and its immateriality*. In the moaning, pressurised bathroom of Room Five-Twenty, Zack had hung on tight to the sink surround, his nostrils full of synthesised lavender . . . *lest I be sucked into the void* – the void full of all-seeing eyes and swirling suspicions. Tightly rolled towels were to hand, each in its own custom-made wooden socket . . . *a cock-rack of carpentered cunts*. He'd looked about and seen . . . *my bits* . . . infinitely regress in mirroring mirrors, while his face loomed large as he squatted under its watchful eyes . . . *Dr Eckleburg, I presume*, and did someone else's business. – The groovy door swings open and a blushing black secretary girl ushers them in, eyes averted. She then retreats behind her desk and ducks right down out of sight. The outer office is panelled with the same bland wood as the rest of the establishment, and on this there's a framed full-colour photographic portrait of a puce-faced, pink-haired *old duffer* with pigskin bags under his rinsed-blue eyes – exactly the sort of baggage . . . *you'd expect the Hilton heir to be carrying*. Put wood int' 'ole! comes from the inner office, and when the Pete-the-Podium-Restaurant-Manager has complied, it resumes: Bring t'dafty in 'ere, willya . . . The sign on the desk reads MR MARSHALSEA, HEAD OF SECURITY, which strikes Busner as entirely apposite, because Mister Marshalsea's head is enormous and secured by a . . . *hairy bastion.* Below this there's snowy shirtfront sliced by snazzy tie, above it are amused eyes which regard him through clear lenses set in browline frames. The beard has a small loudspeaker behind it, which crackles into life: You can't wander round my 'otel wi' nowt on but your birthday suit, old chap – Pete here says yer 'ad yer tackle confused wi' t'chipolatas. Are you A BIT CONFUSED, SIR? CAN YOU REMEMBER YOUR NAME . . . OR YOUR ROOM NUMBER? Oh, yes, Busner thinks, I remember my room number well enough – remembers, too, the ghastly spluttering as he'd let go and accented the white page of the commode with acutes, graves, circumflexes and cedillas of liquid shit. When he'd risen to wipe, Zack saw this lexical explosion, but also a *splatter pattern* . . . on the white tiles to either side . . . *a crime has been committed here.* He'd sighed, Ahhhh! – and continued to alternate between Ahhhs of disgust and those expressing a strange sort of satisfaction with his own incontinence, as he wadded toilet paper and mopped the mess up, conscious all the while of the swollen and hurting *rosette* . . . pinned to my . . . *fundament.* Zack'd seen then – Busner reviews, now – the White Hart Lane stadium . . . *late forties, I s'pose,* net curtains of drizzle hanging down from the floodlights, the pitch a muddy morass, and the players in long white shorts and bulbous boots calling to one another as . . . *they pushed and ran.* Nicholson and Burgess marauding at right-half and wing-half – Bailey, the cheeky chappie, out in front needling the visitors' defence, Ted Ditchburn, stolid and sideboarded in the goalmouth, while the General strolled about in midfield, barking orders. Phillips, the chauffeur, drove them over from Hampstead for the home games in the wizard new Bristol Four-Oh-Five. Maurice kept a hip flask full of sloe gin in the walnut-burled reticule, and, once they were standing on the frigid terraces, breathing in the Bovril breath of the multitude – the men mufflered, capped and swaddled in gabardine macs or old army greatcoats – he'd withdraw it from his own beautifully tailored cashmere one and surreptitiously pass it to his eleven-year-old nephew . . . *juniper fumes and white rosettes* . . . thousands of them . . . *puckering up*. At Camilla's Kilburn flat, where, once wine has been poured . . . *we'll watch pretty much anything*, the trio slumped in front of a show called Extreme Makeover . . . *or somesuch*, and stared right into a shameless sphincter, Zack marvelling at a world in which there could be such a procedure as anal bleaching. *Your starfish* is how the Hollywood quack had encouraged his patient to cultivate his anus – but as he'd goggled on Zack had sensed the leviathan skulking in the depths of his own underpants. – Once he'd worn a white rosette pinned to the lapel of his blazer, but the frenzied baying *Come on youuuuuu yiiiiids!* had long since died away . . . *I'm a Red Devil now*, and, if any further proof were needed, *there's something diabolical down below*: a red rosette – so red and swollen that when he'd parted his legs in Room Five-Twenty and tentatively applied the square of toilet paper, he'd dared not wipe but only . . . *dab*, then brought this swab

47

up for examination. There they were . . . *and by no means for the first time*: bloody-shitty interlocking rings – a sort of . . . *anal smoosh*, or, more fancifully . . . *lavatorial lemniscate*, at any rate proof positive this was by no means his first . . . *date with infinity, now* — back to square one: I'm in Room Five-Twenty, he says to Mister Marshalsea, here's my key card. He fishes the thing out from his jacket pocket and passes it across the desk. Marshalsea's limpid eyes flicker in their tanks and he says, Fair enough. The Mancunian accent has evaporated – clearly it was intended to twit the others – who remain, awkward presences in an office that's nothing special: desk, blotter, brown-vinyl-chair-grouping, framed awards and certificates, but . . . *no windows – there're no windows . . . He's a tough-guy, this one . . . he's going to tear off my rosette and punch me . . .* Marshalsea resumes: That seems in order – but what about your name, you do have one, don't you? In the silence that yawns between them comes the low whistling of the secretary girl, who's on the phone in the outer office: There's a fire alarm what's been set off in Seven-Fifty-Seven . . . Busner wonders whether he should say this to Marshalsea: Designations – and names especially – rarefy concepts, which can lead to attachment to those self-same concepts, but the way of the Sannyasin is to let go of such attachments – with all this entails . . . but thinks better of it and ventures, Um . . . yes, I s'pose so – most of us do, I believe, but I'm afraid I've temporarily forgotten it . . . I do have these little episodes now-adays, postural hypotension, y'know. He staggers, but Marshalsea, unimpressed, clicks a keyboard with *beautiful nails* . . . his eyes swim to the monitor and he intones, Doctor Zed Bisner, Forty-Seven

Redington Road, London Enn Double-you Three – this you, old boy, is it? A thread of old school tie dangles from Marshalsea's rigging . . . *don't like the cut of his jib.* Not a terribly doctorly thing to be doing, Doctor Bisner, is it, mind . . . the Head of Security has a frank look, but, unabashed, Busner simply says, I'm retired. Just as well, Marshalsea rejoins, I hardly think the GeeEmmSee would take a positive view of doctors who wander around hotels stark naked. Technically speaking, Busner back-snaps, I'm only half naked – then, rubbing his palms on his tweedy belly, he intones, The Munis, girdled with the wind, wear soiled garments of yellow hue, they, following the wind's swift course, go where the gods have gone before –. All right, all right . . . Marshalsea flops a *surprisingly camp* hand, the forefinger and thumb of the other dive behind his lenses to massage his *jellyfishes* . . . I don't think we want anything more out of you just now – bona fides and credit rating notwithstanding, I could have you nicked – or, if you are as batty as you seem, call an ambulance . . . *ZACKERGHASTED*: But, Mister Marshalsea! I was only preaching a silent sermon, in honour of the Lord Buddha – he held up a flower, my own man- one has been less . . . *RHEUMY OLD EYES SADLY CAST DOWN* . . . upstanding. Marshalsea's tone softens: Look, I realise this must be distressing for you as well, so, this is what I suggest: Pete here will accompany you to your room and help you get packed up – in the meantime I'll get on the blower and see if I can find a family member to come and pick you up – I'm assuming you've an emergency number in that phone . . . You can leave it with me? But no, Zack wouldn't like to leave his phone with Marshalsea:

he loves his phone, loves the shiny-black inscrutability of its unawakened screen, reverences the smoothly rounded corners of its steely casing, admires the *leadfeather* heft of it in his hand – adores the mild shock when it throbs into life ... *Shock Your Friends with the Amazing Hand Buzzer! One-and-Sixpence plus Fourpence Post and Packaging* ... He's still gripping it when he's brought back to earth by the lift's upward surge. They must've obtained a towel from somewhere, because he's girdled with one ... *of a white hue – a robe readying me for my ascension to* ... Cloud Twenty-Three ... *Manchester's most iconic cocktail bar ... sophisticated ... stunning ... stylish ... minimalist* ... There's a little voice sing-songing in the corner ... *You got me slippin', tumblin', fumblin', sinkin'* ... as they rise – Who, Zack thinks, will come to pick me up? He sees himself standing on the apron of paving outside the Hilton, looking forlorn, his trunk beside him, his school cap crammed down on his time-buffeted old head. He sees ... *the ghost ship* of the Bristol rolling down Deansgate, Phillips's corpse behind the steering wheel, Maurice's cadaver propped up in the back seat. — If he goes, Zack had shouted at his own bullying and ungrateful progeny, I bloody-well go with him! Daniel, quick, slight, dark ... *and pretty like his mother*, Oscar ... *with my own flabby face-mask*, Lottie and Frankie – the former *a mutation*, the latter *a clone*, of their etherially beautiful mother, Lalage herself ... *boss-eyed and bamboozled*, stolid social-working Pat and *venal, conniving* Vigo – they'd all stopped yakking and *freeze-framed* with mouths stretched, arms and legs akimbo, a jumble of *shattered spars* and *tangled emotional rigging*, at the centre of which *I sprawled*, accepting it all:

Kiss me, Hardy! And roll out the brandy barrel! It being the Euston School time of year, Zack had been wearing all three pieces of his earthen suit. Just as well – the speech he'd delivered required the accompaniment of thumbs hooked in waistcoat pockets: And by go with him, I mean go entirely – that's right! I've had the papers drawn up for some time – they're at Marcus Rotblatt's office, I went by this morning and signed them – yes! Signed them! All of you – especially you, Lottie – have now got what you wanted: the house will henceforth be jointly owned by you all, with Mark's share held in trust, managed by Rotblatt on his, Camilla's and Ben's behalf . . . As he'd been speaking – and this was sort of *heavenly* – after decades of listening to them squabble, shout at him and, in the boys' case, swing the occasional mistimed punch or roundhouse kick, he realised he had their full attention – that it'd taken the gift of an entire desirable London property to obtain seemed . . . *appropriate*. You've all seen the changes I've been making these past few years – unburdening myself of possessions, giving up my ex-officio consultancy at the Heath, withdrawing from worldly affairs, and yes, slipping from social conventions . . . Well, this process has now reached its logical end-point: I have achieved the life-stage of renunciation and become Sannyasa! Then . . . then . . . nothing – *sod-all*: they'd just gawped at him for a while, until Daniel, tugging at the fleshy folds of his chinlessness *he did it as a child* . . . stammered out, N-Nothing will c-come of this – n-nothing g-good at any rate. Nothing good can come of something so . . . so . . . nothingy. Zack had stood staring at his second son – it was difficult not to pity him: at his age I'd already been a consultant for a decade – despite my disciplinary problems . . . while he . . . he has no specialism . . . picks up locum jobs where he can – and there was that murky business of the anorexic woman who complained to the trust . . . So many children he has the notion he's some sort of patriarch, so he tries to patronise me. Are you saying, he'd flung back in Daniel's sententious face, I don't know my own mind? Oscar then entered the lists, sneering: Well, you only just now reminded us you've given up your practice – your only insights into anyone were professional ones. Now you aren't a psychiatrist any more, you can't even look inside your own shrunken head . . . And after this Simon had . . . *stuck his own oar in*: Smarty-arty-leathery-pants here – he's gotta point . . . Iss like . . . Iss like you've unwhatsitted yourself of all this stuff, including your own mind, yeah – and your mind's sorta grown legs and put poncey leather keks on 'em, and grown a dumb hipster beard making it look like A FUCK-ING ARSE! – And after this things had got *rather out of hand*, with Oscar screeching, Yeah? Yeah! Who the fuck're you to tell me who I am, you fucking homophobic bastard – what've you got going for you, an ex-bloody-squaddie with mental health prob-lems! And Simon shouting back: I served my country! I served my fucking country! What're you, jeeze: fucking nothing, a big fat zero still living off your old man in middly-bimbly-bumbly age! In the lift, remembering the unpleasantness, Busner shifts from sole to sole, *toenails grow when you're dead . . . therefore . . .* If it'd only been a person-to-person row, it might've been contained . . . *but we had a party line*, and Lottie had then chimed in: Whaddya mean, Dad, especially me? Why especially me? And her father had flustered, You're always saying you want to have a child, Lottie, but you've nowhere suitable to bring one up. Now, I thought . . . well . . . I thought you could do it . . . well, here. She'd groaned theatrically, Ohhhhmyyyygaaawd, and, grabbing fistfuls of tumultuous blonde curls, inveighed, You know nothing about my life, Dad – fuck all. I'm with Oscar on this: I've been trying to get pregnant by donor-insemination for months now, a small fact you're in complete ignorance of. As for having my baby here . . . up she went an octave, across the Atlantic and into a cartoon: *I don't think so.* You may be blissfully free of troubling memories, but for me and Frankie this is a house of horrors . . . She'd rounded on Lalage: Always late picking me up from school, always stoned . . . Nothing in the fridge but your flying-fucking-diaphragm on a saucer! Whereupon Lalage . . . *histrionic as ever* had begun sobbing hysterically, I tried my best! I tried my best! I tried my best! Rooted, Zack had reeled as his adult children turned on each other – but while he watched, slightly awed, his progeny had ceased bemerding him, and instead *moulded their mud* into offers and counter-offers that they slung at each other with increasing force and velocity, simultaneously using the calculators on their mobile phones to make extempore valuations and mortgage calculations. It'd been, he thinks, a fine small-scale re-enactment of . . . *the fervid London property market.* And as they factored away their patrimony, he'd stood there murmuring, Who am I? Who am I? Who am I? a sort of wondering mantra, that, as it persisted grew in volume, Who am I? Who am I? WHO AM I? until he was belting it out: WHO AM I?! WHO AM I?! and they all fell silent. Who am I? he'd then asked them . . . *calmly, quietly, professionally,* because I don't know the man you're all railing at – do any of you really know him either? It can't be dear old Zack Busner – can't be him . . . He's a jolly sort of a fellow – bit of a duffer, p'raps, but basically sound . . . No . . . (small moist sniff) . . . can't be him . . . Daniel had been moved to hug his father . . . *although I sensed his flesh crawling as he did so* and say a few calming words . . . *the way I once did to him –.* How-ow-ow! Busner cries aloud in the ascending lift, How-ow-ow did it come to this? For he remembers a dear little bundle of curls – its eyes wide and fixed on the odometer as . . . *we all willed it to click* from thirty-nine thousand, nine hundred and ninety-nine to . . . *forty thousand* . . . How-ow-ow the world turns! Zack had stood there, his son's arms around him. He'd smelt his son's hair – could it be true that it had the same musty, floral aroma as when Daniel had been a little boy? Can it also be true that this remains embedded, deep in the most primitive part of my rhinencephalon, while all the rest of my brain is being choked in a convolvulus of neurofibrillary tangles . . . ? He'd stood there some more, while his children and their partners fell silent – then he'd gently confided, D'you know, I think I might be losing my marbles . . . After which a different sort of hell broke loose: all of 'em weeping, wailing . . . *gnashing their fluoride-preserved teeth* . . . Ting! Teeth – or so they say – carry on decaying after you're dead . . . *therefore I must be . . . dead.* There're sheaves of flimsy disposable toothbrushes on top of the maid's service trolley, together with a pile of fluffy-white towels, a wad of teabags, and a tray of individual shampoo and conditioner bottles – everything, in short, necessary to restock these hundreds of little luxury cells, each one of which has been the setting for . . . *a thousand scenes of provincial life.* Waywardly, Busner wants to examine the shoeshine machine next to the lift. C'mon, you daftie, says the remaining security guard, I'd've thought you'd want t'get yer keks on an' clear out. But no – Busner shrugs him off and, sticking one bare foot under the brush, lifts the other to shakily depress . . . *Button A.* The sensation isn't unpleasant: a scratchy buffeting – *No! Buffing – No! Buffering* . . . for, seen side-on, the whirring brush would look like the strange on-screen circlet, ever composed and recomposed by . . . *sheaves of flimsy disposable lines.* So there's no alternative but for everyone to wait . . . *until the buffeting, buffing, buffering* stops – C'mon, feller, you've not even got yer Salfords on – you'll mess yer feet up something terrible . . . Their arms linked in both of his . . . *le canard enchaîné* . . . the odd trio waddles on, Busner thinking of all the corridors he's ever escorted *the distressed* down – corridors sunlit or neon-irradiated, corridors latterly with piss-stained cork, rubber or linoleum tiling, *but to begin with* pock-marked herringbone parquet. Now the escort has become . . . *the escorted*, yet Busner hears in the Mancunian whine the faintest of after-echoes, borne in the slipstream of fugitive memory: *Knick-knack paddywhack, aye, thass a funny old rhyme right enough – lemme tell ye, Doc, down on the farm they know what it means – taught me, too . . . There'll come a time, Doc, when dottelt or no, you'll remember all I've told you – then . . . then . . . it'll be the end . . .* There are trays piled with dirty dishes outside some doors – others have newspapers rolled up in *condoms* dangling from their handles. Busner breathes deeply, drinking in old perfume, stale air-freshener, rotten cigarette

55

smoke – and other *more cloacal* odours, as the great battle rumbles on *between sepsis and antisepsis . . . toenails grow when you're dead – therefore . . .* They pull up short in front of Room Five-Twenty, and *my prop-forward* says, Get yer key card out, man. Busner fumbles in his jacket pocket . . . *smooth and smoother*, pulls it out. The security guard says, Awww, thass not yer card – it's yer bloody phone! And to underscore its significance *eyearrdoubleyou . . .* the obsidian screen shines NO CALLER ID, and the old black Bakelite phone the Superintendent kept in the dead-centre of his resonating desk rings and *wrongs* and rings some more, down all the cobwebbed corridors of Busner's mind . . . C'mon, answer the bloody thing, will yer! The security guard tries to snatch it – but Busner's too quick: thrusting the phone back in his pocket, he discovers the key card with the same grope *this old man came rolling . . . home –*. Christ! It's mingin' in 'ere – and 'angin . . . Pete-the-Podium-Restaurant-Manager screws up his eyes and grimaces into the glare blaring from the full-length windows, while the security guard – who, Busner now realises, is . . . *a very young man indeed* – slumps against the wall, clamping a hand over his mouth and nose . . . *he played knick-knack on my thigh* – which is what sensible Pat had done that afternoon at Redington Road: sat him back down on the sofa, soothed and stroked him. The others then came forward sheepishly, one at a time, and offered their own instances of his forgetfulness and otherwise aberrant behaviour, so's to confirm . . . *my own self-diagnosis.* Realising how subdued he was, they drew closer and . . . *chewed over my misfortune.* For a while he'd been content to sit there, *sopping it all up. . .* Oscar, tears in his eyes, describing some strange charade Zack had performed for a posse of outraged mummies in the Starbucks on Hampstead High Street – miming the thing he'd just done in the smallest room . . . *with the largest commode*, because he'd temporarily forgotten the name of it. Pat, still patting away, felt it incumbent on her – as a qualified, if under-employed, psychiatric social worker – to give the rest of the family a potted lecture on Alzheimer's, its etiology, progression and – she'd been weirdly gleeful – *inevitable outcome*. He'd withstood being *Patronised* for a while – then began struggling to rise. Lottie had hung on one arm, Frankie on the other – for a moment it'd seemed they'd . . . *forcibly detain me*. Staring at the bright light of . . . *the void* outside Room Five-Twenty, Busner remembers this uncanniness: a black crow flying past the tall windows by the staircase. Zack had thought then – Busner thinks again, now: This isn't my true home . . . I've got a home on high . . . For years I've run my eyes along egg-and-dart cornicing . . . *L'Origine du monde*, but there'll come a time, surely, when I'll be . . . *reborn*. But Lottie's words had seared him – are searing him still: You – You can't possibly be allowed to sign away all your assets when you can't even remember where your mobile phone is! The effect on her father had been violent: I hope not one drop of the semen they pump into you is MOTILE! he'd bellowed – then, in the ensuing ruckus he became aware of . . . *pill-dust* . . . *fag smoke*, and Simon's arm shielding him from the warring factions of . . . *my own family!* Pat, Daniel, Oscar and Lottie pushed for him to be removed, post-haste, to a place of senile sequestration, there to be confined to a sun lounge . . . *for the rest of my natural life, and may my insurers have mercy on my soul!*

Frankie and Vigo had at least cavilled at such outright cruelty, because: If you lot seriously believe Dad's senile, then legally speaking whatever bit of paper he's signed is invalid! Yes, indeed – yet Busner fears his invalidity is more profound than mere legalities: looking at the chubby blonde woman in her arty and asymmetrical clothing – felt patches, crocheted squares and woolly panels, all in shades of utter, beige neutrality – he'd been unable to suspend disbelief . . . *Is she my blood-relative?* Even as she stamped her well-shod foot and fulminated, he'd seen her *regress and regress*, until she was small enough to be smeared with sun cream and tears and placed in . . . *that paddling pool we had – the red one.* Lottie had always had the fairest and the thinnest of skins: *Daddy! Daddy! She took my* – But, really, had her childhood been that bad? Could any of my own derelictions, or her mother's dopiness – which at least had the virtue of being utterly consistent – be a justification for this, his own daughter, shouting at Zack in what'd been the family home since her Great-Uncle Maurice bought it in nineteen forty-six for three thousand and seven hundred guineas: Let him! Let him give it all away! So what if he's only doing it 'cause he's bloody senile – he never paid any attention to us when we were kids – now, at least, we'll benefit from his pathological inattention . . . Simon must've secreted them somewhere nearby, because he'd simply handed Zack his staff and begging bowl: it'd been time to go. Vigo came out into the road after them and tried remonstrating – not profound and heartfelt entreaties, though, only . . . *the sort of ineffectual twaddle you'd expect from a Danish acupuncturist,* who, for what seemed to Busner to've been *aeons,* has been . . . *my son's bum-boy . . . toenails grow when you're dead . . . therefore this old man, he played five, he played knick-knack on my . . .* For Christ's sake! Will you answer that bloody phone? But no – he won't answer it in Room Five-Twenty, any more than he would in the Podium Restaurant, the lobby or Mister Marshalsea's office. Instead he stands in the debris of the hotel room – for it's been comprehensively wrecked – and stares down at the blinking, pulsing BEN CALLING . . . BEN CALLING . . . BEN CALLING . . . not seeing this writing on a small and glassy wall, but the cold and drenched privet hedges he'd slashed at with his staff, as, together with his ragged company, Zack had *jingle-jangled* towards the Heath, passing beneath the curtained eyes of other . . . *highly desirable detached properties.* BEN CALLING . . . BEN CALLING . . . BEN CALLING . . . or is it London? He remembers going to view the house with Maurice for the first time – there'd been an Anderson dug into the sunken garden and nothing entertaining in the bomb-damaged minstrels' gallery. Built before the last war, Maurice had muttered as he prodded fallen lumps of plaster with his shooting stick . . . *the shooting stick!* Busner saw him now, propped up by it in the corner of the hotel room, just as he'd once been in the paddock at Plumpton, ogling the jockeys, *so seductive* in their bright-billowing silks. *In the twenties this would've been a family home for some prosperous broker or bon-bon manufacturer . . .* Maurice had crunched over the broken glass in his immaculate handmade shoes . . . *never skimp on shoe leather, my boy – begin polishing at the sole if you want to shine when you're on your uppers . . .* And Zack, aged eight, had crunched after him in his own serviceable winter boots, his navy-gaberdine school mac tightly belted. Maurice had

59

gone on: Then came the slump, and some flash-Harry developer must've carved the place up into flats – but it's taken a pasting, it'll need a great deal of work . . . They'd been standing in the shattered scullery by then, Busner thinks . . . *suetty stuff rotting in an enamelled basin – mangled mangle toppled on its side . . . incy-wincy spiders picking their way over peeling paint . . .* but anyway, his uncle's clincher had always been the same: It's a keen price . . . *a very keen price indeed.* – She's a snake, that daughter of mine – a duplicitous snake! He'd made this judgement, Busner imagines, as they'd gained the brow of the hill and begun stumbling down towards the massy blackness of West Heath. Ann had been dragging her feet in the gutter – she wore bargain-basement jeans and a charity-shop hooded top. She'd stopped, turned her raw pink nose up and sniffed the evening air judiciously . . . *posh woodsmoke from decora-tive stoves – cloves and other esters of mulled wine . . .* And? she'd queried, And? It'd been this *And*, he thinks, that . . . *spurred us on*, compelled them all to keep on going, joining one defunct moment to . . . *the next dying one.* Yes, And! Zack had expostulated. And I happen to know she and Daniel had a valuation done before Christmas . . . I saw the letter – usual estate agent bullshit: Six Beds . . . Five Recep' . . . Games Room . . . Windows Leaded Lights . . . Unique . . . Premier Hampstead location . . . Former Literary Residents . . . Superb Views . . . Surrey Hills to the south . . . Sunken Garden . . . Generous Three-Car Garage and turning-circle drive with original brickwork porte cochère – And? the very picture of pathological entelechy had . . . *put in*: And? So that Zack had counter-queried: And? Leading Simon to interpret: She wants to know what the asking price'd be if it was put on the market now, like . . . Months later, standing in Room Five-Twenty, looking down at the little slab in his hand graven with BEN CALL-ING . . . BEN CALLING . . . BEN CALLING . . . Busner considers that of all the oddities whirling around his foggy-old head recently, this has to've been the strangest: the preternatural sensitivity to fluctuations in the fervid London property market of those . . . *diagnosed with peetee-essdee!* But at the time he'd simply told them: Eight-point-five million pounds! No, really – a cool eight-point-five million quid! He'd cried it out to the cricked necks of the streetlights – shouted it into their mistily haloed faces, not forget-ting to add: Or near offer! – And he'd gone on . . . *of course I did*: Which means, together with a seventh part of Maurice's entail – which I may not've added to, but I haven't subtracted from – all of the ungrateful whelps are as RICH AS BLOODY CROESUS! Whereupon Simon had sniggered, If you were my patient, Doctor B, I'd've you shot up wiv enough 'aloperidol to stop a bull-elephant in 'is tracks. Why? Zack had shot back. To treat me for what, precisely? A smile plays around his froggy lips, as he stands in the swampy mess of Room Five-Twenty and summons up Simon's foolery: Not to treat you, Doctor B – to punish you. Punish you for lettin' yourself go, man – big cheesy-thing you are, emi-whasit . . . eminentish . . . Should be dingifacky-facky and imposing, like. 'Stead yer actin' like a fuckin' idiot – eight-point-five million squid? Thass a lot of Big Issues . . . Whereupon Ann, who'd been standing stirring leaf-mulch with the toes of her trainers, said, And? – What the hell did you do in here? Pete-the-Podium-

Restaurant-Manager really is *holding his nose*. This place is a shit-hole . . . Indeed it is, Busner concedes, peering at the stripped bed: the top sheet, *a creased canvas*, has been painted with brownish *arse-strokes* and reddish blood-ones. Pete-the-Podium-Restaurant-Manager and the cauliflower-eared security guard advance along the short corridor into the main body of the room: *inexperienced gallery-goers* . . . looking for some sort of plaque that will explain . . . *what the hell it is they're looking at.* Drained gin miniatures and the jars which once contained a selection of Mister Porter's Luxury Nibbles are scattered across the long strip of desk, skipping over the rope of the hairdryer's flex – which is still on and whirring away, its warm jet agitating the quiver of slim, white cigarette butts in the ashtray, each bearing the *smoosh* of scarlet-painted lips. Busner's aware of a vernal riffling, as of fresh foliage in equinoctial breezes. The Gideon Bible has been removed from the bedside table, shred-ded, and its pages stuffed into the air conditioner's grille – it's a leaf-riffling reminder, he thinks, of life on the bluey-green dirt-ball *for those of us who plunge through outer-space.* A reminder, too, that no matter how far I may wander I'll never arrive – I'll always be there, on . . . *the blasted Heath!* – You know what they get up to here, don't you, Busner had remarked as the trio reached West Heath Road, crossed it and walked on between the lowering trees with their branches clattery in the chill wind. 'Course I bloody do, Simon had said . . . *or words to that effect*, it's the poofs' adventure playground – the turd-burglars' Arden . . . Busner was on the point of admonishing him for these cruel epithets, which might – just might – have been understandable in *one of those* eras, but no longer, when Ann had squeaked, Look! A centaur in the forbidden forest! It was: a snuffly, smoky-breathed, four-denim-legged, leather-torsoed and tremulous beast that, as they drew closer, metamorphosed into . . . *two well-spoken men*, one of whom wished them a polite good evening, even as his conjoined companion cracked an ampoule, releasing . . . *the locker-room chemistry* of amyl nitrate fumes. Zack had retched, staggered – might've fallen were it not for Simon's supportive arm: You've fucked up, Doctor B, he hissed: you're a time perv' – you've messed about with time, groomed it – got it to put its slim young hands on your big old cock. You're like all the others – Jimmy and Rolf, Max and the It's-a-Knockout geezer – 'stead of growing older and wiser, you've stayed stupidly the same while yer knackers've gone . . . south! Ann, her puckish face networked by the shadows of *twiggy intricacy*, had stopped *shushing* through the leaf-fall. And? she'd queried, to which Zack had replied: And my postural hypotension, and my raised cholesterol, and my lipids – and my bloody blood pressure! And that gall bladder flare-up I had a couple of years ago, and the benign melanoma they scraped off my neck at Tommy's . . . *And, And, And, And!* On his last trip to the Bartholemew Road Heath Centre, Doctor Zarqawi hadn't been available. It'd been a matter of honour, of course, to take whichever hack of a locum, or wet-behind-the-ears junior, he drew in the appointment lottery at the local group practice. Still, *sod's law*, he got a dew-picked young Cheltenham Ladies' College graduate: Oh, dearie, she'd said . . . *or words to that pitying effect*, and he'd searched her bright face for a scintilla of embarrassment, while she, fingers arranged, waited for him to detail his symptoms so she could . . . *initiate data-entry*, so allowing a more clinically experienced algorithm to . . . *feel me up.* I want to die . . . he'd begun, and hilariously she'd struck a few keys before pulling up short: I'm sorry? What's that you said, Doctor Busner, you want to die? He'd concurred: That'd be the ticket, my dear – problem is, I'm just too damn healthy . . . It'd taken a while to manoeuvre her into the right psychic position, but soon enough she was reassuring . . . *me I was perfectly unhealthy*, running through his various chronic complaints, reminding him of all the medications he had to take, and eventually summoning on-screen his Over-Seventies' Patient Plan, just in case he needed refamiliarising. Yes, yes! I know all that, he'd cried, but why aren't I iller? I've lived a life – smoked, drank, drugs even . . . Eaten what I wanted for years – exercised precious little . . . Surely you can come up with something that might actually *bump me off . . .* But no, there was nothing – nothing but his unnatural vigour, which, despite his abandonment of the little blue pills, continued unabated . . . *I still burn with desire!* A stinky-old-socks-potassium-permanganate sort of desire – a lust cooked up in a beaker over a Bunsen burner, drawn off with a hypo' and injected directly into . . . *my left circumflex artery,* awakening him *again annagain* to the grotesque recurrence of . . . *my lustful and virginal self!* In the wood, with his ragged company, Zack had stood and bayed at the fingernail of new moon snagged in the Terylene clouds: Oh no, not this – anything but this! I can cope with disease – death would be a relief . . . But not madness, I can't cope with THAT! His view halloo had been more evidence . . . *of my time-perving,* since it preceeded the phenomenon

it should've been a response to: several more faunlike figures hobbling from ferny cover, their trousers dropped, their hindparts . . .
pale, gibbous, cloven. But the real shock had been that of . . . *the old.*
In the moonlight their faces were corpse-grey, while their hands
shook as they girded themselves up. Don't worry, lads, we're not
the Old Bill! Simon had shouted after the elderly cruisers as they
limped away towards Golders Hill Park, while the instigator of the
rout spat out . . . *more despair*: When you're old and infirm, no one
expects you to turn up for life . . . it's understood: you're not you any
more once your body takes revenge . . . Revenge on your mind
for forcing it, year in, year out, into these humiliating postures!
Simon had said something about how cruising was a declining
sport, really, bit like county-level test cricket – but Zack wasn't
having any of it: It's a curse or a spell of some sort, he sobbed, stop
my life – I want to get off! *But toenails keep growing after you're
dead . . . therefore I must be . . . dead* — Must be, because Busner's
going towards the white light, while the angelic, green-uniformed
angel *trumps*, Youse a mucky little pup, aintcha, old timer . . . as,
nose pinched, he plucks Gideon Bible pages from the whiffling
vent . . . *the Spirit of God moving upon the face of the waters.* Busner
stands there, an old and incontinent man – but Pete-the-Podium-
Restaurant-Manager has seen it all before, he knows how to evaluate
a wrecked hotel room for material rather than moral damage.
He ignores the ripped-apart cushions, he disregards the witch's hat
lampshades that've been removed and married together on top of
the glassy table. Next, Busner hears his gasp from the bathroom,
Fucking hell! There's more shit on the walls in here than there is

down the bog! He's back – and spots something under one of the bedside tables which he stoops to examine, then recoils from: What the fuck! Used condoms! Can't bloody believe it – you 'ad a tart up 'ere, old man, didja – or what? *Or what? Or a whatnot – or a poin-what-settia on a thingamajig . . . a whatnot . . .* — She must've felt his eyes on her, because as she'd turned from the window he'd been appalled by her pallor . . . *and her pride*: Juss 'cause you're on the game, don't mean you can't keep fings nice . . . Terrified he'd soil himself – and by extension the room – Zack was forced to concede that *fings*, as they were, were perfectly nice. Your first time is it, love? she'd flung over her shoulder as they clumped up linoleum treads to where a gas meter hunched . . . *clucking*, on a small shelf beside the door that she unlocked and opened to reveal her carefully dusted . . . *fings*. Missus Fitz's treacle tart, baked Alaska and jam roly-poly were all . . . *nice enough*, but, aged seventeen, intellectually and experientially omnivorous, well aware already of his uncle's illegal predilections, Zack wanted his . . . *just desserts*. Yet the pathos of Daily-Express-reader-offer china statuettes ranged on the windowsill and a glossy photo of the Princess and the Captain, snipped from a magazine and framed courtesy of Woolworth's, reduced him to nothing but . . . *intestines and lachrymal ducts . . .* When he'd spotted the tartan slippers on the oval crocheted rug beside the single iron bed, he'd been almost . . . *completely undone*. Especially when he should've been in Wembley with Godley Godfrey and some of their other friends, who, out of sheer curiosity rather than any quest for salvation, were heading for the stadium. During what had followed – *the business*, because that was the word she'd flung into his mind on Romilly Street: *Business, love?* – he'd tormented his conscience with visions of the paradise he'd abandoned. The torture had begun as he removed the trousers of his twelve-guinea suit . . . *you can never go wrong with three made-to-measure pieces*, folded and shakily draped them over a bentwood chair. This much he recalls: *they slid straight off!* His contemporaries had got their first suit for their first job, or their confirmation, or their bar mitzvah . . . *mine was for my first fuck.* In Croydon, the Great Awakener's carefully crèmed hair was a cross planted on the Golgotha of his bare brow, and his index finger admonished as it kept time for the heavenly choir: We're longing for a creed to believe! *Pom-pom!* We need to sing to believe! *Pompety-pom!* A song of salvation! *Pom-pom!* So we may turn in repentance of our sins! *Pom-p'pom-pom-schshhhh!* Zack had waited in his underpants while she disrobed behind the half-opened wardrobe door. He heard rustling, oofing, the snap of a suspender. But when she emerged she was in a floral-patterned housecoat, of which, as she arranged herself over his prone form, she parted the sides, exposing her deflated breasts, their nipples heavily recessed, and the *machine-gunned barrage balloon* of her belly. Rubbing against him, mouth open . . . *and opener*, her face was blanched in the light of an indifferently shaded bulb. Struggling up, Zack had attempted to place his mouth against hers – she'd administered a deft slap, together with words . . . *I'm not your Locarno sweet 'eart, love* . . . that remain with him to this day, while simultaneously and expertly fondling on the French letter, a prophylactic he couldn't remember her retrieving from pocket or purse – a prophylactic he wishes had been stretched and stretched and stretched, until its chalk-dusted manifold encased . . . *all space, all time* — so affording him *complete protection* from Pete-the-Podium-Restaurant-Manager's fulsome and ever multiplying contempt. For, even as the Romilly Street tart begins to seriously *rock 'n' roll: Well if you wanna ride it you gotta ride it like you find it*, he holds up two of the sad saggy things, wondering: What've you done with these johnnies, mate? They look like fucking elephant's ears . . . Then his eyes slide to Busner's exposed crotch area, and, despite all the smelly dreadfulness of plastic-laminated info-sheets torn from their ring binder and shit-smeared, he summons the *fine muscle control* needed to lift a single eyebrow. Standing, preposterously, on his dignity, Busner remarks, I'm a grower – not a shower . . . Balling and dropping the condoms into a waste-paper basket, Pete-the-Podium-Restaurant-Manager becomes all . . . *business*: You do realise, don't you, that it's illegal to pay for sex on licensed premises? Shalluz phone the dibble, then, Pete? interjects the security guard, who won't be happy . . . *'til I'm led away in chains*. But his superior remains so: But, given your age and medical condition, and having established there's no permanent damage to fixtures and fittings . . . *to fings, you mean* . . . I . . . Well, I'll have to run it up the chain, but I reckon they'll back me up. Back you up concerning what? Busner says guilelessly, as he drops heavily down on to the mattress, and head in hands contemplates their . . . *unnatural persistence in growing*. My decision, Pete-the-Podium-Restaurant-Manager says sententiously. Which is? – Which is exactly what Mister Marshalsea decided when you wouldn't give him your phone: pack up your bits and bobs, put your bloody trousers on and GET THE FUCK OUTTA MY HOTEL! Busner is conflicted. Shouting at an old man – a paying guest, no less – isn't what you expect from the managerial-level employee of an international hotel chain, but then it occurs to him – for the first time since he materialised to find his *grower* resting on the breakfast buffet – that before he protests he should at least try to remember exactly what did occur in Room Five-Twenty the night before. The past, Busner thinks, is an international hotel chain: it doesn't matter where you are in the world, the corridor looks exactly the same – simply consult the little card-folder your key card's in to find out which room you were allocated . . . The world of yesterday seeps up from the soaked mattress, and Busner sees himself doing the things he so recently did: taking the lift from the lobby, reading the advertisement for the cocktail bar, buffing old brown brogues . . . *not bare feet*, inserting the key card, opening the door, and encountering a homogeneous mass of cushions, upright lampshades, the taut, navy-blue cover of the tightly made bed and the beautifully bound Gideon Bible . . . *no thought for the morrow, for the morrow shall take thought for the things of itself.* The O'Keeffe parody had been securely on the wall, the minibar chock-full and the ashtray empty. The television had softly sung, You got me slippin', tumblin', fumblin', sinkin' . . . until he found the remote control, read the on-screen salutation: THE HILTON DEANSGATE WELCOMES DR Z BISNER, and, after much *fumblin'*, negated its inhuman error. It'd been late afternoon when he'd first entered Room Five-Twenty, and, for a long while, after he'd put down his staff and bowl, he'd stood by the floor-length windows staring down at the men wearing white hard-hats who, four storeys below, were doing things on the scaffolding attached to an old viaduct. What exactly is it they're doing, Busner had wondered – and, still more superfluously, P'raps I could do that? For the past two or three years, in line with his preposterous physical rejuvenation, he'd experienced an equally bizarre resurgence of this adolescent omnipotentiality . . . *gissa job – I could do that* – and do it well, rising up the professional ranks, despite natural disadvantages of birth – and now age – at a meteoric rate. Doctor, lawyer, deep-sea diver – all were possible. But no – he'd been laid off, and this was therefore *the dropping-off point*, when, all the inertia of a lifetime's Sunday afternoons having finally accumulated, he shot down *the sickening and fatal slide . . .* In Room Five-Twenty . . . *then, as now, doubly exposed*, he despairs: What am I doing in Manchester? A city with which I've no great connection . . . Then, *as now*, his grandson's breathy instruction had returned to him: *When in any doubt about what you're doing or what you should be doing . . .* and returned to him again: *When in any doubt about what you're doing or what you should be doing . . .* together with the rest of his tutorial: the detailed schedule, stored in the phone's diary function, was itself interactive, so he could *finger out* more facts about the future. Ben had also told him that programmed into his own computer, at home in Kilburn, were instructions to send his grandfather's phone *nudges . . . alerts . . . pulses – pushes . . .* and even to make automated calls. It is of no account, Gramps, how the symptomatic panoply manifested by Alzheimer's affects you, so long as it remains the case that the phone is in your possession . . . *so long as it remains the case that the phone is in your possession . . .* Did

70

he truly speak like this? Yes – yes, he did . . . *and does*, an odd mix of profundity and pretension that in anyone else would be ironic, but which for Ben seemed to be a sort of . . . *collaging*, the bits and pieces of his idiolect snipped from newspapers, textbooks, broadcasts and, latterly, the web, and rearranged into communicative bursts *so long as it remains the case that the phone is in your possession* . . . It'd been Ben who'd counselled the rest of the tumultuous Busners to accede to their patriarch's self-abnegation and cease blocking his mendicant path . . . *tumbly-tumbly, neatly bumbly, slippin' . . . slidin'* . . . Not by appealing to their sympathy, nor their reason – and certainly not to their own dormant spirituality, but simply by shouting: IT'S FINE! I'LL GET HIM TO TAKE A PHONE! Then . . . *as now*, in Room Five-Twenty, the senile and electronically-tagged former psychiatrist wiped, swiped, then entered . . . *my significant year*. A home screen appeared . . . *I've got a home on-screen*, on this a Pietà: Mother, Son . . . *and the wholly ghostly* – Mark, temporarily discharged from hospital, his smile fat with chemical fatuity, one bloated arm slung round Camilla's shoulder, the other dolloped on his seventeen-year-old son's weighty shoulder. Behind them Busner could make out the monumental shelving unit that half blocked the bay window in their front room . . . *then, now – perhaps forever* . . . the companion of the units in Ben's room, and two further ones in the strangulated hernia of a corridor. This shelving unit – then, *as now* – presented to the camera's avaricious gaze yet more stuff: a tight joinery of seedees, deeveedees and other seepeeyou disks – the buff grain of piled newsprint, the shiny clapboard of magazines – stacking crates full of plastic animals and figurines, cardboard boxes jumbled up with battered toys – black plastic bags bulging with hanks of old electrical flex. The photo had been taken ten years before – change, if it could be called this, had come solely in the form of more stuff . . . *and less Mark.* Associative mating, they called it: obsessive hoarders attract, mate, and so solder together the *hanks of their old electrical flex*, out of which is sparked a still more obsessive hoarder – but also one who *catalogues* . . . Not by anything intelligible, such as type, genre, artist or subject – instead, the hyperactive little boy, shackled into his high chair, had crumbled his rusks and sorted those crumbs according to size, weight, colour, consistency, and minute gradations of taste and smell discernible only to him, but nonetheless of such epochal importance that, were they to be disordered in any way, he screamed and screamed *for . . . aeons.* This had been the first symptom . . . *if that's what they are* his grandfather noticed. His mother, however, what with her zest for seeking out *reasons to be anxious*, had read all the books, and pretty much as soon as she'd pushed the blob out – putty-faced he was, and with a visibly depressed fontanelle – began saying, He won't look at me – he looks past me. He always looks to the light, Gramps – do you think he might be an angel, fallen to earth amongst us? And Mark, an upsetting presence, had chuckled maniacally: Angel? I don't think so, Milla – he's more like an alien. You're a star man, aren't you, Mandinkulus? Chucking the baby under the chin, making toothless gums *click*, its father's expression had been . . . *worrying.* Ever since then, Mandinkulus is what Mark calls both his son and the supreme leader of the confederation that rules a distant star system. Mandinkulus belongs to an aggressive and brilliantly inno-vative species whose deep-penetration agents – having been long resident on earth, playing the part of surgeons and anaesthetists – had, during Mark's tonsillectomy, aged fifteen . . . *Why did I spout anatomy at him when he was a child? Because he showed such fascination for it* . . . implanted a galactic hyper-beam transceiver in his sphen-oidal sinus cavity . . . *It hurts, Daddy – it hurts* . . . enabling them to give him instructions in real-time, while he could send them back – by speaking very fast in a hushed and monotonous whisper – what he called humint. It'd taken a while for Mark's father to realise that humint was in fact human intelligence – another irony to further ironise an experience of paternity which was, taken in toto, *ironical*. And never more so than when it came to his eldest son, who, rather than flamboyantly breaking down like his Uncle Henry, instead had little bits and pieces of his psyche drilled away by distress until . . . *he was a pile of psychotic pieces*. That his own son's malady had been, at least in part, the inspiration for Busner's principal aca-demic contribution to the understanding of mental illness wasn't ironic – it was *and is* . . . *monstrous: I sectioned him myself!* kept him under observation and . . . *took bloody notes!* The Quantity Theory of Insanity may have made the names of Zachary M. Busner and his young colleagues . . . *a reputation I squandered soon enough*, but, while *blinkered by my own paradigm*, he hadn't doubted the purely circum-stantial character of Mark's distress . . . *there simply wasn't enough sanity to go around*. As the years passed and hospital admissions or arrests followed high-street fracas with . . . *unflagging regularity*, so Zack had . . . *despaired – what'd I done? Oh, good kind God – what'd*

I done? My poor baby . . . Schizophrenia – if that's what ailed him – had made of Busner's bright darling prattling boy . . . *a dull and unlovable man.* It was Mandinkulus who called the tune – Mark merely sang it. It was the sheer crassness of the illness that most appalled his father – the way it crudely remodelled his son's charac-ter, misshaping all its finest features, so that Mark became a dullard with . . . *dreadful taste* who watched ice dancing, horse racing, election specials – whatever was on the box for hour upon hour, and who used a Sainsbury's shopping bag for an attaché case . . . *I have some photocopies here of the alien star fleet's battle order – they're clean . . . they're fresh* . . . and ate with his mouth agape . . . *Oh, love, love, love – why did you abandon us?* Miriam and Zack, Mark's hippocratic-hypocritic parents, never abandoned him, though. Miriam, who died a couple of years ago . . . *or possibly five*, went to Golders Green Crematorium still convinced he'd be . . . *cured, bless her.* They may well've used balled-up pages from the British Journal of Psychiatry to light her pyre, because she was still searching it for signs of a breakthrough up until the moment she expired. Poor Miriam! Who'd carried on practising but never reached any perfection – who in her latter years had sunk into a slough of semi-senility, only to be lassoed by the phone line and hauled back into that practice by a referral. Each new client was her renaissance, and for a few months – perhaps a year – she'd reconstitute her being around the work . . . *soul-after-puling-histrionic-arsehole*, until eventually her body gave out. Meanwhile, Zack, despite age and infirmity, kept on hobbling after Mark, picking up the pieces of his . . . *shattered mind. Oh, Miriam!* he'd loudly sobbed last night – sobs silently now, and adjured himself: You should've gone with her – should've been there at the crematorium . . . should've climbed on to the conveyer belt. And if not that *should've put a telephone in there with her*, because it was frankly preposterous that the young woman he'd once made love to with such carefree abandon was now a heap of cremains . . . *I shan't believe it until she calls to confirm*. For a long time Busner viewed Camilla – even Ben – as simply more of these *shattered pieces* . . . Mark and Camilla had got it together in a manner familiar to his father from decades of observing the strange ways of the . . . *severely distressed*. One minute the one-bedroom flat they'd found for their eldest son on the small cottage estate in Enfield had just the one tenant – who sat there at all hours, and throughout all seasons, with the thermostat . . . *cranked right up*, the old family picnic rug over his knees, rolling up and sucking down one limp cigarette after another – the next, arriving armed with tins of beans and tobacco, and *shielded by my chequebook*, Zack discovered a heavily pregnant young woman in the kitchenette. She was wearing bib-and-braces overalls, and as they'd made . . . *the paltriest* of talk, she'd rearranged the thick coating of grease on the hob with a wadded Jey-cloth. Soon enough, though, she'd . . . *dropped her bombshell*: My name's Camilla, she'd said – and, running a small, scuffed hand over her burgeoning belly, added: And this is your grandson, Ben, Gramps . . . It'd been his first Gramps, and he'd borne it stoically while wondering how the hell a man that full of haloperidol, Stelazine and Largactil could possibly . . . *get it up*. But then he'd been puzzling over his patients' sexual misadventures for decades by then – ever since, in fact, his first psychiatric residency.

Over the years he'd seen female patients fall pregnant by drinking fluoridated water, dallying with ducks or simply having the misfortune to be standing in the path of the great sperm-generator that orbits Betelgeuse shooting out a tightly focused beam of X-chromosomes . . . *for thousands of light years.* Just as no explanation for their condition was too wacky, so no location was dispiriting enough to dampen their crazed ardour: he'd come upon patients engaged in coitus on garage roofs, in water butts and in medical incinerators. At the other extreme, on one notable occasion, passing by the cryogenic tissue storage unit in the basement of Heath Hospital, he'd heard the faint yet unmistakable sounds of mammalian mating. When they'd been prised apart, *all her lips were blue!* While his penis had had to be amputated. Yet if Mark and Camilla's coming-together had been mysterious, still more incomprehensible was their remaining so. Oh, no, no, no, noooooo! Busner had howled into the stalely fresh confines of Room Five-Twenty the evening before, as the great reservoir of grief slopped about inside of him: How many more generations of Busners would be passed the pathological baton? Looking once more at the Pietá resting in his palm . . . *give the dog a bone*, Zack had chewed over the matter of autism, along with handfuls of Mister Porter's Luxury Nibbles, a jar of which he'd extracted from the minibar and opened . . . *with no conscious thought whatsoever.* Both nibbles and malady were so *moreish* . . . perhaps because autism's credentials as an organic dysfunction were even more threadbare than those of schizophrenia. This may've been why both Leo Kanner in Baltimore and Hans Asperger in Vienna had toyed with the notion that the peculiar children presented to them by perplexed parents were afflicted with . . . *a juvenile form of schizophrenia.* A wild analysis, indeed – and one it'd been impossible to sustain for long in the ataraxic face of the . . . *innumerable facts.* Facts that scuttled about all over the shop – facts that dressed down in the faded denim of hearsay – facts that refused to form up into verifiable data-sets. Busner, who still read at least synopses of the clinical literature, had seen theories come silver and thrashing, and theories tossed back in the sea . . . *inert, dulling.* The Big One always got away – while, from a strictly scientific point of view, it all . . . *smelt fishy.* The conflict between mentalist and physicalist accounts of psychic dysfunction had been going on throughout his professional lifetime, yet he'd never seen anything quite like this: a stealthy purge of all the talking therapies – their suspect practitioners rounded up at dawn and exiled to the Siberia of breakfast television and the advice columns of women's magazines, leaving the treatment of vulnerable, confused, *distressed* patients wholly in the hands of the box-tickers and the pill-pushers, who in turn appointed clinical psychologists *wet behind the bloody ears* to deliver partial explanations of poorly understood psychic phenomena . . . *as if they were matters of organic fact!* He'd considered the very essence of his metier to be this: not so much the privileging of mind over matter – for all dualists are, by definition, *Divided Selfs* – but convincing his patients . . . *my children, my lovers* that changing their minds did at least . . . *matter* – and that such changes could be effected without chemical assistance or bullying behavioural modification. What they were now calling Autistic Spectrum Disorder is – he believes – a *canary in the coalmine* of the human condition, its cheeping heralding a decisive shift away from the human psyche's attempt to understand itself . . . *by itself* to the conviction that enlightenment could be gained . . . *from the screens.* Really, autism was a misnomer – the so-called selfists were really . . . *machinists*, snipping, then sewing the long threads . . . *one-zero-zero-zero-one-one-zero-one-one-one-zero-one* . . . of their own *didginess.* Could it be any surprise that theories spun from this stuff were similarly digital, and so reduced the entire cat's cradle of infinitely subtle qualia . . . *bevelled edge of glass* to an ugly string of algorithms? His grandson, the lethally double-barrelled Benedict Whitehouse-Busner, raged against metaphors . . . *They're lies!* . . . while breathily believing many things . . . *yet he has no faith – only the facts will do*: There've been four studies conducted in the YouKay, forty-three in the YouEss – a meta-analysis of outcomes by Professor Subrata Gangooly at Stanford demonstrates conclusively that between three and four hours of interaction with digital media devices per day can enhance performance across a range of cognitive functions – processing, executive, short-term memory – by factors of between seventeen and twenty-two per cent. See here . . . here . . . and here . . . Busner hears each dull tink of Ben's forefinger against the glass, as his grandson's strange voice – its timbre simultaneously breathy and mechanical – *a baritone kazoo blown by an air compressor* sounds in his inner-ear, exactly as he remembers it sounding the previous evening, slumped down on the tightly tucked counterpane. Then, *as now*, it came palilaliacally again: . . . *can enhance performance across a range of cognitive functions – processing, executive, short-term memory – by factors of between seventeen and twenty-two per cent –.* Stop! he'd cried then – cries again now with such vehemence that Pete-the-Podium-Restaurant-Manager ceases his rootling about in the wardrobe, rounds on him and says, Stop? Stop what, cock? – *Stop this relentless verbigeration! You can't just reel off figures like that, Ben darling – you need to know a lot more about the trials' methodologies before any of this data becomes meaningful – let alone a basis for a therapeutic approach!* They'd been sitting in Ben's strange cranny of a bedroom – as they so often did: the old fool and the silly young savant. Both of them *wadded* down at the far end, where the trestle table's wedged against the permanently shut window, and his grandson's plastic bags and crates full of ring-pulls and ragdolls, cider bottles and shell ornaments, reach a sort of . . . *crescendo of stuff.* This much he remembers: Ben, hunched over the keyboard and rapping out as he'd tapped, Promise me, Gramps – promise me you'll be doing the things I have instructed you to do and following these instructions . . . *instructed you to do and following these instructions* . . . Camilla had entered at this point and picked her way carefully from patch to patch of vacant floor, the mugs full of tea on her tin tray . . . *slopping.* She was a bitter woman nowadays – trapped in the third act of her own self-penned . . . *tragic narrative,* the living, breathing *typing* proof, if any were needed, of the fantasies which can be engendered in fervid minds by a week-long residential course . . . *in creative-bloody-writing.* To be honest, Gramps, she'd said, I don't think you grasp the seriousness of your situation – if you keep on hanging out with ragamuffins like Simon and Ann, Dan's going to have you put away . . . *Put away! Ragamuffins!* The fusty locutions his daughter-in-law employs – well, they summon out of retirement his own superannuated slang: *Oh, will you button your lip, Milla!* And place him in the same old steamer trunk as her parents – whom he's met several times over the years, most horribly at their children's bizarre wedding, performed at the Register Office in Judd Street. Busner types them as . . . *county people*, the Pettigrew-Whitehouses – and, although they're a decade or so his juniors, Busner's queer position as the de facto father to their grown-up grandson means he cannot stop . . . *looking up at them* with contemptuous, juvenile eyes. They are, he imagines, the master and mistress of a wet-nosed retriever, the drivers of a mud-spattered estate car. The organisers of charity carol concerts – somewhere in the draughty depths of their detached and faintly dismal house there'll be a chilly vestibule choked with muddy wellies, old shooting sticks *and the golf club Pongo saw the burglar off with*. They may've exiled their only daughter to boarding school, yet in the aftertones of their honking and braying he's detected . . . *fugitive elocutionary echoes – they probably decant their cornflakes into Tupperware boxes . . .* At any rate, as their grandson had grown, the Pettigrew-Whitehouses proved entirely lacking in the savoir faire needed to deal either with him or with his distressed parents. No – that'd been left to his other grandparents, not that Busner had cooperated much with Miriam, the patterns of shared-parenting having been for so long in place: the pick-ups and drop-offs, the *iniquitous* entrances and *transgressive* exits, timed to avoid farcical collision – they were easy to apply . . . *unto the third and fourth generation*. Had he done right by Ben? Busner's grandson was now twenty-seven – he'd picked up a little work at last – *online, naturally* – calculating sporting odds for a bookmaker, but, apart from family affairs, his social life remained non-existent . . . *a house cat – he shits on his mother's tea tray*. And recently . . . *worryingly* Ben had begun mouthing – and remouthing – strange, oracular statements: *The time is coming . . . The time is coming . . . When the weak will be made strong . . . When the weak will be made strong . . . So it has been written in the code . . . So it has been written in the code . . .* In Room Five-Twenty, on the evening of his arrival in Manchester, Dr Z Bisner, *sic*, had slumped on the *drumskin* of his bed – and, although his grasp on the finer detail had been *shaky*, this much he did recall with painful clarity: Simon's hands on Oscar's throat – Simon shouting, You bone cunt! You total fucking zero! If you weren't one of the Doc's kids, I'd kick the shit out of you and use it to paint your fucking poofy khazi! As he'd sat there on the bed, Zack's fingers had gone all fidgety – as nowadays *they so often do* . . . and photo had succeeded photo on the phone's screen, each a precise vision of . . . *another screen*. And he'd thought: There's a fateful symmetry here between these images-of-imaging obsessively recaptured – Ben had taken thousands of screen-shots of his own gaming – and my own rejection by the flesh-of-my-flesh . . . For Zack the conclusion had been inescapable: they preferred the virtual him to the actual one – preferred images and video-clips of him to his physical presence . . . Preferred digits on a bank statement or a house-price index to taking any responsibility for his care . . . Fair enough. Possibly Zack's behaviour had been *a little outré* – inviting Simon and Ann to stay with him while he was flat-sitting for Oscar and Vigo, but the lost cat had been nothing to do with them: one moment it'd been there – the next gone. Had he put the creature out? Or even down? That Oscar and Vigo's baby-substitute was called Schrödinger should've made its loss predictable, since you didn't have to be a nominative determinist to believe they'd been *asking for it* . . . Simon's hand cinching his windpipe, Oscar had screeched, I'm not throwing them out! I'm not throwing them out! While his poor old father roared in reply: If they go, I go! *againannagain*. How could he have known Schrödinger was a house cat? He'd never heard of such a thing before – and now nobody knew if the dumb moggy was *dead or alive* . . . Released by Simon, Oscar had sat and wept: I told you not to let him out – told you very carefully . . . left a big bloody notice taped to the back door to that effect! While Zack shook his time-buffeted head, aghast that the flesh-of-his-flesh should privilege *fur over blood* . . . There'd been no formal arrangement, but Busner had thought everyone . . . *understood one another*. Now he'd reached the life-stage of renunciation, and was divesting himself of all his worldly goods and obligations, he considered it *well within my rights* to *pitch up for a few days* . . . *as and when* . . . *as the mood takes me*. There were plenty of spare rooms at Redington Road – Frankie had one, so did Lottie. There was a put-me-up at Camilla and Ben's, while Oscar and Vigo were away most weekends . . . *antiquing in the provinces*, which was surely a suitable fate for non-breeders . . . *put a few coats of varnish on that – no one'll know it ain't Chipperfield* . . . There were so very many of Zack's progeny: if he outstayed his welcome at one establishment, he could simply pick up his staff and begging bowl and . . . *move on to the next*. Obviously, given his advanced years and his health issues . . . *shat myself – nothing worse*, it would've been folly for him to set out on the noble path during the damp and chill months – but the plan had remained: he'd do precisely this once spring came . . . *lest you think I never can recapture, the first fine careless rapture.* He'd had old Lionel's boy, Dave Wax, make him a suit of yellowish tweed. Zack had told the son: The Munis, girdled with the wind, wear soiled garments of yellow hue. To which the ageing schneider replied, Dunno 'bout all that, Doctor Busner – but this is a most distinctive piece of cloth, I'm sure you'll agree. He'd hobbled along to Smith's on New Oxford Street and bought a suitable staff – really a shooting stick, so he could prop himself up . . . *from time to time.* Then, on the way back to Oscar's in Belsize Park, he stopped at Heal's and purchased a rather nice wooden bowl, which looked to have been roughly adzed from some tropical tree and felt pleasingly abrasive to the touch. He was still pleased when he reached the cash register – but then: seventy-nine pounds and ninety-nine pence for a bowl! A bloody tribal salad bowl – whatever the fuck that means! It'd been, he thought at the time, a perfectly reasonable response – although when the ambulance returned him to Redington Road he'd had to concede things had . . . *really got rather out of hand.* It was incidents such as these . . . *mere contretemps* which Daniel and Pat, Oscar and Vigo, Frankie and Lottie, all said were . . . *forcing our hands*, exactly the sort of idiom you'd expect them to use, grownup babies that they undoubtledly are – Daniel, tiptoeing now into the hushed zone of retirement, still addresses his father with a mixture of cravenness and aggression *Daaa-aad!* that's achingly adolescent. *Toenails grow when you're dead – therefore I must be . . .*

down there in the cold earth, with them uncurling from the ends of my rotting feet . . . questing up towards the surface . . . strange growths . . . Get with child a mandrake root . . . Sitting on the bed the previous evening, he'd felt sanguine enough about it all. They didn't want him – fine, he'd gone. As Maurice would've said, Nothing is worth having that isn't . . . *freely given – four quid for water! Four-fucking-quid!* But in the night, once Niraga – or Nikki, because that's what she'd called herself: Nikki! – had left, Zack's mood darkened . . . and darkened some more. From behind the counterfeit O'Keeffe there'd come cough-cough-cough-*coughulations* that'd *tangled up my mind* and *choked sleep to death* –. – Whozzat? Didja say sumfing, old feller? The young security guard looms over Busner, his fresh face beaming with malicious glee: Nikki? Didja say, Nikki? Was that the name of the brass what you 'ad up 'ere last night? Your girrrrlfriend, is she – your little bit of fluff? And the old man hadn't the wit to contradict him . . . *I'm an orphaned child still – a rat-baby crawling up a rusted drainpipe . . . I'm the scale accumulating in a kettle . . . the mould on a Wonderloaf – all things crusted . . . and obscene . . .* although he knew then – remembers now – the name of the young British Asian social worker, who, moonlighting as a prostitute, had come to him in Room Five-Twenty, and who would always be . . . *without passion*: Niraga, he burps – and the security guard rears away, while all the push-and-pull of last night's vaginal exam . . . *corkscrews into me. — Pop!* Camilla had poured her Gramps a glass of supermarket plonk and commiserated. – I've only just this minute hung up on Dan. He and Pat've found you a retirement community nearby – Rosslyn Hill, I think. Anyway, unless the two of you can convince

them this'll work they'll do everything within their power to stop you going . . . *This much I remember*: Camilla setting down the two wineglasses in two neat loops of the computer cabling festooning Ben's desk – Camilla, kindly and concerned and capable of great attentiveness so long as she isn't off . . . *capering* in the rosy bower of her . . . *vast and improbable love.* So, she'd continued, you'd better pay thorough attention to what Ben's saying, whether or not you're willing to admit that you're getting rather . . . um, forgetful –. I am! Zack interrupted. You are? She'd peered at him with her kindly eyes. I am, he'd agreed, I am forgetful – it's true. I'm also, er, highly emotionally labile – this I cannot dispute, Milla. But I've spent my entire career trying to impress on my colleagues, my patients and, especially, their relatives quite how damaging putting a label on someone can be. It's one thing to adopt a term such as Alzheimer's – or autism, for that matter – as a heuristic . . . an interpretative device, a way of explaining . . . things – but when you say, He's got Alzheimer's. She's autistic . . . it's so definitive – a label – it makes people behave in certain rigid and unthinking ways: You're senile, You're on the spectrum, therefore you're like this, and you've got to take these drugs and live there and do that . . . He had, he now concedes, probably grown *rather emotionally labile* at this point, but Camilla, instead of blurting out, *Oh, Gramps, you say things like this all the time*, checked herself . . . *She's read the patient information leaflet* so knows better than to upset someone with Alzheimer's by . . . *drawing their attention to their own forgetfulness with a knick-knack paddywhack give a . . . give a . . . give a what to who precisely?*
— Put these on, you nutter, says the security guard, handing him

his tweedy trews. And as Busner stands, angling his foot, he teeters . . . totters, and might fall were it not for Pete-the-Podium-Restaurant-Manager, who, taking his elbow, dismisses his colleague: There's no call for talk like that, Dave – this man's still a paying guest, you can get back to your other duties now, I'll manage Doctor Busner just fine. Once the door to Room Five-Twenty has shushed shut, he resumes: Better do up your flies . . . You aren't too steady on yer pins, are you, I'm surprised your people let you run around like this . . . And Busner, once he's succeeded in fastening his trousers, waistcoat and jacket, feels sufficiently *buttoned up* to reply: I'd rather have bruises than bedsores, young man – and yes, my people are trying to get me put away, you're right on that score . . . He sees the his staff poking out from behind the counterfeit O'Keeffe, and, stooping to retrieve it, adds, If it weren't for my grandson they'd have me in a bloody care home . . . He struggles back upright and flourishes it: He's an utter whizz at computers, my Ben – he's devised this system for his old Gramps, it's all here on this mobile phone . . . Busner summons the talisman from his pocket – holds it up so Pete-the-Podium-Restaurant-Manager can see . . . That's him, together with his parents, anyway . . . *Anyway, Gramps,* Ben's words return *breathily,* Anyway, Gramps, it don't matter 'bout labels an' stuff – not now. Thing is, s'long as you don't forget the phone you won't forget anything else – 'cause it's all in the phone . . . All of it: what you gotta do – when you gotta do it . . . *what you gotta do – when you gotta do it* . . . Actually, speaking with the precise meaning of semantics, Gramps, it isn't all in the phone – it's there, it's here on my computer, it's spread throughout the entire world wide web . . . *spread throughout the entire world wide web* . . . 'cause they all sorta interact, right. So, my computer'll send your phone updates . . . pushes . . . alerts. The phone'll vibrate, and all you gotta do is touch this button with your thumb and there it'll all be on the screen . . . *and there it'll all be on the screen* . . . But here's the really cool thing . . . Ben had petted the mouse, his eyes *slippin', tumblin', fumblin', sinkin'* down the screen as he thrilled: See here, these're all the cognitive exercises I've put together for you. Some're simple sorta tests – general knowledge, crosswords and acrostics, Sudoku-type puzzles . . . *crosswords and acrostics, Sudoku-type puzzles* . . . And if you look here – here're more interactive games-type things, with these you can improve your hand-eye-coordination . . . fine motor-control . . . that sorta thing . . . *hand-eye-coordination . . . fine motor-control . . . that sorta thing* . . . Zack had studiously maintained eye contact with Camilla while addressing them both: So, so long as I've got the phone, it's like you're looking after me? Ben nodded – rapid little dips of his big head: Yeah-yeah, always connected – plugged into and rooted through the great mirror of being . . . Always connected . . . *Always connected* . . . I might be wandering, Busner thinks, terribly confused, yet I'll still be sending that craziness back, *with hey, ho, the wind and the rain*, to the big executive brain for which all foolish data is . . . *but a toy*. There is, he thinks, a certain retributive justice about this: it is, perhaps, a fitting punishment for the self-absorbed *knave* they . . . *shut their gates 'gainst*, for the terms of endearment have, he realises, been *completely reversed* . . . With all his children, at some point in their adolescence, lying awake in the master bedroom at Redington Road beside the *wife du jour*, he'd experienced this dread awareness: the child was out there in the world, its burgeoning sexuality a sort of barrier, or . . . *firewall – that's what they call it*, cutting off the intense physical sympathy he'd had for them in earlier childhood, when he could make-believe his hug would protect them from all humanity's evils. Now this child was exposed to it all – yet still vitally connected to him by a tendril, a feeler . . . *a pseudopod*, which had extended from the ruptured cell of the family to probe about in the wider world. A pseudopod he'd no way of controlling any more – yet which sent him back confusing perceptions. Data he would analyse and find constituted experience, occasionally of pleasure, but often of . . . *pain*. It had been agony! Yet it was altogether just – for what were relationships between parents and children if not passionate love affairs experienced in reverse? Liaisons that began with the most intense physical intimacy – and ended, decades later, with the parties involved sighting one another, at a dull party, across a crowded room, and thinking . . . *She looks vaguely familiar*. His children had gone *slippin', tumblin', fumblin', sinkin'* into emotional quagmires and pub brawls, regardless of the thick hanks of nerves still . . . *plugged straight into my cerebellum!* He'd writhed, he'd sweated and, ignobly, he'd longed for the day when they'd receive just a little of his own . . . *desolate data* – for this, too, was an agony, this slippin', tumblin', fumblin', pissin', crotch-dampenin', stumblin' *sudden* old age. And his mind – what was it now, save a whirlpool in which past-present-and-future all revolved, together with a mess of shit-and-piss-and-shit-smeared-paper, leaving his body squatting here in the moment. – They look like a nice lot, says

Pete-the-Podium-Restaurant-Manager. Now, if you've got all your bits, we'll get you checked out – 'less you've changed your mind, and you'd like Mister Marshalsea to get hold of your folks . . . *Get hold.* Indeed, because *getting hold of people* and, still more pertinently . . . *being held by them* was all that mattered. Last night, when he'd poked the words escort agency into the search engine on the phone – having tried prostitute and been directed to a Jaystore research paper on aitcheyevee transmission rates amongst preoperative transsexual sex workers in Manila – had his grandson been looking through his eyes as he hungrily examined the caramelised flesh *I'd no real appetite for?* And was this why Ben had been ringing so obsessively this morning – not taking REJECT CALL for the unambiguity it so clearly was? *Being held by them* . . . the door to Five-Twenty whooshes shut and Pete-the-Podium-Restaurant-Manager cups Busner's elbow in his obliging hand, then they stump along the corridor. Last night, when Nikki left, did she still feel . . . *held by me?* Did she still feel the pressure of his fingers deep inside her . . . *my breath on her belly?* Some newly shined shyster must've only this moment taken the lift, for in the lobby the brushes still whirr . . . *buffing nothing.* How many minutes and hours had they spent together in Ben's bedroom, watching the little circlets whirl into and out of being? An ouroboros that fed on its own inanition as it ate its own . . . *inexistent tail.* Buffing and buffing and *buffering*, until: *This much I can download.* – Nikki – who was café-au-lait, not caramelised – *frothing* in the bowl of blue easy chair by the off-white drapes, her legs tucked up and chuckling, Yeah, I got this job, right, and the agency, right, they're none too sussed 'bout security, right,

send you wherever, whenever . . . meant to check out the client –
check his landline's registered, or his mobile – izzooeesezzeeizz . . .
'course they don't bother . . . Mostly don't matter, but this old
feller – must've been married or summat like that, right, gives a
false whatsit, right, then 'e only goes and dies on me, don't 'e –
no, really – right on top of me, right on the bloody job! Nikki,
who wore a tight black dress with a plunging neckline made of
some stretchy material . . . *a sling for her breasts to swing in* . . . had
seemed amused, but Zack – who'd been sitting on the bed, sipping
from one of the glasses of wine he'd poured out, was suitably
shocked: Oh, you poor girl – that must've been terribly upsetting –.
– It bloody well were . . . She'd run on: 'is place were right up on
Saddleworth Moor, so off the beaten track, sat-nav couldn't find it.
It were winter, too. He were a sweet old feller, but he moost've adder
art condition or summat like that, 'cause I saw him, right, take the
little blue pill . . . Then we were gassin' fer a bit – like uz, now – and
joost gettin' started on the main business, right, when 'is face goes
all blue an' 'e sorta flops right across me, right, stone-bloody-
dead . . . Zack had petted and stroked the idea of Nikki before
he encountered the gigglingly winsome reality. Once the correct
euphemism had occurred to him . . . *That's what she did – escorted me
from Romilly Street to her bedsitting room*, a simple search yielded
scores of escort agencies with names such as Red Orchid Girls and
Chelsea Courtesans. He'd pressed a phone number on the screen
and within seconds was talking to a woman who sounded the hard-
bitten part – he'd pictured coral lips, and a lacquered tongue which
poked and prodded him through all the options. So he'd sat,

employing capacitive touch to examine the photographs and vital statistics of young women he lacked the capacity to . . . *truly touch*. When he'd made his choice, hung up and was sitting there waiting, he'd wondered at his own weirdness and . . . *audacity*. Then he'd gone to the bathroom and checked the plastic bag in which he kept a few essentials – wallet, reading spectacles, change of underwear, medication, but . . . *why did I bother?* He'd voided his own little blue pills into some other toilet bowl ages ago – while the preposterous priapism he'd experienced during his affair with Athena had long since *withered on the vine*. Had he been testing or taunting himself? Perhaps it was his own deeply penetrating sadness that had persuaded him he might be able to brandish a puissant pork sword rather than *a sad little cocktail sausage*. None of this carry-on would be appropriate for a Sannyasin – unless, that is, he belonged to one of the Shaiva Tantra schools, which view sexual activity as part of . . . *the liberation process*. At least, Zack had said, he died in a state of happy anticipation. Whereupon Nikki chuckled, What about you, Zack, are you in a state of happy anticipation? When he'd swung open the door of Room Five-Twenty and seen her standing there in the corridor, with its sickly stink of air-freshener, he'd been nauseated – his pulse drumming in his ears *dum-bumma-dum-dum, dum-bumma-dum-dum, dum-bumma-dum-dum! Love is in the air! Daaa-da-d'daaa-daaa! Love is in the air* . . . But Nikki had immediately taken control of the situation: stretching up on tippy-toes, pecking him on the cheek – and then, when he stepped aside, swishing slinkily past him. Why had he done it? Why'd he ordered up a thinking, breathing, feeling human creature . . . *as if she were a pizza?* To settle the matter of his un-reasonable and – following contemporary usage – *unsustainable* lust? Certainly, but the prompt had been utterly prosaic, namely . . . *my pass-code for the stupid phone – this much I do remember:* it was the year commercial television started up . . . A *whiter-than-white* year – skins, underclothes, women's reputations *unless they wanted to end up kicking on the end of a rope!* The television cameras of the era softened the Great Evangeliser – his hair was suety, his complexion floury, his accents . . . *rose and rose*: The wa-arp and we-eft of this gre-at na-ation is fra-aying! For social action to wo-ork it must be a-cc-o-m-pan-ied by spi-ri-tu-al re-vi-val! Indeed. – Hunched over the phone's tiny screen, Zack had marvelled . . . *for the umpteenth time* at its painful clarity: the digital cameras of today hardened everything, mineralised it all: hair, skin, inexpressibly affecting dimples alike. He'd scrolled down, read the *fuck FAQs* and so had *the readies* – ten new machine-ironed twenties – ready, and was prepared himself: showered, shaved and his remaining teeth brushed . . . *the EssArr way*. The procuress's cellophane accents still crackled in Busner's hot head. He'd asked if Nikki – Age twenty-seven, Five-foot-two, Size Six, Bust thirty-eight Dee natural, Nationality British Asian – was the chatty sort, and she'd crinkled, Ha, ha, ha! Nikki, love? It's hind legs and donkeys with that one – you won't get 'er to shut 'er mouth 'less you put summat else innit. Not that she isn't demure, Nikki – she's ever so demure, ever so respectful of the older gentleman . . . and his needs . . . On she'd gone, perfectly illustrating the very characteristic she sought to describe – while the older gentleman took flight in a Vickers

Viscount and jetted back to an era not so much innocent as *grotesquely gauche*. Maurice was no prude, and, toilet walls being available to all, Zack, aged eighteen, had been acquainted with the biological facts – but the etiquette, the form – this was hardly something you could . . . *Ask Pickles about*. It didn't matter, though, because what's-her-face with the what-not had been quite devoid of the social graces: *I'm not your Locarno sweet 'eart, love* . . . Love! Love! Money may make the world go round, but love makes it go . . . *back and forth*, so driving the flywheel which goes round and round, again annagain, so generating the *business, love?* cycle. Months later, in one of his first anatomy classes at Heriot-Watt, Zack had had an odd revelation: she hadn't put him inside of her at all, only gripped his *membrum virile* tightly in the runnel of her crotch – which was fair enough, given he'd *shot off in seconds – Spunknik!* Despairing, all lust instantaneously exchanged for shame and depression, his fingers had read the pimples in the dip of her spine . . . *signifying nothing*, while the bedstead went on creaking and his nostrils filled with the smell of . . . *coal gas and TeeSeePee*. Looking fondly upon little Nikki, coddled in the easy chair, hair glossy, lips and nails glossier, skin seemingly . . . *flawless*, it was that nameless – and now doubtless long dead – other's dermis that'd returned to him . . . *growing, spreading*, a sickening and doughy tegument, sealing off Nikki's mouth, her eyes and nostrils . . . *semolina – rice pudding*, which, if he felt it beneath his fingers – let alone his lips – would make him *screamandscreamandscream* until he was indeed sick. Skin, which is . . . *the state we're in*. It covered Zack then – covers Busner now, as he and Pete-the-Podium-Restaurant-

Manager board the lift, and, together with a freshly shaven trio of middle-level executives, go *slippin', tumblin', fumblin'* and *sinkin'* down to the lobby. Busner peers at his shining brogues and has no memory of buffing them. In there – in the woolly sweaty darkness toenails are growing, which is something they do . . . *when you're dead.* Not skin, though – skin only grows when you're alive, grows and then dies, so that at any given point you're walking around with life-and-death *slippin' and fumblin'* each other. Ach! Skin! It touches everything – and worse still *touches itself!* Hangnails hook into hickeys – pimples popper-into the pits of their predecessors, until the entire flexible territory self-surveys itself into existence: a map of the territory . . . *made of the territory itself!* Not that Busner has ever had any problem distinguishing the workaday tarpaulin from the silkily seductive stuff – a duffer at dissection he may've been, yet, during his time as a houseman, he'd needed no anatomical know-ledge for lumbar punctures, blood-sampling, dilation-and-curettage and other *fiendishly delicate* procedures. Zack had had . . . *the feel for it*, and, despite a career hardly typified by the laying on of hands, after last night Busner realises . . . *I still do!* Because this much *I do remember* . . . Nikki prattling on about the dead punter as she'd sipped her Chardonnay: It were right heavy, right – no question, but better it 'appen to uz than one of them uther numpties, right . . . on account of the training, right . . . Which had naturally solicited an enquiry as to what this training – which had so prepared her for having old men die on top of her during coitus – might be? Nikki had preened a little: I'm a social worker, right – qualified as a psychiatric one, right, but mostly I take agency jobs dealing wi' normal clients – not that they're that bloody normal! Zack's relief had been pathetic: no longer was this a sordid meeting between a damaged young woman and a much older and abusive man – instead they'd been engaged in a case conference, albeit a highly unorthodox one. It'd all vomited forth: how he'd been sick with anxiety – the concierge might've seen her entering the lift, or, when the Madame had called to verify that a Doctor Bisner was registered, the receptionist might've realised ... *what was going on.* Since he was now retired, there was no reputational damage to consider – but there were his family's feelings, and his own, admittedly ridiculous, spiritual pride: such antics hardly suggested the renunciation of all worldly pursuits required of a Sannyasin ... While he'd been speaking, Zack had noticed Nikki's face growing darker – far from his revelation summoning up an enthusiastic cross-cultural dialogue, she'd exploded: You've a fookin' nerve, Doctor Boosner – y'think I want folk knowing I'm on t'bloody game? What about my career, my family – I've a fiancé, y'know! Yet as soon as these thunder-clouds had gathered, they dispersed: I don't mean t'be skrikin', but if you think you're the only wun 'ere wi' a reputation to protect ... well, give yer 'ead a fookin' wobble! He'd fallen from the bed to the maroon carpet, then set off *knobbling* towards her. This much he remembers: the *bird's wing* of her slight shoulder in his hand – somehow they'd ended up kissing, but this had been no sensitive survey of tongues mutually undertaken. He remembers now – remembered then, too – the first French kisses of his life, tongue-feeling-tongue-feeling-tongue, such that ... *we became one* – and such a one! Our flexible members ever shaping and

reshaping their own mutual awareness – *a good analogy*, he thinks
. . . *for consciousness itself.* But after a little dabbling they'd broken:
Yer 'eart's not really innit, is it, love? She curled back into the chair's
concavity, smoothing her skirts, while he'd sat back on his heels,
watching the old man, with wild white hair sprouting from his
scalp, sitting back on his heels, his belly bulging as he'd squatted
out there, five storeys up . . . *in the glassy darkness.* He'd heard then –
hears again now – the farty rasp of a saxophone, the circus-top
jiggy-jiggy of a hack band. He'd seen then – sees again now – the
unfunny little man's festination as he chases after the scantily clad
dollybirds . . . *King Leer!* But with no kingdom any longer to rule
over with his surreally melting sceptre. No, he'd conceded, I'm
afraid neither my heart nor the rest of me is, ah, in it. So, he'd
decanted another little bottle of Chardonnay into their glasses, sat
back and listened to her tale. Nikki's real name was Niraga: Which
is a bit ironical, right, 'cause it means without passion . . . Then had
come a lament for her parents: her father, laid off from the mills in
the eighties, had picked up only odd jobs ever since – odd jobs and
odder pills, as he'd passed all the required tests, and had eventually
gained a full-time position as a clinical depressive. As for Niraga's
mother, a bartered bride from Uttar Pradesh – she'd never learnt
English, too fearful of those . . . *alien tongues* – she lived out her
days in a grim little house on a great big estate . . . *out Wythenshawe
way.* As for Niraga's brothers, all four of them had fled – South to
university, then on into the professions. When you hear their voices
on the phone, she'd told him, you can't even tell they're Asian . . .
Niraga had a loft apartment in the Northern Quarter, all paid

for . . . *cash on the bloody nail* by her earnings from alternate shifts as sex- and social-worker. As she'd spoken, Zack had become aware of an insistent itchiness – not, for once, his own flaky old coat but her . . . *fresh lick of it.* Niraga wriggled prettily in her chair, her hands ceaselessly mobile as they'd fluttered up towards the labial folds of the fake O'Keefe, then down to her lap. Have you . . . ? he'd at last ventured . . . I mean, I don't mean to . . . pry, but is there something troubling you? She'd guffawed – a wholesome, hearty laugh: I'll say! Me fanny's on fookin' fire – might be a rash or mebbe cystitis coming on . . . Occupational hazard, right – did some creamin' 'fore I coom out, but it's still fookin' burning . . . s'pose I shouldn't've, but she gets right bollocky, right, if you turn down a job . . . While she'd been speaking Zack had made gentle soothing noises, expressive, he'd felt, of paternal concern – then he'd stammered: It m-must b-be awful – having to do this . . . this – he'd gestured wildly with his phone – sort of thing. I mean, it must be bad enough coping with it psychologically, without physical problems as –. Fook you! she'd bellowed, I tellya, right, when I get fed up wi' me own old folks – who're on me bloody case night and day – and fed up with me normal-type clients, right . . . well, it's you lot who keeps me fookin' sane. You lot who actually gi' me a little tee-elsie . . . Tee-elsie, eh – a shocking abbreviation that Busner remembers only too well falling from the mean mouths of EssArrEnns on ward rounds – hatchet-faced women who wouldn't know what tenderness was . . . *if you beat it into them with a meat-tenderiser.* He imagines that nowadays any reference to tee-elsee would soon enough be followed by its sinister conspecific, *dee-ennarr* . . . It could've been this chilly intimation that provoked his crazy proposal: Um, you wouldn't like me to . . . um . . . take a look? I mean . . . he'd cantered on *whinnying* . . . I realise it's pretty unorthodox, but I am a qualified medical doctor . . . and when I was in psychiatric practice I always took care of my patients' minor ailments – I felt it brought me closer to them, assured the most distressed amongst them that I really . . . cared. Niraga hadn't been in the least put out – only preoccupied by . . . *practical matters*: You've no endo-whatsit . . . no speculum, right – and no roober gloves neither . . . Zack's eyes had dibbed about the hotel room before alighting on a *corkscrew!* which had two curving, spatulate prongs between which – for the cork at least – the pain *stops and starts* . . . All he'd to do was to remove the steely screw and, hey presto! He'd waved the thing aloft, saying, Here we have an instrument which very much resembles a speculum – but what about some rubber gloves? It was then Niraga's turn for a brainwave: she'd snatched up her handbag and, rummaging through its soft and perfumed interior, came up with a box of condoms. Well, she'd said, they're antiseptic – and lubricated . . . I dunno – s'pose you were gonna get a look at me bits one way or the uther . . . Mebbe you're a perv – get yer kicks that way . . . What evs – yer know what a speculum is anyways . . . Then she'd uncurled from the chair and padded towards the bathroom on stockinged feet, calling over her shoulder, I'll joost get outta me things, Doc . . . While she'd been gone, Zack had stripped the bed, boiled the electric jug, sterilised the corkscrew-speculum, then arranged all the pillows and scatter cushions into a supportive pyramid. Next he'd fiddled with the foil sachets, so that when Niraga returned, wearing the monogrammed terry-towelling robe, she laughed, Yer 'ands look like big bloody claws! And the lobster man had reassured her: I do know what I'm doing . . . Niraga did as well: she positioned herself sideways on the bed, back against the pyramid and with her knees drawn up. Zack had got down on his knees by the side of the bed – peering in, he'd been momentarily shocked by her shaved pubis: Are you sure you're comfy . . . *with that stubble*? To which she'd replied, Bloody 'ell, crack on, willya . . . *Clitoris, labia minora, urethra, Skene's glands, vagina, Bartholin's glands* . . . you don't need to have any anatomical competence at all to identify *the origin of the world* . . . With one pink, fruit-flavoured pincer, he'd parted her labia and performed the visual exam. I'm going to do the bimanual now, he'd said, rearranging his fingers . . . *Aaa-ke-laaa, we'll do our best!* Then he'd worked with intuitive despatch to . . . *push Button A* and isolate her cervix. She'd groaned . . . *without passion*, but there'd been no spasming, no clutching. He'd asked: Not too much tenderness when I palpate like . . . this? She'd grunted affirmatively – he'd reassured: Okay, I don't think there's any likelihood of pelvic inflammatory disease. The *glove puppet* had hurried about in there – while the *human dummy* ventriloquised: I'm palpating the spongiform uterine tissue . . . your fundus . . . No sign of adnexitis, he'd muttered – and Niraga said, Tubes 'n' eggs good to go, issit? Withdrawing his pincers, Zack had looked into her frank, open face *as if for the first time* . . . Who is she? he'd thought. Who is she, and what has she come to tell me? Then he'd once more bent to his task, picking up the defanged corkscrew and flexing its plastic pincers. Niraga had guffawed: 'Ow yer gonna see what's what up there, right? I mean, it's dead dark, innit . . . but Zack had the answer: My mobile phone's got a torch. – And, leaving her wide open, he fetched it from the glass table. Climbing back down on to his knees, he got to work . . . *Push Button A – push it, I say!* Pressing his weepy eye to the corkscrew's threadpiece . . . *I shrank and shrank* until he was about a foot high: then he walked down the *little passage* – and THEN he found himself at last *in the beautiful garden, amongst the bright flowerbeds and the cool fountains* . . . Bringing the torch's pencil-beam to bear, he'd seen a sprinkling of pinkly glistening papillomata stippling the roseate ribbing of her vaginal canal. *Highly unprofessionally* . . . he'd inhaled deeply, savouring the *fishy-mysteriousness* of her mucosa. Mmm, I think you should probably get a smear test post-haste, he'd said, carefully withdrawing his improvised tool, slowly straightening, then clambering back up . . . *to my actual size.* – It's looking, um, fairly squamous in there – prob'ly perfectly benign, just a touch of pruritis – which I'd imagine is, ah, something of a . . . professional hazard. – And if this was all there'd been to it, well . . . He stands back in the twittering aviary of the lobby . . . it would've been strange, certainly – highly unorthodox behaviour, is what a supportive colleague might've said, but the GeeEmmSee would . . . *have you struck right off!* – C'mon, says. Pete-the-Podium-Restaurant-Manager, manoeuvring Busner so expertly through the press of suits and wheelie-bags by the reception desk that his cup-of-elbow . . . *doth not runneth over.* All is as it was, Busner thinks: and when at last I get back to where I started from? Yes, if the GeeEmmSee knew they'd have his licence to practice taken away . . . *if I'd bothered to renew it.* – Can I get me things back on now, Doc, or d'you wanna take anuther gander? Such light words, yet they'd fallen heavily on him, pushing his eyes back in through . . . *the skirting board* to the compartment full of complicated old mechanical switching equipment: gearing, cogs, tensioned wires and glowing valves . . . *Push Button A! Push it, I say – Oh! Confound the dunderhead* who'd remembered a cut-away diagram from a copy of Knowledge he'd pored over circa nineteen fifty-one, and so looked for too long into that organic abyss: saw labia harden into a Bakelite receiver, clitoris curl into coil assembly, labia minora crimp into a papery disc which wondrously *self-perforated.* He'd felt an unspeakable urge to . . . *press my ear against her,* synaesthetically seeing . . . *what I could hear: Hello? Hello?* coming down this primordial telephone line, one which went all the way back to the . . . *dawn of time,* cunt speaking unto cunt, a doubly lubricious phonology of *sucks, slurps and small farting noises* which communicated the whole truth of . . . *our metempcuntosis – I should've listened!* Listened to the lessons taught him by . . . *the lives of others:* Your dharma? What the fuck's that – nothing but dung dropping from the world's arsehole . . . the cosmic law of eternal recurrence ordains there be dog shit in the streets, that you smell it – glove your hand with a plastic bag and pick it up . . . that you carry it home *again annagain.* As for Moksha – ferrrrgeddit, there's only a mocha-coloured stain *spreading through the gusset of your underpants* . . . But Niraga, whose full bottom lip and ever widening eyes had reminded him at that late hour of . . . *Milla!* had simply got up and unselfconsciously dressed, snapping knicker elastic, jumping to yank up her tights . . . *a girl alone in her bedroom*, then simply sat beside him on the bed for a few minutes, simply chatting: So, right, Doctor Boosner, it's me uz should be paying you fer your services . . . To which he'd gravely replied: I've no need of your money or anyone else's, young lady – I'll be checking out of humanity's hotel soon enough now, and forever. No, you're better off spending my fee on regular essteedee screening – go private, if necessary . . . And she had gone private – she'd gone into the privacy of the night-time, leaving Zack sitting there on the stripped bed beside the pillow pyramid. A bit later he'd filled his wineglass with a couple of Gordon's miniatures before slumping down, warily watching his whey-face floating in the Mancunian murkiness while he . . . *sopped up the spirits*. Later still, the near-homonym of Viagra had been . . . *longer gone*, while, coldly and *without passion*, Zack began to berate himself for being . . . *a pervert, a weirdo – almost a paedophile!* Worse still, although a vaginal exam might be *meat and potatoes* for a proper doctor, for a retired psychiatrist? Well . . . he'd been . . . *gorging on trayf.* On he'd gone, plying the lash as he made further inroads to the minibar, guzzling spirits, wines and beers indiscriminately. He'd regretted not bringing his lovingly assembled exit kit: diamorphine ampoules, sublingual morphine sulphate tablets, capsules of Valium and Tuinal, more than enough to . . . *do the job.* Who gives a flying fuck about Pikuach Nefesh! he'd raved into the bathroom mirror, flailing at his bared arm with the improvised speculum. Then, bloodied and mindless, he'd embarked on the systematic destruction of Room Five-Twenty: unsheathing the rolled towels from their scabbards and soiling them, removing the tall tapering *Klu Klux Klan* lampshades and mating them, ripping out the plasticised info-sheets from their ring binder and frisbeeing them over the wreckage. In his hysterical and drunken distress Room Five-Twenty had been transmogrified, becoming *incarnate!* The carpet writhed with muscular spasms – the wood panelled walls rose and fell, panting in time to the air conditioner's breathy whoosh . . . *and the petals!* Those bilious, badly brush-stroked petals, torn from Georgia O'Keeffe's corpus, they swelled and grew slick with secretions *most prettily* . . . What're hotel guests? he'd soliloquised, as he waved a tumblerful of Courvoisier in the blank faces of a non-existent audience. Surely only the barely vital sparks who check into these meaty prisons for a night or three, to animate them with our lonely frenzies as we *pull our fucking pork!* But he – he had no pork to pull: I can't get it up any more! he'd bayed at the absent moon before collapsing and sobbing at the harsh terms of his dotage. It was bad enough to be a fractious child once more – sent up to bed early, to wait out the interminable summer evening in the suburbs – but it's worse, far worse, to have your own children changed by this change into your . . . *absentee parents*. He cried and writhed and bled and pissed and shat, until, at some point in the hateful hours after dawn, with the new day insulting him with its sunny youth, he'd arisen, newborn, for his twenty-eight thousandth, seven hundred and thirty-seventh day on earth. *I'd risen . . . I rose . . . I rise – I'll rise again . . .* to put on his rancid T-shirt, his ruinous tweed suit – to pick up his staff and a *lonely hunt is all I desire!* the Butcher mimes along in English before continuing, raucously aloud, in fluent, perfectly accented German: Eh noch

Aurora pranget, Eh sie sich an den Himmel wagt, Hat dieser Pfeil, Schon angenheme Beut erlang-lang-langet! The Butcher waggles his own *arrow* in time to the lang-lang-lang of erlanget, seeing not his pale form dancing in the semi-darkness of the hotel room, but the ruddy faces of the Duke of Saxe-Weissenfels-Querfert and his retainers . . . *dangling in the candlelight*, so many . . . *long plums*. And the Butcher hears not the distant rattle-and-hum of the big building he's entombed in, but the sidereal airs of violones, violas, violins, bassoons, oboes, recorders and . . . *horns!* An instrumentation that, as he keeps on *dancing and romancing, oh keep on* . . . crumbles, then disintegrates – strings a-pingin', wood a-crackin', brass a-bucklin', until all that remains is a single softly melodic piano line, coolly insinuating itself into his hot head: Schafe können sicher weiden, the Butcher thinks, Wo ein guter Hirte wacht – not that you were ever a good shepherd, Mummy dearest, while as for sheep, there are two or three in the family, but I'm not one of them – and more to the point: nor are you! Suddenly gripped by burning hatred for his *Mutti-munschen, wavy-gravy-Maeve*, who sits forever in the stagnant green tank of an interminable summer evening in the suburbs – sits with the curtains open, sits before the Yamaha electric organ she bought for her favourite, the youngest, her fat and beringed fingers slickety-clicking as she teases out Bach's sublime melody *doo-d'd'doo-d'd'dooo-doo-dooo-doo*, to the accompaniment of a *da-dum-dum-dumb-fucking-rumba-beat!* Because the da-da-dumb little keyboard broke within weeks of its arrival at Colindale Avenue, this being the way of the family . . . *our touch of De'Ath*. Anger twangs the Butcher – he pirouettes on his long, lean *lallies*, then tucks his *erlang-lang-langet* between his thighs to give himself a . . . *fanny just like Mummy's.* Which means now he is Mummy, because *my razor-sharp mind has skinned that fucking hump* so he wears her tromboning tits and kettledrum belly as, shamelessly deranged now, he stilt-walks about the room, caressing the *thunderhead of her pubes* . . . Snatching up the hairdryer from the shelf beneath the mirror, he hearkens: the rumba rhythm *snickering* in his ear thickens – deepens, skips a half-beat, and he sings: Young man you too girlie girlie, You jus' flash it round the worldie . . . then squats abruptly, releasing his arrow so it quivers in the mortuary illumination of the single fluorescent tube screwed to the bed's fake-wood headboard. He turns back to the mirror and addresses these disembodied features: the *spare ribs* of his cheekbones, the *giblets* of his full lips, his *none-too-parsimonious* nose, the slice of his *tongue* with its *meaty papillae* clearly visible. – Have you met the Butcher? No, really – have you made his acquaintance? His voice is unusually flat and unemotional – his accent neutral, without trace of class or regional affiliation. He drones on: If not, it's perhaps best to encounter him – he runs his elegant pianist's fingers down over his chest, splaying them as they reach his belly – in his own skin rather than someone else's –. There's a hesitant tapping on the door. The Butcher sends expert eyes to search the ill-lit room: the Walkman and laptop computer sitting on the bed are innocuous enough, as is the Gladstone bag lolling open beside them – but the snub-nose revolver lying on the left-hand pillow beside two gold-foil-wrapped Bendicks Bittermints and an envelope addressed to one of the Butcher's other skins are less so . . . *Mister Blah-Blah*

would like to welcome Mister David Pottinger to the Britannia Hotel.
Which is exactly the sort of greeting the Butcher likes, given he's an
illegal to the very tip of his *erlang-lang-langet*: a furious skinner of
humps, and an instant and invisible tailor when it comes to *personal
alterations – my name is Legion, Terry Legion of Telecoms Solutions . . .*
The revolver appears to be a Colt Detective Special: *a lethal little
beast – easily concealed – point-three-eight round – take your fucking leg
off,* but he knows it's really only a strap he got for a pony from an old
armourer who prob'ly . . . *filed the bar himself.* Still, it'd fire at least
once before jamming – besides, the Butcher only needs it for show,
although not this show, so he scoops it up, takes two long strides
into the tiny bathroom, yanks a hand towel from the rail, wraps
the gun in it, pliés to the cupboard and puts it far back on the top
shelf . . . *tits out for the lads!* He grabs a bath towel with which to
cover his own *firepower* – then he's staring into the still-murkier
corridor, where a tubby old woman in chambermaid's navy nylon
uniform observes him, her worn, wary face sandwiched between a
whitish perm and *a whiter shade of* collar. Turn-down service, sir?
The Butcher swings the door wide open so she can see all of him . . .
so lean and limber in my lunghi – see also the Bendicks Bittermints
and the triangle of turned sheet. Someone's beaten you to it, he
smiles thinly, half expecting *the old bat* to *swoop on me* . . . which,
while not the usual hotel order of things, has been known to happen. But she only wheezes, Sorry, sir, while backing, then turning,
and so goes, *shushing* her nylon shoulder along the flock wallpaper.
The Butcher raises his sharp muzzle and sniffs old oatmeal, stale
cigarette smoke, and the esters of Obsession long since evaporated

from the cleavages of those . . . *no better than she should be.* He looks quickly and intently to the right and the left – there're no Bosnians, buggers or *Bashi-bloody-Bazouks*, just trays piled high with dirty crockery and glasses. The Butcher withdraws, muttering, Hotel? I don't think so – more like a twenty-four-seven knocking shop. He shuts, bolts and chains the door . . . *Prince Albert? Be awkward when strip-searched* . . . *Flash-to-bang* the whole encounter took seconds: Have you met the Butcher? he asks of the Queen-sized sagging centre stage – asks also of the purple-brown carpet and the surpassing-grim wallpaper . . . *sooner or later one of us will have to go* . . . and asks most especially of a panoramic photograph showing the Manhattan skyline by night that's pasted on the opposite wall and uplit by another fluorescent tube concealed behind a trompe l'œil sill. It's this oddity – a false window on to a fake world, with real red drapes swished to either side – that led the Butcher to request this particular room when he checked in. Not that he wishes to pretend he's on Park Slope rather than two hundred yards from Piccadilly Gardens, it's rather that the room's windowlessness – a function of its position, deep in the core of this big and surpassing solid old building – means it'll be . . . *impossible for the office to reach me* . . . No, really, have you? He advances, semi-erect penis dowsing, towards the blunt brows of the World Trade Center's twin towers . . . Because if you haven't, you may well be finding this propensity he has for speaking of himself in the third person rather . . . arch? The Butcher allows the towel to slip from his adorably slim hips – so his long slim cock springs up, head questing . . . *eye seeking*: But, really, you mustn't be annoyed . . . he strokes its silky shaft, its velvety tip . . . Squilly will explain, won't you, Squilly? Be a dear, Squilly darling, and . . . oblige? The Butcher's slightly rubbery features quiver in the New York night-light – he's one of those handsome yet nondescript men who can transform their appearance . . . *with the slightest grimace – or merest moue.* The only feature that cannot be annulled is the warning triangle of his isosceles nose: mornings, shaving, the Butcher pushes this *dorsal fin* to one side, relishing its cartilaginous *squeak* and steadily slices . . . *flesh out of foam – blood in the snow . . . Schafe können sicher weiden, yeah, right* . . . Squilly, by contrast, is a wary creature with hooded eyes, who speaks with a slight lisp, his words dragging themselves over his drooping bottom lip and past his nascent jowls. He's also just a little bit more *top drawer* than the Butcher – with a hint of clipped nindeteen-fifties diction clinking in his moist mouth. He says, I shall oblige, Butchie . . . then goes on . . . Well, the Butcher here is a confirmed illeitht –. Can't you ever say anything properly, the Butcher interrupts. It's illeist – illeist! Unperturbed, Squilly resumes: My extwemely close and vewy dear friend the Butcher, here . . . As I thay, he had a difficult childhood – some might say traumatic. There was neglect, certainly – abuse, too. His mother was an intruthive – not to say manipulative – prethence, while his father –. Okay, okay . . . the Butcher breaks in again, I think we're all perfectly aware of what went –. – While his father was a still more manipulative absence, nowhere to be seen while poor ickle Butchie was getting fiddled about with by the bad mens –. – All right, all right, Squilly! That's quite enough –! – My theory is it thorta fractured the poor little mite – thplit him in two –. – And that's what created you, Squilly, isn't it? – Yeth, that's what created me, Butch, I'm your thub-personality, born in the bathtub at Colindale Avenue on the thirteenth of June nineteen thixty-seven – d'you wemember, Butch? – Yes, yes, I remember . . . He remembers his mother, Maeve De'Ath, spread-arsed on the toilet wedged between sink and tub, *I remember* . . . the string of amber beads *spawning* on her stagnant bosom, *I remember* . . . the prominent mole on her prominent chin . . . *an inedible niblet* . . . Ooh! she cried, your willy's squirting! She lunged awkwardly forward to give the offending member a light slap . . . *almost a caress*. She did it again *annagain*, while sing-songing, Squirty-willy, squirty-willy, squirty . . . Steam curled, rubber ducks whirled – *Actaeon was torn!* and *Squilly was born!* How does it feel, Squilly . . . the Butcher oozes sarcasm . . . to've been conceived through the union of two such infantile words: squirt – and willy. Really, you're nothing but a baby-name for a little boy's penis. – Weally? Weally, Butch – weally? If I'm that, what're you, weally, if not a typical sex-obsessed man who likes nothing better than talking to his own perthonified prick! Come, come, Squilly, the Butcher says, still stroking the rapidly engorging . . . *matter in hand*. You better than anyone understand there's far, far more to it than that, don't you? – Oh, yes, I do, Butch – of course there ith. – 'Cause you were the one who first talent-spotted me, weren't you, Squills? You got to me long before that stuffed shirt, Doctor Opie, didn't you? – Yeth, I spotted your talent, Butch – and I was your first handler as well, helping you into your firtht thkin when you were knee-high to a coffee table. You remember it, Butch? – How can I ever forget it, Squillster . . . The Butcher shivers deliciously: his penis is fully erect now – a great curving prong, fully ten inches long, which quests for . . . *There's no ac-tion! Every time I phone you, I just wanna put you down!* The silent scream winds around the Butcher's head – *and Squilly's.* – I wecruited you, that's true – and I've handled you ever since. I'm handling you right at this moment, as it happens . . . He is: he's handling the Butcher, even as the Butcher is handling Squilly . . . but there's more to it than that, isn't there, Butchie-dearest? There is indeed a great deal more to it than that – for they contextualise each other, the Butcher and Squilly, filling in all the background details of whichever scene they happen to be . . . *acting out.* Narrative, too, they *doo-doo-doo* for each other, so propelling their partnership forward in a wobbly bubble of their own repartee: along strip-lit corridors, down dark roads and up narrow streets – into hidden doorways, up back stairs and into . . . *hell's darkest chamber.* – And all the while, one or the other of us keeps on *Boughing out* the commentary – there has to be a commentary, has to be a mannish boy in a sheepskin coat with a microphone . . . You're listening to him NOW! Don't sit there with your mouth hanging open like a fucking MONG! 'cause he might put that THING! in your ARSE! or your CUNT –! Arse for preference, though, Butch, Squilly says – and the Butcher momentarily stills, legs prettily parted, one shoulder back, beautiful face downcast. Oh, my Antinous! Squilly exclaims, grabbing for his cock – but the Butcher slaps his hand away. – That's not something we talk about! Besides, we don't want to die of fucking ignorance – now do we? To which Squilly throws back his head and laughs. – Look at us – dancing licentiously in the noddy, swirling round in a cesspool of our own making –. He breaks off: the Butcher's hands are at his throat – he can taste the Butcher's *dogged breath*. – Not now, Squills, that's not something we talk about at all openly, is it? That's p-perfectly c-cowwect, Butchie, Squilly stutters, and, relaxing his grip, the Butcher continues: We only talk of such things in our safe place, after we've thoroughly swept it. Our safe place, where we arrive separately, leave separately, and no one ever knows we've been . . . You've handled me for years now, Squilly, so you know this better than anyone . . . He falls silent, and the two stand looking at nothing through the same pair of empty eyes. Eventually, Squilly says, I turned you, Butch, didn't I? And the Butcher concedes: You did, Squills – you turned me because you're older and wiser. You understand the ways of the world – and, most importantly, how to keep those ways secured, for we are the wise shepherds and our job is to watch over them all so –. Schafe können thicher weiden, Squilly lisps – and the Butcher translates: So sheep may safely graze is about the size of it – that's why you turned me, Squilly. You turned me this way . . . He begins to execute his own version of a piqué turn . . . and you turned me the other way . . . he reverses his twirl . . . and now I don't know any more if I'm an agent or a double agent, or a triple one, or . . . the Butcher spins faster . . . *Baryshnikov – but ballsier!* He starts singing: You turned me right round, baby, right round . . . His penis audibly whirrs, *a rotor*, slicing the flock wallpaper and the Manhattan skyline *to shreds* . . . The Butcher sees *bollocky bags* full of dead bodies lifting off from a dull and dusty plaza – sees the PeeEllAy helicopters hover over the Western Hills – sees the *scrotums* slashed and the bodies ... *fall.* He slumps down on the bed, his head crammed full of writhing flesh, blinded by fear flashing from dying eyes, deafened by howls and the poppling of small-arms fire. Squilly says: C'mon, Butchie – you've gotta bweak a few eggs if you want to make a weally lovely omolette aux fines herbes, you know that ... But the Butcher says nothing, only sits massaging his synthetic features, his blue-black hair twined in his pianist's fingers. Squilly's having none of this: What is it we always thay, Butch, when we're feeling a bit queathy? Fuck off, Squilly, the Butcher grunts. Thay it! Squilly barks, Thay it with me, Butch – thay it! And then they chant in unison: The pro-fess-ion-al skill of esp-i-o-nage con-sists en-tire-ly in the ex-ploi-tat-ion of hu-man weak-ness ... And when this is done the Butcher finds himself standing by the wardrobe wearing clean white *Calvin Kleins* — which was how he'd introduced himself to the greedy little woman in the big ranch house ... *out of South Fork via Chester* earlier that day. When she'd the temerity to laugh, the Butcher encouraged her hilarity by retrieving from his pocket the folded page he'd torn from a magazine, unfolding and holding it up so she could see Mark Wahlberg, naked except for his Calvin Kleins ... *hand on his squilly.* Ha, ha, ha, she'd chortled, don't be ridiculous, that's not eyedee. When the Butcher next spoke they'd been in the oppressively fitted kitchen and the dodgy strap was in his hand. How d'you know anyone is who they say they are? he'd remarked conversationally, Because they've got a photograph with a name written underneath it? He sighed heavily: C'mon ... logically speaking, there's no reason why the name should designate the photograph –

let alone the person the photograph's of . . . This critique of the lazy inferences afforded by sight had been lost on the greedy little woman, since by then she was slumped down between the dishwasher and the deepfreeze, altogether disconsolate since her tell had been . . . *so fucking simple.* After he'd flashed the strap and begun backing her down the hallway, he'd heard a radio playing in an upstairs room: JayWhy, programatically sucking *ministerial cock.* The woman was an uneasy listener – her eyes roving hither then thither. So they'd detoured to recover a large bundle of dollar bills wrapped in clear plastic and duct tape from the dirty-clothes hamper in the airing cupboard, and a much larger one of Swiss dinars . . . *scimitar-wielding horsemen riding through a calligraphic cloud . . .* from a hatbox in a walk-in wardrobe. Both packages were lying on the breakfast bar . . . *What's the recipe today, Jim?* when the Butcher said his piece: Here's the thing about people like you – stupid greedy people like you. Y'see, you can't help thinking you matter, and that the world is there for you to exploit as you see fit. Of course, even a stupid greedy person like you understands in her heart of hearts that she doesn't and it isn't – but it's damnably hard to maintain objectivity, isn't it? We-ell, you relax, pet, while I tell you how things're going to be from here on in . . . – But the greedy little woman couldn't relax – she rocked back and forth on her *fat arse*, she pulled up the leg of her naff slacks to scratch at the blubber barely contained by her . . . *pop socks!* The Butcher had almost relented – told her the revolver was nothing of the sort, its chambers quite unable to spin *round, round, baby, right round . . .* He'd almost relented – but didn't, because he's the Butcher, and no

self-respecting butcher ever undertakes a job *without his chopper*...
Outside, it'd been an early-summer afternoon in well-to-do outer-suburban England – the ranch house was set back from the road and there were no eyes on. He'd opened the door of the double garage to find a crappy old Austin Metro ... *the little lady's run-about*, and a brand-new metallic-black Three Series Beamer ... *his work car when he's not abroad*. Well, well, well ... the Butcher thought ... they are doing ... well. His own work car was parked half a mile away on a busy thoroughfare – it was a bog-standard rental hatchback he'd rendered still more inconspicuous by suckering a stuffed Garfield-the-Cat to the offside rear window. He'd driven it back to the airport, and in the car park – butcher that he is – gutted Garfield, removing a small veeaitcheff transceiver and replacing it with the wads of currency. As he'd done so, he'd *run the plays*... What would happen to the stupid greedy woman – and Fechner, the marginally more clever operator who'd set up the front companies to buy the precursors, organised the supply lines and done much of the laundering? The stupid greedy woman was undoubtedly *too stupid* to work out who the Butcher was working for – let alone whether his employers had authorised his house call. By the time he'd left she'd been whimpering, pleading for mercy: it was ... *most unsavoury* – especially when she'd grabbed his free hand and pressed it against her *sad sack*. She might, the Butcher hypothesises, kill herself – or Fechner's partners in the enterprise, a nasty bunch out of Skopje, could well oblige once they found out about her *sloppy accounting*... It was possible Fechner hadn't simply been using her, but had some sort of emotional investment – in

which case there's a possibility they'll make a run for it. The Butcher pictures the odd couple, gone to ground in a guesthouse in a far-flung market town . . . *China Pekes on the fire surround – Will you be wanting tea in the morning?* Any which way you sliced it, there was a zero-probability of any blow-back – so, as he'd stood there in the kitchen, wearily regarding a poster of a demi-nude hunk cradling a naked baby in his denim lap, he'd shown her some snaps of his own: tiny whey-faced bundles dumped at the foot of a mud-brick wall, somewhere in a patch of *ochreous nowhere*, while he let Squilly do the talking, because there's something about Squilly's *bweathy lithp* that really *puts the wind up 'em* . . . The Squillster had gently pointed out that her greed had contributed, in part, to the deaths of an estimated three thousand children. She didn't know . . . ? Hadn't realised? Oh, dearwie, dearwie me, Squilly had said, waggling his slack old thespian's face, I do tho hate to be the bearwer of bad tidings . . . Fortunately, he was able to suggest something she could do by way of expiation . . . Taking the woman by her crimped and greying-out-at-the-roots scruff . . . *orf we jolly-well went*: the Butcher led her about the ranch house, pointing out its suicidal features: the big pot of jellies in the bathroom . . . *I knew would be there*, and regarding which he gave her clear instructions about . . . *exceeding the stated dose.* Back downstairs, he'd jerked her along to Fechner's gun cabinet – which he'd already located . . . *in the obvious place.* Hunched up in the utility cupboard, to the accompaniment of a ticking meter, the Butcher had expertly cracked its combination lock . . . *doddle for a man who can do a Number Four Manifoil in seconds*, before giving the stupid greedy woman a brief lesson on

cocking, loading and firing an over-under shotgun. The Butcher
had let Squilly divulge the most important bit of know-how: Tuck
the muthle here, in the hollow of your thwoat – you've vewy
short arms, so it'll be awkward getting the barrels in your mouth.
Don't on any account put 'em here . . . The Butcher had nuzzled
the smooth, blue-grey snout against his own fashionably stubbly
one . . . or here . . . he shifted it to his forehead . . . because the
wecoil will dislodge it, and you'll end up paralysed, pithing yourself
in adult-fucking-pull-up-panth . . . The stupid greedy woman was
rather upset by the time they'd finished with her. As he'd taken
his leave, the Butcher drily observed: It's the Roman way out –
you shouldn't feel too bad. After all – all any of us ever have
are moments, and we lose an infinity of them every second. Think
of your entire life as simply another moment – and appreciate whatever beauty it may've possessed was purely a function of its . . .
ephemerality. Reflect on how boring a film, a fuck or a conversation
can be if it goes on . . . *too bloody long!* Wise words, he'd thought –
comforting in their way, although she'd shown no sign of being
soothed: her lips stretching . . . and stretching . . . until her warped
mouth resembled *an infinity symbol* — In the cab back from the
airport car hire, bumbling through worn-out Wythenshawe, dowdy
Didsbury, and all the rest of Manchester's pebbledashed sprawl, the
Butcher had a petite crise, but Squilly took him in hand: Now, now,
Butchie – ever since you were an ickle-lickle boy, you've understood
you mutht operwate at two levelth: the perthonal and the political,
and when they conflict you mutht always opt for? The political, the
Butcher had conceded. – Quite so: you mutht always choothe the

political, which I know is painful for you, Butchie – no one likes to deceive their nearetht and dearetht. At this the Butcher had spat back: Unless they're a fucking psychopath! And Squilly had soothed on: Well, we both know you aren't one of those, Butch – you're a tholdier, and perfectly dethent soldiers feel utterly bloody about killing, even in wartime. But I don't kill, Squilly, the Butcher had protested. I've never killed anyone, only let them . . . ah, die . . . What the Butcher hadn't aired was his long-nurtured ambition – not to be a murderer, but at least to feel what it's like. In the Butcher's view, murdering always got rather too bad a press – which was only morality's marketing department *working overtime.* Murderers were always portrayed – in books, in films, on television – as either insensible psychos or conscience-stricken – thrust out into a lonely, outer-darkness by their dreadful crime. But what if the opposite was the case? What if by taking a human life you stepped from the shadows into the bright light at last – felt the rush as it suffused you, and you realised you'd finally become *who you were truly meant to be?* Nearing the city's dark heart, caroming past the blackened shells of old warehouses and mills, the Butcher hadn't seen the pustulant back of the cabbie's neck – but his father's face, its expression as usual *soft and conciliatory* . . . And now, in the windowless room in the dark heart of the Britannia Hotel, the Butcher recalls the myriad vengeances he used to plan for Kins during the white-hot years of his own adolescence: the bombings, stabbings, poisonings, garottings and dismemberments. The carving-up, then cooking-down, in an *acid bath* . . . he'd plotted to the last detail, before he began to cool – becoming conciliatory, content not to terminate Kins, but simply to *let him die* . . . Not that Peter De'Ath showed any sign of expiring: pushing seventy, retired, effectively neutered, he lodged in his cubbyhole of a study, in the bungalow on the outskirts of Hemel, scratching away at yet another book on the theory and practical organisation of local government funding that no one – *repeat: fucking no one* – would ever read. But then that was Kins all over – his weakness was mental quite as much as moral: he could concentrate only on one thing at a time. Whereas his eldest son, with his *Cheops* of a nose – inherited from earlier *dynasties of De'Aths* – had been able, for as long as he could recall, to *do at least three*. The Butcher had only to look at a page of text for its content to be *ever accessible* – only to run his limpid eye down a column of figures for them all to be *known to me*. If the Butcher overheard a conversation, he was able to repeat it, verbatim, whether hours or months later. Moreover, these mental feats didn't so much as perturb the smooth flow of his physical actions – the Butcher could time a soft-boiled egg to perfection, while reading a newspaper editorial and . . . *taking notes*. He knew he was different – and he liked it. But he saw what happened to children deemed different – and that he didn't like. Kins, whose own father had been something of a savant, had been gently reproachful: I dunno know why you don't do something with these exceptional abilities of yours, Johnny. Sirbert was able to bootstrap his way from dish-washing to running the Woolwich Arsenal in a few short years, and went on to have a brilliant career in the civil service simply because he was able to *marshal the facts*. Which is presumably what Kins thinks he's doing as he scratches away. He is, the Butcher thinks, a pathetic sort of hobbyist – a trainspotter, or possibly a model-railways enthusiast – for whom the truth . . . *is always timely*. Standing before the strip of mirror screwed to the inside of the wardrobe door, the Butcher cultivates his contempt: Kins may be a ridiculous epigone – and a piffling lefty to boot, full of the same useless spume as *the Welsh windbag*, but, while Squilly recruited the Butcher . . . *it's Kins who taught me my tradecraft*. The Butcher pulls on charcoal-grey trousers and worms his way into a tight T-shirt bearing a single black, blocky word: RELAX. Quite possibly a little recherché, but then *these are the provinces* . . . Next comes a mid-blue shirt that someone . . . *me, actually* has beautifully pressed. He buttons this to the neck, hiding the T-shirt's collar. Next comes a reversible jacket the Butcher had his tailor . . . *run up for me*. There've been bonuses – certain little perks – along the way: Pira drug money chanced upon in Gib' . . . *of all places*, a Czech would-be defector's Meissen bribe – and, most providentially, an old postwar câche dug up in the woodlands beside the Neusiedlersee that, besides containing some rather antediluvian weaponry, also furnished him with krugerrands, which, *once the service wash had been paid for*, realised over twenty thousand . . . *They'd all do it, if they'd the balls* – if they had the balls, and if *they had to*. But the Butcher's colleagues are God-blessed children: *they've got their own* . . . Daddy and Mummy having put them down for Eton at birth – Daddy having taken them along for their first fitting aged fourteen, so, by the time such stock phrases were required of them, the *toffee-nosed tossers* were well able to casually *toss off*: D'you like it? I had it run up for me by my tailor in Savile Row . . . But then, so far as the Butcher's concerned, all of his fellow intake are cocktail-party fodder – softly powerful pen-pushers, who, if they got their hands dirty running an agent . . . *went crying all the way home to VeeBeeArr.* Whereas the Butcher knows only too well what it's like to live your entire life . . . *in the target country,* to all intents and purposes just another worker bee, when in reality you're *an agent of deep penetration.* These words, *deep penetration,* remain bright in the Butcher's greige mind as he fetches plain black leather shoes from the wardrobe and plain black socks from the Gladstone bag. Sheathing his feet, he feels his cock stir in his jockeys . . . *deep penetration.* He stands, does a little jig – gives voice: Was mir behagt, Ist nur die muntre Jagd! For Manchester, on a warm Friday night in June, is surely a perfect hunting ground – a lush pasture where, disoriented by alcohol and maddened by lust, no *Schafe* whatsoever may *sicher weiden.* From the chest-of-drawers the Butcher retrieves an American soft pack of Marlboro, a fliptop box of Mates condoms, a brand-new Nokia One-Oh-Eleven mobile phone and a small tube of lube. He hefts the phone lightly – it's strictly for non-professional use: the Firm's dragging its feet when it comes to equipping its employees with encrypted cellular phones, although at Vauxhall – almost as much as at Langley – briefings are becoming increasingly visual – so much for the meticulous report-drafting skills new EyeBees received instruction in. In their nouveau-postmodern ziggurat of a home, seeseeteevee and satellite footage are relayed to the officers' desktop computers, where they're displayed alongside plans and diagrams. The Butcher wonders if he alone can see the invisible digital threads binding together these shining screens ... *the jade armour of a new underground army*, and, as he sends his short-burst veeaitcheff transmissions, or uploads SeeEx from his encrypted laptop to the burgeoning Service intranet ... *I follow the data*: I go with it, Squilly (Weally, Butch – quo vadis, pwecisely?), I go into some weird origami realm, Squills, where face and form fold into psyche and self – where consciousness spreads out, then's cut on the bias into strips of impossibility which're also the form-fitting perturbations we call electromagnetic waves – it's these that enfold me in their diaphanousness, Squilly: the very bella figura of the future! With his reversible jacket and interchangeable shirts, the Butcher is ready and able to for the chase. First, however, a stirrup cup must be drunk. Into the dim and dust-furred recesses of the big old hotel pop is being ... *inappropriately piped*, and it's to the accompaniment of EmmSee Hammer's latest that the Butcher descends the wide staircase. Gold paint is oh-so-slowly flaking from the mouldings high overhead – but he sashays to the right, to the left: so Croesus's dandruff can't ... *touch this!* The large lobby area wells up: a purple-brown lagoon of carpet and flock wallpaper, ill-lit by huge fake chandeliers *prob'ly left over from some seventies refurb'* ... In the reception area late arrivals are checking in, while in the bar a few desultory adulterers sit sipping duff cocktails and *diddling with the dry-roasteds*. As the Butcher descends further a group of young men comes into view – they're slumped in mismatched rattan easy chairs they've dragged around a table in the very furthest corner of the bar, beneath a large and artificial palm. It's all part, the Butcher realises as he goes still lower, of the hotel's feeble stab at a raffish,

Raffles makeover. At the bar he orders a dry vodka martini, impressing the correct proportions on the barman: One part of vermouth to six of the hard stuff, please . . . I s'pose, the *old trouper* says, shooting his grubby cuffs, you'll be wanting that shaken, not stirred? And the Butcher, taking a chilly gulp, shivers back: How'd you know I've got a licence to swill? Then, drink paid for and Marlboro lit with a flick of his rolled-gold Dupont, he begins his approach – stalking from the cover of one porphyry column to the next, until he *gets alongside* and receives enough *audible take* to establish that they're . . . *junior officers!* They have to be – what with their brutal barnets, freshly aired faces and frumpish civvies – heavily creased from having been stuffed at the bottom of their bergens for the entire . . . *training weekend.* The Butcher knows the drill full well: wrenched shivering from your fartsack at dark o'clock . . . Hot locks from the field kitchen: congealed eggy-mess, bootlace bacon, orangey baked-beanishness – all of it wolfed down in the star-studded pre-dawn. Then up into the hills for a long day's yomping, fantasising they're Colonel H taking out an Argie machine-gun nest. Survival kit in a matchbox – flint and tinder, bracken-boiled brews and burst blisters – then capture by other dumb mummers blacked-up with boot polish. Held in a sheep pen – taken away one by one and subjected to – A t'riffic beasting . . . chimes in one of the young men, hunching forward excitedly in his creaky chair . . . I mean, I only gave 'em the big three, but they were fucking agg', weren't they, Tizer? D'you think they coulda been green slime? The Butcher, who's established his listening post at a table ten feet away, is able to analyse the group's pecking order from this nig's manner alone: his self-conscious use of military slang – his adoring eyes, it all leads to one conclusion: *Tizer's the top-dog here*. He's probably as pedigree as the others, this Tizer – although he has the tight brown curls and block-head of a British bulldog, with huge raw-red paws to match. He sits in judgement, does Tizer, a lurid rugby shirt, quartered yellow-and-pink . . . *Battenberg ArrEffSee*, stretched over his huge frame. He *sips in judgement*, does Tizer – tilting his face back so it shines in the bar's winelight. And he smokes in judgement as well: sucking on a roll-up at length, then pooting this out: Dunno about that, Anderson, prob'ly just some staff twats who fancied themselves and did it for the sheer fucking badness . . . Anderson collapses back into his chair, *crushed*. Poor little fucker, the Butcher thinks – such a runt he doesn't even have a nickname. Tizer rises . . . *Christ! He's a big bastard*, his bottom half clad in the *virulence* of stonewashed jeans. He waves his half-full pint about, declaiming, Lads, lads . . . it's gone twenty-hundred and none of us are remotely pissed yet – minibus heads back to aitchqueue at oh-eight-hundred, which only gives us twelve hours to get COMPLETELY FUCKING MULLERED! Tizer's words wing up to the gilding, and the Butcher thinks: If he didn't have a posh accent he'd be out on his chou-fleur ear . . . Thinks this, although the majority of his attention belongs to Squilly, who's delivering his first contact report: They've been on exerthise in the Beacons – now they're on the razzle in Manchester – there's a minibus heading back to their wegiment . . . Only outfit that fits is England's Knights of the North –. So, the Butcher interrupts, they're Yorkshire Hussars, then . . . ? Pwecisely,

Butchie-dear, Yorkshire Hussars, who're currently stationed at Catterick – although they prob'ly wish they were in Mogadishu taking out Aidid. That's a job for the friends and their helicopter gunships, says the Butcher drily, not this bunch who're wet behind their lugholes. But this is what he says aloud: Allow me, lads – lagers all round, issit? The muzak mysteriously mutes – five pairs of eyes swivel towards the Butcher and *lock on*. He laughs: Okay, okay . . . don't worry, I'm not trying to muscle in – I'm just a weekend warrior, a gung-ho stab who'd like the honour of buying the real McCoy a wet . . . In order to avoid any awkward questions later, should his tactics work, the Butcher sprinkles his words with *söme öpen Nörthern vöwels* – he's still left *in the stress position* while the five pairs of eyes . . . *pat me down for Semtex*. At last Tizer speaks: How the fuck d'you know who we are? Well . . . the Butcher is placatory . . . you did mention your aitchqueue – but lissen, I get what you're driving at: you gotta be careful, what with the fuckin' Paddies on the warpath again . . . The air whistles from Tizer's inflated chest as he says, Glad you appreciate the sitch, mate – we're under strict orders to keep mum and go quietly since the Warrington ones . . . Can't even wear a blazer or tie –. Careless talk costs lives, the Butcher puts in. So, what about it, lagers? Or lager-tops for the girlies? Or does you does or does you don't you desire a pint of proper fucking Northern heavy? Half a pint later the Butcher has his *plates of* under their table, and is wondering if there's . . . *any meat for dinner.* Neither top-dog Tizer nor runtish Anderson is in the last bit appetising. There's Shabba, so-called because he's come up through the ranks *ha-ha* . . . and Potso, who's *over-bitingly* posh – then there's the other one, Greeny: a blond six-footer with a medium build who gives as good as he gets – although, when the banter dries up, the Butcher catches a glimpse of the young cavalry officer's true nature: shy and defensive . . . *he's something to hide – quite possibly, the thing.* So . . . Mike – it's Mike, is it? Yeah, well . . . Mike, y'know the score, do you? Tizer asks the Butcher, who's given them the first name that occurred to him . . . By which I mean not just where does a man go in this town to get a skinful, but where does he go to be in with a chance of getting his leg over! The Butcher, who's skulled his martini and switched to lager . . . *one of the boys, that's me,* is thrown for a moment – thrown into *the flesh pit* of the Eagle's back room, where the high-energy pumps and the leather-clad bodies *writhe* . . . He sees faces slick with secretions – mouths howling out demonic lust as the dancers struggle to stay afloat in the *great moaning ocean of the un-fucked* . . . Well, he says, for starters you wanna give the club in the basement here a miss – we're talking terminally dull middle managers and their secretarial squeezes out for a hop and few glasses of cheap fizz. (*LAUGHTER*) Ditto the Haçienda – whatever you may've heard about Manc' raver chicks off their tits on ecstasy, truth is, they may be all touchy-feely on the dance floor, but head back to their place and you're in for a long night grinding your teeth while she yaps on about the meaning of fucking life . . . (*MORE LAUGHTER*) Nah, best bet is, have a couple more bevvies here, then round the corner to Twenty-One Piccadilly – check out the cattle market, hear the Manc' moo, but keep yer heads down, lads – it can kick off. So, if there's no action there you're best off making a tactical withdrawal to the Circus Tavern, which is by way of being a perfect stag, since it's the smallest pub in the entire fucking world! (*UNBRIDLED HILARITY*) You can plan your next move there, but, I've gotta say, Tizer, your gear ain't exactly in order for this sorta op'. You what? Tizer grunts. Manc' birds . . . the Butcher explains . . . well, they like a well-turned-out bloke. You lads'd score in seconds if you had your number ones on – split-seconds if you were in dress. What's yer badge by the way? The young cavalry officers look oddly at the Butcher, who wonders if he's overdone his little act – though it's always easier to stay in character if *you're a bit of a character*. Then the blond called Greeny pipes up: Sorta sheep thing . . . big sheep thing – sorta ram rampant . . . (Ooh! Squilly flutes, The pathos of the tiny old acne scars pitting hith downy cheekth!) Here they are, Squilly, the Butcher says: here are the young men. (Oh, yes, Butchie-dearest, but there can't be much weight on their shoulders – not with thuch empty heads!) . . . Anyway, Greeny persists, what about later on? And the Butcher, noting the furrowing of his forehead, thinks: Not your scene at all, now is it, boyo – because it takes an imposter to spot *a heterosexual-impersonator* . . . but he only says: Legends is good enough for a stomp, but don't get too sweaty 'cause then it's on to the New Conti, where you brave warriors will hit gash-fucking-gold: nurses, social workers, speech-fucking-therapists – wall-to-wall bleeding hearts, any one of 'em ready and willing to offer up their rarebits for a bit of pork scratching! (*LAUGHTER, APPLAUSE, CRIES OF ENCORE!*) For real? Greeny asks, putting down his pint on a coaster he's carefully aligned with the ashtray. Cautious . . . a little obsessive . . . the

Butcher thinks . . . but doesn't understand himself. One of those slightly plodding types who'll practise and practise 'til they can do it so competently they don't know they're doing it at all . . . The flock walls of the Britannia's cavernous bar recede, leaving the Butcher with his sweaty back against a slab of corrugated iron, watching two boy soldiers who sit opposite one another on the dusty ground, disassembling their AyKays, reassembling them, snapping the firing pins, slotting in the magazines, aiming, firing . . . *small arms for the fucking eighties, eh* . . . Yeah, for real, the Butcher replies: For real – for unreal, for all that's fucking righteous and pure. They'll lead you by the todger, gentlemen, and screw you 'til you cry out for your Home Counties mummies . . . You'll be coming, will you? asks Greeny, and the Butcher's melting heart *runneth over – ah, diddums!* For it's awfully hard to picture this well-scrubbed and freshly shaven young man knocking on the door of hell's darkest chamber and requesting admission – not with that provincial middle-class accent. The Butcher has a question of his own: Um, Greeny – what's that about, mate? And the junior officer blushes – *Blushes! Oh, my heart will burst! Pyrois, Aeos, Aethon and Phlegon gallop across the fiery skies! He's the One, Squilly – the One!* Bit naff, Greeny says – the nickname and the real one. Then he sticks out his hand: Gawain, he says, Gawain Thomas. The Butcher takes it, and, noting the others are distracted by Lineker and goal difference, queries, As in Gawain and the Green Knight? But doesn't let go until the other . . . *loosens his grip* and, blushing still more furiously, says, Pardon? I mean – is that it, the poem, I mean? I mean, I've never actually read it – should, I s'pose . . . Well, the Butcher counters, you should certainly read enough of it to put this lot right – the Green Knight's the chap in the other corner . . . While to Squilly he exults, Pardon! Pardon! (Yes, yes – the very signature note of English good manners, useful in such commonplace phrases as, Pardon me while I put my cock in your arse.) The blond peers at him from under puckered brows, *but I don't think I've been blown* . . . and repeats, You'll be coming with us, will you? The Butcher chuckles, holding up his ring finger . . . *Brr-Brr-Bravingtons nineteen ninety-nine*: No can do, mate – if I'm not indoors by nine the ball'll start yanking on the chain. He pulls out the Nokia and shows it to the junior officers: Made the mistake of getting one of these – now she can reach me anywhere. It's the shape of things to come, lads – privacy'll be a thing of the past . . . Over by the revolving doors they say their adieux. Tizer, Shabba and the slunk they call Potso have all been back up to their rooms, and are now sporting blue blazers with regimental crests on their top pockets . . . *Poontang trumps Pira every time.* You'll be all right in the pubs and bars I've mentioned, lads, admonishes the Butcher. But if you want my advice don't go off-piste – on a Friday night there'll be loads of squaddies out and about. You know the drill: once they're mullered they can't recognise an officer – least, that's what they'll claim when they're up on a charge for beating the shit out of you . . . There are manly handshakes all round – and "Mike" is gone . . . *dematerialised – else-where: me jus'a flash it roun' the worldie* . . . They go right – he goes left, the *bummadum* beat from the Britannia's duff disco vibrating through him as he gains the corner, turns it, slips out of his jacket, turns denim inside out of worsted, puts it back on again, unbuttons his shirt, takes out a small tin of Vaseline, combs the short hairs above his perfect ears, replaces it, gets out a Marlboro, lights it and stalks on, his mane shining . . . *born free, and life is worth living!* as he prowls into the gay village. Where he sees *slappers* with grazed legs and sore mouths stumbling around the bus station, scallies in shell suits *crackin' on* and ruffled little chickens, weepy-eyed from the exhaust fumes and *waiting to be plucked* . . . Not that the Butcher's going to do the plucking: *I'm not a fucking game dealer.* A dosser limps towards him, tucked under one arm the Big Issues he's mostly nicked from some other seller. Big Issue, mate? The Butcher stops, takes in torn and stained shirt, shat-upon trainers and a water rat's drowned face. Big Issue, mate, he pipes up again – *Pipe down!* Kins would eventually shout when the Butcher and his brothers grew too rambunctious. – D'you remember that, Squills? (I do, Butch, of course . . .) and to the dosser the Butcher says, The really big issue is whether or not you can score – can you? The dosser's eyes frisk the Butcher, patting down his reversible jacket, pulling out his wallet . . . *checking to see if there's a warrant card.* What's yer game, mate? the dosser wheedles, I mean, 'ow do I know you ain't some jarg cunt? (Most perspicacious of him, Squilly purrs, given you're probably the jargest cunt he's ever clapped his piggy little Scouser eyes on . . .) But the Butcher simply says: I'm gagging for some brown, mate – rocks as well. I've got the readies . . . he pats his breast pocket . . . I'll see you right for a bag. Which, to the casual listener, might not be the most obvious incentive, since the dosser already has a sleeping one draped round his scrawny neck. — They walk south on Oxford Road, the dosser moseying ahead, tripping into and out of the gutter to avoid the students milling outside the pubs and clubs. The Butcher is in his element: perfectly attuned to the city and its febrile inhabitants. He lights another Marlboro and breathes out: a centuries-long exhalation, laden with coal-smoke and cotton fibres, which wheezes through the rusted ribs of derelict warehouses and the perished brickwork of old viaducts. *The chase is on!* and *der Freischütz* feels not only *dry-cleaned* but positively *sand-blasted*. Who am I, Squilly? he asks, and Squilly obliges (You're your father's son, of course). They stump under the ring road and emerge into . . . *a different limbo*: the paler brick and beiger concrete banalities of the University area, the Butcher seeing not the junky Virgil tripping along before him, but Kins – Kins sitting on the lavatory at Colindale Avenue, grey flannel trousers and bilious underpants down round his lumpy legs. Kins, with an Ordnance Survey map crumpled in his lap – a relief landscape he pores over through horn-rimmed reading glasses: *the Fat Owl of the Remove, who was yet so very . . . elusive*. If the Butcher is his father's son, then Kins – or Peterkins, or Peter De'Ath, or *whatever cover name he operates under* – had also to've been playing the double-game. The preternaturally gifted Butcher realised this when he was very young – he carefully logged his father's absences, then analysed their pattern. He found evidence in the seat wells and glove compartments of Kins's Rover – the strange *Lifesaver* of a rolled stocking, alien hair grips, a copy of the Bunty he'd leafed through with great absorption, eager to discover what became of . . . *the Spectrum Girls*. He sniffed the perfume that clung to his father's tweed jackets, together with the faecal aroma of stale cigarette smoke and old *whiskybreath*. It was his mother's complicity with his father's subterfuges that'd struck the Butcher most of all – her complacent sigh, each time he announced he was *running over to Hemel to pick up one or two . . . things*, when she knew – *we all did* – he was going somewhere else entirely: a dead-letter drop, from which he always returned *empty-handed*. Had Kins been running Maeve or was she running him? The precocious Butcher understood unhappy marriage from infancy – it was not a sector in which intelligence can be gathered. Rather, the distorted intimacy of a divided couple is typified, he'd realised, *by counter-intelligence*: both parties knew those closest to them had been *turned*, yet they continued to run each other, on the basis that, were they to stop pretending to be a good and faithful spouse, the opposition would *roll up the entire network . . .* – Then there'd been the momentous and windy day when Kins had at last taken the Butcher with him on a mission. The Baker and the Candlestick-maker must have stayed at home in Saint Albans with Maeve – at any rate, the Butcher remembers there being plenty of room in the Rover for the woman and her two children: the girl the Bunty must've belonged to, who was the same age as him, with wild brown curls and wicked black eyes, and a littler boy of six or seven, who'd sat solemnly between them on the back seat, one hand squeezed down the front of his tight shorts . . . *hanging on to his Squilly*. Kins introduced the woman as *a colleague of mine who's doing some very interesting work with handicapped and disruptive children*. She didn't look like other colleagues of his the Butcher had encountered, who seemed *half dead*. The woman – who, *true to type* – had dyed-blonde hair and exaggerated makeup, was twice as alive as anyone the Butcher had ever encountered before: as Kins drove through the outskirts of Hemel, she'd chatted away non-stop, deploying a choice vocabulary of fucks, bollocks, wankers and even a . . . *cunt!* She'd seemed quite as disruptive as any juvenile delinquent – but Kins hadn't urged her to . . . *pipe down!* When they'd arrived at the comp' – a collection of one-storey concrete-and-glass hutches – Kins canted awkwardly around and lectured the children from the pulpit of the front seat: This is the very first unit for handicapped children to be opened as an integral part of a new comprehensive school – we should be very grateful for what Missus *Whoever* has done, she's a remarkable educationalist and *a real battler for change* . . . A real battler indeed, Squilly! the Butcher carps as their odd trio marches across the dual carriageway and on into the Hulme *war zone.* And remarkable, if only for her ability to keep my father stuck in her honey trap for so many years. The gala opening for the new special unit remains *enzoed* on the toughened glass of the Butcher's painfully clear mind, even after all these years: the wind kazooing through the struts and bars of the playground equipment – the girl with the black eyes taunting the Butcher, then running away. He'd pursued her. Peter and Maeve De'Ath were drinkers, certainly – and the sort of Francophiles who thought it the dernier cri in sophistication to serve their sons watered-down wine – but this was the first time the Butcher had been truly, madly . . . *deeply* pissed. The girl-with-the-curls had nicked a little bottle of gin from the table where the tombola prizes were arranged – Quality Streets, a tin of car polish, Crabbie's Ginger Wine – and led the Butcher by his *beautiful, aquiline* nose into the dank and dripping lavatories, where she tried to get him to touch her between her pasty-white thighs. When he wouldn't, she'd made a grab for . . . *Squilly*. After that the Butcher did as he was told, knocking back gulp after gulp of the gin. until he lapsed into a sense-manging swoon: *I could taste her maniacal giggling* . . . He'd followed her back out into the windy afternoon – the grown-ups were all gathered by the chainlink fence on the far side of the playing field. The goal nets, the grass, the banner announcing the grand opening, the women's ugly smock dresses, the woolly clouds stampeding overhead – all of it had rippled . . . *seethed*. The naughty girl had egged him on – *I smelt hot egginess* . . . The witch's hat roundabout squealed and clanked – the rocking horse *neighed and curvetted* . . . The Butcher put one hand on the cold climbing frame . . . *and smelt old dried blood*. Next, he'd been standing at the very top, crêpe soles planted on the highest parallel bars – and the girl was beside him, her Medusa curls uncoiling to *hiss* in the wind. She'd smiled at him – and at last the Butcher had wanted to touch her, touch specifically . . . *her bum, and her shrinking-little-violet arsehole*. Then they'd both opened their bitterberry lips and the scream that's forever screaming – the silent scream of entropy itself – streamed out from them. Then they were tumbling down through the climbing frame: Bong! Bong! Bong! For Jonathan De'Ath, aged ten, this news bulletin had been all about control: getting it, maintaining it, losing and regaining it. When he'd clambered back up into consciousness, the Butcher was laid out on a white trolley in a white-curtained booth, and Kins had been sitting beside him, holding his hand, his usually burgundy face . . . *drained* –

white. Only much later, when he'd fully recovered, had the Butcher grasped what must've happened: Squilly, who was made of rather sterner stuff, must've woken first. – You gave him what-for, didn't you, Squills . . . (I told him a few, ah, home truths concerning his extra-marital activities, that's true enough . . .) Wo ein guter Hirte wacht, Squilly (Schafe können sicher weiden, Butch . . .) At home, in Saint Albans, in the semi in the very crook of Colindale Avenue, the Butcher's younger brothers – the Baker and the Candlestick-maker – did just that: safely grazing their entire childhoods away to the electric piano's bossa nova beat. But the Butcher, while he may've joined in with the orienteering, thwocked tennis balls on clay courts and sealed valentines *with a loving kiss*, had already fed on more piquant fare: the ambrosia of . . . *betrayal*. He surveilled his father with great care, aware of Kins's tradecraft, but still unsure of his motivation . . . *who is he, my father?* On the rare occasions the De'Aths went into London to visit the children's grandfather in Blackheath, the Butcher saw another side to Kins. With his own overbearing father, the ruminant plate-glass lecturer nonetheless *gave as good as he got*. But old Sir Albert – known familially, although not affectionately, as Sirbert – brooked no opposition: he beat on his sheepily synthetic son with a big analytic stick of facts, facts and still more statistics. They'd argued about everything, Sirbert and Kins – sitting at either end of the oval mahogany dining table, beneath ovals of oil paint, out of which swam the oval faces of the De'Ath Family's grand-maternal line, who'd been the sort of mild-mannered minor prelates with modest rural livings whom Kins revered: The cleresy is what old Trollope called them, he'd say – before always adding: Y'know, I rather think I'd've been perfectly happy living a hundred years ago – a country vicar, with a quiet parish. Whereupon Sirbert would snap: You're deluding yourself, my boy – what about the Origin of Species, or the Black Hole of Calcutta for that matter? No, there's never been an era when even the most devout are entirely without doubts or other conflicts of conscience. To the Butcher, in his perspicacious early teens, this seeming abstraction had been just that, for lying beneath their superficial badinage he detected the presence of a far more solid rancour *heavier than Missus Haines's chocolate cake.* Understood this, although he struggled to calculate the peculiar parabola of his grandfather's . . . *precipitate rise.* Sirbert, who sat in his wing chair, in his imposing heath-top house, surrounded by all the stuff he'd acquired during his lifetime – hobbyists' gadgets and ministerial gifts, heavy old furniture and silver-framed photographs showing foreign delegates warily clasping his massive hand. Sirbert, perfectly bald in speech as well as tonsure . . . *no politesse,* whose many degree certificates – awarded extramurally by the University of London – papered the walls, had been an autodidact before he was an autocrat: a beneficiary of the Northcote–Trevelyan principles, whose ever-so-'umble origins in a Fulham slum had been left far behind by nineteen sixteen, when he found himself in charge of the Woolwich Arsenal's shell production, and, if you added collateral damage and friendly-fire incidents into the account . . . *the true victor on the first day of the Somme.* By the time the second war screamed into view on swept-back wings, Sirbert had become Beaverbrook's permanent undersecretary and responsible for the island-fortress's production of . . . *finest fighter-aircraft.* In the fifties, up until his retirement, the Butcher's grandfather headed up the Electricity Board – head being . . . *the operative word.* As a child he'd pictured the humming and crackling high-tension cables of the National Grid radiating from Sirbert's *condenser,* the shiny dome upon which the old man often arranged several pairs of spectacles with different lenses, the necessary corrective – or, so he assured the Butcher, for the strabismus . . . *we both share.* Yes, the Butcher thinks as he follows the dosser on into the Mancunian night, Sirbert and I are the same: deprived of binocular vision, we're unable to perceive depth intuitively, and so are condemned to . . . *gather as much data as we can.* On the plus side, both grandfather and grandson had forever this *beautiful aquiline nose* before them – and if you can always see your nose, there's very little possibility of your *being led by it.* — There are grafitti tags sprayed across buckled garage doors and splintering benches – they turn a corner and start down a road between two long façades of scabrous chipboard. Every third or fourth boarded-up house has been charred by *scallies equipped with low octane . . .* On the corner there's a carbonised Methodist chapel . . . *in my father's house there's no insurance policy.* Still the dosser limps on – still the Butcher prowls behind, pausing now and then to sniff the night air judiciously: the hoppy reek from a nearby brewery overlays poverty's rancid fermentation, which *bubbles up from the bottom of the melting pot.* Crossing an empty esplanade edged by a shitty-little shopping parade – bookie book-ended by bakery and hole-in-the wall bar – there're eyes on from an aerial walk-way, others from a parked Transit – but it's only idle dicking . . .

Manchester rules – not Moscow's. He walks with one hand in his jacket pocket, fondling the mobile phone, turning it over and over, his fingers seeking out the ebony keys and playing soundless serenades on them ... *but who should I be serenading?* At the office, where the Butcher's flash apparel is often noted *nice tie, Jonathan – silk, is it?* his cover story is a bestseller that entirely suspends his colleagues' disbelief: *Young man, you're too girlie-girlie* ... The Butcher is the EyeBee's most celebrated lothario, and the tales of his chasing are endlessly retold. How the Butcher managed to score not once but twice on the new entrants' course at Fort Monckton: both a fellow officer – and a civilian actually during a training exercise. He picked her up in a pub in Fareham, accompanied her back to her flat, bonked her – and relieved her of her passport details, which had been his real objective. Legend also has it that, such was the Butcher's sexual artistry the girl didn't even cavil when he rose pre-emptorily from her futon to spend a full half-hour in her tiny bathroom showering, shaving and generally grooming, so when he arrived at the arrvee to be picked up by the minibus *right on time*, there wasn't a hair out of place on his gorgeous brow. Legend has it right – and, although he was mildly censured by the head of the controllerate along these lines – The whole point of the bloody exercise is to extract information without leaving any evidence behind! – the Butcher's insouciant reply – Sir, I'm not a rank amateur, I used a condom – has also become *legendary ... One in Hanover, One down a vere, One she's a lawyer, One she's a doctor ...* Melissa is indeed a doctor, isn't she, Squilly? (She is, Butch – a highly competent general practitioner, I believe.) When the Butcher met her she was the embassy's doctor in Geneva – but he didn't start fucking her until they were both back in London. He enjoys booking her last appointment of the day under an assumed name. She'd be expecting a Mister Hemmings – who was sorely troubled by his haemorrhoids – but would receive instead . . . *a delivery from the Butcher*, who'd peel away her filmy wrapping before . . . *chopping her up into choice cuts*. The Butcher considers Melissa to be one of his least irritating beards, and so hardly worth the bother of *shaving off* . . . But although, in office parlance, she isn't remotely . . . *conscious*, her EffSeeOh experience means she smells something *just a bit off* about the Butcher. It is, he thinks, the most tender and trusting of movements, a gesture performed with legs and buttocks: the beards rising up so he could smoothly remove their knickers. With men it's different – you have to *yank their keks offa them* . . . Melissa's head dangling off the examination couch, the Butcher pauses, admiring the smoothness of her professionally depilated thighs. It isn't that he needs to fantasise in order to sustain his erection . . . *it just adds a little seasoning* to see her soft and lightly furred cleft as . . . *an adorable tush*. Gripping the vinyl to either side, the Butcher cranes over and applies tiny tongue-dabs with consummate artistry. Melissa moans, arches her back – thrusts against him as he simultaneously eases thumb into vagina and index finger into anus, then . . . *all hell breaks loose*, which is as he intends. The Butcher takes his time basking in the ruddy conflagration of her climax – looking at patient information posters pinned to the consultation room's walls, seeking out crude diagrams of the male form and embellishing these with *all Tom of Finland's skill*.

Honestly, Squills, he'll remark, as they step down from the portico and proceed along the north side of Cadogan Square towards Sloane Avenue, I do believe I could be aroused by a stick-man – if, that is, *he had a big stick-cock . . . It's closing time in the beer gardens of the West . . .* and an ancient couple exit the hole-in-the-wall bar, the man leading a Scotty, its front half sheathed in Celtic shirt, while the woman *the mummy of the mummy who cursed the fucking mummy,* says, Gorra nice bit of gammon fer 'is tea . . . a scrap of dialogue the Butcher leaves floating in the dirty swill, beneath the bench, on the cracked hardstanding . . . *at the world's end.* As he mounts the first of the short flight of steps leading up to MENLOCK COURT, he has a vision of a different dish altogether: his father's brawny face, on one particularly alcoholic afternoon . . . *I should've sat in my room,* not encountered him on his tenth stagger back from the car . . . *where he kept a half-bottle of Vladivar.* Kins, kneeling in the hallway, his pullover unravelling, a fag fallen from his insensible lips burning the Axminster runner. He'd grabbed his twelve-year-old son's shaky thighs . . . *strictly speaking that cut is the loin,* and sobbed and sobbed, and sobbed some more. But he never talked – *he didn't break,* because – as the Butcher is now prepared to acknowledge, *he was already broken.* So's the lift – its doors attacked with the same tool used on the front ones, a crowbar or possibly a jack-hammer, which punched through the metal sheeting so it could then be kicked in and yanked out. Cables severed, the lift car's wedged at a queer angle in the shaft – its tilted floor supports a large fresh sweet-smelling human turd, so neatly coiled the Butcher imagines its creator squatting, his hips gyrating . . . *an artist will be judged by the resonance of his solitude* as he iced an invisible cake . . . *or the quality of his despair.* There's no electricity in the block: this is a realm of fire and water – the ruptured tanks on the roof are still disgorging so that a rill runs down the emergency stairs the Butcher's Virgil leads him up, and, at each landing, he sees through shattered glass . . . *another circle of hell.* If this were the Texan bad-lands – or some north-western, evergreen waste – agents wearing crisp, navy-blue windcheaters would be leaping limberly for cover. But this is Hulme, and there's only the Butcher, who isn't even *equipped.* Anyway, s'pose he were – he doubts he'd have the sheer balls – as his young soldiering friends might put it – to stop what he sees going on as they make their way through the flickering obscurity of the fifth floor: mutant bikers sporting blood-soaked colours, who've got hold of some . . . *poor spade* and are roasting his feet over a fire of chopped-up fire doors . . . *l'amour est un oiseau rebelle.* His cries follow them as they pass more of these lurid vignettes: a girl lying naked and bleeding – a second being . . . *sorely used* – children huffing glue – others lying unconscious. It is, the Butcher thinks, a sort of *depravity calendar* – and at the end of the corridor . . . *it's Christmas*: a heavily barricaded door in which a crude serving hatch has been hacked, in front of this a perfectly orderly queue . . . *whatever else we may be, we're still British!* which they join, the dosser whispering in the Butcher's ear, Gear's in tens, twennies, quarter-gees – rocks're twenny . . . They shuffle slowly forward, eavesdropping on the he-nicked, she-whored of *ordinary decent criminals.* The Butcher takes his turn at the hatch, whispers his order and passes through four twenties, he receives four cling-filmed *black pearls* in return. Next *we repair to the smoking room until it's time to rejoin the ladies* . . . They climb up to a flat at the very apex of the derelict block, where crack- and smack-heads recline on slashed sectional sofas *vomiting foam* . . . looking out through the mangled windows at the speedily receding city's *redshift*. The ping! of the spark-wheel from a lighter lit so long *it's lit itself* alerts the Butcher to the matter of timing, and he checks his Omega Seamaster. (Time to go, says Squilly, if, that is, you're wasted enough . . .) He is: five authoritative hits on a crack pipe fashioned from a thirty-three see-el mineral water bottle have transported the Butcher to . . . *Avalon*: a sanctuary lying behind *seven veils of subterfuge*, where, undistracted by his clamorous informants – Agents Sight, Sound, Touch, Taste and Temporality – he can get on with *analysing the data*. (Where d'you think they'll've got to, Butch?) And the Butcher answers, They'll be downing their pints preparatory to leaving the pub. (So we'll catch up with them at the New Conti, shall we?) Indeed we shall, Squilly – to which end: Any fucker in 'ere got any downers? I'll pay a fiver for Rohypnols, a quid for jellies . . . The crack- and smack-heads stir, scratch and whine – one rolls over on to all-fours and crawls towards the Butcher. She's a young half-caste girl, her *Deputy Dawg* muzzle defined by a dark *suffering* line. Annamit, annamere, gissitere . . . she mutters, tipping two blue-and-white capsules from a matchbox into his hand. — Looking up from the front steps of MEDLOCK COURT, the Butcher sees the dosser's pinhead pricking out of a window on an upper floor: Oi! Oi, mate! floats down into the abyss – and the abyss, who's already divvied up one of the black pearls by way of commission, shouts back, Fuck off! Come after me, an' I'll carve my fucking name on your spotty-fucking forehead! After that the Butcher's striding across some waste ground, with Gustav Doré griffons scrambling behind him – lifting off into the orangey darkness, their skins *stinking . . . warty . . .* their wings *shit-smeared*, their clawed feet wrapped-around with lengths of chain, the links wreathed in *hanks of greasy hair . . .* Squilly's turning cartwheels inside the Butcher's head, and it's this gyroscopic motion which . . . *powers me on.* He sees a burnt-out Ford Fiesta with a dead crow spread-eagled on its buckled bonnet – he feels inside the great *lens* of his crack high, which magnifies . . . *every thought and sensation*: a fragment of dry-roasted peanut, lodged between molars at the Britannia, breaks free and becomes . . . *a boulder*, rollin' and tumblin' around his salty mouth. Poised between fight and flight, the Butcher has an infinity in which to discriminate between the sound of a car backfiring as it screeches round the corner of Spruce Street and *Serbian sniper fire . . .* Plodding on past the King-dom Hall, he remembers this *Armageddon*: Searchlights fingering shattered brickwork – the miserable whimpering of a dying human animal – a pool of blood and guts in another dark and smelly hall-way – the b'b'boom-boom, b'b'boom-boom of his trip-hopping heart as he mounts another flight of stairs, in another faraway land of which . . . *we know fuck-all.* Then knocking on the door in a still more stygian hallway, and *pushed to the limit we dragged ourselves in.* Where've I been, Squilly? the Butcher asks – but when Squilly begins sing-songing a full list of his postings since he joined the Firm (Londonderry, Geneva, Tehwan, Thawejevo –) he screams,

I meant RHETORICALLY! A cry which fills the motorway flyover's chilly cavities – for by now they've stumbled back into town . . . *just like a sacred cow.* Christ, I'm high, Squilly (Too high to hit your quarry, Butch?) Oh, no – you know me better than that. (Was mir behagt . . .) Is the lively hunt! Always, Squilly, always! With this noble cry, the Butcher slips out of his reversible jacket, rereverses it, enters a spit-and-sawdust pub, strides to the bar, orders a large Scotch, knocks it back for *a quick straightener – no shit-stabber, me* . . . then leaves, making his way, via Charles Street and Princess Street, to the New Conti, where he loses himself in the goose-bumps on the back of a plump girl's thighs until it's his turn to be inefficiently frisked, *no professional, he*: Knockier izzit, mate? the bouncer asks, hefting the Butcher's mobile phone. Dunno why yer bother – I mean, oo yer gonna call, Ghostbusters? Then the Butcher's in, *watching from the wings,* scenes he's seen played, replayed and played yet again: Bodies are, he thinks, big hands – which makes of dancing . . . *a frenzied gesticulation.* The bass line shudders through panting flesh: They call me Mister Loverman, they call me Mister Loverman! and the Butcher thinks, You wish! Observation is the key to successful hunting – soon enough he spots Tizer, whose bull-head rises above the maelstrom, tossing in time. After that the other junior officers are easy to locate: Shabba, giving it his all . . . *since it's his theme tune,* as he throws some shapes in the moon-face of a seriously fat girl – Potso limboing under the disdainful eyes of a black one. Even Anderson has a dance partner – a plug-ugly Pee-wee Herman of a thing, with whom he's attempting to jive, swinging her so vigorously she slams into the other dancers.

But there's no sign of the Butcher's quarry, as he edges along a wall papered with old flyers . . . *Gerry prob'ly needs a pacemaker by now.* Come Monday morning, the Butcher thinks, I'll swipe my card against the sensor, punch my number into the keypad, go through the electronic gate, say good morning to Gardiner, cross the atrium, ride the lift to the lucky seventh, turn right at the Stubbs, then left at the Landseer, unlock the door to my office, lock it behind me, go to the cabinet, spin the Manifoil, get out the office laptop and begin writing up a version of the last few days' events . . . *for Cumming's exclu–.* (There he is!, Squilly interrupts) – he's spotted Greeny over by some dusty drapes in the far corner of the throbbing room *which must hide the doors to the bogs.* 'Scuse . . . 'scuse . . . 'scuse . . . the Butcher makes his way between the disco dancers. By the time he unzips, Gawain's *splatteration* is already counterpointing the cistern's gurgle. Their shoulders touch and he double-takes, Oh . . . it's you. The Butcher reminds him, Mike, but let's just shake todgers rather than hands on this occasion. How're you getting on? Your mates must've got lucky . . . The junior officer gives a doggy shiver, tucks in, zips up, mumbles non-committally, goes to the slimy sink and begins . . . *washing his hands!* Oh, Squilly, I do so hope he doesn't have to do that every time he touches a penis! Staring at the unexpected benison of a splodge of liquid soap, Gawain is nonetheless petulant: Thought you said you had to get home . . . Said you were married – wife's a ball-breaker . . . that's what you said. He soaps his hands methodically, and his pursuer purrs, What say we get the fuck outta here – go somewhere we can really let our hair down? Gawain's breath smells of humbugs – confectionery the

Butcher also uses to . . . *hide my own hypocrisies.* But since he's in the cavalryman's face, he takes his time examining it: a soft and sandy complexion . . . *he'll freckle in the sun – ahhh!* standard-issue blue eyes . . . *a little gweilo for my taste* . . . an honest, dimpled *manly* jaw, surprisingly full *kissable* lips and *a perfect nose! He's the one, Squilly – the one!* A one, moreover, who, although trapped in the malodorous corner of a bog by a man barely known to him, makes no attempt to *break free!* Dunno, he says, early start tomorrow – and I've a match in the afternoon . . . Football? the Butcher asks. – No, rugby . . . Rugger! the Butcher exults to Squilly (And you imagine he has whyming proclivities, do you, Butch?) Well . . . he adopts his most sincere tone . . . we wouldn't want you underperforming on the pitch. How about this: I guarantee to get you back to the Britannia in one piece by oh-three-hundred? Fit bloke like you – shouldn't be too much the worse for wear . . . 'Sides, you know you'll be kicking yourself tomorrow if you pass up the opportunity – I mean, when're you gonna see some proper action again? In the street the Butcher considers his options: he could take Gawain to Manto's for a few rounds – but the place will almost certainly be ram-packed with *Nellie queens* . . . Instead, he ducks into a Pakki shop, buys a can of Coke, snaps it open and, while Gawain's distracted *Superman* steps into a phone booth, gets his stash out and deftly transforms the soft drink into a cocktail of hard drugs: two parts of emmdee-emmay to one of Rohypnol . . . *don't want him going under before he's come up.* Then they're trolling on down the road, Gawain's Adam's apple rising and falling as he guzzles from the can. They pass by young women tottering on high heels – one's collapsed altogether by some wheelie bins, her skirt having ridden right up, while her lucky pants haven't proved to be fortunate at all – although she remains *a very shapely lass.* Gawain's eyes take in bare, splayed legs, but reassuringly . . . *don't linger.* It's only a hop, skip and *glug* to the Paradise – the Butcher wonders whether to persist with his false flag operation, or if Gawain's sufficiently out of it by now to risk making him conscious his companion is one of those . . . *boys who like girls who like boys who like boys.* It's well past midnight yet the venerable Victorian buildings still *heave and pulse* – synthy skirls, over-revving car engines and frequent bestial howls rend the filmically bright darkness. Manchester, the Butcher speculates, has been camouflaged *by itself:* a vast sheet has been thrown over the city, one patterned with towers, domes and cupolas – all the superfluous ornamentation you'd expect to see if you were arriving by camel *for Belshazzar's feast.* He relieves Gawain of the Coke, slakes . . . *my dreadful thirst,* and, backing him into a doorway, breathes *sweetly* into his expectant face: You, um, require a little . . . adjustment, Lieutenant. Where we're going the dress code is as strict as any mess, but . . . um, messier. The Butcher gets out his little tin of Vaseline, dabs his fingers, musses the *adorable* sandy-blond hair, exulting the while, because: *He doesn't flinch!* Which gives the Butcher further licence to yank Gawain's shirt-tail from the waist of his preppy chinos. There's nothing he can do about the dreadful blazer – although it might count in their favour, since: All the nice girls love a soldier, All the nice girls love his Glock . . . the Butcher sings as they troll on . . . 'Cause there's something about a nine-millimetre semi-automatic pistol that reminds them of a man's –. This . . . this is . . .

Gawain breaks in . . . a gay club. Which is, the Butcher, thinks, not terribly observant for a man trained in long-range reconnaissance. They've joined the back of a queue mostly consisting of pumped-up clones in tight white T-shirts, who jitter-jig to the chukka-chukka ah-ahh spilling from the doors . . . *love's gone mad again.* An outrageous figure wearing a green lamé dress and leggings teeters between the clones on nine-inch heels. His/her face is plastered with white pancake and fissured by blood-red zigzags. Perspex fragments embedded in this car-crash maquillage glitter as he/she approaches, while the small battery-powered toy car he/she sports in lieu of a toque spins its wheels rrrrRRRRrrrrRRRR . . .! in his/her bleached-blond/blonde bouffant hair-do. He/she waves a windscreen-wiper wand, bestowing a blessing on this clone: You're in . . . and anathema on that one: Off you jolly well fuck . . . Cuddle up, soldier, the Butcher hisses, sliding an arm under Gawain's blazer and round his *gorgeous hips* . . . He won't let uss in if he thinkss we're sstraight. Why? Gawain hisses back. Why do we want to get in? Because, the Butcher *insistss*, it's only the besst place to pick up birdss – no competition! – Ooh! the walking car crash has reached them: Somebody can't keep her hands on her ha'pennies, he/she says, *shaving* Gawain's cheek with the rubber blade. The best a girl can get, eh . . . Okay – you're . . . in! *In! In! In!* In to three storeys chock-full of . . . *abandonment*: the dance floor's a heaving mass of bare and sweat-slicked torsos – and the Butcher dives in, dragging Gawain behind him. The house music's satiny fabric, stitched together with repetitive beats, enfolds their bodies. Gawain's gyrations – the Butcher coolly notes – are part parade

ground, part assault course: his hands reaching for invisible holds –
his feet marching . . . *on the spot.* The regimental ram embroidered
on his blazer pocket is rampant, then couchant, then *rampant
again . . . annagain.* The Butcher thinks of sheep he's seen grazing
aloft in scrubby trees . . . *astonishingly agile.* The packed dance floor,
a single entity, throws its arms up . . . *and out!* We're all Action
Men, the Butcher thinks: drilled to perfection and capable of adopting . . . *any pose.* Look at the cavalry one, full of pharmaceutical
fodder – see him canter amongst the clones, his eyes rolled back in
their sockets . . . *whitely sightless.* See his muzzle, flecked with foam
as he whinnies along with the rest of the prancers: In dance floor
stag! In leatherman drag! Dressed to please! Stripped to tease!
Strip for me 'cause I WANT YOUUUU TOOOO! The Butcher,
conserving his *energee,* shuffling on the spot, watches as Gawain is
flayed by the flailing arms – first his blazer, then his shirt – until
he's *like all the rest.* Still the sonic earthquake *rumbles on . . .* Still the
beat doubles and . . . *redoubles,* whipping the dancers into yet more
frenzied gyrations . . . *round annaround, again annagain,* until the
lights start strobing and the hellish inferno of the Paradise Factory
suddenly . . . *stills.* They're stills, Squilly! the Butcher cries. Nobody's
really moving at all! Gawain hunched over, digging a flagstaff into a
pile of corpses – Gawain bow-legged, riding an invisible horse along
Whitehall – Gawain, arms outstretched, running down a Vietnam-
ese road, his skin . . . *hanging off his back.* As the Butcher slots these
stills into his viewfinder, he edges closer and closer to a revelation
concerning . . . *perception itself* and *what it is to truly see!* (Who the
devil d'you think you are . . . Squilly speaks from out of the *burning*

bush – thome thort of philosophucker?) Then the house music begins to fade, the house lights come up, and the Butcher sees his quarry being led by the nose towards . . . *a bottle of fucking amyl!* Now then, now then – lads-who-love-lads and lasses who love other . . . lasses! The car-crash trannie is back, standing on the low stage in front of the speakers. Enough of yer bloody skrikin', he/she cries, there'll be time enough fer love when I've made the announcements . . . Thank you, Dave Kendrick, fer spinnin' the discs that risk . . . Now then, now then . . . there're representatives from the Lesbian and Gay Switchboard in da house handing out da rubbers – he/she tosses his/her car-crash head – C'mon, it's not rocket science – jus' roll one on your rocket, when yer get it outta yer . . . pocket! The Butcher, becalmed at the side of the dance floor, sees eyes-on from the balcony: Obvious plods, eh, Squilly . . . (Plain as the pwoverbial pikestaff, Butch) Prob'ly looking for dealers, eh . . . (Prob'ly – are you bothered?) I'm not bothered . . . (Well, you should be.) Why? They're not Branchers, are they – 'sides, I've never been declared *oop North* . . . Gawain appears at his side, balled-up shirt and blazer clutched to his bare and heaving chest . . . *rubimdownallfoamyinthestableyard*, and the Butcher says, You look like you could use a little rest and recuperation. They mount through dry-ice clouds, past Fred Perries feeding on each other's faces, into a *World of Leather*: a chill-out room full of the sort of queens the Butcher hasn't seen since the glory days of . . . *the Motor Sport Club*. He pilots Gawain to a banquette and they slump down – opposite are *a matching pair*, peaked caps, complete with Totenkopf insignia, shading rouged cheeks and eyelids caked with mascara. Gawain, his eyes bugging out, struggles gamely back into his red shirt. BEYOND THIS SIGN, the Butcher thinks, YOU WILL BE DOWN RANGE. Slumping down into the stinking vinyl, Gawain struggles to articulate: I . . . I . . . I'm . . . and, despite a finger pressed against his lips, he won't be silenced: I'm . . . I'm engaged to be marri–. Until his gob is stopped . . . *with mine.* Tongues are ropes with which we bind our lovers, the Butcher thinks, as he *skips around* in Gawain's salty-sweet mouth. Focused intently on all the data streaming into him through his nervous system, the Butcher is nonetheless assailed by odd images: a dropsical fake-gold watch *time-swollen*, and hanging by its wristband *from a mechanical claw* . . . An open telephone junction box – its multicoloured tangle of conversation being *invisibly combed* . . . He hears the icy chimes of the chill-out music *shining* somewhere in the clubbable hubbub – hears also the harsh *Alllouaahhh Akhbaaaarrrr!* of an amplified call *to submission* – all of which seems perfectly appropriate for a first kiss. At first tentatively, but then with greater authority . . . *it's the habit of command!* Gawain leans into him, forcing the turncoat to . . . *swap sides!* I was gagging for it, Squilly (So you were, Butch – now you're gagging on it.) Next, Gawain's hand is probing the Butcher's crotch – Whoa, Soldier, didn't you hear mein poofy host – keep yer hands on yer ha'pennies, not mine: this isn't some glory hole . . . and for long moments the Butcher recalls the haul through *crotch-stinking darkness* . . . his only handholds . . . *greasy poles.* Gawain's eyes are shut, his expression is utterly guileless – compellingly vulnerable. Right now, Squilly, I could get this man to do anything – anything at all. And betray anyone –

anyone at all. (It's been a thuccethful appwoach, Butch – no one would deny that. But have you given any thought as to how you're going to wun him?) Oh, it's deep penetration for this one, Squills – he's a keeper, a sleeper, a midnight creeper – (Wooh-wooh, Butch, wooh-wooh!) Despite the drugs, the heat and the animal frenzy, these are militarily trained men *who crave routine . . .* So for the next couple of hours they alternate between marching up and down on the dance floor and feeling each other up in the chill-out room. At about four ayem the car-crash emsee returns to the stage, the music stops, and, taking the mic, he/she delivers a little homily: Ooh, yer all a little overexcited, children, aren'tcha . . . No . . . well, seriously now, lissen up! There's stuff going on out there in the real world you lot should pay attention to . . . But the strung-out ravers aren't paying attention to anything much – just standing around snapping each other's bovver-boy braces. The Butcher, looking at Gawain's top pocket, thinks of the Green Slime's regimental crest . . . *a rampant pansy resting on its laurels.* – Lissen up! I'm dead-blüddy-serious . . . He/she holds the mic against his/her revved-up hairdo, and the amplified whine winds them all in. We're boy-racers, us, the Butcher thinks, powering towards the next century – the enemy's out there, but we don't know *who he is any more . . .* – This feller in Texas, 'spect he were a bit of a nutter – but they didn't have to send in them Swat teams an' whatever, an' machine-gun 'em all to death – kiddies, too. No, it should make yer think – there're all sorts in the world, so what's so funny about peace, love an' understanding? What indeed, the Butcher silently cavils. Problem is they're all in short supply. He wonders what would happen if the emsee turned his/her fissured and glittery cheek to those Chester ranchers? There's a great big worldful of war, hate and incomprehension between wolves such as them, hunting down nerve-gas precursors for brutal dictators to use on their own flock, and these *dipped sheep*, who're standing about wiping the fungicide from their eyes *with bar towels* . . . (Wo Regenten wohl regieren, Butch.) Kann man Ruh und Friede spüren, Squills . . . The Butcher turns to Gawain, who stands slope-shouldered, head hanging, his sweat-soaked shirt *a red rag on a knackered bull*. He examines the cavalryman's superb musculature – the Chobham armouring of his broad chest and the steely linkages of his sinewy arms. He considers the vast amount of tax payers' money which has been expended bringing this young man to a peak of physical perfection, and filling his head with tactics and stratagems. Yet here he is, waiting and waiting . . . *for the next Kuwait*, whereas the Butcher – whose business is, after all, target acquisition – well, *what am I waiting for?* Soon after, the club shuts, and the emsee drives them all into the street with: This may be paradise, my little angels, but you can't stay here fer eternity! The punters gather together for a few minutes, pairing off, swapping phone numbers, and speculating as to where another drink or drug can be found – then they scatter. Gawain staggers, and the Butcher supports him: a heavy weight *on my shoulders*. The junior officer's right out of it now – way out at the end of the galaxy's spiral arm, and babbling thoughtless bubbles: Light colours . . . in the tepee . . . Daddy said . . . hang it from the ridgepole . . . ups-a-daisy . . . (EmKayUltra should've known about this little cocktail, eh, Butchie?) Possibly, Squillster – however, as we know only too well, the problem with truth serums is that, while they may innoculate against perfidy, the product itself is often – (Well past its sell-by date?) I was going to say, decidedly off. Materialising underneath the arches, opposite the Ritz on Whitworth Street, the Butcher remembers watching live footage of target acquisitions at Langley, one of the shows the Agency likes to put on to impress their friends: the camera-eye, zooming through cirrus shreds to trap a racing technical in its cross-hairs – a vehicle which, no matter how fast it travels, *can't replace the fear – or the thrill of the chase* . . . He slides his hand down Gawain's chinos and into the sweaty groove between his buttocks – the cavalryman *whinnies* . . . Next they're grazing on each other's faces in filthy meadowland on the crumbling bank of the Bridgewater Canal . . . *where have we been?* Dawn has come – a fireball exploding over the Manchester Riviera, and diesel-powered ducks leave detergent wakes as beer cans bob-bob-bob about in the . . . *Boddingtons.* Dawn has come – its rays lasering down to etch this precise and frozen image: a slim, dark man in anonymous clothing lying on top of a bigger blond man who's half naked, his washed-out, paisley-patterned boxers pulled down to expose his . . . *boneless rump roast.* The Butcher yanks them down further – then, *pushed to the limit*, he rises up, drags down his zip and unleashes . . . *Squilly!* who sniffs the fresh morning and the stale canal, then quests towards his quarry. This time the Butcher leaves a deep thumbprint in the little tin of Vaseline – he briefly considers the box of condoms he pocketed at the Britannia, but realistically *what're the chances?* Gawain is undoubtedly *one of us*, but the Butcher is a past master of such tradecraft and intuits Gawain has never, ever gone beyond *prep-school circle jerks* – why, despite the lateness of this early hour, his handkerchief is still perfectly aligned in his breast pocket, so all the world can see . . . *just how fucking straight he is.* No, no – this is a faggot who's *never been ignited,* who's got his jollies up until now on the playing field – the Butcher kneels to *feed the ball in,* hearing twenty-year-old changing room jibes: *Woolly-woofter! Fucking poofter!* and feeling Mister Marshall's wedding ring snag on his waistband as the Deputy Headmaster checks to see if De'Ath Major is wearing underpants under his rugby shorts, in direct contravention of the school rules. Coaxing Squilly into full and majestic turgidity, the Butcher takes a moment to ruminate bitterly on the legalistic fig leaves with which paedophiles mask their proclivities . . . *Hold!* before uttering a small prayer of his own devising: Soon to be dearly beloved, I do hope your back passage is . . . uncluttered. *Hold!* The world strains all around him – he feels the undergrowth writhe, every blade of grass is neon-edged, thistle-down floats through his yawning eyes – eyes that see not this colossal incongruity: two of Her Majesty's upstanding servants lying on a canal towpath preparatory to performing a sodomitical act – but . . . *Kins!* Specifically, his father's bloodhound visage, its heavy jowls and lacrymal bags. Poor Kins! He too has been *a smoker . . . a joker . . . a midnight toker* – he, too, has been nailed up on the cross of a forbidden love. Kins, at Colindale Avenue, standing by the French windows, peering out at the lawn-shaped patch of mud, sown with hoppers and choppers . . . *deflated and rusting.* Kins, who, his eldest son acknowledges for the first time,

I'm alike, in this respect at least: both of them, whatever they may say or do, are fated to remain homeless, especially *when we're at home* . . . *Hold!* Gawain groans, perhaps anticipating the bite of the Green Knight's axe-blade . . . *Hold!* a dying fish up-plips in the moribund canal . . . *Hold! And* –. Diddle-ooh-doo, diddle-ooh-doo, diddle-ooh-doo-doo! The throb in his pocket is insistent – more insistent yet than Squilly (What the fuck, Butch?). He fumbles the Nokia from his pocket and squints at the tiny screen: number witheld. Indeed . . . *all their numbers are withheld – they're very withholding people* . . . *Hold!* The Butcher hits the necessary button and the ooh-dooing *diddles away* . . . he rubs the glob of Vaseline expertly into and around Gawain's anus . . . *and* Engage! The scrum-half feeds the ball in so fast Gawain curses Trooper Pythian – F-F-Fucking dickhead! – who, as ever, hasn't sufficiently engaged with the front row. As his arm slips from the Pythian's sweaty hips, Gawain braces his shoulder against the Lock's buttocks . . . *taking up the strain* in this push-of-war. The patch of cratered mud bucks and heaves before his own fanatic face – boots scythe into view, steel studs scrape on shanks and shin pads. Cartilage grinds against bone – behind him Tizer grunts, Steady, lads . . . steady, as the thirty-two-legged *creature we've become* crab-walks across the sodden ground. Gawain hears the seagulls . . . *our biggest fans* flapping about the touchline, while into his shoulder pumps all the tension in Pythian's buttocks and haunches – together with all the pushing and pulling of interlinked arms, the thrusting of legs, the . . . *butting of heads*. Steady, lads, steady . . . Beyond the wheeling scrum range the loosening line of backs, each man, Gawain thinks, vitally connected to me by eyeline and anticipation . . . Steady, lads, steady . . . The SeeEssEmm is killing his hangover with a sneaky can of Tennent's behind the home goal posts – he, too, is vitally connected to Gawain by *the chain of command*, the links of which join all the men on the establishment – gunners and tankers, Yorkies and Scotties, Queue-men and blanket-stackers – into one enormous dutiful and purposive creature that longs *only to serve* . . . A creature which is itself only a part of a still greater *body of men* . . . Steady, lads, steady . . . the ball flips back – Gawain slips, knee-knocking it forward into the melee. Fuckinell, Greeny, Tizer grunts – but *without malice* . . . At the Academy, five weeks in and fitter than he'd ever been, what with daily log-runs and increasingly frequent bad-boy badge parades, Gawain was *legless* with fatigue. Slumped in a War Studies lecture, drowsing fitfully while a tweedy-old pipe-puffer droned on, he'd had this epiphany: I belong – I truly belong. Each beat of Her Majesty's loyal heart *pumped* life through mysterious constitutional mechanisms into the grey matter of Her Government – which in turn animates *all of us*: a hundred thousand highly trained bodies, knitted together by our instinctual drive to *fight!* It was this he'd been fleeing to from . . . *the Welsh desert.* This he'd yearned for on the sodden afternoons of his childhood when he wandered the *sodding* lanes around Nantyfynn: a family that was, above all, functional – while as for the other thing, the *breaking free from your lies, you're so self-satisfied* . . . well, he didn't need it – didn't need the fauny figures in their slinky green leotards hefting him aloft to the camp tootling of their massed synthetic horns. Although, aged eleven, hunched up with his siblings on Missus Price's parlour couch to watch Top of the Pops, he'd feared he might *explode with excitement*. – Go, Greeny! Go, you fucking bell-end! The ball – hooked back to Tizer, knocked back again by him – lies at Gawain's feet, its voluptuous form *so huggable*. He boots it forward, eccentrically oscillating – and, breaking from the scrum, *catches it on the fly!* He scopes out the killing zone between him and the touchline: the Welsher's full-back, together with the rest of his brick, are spread out between Gawain and the touchline. On the range there's a *catch in the Rarden's throat* before it begins to hammer out thirty-mil' rounds. On the hoof, Gawain hesitates for a moment, calculating his trajectory – then, roaring, he begins a charge that ends . . . in the changing room: Nice one, Greeny . . . Blinder, Greens – fucking slotted those Taffies, didn't we . . . Christ, we're pure. Awaaay, away away awaaaay! We are the sheep-men – we are the Fighting Rams! Gawain joins in with the pink and steaming choristers: No ifs no butts, we're the Rams! Baaa-baaa-baaaa! Ha-haa-haaa! Alll-right, Greeny – room for one more on top! Don't bend over for the soap, boys . . . ! Agitated by muddy rivulets snaking across the white tiling, a single, wiry *questioning* pubic hair interrogates him: What are you, Lieutenant Thomas? And, as he rubs the suds around his cock and balls, Gawain wonders, Will the harshing ever cease? Back at the regimental lines, flushed by his rubdown, exhilarated by their victory, he runs into Blakey, who sniffs self-importantly: Gawain, this briefing this afternoon . . . Turns out it isn't just normal slime – SeeOh wants full opsec, dry run. We've the real McCoy coming up from London. – Meaning? – For fuck's sake,

Gawain, what an utterly bone question . . . Captain Blake's pinched, white face darkens, *why's he always so bloody angry?* – As my Two-EyeSee, I need you to be a little bit more on the actual ball – not just the rugger one. Rumour is we'll get our movement order any day now. Taffies still here? Gawain grins: They're in the canteen, Phil, hoovering it up – prob'ly not a lot of scran back in Taffy land. – Well, you'd know all about that, Lieutenant Thomas – anyway, chivvy 'em along now, get 'em off our patch. I want everyone in the briefing room by fourteen-thirty, okay? No excuses – no bullshit: everyone. Captain Blake swivels neatly on his heels and stamps away. It's a clear, sharp Saturday afternoon in early October and the wind is stripping the leaves from the trees. There're kids mucking about in the playground behind the married personnel's accommodation – boxy little brick semis with white-painted aluminium facings which wouldn't look out of place on any council estate, on the outskirts of any British town. Gawain pictures Fiona sitting inside one of them – sitting knitting, a Moses basket by her side. He hears her needles *ticking away*, smells the furniture polish and sees the future ahead: *years will rotate – nothing will change* . . . He calls after the stiff, retreating back: I think Pisspot and the SeeEssEmm were out on the lash last night, Phil . . . Stiff back turns to *soft belly* and Captain Blake scowls: I don't give a ruddy fuck about that, Gawain. In less than a week we may well be under fire from some Serb scum who haven't troubled to wade through all thirty-two pages of Unprofor's rules of engagement – our blokes need to be completely clued-in. So see to it, Gawain – that's an order. He does his habitual finger-fidget, intended to solicit the salute which Gawain grudgingly sketches – then turns away again. Noting the *forty fucking Walnut Whips* on each of his SeeOh's hips, Gawain thinks, He won't pass the physical if he doesn't put a sock in it . . . – Oooh, yeah! Boo-yaa! Greeny! Greeny! The cries go up from the men seated either side of the long Formica-topped table as Gawain bashes through the swing doors – it isn't the first time he's scored the winning try, but this is a different sort of victory: he feels held, embraced, by *my brothers in arms . . . a t'riffic relief,* given that ever since he joined the regiment Gawain has struggled with . . . *distance.* At the Academy, together with the rest of his peers, he'd cheerfully ignored the small mauve-jacketed book which had been left on top of his bed-block: *Serve to Lead, eh . . .* Okay, agreed, he'd flicked through, pausing to read the odd fragment: *Success in battle really comes from a combination of the skill and daring of the leader and the skill and confidence of the led, and we, the British . . . He was open-hearted, manly, friendly, and independent, a most gallant and zealous officer, and much devoted to his own corps . . .* then chucked it aside – after all, this was the sort of guff he'd heard since childhood from his own father. Heard it right up until Derek Thomas left the army and *went postal . . .* But on the morning Gawain first strode out on to the parade square, and saw H Company lined up before him – thirty lairy young men, their wary eyes *frisking* the nig Rupert to see if he'd *anything to hide* – he'd had a mad urge to rip the pips from his shoulders, cast his peaked cap aside and throw *myself among them.* Because that's you all over, isn't it, he admonishes himself as he takes his place on the bench, between Pythian and one of the Welshers . . . you pathetic little poofter – you'll do anything, repeat

ANYTHING, it takes to be *one of the boys*. And, just as at the Academy, where he'd floundered at first to *make my mark*, so he'd realised his future with the Hussars would have to be cemented in the churned-up mud of the rugby pitch. Better he should be known as a fully fledged rugger-bugger *than the other sort*. Better he should assume the habit of command than hearken to his *finer feelings*. But it remains difficult – damnably difficult. It's entirely possible, he supposes, for a man to be *as hard as nails* and *as bent as a nine-bob note* – his curse is to be not exactly a gentleman, but very definitely *a gentle one* . . . and, seeing some seventeen-year-old Geordie holding back the tears, Gawain still longs to put an arm around his shaking shoulders, bestow a kiss on his spotty forehead. *Objects in the mirror may appear larger* . . . which is why it's so damnably difficult to *keep my distance*. Then again – there were tales enough of unbending Ruperts, who bore down on their men with all the weight of their entitlement, so were subjected to *creepy mind-fuck*: brews adulterated with salt, whispering campaigns during briefings, salutes so sketchy as to merely suggest what a salute might be like, should the subordinate disdain to bestow one on his superior. Which is what, Gawain reflects, unloading his tray, I was doing to Blakey. Poor Blakey – shackled to his harridan wife. Passing by their quarters, once, Gawain had heard them *hard at it* – and she's the very picture of a long-haired general: a big, gawky woman in dated, dull clothes – calf-length skirts and blouses with piecrust collars – who's present at all the regiment's carefully orchestrated disco-dances and church parades, manning the refreshments table or handing out the hymn sheets – sticking her lantern jaw into everything, desperate to shed some light on her husband's prospects for promotion. Will it be like that for Fi and me, Gawain wonders, pushing a small bow-wave of gravy across his plate with a perfect hemisphere of boiled potato, the greasy wake *spreading out behind* . . . But what's ahead? Nothing but scraps of overcooked roast lamb . . . *quite indigestible.* Standing outside the Admin Block with the rest of the team and a few hangers-on, Gawain waves as the Royal Welshers' coach sweeps round in a wide circle, *whisking all the whey-faces away* . . . There's poetry in that, Gawain thinks – poetry in most things if you stop to think about it. Poetry and artistry in military manoeuvres as well . . . *hard edge, light touch.* Artistry, too, in the cell Blakey's placed on the overhead projector's lightbox – the original political boundaries having been repurposed with felt-tip pens of many different colours. He steps away from the lectern – and the Chief steps up, a fine figure of leadership: strapping . . . *he could beat me to a pulp*, his features razor-sharp, his laser gaze targetting far horizons. The Chief doesn't exactly drone on – but Gawain, his belly full, his muscles dully aching, finds it hard to concentrate on all the divisions and subdivisions: the Bosniaks and the Croats, the Bosnian Serbs and – for all he knows – the Serbian Bosnians . . . Basically, the Chief *drones on*, our job's to keep the bastards apart – tricky enough under the best circs, as those of you who were along for the Cyprus deployment will know full well. But the situation in the former-Yugoslavia appears – at least to me – wilfully complicated . . . The junior officers at the front of the room stir, amused by this very typical *Chiefism* – because Lieutenant-Colonel Roger Renfrew refrains from the soldier's habitually fatalistic attitude towards a world which . . . *refuses to follow orders*. For him there're no impersonal shitstorms, snafus and embuggerations – only situations in which, had the Fighting Rams been to hand, the malefactors would've been *brought to heel* – which was another Chiefism, covering everything from pacifying bolshie civilians to reducing Her Majesty's enemies to *human purée* . . . given each territory has its own embattled ethnic minority – which is more often than not supported by an ethnic majority in the adjacent territory, who in turn are giving merry-hell to a different ethnic minority . . . Gawain observes Lieutenant "Tizer" Townshend in the front row – must be tricky being quite that big, makes it easier for you to be spotted when you're . . . *grabbing forty winks*. But it's fair enough, really – Tizer gave his all against the Welshers . . . *as did we all*. At times – and this is one of them – Gawain indulges in the fantasy of living entirely in a parallel rugby-union universe, where all his adversaries are gentle-manly and *play by the rules* . . . Yet he can never sustain this vision – he's always out there, receiving a perfect pass, getting his head down and charging – only to realise that the last defender between him and the touchline has . . . *long hair and breasts!* It wasn't exactly repulsive, kissing Fiona, but *it's dreadfully cramped and fiddly in there* . . . so he smoothly re-enters this messy and chaotic world, right on cue: Gawain, you're responsible for the B Company rota – have all the men cycled through? He smiles at his prospective father-in-law and replies, Troopers McCruisken and Fellowes still to complete, Chief . . . then Lieutenant-Colonel Renfrew *smiles back!* Smiles so warmly his prospective son-in-law glows. It occurs to Gawain – not for the first time – that the Chief *actually likes me*. This isn't the benevolent tolerance of senior-to-junior officer, but *genuine affection*... Fair enough, Renfrew says, but see to it, there's a good chap – time is of the essence. Now: I know some of you will still be thinking this'll be just another Cyprus – but there's tricky, and there's seriously bloody tricky ... He lays his green felt-tip pen down on the cell ... In Cyprus we had a long-established and completely secure base, hot-and-cold-running water – regular bulletins from the bloody News Bunny, so far as I could make out. But in Bosnia our billet's going to be a little bit more ... commando. Lesley? – This is the cue for Major Hirst, the Adjutant, who runs a hand through his sparse hair before taking his place at the lectern: Well, Chief, it's certainly pretty basic – and there's been pretty fierce activity in the immediate area, but I'm hoping it hasn't been used as a bloody mortuary. In a nutshell, chaps, the Unprofor bods – in association with the local commander – have, out of the goodness of their hearts, commandeered this highly des' res' for us – he snaps off the overhead projector and snaps on a slide one: a long, low concrete structure appears, sited on a densely wooded hillside – which was, up until hosilities commenced, a ... um, paint factory. Someone in the back row whispers, With Dulux once is enough, but the Chief, hands on hips, ignores this: We'll be on lock-down after dark – full stag, obviously. We may not be able to undertake offensive ops – but we're bloody well going to defend ourselves. On that very matter, Captain Anselm is here from EmmEye to give us some up-to-date intel' on who the players are and what capabilities they have – and for those of you thinking there'll be sod-all productive for us to do, Anselm's brought a . . . um, friend with him from London. Apparently – the tip of the Chief's nose *grows* – his, ah, friends' friends – *no Pinocchio he* – are keen to find out more about our Serbian chums . . . Lesley, will you ask them to come in? In the corner of the briefing room, between the desk with the projector on it and the door, rolled-up maps have been deposited, together with the seats of broken plastic stacking chairs. The seats of plastic stacking chairs have been deposited in the space between the door and the desk with the projector on it, together with rolled-up maps. All the Rams' officers are looking at the door – looking towards its little window of toughened glass. Gawain thinks: That's where I'll always bloody be – not inside, not outside . . . Always at the door, piled up with the rest of the broken stuff no one *can be bothered to get rid of* . . . The door's pneumatic arm whistles, summoning *the knowledge that gives us strength*: Anselm, who looks like *typical slime* – a killer-nerd with blue-tinted glasses and a conspicuous stain on his jacket collar . . . *ally as fuck*. He's an odd smile about his lips as he pushes the door wide open so the man Gawain knows as . . . *Mike!* can enter. He's wearing a beautifully cut pinstripe suit and carrying an expensive leather briefcase. He hesitates briefly – and Gawain sees him, standing in a cloud of thistledown . . . lifting one slim white foot so he can lasso it with the slim white loop of his . . . *Calvin Kleins*. Without any preamble Anselm begins running through the dispensations and strengths of the various forces: Essentially obsolete platforms . . . Such-and-such artillery . . . Restricted mobility . . . and so *predictably* on. Gawain's aware of some of his brother officers taking notes –

164

but he can only sit, mouth open to catch the *flies* that buzz out from Mike's piercing pale blue eyes. He is, Gawain glories, *so much better looking than I remember* . . . But as he stares – and Mike stares back – a clamminess overtakes him, for fingertips . . . *pencils – penises!* are rubbing the man's perfect skin *on to mine* . . . transferring the decal of his identity . . . *to me!* I'm pleased, Captain Anselm says, to tell you we've someone here who knows a great deal more about Ratko and Radovan than I do – Jonathan? The man previously known as Mike takes his place at the lectern and snaps off the slide projector – the former Yugoslavia is *just that.* Through the after-image of the Balkans swim these *fishy words*, last heard in the *South China Sea* of the Britannia's bar: Okay, okay . . . don't worry, I'm not trying to muscle in – I'm just a weekend warrior, a gung-ho stab who'd like the honour of buying the real McCoy a wet . . . By his kit and clobber Gawain would've eyedeed him as ex-public school – and quite possibly Oxbridge – but then there's the odd colourlessness of his accent – which was surely . . . *Northern, I'm falling* . . . Falling, as undigested chunks of roast lamb rise up his oesophagus – falling . . . no! *Plunging into* . . . *the abyss*: What's he doing here? It can't be a coincidence – and who the fuck is he anyway? A friend? A friend of a friend of friends? He's certain *bloody friendly* . . . The situation is fluid, as you're all well aware – Colonel Blake tells me you'll be based at Vitez, but, with the AitchVeeOh and the Serbs now in cahoots, it may no longer be possible for the Bosnians to hang on to the Maglaj finger – which really, since the combined forces launched their attack in July, hasn't properly been a finger of territory at all, only a finger of . . . fudge, which isn't enough. – The junior officers in the front rows chortle obligingly – not that the man calling himself Jonathan is ingratiating, his is an unforced charm . . . *people say yes before they know what they've been asked to do.* Listen, he continues, we're obviously not asking you to do our work for us – that'd be in direct contravention of your peace-keeping status. But in a three-cornered ruck like this . . . well, all sorts of interesting stuff comes out of the woodwork . . . But why the fuck, Gawain silently interrogates him, why the fuck have you come out of the woodwork? He thinks back to that summer morning in Manchester – consciousness dribbling into his gritty head along with the cold water piddling from the duff shower rose. Tizer and Shabba must've hauled him bodily from the bed, where he'd been crumpled in his soiled clothes, and dumped him in the bath. As Gawain spluttered into life . . . *a cold start – too much choke*, he'd heard Tizer reading aloud in the next room: Hope you enjoyed yourself, Greeny – and don't worry, what happens in Manc' stays in Manc' . . . cheers, Mike . . . Then Tizer had been standing in the doorway, looking down at him: What the fuck, Greeny . . . sounds like you met up with that bloke again – the stab. Also sounds like you got up to some serious monkey-business – got laid, didja? *Did I? Did I?* Appalled, Gawain peers intently around the briefing room, seeking out the faces of his Manchester companions. Surprised? Yes, they are – obviously, but, apart from Lieutenant Townshend, who's sitting forward and staring hard at Mike's *Jonathan mask*, none of them appear that *suspicious* . . . – We suspect there're some players behind the obvious ones – but, given how chaotic the situation is, it's next to impossible for us to get intel' in any of the usual ways. Now, I'm not claiming there're Spetsnaz commandos running around in the woods – but someone's putting the lead in Ratko's pencil. They may be well on their way to becoming a second-class power, but the Ruskies still regard this as within their sphere of influence . . . Mike-*and-the-Mechanics* . . . *Iron* Mike *Tyson* . . . *George* MIKE*al* . . . what's his sphere of influence? As he chats on – casual, laid-back – despatches keep on arriving at Gawain's *aitchqueue*, which are breathlessly delivered – they bring indisputably accurate intel' that must've been gathered *by an eye in the sky* . . . How else to explain these satellite images that're nonetheless close-ups? Gawain swigging from a can of Coke . . . *He drugged me!* Gawain on the dance floor of . . . *a screamingly queenie club*, shirt off, chest wet – and, still more disturbing, Gawain, face down in a patch of weeds, his buttocks naked and . . . *raised*. It's all as bad as *bad can be* – yet the utter badness of it is concentrated into this explosive realisation which . . . *shatters my mind*: When he thrust into me – *I pushed back* . . . – It's a situation that may indeed change as new players push into the Balkans – Captain? Anselm's been fiddling with the slide carousel, and now an image wheels on to the screen as Anderson springs *puppyish* from his seat to hit the lights. His ghostly face *wood-grained*, Mike/Jonathan continues: This is just one of scores of crates the Dutch contingent have intercepted during their deployment – you'll observe that the AyKays are of all sorts. Some old, some new. Some're of Soviet manufacture – others've been bodged up by metal-bashers in the Kandahar souk. They're crated and freighted by Macedonian and Albanian gangs – but the consignments are paid for by the same

dissident Saudis who funded the Mujahideen in Afghanistan –
Captain? Another slide click-clacks into view, and he continues:
You can see here that the Kalashnikovs have been interspersed with
layers of these books. – The Rams see mauve-covered volumes,
strewn with golden tangles of Arabic script, and Second Lieutenant
"Shabba" Sharples calls out, Serve to Lead! – a reference the spook
effortlessly incorporates into: In a manner of speaking you're right –
it is their manual of leadership, since the literal meaning of Islam
is submission – submission to the will of God, or your SeeOh,
whoever's closer to hand . . . I submitted to him, Gawain thinks,
does that mean he's my god? . . . Anyway, we're not entirely sure
which bothers us more – the guns or the godliness – but one thing's
certain, with their adversaries in 'Stan out of the way, these Saudi
fighters are looking for other Muslim populations to mobilise. This
is a serious matter, gentlemen – intelligence assessments can take
some time to analyse thoroughly, and this isn't even necessarily
for Whitehall consumption, but at VeeBeeArr we're getting all
sorts of credible intel' which points to the same ugly conclusion:
Europe is going to be the new front line in their global holy war . . .
A global holy war, eh – this is enough to get every red-blooded warrior
in the room's attention . . . *and we all start fantasising.* Gawain sees
illustrations from one of his old Ladybird books: in the first,
Richard, Cœur de Lion, cleaves an iron bar in two with the edge of
of his mighty broadsword – in the next Saladin bests him by slicing
a silk scarf into two shimmery and exact halves *with his scimitar* . . .
Half an hour later the briefing closes with predictably professional
questioning: Will there be a two-can rule? But by then Captain

Anselm and his personable friend are *long gone* . . . Spilling out through the Admin Block's swing doors, the junior officers spark up and form a scrum round their match-winning flanker: Wotcher reckon, Greeny – can't be coincidence . . . Your spooky pal come to look you up, hasn't he . . . Yeah, Greeny – he's got your bum under surveillance . . . Time out! Round two, is it, Greenster? He stands, head down and lowing pitifully in *my secret barn* . . . No Fighting Ram, but a veal calf, kept in the dark for its entire life, then *led out to be slaughtered* –. Aye, aye, lads, Lieutenant "Potso" Ponsonby sings out, what's this at ten o'clock? And they turn to see the Chief, together with the EmmEyeSix man, rounding the corner of the mess. The Chief's face *is a picture* – albeit one executed by *an unofficial war artist*: on its veiny canvas disgust and delight are *battling it out* . . . Bit of a turn-up, Potso says as the odd couple draws near, you, ah, turning up like this. The Chief grimaces: Ah, yes . . . Jonathan here told me about this strange coincidence – says he had a drink with you chaps in the summer, in . . . Manchester? Bit more than a drink in Gawain's case, Chief, Tizer puts in. Really? The Chief turns to his prospective son-in-law: How's that, Captain Thomas? And from somewhere . . . *or someone*, Gawain receives the gift of light-hearted charm: Oh, y'know, Chief – far too much booze . . . Dancing, yes – but rest assured, no romancing . . . He darts a look at his canalside ravager, but the EmmEyeSix man's expression is as sunnily unclouded . . . *as that morning.* Shocked, Gawain realises: It's routine for him – absolutely bloody routine. Picking up a man – getting him drunk then drugging him . . . Taking him somewhere and . . . then . . . Chop-chop . . . bag the chops . . . *That'll be two twenty-five . . . pay at the till, please . . .* The halo of a white nylon trilby encircles the spook's beautiful brows – a white apron shrouds his slim form. His hand no longer holds a wisping cigarette but *a dripping cleaver!* Because he's a *butcher*, this one – not a killer – which, when you stop to consider it, is really a perfectly honest job description if you're a soldier. No, he's the man down the chinking line, who drags the upended beast along the rail by a length of chain tied to its leg, then sticks a billhook in under its ribcage, and, with a sharp yank, *unzips my belly.* Blood and guts hosed away, he sets to work cutting and trimming *prime cuts* . . . I don't know about you . . . Gawain keeps it up and light . . . but that was the worst hangover I've had in ages – took me days to recover . . . The *Butcher* smirks – and the Chief *carries on*: Well, carry on, then, Gawain – er, Jonathan here says he'd like a look-see round the establishment. Bit bloody odd if you ask me – there's bugger-all to see –. You can never, the *Butcher* cuts in, have too much information in my line of work. The Chief sucks his *shit-coated* lower lip: And I s'pose you've clearance? The Butcher raises one elegant eyebrow, summoning a gruff: Will you do the honours, then, Gawain? Already ten yards off, the Chief turns back: And thank you, ah, Jonathan, for a most illuminating overview – wasn't it, chaps? He strides off, while his chaps wait until he's out of earshot, before: So, Mike – or Jonathan, or whatever your name is, mate – you the full biscuit, or what? Tizer lowers over the *Butcher*: EmmEyeSix, issit? EssEyeEss? And Shabba joins in: Oi, Mikey or Johnny, or whatever your name is – you gotta pen what fires bullets? The spook's unruffled: As a matter of fact, I do, he says, withdrawing a fat fountain pen from his inside pocket. See, to all intents and purposes, an innocuous – if rather expensive – Mont Blanc – he unscrews the cap . . . the expected nib – but remove this – he does so – and you'll see that instead of an ink cartridge there's a, um, secret chamber – it's rifled, and takes a nine-millimetre cartridge . . . Shabba says: Did Q demonstrate it for you in his underground lab? The Butcher laughs indulgently: Yeah, well, it really is called the Q Section, and they do give us gadgets – stuff we use out in the field. But we're talking secure comms mostly. Not to shit on the Firm's mystique, but it's a stone-cold fucking fact: no Intelligence Branch officer has so much as fired a weapon on assignment since the Second World War . . . He reassembles his *mightier-than-the-sword*, seemingly oblivious to the five pairs of eyes intent on his every move. *No ifs, no buts* . . . we're all, Gawain thinks, thinking the same thing – although it's him who says: Same diff' . . . for the regiment, I mean. We missed out on Granby – Desert Storm, that is. Haven't even had a Paddyland tour . . . All we've done in years is a blue-hat job in Cyprus –. And now this Bosnian bollocks, Tizer interjects, but screw that anyway – what's the story, matey? Bit far-bloody-fetched, you turning up like this on our patch – you and Greeny here gotta thing going on –? Oh, keep on, Shabba sings, dancin' an' romancin' . . . Yeah, the *Butcher* says, *mincing* his fag butt with the sharp toe of his handmade shoe, we've got a sort of thing going on – obviously I can't tell you lot anything about it. Why, Anderson says, why not? I mean, we've all signed the OhEssAy . . . Oh, shut the fuck up, Tizer yawns, he isn't remotely serious – they're just lovers, that's all there is to it. But listen . . .

seriously – all that stuff you were saying in there, d'you mean it? D'you really think the fuzzy-wuzzies're going on the offensive? The Butcher's tone darkens until it's *well done*: Absolutely. We're in a chaotic new world, gentlemen – anything you pick up while you're out there – he reaches into his inside pocket – either kick it up through your own int' sec' to Brigade Command – he pulls out an *oxblood* leather wallet – or you can reach me directly at Vauxhall Bridge Road ... and deals the cards out *croupier*-quickly. Tizer snorts: Who the fuck would we ask for? There's no name on this – just a number. The Butcher remains the very epitome of sang-froid: Our political masters may've in their infinite wisdom decided that the Service, as a whole, should be publically avowed – but that doesn't mean any individual actually ... exists ... He wiggles his manicured nails either side of his face. – Spooky, eh? He laughs, Fuck's sake, chaps – we're not a bunch of plods yanking diplomats from under whores' beds, that's Stella's outfit. We've a bit more – he drops an octave – class. Now, Greeny? Gawain knows that to check if a joint's ready to serve, you thrust a carving knife right in – hold it there for twenty seconds, then withdraw it. If the tip of the knife is too hot to touch ... *the meat's done.* They're strolling perfectly casually away from his brother officers, and he's saying to the Butcher *perfectly casually*: I've no idea where to take you – the garrison's absolutely vast, but it's just a dull little town, really – shit shops, tacky facilities ... He falls silent, conscious of the lithe body loping pantherishly along beside him. I want to break free, he thinks, but *he already is* ... How 'bout the gym? the Butcher says, and Gawain *piffles*, Pardon? The gym, the *Butcher* persists.

The gym-na-si-um. Y'know, where the young men lift the weights from their lovely strong shoulders. Dunno 'bout you, Gawain, but there's nothing more likely to, ah, divert me on a boring Sunday afternoon . . . *Silence*. They walk on in . . . *silence*. Their footfalls striking the tarmac drum, they gradually synchronise, until it's a comradely *march* . . . Gawain remembers SeeEssEmm Rowley at the Academy – recalls standing before him . . . *no time to take a shit*, so one was still . . . *chambered*. He feels the spatter of Rowley's spittle on his cheeks – hears the martinet's strangulated cry: *There ees sheet drill, Thomas, and there ees be-you-tee-full drill!* But this drill they're doing now – it can never be beautiful. Never be beautiful because it's being performed by a couple of . . . *bum-boys!* Squad, left turn, Gawain involuntarily mutters – and is thrilled when the body beside him does precisely that. They march along a concrete path between stunted military hedging – they bash through swing doors, bounce on springy floorboards, bash through a second set of doors and find some young men weight-lifting: one lies supine, arms bent, shoulders bulging, the bar inches from his *giblets* face, while the *underdone* one hovering above says, Point . . . Point . . . Gawain and the *Butcher* march past their *sweatcloud* and *Squad, right turn!* bash through a third pair of doors, into a *padded cell* . . . Rubber mats are draped over wall bars – and there's a tickly stink of sisal, liniment and more sweat. Gawain slams the *Butcher* up against a vaulting horse that's *ready for the knackers* . . . Your game – what is it? What's your . . . f-fucking game? The *Butcher* remains imperturbable – apart from his eyelashes. He has, Gawain observes, the longest silkiest eyelashes – and they, they are perturbed by . . . *my breath*. The tip of the *Butcher's* tongue pokes between his pursed lips. He gives a little wriggle – which somehow relaxes Gawain's grip so that . . . *I'm caressing his shoulders.* The eyes implore Gawain to *Kiss me!* And then there's a rainbow trout, tickled from the Wye, thrashing about . . . *in my landing net.* Gawain has been trained to perfection in the art of tank warfare – as a light reconnaissance unit, the Fighting Rams are deployed to probe the enemy's defences, and where possible *thrust forwards* . . . He struggles at first – then, advancing a knee into the defile between the enemy's flanks, he begins to reverse . . . *the tide of battle.* Following Sunday lunch, the Chief will be drowsing in his armchair, slowly drifting down Jacob's Creek while Missus Renfrew wipes the place mats and puts the napkin rings away. Upstairs in her attic bedroom, beneath the dormer window, Gawain's straight doppelgänger sits with his fiancée . . . *a man who never was.* She's showing him the pictures she's cut out from glossy magazines and inserted in the plastic pockets of a ring binder, because she's a well-organised bride-to-be: *Obviously this isn't my corsage, Greeny – you won't see that 'til the Big Day . . . But I thought maybe this one . . . or these – for the bridesmaids, and my maid-of-honour . . .* Gawain likes it when Fiona calls him by his Rams nickname – it makes him feel they're shackled together: another ball-and-chain linked in to the chain of command . . . *We're good mates – we are.* What he likes a lot less is the clanking of their interlinked and insufficiently oiled tongues – that, and the oppressive smell of lavender rising up from her clothes, her hair . . . *her skin.* When I've left, he often thinks during their clinches, she'll fold herself up and put herself neatly away in her hope chest. But here, in the gym's store-room – in amongst a tangle of ropes and a jumble of obsolete equipment, leaning up against the only horse this cavalryman has ever ridden, Gawain abandons *all hope* . . . and groans into the *Butcher's* avid mouth, even as he feels his *joint, too hot to touch*, against his thigh. Stubble rubs stubble, adding to the heat of their passion – passion which *boils my brains* . . . producing a steamy pungency that swirls and curls through the gap between the swing doors. Soon enough, Gawain thinks, some roided-up muscle freak will smell us – and what will happen then? As their tongues tackle, he sees their stripped-sapling bodies dragged across the muddy pitch – sees their incriminating erections waggling in the outraged faces of the court martial . . . *Lieutenant-Colonel Roger Renfrew presiding*, senior officers who ceremoniously order the miscreants to be *poleaxed with our own choppers*. Cut it out! His cry, shouted into the *Butcher's* mouth, escapes – and they break to stand facing each other, rocking a little on the worn old floor-boards. For . . . years . . . now . . . the Butcher pants . . . the lively hunt has been all I've desired – he wipes his *greasy* mouth with the back of his hand – but now I've met you, my love – he cups Gawain's cheek – the sheep may safely graze, because I've tracked you down, dearest – and now you're at bay . . . And his love *bleats*, I don't even know your name. Laughing, the *Butcher* sticks out his *cleaver*: It really is Jonathan – Jonathan De'Ath. Gawain – straightening his tunic, adjusting his belt – *whines girlishly*: How do I know you're telling the truth? The *Butcher* laughs some more – then answers sincerely: Well, De'Ath – hardly a viable alias, is it? I mean, when we do a natural cover operation – that's assuming a false identity – it's got to be credible, so Requirements select the name on your passport, driving licence or whatever carefully . . . Make sure it's not likely to raise eyebrows – or hackles for that matter . . . They hear boots giving the corridor *a good kicking*, and Gawain blurts out, We've gotta geddout of here! Then they are, striding down the somnolent lanes lined with ticky-tacky boxes: *Alamein Avenue . . . Blenheim Crescent . . . Malplaquet Mews . . .* Every single schoolrun, Gawain muses, will be a campaign that lasts for . . . *centuries.* Trooper Winters from Gawain's own section is manning this, the quietest of the checkpoints on the entire peri- meter. But if he's surprised by this sight – his SeeOh *bugging out with some pinstriped ponce* – he's too fixated on his victorious future to show it, only saluting smartly as they swing past the sentry box's tainted Perspex. *Squad, le-eft turn!* A boot between the bars and it's *oop 'n' over.* Then they're standing on a patch of piebald turf surrounded by moulting hedges from which tattered crows lift off *kraaarking* . . . Jonathan raises one black sole and then the other. This, he says, is gonna trash my Grensons. Gawain, walking ahead, hears the swish-past of weekenders' cars heading home down the AyWun, and throws back: We won't be overheard here – your lot haven't got an eye in this sky, have they? He turns to confront his pursuer, and the rage that's been building inside him bursts out: In Manchester – that night . . . Did you? Catching up, Jonathan grabs his arm – and, looking straight into Gawain's eyes, asks, Did I what? Did I? It would've been rape, y'know – rape. You were completely fucking out of it –. And who was responsible for that! Gawain bellows. The Butcher shakes his pretty head: Not me – not

176

my style at all. And of course I didn't . . . take advantage of you –
are you crazy? So heightened are Gawain's senses he feels each
hot snort of indignation on his *quivery* top lip: N-no, I'm n-not
fucking mad – I'm about to go to staff college. I'm a Fighting
Ram – a Yorkshire-bloody-Hussar. And I told you – I fucking told
you – he has a fistful of red knitted-silk tie and crisp white shirtfront – I'm engaged by the hedges – which are in bud and greenly
streaming past the car's windows. Mark's lips are moving schizily
as he *tosses his word-salad* – which is Camilla's own coinage. She
catches, Tossitupin theair, and also: Felltoearth nowherenear . . .
Followed by, Inmyfuckin'arse – halloperidolly, gotta sweetie –.
I'm NOT TALKING ABOUT YOU! she snaps, and he falls
silent – silent enough for her to hear more burbling coming from
the back seat: Fivehunnredanfiffy, fivehunnredanfiffywun, five-
hunnredanfiffytoo . . . painfully audible despite the Vauxhall's
growling engine and the wind whistling through the windows' perished rubber seals. At least with Ben there's never been any How far
is it, Mummy? or When will we get there? No – no! She checks
herself: Not at least – if only, if only he'd say those things over and
over again like normal children do! Not that Camilla actually
knows what normal children of his age do, not having spent much
time around them. But it had to be better than these fivehunnredan-
fiffynine *egregious stereotypies* – not her words, but those of Mark's
father, *tossed* to the top of her own *word-salad* . . . She shifts her
hips in the warm vinyl, adjusts the rear-view mirror . . . *could be
worse – I've all my own teeth*, and feels the fart brewing beneath the
gastric band of her seat belt. When she was loading up the Vauxhall,

preparatory to their departure from Bamburgh, she'd found Ben already belted up in the back, the road atlas open on his lap: he was consulting the distance table on the final page. She's no idea what it is they've passed fivehunnredansicksyseven times since then . . . *telegraph poles* . . . *lamp-posts?* but knows whatever they are her son will've used them to calculate fairly accurately *where we are* . . . White-out-of-green lettering CATTERICK GARRISON TWO MILES swims into view . . . *right on cue*, followed by a slip road they grumble past. The fields to either side of the motorway are flaring bright under the late April sun . . . *I was raped inna rape field*. Were you, Milla? she quizzes herself: And by who? The reply comes back: By a rapist – obviously. Rapist, Papist, therapist – I was raped by the Papist rapist of my therapist . . . *inna rape field* . . . The syllables form and reform in Camilla's aching head as, unable to resist, she's dragged back into the hateful memory: the oily stems of the plants she grabbed at as he dragged her by her ankles along the muddy furrow – the putrescent smell of the drenched vegetation and the still shittier stench of . . . *my fear.* I'm traumatised, she thinks. That thing he did to me, he did, ooh . . . twenty years ago – and for all of my adult life I've been *t-t-t-traumatised*, like when you hit your head really hard and for a while the whole world's ringing and singing the painful vibration that's you . . . Fivehunnredanseveny-free, fivehunnredansevenyfaw . . . Which is why I've ended up like this: vibrating in time to my son's monotonous voice as he *speaks the distance* . . . He's a human milometer – or metronome, and I'm shackled to his . . . *pendulum*. Shackled to it – and by extension to his father, a man who's so out of it on sedatives, hypnotics and antipsychotics he can't so much as put a hand on my knee – *let alone rape me . . .* The Vauxhall rises and falls on undulating tarmac waves – while Camilla, *falling – falling – falling* along the interminable road, cannot wait to touch down in the sanctuary of their Kilburn flat, where at last the shelving units piled up with her son's ever increasing stuff will shield her from this radioactive landscape, and her memories, which burn brighter than *ten thousand suns – he got out a penknife, opened it quite casually – cut the hem of my dress and tore it wide apart . . .* Rolling and tumbling past the slip road to another motorway services they can't afford to stop at, Camilla feels the fart swell more – then mutate into the familiar nagging pain of her *endo . . . endo . . . endometri– Fuck it! Woman's trouble –* which is how her own mother had referred to the affliction six-hunnredanwun times a day, as she'd squeaked about the house in her . . . *plastic knickers.* Camilla – weighed down and *wonky-donkey* that she is, with her autistic son in one straw pannier and his schizophrenic father in the other – wishes she had one of those hands-free earpieces so she could talk to the *psychiatric grandaddy of us all . . .* She sees herself sitting at her trestle table in the bay window, with the dustballs draggled into being by the long blackout curtains *tickling my ankles.* She feels the handset pressed so hard against her ear the cartilage *crackles,* and she hears herself going *onanon,* recounting the deranged doodles and crazy shading of *his male line . . .* Yet he never displays any impatience, *my father-in-law –* which is how Camilla mostly thinks of Zack – unsurprisingly, since their relationship is so often resolemnised, as they jointly make their signatures, giving consent on the same miserable pro formas

179

which authorise this test or that futile intervention. He never shows any irritation – and this, despite his own chaotic domestic situation: an ageing man who has to wrangle small children of his own – coordinating lackadaisical au pairs and rushing from hurried consultations so he can do the schoolrun. And all because the *lady loves getting laid* ... An ague of hatred for her father-in-law's errant third wife, Charlie, grips Camilla – her hands grip and twist the steering wheel, while through her sudden tearfall she sees this threatening vision: Zack's full and froggy features floating above the middle lane. Keep two chevrons visible between vehicles and phantoms, she says aloud, easing off on the accelerator, lest she collide with ... *the eyes of Doctor Eckleburg.* Yes, tomorrow morning she'll be at her table – and he'll be sitting at the counter in the well-fitted but forever-messy kitchen at Redington Road, spooning up Cheerios as he listens to her *serial woes* ... Recently, Camilla's been unable to prevent this relentless punning sixhunnredanthirtyayt times a day – it's become *a sorta psychic tic what ticks all the boxes.* Zack has always urged her to view Mark's wordsplurge as *ebulliently productive* – but she's been listening for years now and it's *tangled up my mind* in an *Alphabetti Spaghetti* of meaning. When the three of them are under the same roof – which is becoming increasingly rare – Camilla still tries to understand. Mopping the dingy lino-leum – picking congealed porridge from a bowl as she receives her sixunnredandthirtynine*th* warning of imminent alien invasion, she'll think, This is your life – and has been for over a decade now. A decade during which Mark must have gone on and come off his medication scores of times, so repeating the same sickening cycle – the slump into silvery, salival somnolence, being the state of her own mind, Camilla suspects, as much as his. Could it be that she unconsciously wills him to stop taking the pills? Because at least when he's crazy . . . *he's alive.* She and Zack share, she thinks, a similar attitude, although in respect of different individuals: for her father-in-law, while not exactly in denial about Ben, nonetheless for a long time rubbished the idea there was anything *much wrong* with his grandson. Then there'd been the birthday party: they were living south of the river in the run-down council flat Mark had been allocated after his last discharge from the Maudsley. She remembers standing with Zack in the concrete trench of the balcony, listening to the gasp of the heating system, but still hearing his son's schiz-scat. She recalls him saying, You're a profoundly unlucky young woman. You fell in love with my son during one of his less, ah, disturbed periods – then fell pregnant. Now you're trying to cope with a highly active toddler and his disturbed father at the same time – it's hardly surprising you're projecting some of your own distress on to the child, so seeing his behaviour as pathological. Frankly, Milla, I don't think anyone would blame you if you felt you had to *choose between them.* Meaning what? Send Mark off to chemical concentration camp forever? Abandon the man who'd touched her so gently – held her so tenderly, whispered to her so . . . lovingly. Had it been Mark's schizophrenia which had made him such a demon lover? Falling into his arms – *falling into the abyss.* His mouth on my mouth – *his mouth on my* . . . Falling down to London *AYSIXTYWUN, SKIPTON-ON-SWALE* . . . My guts falling out . . . *of my fanny.* A fallen woman, Camilla thinks, that's me. She glances over at Mark, slumped in the passenger seat, angelic face distorted by his *diabolic muttering*: Whykaytooyouwant-mesixsixsicks? Choose between them? How could Gramps've said such a thing – yet he did, and lots more besides. Because he'd always been *sorta schizy too* – full of warmth, affection and concern, but at the same time coldly, clinically observing his grandson. And Ben had been the *terriblist toddler* – a frenetic ball of blond curls and brown stains . . . *from the Marmite*. Didn't matter how carefully she hid it – he found it, got it open and *smeared it* . . . Mark does exhibit some *egregious stereotypies*, Gramps had said, standing there in the trench, peering through two layers of dirty glass at his son. Mark would've been wearing a Power Rangers mask – which, he used to say, shielded him from interstellar surveillance – while Zack's grandson *wouldn't keep his clothes on 'til he was four*, so ran around annaround, naked except for an ugly tan biodegradable nappy. Camilla sees her son as he was: hunched over his meticulously lined-up toy cars and holding both hands, fingers spread and fluttering, before his startling blue eyes . . . *please fly away forever, Peter – fuck off for good, Paul*. He does it all the time, is what she would've said to his grandfather . . . *'cause I said it all the time*: He does it all the time – and if he isn't doing that, he's spinning round annaround 'til he's so dizzy he falls over. Or else he's pelting up and down the hall – then charging into the kitchenette and banging his head against the fridge – see? See? You can see the big dent he's made in it *from here* . . . Yes, you could see the dent from the balcony – see it also from the AyWunEmm a decade later. See it, and see as well *meticulously lined up* all those occasions when she'd pleaded with Zack: You see that? You see what he's doing now? See, see, see! Sixhunnredanfawty times every bleeding day, *or hour . . .* It's been her fate, Camilla realises, to be compelled always to look at her fidgeting, rocking and rolling son, while he never so much as glances at her *for a second!* At Heath Hospital, shortly after Ben's bloody becoming – wrung out, *a soiled dishcloth* of a woman following thirty hours of gas-tank-deflating and botched-epidural-inserting labour – it'd been Zack she'd babbled to: H-He, w-won't look at me . . . Staring down at the baby's whorl of mucus-lacquered hair – *Where?* Where'd Mark been? Out of sight, and . . . *out of his mind. Tush now,* Zack had said, or words to that effect: Tush now, newborns don't focus right away – it takes days, sometimes a week or more for their eyes and their minds to fully connect . . . *G'dunggg! G'dungggg! Khhssshhhkkkkhhhhssschhhg'dunggg! ESTABLISHING NETWORK CONNECTION . . .* Who knows what this little chap's seeing right now? P'raps it's some other reality altogether. But when they do focus for the first time, it's always on their mother's eyes. Little Ben will see you, Milla – and he'll see that you're seeing him, see also that you're focusing on other things, other people . . . Camilla often didn't have the *froggiest* what *Frog-face* was banging on about . . . *but I got that.* Our bubble-worlds, her father-in-law had speculated as he peered into her teary eyes, are so very delicate – so easy to pop. Nevertheless, we pierce them thousands-upon-millions of times . . . Pierce them, then sew them together with our *sight-lines.* That's how we know what someone else is thinking about – even before they speak . . . *I was raped once – inna rape field. Around this time of year – a flowery torture. He – he looked lovingly into my eyes the entire time he was . . . punching me in the face.* It'd been the middle of the night when her son was born – Zack had taken a banana from the bowl on the windowsill and held its up-curving and sweetly-rotten-smelling prong against *the cold black glass – he punched me in the face, and kicked me . . . down there.* Zack had said, Mummy looks at the banana – baby thinks: She's thinking about the banana. The way they perceive the actual physical object may be radically different – but the mental object they create together, by definition . . . *it's the same thing.* Bananas and babies, Milla – atom bombs and Arthur Askey. Have you ever wondered how it is that the world, in all its confusion and complexity, is nonethleless entirely legible to us the moment we attempt to read it? From earliest infancy our perception has this fluency – p'raps it's because the world is a book that's been read by us before . . . A month or so later she'd revisited this conversation – and asked Zack to write down what he'd said so she could get to grips with it. He'd searched out a jotter from his corduroy pocket, each page of which carried the same exciting news about an ulcer drug, and set this down: Ultimately perception isn't individual but collective, and the world which is its object is nothing more or less than the analogue of all those myriad moments when we look into another's eyes and see them *looking elsewhere — I'm gonna shit myself – we've got to stop! My legs!* are magically unscrewing from their threaded sockets, while *My ribs . . .* Camilla lifts a hand from the juddery steering wheel, clutches her breast . . . *are popping one by one from their cage* – until there's *nothing to spare . . .* only a jumbled slurry of bones and guts *rollin' on down the road* at sixhunnredanfiffyfive miles an hour. You can stop, she commands her chanting son, 'cause we're gonna stop – I've gotta go to the loo. But he goes on relentlessly enumerating – just as the pile of persistence in the passenger seat keeps *tossing his word-salad*: Machine stops – planesfallouttathesky . . . Squashed-peopledie – death'n'destructioneverywhere . . . Eyewarned'em . . . The signs charge towards them: WALSHFORD . . . *washed up*, HUNSINGORE . . . *hunting gore*, WETHERBY – which sounds familiar in a Northern accent: *Where-there-bee*, which also sounds like a kazoo up yer 'ooter, or buzz-buzz-buzzing about in your beehive 'airdo spend! Spend! Spending! even though you *ain't got it*. You go swanning along the high street, underneath the striped awnings, avoiding the bat-eared boys in cloth caps playing with the metal-hoop-type-thingies from barrels. On their way up to Ma Peggotty's place: *Get it inside you, boy, and y'ull be goin' oop that hill as quick as you coom down* . . . *Where-there-bee – wheaty-germ* . . . Ben had been *Ay. Layt. De. Vel. O. Per.* Not when it came to talking – that'd come quickly enough . . . *that'd come quickly enough* . . . But he wouldn't read until Gramps had bought the seedee for him: Bobby the *buzz-buzz-buzz* Bee and his Jollyphonics. Bring your Bee-Bee-Bat and your Bee-Bee-Ball to the park. Little Ben, sat up on a high stool, demonstrating *dynamical movement and gesture* as he *ham-ham*-hammered away at the *Bee-Bee-Bee*-buttons helping him to *develop the ability to hear and discriminate the forty-two-letter sounds in the English language.* Little Ben, a strange smile on his Marmite lips as he played upon his *dee-dee-dee*-drum. No Powder Puff girls for Benny – no desire whatsoever to *catch 'em all* . . . His only friends Bobby-the-Bee and his great pal, Phonic-the-computer

– his hands never still – always *ay-ay-ay*-agitated, 'cause he'd got *ay-ay-ay-ants on my arm* and they were *causing me alarm ...! Where-there-bee ... what?* As the Vauxhall *sambas* off the motorway and on to the slip road, Camilla envisions Harold Shipman lookalikes walking arm-in-arm with Myra Hindley doubles. Sees their trowel-shaped beards and cold complacent eyes – sees them munching on Eccles cakes and brushing crumbs from the lapels of their waterproof jackets. Sees them laughing *all the way to the blood-bank – I haemorrhaged ...* And the worst part of it had been *I gorra lorra blood ...* the phonics rattle around in her head *jo-lli-ly*, as the car rushes between vernal hedgerows. Camilla spies a lonely phone booth ... *Hello? Hello? Where am I? Inna phone booth inna rape field*, which may be postcard pretty from a distance – but up close it's rotten and slimy, the oilseed rape – *where I was raped.* Did I tell you about that, Doctor ... *Who?* Yes – yes, she'd told him all right – told him very early on, in the kitchen at Redington Road, which was where Mark was staying the night he'd picked her up at the poetry reading – a wild and wordy night of *phonics and philthy phucking – up the stairs, past the stained-glass windows, up my back passage. Preferred it that way – felt less violated ...* Can't've been more than a fortnight later – Mark prob'ly upstairs in his child-hood bedroom *slopping about in a tank of Stelazine*, while he stared sightlessly at the cut-out-and-keep posters still stuck to the walls: sharks, Second World War aircraft, Cold War spying gadgetry. Downstairs, over a bottle of plonk, Zack had probed Camilla, and she'd *thrown up right away: I was raped once ...* inna rape field ... an I s'pose you're gonna tell me that explains everything ... She pictures him eating toast – *he's always eating toast*. Hears this low *crumbling*: Not everything – but some things . . . I'd imagine. I mean, you realised very quickly, I think, that my son is "mentally ill" . . . The quotation marks are always present when he uses such terms, two crooked fingers *shoved down the throat of the conversation* . . . Up he'd chucked: It's purely speculation, but I'd imagine you were drawn to him – albeit unconsciously – by this fact alone: for him – for you – *the worst has already happened* . . . The Vauxhall idles noisily at a pelican crossing, and Camilla hearkens to its costly clatter – its nuts and bolts and cogs and cables are all *my responsibility* . . . The outskirts of Wetherby are grim – stony-faced buildings on all four corners, their narrow eyes *snow-blinded* by net curtains. Two elderly women cross in front of the car . . . *the halt leading the lame*, who in turn leads a wicker shopper . . . *closest she'll get now to a beehive*. The lights *bleed out* to orange, and Camilla eases down the accelerator . . . *Endometriotic lesions develop their own nerves*, Zack had told her when his grandson's difficult birth was followed by . . . *further complications*. And she'd flung back: My geepee already told me that! The truth was, no doctor – not even a consulting time lord – could've dreamt up such freaky sci-fi stuff: the lesions not only grew their own nerves, but those nerves were then plugged directly into her central nervous system . . . *G'dunggg! G'dungggg! Khhssshhhkkkkhhhhssschhhg'dunggg!* So there was the disease's pain to endure, plus the pain of the symptoms it'd *given birth to* . . . Camilla couldn't eyeball the lesions deep inside her womb – but she could see the eyes that'd been torn from it. It was *featherweight*, Ben's gaze – it wafted away from her heavy scrutiny.

He won't so much as look at me! she'd said again *annagain* – to Zack, to Mark, to all the other members of the disorderly family she'd drunkenly fucked her way into. He won't look at me – it's not normal! All the other babies at the mums-and-toddlers group – all the other babies in the world! That's what they do – stare into their mother's eyes . . . that's how they bond – that's how they know *who you are* . . . A decade ago, standing in that concrete trench, watching her son twitch and flail, she'd shrugged off her father-in-law's assurances for the *sixhunnredansixtysixth* time. You don't get it, Zack – you just don't get it, she'd sobbed. Sometimes I think he's like that kid in the horror movie – Damien. I start thinking he's possessed – that he's the . . . Devil . . . The handbrake creaks ominously, the engines dies. There's the silence . . . *of the grave*, but none of the peace, for father and son are out of the car before Camilla's had time to undo her seatbelt – out of the car, and both striding across the supermarket car park towards the same set of sliding doors, despite following radically diverging trajectories . . . *they're never together.* She remembers the conversation on the balcony so well because Ben had been exactly two and a half – and she'd organised a half-birthday party for him. Back then she'd believed she could jolly him into sociability with party poppers and Hula Hoops – but he'd been perfectly indifferent to the three or four toddlers and their mothers, who Camilla had *artily . . . craftily . . .* lured up from the One O'Clock Club in the concrete bunker ludicrously named *the William Morris Community Centre.* Ben's father had shut himself up in their bedroom – remained there the whole time, sulking because she wouldn't let him wear his Power

Rangers mask. It was left to Zack to dole out cartons of Um Bongo while Camilla wrapped up the pass-the-parcel – left to Zack, as well, to make conversation about the drains . . . *rancid sewage smell fluting through air vents poxy with congealed old paint blobs* and the DeeAitchEssEss – both of which he'd been suprisingly well informed about. As the afternoon wore on, the mothers – three stolid and near-pyramidal Ghanaian women – had grown warmer and more garrulous, while the half-birthday boy retreated further and further into . . . *himself.* Ben had ended up sitting in the dirty clothes hamper and screaming as if it were him – not some gilded-bloody-princess – who was *the most hunted person in the world* . . . The Ghanaian mother who tried to pick up Ben to comfort him got a Hot Wheels in her eye for her trouble. Eventually, Zack gave him half a Valium crushed up in some Um Bongo . . . *not strictly speaking ethical, that* – another of his phrases which, over the years . . . *has caught me, too.* Ben ended up half awake, slumped on a grubby sag-bag, and clutching the toy car in one hand while the other expertly manipulated the buttons which thrust the little plumbers up on to moving platforms, or made them jump down into yawning ravines . . . *he was only two and a half!* Perhaps it was on that miserable occasion, after Zack had got a half-bottle of whisky from the offie, to stifle their own more silent screams – but it might've been at any point during Ben's terrible second year, his thunderous third or his *fucking dreadful fourth* – that this lecture was delivered: Autistischen Psychopathen, that was Hans Asperger's term for the odd children he saw in his clinic. He also described them as intelligent automata – and he was a humane practitioner!

A saint compared to Kanner – who I met at a conference once and found to be a bumptious-bloody-blowhard . . . Manipulated his trial data as well. As for Saint-bloody-Bettelheim – well, it's all coming out now. Far from his "Orthogenic School" being some haven of creativity and self-expression, turns out it was an abusive snake-pit – while he was just another self-hating Jew turned *Konzentration Kamp Kommandant* . . . — The sign on the car parked in front, BABY ON BOARD, is boring into Camilla. Her hands still gripping the steering wheel, she sees the baby – not bored, but hysterical *inna rape field* . . . Lying there – convulsed, puce, scream-ing the way only babies can, on and on, their razor-sharp tongues revolving mechanically as they process this misery-food. On and on – *boring into you*, on and never off – *can't turn 'em off, no off-switch* . . . Can't turn 'em off-and-on, *which usually fixes the problem* . . . *You're not bored, though?* Sorta *phonics* he'd come up with – and not *fee-say-shuss-lee* . . . Bored? Her voice, her words – spoken during a summit meeting they'd held at the peak of one of Ben's crises: Bored? I'm not fucking bored, Zack, it's gone way beyond boredom – *I'm gonna kill myself* . . . Her baby is always on board – suckered to the windscreen by its Um Bongo-sticky hands . . . *they kill them in the Congo.* Suckered there like one of those dumb stuffed Garfields there was a craze for – sending out short, savage *bursts* of misery and distress *only I can receive* . . . Ben, aged twelve, still sleeps in her bed – and on one . . . or several . . . loathsome occasions, Camilla has woken in the night to feel the hot tip of his rigid penis pressed against her thighs *inna rape field* . . . Can she bear to be bare behind flimsy partitions . . . *smearscrape-moppitupp?* She can – she must.

Squatting and *squitting* in the cubicle, she hears, Loadsa love –
chat t'yer later . . . And thinks, Coming soon! To a rockin' Portaloo
near you! An epic tale of luv-'n'-loss *in fully-phoney Dolby Surround-
sound!* – *We do have money behind us, you know* . . . Such an odd thing
to say! Camilla remembers him saying it for the first time in the
Sainsbury's near Brook Green. Would've been a couple of years
after the Power Rangers party, and their fake little family had
moved to a sheltered block run by a mental health charity near
Ravenscourt Park . . . *Ben at that age* galloping *round annaround*
under the railway arch, his outstretched arm waggling, his hand
circling, his fingers flickering as he'd . . . *stimmed.* Dollops of duck
and goose shit all over the sad lawns surrounding the milky-watered
pond *never forget it* . . . Ben sitting on a badly carved wooden
wombat, momentarily stilled – a carton of juice in one hand, a
flapjack in the other, a mumble of cabbalistic numbers *sixhunnred-
ansixtysix.* . . slipping from his sticky lips . . . *We do have money
behind us, you know.* Such an odd way of putting things – then, as
now, Camilla had pictured a game of Gramps's footsteps: *load-
samoney* creeping behind her – a rustling wad, ill concealed in a hide
woven from banknotes. He'd also said things like, You're not too
proud? To which she'd snorted: Don't make me *laugh-arf-arf!* and
clapped her flippers in the Sainsbury's salad aisle, as Zack turned to
her, a ready-made one in his hand, his *puckered facebag* full of healthy
concern. He remains, she thinks, *endearing* – the word appears in
her hurting mind, as she rocks and rolls and *squitsan'shits*, its letters
wreathed in radicchio and rocket leaves. Back then he'd still been
in his prime: a figurehead of Psychiatry, in his habitual corduroy

jacket and grey flannel trousers, bolted to the prow of . . . *a shopping trolley*. We – the family, that is – have money behind us . . . To which she undoubtedly would've replied: You've always paid our rent – we're very grateful. To which he would almost certainly have countered: And am happy to do so – and to offer more help, if required. More! Yes, more! That's what little Ben had needed – more high-dose vitamin supplements, more minerals and enzymes – more probiotics and anti-fungals, more Bio-Chelat rice bread spread with yum-yum almond butter, more glutathione cream rubbed on his swollen tummy – and especially more Risperdal crushed into his first morning spoonful of Marmite, a practice that – when his Grandfather got wind of . . . *he blew*: D'you know what this rubbish is? Shaking the pill pot to a *bossa nova beat*: It's an atypical antipsychotic developed for the treatment of schizophrenia in adults – if anyone should be guzzling this dangerous pap, it's Mark, not Ben . . . Such conviction, she believes now, was only born of confusion – those first few years of Ben's life . . . *we were all making it up*. It was a burgeoning subculture – it wasn't only the Whitehouse-Busner Family who were dancing to the autists' beat: there were all the other parents, carers and assorted practitioners who'd to tend and toilet their ceaselessly self-stimulating toddlers. In waiting room after waiting room, with Ben squirming on her lap, she'd bitterly ruminated: For once I'm trendy – hip, even . . . Too young for punk – too old for acid house, Camilla had cleverly managed to give birth to . . . *my own rave scene*. But then, that'd been before the rumours of a new and devastating form of autism, one marked by the most dramatic behavioural regression imaginable. Panic ripped through the online forums she didn't so much frequent as . . . *lived on, the whole fucking time!* Late at night, staring into the ghostly furniture of their back-lit pages, she read about children who'd once prattled away now falling stonily silent – others who'd seemed quite continent *shitting themselves in droves* . . . What frail hope Camilla had rested in Ben's *Jolly-fucking-phonics*: he spoke – and not just the sporadic words and disjointed phrases to be expected at his age, but entire, well-formed sentences . . . *Tarzan was a very good film, Mummy*, and precociously early: Moreover, if he was "high-functioning" for a child with Asperger's – a term beloved of the clinical psychologists who ticked boxes and flipped charts *for a living!* – he was also well in advance of his "normal" peers, who were gooing and gaaing while he was already issuing precise bulletins from his metallic world: *These are vee-eights and they're super-fast – these are special rockets and they fly very high* . . . and issuing them again: *and they fly very high* . . . He might look straight through her a thousand times a day, but he gave her the gift of his words – which had been a . . . *relief*. Relief! She tenses her buttocks experimentally, feeling the sharp-edged corona of the flimsy toilet seat . . . *cutting into me*. All done? Yes . . . yes, she *clenches*, she might well be . . . *done*. Mute and moaning – that was the alternative: she'd seen those autistic children who took the crooked roads that led to cul-de-sacs of *incommunicability*, where they rocked and rocked – and rocked some more . . . *but never rolled*. And now the internet was seething with speculation: This doctor – at Heath Hospital no less! had definitively established a link between the emmemmarr and autism. The publicity given to his study had produced a great *howl* of new cases – parents who screamed that within heartbeats of their children being immunised their little bodies had convulsed, and it was *closing time* as their minds . . . *their spirits – their souls . . . whatever* . . . went . . . *west.* When their parents got them home, instead of the light fever expected, there was a heavy one – hallucinations followed . . . *Fimbles fumbling – fucking, I dunno* . . . and when the poor mites finally recovered themselves, that was all they had: *themselves* . . . Now the online forums resounded with the despair of parents whose once lively, outgoing and empathetic toddlers were imprisoned in the most terrible solitude, locked up inside in the red plush padding of . . . *their own brain cells* – Hullo? Yes? Hi – sorry . . . we got cut off . . . again . . . reception's . . . patchy . . . Well, indeed! Why wouldn't the reception be patchy if you make a phone call right beside a woman *doing a shit!* The night after Ben *got shot*, he'd galloped up and down the trench of the balcony, around *annaround* the cramped little flat – a headless horseman, neighing and neighing and *neighing some more – Oh, Christ-fucking-Mary-Maclary-from-Donaldson's-Dairy, why did we DO IT!* In the resonating toilet stall, in the rockin' Portaloo, in the grim-faced Northern market town, the distressed woman rolls around on the toilet seat. Camilla knows she isn't truly ugly – she thinks: I'll see it when I've wiped myself, pulled up my knickers and tights, pulled down and straightened my dress, unbolted the door and am standing in front of the soap-smeared mirror – see my fat cheeks, snub nose, thin lips and yellow-bloody hair. Camilla has – or so she's been told – *lovely eyes*: wide, bountifully lashed and *baby-doll blue-ooh* . . . She'd once been chucked on the barbecue of male regard, they like their flesh . . . *flame-grilled*. But now? Camilla sobs – and then plops: healthy round-sounding pebble-dropped-in-a-pond plops. But when she rises *Look behiiind youuu!* there're blood and mucus in there as well. Pretending it doesn't exist, she knows, is not an option – but living in the full knowledge of it doesn't make things any easier, given the condition . . . *isn't, I'm afraid to say, treatable – unless you're prepared to have a hysterectomy – although we can provide quite effective symptomatic relief.* These last the words of Doctor Glazer, a specialist who billed pretentiously in guineas and consulted floating high above the leafiness of Montagu Square. Not that Camilla ever saw the bills, because . . . *we have money behind us.* Paying her and Ben's private medical bills was something Zack candidly admitted he would never – could never – do for his own children . . . *not strictly speaking ethical, that.* Doctor Glazer specialised in the laying on of his own long and waxen hands – but the premium price-point was determined by his *plumminess.* My patients don't die with endemetriosis, Mzz Whitehouse-Busner – let alone of it. No, my task is to make it possible for you live with the complaint until, in the fullness of time, you reach the menopause, and are naturally relieved . . . *the fucking shit.* Framed degree certificates and watercolour sea scenes of . . . *dumb Cowes,* and mood-music tinkling from concealed speakers. Glazer had thrust his tapering fingers into Camilla's tummy and tum-tummed along to Pachelbel's Canon – *I'd've liked to've lashed him across its muzzle and fired the fucking thing!* Which would've been a sweetly melodic death, and *far better than he deserves* . . . Standing in the chilly-damp Portaloo, staring directly into her own exhausted eyes . . . *without flinching*, Camilla is able to muster a certain objectivity: And you, she interrogates herself, what exactly is it you deserve? She'd tried her best – she'd loved her son, and ministered to him assiduously . . . *my little Tamagotchi*, responding to each and every one of his electro-peeps and synthesised cheeps. So caring had she been towards this *intelligent automaton* that she'd neglected to . . . *keep myself alive* . . . It'd been a rigid corpse of a woman propped up in the passenger seat of Charlie's BeeEmmDoubleyou, as Zack had piloted them through the London traffic, en route from *one bloody charlatan to the next* . . . You should be grateful, he'd said – or *phonics to that effect* – because even thirty years ago, the recommended treatment for children like Ben was –. *I know! I know!* She soundlessly shouts down this voice from the past: I know – *parentectomy*, the removal of the child from the evil refrigerator mother who's completely frozen her own child's emotional development. Which was why, whenever Ben was surrounded by happily laughing children, he . . . *screamed and screamed* and couldn't wait to be alone again. Camilla remembers how confidently Zack had circled the steering wheel with one hand, so the car slid across Park Lane and slipped round *annaround* Marble Arch – strange *you're such a good driver* . . . She recalls saying to him then – and *againannagain*: Yes, he wants to be alone – but alone with me. Which was certainly true, although when they were alone together . . . *he scarcely noticed me*. Or, rather: Ben only paid attention to his mother when she was trying to give him the latest *guaranteed therapy*. Which consisted of holding him tightly in a secure, mummy-bear-hug, for four separate periods of thirty minutes each, spaced throughout the day. This had been just one of the rigid prescriptions she was . . . *unable to fulfil*, because, aged four, her son squirmed, kicked, punched and finally held his breath until . . . *he blew it all back in my face!* A malty blast, stinking of *all the shit we made him swallow* . . . But really, she admonishes her mirror-self, *I mean me* . . . Zack always urged caution: I've been around the block enough times . . . he'd say as he drove the three of them around another block, a further time . . . and I've seen so-called new mental illnesses and conditions emerge throughout my professional lifetime. Arguably, the naming of our distressed parts is all psychiatry consists of nowadays – that, and doling out the drugs which allegedy alleviate these symptoms . . . Anyway, every fresh malady comes flanked by its own team of would-be experts . . . *and I was the striker!* She remembers visiting a special school with Gramps and Ben sometime in the early nineties. Aged four, her son was *conspicuously failing to integrate with the group* – the jargon of the head teacher at the local primary, who'd presumably been on a course of some kind, where they'd filled her head with this gibberish. But when Camilla waited, peering through the school gates at the realm of asphalt and white lines, she saw no group for her son to integrate with – only furious little bodies charging this way and that, following intercepting trajectories which sent them smashing into each other – a strange enactment of . . . *the strategic defence initiative.* At least these children were all together – not alone. Not alone like her Ben, who sat in the far corner, underneath the rubber-tyre swing, beside the bin. He was so alone – so profoundly and fanatically alone, lonelier than the loneliest pine . . .

on the remotest hillside, his face a vacancy blurred by his whirring hands' . . . *stimming*. Which is what Camilla learnt to call his calming of his mind by the agitation of his hands – just as she's more recently learnt that her son doesn't suffer from autistic psychopathy, or childhood schizophrenia, but rather is *neuro-atypical*. This sounds pretty harmless – maybe even better than that. In the last couple of years Camilla's begun to read blogs – online diatribes, really – written by defiant autists, who're introducing into the established lexicon terms she associates with the *wonky-donkey* feminist groups she attended during her short spell at university . . . *dropped out . . . plop-plop-signed on a sheet of bog roll* . . . These militants speak of becoming *empowered* – of exercising their *rights* and actualising their *autonomy*, thereby freeing themselves from the *patriarchal attitudes* of the boringly *neuro-typical*. These zealots preach the New Gospel according to Temple Grandin: they aren't mentally ill, but share with this high-functioning designer of abattoirs and other animal-husbandry equipment a certain *handicap* . . . Although that's not to suggest . . . *they bang on*, that all aspects of neuro-diversity are negative. On the contrary, it's precisely the wide variation in *cognitive styles* between various *phenotypes* which allows for the emergence of prodigies and savants – some showing extreme aptitude for mathematical reasoning and calculation, while others are amazingly gifted linguistically, and still others – such as Grandin herself – are capable of astonishing feats of visualisation and . . . *spatial imagining*. Spatial imagining is what Camilla thinks she's doing when she reads on, deep into the Kilburn night . . . *drunks barking at foxes*. Sitting in her curtained embayment, in the submarine glow of the opened clamshell – a laptop computer which was yet another Gramps gift – she stares and stares, as if gazing alone could . . . *make me understand.* She stares and stares until the slickly machined info-panels grow rough and organic – and the words themselves . . . *hairy: Just as physical diversity is understood to be one of the engines of evolution, so may be neuro-diversity. Indeed, without significant neuro-diversity the human genotype might never have been able to make the leaps in cognitive functioning necessary to bring about the information revo-revo-revo-revolution . . . go round and round, round and round, The wheels on the bus go round and round ALL FUCKING DAY LONG!* While Camilla's enviably long and silky *wipers* go *swish-swish-swish*, as she bats them coquettishly at the wrung-out *drab* staring back at her from the mirror. I have, she thinks, really let myself go . . . and, receiving the little spurt of spunk-soap, she's at once pregnant with resentment: Who is there to primp and preen for – father, son and grandson, too – none of them sees her as a woman, let alone *a sexual object* . . . She's just a maternal, caring wonky-donkey, who plods around the Kilburn flat all day, following a course plotted for her from Ben's nook to Mark's hidey-hole: silvery space blankets draped over a clothes rack to deflect the . . . *death-rays.* Round *annaround* in a figure-eight that describes her own . . . *hour-glass figure.* And now – her time's *run out!* There's no telling what the pair of them might get up to in the Where-there-bee Tesco's – Camilla has often returned from *toileting myself,* only to be very publicly inconvenienced by their behaviour. Mark's freakouts are easier to take – *flamboyant,* his father calls them – he bays operatically, snatches up whatever coverings there are to hand and, draped in these, crawls under counters, tables or chairs. There he'll remain, curled up in a foetal ball until she arrives to coax him out. But by that time his nimble-fingered and tech-savvy son will've got into whatever electrical equipment there is to hand and . . . *fimbled about*. Two years ago, when Ben was just ten, Camilla had been *bleeding out* on the toilet at South Mimms services, when she heard: Every girl . . . every boy . . . Come and open up your eyes . . . ! belting out from the public address system – and by the time she got back to the soft-play area where she'd left them, she found a crowd of fellow travellers who'd hearkened to the call, and were indeed staring at a *world of wonder and surprise*: Mark and Ben, piling up a great teetering pyramid of foam bolsters and vinyl cubes. Spotting his mother's appalled face, Ben had cried out: You're back . . . ! *You're back!* before adding under his breath, But not in a roly mo . . . *But not in a roly mo* . . . As she'd struggled with his frightened father, he'd explained to the gawping spectators precisely how he'd rewired the system so that it played . . . *Fimbles . . . Fimbles . . . Fimbles . . . We're the Fimbles* . . . the ditty's very repetitiveness another dismal reminder of his own palilalia. Then there was the time in the Dixon's on the Kilburn High Road, when Camilla left them for a couple of minutes while she popped to the chemist's next door, and on returning found the shop window . . . *full of gurning Mark-faces*. Ben had managed to wire up very single television and computer screen to a seeseeteevee camera focused on his *flamboyant* father. She'd stood there, fighting down the urge to scream – for wherever she'd looked on the cluttered sales floor, Mark's unseeing eyes were staring back at her, while his mouth hung open in just the way she remembered it doing when he came, so impregnating *stupid, drunken me* with the creator of this *wilderness of mirrors* . . . It'd been this way as soon as Ben could crawl – he made straight for the television. Not to watch, but to *fimble about* with it. I'm a worm . . . *I'm a worm* . . . Ben had said to his mother on his fifth birthday – he hadn't meant a grey, wrigglingly divisible one, but the new inter- net variety: I was born the year Robert Morris created the first internet worm . . . *created the first internet worm* . . . was simply a statement of fact – the little boy didn't play the part, didn't wriggle or cry out he was being chopped in half, any more than he played at being anything. There was never make-believe for Ben, only the facts on the ground – *and up in the sky*: In nineteen eighty-nine the first twenty-four satellites of the Global Positioning System were placed in orbit . . . *were placed in orbit* . . . and Intel released the eight-oh-four-eight-six microprocessor which contains more than a million transistors . . . *more than a million transistors* . . . Such pre- cocity hadn't been altogether a surprise – it was a difficult pregnancy: she'd felt him *stimming inside of me*, and, although she'd wanted a home birth, in the event it'd been . . . *a phone one.* The ringing baby was yanked from her and held up to the obstetrician's ear so he could establish whether Ben was . . . *alive.* And now, stepping down from the rockin' Portaloo, making her way under the glass canopy between the Wetherby shoppers, Camilla is presented with another version of her predicament: a purple pony, which plunges up and down, eyes flashing as it gallops on the spot to the accompaniment of synthesised hurdy-gurdy music . . . *I'm going nowhere.* Last night, at first crouching in the porch of Mona's cottage, she'd then subsided amongst the muddy wellies and grass-stained waxed-cotton jackets. Funny thing about Barbours, Mona's feller had said over supper, they were actually invented on Tyneside, for the dockers who had to be out in all weathers ... And Camilla quipped: Stupid middle-class people – carrying coal-coloured jackets to Newcastle ... a feeble joke, but then *I'm enfeebled* ... She'd been exhausted as well, after a blowy trip out to the Farne Islands, where, according to the boatman-cum-guide, ancho-whatsits had clung, praying, to the shit-splashed rocks. All around the boat waxed-cotton heads had risen from seaweed-swirling swell ... *Ark-Ark!* Such trust in the Labrador eyes that held hers for long moments – such *empathy*. Look at the seals, Ben! his mother had cried. Aren't they fab? But Ben had the collar of his borrowed wax-cotton jacket buttoned up right over his head, so he could sit in his one-boy tent ... *playing his fucking Game Boy.* The sweetly *smeggy* smell of the mussel broth she'd slurped for supper followed Camilla into the porch, where she turned this way and that – as she'd been instructed. For a moment *or more* ... tired heavy breasts had rested on knees *creepy-crêpey*, yet *I didn't exist* ... for without *reception* there could be no *perception*: no mussels, no Mark, no Ark-Ark! No Ben – *no number ten* ... until the smallest of the three connection bars on her mobile lifted its blocky head *a tiny bit* ... lofting her with it *towards the white light* ... It's our fault, she'd gasped into the shingle-shifting ether. We did it to him – I feel so guilty, Gramps ... I think ... I might die of guilt ... For a long while he hadn't spoken, but at last his plummy voice squeezed from the

handset: Nonsense, utter balderdash – I don't know this man personally, Milla, but he works for my Trust. I've already made
enquiries, and there's a lot more to this than meets the –. Stop it!
she'd cried. Will you please, just for once, stop lecturing me!
Camilla – who ran away from her convent boarding school at sixteen and never went back – has only the haziest understanding of
the maze of communications *we're stumbling through.* When Ben
was little, she'd made him a tin-can telephone – which entranced
them both. She'd been well prepared – she thought then, *thinks
now* – for these straitened circumstances. Her parents' parsimony
had extended to ironing brown-paper bags and keeping them in
kitchen drawers – they scrimped their only daughter into private
education, choosing a Catholic school not because they wanted
her soul saved, but because it'd been *all we can afford . . .* Their
shitty words – parsimonious pebbles, dropped *plop-plop* somewhere
else . . . *in space – in time* – yet still rippling the world. Rippling the
electric pony's purple mane – rippling the four identically freckled
faces plastered to the adjacent photo-booth. But these are her words,
spoken here and now . . . *person-to-the-person that's . . . me*: What
do you want to be when you grow up, Milla? – Me? Why . . . I'd
like to be a carer to a schizophrenic partner and an autistic son,
getting by on benefits and hand-outs – after all, that's what my
upbringing has prepared me for . . . Camilla had enjoyed the tin-can
telephony, because, once freed from the oppression of his mother's
gaze, Ben had prattled away, not exactly to her, but at least *in my
general direction.* When, a year or so ago, his grandfather had bought
one of the brand-new eyeBooks for both of them, it'd been Ben who

set up their internet connection – the cement-mixing, miniature-anvil-bashing, feedback-howling which rapidly gave birth to his first written communication, and to her first experience of the merry chirrup: *You've got male* – which was how she's heard it ever since. Ben's email also consisted of three short misspelt words . . . *sounds that became signs that become sounds that became signs* in his mother's ever bleary, ever teary eyes: *by me mobl.* Well, perhaps I will . . . Among the Wetherby shoppers Camilla sees plenty of teenagers with mobile phones . . . it might do the trick – he might talk to me normally at long last. *It's Good to Talk!* and listen as well. Last night, her conversation with Gramps had ended with wave upon wave of static carrying the frail barque of their conversation further and further away: You're breaking up! he'd cried to her. You're breaking up, Camilla! Which had indeed been true, because when she returned to the cottage's sitting room, where Mona and her bloke were curled up on the couch . . . *I was in bits.* She'd sat there watching them cuddle. Sat there looking at the fishing net pinned to the perfectly plastered wall – sat there looking at its catch of dried-out starfish, scoured seashells and a bottle-green glass float. Sat there, not envying her dear, dear friend . . . *not envying her at all.* Certainly not envying her paradoxical post-partum bum – *she's childless, but fully gravid with his come* . . . Or envying their relationship . . . *don't fancy anyone any more*, yet hating herself for the *Ralgex* jealousy she'd felt burning on her tummy and . . . *between my thighs.* She didn't fancy anyone any more – but it'd be nice just for once to have someone in her life who, gently and tenderly, would rub an embrocation into the lovelorn lesions *that have grown their own* . . .

nerves. Camilla can't see her wayward menfolk anywhere. She goes into the supermarket and walks hurriedly along beside the check-outs, scanning each aisle in turn: *BAKERY, READY MEALS, DAIRY* . . . Her frigid parents are due for the first of their two, two-day annual visits tomorrow . . . *should I stock up now?* At Victoria Coach Station they'll be waiting for her right where they've got off the Birmingham service: two sedentary and apprentice *old folk*, wearing early-retirement-uniforms and shoes with enhanced grip. In the coldly echoing, diesel-stinking, corporately liverish coach station, they'll be standing with their ironed-brown-paper-bag hands *folded.* Coldly they stand, in the diesel-engine-echoing coach station – and *they stink.* If you were to unfold their brown-paper clothes they'd release the exhausted reek of . . . *parsimony: Would you like the parson's nose, Camilla?* Said with the only genuine feeling they possessed . . . *as if, as if* . . . a greasy blob of chicken arse could make for . . . *any of it.* There's obviously no room for them in the Mowbray Road flat – even if there had been, they'd never sleep under *my immoral and Semitic roof.* Not that the Pettigrew-Whitehouses are especially pious or bigoted – it's more that they're creatures of habit: for years regular attendees at the local See-of-Ee church, Saint Alphege's, a millennium-old *aircraft hangar,* they have, in recent years, transferred their loyalty to the *evangelical potting shed,* which opened for business at the end of their road. Here they stand, Sunday-after-Sunday, listening to the rasping of their fellow worshippers, as they speak in *sandpapery tongues.* They'll be at it now, Camilla thinks as she moves towards the exit, buttoned-up tight beside charismatics who wave . . . *one wooden arm aloft.*

Then, tomorrow, they'll take the bus into Birmingham to catch the coach – yet another thrifty feat, that, if unacknowledged by her, will summon from her father . . . *Aren't I clever, Milla, darling?* This, perhaps the most deranging of Mister Pettigrew-Whitehouse's many foibles: his self-referential endearments – and his hand-me-down vocabulary: the *darlings, awfullys, beastlys* and *napkins* of his genteel upbringing, all of which Camilla carried with her to school and . . . *flushed down the lavatory – NEVER the toilet!* How exactly her father came down in the world, while her mother rose, Camilla had never found out. For a while, in her Milla Tant teens, she'd torn at their weedy gentility, trying to expose the rusting social seesaw they'd sat on – but then it happened *inna rape field*, and happened again *inna squat*, after which Camilla's origins seemed a lot less important to her than *the shit I was in* . . . Twice-yearly for two days. They put up at the Kerry Guesthouse on Mapesbury Road, run by that *Whore of Babylon*, Missus Donleavy, who, besides being *endlessly obliging*, hadn't increased her rates for years. Four days *per annum* – two of which were Sundays. A break in routine for the Pettigrew-Whitehouses, who, instead of receiving communion, ate dry, tasteless and wafer-thin chips at the Golden Spoon on the High Road. Joyless meals they paid for with coins slid out, one by one, from the recesses of her father's horseshoe-shaped leather purse. A break in Camilla's routine as well: twice a year she got to sit in silence across from her parents, instead of having to share the long one, which, every other Sunday, stretched from pole to pole all the way from Solihull to Kilburn. Camilla made these calls sat on the crocheted blanket she'd thrown over the squashy old divan she and Mark had dragged back from the People's Dispensary for Sick Animals' furniture repository in Cricklewood. Camilla prodded the buttons, and waited until one or other of them stirred. Then waited some more. News of their grandson or Mark – which was seldom jolly, although occasionally amusing *inna bleak kinduva way* – left them as it found them: *cold* . . . It was understood by all three – although, in common with so much else, never spoken of – that it was Camilla's responsibility to call them, never the reverse. After all, it'd been her who'd run away – dashing along dirty verges, scampering through the spaghetti of arterial roads, to a rendezvous with *a man from the motor trade* . . . Lucas Industries in Shirley, to be precise, which ran a restart programme for youngsters who'd dropped out of secondary education. Camilla sat in an office block beside the EmmFortytwo construction site, itching her bare feet on nylon carpet tiles and watching as the whiteboard filled up with numerals and brackets *I could never factor in* . . . She'd met Mona on the restart programme, and gone with her to Warwick University, where Camilla lasted only a year. Zack says supportive things such as, *You've got a good mind, Milla*, and, *I really think you do yourself down* . . . Yes! Down! *Down-down, deeper and down* . . . to where greasy locks toss between denim thighs. No – she'd lasted only a year, and she doubted her father-in-law's estimation, because the thick syllables and crusted consonants of Middle English . . . *stuck in my craw al stuned at his steven and stansil seten* . . . *In a swoghe sylence through the sale richei.* She hadn't done anything as dramatic as dropping out – only *drifted away* . . . behind the whitewashed window of a defunct sub-post office in Leamington Spa . . . *rubber stamps and rubber bands scattered on the parquet* where she writhed with an unsuitable boyfriend. The following year saw her in a squat in Ipswich, with one still more so – which was why . . . *inna rape field – I won't . . . ever again . . . think his name . . .* Last night Mona had sat up on the couch and *Ark-Ark!* asked, Did you get through? Then Ben – who can hear with spooky acuity *when he wants to* – looked up from his Game Boy and said, Numbers of confirmed autism cases increased significantly in the eighties – long before the introduction of the combined measles, mumps and rubella vaccine . . . *long before the introduction of the combined measles, mumps and rubella vaccine . . .* That'd been it: Ben's first and last words on the subject of himself. His mother took them to be his way of *reassuring me.* Yet how much better it would've been if he'd put his arms around her – if only for a moment – and said something like, It's okay, Mum, it's not your fault – 'sides, I'm happy with the way I am. If I weren't like this I wouldn't be . . . me . . . *I wouldn't be . . . me . . .* But this is, she thinks, all bollocky-bullshitty-wishfully thinking on her part. Pacing up and down under the portico of the *Where-there-bee* Tesco's, staring with mounting anxiety into the Perspex dome of the gumball dispenser, then at the multicoloured scraps of foil beneath her sandalled feet – the scrabbled shells of Cadbury's Creme Eggs. Because it's Easter – and a time of rebirth, when *fluffly little lesions* grow new nerves, and start to *peck-peck-peck at your underparts.* Reaching the end of the glassy portico, Camilla hears shtooms! and peeeowws! and k'tannngs! On the far side of the road, she sees scraped out of the black paint slapped across a shop-front, the letters H-O-L-L-Y-W-O-O-D-A-R-C-A-D-E pulsing with the lights flashing within. Inside the noises are far louder – and there's also the clackattack of air hockey and the whip-clop!-rumble of pool. Gormless Northern lads loiter, just this minute hatched from their *cracked* shell suits – because it's Easter and a time of rebirth . . . *when you spend your child-support on cheap booze.* She finds her own chicks in the far corner, between Maximum Force and Licence to Kill. They're in profile: cradling their plastic machine-guns, and she sees the family resemblance which otherwise eludes her: bulbous tips to noses big and small – the froggy lips they share with *wide-mouthed Zack.* Mark's smoking one of his toothpick-thin roll-ups, while his son sucks on an actual tootmhpick – of which he has a score about him at any time, available to be twirled in front of his startling eyes for *yet more stimming.* Both are furiously con-centrating – trigger-fingers twitching out cheeowww! cheeowww! cheeowww! until a deep American voice bellows: RELOAD! and they pivot neatly to the right and the left, POINTing THE CON-TROLLER OUTSIDE THE SCREEN TO RELOAD! then pivoting neatly back to resume their carnage. They are, Camilla realises, utterly unaware of me – I could collapse on to this grubby carpet and they'd never notice . . . She peers closer, trying to make out what it is they're killing so concertedly, and sees cartooned body-builders with bandanas wrapped round their fat heads leap from helicopters and tumble from tanks – RELOAD! and her menfolk carry on dutifully *culling the beefcake* . . . Yesterday after-noon the boatman landed them all at Seahouses and they'd plodded along the beach back to the cottage, Mona and Camilla arm in arm, the three males in their party . . . *not really with us at all*: Mona's bloke way ahead – Ben far behind, and Mark slopping in and out of the wavelets, his wellies crunching a wrack of mermaid's purses and mineral-water bottles, his plainchant borne to them on the breeze: *And this little piggy's brain rotted 'cause it's tummy was fulluv roast beef, whee-whee-whee . . .* or words to that dismal effect. Her arm tightening in Camilla's, Mona had said: He picks up on things, doesn't he – I've noticed that. What he just said then – pigs eating beef . . . We bought the cottage the year of the bee-essee crisis . . . mind you, that was beef eating itself. Anyway, when we were walking along this beach late that summer, inland there must've been, ooh, I dunno – twenty, maybe thirty . . . Loads of big fires – or pyres. Locals were pretty cynical – said farmers were loading their cattle on to transporters and driving them from farm to farm, hoping to pick up the virus. Said there was more to be gained from government compensation than at market . . . Camilla had looked at her friend – the only one she's managed to hang on to from her youth: was Mona making some sort of elliptical comparison? Saying Camilla, by analogy, was also a farmer, driving her diseased *beefcake* from hospital to therapist, and in the process picking up . . . *Zack's compensation*, which was what Mark's dour and darkly beautiful mother, Miriam, insinuated when she deigned to visit the Kilburn flat? But no, all this had simply been a preamble, because Mona had then blurted out: I just don't know how you cope with it, Milla. I honestly think I'd have a breakdown if I had to deal with a fraction of the stuff you do . . . And Camilla, her eyes on the fantasia of Bamburgh Castle, shimmering through the sea fret, had gasped romantically: I-I love him – and I hate him . . . She wonders now, as she watches the surreal slaughter, if she could ever explain to anyone – even Mark's father – how, as she bent and shaped her affection to match the distortions of his psychosis, so it had become *two-sided*: love and hatred were now inseparable . . . *just like us.* RELOAD! The plastic muzzles swing away from the screen then back in . . . *perfect harmony.* They find each other, Camilla thinks, in this neon jungle – they're content so long as they don't have to be themselves at all, only fellow Rambos – RELOAD! But this time, as he swings Ben sees his mother and *the spell's broken.* He carries on slaughtering but his actions are mechanical, as is his speech: Dad's pretty good, but I always beat him . . . *I always beat him* . . . 'cause he doesn't understand how the machine's been programmed . . . *how the machine's been programmed* . . . The attackers come from different places, but they always end up in the same bit of the screen . . . *in the same bit of the screen* . . . All you gotta do is keep moving the gun like this as you fire it . . . *like this as you fire it* . . . You don't have to aim it at all . . . *have to aim it at all* . . . But you get just as many . . . *just as many* . . . GAME OVER! Camilla says, C'mon, you two, we've still got a long drive ahead of us. Back in the Vauxhall, with Ben inserted into the envelope of his laptop and his ears plugged to it, Camilla begins to ask Mark: D'you think that –? then stops, because her question would require him to think about *now* and *then*, and at the moment there's nothing more aggravating to Mark's condition than . . . *time.* He howls at any reference to the past or the future, for as far as he's concerned . . . *they don't exist.* It's always now! he screeches, curling into a ball and rocking on his bony fulcrum. It's always nooooow! *The alarm call of the wild* is what she privately calls it – and it's a near-daily occurrence, yanking her forcibly back from past regrets and future anxieties to this: the groan of the car's engine . . . the moan of her own troubled guts – and the flickety-click of her *lost boy . . . fimbling* around in virtual space. The motorway ahead darkens – onrushing cars and lorries in the other carriageway shrink to small, white *dots*. The screensaver on the first computer Camilla ever used – in an architect's office where she was temping – returns to her now: Interstellar Voyage, it was called – but, planted at a mushroom-coloured workstation as she bored into outer space, Camilla – then, as now – had been boldly going . . . *fucking nowhere*. What is it she wants to ask Mark? Yes . . . Can he remember – even roughly – when it was their son had *got to third base* with his beloved computers? No longer simply *touching them up*, but shoving his grubby fingers *right inside*. Friends – well, Mona – say there's virtually unlimited pornography out there . . . *in there?* Camilla's eyes slide to the rear-view mirror, which frames Ben's square face and straight blond fringe. He's ripening, perhaps . . . but isn't oily yet, not yet matted-*shatted, shit-heel – yeah, yeah, inna rape field shit-heel – You lookin' at me, shit-heel? Walking in through my eyes, shit-heel – dragging in with you all the shit you picked up in that rotten rape field* . . . Christ, Camilla concedes, I feel rotten. But no, it wasn't some *Botty Venus* Ben slammed the clamshell shut on when she sidled up behind him, but the numerals and digits striping its screen. What're you doing? she asks him, and every time his answer is the same curt, Coding, Mum. His mother remembers boys putting little plastic pegs into little plastic peg-boards – Mastermind or Mindmaster they called it. And what about the girls? *We skipped it and skipped away* . . . They played all sorts of code-breaking games back then – spying was sorta sexy: secret agent running across the fields with a girl . . . pulling her down . . . down to the ground . . . *inna rape field* . . . No, no – not sexy at all, with his wiry chest-pelt and grease-painted-brows – but no commie toff, that one – not numbered third, fourth or fifth man, nor letter-designated – Colonels A and B, Informants C and D like Ben's First Word Book, *Dee-dee-dee we bang the drum! Dee-dee-dee!* It'd been more than ten years since the Wall crumbled . . . a victory for the spooks but no retirement plan. Ha-ha, turns out his Dee-BeeFour was on the aitchpee – he's no vee-eyepee status any more, so he's shaken *the shit-stirrer – the shit-heel, onna crushed cardboard box, flap in hand, FORMER SPY. I HAVE NO HOME AND NO SHELTER. PLEASE HELP.* Fat chance – evil fucks. Any-way, that's not what Ben's up to – he's only fimbling about in there, fimbling about with strings of letters, piles of digits . . . lifting them . . . sifting them . . . through his . . . digits. Harmless, really. When he was very small boy it was sharks, Star Wars, birds-of-prey, all normal – perfectly normal. True, he was a bit obsessional – had to know every last thing about his chosen subject. Had to take him up to the Charing Cross Road. *Foyles.* Had to buy him a book on ospreys. Specialist book costing thirty-four pounds and seventy pence. Had to. To the credit of his *customised* brain, he got it down pat, and pattered along beside her for weeks – *weeks!* She'd had a smock dress at the time. *Quite nice.* With frogging at the breast – he hung on to the hem. Never got the shape back. Seen in flight from below the osprey has white or mottled underparts . . .

white or mottled underparts . . . Which was how, aged four, he must've seen me, staring up from below at my face, mottled with angry red patches. He was a junior spy forever *birdwatching – So it goes on*, the acid-yellow rape fields sweeping past the Vauxhall's *mottled* windows, then the *lardy-arse* cooling towers of the power stations clustered around the Humber . . . And then, not exactly nothing, but an increasingly maddening confusion of signs and lanes and slip roads. They have a *wee-pit-stop* before the still more maddening drive down through Mill Hill and Hendon, until they're meshed together on the North Circular with all the *Chiantishire cunts* rollicking home from the second homes where they doubtless also spent the Easter bank holiday sopping up . . . *mussel broth – Ark-Ark!* Camilla rests her forehead on the steering wheel, feeling the heat the mile upon mile of friction has rubbed in . . . *down below – the Vauxhall . . . and I.* She digs at the brake, then the accelerator – the car *hiccups* along in the jam. Is she rested after their little comfort break? *Am I fuck* . . . This evening she'll have to spend hours getting Ben ready for school tomorrow – his very ordinary school requires very special preparation, although his lunch cannot have anything so conventional as *being prepared* done to it. No. It must be *assembled* as she imagines computers being assembled under surgical lights by neat-fingered women – hairless women, their brows and pubes shaved, too, who wear white nylon snoods, face masks and gloves . . . *somewhere.* The lunch's component parts are: Marmite painted on pumpernickel, a necessarily straight banana, a carton of coconut milk, kelp-flavoured root-vegetable crisp bits. The latter components must be sourced from obscure yeast-stinky health food shops all over North London – curse the *fucking internet* for making the boy aware of such things. Camilla stands behind Ben as he stands behind his avatar, *but I've no control*. She's stood there for much of the last couple of years, watching the web pages download: multicoloured strips of *consumer choice*. Ben doesn't explain to his digitally migrant mother about modems, bit-rates and connection speeds – he acts them out on all-fours *such womanly hips*, snuffling at the skirting boards, picking cable-clips from perished plaster, as he *fimbles* with the information superhighway. His nails are filthy and need clipping . . . *osprey's talons, really* . . . She looks up. Overhead the April day is fading – the enormous concrete *tangle* of the gyratory system *unravels* into the sunset. Beyond the Vauxhall's bonnet mud chunks drop from the crusted axle of a dump truck. It's a nightmare getting Ben to have a shower – while a change of clothes requires protracted negotiation. They made a *Good Friday Agreement* that he'd begin the new term in new clothes, and ditch the fraying grey hoodie and Asda jeans he's been wearing day in day out for months. But now, as the car's blatting past the Brent Sidings, Camilla remembers: *I left a load in the machine . . .* She'll have to run a full cycle again, then try to dry them before morning – else there's no guarantee of getting him to school at all. And even if he does go to school, where will that lead? What sort of job will Ben ever be able to do – can she see him working in a butcher's – this one, for example, where two black men dispute over a tray piled high with bloody pigs' trotters? Clearly this is no simple conflict over price or quantity, but something altogether more sinister – the disputant's face is grey with anxiety, his spittle drips down on the trotters . . . Gramps says all immigrant communities – no matter where they are or where they've come from – have much higher rates of schizophrenia. Not that he uses the s-word . . . *I prefer schizophreniform disorder – although not in the sense that DeeEssEmmFour uses it* . . . No wonder Mark's so at home here – back with his crazy peeps. Back in *our London*. He stirs, unshaven neck twitching in the collar of the cagoule he hasn't removed for the past four days, and mutters, Shitters . . . up to their necks innit – blood 'n' guts . . . ox-heart speaking in tongues . . . He. Can. Look. Inside. My. Soul! He starts whimpering as the car pulls away from the lights, so she shifts her hand from the gearstick to his knee . . . *mechanically comforting*: Home soon now, love, and I'll put the kettle on for a nice cup of . . . *chlorpromazine*. Yet . . . yet . . . she's been comforted by them both in the past – received physical succour. When Ben was littler there was the holding therapy – he may've punched and kicked . . . *but we were connected* – and before that they'd shared the queasier intimacies of toilet training . . . *for months – no, years!* Training didn't cut it: this was toilet further education – an aitchenndee in shitting, a bachelor of *piss artistry*. So very long had it taken that Ben was able to comment on his bowel movements long before he could control them: *Look at that great big poo what I done, Mummy* . . . he'd remarked, aged thirteen months, stretched out on his sheepskin, legs akimbo, the poo in question coddled there: a great and glistening toffee-coloured *roc's egg*. So great, and so glistening, it might conceivably have been *another newborn . . . can we fix it?* No, she's forced to acknowledge for the *sixhunnredansixtysixth* time, no, we fucking can't. Even when a bribe worked and he stayed on his potty, it was only on this further condition: he was allowed to *suck on my tit*. The thick green roll-neck woolly he wore *'til it rotted* – the relentless suction of his jaws clamped on her smarting nipple, his cheeks ballooning as he *drank me down*. Christ! Christ, she's tired – the Vauxhall groans up the modest incline of Shoot-Up Hill, and Camilla can no longer distinguish between the slap-a-tat-tat of its fraying fan belt and the disintegration of her own *insides* . . . Ben seems to have no anxieties – he just gets on with sucking and stimming and shitting . . . *a remarkable child*, is his grandfather's view: *He really is able to do to do three different things at once – reminds me of some of the autistic savants I've come across over the years* . . . But not, it would seem, of his daughter-in-law, who does three things at once . . . *all the fucking time. Yes*, and one night at Redington Road, when Zack's own youngest children – Ben's twin baby aunts – were tucked up under their thirty-two-tog duvets, he'd opened a bottle of wine and held forth: All my career, he'd said, I've followed Ariadne's thread, followed it through a maze of conflicting theories, hoping it would lead me towards the clear light of understanding . . . It had been a testimony to the respect Camilla had for him, and the gratitude she felt, that as they sat and sipped and listened to Ben riding his trike round *annaround* the conservatory, she didn't throw back at him: Why don't you, for once in your pontificating life, take a bit of Ariadne's thread and *sew a bloody button on with it –!* Mum! Mum! Ben's face, thrust from the foreskin of his hoodie, fills the rear-view mirror: Mum, you've missed the turn again! And she has – they've been living in the Mowbray Road flat for seven years now: seven long years full of frantic activity . . . As to progress of any kind, when she considers the matter, it seems she's merely been sitting stock-still in her bay window, with the days and nights *flickering on my face*: a woman fallen to earth, in an alien world. She isn't yet – and perhaps never will be – at home he'd be angling his scraggy saggy unshaven neck, at the end of which was his scraggy saggy unshaven RED face, towards the cocktail cabinet, a kettle-drum-shaped contrivance of mirrors and marquetry which stood on three peg-legs. Maeve had brought it back from a church jumble sale. The Butcher had been sixteen and *sour* . . . seated at the kitchen table reading Cicero's defence of Sulla . . . *that he would've been amongst the most virtuous of our rulers were it not for his choleric and fanciful disposition* . . . which had probably been translated by some *kiddie-fiddling classicist* who taught at a prep school where they *dipped* the little lambkins rather than bathing them. Ever a martyr, she'd've humped the ghastly object awkwardly in through the side door, and the Butcher prob'ly said, Let me give you a hand with that, Mum. To which she undoubtedly would've replied, Oh, no, that's all right, Jonathan, you *get on with your book* . . . Ach! the flabby-mindedness of the woman! The Butcher inveighs (You're inveighing again, Butchie, I've warned you about that.) For Maeve De'Ath the classics were a household chore you *got on with*. As for "Jonathan" (Where to thtart!). Absolutely, Squilly – ab-so-bloody-lutely: Jonathan is long gone – and Kins has *dearly departed*, but the cocktail cabinet remains. It's no longer hunched in the bay window of the room Maeve De'ath insisted on calling the drawing one . . . *prétentieuse, elle?* Although, to be fair (Which in her case you've always found rather difficult, Butchie), drawing did get done there – not by him, but Oliver and James De'Ath could sit and draw at the same time *the clever little wankers . . .* which is how their elder brother referred to them then *and still does*. Their mother – being the woman she remains: hollowed out by her own chippiness, a bag of sawdust *where her guts oughta be* – always refers to her sons by their given names. As for Kins, ever since he was made conscious he'd taken to calling his sons – albeit only in the confines of his own deeply prosaic mind – *the Butcher, the Baker and the Candlestick-maker*. This would be fair enough even if only sixty-six per cent of his progeny exhibited the appropriate tendencies – a vocation, say, for cake, or a certain facility with an awl – but, as Ali Hassan al-Maji's pilots swooped low to dump another helicopter gunship-load of napalm on the fleeing Peshmerga fighters, Oliver De'Ath began working at a craft shop in Wantage – not (We hathen to add) a mere purveyor of knick-knacks and amusing tea towels, but the going concern of a notable woodworker, who sawed and planed table tops, and turned both their legs (And candlethticks) for the discerning public. That's nice, dear, Maeve De'Ath would say, every time her youngest presented her with another newly varnished chip off his workaday block, but her tone was flat . . . *disappointed*. As for the Candlestick-maker's immediately older brother, he, too, was notably deficient when it came to *getting on in the world*. At the local EffEee college James had been adjudged inadequate – and so he took to the back bedroom of the Colindale Avenue house, where, in the walk-in cupboard, he grew marijuana under lights. A few years later he emerged, and floated into a job at the Crusty Loaf

Bakery, a Saint Albans tea shop that prides itself on homemade cakes, bread and pastries *vente à emporter* . . . His younger sons' lack of career progress had never bothered Kins, who, epigone that he'd been, was always a *ferocious under-achiever.* So long as his boys accompanied him on long rambles through the surrounding countryside, listening the while to his lectures *full of longueurs* . . . so Kins was content. Were you happy, Dad? the Butcher thinks, staring down at the semi-reflective surface of the Baldwins' brilliantly clean kitchen table – and seeing there his father's *scraggy saggy unshaven RED face.* Are you happy, Dad? He'd posed the question to Kins when they were still close – when they still did things together, before *the incident.* Posed it, because, even if his own *data-set* was already heavily restricted, the Butcher still admired his father's tradecraft – his skulking, tail-between-his-legs (Until needed!) insouciance – and needed to be told it hadn't *all been in vain.* Happy? Kins speaks from the Other Side, his full bottom lip moist with his own *never-ending self-deprecatory moue.* Happy? Dunno 'bout that, old bean – whenever it occurs to me to wonder if I'm happy, I always think of my old history master at Lancing –. – The Ape. – That's right, the Ape. He always used to say, Happiness is a by-product of life, just as coke is a by-product of smelting steel – you can't go at either of 'em directly – you've chopped up that garlic. You do still want to help, don't you, Jonathan? Vron Baldwin asks. She's hovering over him, a brittle-but-natural blonde of his own age, wearing a peach-coloured wool suit under her blue-and-white-striped *ouvrierist* apron (A word here about the Butcher's mnemonic capacity: with each new generation of recording devices – for text, for image, for film and audio – so his vast internal database has been appropriately upgraded. The two-by-four file cards on which he set down details of informers, suspects and agents have been transferred successively to automatic document carousels, then to magnetic tape – and now digitised, along with the enormous stacks of five-by-eight black-and-white prints, blown up from microdots, which picture just about everyone he's ever seen, and everywhere he's ever been, and all the reports he's ever read. When, a couple of years ago, Pople and Kohn won the Nobel for their work applying the complex equations describing quantum chemical processes to determining the three-dimensional structure of molecules, the Butcher found he was immediately able to employ similar techniques to build his own nanomachines – tens of thousands of micron-sized robots, each of which could be programmed separately to labour on the great and never-ending data-harvest. The Butcher is only too aware of the curious correspondence between these technological metaphors for his own mental processes and the paranoid fantasies of schizophrenics, which also have a built-in obsolesence – the death-rays aimed at them being decommissioned as laser beams are installed. The Butcher's also always been conscious that, should he reveal the full extent of his mnemonism, he would become an object of fascination, fear and cack-handed medical intervention. As a child he'd had before him an example of what a superior mnemonist might do with their life, in the form of his grandfather, who came of age before the normals began netting entire populations with their crude metrics. Sirbert had been viewed as eccentric, certainly – but never pathologically so. His grandson would do better, and actively conceal the existence of his database, with its banks of winking EyeSeeEl mini-computers, wired in series, which had been installed in the sub-basements of his enormous Mycroftian mind. Conceal this – and hide also his equipment: the superior perceptual mechanisms enabling him to gather such huge quantities of visual and audio take, computer and telephony metadata. It was wearing, of course, running this ongoing surveillance programme with only the one agent in the field – and the relentless cerebration can at times seem a little like psychosis: all those numerals and letters swirling inside his tired eyes. Surely, under such circumstances, it's understandable that even the most conscientious and effective operator has recourse to chemical assistance – strictly under medical supervision, of course. Since the in-house medics introduced random piss-testing, the Butcher has reluctantly forsworn illegal stimulants in favour of forty to sixty milligrams of methylphenidate daily, which not only calms – enabling the sequestration of clamorous intelligence-gathering from the normally quiet business of life – but also, paradoxically, enhances episodic, working and long-term memory. The Butcher has a hunch prolonged use of this nostrum may be implicated in the restructuring of his own neurological architecture: a process that's gathered pace in the past decade or so, in line with the boom in middle-class house conversions. Obsolete partitions are being knocked down and unused attics pressed into service – all is becoming rational and open-plan. Which is why at Sunday lunches, in conversation with gently whinnying Tories, the Butcher would add his own phatic forgetfulness to their general amnesia, referring always to what'shisface or thingummyjig – while ever unable to retrieve the relevant information, despite it being *on the tip of his tongue*) and holding a paring knife in one hand and a bunch of parsley in the other. Her purple lips purse: Not a lot of point in your pitching up early if you're just going to sit there daydreaming – the others'll be here in half and hour . . . no doubt famished. No doubt, the Butcher thinks, but he says nothing, only chukka-chukks the clove on the chopping board with his own paring knife. From deep in the recesses of the Baldwins' large hilltop house comes the unmistable yapping of the Simpsons, and for an instant he sees himself: adipose, jaundiced, *naked* – wandering through a *dooo-doo-doo-do-d'* two-dimensional world *not unlike this one*. There will be children watching – the Baldwins have a brace . . . *possibly three*. If the Butcher's ever in real danger of blowing his cover, it's in the presence of . . . *junior spies*. He'll be forty this year – an age at which even the most committed of bachelors begins to be *stripped bare* by mortal anxieties, so chucks chins, tousles hair, hands out bigger tips – all preparatory to dutiful insemination. The Butcher sips the vagina of Sally – his longest-growing beard – as any connoisseur might savour the nose of a grand cru – but the information he seeks concerns progesterone and estrogen levels. He hears Sally's laughter now – the trying-too-hard cluck of the *seriously broody*. That's your Sally, isn't it, Jonathan? Vron Baldwin says, with an irritating emphasis on "your". Yes, the Butcher concedes, and, glancing at the kitchen clock – a doubly predictable Swiss Railways Mondaine – wonders who the Baldwins' other guests will be. A couple of Nick's colleagues will attend, *no doubt*. It's been over two years since their great defeat – and it's amusing enough to observe some of them relaxing into opposition by becoming *moister* and more heterodox. It's the wives who tend to be the most absorbent – at well-set tables in Wiltshire and Gloucestershire the Butcher has heard the words *as a feminist* spoken with no irony whatsoever. (You've also heard colleagues weferred to as gay with little or no opprobrium attached – but that's something you don't like to dwell on, or to acknowledge at all.) Can I have a go? Sally says, making her entrance behind a boy of about eight . . . *Sam, possibly – or Arthur?* who's manipulating the levers of a remote controller, so sending a model car racing across the phone-box-red Amtico, round the massive, granite-topped kitchen island and out the far door. *Dear Sally . . .* he sees her as she was at dawn, arranged, naked and bamboozled on the tightly tucked five-hundred-thread-count dais of his *chopping block*, her paler and depilated pubic triangle a point of maximum vulnerability, her *Lanzarote* legs bent back. What was it Kins had called her? A sporty girl – that's right: *a sporty girl*. His euphemism for a girl limber enough to be *bent any which way . . .* without disturbing the Cindy-perfection of her hair. Longest-growing beard, Sally is – and consequently *ticklish . . .* Two steps and she's on him, her lips nuzzling his ear, her pearlescent teeth nipping its lobe, her Prosecco breath whispering, That man Fiddes, Jonathan, such a bloody bore – I've been forced to play with the children! She scampers away and strikes an illustrative pose in the doorway: one leg cocked at the knee, a finger to her pouting bottom lip. She's wearing long white ribbed socks, a pleated navy skirt, a pale blue linen blouse and a nautical scarf – and, as she *weighs anchor* and sets off in the child's wake, the Filipina marooned on the kitchen island cannot prevent her entirely justifiable expression of . . . *contempt*. Whatever the wipeable, durable and impermeable character of contemporary kitchen worktops, there remains *a crack in everything* . . . through which . . . *the derision gets in*. How old precisely is Sally? To say *forty if she's a day* would be to make of yourself precisely the cliché she's fast becoming: a sporty girl, who, by all that's right and proper, should long since have had a pair of her own sporty girls, with blonde forelocks of their own, whom she could trot along to gymkhanas and all the other *dressage* of contemporary upper-middle-class English social existence. Of course, it's precisely, painfully, *paradoxically* because of this that she's the Butcher's longest-growing beard: Sally fits in – she's sporting as well as sporty – her county accent precisely counterpointing his own colourless tone. Blended *we are* into the right Farrow and Ball shade – fitted *we are*, bespoke even: and perfectly coordinated with the increasingly threadbare British class system. Cheltenham Ladies' College? Absolutely! But not a Registry Girl. Even for a funambulist such as the Butcher, this would be too taut a tightrope to toe – or strip the Rigby and Peller lingerie off . . . *Oh! Really, Jonathan – really!* Her response to the subtle scrape of the bedside table's drawer is Pavlovian: a puckering-up of her shy little *starfish*, long before the *sharkish* finger, slathered with Vaseline, angles in *for the kill* –. – Bloody hell, Jonathan, I see the wife's got you on cookhouse patrol! Right on cue *Le Bourgeois Gentilhomme* appears in the opulent kitchen, and stands twirling the handle of some Starck-new corkscrew. Nick Baldwin is a lanky, *twisted* nervy figure – bald by nature as well as name. Wouldn't you, he asks, be interested in doing something a little more interesting? Which is exactly what Doctor Opie, the Butcher's tutor for Sub-Saharan African Politics, said to him at the end of their last tutorial before his finals, sitting in his opulent study at Saint Antony's. A little more interesting than what? he replies now, *as I did then*. More interesting than chopping bloody garlic! Baldwin *spumantes* – he's had a few . . . he'll have a few more. The Butcher, while careful to control his own alcohol intake in operational contexts (Of which this is surely one . . .), *Thank you, Squilly*, nevertheless appreciates the effect it has on British policymakers – without its heady fumes to cloud their judgement they'd never do anything at all. *Don't just do something . . .* would be their motto . . . *sit there!* Honestly, Baldwin spittles on, I don't know why Vron insists on dragooning our guests into performing these, ah, menial tasks . . . Possibly – the Butcher is judicious – she thinks it's a good idea for us to undertake at least some of the practical work required to put meat on our tables – and clean clothes on our backs for that matter . . . Every time Gawain takes off his shirt, his lover marvels once again at the beauty of his *rumsteck*. This is the moment the Butcher savours the most: the piquant taste of Gawain's skin as the tip of his tongue circles the scattering of brown moles between his *basses-côtes* and his *queue*. Fancifully, one hand firmly encircling Gawain's penis, the other stroking his back, the Butcher imagines them *one and the same* and so cranes to kiss *his blushing glans* . . . You're sounding distinctly pink, Jonathan! Baldwin guffaws, and the Butcher answers his host levelly: My father always made a point of polishing his own shoes – he did it, ah . . . religiously. On religiously he runs his hand through

his thick, lustrously blue-black and perfectly coiffed hair – a sub-
liminal command Baldwin responds to by smoothing his own
smoothness. This purely physical act encodes the secret message
of . . . *superiority – we're devious, aren't we, Squills* . . . (I prefer to
think of it as good tradecraft, Butch). *Explain?* (It's not just her
accent you prize Sally for, Butch.) *Go on.* (Every time you sneak
into White's, the Beefsteak or the House of Lords tea room . . .)
Sensational crumpets . . . (. . . you're dangling beneath her, and the
cyclopean knob-head standing guard feels the cashmere back of just
another Fighting Ram.) *Cashmere comes from goats, I believe, Squills.*
(Whatever . . .) Whatever, indeed. – The Butcher looks up at his
host. He's been in meetings at which Baldwin has been present –
just another of the semi-conscious drones the Butcher's introduced
to as "a friend" (A friend indeed!), and thereafter referred to – as
friends usually are – solely by his Christian name . . . *Jonathan,*
perhaps you've something to add? There are, of course, those at the
EssEyeEss, at the EffSeeOh – in fact, throughout AitchEm-
Gee – who know De'Ath's pater was . . . *a bit of a pinko*, while his
mother, despite all her striving, remains very much . . . *bottom*
drawer. Then again, it's those selfsame Westminster Village gossips
who also know his grandfather was Sir Albert De'Ath – Sirbert to
his intimates (not that he had any beyond the family), at one time
Chairman of the Modern Churchmen's Union, a lay preacher and a
mandarin of unimpeachable standing. Sirbert had been responsible
for shell production at the Woolwich Arsenal during the first show,
then, as Beaverbrook's permanent undersecretary, oversaw aircraft
production throughout the second. As a child, the Butcher was

always a little perplexed by the obvious pride Kins displayed when referring to his father's KayGee – it sat oddly with his professed egalitarianism. But, as the Butcher grew, acquiring his own sensitivities, he began to understand that even the most pacific English vegetarians retain *a lust for blue-blood* . . . just as the English upper class are always gagging for *cockney claret*. Rightly so, since without regular infusions they're ever in constant risk of being choked by the ingrowing branches of their own . . . *family trees*. That his grandfather had been a Knight of the Garter – a member of a select band, numbering only twenty-four at any one time, and personally appointed by the Sovereign – would've buoyed the Butcher up as well, were it not that every time it reoccurred to him he saw this same childish vision: Sirbert, half naked in some golf club changing room, yanking up a thick, hand-knitted woollen sock and snapping it into place with . . . *a frilly band of elasticated white lace –*. He was a religious man, wasn't he, Jonathan? For a moment the Butcher's flummoxed – who can Nick Baldwin be referring to? Moreover, why such an intimate tone? As the years pass, and the Butcher's vast data-set grows exponentially, he occasionally has difficulties with *random access* . . . and so for fractions of a second forgets the precise tenor of long-standing relationships, whether professional or only *semi-so*. He's known Veronica Baldwin (née Prodger) since they were at Oxford together – I punted her up the Cherwell a few times, true enough (And wore her as a beard to the May Ball in 'eighty). *Thank you, Squilly.* No wonder her bird-brained husband knows about Kins's slow-hand-clap Christianity. So, to Baldwin the Butcher replies: Yes, fairly God-fearing – though he was rather better at keeping his shoes immaculate than his . . . soul. Baldwin laughs – a gurgling catarrhal laugh suggestive of . . . *Macmillan nurses to come* – and spills out, All right for plonk, are you? Which the Butcher sops up with a simple, Fine, thanks, before bending back to his task – anything's better than looking at Baldwin's idea of Sunday casuals: a pink shirt from Pink's, equipped with white collar and cuffs and savagely tucked into a pair of viciously ironed black Levis, no arbiter elegantiarum, him. The Butcher thinks of that *cracked actor* the PeeEmm. Richard dragged the Butcher along to one of his Downing Street briefings . . . *tepid, over-stewed cafetière coffee and Duchy-fucking-Originals.* Then, because TeeBee was in a frightful rush (But really in order to spook the spooks, eh, Butch . . .), he asked them to go with him in the car to Northolt. The Butcher recalls TeeBee clambering up into the back of the armoured Range Rover and arranging his mannish boy's mush *in the best possible light* . . . TeeBee and Richard carried on about Kosovo – could they square the circle? Was it significant that Khaled Sheik Mohammed was thought to be operating there? Should Blix's appointment at Unmovic be seen as a good . . . or a bad thing? From time to time, one of them would turn to the Butcher and ask his opinion – and he punctiliously obliged, while TeeBee stared covetously at his two-button French cuffs. Once or twice, the Butcher had thought he was about to ask *where I'd had my shirt made* . . . (Fucking Charvet of course – he's such a big girl's bloody blouse). Richard, by contrast, was utterly enthralled (And enthwalled by how enthwalled TeeBee was by him – I think this is the beginning of a beautiful friendship). *Khaled and Kosovo . . .*

The Butcher remembered then – *remembers* now – Gawain's gruff accounts of his YouEnn deployment almost a decade before: the tight joinery of frozen corpses on the back of a lorry, blue tongues stuck in bluer grooves . . . His SeeOh so pissed that one morning out jogging he fell headlong into a ditch. The Fighting Rams had been penned up in an abandoned paint factory. One night the Three Degrees arrived to entertain the troops: Sheila Ferguson shoving her spangly bits in all those hungry faces (When will we share precious moments, eh?). *Onanon* went the world leader to his spymaster – but the Butcher was more taken by the odd gyrations of the PeeEmm's security detail. The two other Range Rovers kept over- and undertaking their own vehicle, *round annaraound* all the way along the constipated Western Avenue. Force protection? More like a *suppository action*, since all the other drivers *shat themselves* struggling to get out of the way. TeeBee talked with his hands – hammy gestures: riffling invisible cards, karate-chopping immaterial bricks, pointing an adamant finger towards the heavens . . . *he'll be at home there.* The Butcher thought of the bubbles in foreign stations – air-gapped little cubicles jacked up on bricks, old railway sleepers – whatever was to hand. Inside, spooks, diplomats and visiting pols would sit *shit-stirring* in the increasingly smelly atmosphere. The Butcher sensed it's like this for TeeBee even more than most prime ministers: he inhabits a bubble-world wreathed in an atmosphere poisonous to all but . . . *sycophants.* Usually, security measures are designed to keep eyes and ears out – but for him they were required more to keep his febrile self-regard . . . *in.* The Butcher has been up close and personal with plenty of those who wield power . . . *or fantasise they do.* In his own tidy, binary mind he classifies them simply either as rulers . . . *or as sheep.* The sheep are indeed a problem (They imagine they may safely graze, don't they, Butch?). *Wo Regenten wohl regieren, Squills – although rather forgetting it's they who're meant to be doing the regieren.* But it hadn't been sheepishness that bothered the Butcher as, in the ulterior light of the Hanger Lane underpass, he gazed upon TeeBee's beautifully glazed chops, but the sempiternal sheen of . . . *sanctimony.* He'd seen it from afar – everyone has – but observing Richard, in thrall, adjusting his donnish style to fit his idea of what TeeBee might want in a spymaster – *all hit-this, cut-that, thrust-there* – the Butcher had been *really rather alarmed* . . . Never more so than when the PeeEmm, in response to a particularly pressing query . . . *It's plausibly deniable – can we go ahead?* . . . which related to one of the Butcher's own assets, graciously inclined his head (Adjusting his bloody halo . . .) and checked to see how this looked in one of the wing-mirrors before answering. The Butcher, seeing TeeBee groping blindly forward into the *unredeemable* future, gripped by the delusion that all is perfectly visible . . . *in the searchlight of Providence,* silently sing-songed, *There may be trouble a-head* . . . — Oh, is that the time? Nick Baldwin's returned, and the Butcher thinks: if the Tories ever want to get back to Number Ten they'll have to haul their fashion sense kicking and screaming into the new millennium . . . You better get a move-on with that garlic, Jonathan, Baldwin says superfluously, Vron wants the lamb in toot-sweet . . . Yes, time is indeed of the essence: when the Firm made its move from Century House, Cumming's clocks went with them. Now,

231

when the Butcher goes to see Richard in his bland new sanctum, the spymaster's own rapidly ageing face *sags* in amongst all these silently ticking ones: I'm very glad you could make some time to see me, Jonathan, Richard had said earlier that week – and the Butcher replied: Timing is my business, Richard . . . Which was true enough, since when the message peeped through to the Butcher's pager he'd been in Chariots Roman Spa watching (The young men lift the weights from their shoulders?), as has been, is . . . *and will always be*, his wont. He'd only fifteen minutes to exfiltrate himself, return to his house, change out of his leathers and back into his pin-stripes, then head along the Embankment to VeeBeeArr . . . *Elvis entered the building* by stepping into the first security gate, stating his name and Service number. Released into a short catwalk lined with steel, trident-topped palings, he then entered a second security gate, where he inputted his pass code *six-oh-six-seven-zero-one* using a steel keypad. The Perspex pod split, disgorging him into a *hideous atrium* – a great echoing volume, filled with the sounds of . . . *silence*: the brothel-creeping of the younger generation of crêpe-soled grammar-school-entrants of whom the Butcher was the *front-runner* . . . Checking his own vintage Longines, he'd realised there were still five minutes to spare, so strolled round the planta-tion of palms and out on to the terrace. It had been a brisk day – the westerly wind sweeping along the river, pushing a scummy tumble of cloud before it. Grim as it'd undoubtedly been, the old Lubyanka also had superb views – the Butcher, who, whether hungover or not, could deal with his admin and draft his SeeEx reports in a fraction of the time it took his colleagues, would often spend hours in his cubbyhole on the fourteenth floor, standing at the window, staring out over Lambeth Palace, Saint Thomas's and the river, while feeling the wide metropolitan world wheel around him. Spies alight here, bus conductors allegedly said as they halted at the junction of Westminster Bridge Road and Morley Street (Not that you've ever had to do anything so gauche as take the bus!). There'd been Sirbert's small inheritance soon after the Butcher joined the Service – and this went into a dinky flat on Kennington Lane, which, watered by the occasional windfall, grew in a few years to become a garden one on Fentiman Road. Here the Butcher remained for several years. Then his upstairs neighbour – a general's widow with large hands who always wore tennis shoes, and with whom he had . . . *an understanding* – inconveniently went and died. Her heirs – a provincial solicitor and his diffident wife – came to introduce themselves, and, spotting the framed photograph on a side table, the solicitor said, Fighting Rams, eh – you a military man, then? And when the Butcher answered, I'm on the Territorials' roll – but that's a hobby thing, my day job's at the Foreign and Commonwealth Office, the solicitor gave him a funny look and said, EffSeeOh, eh . . . That was all – but it was enough: his cover was blown. The Butcher put the flat on the market the following day. He found an ex-council house on the oddly sleepy lane which is all that remains of Lambeth High Street, in between a scrap of park and the Fire Brigade's headquarters. It felt familiar, being of the same vintage as the Hertfordshire University campus where Kins had *bloviated for a living*: a system-built affair assembled using concrete, painted panelling and unplasticised polyvinyl chloride.

233

The month the Butcher moved in Stephen Fry was opening in a play about George Blake's time in the Scrubs – the Butcher had a thing for Blake (*You identify with him*). *Identify! Puh-lease, Squills* . . . so booked seats for him and his then current second-string beard, Lucinda, a broad-shouldered girl with a wild tangle of dark hair, who he'd spotted fighting to control it, beside a yucca, on a half-landing, at the new offices of the new Department for International Development . . . *aim high – shoot low*. But by the time they pitched up, Fry had already fled: hotfooting it to the Continent, in emulation – the Butcher suggested to Lucinda, who was *no fool* – not of his real-life character, who'd been spirited away in a fellow traveller's Dormobile with his kiddies sitting on top of him, but of Oscar Wilde – Wilde had made a run for Dieppe and Bosie as soon as the gates of Reading Gaol swung open . . . Fry's problem, the Butcher suggested, was the same: he *lacked the courage of his own perversions* . . . Of the play, the Butcher remembers little, save what the playwright *got wrong* . . . This is a scene, however, that he retains: Lucinda, standing naked by the blank, black windows of his new and very empty house . . . *a silvery spunk-trail trickling down her thigh*, and staring towards where the singed bricks of the firemen's practice tower would, when the sun rose, block out the light. She'd gently remarked, Maybe that's your problem, too, Jonathan . . . So, despite the fact he enjoyed her company and found her vagina *quite orderly* – he fired Lucinda the next day, via email. It was, he thinks, one of the first he'd ever sent – and, although he'd used his private account, it required an effort of will to resist the deadweight of the drafting pro forma all EyeBees had used for . . . *mind out of time*:

three lines at the top in summary, all surnames capitalised, conversations indicated by (cons), colleagues by their alpha-numerical designator and emphasis conveyed by a bracketed (LWU), meaning last word underlined. So: Sexual relationship between Jonathan DE'ATH and Lucinda PHILLIPS. Possible agent compromise due to source's superior gaydar (LWU). Discontinuation advised forthwith (LWU – or even fiftwith, Butch – but don't divagate so, you were thinking about time, and Tony Blair, and black Levis . . .). So I was, the Butcher thinks, so I was . . . (Or is it, perhaps, that Sally's finally due for discontinuation?) He looks up at last from the macerated garlic – further off, in the tiled hallway, he hears the tinkle-bray of . . . *incoming Tories! Tories! Tories!* In the Chief's office the form is that the suppliant sits with his back to the Tate Gallery – averting his eyes from art and setting his face *to the future.* The Butcher's current duties include some responsibility for overseeing the Firm's own large data-set – there are regular trips to Cheltenham for meetings as dully predictable as *electric clocks.* Cumming's clocks are, he thinks, at once glass-spiked Sputniks orbiting the woody heavens of the generously appointed office – and blank faces, behind which large cogs gear into smaller ones . . . *with an inexorable logic.* He'd been hoping for an overseas posting – a little troubleshooting, perhaps, in the Gulf, or the knitting back together of one of the Firm's unravelling Far Eastern networks . . . *no such fucking luck.* A Parker fountain pen had been laid ostentatiously on Dick's blotter – beside it a pot of green ink: The world is enough . . . he'd said. What the fuck does that mean? It'd been a rare instance of the epithet issuing from Dick's smiling-upside-down lips – even when the spooks are *pissed outta our minds* at the near-obligatory Friday-evening drinks, they remain well-spoken and close-mouthed for . . . *cracked actors*: What's he going to be when he grows up? the Butcher thought then – thinks now: Sydney-fucking-Greenstreet? For he's swelling, Dick is, sitting for day after day beneath those sanguinary clock-faces as they . . . *haemorrhage time*. No doubt the Firm's first Chief saw his hobby as a metaphor for his métier: the careful assembly of the secret mechanism that lies behind (. . . Events, dear boy, events). Thank you, Squilly, the Butcher murmurs – standing now at the kitchen island, the Filipina looking on, as he stabs expertly at the leg of lamb, making a series of utilitarian . . . *wounds*. But really, even if there ever was any calibration between the covert mechanism and *the way the world turns*, it was trop en retard now: the Mad Hatter's dropped his half-hunter in the teapot, and, for all the dancing of sound into light, and the shimmying of light into sound, there remains a profound sense, here, at the Zero Meridian, that time's . . . *going nowhere*. Which means, in turn, that events are being *stillborn*. Yes, the West's enfeebled events – jizzing up the Chinks after the duff run on Belgrade, then all those other sorties: bombs dropped not on some far-away-country-of-which-we-know-little, but *right in our backyard*. Still, they made no sound – these congenitally deformed events. Soon enough – the Butcher thinks, as he begins methodically to insert small wedges of garlic into the gashes – in order for anything to happen at all, it'll need to be . . . *outsourced to the developing world*. And to the Chief he'd said: The world is not enough, Dick – not enough, then he turned back to the window. So the Chief had been compelled to address his beautifully tailored back . . . (Five fittings at Kilgour's – you spent more time in Thavile Row that month than at the office). The faint reflection of Dick had removed its glasses and massaged its translucent eyes . . . – D'you know that repulsive little ginger nut the Foreign Secretary? I've run across him, the Butcher conceded. – Well, he only went and let the film people use the building as a bloody backdrop for this flick without consulting me at all! The Butcher hadn't altogether believed what he'd just heard: Dick, who'd been *pretty fearless* in Geneva – personally setting up letter-drops and brush-contacts, carrying some of them out himself – even getting up to a bit of rough stuff with the increment . . . There he'd been, high on this petty dudgeon. The Butcher takes the bundle of fresh rosemary from the Filipina, releases its constraining rubber band and begins spearing sprigs into the joint. Gawain will be nearing London by now, driving his shitty old Volvo. The thrusting tank commander may be able to direct a long-range reconnaissance mission deep behind enemy lines, but London traffic confuses his *dear, woolly head*. He'll park up in Hendon and take the Northern Line into town. Sunday afternoon is perhaps the most difficult time for him to get away – after the obligatory roast there's mandatory home-work, and all the squalid demands of a breeders' household with three young offspring. His cover story these past few months has been water-tight: although recently promoted, Lieutenant-Colonel Thomas was passed over for Regimental SeeOh. Aggrieved, he's applied for secondment to the DeeEssOh, which has necessitated his travelling down to London for various selection panels ever since. Each trip requires an overnight – or so Fi believes. *If she's still that complacent* . . . The Butcher will find out soon enough, lying in his lover's arms. Surely she suspects by now? Surely she has at least an inkling? She's woman enough – at least biologically – to have some sort of *feminine intuition?* The lovers discuss the personality they're betraying in obsessive detail, running their mental digits over its confusing contours. Both men are meant to be experts on human psychology – their respective professions would seem to demand nothing less. Yet, when it comes to Gawain's wife, they're stymied: they can see the shape Fiona impresses on their own lives, yet have no idea *how she makes it.* Is that the time? Vron Baldwin cries, re-entering the kitchen. C'mon now, Jonathan, that joint should've been in yonks ago . . . The Butcher hefts the roasting pan and the lamb slithers about on its extra-virginal . . . *piste.* (Wo ein guter Hirte wacht, eh, Butch . . .) Vron opens one of the oven doors and he slides the tin into the hot socket. Basted by orangey light, the joint glistens, and the Butcher thinks of last New Year's Eve. Disdaining such a staged saturnalia, he'd sat at home and listened to the evil buzz which vibrates through his house, while watching the festivities on television, half hoping planes would indeed . . . *fall out of the sky,* for what fitter solution could there be to humanity's great third-act-problem than a digitally induced mass suicide? When the estate agent had shown him round, the Butcher had been sizing him up for . . . *a little amateur conveyancing* when he registered the buzz. The estate agent had blushed charmingly: It's the electricity substation, I'm afraid: it's directly adjoining the house – to be honest, it's put quite a few potential buyers off, and I think the vendor might be prepared to accept a considerably lower offer . . .

The vendor had – and the Butcher considered it *a win–win*, since he positively enjoyed the buzz, glorying in the way it enfolded his svelte form in the great electro-magnetic go-round which, when you stop to consider it, *is* everything. Towards midnight, as the crowds were gathering, and – if the media was to be believed – the Thames was about to be infused with Greek fire, the Butcher snapped on the television. There they'd all been: the flock of the great and greedy, hungry for preferment, and penned in a measureless concrete canyon, such was their desire to drift downstream with Their Royal Highnesses and experience the rarefied delights of TeeBee's pleasure dome. The Butcher actually caught a glimpse of Dick, John and Gerry, blinking in the unaccustomed limelight, and fully apprised of the terror-threat, flinching rather more than the other vee-eyepees whenever a rocket went up. The fundamental error in the lives of almost everyone, the Butcher thinks, as he allows Vron to tuck his arm under hers, is to place themselves at the very centre of things . . . I'll do some introductions in a minute, she coos, but first I'd like to ask you for a little advice. Her sagging udder has him trapped and: *I doubt very much she did her pelvic-floor exercises before pushing out little Sam* (Or Arthur – y'know, I think he may be one of your godchildren, Butch). In the airy hallway she wheels him round, and he sees not the pale oak staircase climbing up past tall stained-glass windows, but the flyleaf of his school atlas: Jonathan De'Ath, Number Four, Colindale Avenue, Saint Albans, Hertfordshire, England, Great Britain, Europe, The World, The Solar System, The Galaxy, The Universe . . . (There was a time when you thought you were at the thentre of things, Butch). So there was,

Squilly – yet how very ignorant I was, as misinformed as any medieval cartographer. But as I grew we slipped, didn't we, Squills – slipped away into the wings, a vantage from where we can see *what actually goes on* . . . – D'you think I should worry about him, Jonathan? The object of her anxiety – Sam (or possibly Arthur) – lies full length on the lush carpet in front of a vast television. He's exchanged one controller for another, and now noses the barrel of an automatic rifle (Looks a bit like a Galil, wouldn't you say?) into an on-screen labyrinth. The Butcher's seen such things before – but, as with the game of life, it's the setting which interests him more than the action. What is this imaginary realm, a cut-and-shut between the Oyster Bar at Grand Central, an Istanbul hammam and a giant public toilet? (Or lavatory – don't forget Mummy!) There are odd brown patches scattered about on the dirty tiled floors – and as they watch, the rifle's sights encircle one of these and its muzzle spews fire. The patch spews red pulp. I can't keep him off it, Vron says, really I can't – Nick was so pissed off with it last week he unplugged the PlayStation and locked it in the garden shed, but clever old Arthur here pinched the key, got it back and set the whole thing up in his bedroom using Consuela's television as a . . . as a . . . – Monitor? – Yes, that's it, Jonathan, as a monitor – but honestly, he's so . . . addicted. Can't be good for him, can it? Look – look at how gory it is. The Butcher looks: it's not gory at all – gory is hot and wet and traumatised. Gory is a ringing-singing-screaming all around you. Gory is an explosion so loud it knocks the top of your skull in and spreads your brain *on the walls* . . . The Butcher looks and sees this: the child lying on the carpet is really stalking along a subterranean corridor, turning to the right, to the left, sliding down the balustrade of a shattered staircase, past twisted rebars beaded with concrete *pilules*. The assassins that come, tumbling from triangular shadows, are projections of Cubist irrealism: all glassy block-jaws and compound eyes that then shatter in the rifle's flash. The Butcher observes this – and recognises a phenomenon he first witnessed at Langley three or four years ago, when he and Colin were given a demonstration of the Friends' latest box of delights: operations coordinated and conducted using pinpoint-accurate satellite locations to obtain audio-visual take from multiple sources, so enabling real-time remote-control of the man on the ground. A little revolted – but mostly fascinated, the Butcher and the then Chief had watched on a monitor, which was directly connected to a camera mounted on the operative's body armour, as he'd stalked along Beirut back alleys. The experience had been uncanny: ducking beneath rusting fire escapes festooned with laundry, scampering across cluttered courtyards, turning to the right and the left, then sliding down and around a shattered staircase, at the bottom of which the *bed-head* of some Mohammed or other who'd crossed the Agency had been turned to . . . *mush.* As he recalls, the SeeEyeAy man who made the kill was cracking open a can of Mountain Dew as he told the shooter where to aim . . . *where to fire.* To the player, whether he be a twelve-year-old soldier of fortune in Hampstead or a middle-aged spook in Virginia, the illusion remained the same: you appeared to be making definite progress – moving forward, scoring points and so acquiring additional powers. But the truth was you were completely and

Medievally static – as static as the warm body you'd abandoned, slumped in a chair. It was the virtual world which revolved around these digi-bodies, not vice versa: a turmoil of zeroes and ones, forming and reforming an ever receding middle ground of mud-brick walls, mosquito-infested puddles, corrugated-iron roofs and unemployed young men. Oh, I dunno, Vron, the Butcher says, tightening his arm in hers in a way he hopes she finds . . . *affectionate?* Boys will be boys and all that jazz. When I was a boy, my brothers and I were pretty damn blood-thirsty – constant diet of war films and comics. Only diff' was we had to use our imagination – but does that really make it any better? Y'know . . . in my mind's eye, Vron, the butchery I carried out was a great deal more realistic than this . . . Vron peers at the Butcher a little oddly – and he knows she's recollecting the story told about him at Oxford: how during Freshers' Week he'd joined his college's vegetarian society and invited its members to meet in his rooms, where he'd prepared a colossal fry-up for them – lashings of rashers, chains of interlinked sausages, slices of greasily gleaming black pudding and two or three bulbous kidneys. The spectacle had caused them to . . . *flee – pissing themselves.* The nickname subsequently bestowed on him was *fairly predictable* . . . although, as they wheel round once more and clack back across the parquet, he does wonder: Has Baldwin been saying things to her? Saying – or merely twittering? They've entered an aviary . . . *full of Tories:* a bright and overwhelmingly floral room – floor and wall coverings both – furnished with large soft sofas and chairs, and equipped with a baby grand upon which are silver-framed photographs of family, friends and the more famous politicos . . . *he wishes were his friends.* There are vases of late daffodils and early irises poised on occasional tables, and, as they advance between them, the Butcher searches the faces that open up to him – Hi, Jonathan . . . Jonathan – what's the news, old chap? D'you know Jonathan De'Ath? – for any indication of . . . *conscious-ness.* At the old Lubyanka, where tea ladies in nylon housecoats pushed their trolleys along strip-lit corridors over dun carpeting, past despairing pot plants and beneath disintegrating ceiling tiles, the scene was so dispiritingly anonymous it had been difficult to visualise the building at all – unless you were actually standing on the scuffed linoleum floor of the reception area. For EyeBee officers of the Butcher's generation, who'd joined the Firm when post-Philby paranoia remained rife . . . *Kall-me-Kim, the Kommie Kunt wore brown suede shoes – keweedee all brown-suede-shoe-wearers are Kommie Kunts,* and London was played by Moscow Rules, there was a degree of security to be gained by this fact alone: their own offices were so woefully under-imagined they were impossible to surveil – whether with the mind's eye or *a sub-miniature Minox.* But now . . . ? Well, since the Service's public avowal, courtesy of *the Currie-stirrer,* the fish-eye lens had been inverted, so, children that we undoubtedly are . . . *with our Secret Sam briefcases and bottles of invisible ink,* we hide in plain view – although remaining exiguous . . . a distortion in full sunlight . . . a spinning *sphincter* implanted in the smooth *screen-skin –.* How're you, Jonathan? says an . . . *affectionate?* voice, issuing from a *corn plaster* the Butcher peels off, exposing the pink face of . . . *that pinko one* (Who's always banging on about civil liberties . . .) *and has been demob-happy since ninety-seven – 'though I've heard he's a weekend warrior. –* Not too bad, David, you? Then the politician does an unexpected thing – rising from his flowery chair, he takes the Butcher's arm and leads him through the open French windows and into the garden. A series of red-brick terraces descend to an oblong ornamental pond covered in water lilies. Beyond this rhododendrons screen off the garden below – for the hillside falls away sharply here, while, from the Baldwins' peak perspective . . . *Nick must be minted – this place has to be worth five mil' and rising,* the Butcher can gaze right out over North-West London, all the way to the leafy streets surrounding Shoot-Up Hill. What a perfect day, David says, and the Butcher agrees: Yes, such clarity – I feel I might look into the soul of Kilburn. David darts him an odd look, then gestures with his flute: Not drinking, Jonathan? They've gained the edge of the first terrace and the Butcher peers down at his handmade Franceschetti loafers and shuffles them a little (Nice sheen!): Bit of a flap on at the office – prob'ly have to go in later . . . Better keep a clear head . . . The politician perks up – and when the Butcher gets out his cigarettes and offers them, takes one, then a light, before striking a macho little pose with this prop and saying, Oh, yes, the office – you mean VeeBeeArr, don't you? David has the look *they always do*: eyes clenching into knuckles, which in turn deliver the lightest knock on the door of . . . *hell's darkest chamber.* The Butcher smiles tightly – but says nothing, only puffs away, thinking of how newcomers to London – natives and long-term residents as well – cannot help but think of the Thames as a straight line, and so are repeatedly surprised by the way the solid bastions of

the North Bank – Saint Paul's, for example – suddenly up foundations and, trailing their . . . *cold stone skirts*, step over its chilly waters.
This grand optical illusion is particularly evident when the Butcher
goes out on to the terrace of *the Aztec Camera*, escaping the airless-
ness of his office to breathe in a cigarette. From this vantage, the
channel separating VeeBeeArr, Tintagel and Camelot houses from
the Tate Gallery, Millbank Tower and Thames House . . . *where
the EmmEyeFive plods swing their limp dicks* appears ruled straight
by Victorian masons. No wonder, he's often mused, the British
political class, despite our numerous betrayals, continues to place
such trust in its intelligence services. Any former imperial power
will have – in the modern idiom – abandonment issues, but
we spooks aren't going anywhere: *Here we are* . . . right beside
them, hiding in plain view, and perfectly located for *upstream data
collection* . . . As it is with the buildings – so it is with their denizens,
who constantly cross over from one side to the other of this, *the most
deceptive bend in the world* . . . Taking the Butcher's abstracted
silence for clamorous engagement, David remarks, I'm just back
from Saudi . . . then goes on to recount how . . . *he walked in marble
halls*, while the Baldwins' other guests nose out from the French
windows, lowing hungrily about the roast to come: When all's said
and done, I'm perfectly happy with chicken . . . David – perhaps
make-believing he's in the field – goes sotto, so his tale of a furtive
princeling, beckoning him away from the Potemkin progress of the
trade delegation, becomes compressed to the width of a news-thread
which unrolls between them: I'mnotsayingthere'sanythingdefinite
therebuthemadeitprettycleartomehe'dbeinterestedinworkingwithus

ObviouslyIunderstandabout . . . andsaidnothingtoindicateIwasany-
thingotherthanwhatIappearedtobe . . . As the EmPee rattles on,
the Butcher allows some warmth to enter his expression – albeit his
mind remains, as ever, coldly calculating: What're such assets
actually worth? Fuck-all, really. I've seen 'em all and done 'em all
myself . . . There're so many of these princelings, swirling about in
the cloacal confines of the court-cum-seraglio – they bob about in
there, slathered in the shit-and-piss of their kickbacks and corrup-
tion, and if you ever try and catch one of 'em by his toe – (He hollers,
I'm the PeeEmm's son! So you have to let 'im go!). So to David
he says, Well, that is, ah, interesting – I'll certainly mention it to
some people who may be . . . ah, interested. The EmPee looks a bit
deflated and shuffles his desert boots on the suburban terrace. The
Butcher considers the many solecisms David embodies – where to
start? Surely with this screamed admonition: *Never, ever, ever . . .
BROWN IN TOWN!* But then it's the baby-boomers who've their
fingers on the brass buttons now. He remembers being in Kosovo
with Dick, who was then head of the Eastern Europe Controllerate.
They'd watched the Great Liberator going walkabout in a crowd of
natives, sporting the same black Levis as this one, together with a
red shirt thrifty Cherie prob'ly bought for him *at fucking Millets . . .*
Watching him bend his smiling, beautifully orangish face to their
frowning hairy brownish ones, Dick had said, We'll wait 'til he's
had his fill, then we'll tell him they're all his enemies . . . Confident
words, spoken cramped up in a whited-out Warrior with YouEnn
painted on its turret – assertions they were more than able to back
up with the contents of the buff folders they'd brought with them.

The Butcher remembers also, how, as TeeBee flicked through the pages, Dick grew giddy seeing the application of the secret cog to the political drive-shaft . . . *ahh, the old in-and-out.* – The Filipina reappears bearing a plate covered with little filou-pastry parcels. What's in these, please . . .? But before David has an answer he's popped one . . . two into his mouth, and positioned a third on his meaty palm. Vron, who comes fussing along behind her maid, says, Honestly, David, you won't have any room for lunch . . . And he offers up: But these look too scrumptious, Veronica – besides, I'm utterly famished. Well, she titters *nervously?* You can blame Jonathan for that – took him forever to chop up a few cloves of garlic . . . She looks to the Butcher for *ruefulness?* but he's yards away – an iridescent dragonfly, flitting over the lilyscape – then miles . . . While the new Chief had sat cosseted by Cumming's clocks, the Butcher had stood at the window looking down at the deceptive river, and remembering the previous year, when the great Ferris wheel had been borne upstream on tugs in prefabricated sections, then assembled and oh-so-slowly winched upright. For at least a day it was set at a forty-five degree angle, its massive clockface . . . *gushing time*: a mighty flow of hours and days, swirling past TeeBee's tit, Canary Dwarf – and all the other *terrorist targets* – and out into the *sea of forgetting*. Thing is . . . Dick had spoken to the hands massaging the Butcher's tender kidneys . . . I mean to say – well, I hope . . . The Butcher rounded on him: You don't seriously imagine I thought I was in contention? There was then some fountain-pen fiddling – so the Butcher went on, quite recklessly: For Christ's sake, Dick, I know what people say –

247

I know what people would think. No . . . he'd dropped down into cockney . . . I know my place. There'd been restrained laughter at this, and the Butcher considered then – reconsiders now – how the mores of the secret world are really an extreme intensification of the reticence, obfuscation and well-schooled evasiveness the English upper-middle classes think of as . . . *good manners*. Manners only intensified by the spooks' tendency towards *selective breeding*. All those colonels' daughters, whinnying and whickering – bucking, snorting, ramping and curveting, their jodhpurs and hacking jackets cast aside, before whinnying some more – until they hand over a leisurely composed note, on a piece of pale yellow notepaper, decorated with a single drooping primrose, which reads: *I think I'm going to come* . . . But *Dick sees Jonathan run – Dick knows Jonathan likes dick* . . . Dick can still remember the fag hunts of the late seventies, when *swishy-swashy, swishy-swashy* . . . they swept through the Intelligence Branch: Dick was trying to tell him *times have changed* . . . trying to *flush me out* . . . The Butcher was having none of it – he waited the moment out: he was to be sidelined – that much was clear. And why not? Another round of cuts was hacking dead and live wood alike from the decision tree, it being so very hard to convince the Exchequer that the bearded weirdos and Turkish smack-runners represented quite the same existential threat as the Soviet nuclear arsenal. Thing is . . . Well, the thing is . . . Dick had eventually stuttered into life . . . I mean, the sort of thing you do at the moment . . . sort of troubleshooting, really – going into a station . . . a whole section as well, and sort of sorting it out. Well, I thought –. – You wondered whether I'd be prepared to keep on with it, now you've taken the helm? – Yes, yes . . . that's right. Would you, Jonathan? Would you do . . . just . . . that? And the Butcher, staring across at the Tate Gallery, but seeing only Kins's *scraggy saggy unshaven RED face* staring back at him from the lead-reinforced glass, had thought, What the hell, one more roll of the dice . . . Dick had then told him about the Chargé d'Affaires attached to the Iranian delegation in Geneva: Might be bugger all, but we've reason to believe he's one of Younesi's. Claims he's an asset well placed to source intel' on Saddam's doubleyouemmdees. I'd really rather it was you who went over and met with him – you've some Farsi, haven't you? It's not that I don't have confidence in Roger, or his people, it's just . . . At this the Butcher turned from the window to confront the man (You must, perforce, call your line manager). Fair enough, Dick, I'll sort out some fig-leaf cover with Requirements and get over there in a week or so – but if you're expecting me to play pat-a-cake with this stuff, put it in an accept-able shape for the PeeEm's bag-man, I'm not playing ball. I won't bypass the usual analysts, and I'm not going messing about with long-established sources – some of whom I recruited myself . . . Given the circumstances, this had been about as pale and yellow a note as he could manage. Vron Baldwin has gone. David stands with that stupid, puppyish expression on his face they all have: those loyal dogs, waiting for their scraps of clandestine preferment. The Butcher toys with telling him what happened to the last EmPee the Firm ran – because it does happen, although very rarely, and only in collusion with the more paranoid prime ministers. He'd been useful enough for a while – reasonable product on the Serbs around Milošević. Then it all got a bit *tainted*, and the Butcher had taken a rather proactive role, working closely with the officers faking photographs, receipts and bookings. He'd shared just a soupçon of his intimate knowledge of London's *nethermost portions*. The EmPee had a moment of madness and ended up for an eternity doing talk radio (In Wales). This time the Butcher plays it differently: The interested people – should they be, ah . . . interested, will want to get in touch with you. Do you know how to go about setting up an anonymous email account with one of the big providers – Hotmail, for instance? The EmmPee's ears really do prick up, and, suitably enough, in his doggy guise he's then called upon by Vron to round up his fellow Tories – who're distributed about the terraces, blinking in poplin jackets and linen sundresses that bear the heavy creasing of a winter's underbed storage – and herd them into the dining room. Where – after baked goat's cheese and balsamic onions – she asks: Jonathan, would you mind awfully carving – Nick's so clumsy, and it is rather your . . . thing? He pauses, serving fork aloft, a slice of steaming lamb speared by its tines. Slowly, the assembled company fall silent – the last audible take being "teak decking", which plops from the mouth of a woman sitting beside *poor old Sporty Spice!* Who's been in post so very long now it was Dick himself who'd said, after several too many at Friday-evening drinks: Jonathan, old man, don't you think it's high time you made that lovely girlfriend of yours a touch more . . . aware? Standing in the hideous atrium at VeeBeeArr, the tipsy spooks wheeling about them, the Butcher had chewed over the unutterable: Absolutely, Dick, she's a right to know – and she's completely sound. Old man was bomb disposal — nearly got his nuts blown off by the Ra. There's only uno problemo with bringing the bigger picture into focus for her — well, two actually: first, she's too fucking thick (lwu) to grasp it, which is precisely why she's lasted this long — and secondly: if I were to jolt her into partial consciousness, even Sporty might have the nous to put together my profession of secrecy *and my penchant for sodomy* . . . I was . . . he looks round at the Tory *sheeple* . . . going to ask which of you would like your lamb rare . . . they moan obligingly . . . But, bearing in mind the old adage you are what you eat . . . their woolly faces grow pensive . . . You'd better all have it well done — unless you never want to be in government again! The Tories baa appreciatively at this feeble witticism, and the Butcher hides his face in the meaty steam. Oh, Gawain! he cries in the bony cave of his own darkest chamber. My noon, my midnight, my talk, my song! And he imagines his lover driving through the Hatfield Tunnel, the light and shadow playing on his boyish features. There's a certain sort of gentlemanly English face — epitomised, the Butcher believes, by the actor Michael York — which retains a youthful mien well into middle age. (Even older!) Senior EssEyeEss mostly belong to the Travellers, but the Butcher prefers the more sedate, and slightly more liberal, Reform, where from childhood — since it had been Kins's club as well — he's seen these faces, ever-green against the worn brown leather of the library chairs. It's said of humanity in general . . . (Thpare us the bloody oracular, Butch — thpare us that!) . . . it's said of humanity in general that the retention of infantile characteristics into adulthood is a measure of evolutionary success: these boyish men and mannish boys, scanning the swags of tickertape draped from the baize-covered boards, or slowly impacting on whitebait in the dining room's old-gold gloom – could it be their biological retardation had been essential for the rapid expansion of the empire they'd served? Kins, too, despite jowly ruddiness, had been a boy-man, delighting in impromptu games, small excursions and all their accompanying *little smackerels* . . . His pacifism, his piety, his local-government-fucking-finance, his rose-tinted utopianism – it'd all been *par for the course* . . . In the large and floral drawing room, the Butcher takes his coffee in a Barcelona chair with Sally, and wonders whether he should ask her away for a weekend . . . *in Barcelona?* At the same time, he taunts her: D'you see him? He nods towards a small, plump inoffensive-looking man wearing a gaudy moleskin waistcoat, who sits in the far corner of the room, his tiny, gold-rimmed coffee cup resting on his paunch, his mild eyes blinking at the gathering from behind thick lenses. You wouldn't think it to look at him, the Butcher whispers, but he's a big DeeYouPee grandee – and implicated in all sorts . . . from aiding Loyalist death squads to kiddy-fiddling at Belfast care homes – if I told you the half of it, Sal, you'd up-chuck Vron's tiramisu . . . But Sal doesn't want to admit the least fraction of such disturbing smut – let alone a half of it. The Butcher has page upon page of witness statements, all available for . . . *downloading*. The blocky Biro of the plods dutifully detailing how many *scraggy saggy RED* old cocks had been placed between how many young, trembling buttocks. But, even if he drilled it into her, none of it would *get through* – any more than it would've to Kins, both being *innocent little eras of their own* – permanent and enduring nows, endless evenings in which the shadows cast across the cricket pitch never, ever lengthen, and the little darlings up in the nursery never grow older, never having been *born in the first place*. You're teasing me, darling, Sally whispers, and that's unkind. Which is true – and hardly his style, so he says, You're right, I'm being silly – listen, I've got to head off in a minute, will you take the Merc', it's a bugger to park in town and I fancy a walk . . . The Butcher does his valedictory round: there's a forthright handshake for Nick Baldwin, and an ayframe hug for his wife – then he's free, striding between the opulent red-brick villas to the crown of the hill, where, with mingled consternation and . . . *nostalgia?* he recognises the woodland below and remembers when, newly passed out from the intelligence officers' new entrants course at Fort Monckton, he'd gone about establishing his own London network: sliding along the sweaty walls of the Bat Cave, slinking into the Pink Panther – plotting up in late-model four-door saloons on suburban streets for hours, until, in the underbrushed dawn, he made his approach. Not that he'd ever been a compulsive cruiser or a committed cottager, but he'd always appreciated the fit between this darkly honest realm and his clandestine nine-to-five. Both espionage and closeted homosexuality depended on good tradecraft – including cryptoanalysis: a mouth slobbering at a crudely hacked hole could mean quite different things . . . *depending on the context*. Both his métiers also required the Butcher to meet with individuals, mostly male, in nondescript spaces located in liminal places: chain-hotel rooms facing on to clogged arterial roads, boarded-up commercial premises behind abandoned petrol stations, mothballed offices above whining dental surgeries. — As he turns right on to West Heath Road and begins the stiff haul up to Whitestone Pond, the Butcher peers back down the long corridor of his life, with its scuffed linoleum and dinted, distempered walls. He sees himself charming Bulgarian cipher clerks and leather queens from Purley – he tastes the dead skin that's dust, and the skins which, once supple and scented, have now turned to . . . *dust*. He thinks of his colleagues, whose sins of omission and commission alike are readily washed away by the tepid tea at a vicarage coffee morning, or the spit of a military band. At Whitestone Pond the Butcher stands looking out over London – the breeze flaps the legs of his raw-silk trousers. Not a great expense, he'd shamelessly tell curious colleagues, I'm bespoken for in the Far East – the tailors in Kuala Lumpur put the Singaporean ones to shame. See the stitching round the collar, here . . . and the individual pen pockets, each one lined with absorbent material? (It's bloody barefaced to talk like that, Butch – they'll think you're queer.) They know I'm queer, Squilly – they've known it for years. (So why on earth do we persist with this pathetic thubterfuge – I, for one, am fed up with lying face down in minge every other night of the week.) The Butcher doesn't rise to this: he's looking at the raddled countenance of London but seeing only that *scraggy saggy unshaven RED face* as it was on that Sunday afternoon in the early nineteen nineties. It'd been around this time of year – sunny, too – and the Butcher was driving back from Oakley in a brand-new Alfa Romeo Spider coupé (Courtesy of Slab Murphy's Libyan paymasters, as I recall – and in the Vinaccia Red livery), which handled like a rocket-powered skateboard and could do a cool hundred and thirty-five on the flat. In all probability he'd been going still faster: whipping down through the elongated chicane the flyover describes over High Wycombe – when he was taken by an urge to see his father, so seized the slip road for the EmmTwenty-five, and found himself within the half-hour looking at Kins looking at the three-legged, kettle-drum-shaped contrivance of mirrors and marquetry, his scraggy saggy unshaven *Vinaccia Red* face burning with desire. For Christ's sake, Dad, the Butcher had undoubtedly chided him, it's not even tea time yet. If Maeve had been there it probably wouldn't've happened – but she was out, answering calls from the suicidal on behalf of the Samaritans . . . *the jolly Missus Jellyby*, as eager to save a stranger's soul as she is unwilling to mop up the . . . *blood on her own carpet.* She did return later, and the three of them had attempted to mend things over homemade banana bread – but by then the damage had been irreperable. (The damage to your English, Butch – is this feeble clichéd psycho-biography the best you can come up with?) What had got into Kins? (He would've been the most virtuous of our rulers, were it not for his choleric, fanciful disposition . . .) Had it simply been a case of his blood-alcohol levels dropping too low, so precipitating this sober assessment of his eldest son: You dress like a prize ponce, Jonathan, the saggy-red face spat. While as for that little German car you drive –. – It's Italian, Dad. – German . . . Italian . . . I hardly think you can afford such luxury items on your salary. You forget, young man, I was a public servant myself . . . His *oyster* eyes *milted* with resentment – his *hamfists* began *acting up*, so the Butcher focused on his own manicured ones. It had been a long time since he'd hit his father, and in the intervening years – what with being professionally trained in unarmed combat – he suspected he'd become a bit better at it. Under the ignorant eyes of a kitschy three-dee Christ, Kins took his poison and administered his medicine: I don't pretend to know the ins and outs, but I read the paper – I watch the news. Your so-called friends have a funny way of going about things, and they like their funny little jokes as well – what're they calling it? The turkey-shoot, that's it . . . Well, I'll tell you what I call it: a shameful massacre – that's what. And you . . . you were in the Middle East last year, admitted as much – hinted, didn't you, that you'd been sorting stuff out behind the scenes . . . Led me to believe, didn't you – 'cause I doubted the Coalition were really going to be that bloody willing when it came to finishing what they'd started – that you and your friends had it all in hand . . . A shameful bloody massacre – that's what you and your pals had planned. All those poor bloody young men – not Ba'athist thugs, mind, just poor young conscripts dragged from the bosom of their families to be burned and bombed and shot to pieces . . . And he'd banged on a great deal more in this fashion – words being the silly old sausage's only ammunition. It'd been an impassioned speech – one the Butcher redacted *in real time*, because what did it amount to, really? Only more of the piffle Kins had come out with after the EePeeVee team had visited him and Maeve almost a decade before – splendidly naive bollocks about the brotherhood of man, the necessity for force always to be tempered by restraint, and the dark paths men disappeared down whenever they made the fatal mistake of imagining their ends could be justified by such means. The Butcher heard him out in silence, refutations and put-downs stillborn, stillborn *slunks* . . . What could he possibly say that would satisfy the simpleton? His tongue was tied – not by the OhEssAy (But because you're gay . . .) Gay? Puh-lease! What the fuck does that mean, Squilly? (I know what it meant to you before the incident, Butch: Hello, my name's Julian and this is my friend, Sandy –) No! Not that, Squills – I beg of you. (Lovely to vada your jolly-old eeks, Mister Horn . . .) Oh, for fuck's sake! the Butcher cries aloud to the Sunday motorists piloting their Jags and Mercs at trotting pace past the clapboard simulacrum of Jack Straw's Castle, but *the little prick won't let it lie*: (I think you'll find – if you analythe your own large data-set properly, Butch – that there was a time when you and your brothers amused your parents by imitating the flamboyantly camp comedians you heard on the radio. It was an era which impertheptibly faded into that brief period when you were –) Out? I was never out, Squilly – you know that! (Maybe not as currently understood – but you forget: I was with you on theventies Saturday mornings when you raced to Mister Martin's shop to pick up our copy of what was then the largest circulation newspaper for homosexuals.) Oh, okay – if you insist on dragging it all up, yes, I do remember. (And presumably remember, as well, that old Mister Martin was such an innocent he thought it was some sort of gazette of good times . . .) Yes-yes – he'd peer at me through filthy lenses and say, You really like to keep abreast of things, don't you, young man? (A marvellously inappropriate turn of phrase, given the only breasts you'd seen at this time were Mister —) Don't go there, Squilly – I beg of you: it's too early in the day. I need a stiffener before I can peer into that dark chamber . . . Although in point of fact, having slid down Heath Street on his Italian loafers, the Butcher is peering into the dark chamber of the tube station, where he can see a little Sally-esque girl with a tangle of blonde curls, who's clutching a helium-filled balloon in one hand – a balloon which bears on its silvery surface Ronald McDonald's disturbing features. The Butcher tries smiling – but it isn't the little girl who responds, but *the balloon!* which is ventriloquised by . . . *Squilly!* (It was an innocently ignorant era, Butch – and you were only fifteen, so you can't be too hard on yourself. Don't you remember – because I do. We'd troll along to all sorts of cranky gatherings – in community halls or rooms at the back of pubs. Meetings called to pwotest the murder of Blair Peach, and the brutal tactics of the EssPeeGee.) Your point being? (My point being that, in amongst all the other fringe nutters who'd laid out flyers and leaflets on the trestle tables, there'd often be a couple of well-spoken and neatly dwessed men from the Paedophile Information Exchange . . .) Oh, Ronald, the Butcher mutters as the lift doors open, and he follows Squilly bob-bob-bobbing along the curving tunnel . . . must you? (. . . who'd hand out leaflets of their own, which, perfectly politically correctly, in the lefty lingo of the day, set out their arguments for the right of all parties concerned to pwactise what I believe they called . . . man–boy love.) The Butcher stands at the very edge of the platform, watching a mouse undertake its daily commute . . . *from condenser to crumpled crisp packet.* Ronald McDonald has been replaced by a beautiful young masked man, naked to the waist, who silently and handlessly beckons to him, mouthing, *No introduction necessary* . . . The

English psycho stands, feeling the great weight of the past on his shoulders – soon he and his lover will be together, but he's not sure *I can bear it much longer* — There's a grunt, a swoosh, a crack and a thwack! as Kins unwinds and drives the ball right at the screen. Then a brief yet disconcerting hiatus, before the ball-playing-the-ball appears, hippety-hopping along the perfect fairway, towards the perfect pin. Y'know, your grandfather wouldn't so much as talk to me or your Uncle Mike until we could handle a golf club properly, is the sort of thing Kins probably said – given he said similar things thousands of times throughout the De'Ath boys' childhoods: a maxim, intended to what? Convince them of the contrasting warmth of his own *hands-on parenting?* There were homiletic tales as well: any request from the Baker or the Candlestick-maker for this or that item of crafty kit would be answered by Kins recounting *for the umpteenth time* how he and Uncle Mike had amused themselves for entire long vacs with bat, ball and bails: out on Blackheath, in the everlasting interwar gloaming – one boy standing in at the crease for eleven men in succession, while the other ran towards him, arms windmilling. Or else it'd be how he and Uncle Mike would be given a shilling by Sirbert to go to the flicks – A shilling, mind, twelve whole pennies. With which the two fanatics could gorge themselves on half a day's entertainment: the Perils of Pauline, a magic turn, a refulgent organ rising up from the bowels of the Roxy *tootling* – followed by not one but two features. The boys wouldn't return to the Paragon until tea time – which they hadn't really the appetite for, having had enough change from their shilling to get stuffed with sugar buns from the Aerated Bread

Company . . . *Christ! He was full of shit.* So full, he'd had to type it all out of him, laboriously on an Imperial Good Companion. Copies of the De'Ath Watch, the homemade magazine these two thrifty boys published in their reclusion, were still extant during the Butcher's childhood, neatly deposited in a tea chest in the old nursery, along with their lead soldiers, their spinning tops and skipping ropes. During interminable Sunday lunches, while Kins and Sirbert were downstairs in the dim dining room, sitting opposite one another at the heavy mahogany table, *masticating* their way doggedly through one of Missus Haines's parched and stringy roasts, the Butcher would be upstairs, flicking through smudged old pages. The De'Ath Watch mostly consisted of his father and uncle's test match scores, and Kins's reviews of such gems as Topaze, with John Barrymore and Reginald Mason, in which the part of Coco – a loose and fradulent woman – was played by Myrna Loy, an actress for whom Kins, aged fifteen, reserved his warmest approbation: "sporty". It'd been the great weight and solidity of this life that had borne down on the teenage Butcher . . . *Oh, won't you roll away the stone!* so the Redeemer can emerge, clad in grey flannel Oxford bags, a thick hand-knitted pullover, a thicker hand-knitted tie, a dense and hairy tweed jacket, and shod in brogues carved from a single, solid block of toughened cow-skin. For hour upon hour, father and son mortified themselves with the stodge dished up by Sirbert's cook, their basal behinds and solid flanks cleaving to the worn leather seats of their hefty chairs . . . *I masticate every mouthful forty times before swallowing*, the Butcher's grandfather was wont to say. The Butcher couldn't've said he knew him well – but, unlike his brothers, he wasn't in the least intimidated by the old mandarin, with his ivory dome, upon which – in his later years – there'd often be poised several different pairs of spectacles. C'mere, little Johnny, the old man would say, beckoning him towards the velvet-lined teak box which lay open on his tartan-swaddled knees. The Butcher goggled at the rows of gleaming lenses, each upright in its padded groove. Sirbert would take one out, clip it in a frame and have the boy peer through while he explained about dioptres and astigmatisms. Sirbert also had a stereoscope – not a modern toy one, in the plastic confines of which you could see Tracy Island, or imagine you were on a trip to Marineville, but a serious bit of old Edwardian kit made of wood and brass: C'mon, put your physog' here . . . Now, shut your right eye, and, if I adjust these knobs, what can you see? The Butcher saw a Beatrix Potter rabbit sporting a green muffler – but when he looked with his left eye, the rabbit had mysteriously hippety-hoppeted inside a wire cage. Y'see, boy, Sirbert explained, his tone, as ever, even, his accent, as ever, colourless: our shared affliction means we lack the attributes of binocular vision – most notably stereopsis, whereby the angle of inclination between the two eyes allows for accurate depth-perception. You might say, little Johnny, that you and I live in a flat and two-dimensional world . . . Yes, a flat world in which information acquired by one eye was then vetted by the other. Sirbert liked showing off his lightning-quick calculating skills for his grandson by factoring the United Kingdom population by the latest farming statistics in order to supply individual dietary data . . . *in seconds*. The old savant saw the makings of a superior mnemonist *in little Johnny*, noting the boy's ability to achieve a *comprehensive visual take* at a glance. Sirbert had hypothesised: *It may well be our ocular peculiarities that make us capable of such retentive feats . . .* He believed he'd found a way to compensate for the affliction by wearing six pairs of differently lensed spectacles at once, so when Maeve told him little Johnny was going to have an operation at Great Ormond Street to correct his lazy eye, her father-in-law had a rare *apoplexy*: *For God's sake, woman! This boy of yours is a prodigy – do you want to take it away from him? Of course she did.* On awaking from the anaesthetic, the world had been a blur, out of which swam this disturbing vision: Sirbert, lying massive and naked, his turtle head propped up against the mahogany headboard of his high, hard bed, while with both hands he *masticated forty times . . .* The Butcher's prodigious memory was unaffected by the operation – but this was something he kept to himself, along with the rest of the skills he was acquiring at around this time . . . *in Doctor No's reactor room.* The tube rolls downhill towards Belsize Park – the carriage is full of American tourists, who look – judging by their short pants and transparent-orange sun visors – to've been for a walk on the Heath. The Butcher, slumped on worn moquette, looks past the careworn face of the woman opposite, to where his own curves across the window: a fleshy blodge that, as he squints, elongates, darkening, until it approximates to Kins's *scraggy saggy unshaven red face.* His father had been, the Butcher now understands, utterly intimidated by the old man – and his compulsive, hand-me-down anecdotage was the evidence of this, as was his hard work maintaining the cult of Sirbert's personality. Driving the Rover back up Green Lanes past the grotty shopping parades of Wood Green, Kins would substitute a younger, slimmer and more dashing Sirbert for the frigid patriarch they'd left behind in Blackheath. Young Sirbert had been a Fulham cockney on the make, his big hands firmly wrapped round the greasy pole of . . . *his exploder*. D'you remember, Kins would say, the story about Sirbert royally besting two higher-ups at his Ministry on the links? Ye-es, Dad, we know! The Butcher, the Baker and the Candlestick-maker would chorus from the back seat – although they also knew it was impossible to switch off this Home Service, with its multiple repeats: He didn't have a full set of his own clubs, only –. A mashie niblick and an exploder! the boys chorused, while, not in the least put off, their father would go on *anon* . . . Above the tourist's head are the laughing eyes of a Sally-alike being *sensitively dealt with* by the British Pregnancy Advisory Service. A voice from the crypt intones: This is a southbound train via Charing Cross terminating at Kennington . . . then continues . . . Sirbert strode to the first tee, armed only with his two humble clubs – the bigwigs waddled along behind, and behind them came their caddies, bent double under the weight of opulent bags. As Kins would have it, Sirbert had taken fifteen strokes off the complacent permanent secretaries – just as he'd taken thirty off the Welsh Wizard and his entire war cabinet, before going on to win the war by advancing single-handedly into the Huns' lines, hurling his mashie niblick and his exploder before him . . . *please do not leave packages unattended*. The Butcher and his brothers had heard many variations of this tale, but he knew he was the only one who grasped its theme. Kins had never made any secret of the fact he'd been a conscientious objector – how could he, when there was always *someMaeveone* there to remind him? Hers was a leftover revenge – a congealed and fatty beef she had with him: Your father in the war? Let him off scot-free, didn't they – I expect your grand-father pulled some strings . . . Anyway, your father heard about this commune-thingy in Lincolnshire, so he went up there to till the land. Maeve De'Ath, *a cheerful soul*, would beam with disloyalty as she undermined her husband: Turned out Kins wasn't quite as good with a hoe as he was with a golf club, so after a few weeks he just leant it against a barn and buggered off back to London. While all his pals – his brother, too – were saving the world from Hitler, your father mooched about the West End poncing drinks and living off an allowance . . . She'd say these terrible things not in his absence but while Kins was mooching about the house – or actually in the kitchen, standing beside the fulminating Potterton, a teaspoon in hand, an uneasy smile seaming his *sad scraggy saggy unshaven red face*. And on the day they visited the driving range in Sunbury, that seam had grown wider . . . deeper, becoming a canyon into which . . . *I fell*. They'd begun sniping as Kins parked the Rover, got out his golf bag, and the two of them entered the low cinder-block structure, with its pancake-coloured and pancake-thin carpeting. (What on earth possessed you?) I couldn't go on, Squilly – I couldn't go on . . . The Butcher had already tried to broach the issue with his mother by alluding to Freddie Mercury . . . *or Frederick the Great*. But that morning he'd finally been explicit. Sat at the kitchen table, his weekly reading material propped against the willow-patterned milk jug, he'd told his own *drab little tale*: I've been going back to

Mister Deane's house after revision tutorials, Mum. He gives me almond slices and tawny port and then he . . . he does things to me. Maeve, who'd been washing up, said nothing – but the Butcher saw her fat back stiffen. It'd been sheer folly – yet he'd pressed on, after all (An ickle boy always wants hith mummy to understand): He says he wants to do other things to me, but I don't want to, Mum . . . I mean, I know you know I'm gay, Mum, but you never say anything about it . . . is it that you . . . don't . . . mind? The thermostat clicked, the Potterton puttered to a halt, the temperature dropped by five degrees – all Saint Albans had been . . . *eclipsed*. Maeve De'Ath had turned from the sink, her hands dripping with *bloody suds*: Have you finished? she'd said – followed by words to this effect: So long as you never speak of this matter again, nor shall I. So long as you make a pretence of being normal, I shan't enquire into how far you've deviated. But if you persist with this sickening effeminacy, or ever speak to me directly of such perversions again, you'll be dead to me – you hear me: dead. The Butcher had sat there at the kitchen table, his head seemingly thrust into Sirbert's stereoscope, where a pink-nosed bunny hopped inside a cage *forever*. That afternoon Kins had locked it. To his father, who'd been preoccupied by balancing his Penfold Number One on the little plastic pyramid there was in lieu of a tee, the Butcher had tried being more circumspect: You must've noticed, Dad, that I get Gay News every Saturday . . . Kins had winched his big torso back upright, waggled his driver, looked towards the faraway nearby of the screen, upon which a sylvan scene had been projected: an avenue of lush trees with a strip of emerald fairway running between them all the way to the flag flickering on the two-tone green. The Butcher wondered then – *and wonders now*, as the tube doors open at Camden Town – how exactly the equipment had worked. The blasé attendant had explained it in general terms: when the ball hit the screen, sensors recorded velocity and trajectory, then transferred this information to its filmic representation – the white *scut* which went *bob–bob–bobbing along* . . . There'd been a grunt, a swish, a crack! and, as Kins's championship ball metamorphosed into an image-of-itself, the Butcher had experienced all-consuming vertigo: the pancake-thin carpet split asunder, while between his scruffy trainers the great yawning abyss of Kins's non-acceptance opened up. Au fond, the Butcher has always cordially detested his mother (We'd never have guessed) – but Kins? At sweet sixteen the Butcher still clung to this sickly illusion: his wayward father would understand *my own waywardness* . . . Yet Kins had said nothing, only gone on whacking balls into the *green closet* while his son looked on. Later the two of them occupied a trestle table outside a riverside pub. Kins – who'd been liberal in this regard at least – bought them both pints, and had doubtless wiped the froth from his wet-red lips with the back of his hand . . . *'cause he always did*, before finally speaking: Have you read Orwell's essay Such, Such Were the Joys? Or Graves's Goodbye to All That for that matter? Thing is . . . I was at prep and public school during the same era, but I never witnessed any such . . . behaviours. The boys I was at Lancing with were a fairly normal lot – mostly civil servants' and clergymen's sons. Some were really rather pious – not least me. D'you know, Johnny, I think on the whole it's very much exaggerated – the sex relation.

It's the temper of the times – Messalina would be right at home. Nowadays, everyone wants to make a big deal out of their sex relation – brute it about. But you've only to consider Cousin Minnie – or Cousin Elfreda for that matter. You can't tell me old spinsters like these were driven by some sort of repressed sex-drive. I don't believe either of them's ever given the matter any thought at all . . . No, no thought: the Butcher's head separates into two whitish blodges, connected by a smear of sentience: *Squilly and me.* He looks to the right and sees the next carriage, rotating clockwise on its coupling. He looks to the left and sees the carriage behind, rotating anti-clockwise on its coupling, as, boring beneath London, the train describes . . . *this eternal figure-of-eight.* A quarter-century ago, at the futuristic golf range on the outskirts of Staines, beneath the screaming flight path: the clocks all stopped, the phone line was cut, and the mutt choked to death in the corner . . . *on a juicy bone.* As he'd followed his father back across the car park, the Butcher looked up to the sky and saw inscribed there by the disintegrating contrails of jets lifting off from Heathrow *love is dead.* The three of them had never spoken of any of this again – not even years later, when accident rather than design brought them together on a Sunday afternoon, *a fine cast of British character actors,* to watch a similar ensemble at the Rex in Berkhamsted. Ra-ra skirts and horsy accents cantering through a succession of country-house hotels, breaking and bonding. Then at the funereal end, a Scots actor with thick eyebrows had intoned, *My noon, my midnight, my talk, my song* . . . and at this moment the Butcher supposes Kins must have glanced along the row and seen his son's cheeks, wet with sentiment. When they were standing back in the sunlight, beneath the cinema's decaying Nouveau façade, Peter De'Ath had turned to his wife and said, quite loudly, I've no idea why anyone would cry over that sentimental tosh . . . Whereupon his eldest son, who'd visited James Pringle House for another aitcheyevee test only the previous week (There's a little bit of the sociopath in all really effective intelligence officers, isn't there, Butchie . . .), bit down on his own *meaty treat*: Why compound his stupid, bigoted father's woes? Why add to the drip-drip-drip of Maeve De'Ath's contempt and derision – an acid rain ever falling on that sad scraggy saggy unshaven red face? Now the Butcher sees them once more in the hall at Colindale Avenue, this time their roles reversed: it's Kins who stands – and the Butcher who kneels, suppliant. While from the ceiling, the architrave, the tiny Artex *pricks* stippling the walls, the drops drip and flow and course . . . *For the rain it raineth every day, When that I was and a little tiny boy* . . . And now Kins had been laid to rest for all eternity in his own narrow closet, courtesy of J J Burgess and Sons, independent funeral directors since eighteen thirty-nine – see them, carrion in cutaways, hauling corpses through the mud at Balaclava, Mafeking, Amritsar . . . *Crossmaglen*. At Leicester Square, the Butcher . . . *comes to man's estate.* (We're reborn! Squilly cries. Rising from the waves! Neptune's Naiads blow a fanfare on their conches!), but the Butcher's in no mood for such locker-room banter: Shut it, Squills . . . (Oh, I see), but the malevolent sprite keeps on as the Butcher heads down the Charing Cross Road (It's like that, is it – you're keen enough on me when you're lonely), weaving between the Sunday-afternoon strollers

(D'you remember our first few weeks in London?). Of course the Butcher does – but he'd rather not dwell on the long nights he'd spent nursing a pint of lager in the far corner of the Pull-and-Dump, watching some Pritt Stick-and-tinsel performer shake his posing pouch in the punters' bored faces. Sitting and watching and longing and fantasising about what he might get up to with lither, more limber and younger men, if only he had the *balls* (You were a sweet boy, really, what with your crushes on Björn Borg and Ilie Năstase – mixed threesomes rolling round on Court Number One). He'd sit out the evening, 'til some sozzled tax inspector or crapulent compliance officer took him back on a night bus, to Pinner, or Poplar . . . *or Palmers Green*, where in his bedsitting room they'd bicker over who should be allowed to put what, where and for how long. When the letter finally came, and the young Butcher arrived at Carlton House Terrace for his initial interview, he practised his voyeurism on the reproduction of The Blue Boy hanging in the corner of the room, until the captious personnel officer returned and asked him needling questions about the OhEssAy, which lay on the glass-topped table in its plastic-laminated folder: Had Mister De'Ath thoroughly read its contents? Did he understand the gravity of a treasonable offence, and the severity of the penalties mandated? The Butcher had displayed *FORTITUDE* then – thinks it now, because he's standing outside the National Portrait Gallery, look-ing at Edith Cavell's Carrara figure, crucified on . . . *a mound of shit*. Fortitude, the Butcher thinks, is what you must have if your career path necessitates running around *annaround* the ragged rock: *FORTITUDE* and the devotion needed if you're to *SACRIFICE* yourself for *HUMANITY*, at dawn in some muddy and foreign field. The hint of stringy-vesting under the personnel officer's white, mixed-nylon-and-cotton shirt had set the Butcher's incisors . . . *on edge*. Half an hour had been twenty-eight minutes more than he'd required to memorise the thirty pages of the Act – nevertheless, Bryce felt it incumbent on him to summarise: EmmEyeSix, as you probably know already, is the YouKay's overseas intelligence-gathering organisation, administered by the EffSeeOh . . . This little briefing – and all subsequent ones – had a nudge-nudge, wink-wink air about them: the smutty talk of naughty boys (Your wife, does she go?). Or were they all aspiring pederasts, these secret operatives: *Do you think you might like to do something a little more interesting . . . ?* To which there'd only ever been one possible answer, the Butcher having long since known that gathering intelligence from secret human sources . . . *was what I was put on this earth to do*. He glances up at the admiral on his recently cleaned *big stone cock*, and angles his own bowsprit towards Admiralty Arch: Yes, gathering intelligence – because there're so many sad scraggy saggy unshaven red-faced *sheeple* in this green and pleasant land – sheeple with *no intelligence of their own to baa of*. Sheeple who, above all, need wise – if unacknowledged – rulers to watch over them, so they may . . . *safely graze*. True, shepherding can be a brutal business – sheeple scream when they're hauled, kicking, to be dipped in the chemical waters . . . *of Lethe*. But it's better for everyone if they forget – better still if they *never knew to begin with* . . . How many times have they met up like this to make love and play house in the seven years since Manchester – scores, certainly. (Getting on for a hundred, I'd say . . .) Sometimes the Butcher heads north, books a hotel or motel room – sweeps it, checks for watchers, and their arvee is as professional as possible: arrivals and departures meticulously synchronised. Mostly, however, things are a great deal more amateurish: *Never shit where you eat* is a maxim the Butcher often retails to his assets – the greedy little men and women who con-stitute his *stock-in-trade*. They seldom listen, though – they'll spill their guts, then take their loose-lipped mistress to an ambassadorial reception. Or they'll receive details of a numbered account in their name and, instead of keeping well away, head straight for Berne or Basle and go on a colossal bender. As for the Butcher . . . well, the rule doesn't apply. Or, rather, since shit is what he in fact does eat there's no way of avoiding the stuff. The poor, prosaic sheeple believe the Firm operates in a physically ulterior realm – secret tunnels and underground command centres, where second-string British character actors demonstrate the latest gadgets. Such places do exist, but, like so much of state's unconscious – a chthonic inner-space where they do indeed plot sex and death – they're for the most part . . . *mothballed*. Besides, an abandoned Cold War bunker is no place to entertain a hard-working soldier. The Firm keeps a number of properties scattered around Westminster and Pimlico, ranging from entire terraced houses – tricked out in what the Alice Band in General Services believe at any given time to be the dernier cri – to cramped council flats on the estates along Lupus Street, and fusty bedsitting rooms up five flights in Victoria. Such is the nature of the Butcher's work – the fixer, the creeper, the sweeper, the cleaner, the *poop-a-fucking-scooper* – he has unfettered access to these hidey-holes. Everyone understands he may need somewhere to park a second secretary or a member of a trade delegation for a few days while he *checks their bona fides*. The lovers have developed their own rituals over the years: the Butcher always arrives first, bringing a few creature comforts with him – perhaps a length of Indian material to throw over a worn pleather couch, if their accommodation is particularly spartan. (Or a thented candle – you haven't forgotten the thented candle, have you?) Definitely a box of Highland shortbread – which Gawain, endearingly, likes to dunk in his tea. The important thing, the Butcher feels, is to create a temporary oasis for them both – a place of succour, with sweet water and sweeter dates, which lies outside of time. (Stop all the clocks, eh . . .) – The Butcher stands in Horseguards, by the Guards' Memorial, where he looks up at the handsome stone faces intended to represent . . . *trauma and degeneration*. Those first few years in London, the leather queens creaking in and out of the Eagle Bar – the denim ones thronging the Coleherne: all seemed larger-than-life-sized to the young Butcher, their faces stony, their poses rigid. (And of course, there was the virus to consider.) Their brutal argot, with its arse-play and bottoming, was repellent to the sensitive lad (You're not forgetting the impact of aitcheyevee . . .), but gradually he got to grips with it. (Hanging on to the cistern while some rhinestone cowboy gave you a booty-bump – what about aids, you fucking moron?) What about it, you evil little prick? The Butcher has spoken aloud, and the Japanese tourist aiming his lens at the Memorial looks curiously at this expensively dressed and foul-mouthed man. Unfazed, the Butcher addresses the man directly: Don't die of ignorance would've been a good inscription for this tomb . . . Then he strolls on, past the pelicans on their ragged rocks. (Doing a little cottaging of their own, aren't they, Butchie?) I was always careful, though, Squills, wasn't I? (Oh, you were indeed, Butch – you brought a rather, um . . . straight sensibility to the business of being queer.) Yeah – there was only the one booty-bump, after all. (Because then there was a long night of whisky drinking and listening to Mozart's bloody Requiem before you went to James Pringle House to do the test. After that you memorised the leaflets and bought Mates bloody wholesale!) Three – three condoms I'd wear. You've no cause for complaint, Squilly. (No, indeed, Butch – besides, life without a little risk is a dish unthalted.) Strolling on towards Petty France, the Butcher ponders the perennial thrill to be gained from a man in uniform, and recalls hearing that first, slyly interrogative cough from the stall beside him, in the public toi– lavatories opposite Saint James's Palace, on the morning after his second interview. Sitting in the waiting room, flipping through the same back number of the Economist he'd flicked through on his first visit, the Butcher idly memorised the dope on Black, the Ra supergrass, and committed to memory the names of all the medallists at the Helsinki games. The colourless character who'd conducted Butcher's first interview had asked him to describe someone he knew. A "colourful character" was how he'd put it, and the jejune Butcher had toyed with describing him to himself – albeit with embellishments. The colourless man may've introduced himself as Bryce – but he quickly admitted this was a cover name for whichever officer was fulfilling the role.

Then, as he was actually painting Mister Deane's portrait for the man – the taut pot belly and prominent yellow teeth, the drip-dry hair and canvas complexion – the Butcher experienced an odd sensation . . . *I relaxed!* Relaxed for the first time since the Sunbury Incident. Relaxed because at last . . . *I'd come home.* Home to somewhere where it was completely acceptable to be . . . *an imposter.* Home to his grandfather's house, with its many papery mansions – Whitehall, that wasps' nest, knocked down from the ancient rafters by Black Rod. Whitehall, with its hexagonal corridors along which rustle the bug-eyed servants of the state, their antennae waving diffidently as they utter qualifications – pozzibly, prozzpectively – but never say anything definitive. At least not to their political masters: the larvae, who are all white, all male and who lie on their red rugs, in front of their coal-effect fires, feeding on the contents of the red despatch boxes open beside them, growing sleeker and fatter with all the nutritious secrecy. And there, at the Butcher's second interview, had been the buggiest of the state's servants: five of them, ranged behind a long brilliantly polished table surmounted by a savage floral arrangement – snapdragons biting the heads off pansies. Looking from one face to the next, noting donnish bifocals and foppish bow ties, for a moment the Butcher had imagined he was back at his viva in the Examination Schools, about to be asked nothing more important than the nature of Montesquieu's influence on the development of French liberalism. But then it began: What did he know about Chad? Did he have any idea what AitchEmmGee should do? Could do? And what about Ağca – did Mister De'Ath have any . . . thoughts? Did he lend any credence

274

to the assassin's KayGeeBee credo? And Jaruzelski's threat to crack down on anti-socialist activities? A bluff, or not? The Butcher, licking his chops, had chewed it all over, then began speaking slowly but fluently, his answers appearing before him as text does on an autocue: superimposed over the expectant faces of the panel, hovering sub rosa – then disappearing, up into the extravagant mouldings. His waspish interviewers had been impressed – yet still they flew at him, their barbed remarks now stinging at his . . . *convictions*. Patriotism! The Butcher stands on a bridge over stagnant and shitty waters, looking towards the Palace. Spooning in Room Thirty-Seven of the Knatchbull Services Travelodge, his hand gently buffing Gawain's erect nipple, the Butcher had listened while his cavalryman told him that when the loyal toast was proposed in the mess, some of his more moronic comrades (More? Is such a comparator really applicable here?) would – should the steward not've removed them in time – pass their port glasses over their water ones. Of course, Gawain had hastened to add, they aren't really pledging allegiance to the Stuart Pretender! (Who's probably a Belgian dentist with a mail order certificate in his filing cabinet.) The Butcher had a certain sympathy for the toasting Rams, for his own loyalty also was proved by his impulse to betray – moreover, following Messrs Childers-through-Le-Carré, surely a conviction that remained forever unchallenged can scarcely be worth the name? So he'd admitted everything to the wasps (Because you knew they'd find out anyway): his youthful flirtations with unilateralism, anti-racism and of course . . . socialism. I was a fervent believer – he'd shaken his pensive head – in the perfectability of Man. (Any man you could lay your hot little hands on!) Why? Well, the wasps would find that out soon enough, too – when their vetting officer went to interview Doctor Peter De'Ath, Senior Lecturer in Politics at the University of Hertfordshire. After the spooks were done with him, the Butcher reeled into the bright noontide, and stood at the top of King George's steps, looking out over the greenery of Saint James's Park towards New Scotland Yard: I've arrived! he'd trumpeted to the traffic rumbling up the Mall – an arrival further celebrated by the loosening of his bowels. In the cubicle he'd spotted a glory hole neatly concealed behind the toilet roll. Unlimbering the holder and removing a wad of toilet paper, he'd placed his eye to the *gunsight*, and been rewarded with this vision: an upstanding member – red-headed, its shaft licked by gingerish and hairy . . . *flames*. Of course, the Butcher had already fantasised for over a decade about what it would be like to get inside a Household Cavalry guardsman's snowy-white pantaloons. (Ever since, in point of fact, you lay with me beneath you, thtiff as the proverbial, and watched the Trooping of the Colour on television.) And now there they were: their front flaps unbuttoned, their soft seams framing the . . . *conflagration*. The soldier's silver cuirass was propped up in the corner of the stall, and, as the Butcher had substituted his eager mouth for his hungry eye, he retained its fish-eyed after-image: white columnar thighs – tensed white buttocks. And as the juicy bone had *muffled my drum* . . . the Butcher heard once more the fugal wheezing of the oldest and most academical of the panel members – a smallish man in a corduroy suit, who throughout the interview held one lit cigarette after another in front of his burnt-out face, but never took a drag: You've given a pretty thorough account of yourself, Mister De'Ath, and I think I can speak for my colleagues – and the Service more widely – when I say we're perfectly understanding when it comes to youthful ideological indiscretions. Nor are we inclined to paint a candidate up with his father's pinkness. However, one sort of carry-on we've absolutely no tolerance for whatsoever is . . . the old spook's eyes watered *a false lustre* . . . drug-taking. So, if you've so much as taken a pull on a reefer – let alone anything harder – we need to know right away. The Butcher had nearly laughed out loud with relief – given the bigoted temper of the times, he'd been expecting homosexuality to fall from those prissy old lips. Lips that surely (Surely!) longed to kiss the roast beef of old England? Meat, meat and more meat – could it be a surprise to anyone that someone called the Butcher is an enthusiastic carnivore? So enthusiastic that when he bends to the meal in hand, rather than tear at it toothily, chew it up and gulp it down, he'll hold the hot gobbet in his mouth, tongue seeking the stippling of papillae between glans and corpus spongiosum. This, he'll think as he licks and sucks, is true patriotism – I'm eating the nation's manhood, and, just as cannibals imagine they can ingest their vanquished enemies' bravery, so I believe these pricks will inoculate me against any moral contagion, for mine is a higher purpose! But at that premature feast the loyal toast could not be made – after ten or fifteen of the guardsman's vigorous thrusts, the meat-counter trainee had been spluttering . . . *choking*. He substituted willing hand for wanting mouth – but the guardsman wasn't having it, abruptly withdrew, then represented the dish in the serving hatch. Ever a quick study, the Butcher understood this gesture well enough – but before he'd time to comply there was door-rattling and breathy childish tones . . . *Daddy, I gotta go.* The guardsman had again pulled out abruptly, clinking and clanking followed as he buckled up, then the bolt was withdrawn, to be succeeded by the chink-ch'-chink of retreating spurs. The Butcher thought he'd earned them. (You think love will last forever – but you're wrong.) I'm not, the Butcher says aloud, as he strides across the blank intersection between Carteret Street and Broadway. (But he's far away so much of the time.) What of it? We'll be together eventually – it may take years. (And during those years you may well be disgraced – someone could get hold of your large data-set, the audio-visual take, the emails . . . the background material. You have it all, don't you?) I have it all, Squilly – every fucking cardboard coaster his lager's dripped on to, every hurried mobile phone call he's made to me from a lay-by. And yes: I've recorded his gentle snoring as he softly sleeps as well. (You're a blithering idiot, Butch – where is it? Where is all this SeeEx?) You know where it is, Squilly – you were with me when I cached it to begin with, you've been with me when I've moved it to safer locations. (Yes . . . yes I've been with you, Butch – with you all the time. Frankly, you'd be better advised to focus your affections on me, your constant companion, than the headless horseman.) Headless? (Oh, c'mon, Butch – can't you even admit it in the privacy of your own head! He's thick, your love object – as thick and as docile as a –) The Butcher, resplendent in dinner jacket and snow-white shirtfront, is a frequent guest speaker at the dinner which marks the completion of the new EyeBees' course. Standing, mellowed by candlelight, at the head of the long table, in the lime-washed former magazine of the Fort which now serves as a dining room, he would recount tales of operations he'd either initiated or conducted – and in many cases done both. His grasp of the details was fiendish – and his pacing and sense of drama highly evolved. The Butcher's rhetorical skills were just as prized as anything he did operationally, while he knew that, despite weeks of being introduced to the utterly routine nature of their future employ, the new entrants' heads would still be full of derring-do and techno-wizardry. (Now, pay attention, Butch . . .) Quite so. But then was not the time to disabuse them. (You wouldn't want to kill the magic light – leave the chamber empty of –) Delighted to've made your acquaintance, he'd say, shaking hands all round, subtly shooting his cuffs. He never stayed the night at the Fort – he wanted to give them the elegant midnight fantasy, not the puffy-eyed morning reality. Powering up the EmmThree in his two-eighty EssEe cabriolet, the misty sprites rising up from the roadway consumed *againannagain* by its sharkish radiator grille, the Butcher would imagine the new officers gossiping about him as they filled in their chits, posted them in the honesty box, then glugged more and tawnier port: He was one of the team that handled Gordievsky, wasn't he? And mixed up in that Gaddafi business – 'though I don't think he likes talking about that one . . . I heard he was also involved in Stakeknife . . . Don't be ridiculous – that's Thames House's beat – them and the EffArrYou. The Province is outside our remit – anyway, I expect he only uses one of those when it's spelt properly – he is the Butcher after all . . . Oh, yes –

he was, is and always will be "the Butcher" to generation upon generation of the huddled, clerkish figures, bent against the wind and grit, who flock over Vauxhall Bridge each morning . . . *ready to undo so many deaths* – or come trotting from under the bricky mess of the viaduct, wearing their chain-store suits and ready for another long day of getting their political masters . . . *off the hook.* No one at the Firm can remember who dubbed him, but no one has ever doubted the nickname's appositeness . . . *least of all me.* Yes . . . he thinks now, looking up at the premises the Firm once occupied above the tube station . . . there are only coincidences – whether sentient individuals or programmed projectiles, their apparent arrival at the same place, at the same time, depends on where you're standing – and what angle you're looking from. And if neither people nor objects coincide? (It'd be impossible to move the action on at all . . .) Contrary to what the trainees might think, the Butcher had been in Belfast in June of ninety-four. He can recall the round-cornered windows at the Europa Hotel – many bearing the test-card patterns of blast tape. Sitting at a wooden pew in a stained-glass stall in the pub opposite, he'd drunk late with Prod plods of various sorts – the atmosphere had been rancorous, and the Butcher, sensing the deep and vicious streak of homophobia running through his hosts, held his (Delicious, mobile, artistic . . .) tongue. In the morning it'd been fitted to his mouth – complete with an underlay of nausea. Why'd he been there at all? Liaison was the bullshit term used for a lot of the snooping around he'd done on Colin's behalf at the time – yes, chiefs might come, and chiefs would most certainly go, but the Firm couldn't do without its high-class, family . . .

Butcher. He'd gone out to Aldergrove with them, then, at the very last second – when the Chinook's rotors were already whipping the drizzle – he'd ducked beneath them, shouting to his colleagues, I've left something at Facilities – I'll get the Stranraer ferry and catch up with you this evening . . . *Oh mist rolling in from the sea, my desire.* The slipstream from this very near miss remained whistling eerily about him for months – and the Butcher can still feel it now . . . *past painted deserts the sunset's on fire.* If he'd've asked his father about it, what might Kins have said? That his son owed his deliverance to his Saviour? The Butcher looks up at the carved stone figure which sits, legs parted, on the cornicing halfway up the office block's façade. This petrified Saviour, perhaps – who has a naked slip-of-a-boy twisted into his arms. The Butcher regards the Epstein sculpture – he's passed it thousands of times but never stopped to stare. (It's not Jesus, Butch.) No, Squilly, I see that. (The broad, saggy, scraggy, sand-stony face . . .) It's Kins – I get that. (Kins – and you, Butchie – you, hugging his neck even as you thrust me out into the world. You're going to betray me, Butch – *you're going to betray me.*) He turns away from the building, thinking of all the buccaneering types who used to hang out here . . . *the camel-drivers*, who'd believed their own Lawrentian experiences fomenting tribal unrest, were the only qualification anyone needed to be *of thecret thervice* . . . *Whatever's happened to Squilly's lisp? I'd swear he used to lisp more* (Lithp). The ickle bunny hops into the cage – its filmic white scut disappears down the long green fairway . . . *hippety-hoppety. I'm late . . . I'm late . . .* Checking his Longines again, the Butcher's isoceles nose is congruent with the rotating triangular sign reading

NEW SCOTLAND YARD. He considers the child's view of West-minster maintained by the generality of sheeple – the papery clichés of . . . *Our Island Story*. Just after New Year, Sally squeaking on his arm, the Butcher had taken a turn on the Millennium Wheel. Mounting one of the softly rocking pods, they'd been slowly winched skywards. It'd been a bright winter afternoon – and this, together with their odd parabolic ascent, gave him the powerful illusion it wasn't they who were moving, but rather London's prin-cipal buildings, which were popping up from their bricky bindings into full and cardboard relief: the candy-striped campanile of Westminster Cathedral unfolded – Millbank Tower sprang forth. Staring out over the Thames's deceptive bend, the Butcher had seen an off-yellow amphibious vehicle chugging through the choppy waters . . . *vomit returning to its dog*. He knew where it was headed: the little notch of beach beside VeeBeeArr, where, under the blind eyes of the statues ranged along the south side of Vauxhall Bridge – personifications of Science, Fine Arts and . . . (A testimony to your pater, I'd say) . . . Local Government – the Frog Tours amphibian would describe its own odd parabola before croaking up the muddy foreshore and on to the concrete ramp. Many are the times the Butcher has sat in his office on Level Five, Blue Zone of . . . *the Aztec Empire* and watched through the obsidian mirror of his lead-glass window as the doughty little craft . . . *does its bit*: moving cheerfully from one element to the other – and on each and every occasion he'd resisted the analogy: I'm not a dual-purpose piece of kit, up-armoured for military as well as civilian use. Yet, left behind on the river's surly surface, were always these: the twin circles described by successive Frog Tours amphibians, slowly inter-linking to form a foamy ... *lemniscate. We. Will. Be Together. For. An. Eternity.* – The Butcher is walking along the cobbled defile of Strutton Ground, past shuttered sandwich shops and heel bars, aiming for the old cast-iron-and-clapboard pissoir on Horseferry Road, where he unzips and unconstricts, *aaaah ... !* I've never had a friend, he moans at the splashback. A gay best friend with whom I could discuss my ... relationship. (You've got me, Butch – I'm right to hand.) Someone who could give me advice, and a shoulder ... to cry on. (There's me: now shake me dry, old chap.) Passing by the Regency Café, the Butcher rubs his sore tongue ... *too many fags last night gottagivvitup* over his ground-down teeth: not long now – not long before it will be describing its own *eternity rings*: beginning at the clitoral glans, swirling around that noble head, licking down the veined shaft, then circling back again *annagain*, until Lieutenant-Colonel Gawain Thomas, TwoEyeSee of the York-shire Hussars, clenches his insides, forcing the very real fingers his ghostly lover has thrust deep into his rectum to close ... *agonisingly ... ecstatically* ... on his prostate. Not long now – and not far either: hurrying along Page Street, the Butcher pictures his sharp, black profile static against the flats' chequerboard façades, and agonises he'll be ... *stuck here forever – stale-mated on this spot-spot-spot*. And when had these pesky ellipses become so ubiquitous? They bedizen the windows of VeeBeeArr, and, turning into Marsham Street, he sees them spattered across the windows of Shepherd's Wine Bar ... *parenthesising the plate glass*. It doesn't matter how vigorously he strides, he'll be caught ... forever ... in this ... hiatus ... *squitting on my square – it's 'Stan all over again —* the tumbled-down mountains of tinkling scree in ancient shades of dun and ochre, the pair of raptors wheeling high overhead in the crystal sky-dome above the Hindu Kush: courting falcons, oblivious to the world below, whose widening gyres almost . . . but never quite touched. At Colin's behest the Butcher had accompanied the team delivering the Blowpipe missiles. He'd been in Slammers anyway – tidying up a pile of doggie-doos done by the Second Secretary, an incontinent idiot who'd been honey-trapped by the Soviets. The Butcher shivers, remembering the long drag in: frigid nights bumping over rutted tracks, headlights off, the EssEff drives bug-eyed in night-vision goggles. The Butcher recalls trying a pair on for the first time, and entering an aqueous realm, across which the heat-signatures of warm-blooded creatures were anonymously scrawled – recalls this, as well as thinking at the time: This is what it must be like for the normals – condemned to try to understand the world on the basis of such meagre data. Their final day-stop was at a hilltop eyrie of a compound . . . *absurdly lyrical* – all around the white-capped mountains swept up . . . *strophe*, and tumbled down . . . *antistrophe*. The Mujahideen who'd been sent by Hekmatyr to meet the British convoy arrived at dawn – and came upon the Butcher squatting and squitting over the cliff-edge, his diarrhoea raining down on the scrubby bushes far below, where sheep . . . *precipitately grazed*. Of course, the Brits already knew the missiles were . . . *shit*: the Butcher had maintained his sang-froid as he wiped himself with the foliage to hand, and adjusted his nondescript salwar kameez (Sooo drab!) before joining the others, who were preparing the demonstration, trudging about on the tinkly scree. Barry from Queue-branch had brought a portable video-camera, and once the ArrEssEmm commanding the EssEff detachment had fired a parachute flare in lieu of a target . . . *he started rolling.* One of Massoud's men – who'd come from the Panjshir especially for this – fired the missile, and a second began fiddling with its handheld controller . . . *sweat-worm – snail-trail, complications of shirt-tail* . . . The Butcher looks up above the wine bar, and sees the missile incandescing between the steeply pitched roofs of *Arse and Crack* buildings – he looks across the road and spots the Mujahideen with the controller in front of the dry cleaner's on the corner of Page Street. The Butcher observes his frantic hands, then follows his desperate gaze to where, in the near distance, the Blowpipe's slim white nacelle flicks, twists, corkscrews crazily, before disappearing in the direction of Smith Square . . . *where it'll probably wipe out a few of Nick's researchers.* The Butcher pinches his nose hard: the insight he'd been given at the Baldwins' hilltop eyrie, watching little Arthur playing his computer game, was nothing new: it'd been the same on that remote hillside – Massoud's men may have been disillusioned with the Brits' kit, but they'd remained confirmed in their *user illusion*: that they were moving things about in the real world, when, as the Firm's team saw for themselves when they got back to the station in Slammers and played back the wonky veeaitchess tape, the reality was . . . *the world turns around them.* (And still does: you've seen the latest SeeEx out of Kuala Lumpur – a summit meeting of the heirs to the pious ancestors.) You know I have! the Butcher snaps, pinching his nose still harder.

(Trying to get rid of me, are you? Fat chance.) Cornering into Herrick Street, he extracts a heavy bunch of keys from his trouser pocket, and, as he enters the courtyard of the block where the Firm's safe flat is located, readies the fob to touch against the panel. The seeseeteevee camera angled towards the door has been rendered inoperable . . . *on a regular basis*. Upstairs he gives the five small rooms a thorough going-over: a bug could well've been installed but not removed – it happens, and the last thing the Butcher wants is for the sounds or sights of their lovemaking to end up, along with all the other secret affairs the Firm clandestinely records, panting and groaning in the huge bank of computers beneath VeeBeeArr. Pausing in the windowless bathroom, a damp sponge tufted with old hairs held before his fastidious face, he thinks of Gawain's neck. When he nuzzles there, bestowing tiny kisses, the Butcher smells sweat and shaving foam, mingled with some duff aftershave the silly sap imagines to be . . . *manly*. Does he still fuck Fiona, much? Put it inside dumb little wifey? (Double standards redoubled, eh, Butch?) In the early days of their affair the Butcher would torment himself – not just with images but entire little playlets. FIONA: Gawain, darling, the kids are all tucked up, and I've bought some rather exciting new nightwear – I'll be ready in the boudoir in five minutes, and you can *tear it off with your teeth!* Sitting on the drum-tight cover of the single bed, the Butcher hears blood beat in his ears – beyond this resonates the soundlessness of an inner-city Sunday afternoon. Waiting for a lover, an agent, an asset – a phone call. They're all, he thinks, fundamentally the same: situations in which you're compelled to be embodied, to consider the world through the media of sweat, hair and keratin, to feel the slack strings of your temporarily unused and fleshly . . . *marionette*. He tries to concentrate on what a psychotherapist, proffering the box of tissues, would doubtless call his "emotional reality": for seven years now he and Gawain have been secret lovers . . . *I tell him I love him – sometimes I mean it. Other times* . . . (It's just words, isn't it, Butchie?) *I feel jealous – and I know he does. He wants me to shave off the beards – says there's no call for both of us to hide in the hippety-hoppety shadows . . . But then poor old Greeny would be really jealous . . . He suspects, of course* (in his purblind, innocent way) *the mountainous peaks of cock I've scaled – the canyons of arse I've abseiled down into. But were I to make a public avowal – well, it'd be like the Firm: I'd only be doing it because the war was over . . . and the next one's not yet begun* . . . Staring out at the plane streets frothing along John Islip Street, the Butcher tries to remain embodied in this questioning moment, where the translucent circle spins . . . *buffering* – but he can't manage it. Hakuna matata, old man, he mutters, seeing the Methodists' rusting corrugated-iron porch, and the entire pride of De'Aths gathered before it on the mossy asphalt. It'd been Maeve's choice – she knew the Minister through her volunteering with the Sams. The Butcher hadn't demurred – what could he have said? (Dump the homophobic old cunt in a landfill – it's no more than he deserves.) The Baker came from outside Bath, together with his hippy-dippy wife and their four children, who, although their tow-heads were reeking of tea tree oil, had still . . . *scratched*. Sniffed as well – because it'd been January, and the white skies over Hemel were raw with rain clouds, while the north wind grazed the skin between the Butcher's viciously sharp collar and his savagely shaved chin. He remembers he'd turned to the Candlestick-maker and said, perfectly calmly, Where the fuck do you get off showing up looking like that ... And the Candlestick-maker, grubbing up some moss with the fraying toe of his espadrille, had said nothing in reply – only given his big brother ... *a zigzagging stoner's grin – where have they been?* As if the funeral weren't bad enough, the sight of his brothers' faces – uglified and inadequately moisturised versions of his own – never ceased to fill the Butcher's black heart with rage ... *and pain.* He remembered then – recalls now – how they'd come back together from school on the Greenline bus, and he'd led them to the very back, where he and Squilly would entertain them by vigorously stimulating each other – the aim being to achieve tumescence and climax ... *in between stops.* As the undertaker's assistants hobbled from the corrugated-iron porch, Maeve De'Ath had staggered *in sentimentality* – and might've fallen, were it not for the supportive son. Through her black leather glove, and his successive layers of cashmere, worsted and Egyptian cotton, the Butcher felt the impenitent grasp of her stubby fingers – in his darkest and most maddeningly addled moments, back in the days before Gawain, and before his Ritalin 'script, it had been those fingers he'd hallucinated, poking out from the off-white walls of his aseptic dwelling and ... *trying to drag me back.* Two visits per year, he'd decided there and then – the others could deal with *all the rest.* Maeve wouldn't mind – she liked nothing better than to be grouted to her grandchildren by *copious amounts of snot*, whereas her own firstborn had remained an enigma to her ... *she's never listened to me.* Maeve De'Ath, a squat *pear* of a woman who for three nights of the week squeezed into the telephone the juice of her *compassion.* This remained the Butcher's abiding image of his mother: her sitting in the dim hall at Colindale Avenue, her face a pale splodge – her hand another, which held the receiver clamped against her skull. So hard and for so long, that the teenaged Butcher, skulking by, entertained the notion that bone and Bakelite had knitted, so creating a strange cyborg . . . *half-woman, half-phone,* which'd remain eternally receptive to the flow of electrical impulses the Samaritans' switchboard piped . . . *into our home.* And then, when Maeve wasn't sopping up the suicidal thoughts of complete strangers, she'd be off on her rounds, from table-top to car boot, picking up a whatsit here – letting fall a thingummyjig over there. The balance of china dogs and old engraved pub mirrors she'd afflict on her menfolk for a few days, before they, too, joined the great lagoon of superannuated bric-à-brac, that, as far as the Butcher could see, surrounded Saint Albans, as the boundless sea surrounds land on medieval maps . . . *here bee junke.* This was her constant complaint: *I don't know why you have to be so . . . critical,* for any sort of analysis was quite alien to her nature, *Your mother has a synthetic mode of thought,* Kins would say – emphasising the syn – *she delights in putting things together, whereas you're very much the analytic type . . .* and the Butcher, sitting there *pulling things apart* with his fine mind, was strongly inclined to reply: What about your Berko bit-on-the-side, is she a synthesist as well? Is that why she delights in your putting your scraggy saggy old cock together with her saggy scraggy old cunt? – The Butcher had given the euology – if it could be so dignified. He spoke as one unaccustomed to do so publicly – asking for his listeners to for-give his inarticulacy, while seeking to imply this alone guaranteed his . . . *veracity*. Kins . . . had been . . . a good man . . . and . . . a good father. A brilliant scholar and . . . a much loved pedagogue, whose dedication to the knotty problems of local government . . . finance had contributed – in ways his eldest son was unable to specify – to . . . public debate. He had been a loving and . . . atten-tive husband – a gentleman in the true sense, whose piety and commitment to pacifism had been strong – (though he never actually got off his arse and did anything!). Looking around the dank tin shed at the mourners, who, although they sat coldly fused to the plywood pews, were mostly *on the way out*, the Butcher had recommitted to the pursuit of a swift and early demise . . . *Then fancies fly a-way, I'll fear not what men say . . . I'll la-bour night and day . . . To be a . . . corpse!* What could possibly be worse than being sprung from your mortal coil as Kins had: winnowed out by cancer, his saggy scraggy old body swollen and yellow from all the bile his diseased liver could no longer process – yet still fluting, *It's too soon, Johnny, it's toooo sooon!* It'll never be soon enough for me, the Butcher had sworn as he tapped his file cards on the lectern. Never soon enough to avoid the inevitable devaluation of my precious . . . *assets.* And when he'd looked up again, there they'd all been: Tehrani taxi drivers, Brazilian petrochemical engineers and Russian hydrologists. He could see Lin Gao at the back, sitting beneath an old framed sampler *Let Me Live in My Father's House, and be a Friend to Man.* The Chinese EmmEssEss operative had been nabbed in a bizarre little hidey-hole they'd managed to contrive in the foundations of the Honkers residency. The Butcher flew in from London and, against the odds, succeeded in . . . turning him. (You turn me right round baby, right round . . .) He was perfectly willing. (He was scared shitless.) After I pulled out – I got him out. (And where is he now, the poor fucker – doing the dishes in a Little Chef outside fucking Wincanton! No, Butch! This mealy-mouthed self-exculpation is beneath you.) At the council crematorium, while the other mourners huddled together in a cloud of breathy commiseration, he stood apart, his hand thrust deep in his pocket . . . *I am the lineman for the County.* He held his mobile phone so tightly – he wanted to *stop all the clocks* . . . send the signal from mast to computerised exchange – and from there to the ring of satellites, ever circling the earth, and the three hundred caesium clocks which precisely calibrate all the events (Dear boy) that have ever taken place, or ever will do . . . *world without end.* Back at the bungalow on the outskirts of Hemel, the evidence of his parents' pathetic diminuendo had been a mute cacophony: the mourners sipped tea from dirty cups – the frayed curtains swayed in the mouldy draughts, the bric-à-brac faded to . . . tat. Unable to take it any more, the Butcher had stepped out into the garden, where he'd half expected to see his father – naked, skipping between the raspberry canes, crying out to the starlings, It's too soon! It's too soon! Which was ridiculous, since he'd been present when Kins was shut up in his own closet of seasoned oak, *with brass-effect handles and casket ornamentation* – present also, only minutes before, when the poor old fucker'd been committed to . . . *the flames of his own obsessions,* since the crematorium was indeed a recipient of local government funding. Sitting on the wonky tree swing, the Candlestick-maker had bodged up for the Baker's children, the Butcher looked up to the sky, where a charter flight en route from Luton to Larnaca was indeed . . . *moaning overhead.* Although the message it scrawled on cold heavens wasn't HE IS DEAD, but, far more disturbingly, HE YET LIVES! Yes, still lives – still lives in the faces of the tourists the Butcher passed by on his walk from Leicester Square – and will still be living tomorrow morning, in the self-satisfied countenance of some dumb Humphrey or other, when he wends the deceptive bend to the Cabinet Office, to progress a batch of Florida warrants. The Firm's rules, as ever, play to the Butcher's advantage: warned never to acknowledge their colleagues in public, its employees are intimate behind closed doors, always seductively whispering each other's given names. It was the Butcher's pleasure to blank fellow officers in the streets, then duck into Chariots Roman Spa and wank a perfect stranger. If a line were to be drawn from the Hoist – an essandemm club underneath the railway viaduct – to the Royal Vauxhall Tavern, and from there to VeeBeeArr, the shape described would be highly congruent with the Butcher's own isosceles nose – and, after fifteen years cruising the inland waterways, he could sniff out trouble anywhere on this island of the odd. (You're over-egging it, Butch – truth to tell, you've scarcely strayed these past seven years.) The Butcher gets out a pack of Marlboro and lights one with his Dupont. Sucking the smoke down deeply, he contemplates his . . . *nicotinous patch*: in his time he's witnessed a precipitate decline in tradecraft amongst spooks and fags alike – the spies are no longer on the lookout for the opposition's leg-men, while the gays have abandoned their own secure comms: their hankies, earrings and cryptographic bunches of keys. Nowadays, they'll stand about in the bus station, trilling at the top of their voices about their formerly covert liaisons. But not the Butcher – the Butcher isn't pleased by these public avowals at all, au contraire, he's shocked to his core. What place is there in this bravely *Blairing* new world for a snobbish, repressed homosexual spy with a taste in fine wines and silks? The Butcher has done his time on the drugs-and-thugs desk – profitably so, since he ran across a gang of Turkish-Cypriots out of Clapton who'd the brass neck to try transhipping a metric tonne of heroin via . . . *South-bloody-Mimms*. It'd mostly been the EnnDeeEyeYou's show – the cream of the copper crop, although that's another thing that's changed: the best and brightest were plodding away from the force – just as spooks were wafting away from the secret world. There's always been some toing and froing between the Firm and its customers – EyeBees who've risen so far but can go no further, might slide sideways into the EffSeeOh or the Cabinet Office. Now this trickle of valetudinarians is becoming a flood. So long as Dick remained Chief the Butcher would be secure . . . *I am the leg-man for the cunty*, but now the jockeying to succeed him has begun in earnest the Butcher feels it – feels a new perturbation in the electro-magnetic waves that pulse through his up-ended shoebox of a house on Lambeth High Street. The buzz is intermittent: five minutes on, five minutes off, twenty-four hours a day. To begin with he'd feared he'd go insane – waking time after time from troubled naps, in which the scrambled letters from old disposable code books, four groups of four, again *annagain*, descended, row upon row, down the back-lit, orange screens of his eyelids. Waking to this: the scrambled letters from old disposable code books, descending, row upon row, down the black slats of the Venetian blinds he'd had put up in the bedroom, the study, the kitchen – everywhere, in point of fact. The floors are black rubber blocks – the walls off-white silk paint. The furniture is minimal and fabricated from metal and leather. To say the Butcher's abode is minimalist would be a gross exaggeration: it's nothingist, voidist – vacuumist, even, since he cleans the place fanatically, wiping, dusting and sucking up every last particle of dust that dares to be motile. He does all the cleaning himself – not for security reasons but because . . . *I enjoy it.* And enjoys especially those deep, deep cleans – the ones where – once he's finished with the steam-cleaner – he takes an old toothbrush to the grout between the bathroom tiles. Finishing up, crouching in the exact centre of the main room at three in the morning, naked save for rubber gloves and earthed by the rubber floor, he feels it more strongly than ever . . . *the buzz.* Feels it, and sees its graphical expression in the wave-form shadows the Venetian blinds throw across the off-white walls. The buzz was all around him – and jangled right through his Ritalin-soused metabolism. The buzz was in his cigarette smoke and his puckered-up ball-sack – the hot juice dripped in fizzing globs from the plugs and light fitments. The buzz held and released him, held him and released him again *annagain* – a steady series of electro-mechanical pulses travelling through flesh and bone, through metal and leather, carrying with them all the multitudinous bites and blips of the digital realm. And sitting on the tartan bedspread in the safe flat, the Butcher still feels the buzz, agitating each and every one of . . . *my particles.* At some unspecified point in the future, he imagines, this oscillation will reach its terminal velocity, and then there'll truly be . . . *the vacuum, the void, the nothing from which nothing comes.* Stubbing out his cigarette, the Butcher shudders – the stasis horrors are upon him, and he can see a future in which *nothing ever happens ever again* . . . He sees them walking down the chiller aisle of some suburban shopping-barn, all their ardour *freeze-dried.* Hand in hand, the formerly civil servants are now . . . *civil-fucking-partners.* The Butcher scrutinises the once-martial Ram – who's become broad-bottomed, careworn and *painfully unsexy* – as he reaches out to grab a bag of cauliflower florets. Then, as they head across the car park, the trolley's wheels skipping and skittering, he sees them: his step-children, pressing their baffled father's *face-masks* against the car's windows: useless assets, who, just like their Uncle Jonathan, should've long since been . . . *wound down.* Stop all the clocks! the Butcher cries aloud: Stop all of Cumming's crappy hobby-chronometers – stop this one, too! He holds aloft the featherweight Philips alarm clock some Registry Girl has left beside the bed, preparatory to hurling it against the rose-patterned wall . . . *for nothing now can ever come to any . . . good,* when there comes a different buzz: the intercom. Lieutenant-Colonel Gawain Thomas has arrived, *comme d'habitude,* exactly on time. Usually the Butcher would already be standing stiffly to attention (Me, too). But the fustiness he'd brought back with him from Kins's funeral has been furring the Fabergé circuitry of the Butcher's diamond-sharp mind – so he sits a while longer, thinking and smoking. Thinks of how, in the course of their affair, while Gawain has grown rather plumper – he's gone in the opposite direction, becoming still leaner and more angular. As a young man the Butcher took a perverse delight in cutting himself shaving – the soap-slicked slip-nick! the shocked hiatus, the sudden crimson bloom . . . and its paining reconfirmation: *Yes, you are the Butcher – committed to cutting up all bodies, including your own.* But now . . . now . . . he stares deep into the flesh-pit, the *great moaning ocean of the un-fucked*, which has tormented him ever since *Mister Kipling fiddled with my exceedingly good cakes* . . . and he sees there only corpses: the corpses of friends and lovers who've died . . . *unacknowledged*, the corpses of assets who'd to be expediently *let go of*. . . Idealistic young men he'd met when working ex officio on the Moscow Desk, who most likely lived out the balance of their forgotten lives tortured by a different and far louder . . . *buzz*. What can it mean, this *Babi Yar* hovering in the limpid, slightly stale atmosphere of history's back bedroom? The Butcher feels at one with the shadowy figures of the Einsatzgruppe, who stand about on the blood-soaked edges of the *hateful hollow*, looking down at the jumble of emaciated corpses, the barrels of their Schmeissers still smoking as they . . . *light their cigarettes*. One of the last things he remembers his father saying to him, on the afternoon when Maeve called the ambulance, and all three of them knew it was going to be . . . *a one-way trip*, had been: Can I bum one of your fags? He'd said it before, of course – it was one of his stock-phrases, a testimony to Kins's stopped-clock idiolect, to which no vocabulary had been added since . . . *nineteen thirty-nine.* In the past the

Butcher would hold his tongue – but on this occasion he'd laughed long and bitterly. Now, taking a final drag on his own un-bummed fag, the Butcher exhales: Hakuna matata, old fellow – hakuna matata . . . The paramedics had been understanding types, and they strapped him to the stretcher still smoking. When they'd gone, all that remained of him had been a few wispy tendrils . . . *snagging on the Artex*. The Butcher went to see Kins a few times in the hospital, and sat there, listening to the machines he was wired up to bleep – watching the globules of saline worm their way down the tubes, and into the *meat* they were *preserving*. The Butcher had fixated on his dying father's hands – the quiver of their tendons, the coiling of their veins, their liver-spotted camouflage. They'd been young once – these hands. P'raps they still were, cosy in these *old pigskin gloves*. It was hard to imagine Kins's clumsy hands – which the Butcher had only seen wrapped around golf clubs or Biros – slim and young and *caressing* . . . Maeve had three equally contemptuous nicknames for her life-partner: Your food's on the table, Professor Branestawm! she'd shout up the stairs on the days he worked at home. He'd had a little study in the box room, where he'd sit, hour upon hour, dutifully filling in the pages of narrow-feint foolscap pads with more facts, figures and opinions about local government finance. Here he is again, Mister-bloody-Hulot! she'd carp, when Kins, the car having refused to start, would stand peering into the mysterious grotto of the engine compartment. Hurry it up a bit, Pooter! she'd taunt from the kitchen window, as he sweated his way up and down the narrow strip of garden, his *pigskin gloves* blistered by the lawnmower's handle. The buzzer sounds again and at last the

Butcher stands, walks to the wall-mounted intercom and summons the footfalls he's been anticipating all day. He's spoken of all this to Gawain – it couldn't be avoided, since Kins's inconvenient demise has messed up several of their rendezvous. But now the Butcher wishes to forget about all that . . . *and play with my teddy bear*, which is how he thinks of Gawain when they lie, his cheek resting on his cavalryman's gingery *belly-fur*. Oh! the dawns of sweet ecstasy when they cuddled, *runny-honey* flowing into one another, in some gay-friendly bed and breakfast in Peebles or Pontefract or Prestatyn . . . *my friend will be arriving late tonight and leaving before breakfast*. Why? Why now, when he can hear Gawain panting his way up the penultimate flight, does this acid and indigestible memory . . . *rise up my gorge*? He'd stood in the bungalow's vestibule, listening to the mourners' burr on the far side of the frosted-glass door, his pigskin gloves in one hand, a cigarette in the other, transfixed as the little plaster pimples bulged and rippled – first the tips, then the entire fingers clawed their way out of the walls: it was Kins . . . *just coming!* Which was what he'd call down from his attic study when Maeve summoned him to the table: Just coming! He'd halve the distance between him and the kitchen . . . *Just coming!* then halve it again – yet never actually arrive. On this point at least Maeve had been in the right: Kins was most profoundly absent when he was standing in the corner of the kitchen, by the rumbling old Potterton, his mind also *rumbling along* until the thermostat . . . *clicked off.* Appalled, the Butcher had stared at his father's multiple and severed arms, all frantically signalling to make . . . *a U-turn out of the grave.* On the trolley, wreathed in the smoke from the fag he'd bummed

off his bumming fag of a son, he'd sobbed, It's too soon, Johnny –
too soon! And his *shit-stabbing, fudge-packing, pillow-biting* son had
taken a moment to snidely reflect: Too soon? What the fuck did
he think about these past few months of his decline – dragging
into the hospital, sitting there, the sour solution dripping into
him, then dragging home again, to sit with the radio on, and the
susurrus of middle-class voices . . . *dripping into him?* Local-bloody-
government-finance, no doubt – and some never-would-be-read-
anyway journal article that will now never be written. The Butcher
had gestured to the paramedics to give them a moment alone, then
he'd leant in to that *saggy, scraggy, jaundiced face* . . . a saturnine
smile splitting his own perfectly shaved one. Do you remember,
he'd hissed, how Mum would call you for supper, again and again?
And each time you'd bellow down the stairs, Just coming! Kins's
eyes had been horribly mobile – the eyes of a frightened child,
but the Butcher remained pitiless: You were always just coming,
weren't you, Daddy-dearest: *which is presumably why you can't get it
into your thick old head that you've finally arrived!* (Or words to that
effect, Butch – because what I actually recall you saying is that,
having come through the great charnel house of the twentieth
century unscathed, he'd lived a pacific life in a semi-detached house
in a semi-provincial backwater – much like his beloved Trollopian
cleresy – enjoying the concupiscence occasioned by wife-and-
mistress, fathering three fine and healthy sons and effectively being
subsidised by the state he'd refused to serve, as he wrote many
books and articles on a subject of great interest to him, but hardly to
anyone else.) Yes . . . yes . . . I s'pose that's more like it – I wasn't

quite so cruel, I did try to reassure him his life had been meaning-ful. It was his eyes, Squilly – his awful, frightened eyes. And he'd no eyebrows by then to speak of – the chemo' singed them off. A pitiful baldness, I thought – a kick in the bald man's bald arse as he scuttles off this mortal coil . . . (But he's not gone, is he, Butch?) Footsteps sound on the final flight and there's a light-but-firm tap on the door. The Butcher puts his eye to the peephole and sees Lieutenant-Colonel Gawain Thomas in the form of a huge tadpole: outsized, sandy-red head – tapering, blue-suited body. He could open the door and right away they'd be in each other's *fins?* – within minutes the tartan bedcover would be tangled up with their shed clothing, and they'd be *spawning with each other* . . . Yet still he hesitates, thinking back to that chilly corridor full of reanimated arms and the odour of reheated puff-pastry: Kins's eyebrows had been gone – but the Scots one, who'd read the poem, had had beautifully thick and black eyebrows. Sitting in the Rex, his mother and father beside him, *plushdust* tickling his nose, *poshlost* tickling everyone else's . . . *fancy*, the Butcher had thought: He's been cast against type – to elicit sympathy, no doubt: so much harder to be gay coming from that sort of background . . . So much harder to quaver, He was my North, my South, my East, my West – yet it's proved just as hard for me to live with . . . *divided loyalties*. Listening to Gawain's steady breathing, the Butcher fears he may never leave that corridor – never leave that golf range either. He'd tried hard as a young man, he believes, to win his father's love – but always it hippety-hopped away, towards the flag at the far end of the filmic fairway . . . *who was he, my father?* And at last the Butcher swings open the door of the room: a beautiful young woman had been standing there – perhaps the most beautiful woman he'd ever seen: a vision swathed in a sky-blue sari chased with some sorta golden embroidery-stuff – its bodice tightly fitting her slim figure. A sandalwood-scented, blue-black-haired vision, with one plucked eyebrow quizzically arched. – Charlie, Charlie One! Conference call commences in five . . . Charlie, Charlie One, do you read me? Conference call in five . . . Awkwardly slumped in a swivel chair, in a Portakabin, in a dusty-dry compound, somewhere close to the birthplace of civilisation, Gawain – tethered by headphones to the radio net – corkscrews up from greenish sleep, only to subside once more into this reverie of the recent past: The Taj Palace Hotel in New Delhi, and the young Indian woman holding the spiral-bound reporter's notebook and dictaphone, who'd said: My name is Surinder Sehti, I am a defence correspondent for the Times of India – if you have a short period of time to spare I would like to ask you some questions about what it is that serving British Army officers are doing here at a time of the maximal tension along the Line of Control? This much Gawain remembers – the repetitions, and the punctilious diction – and he also has a vague recollection of slim white columns forming vanishing perspectives, their pediments and capitals merging with geometrically patterned floors and walls. Each time he'd quit his room, heading out to the arms fair, he'd be caught in this maze, while in the mid-distance he'd spot the peacock's tail of a porter's shako disappearing behind a slim white column. He'd stood there in the doorway – pink after his lukewarm shower, his terry-towelling robe open to the waist, and he'd thought:

Yeah, what the hell are we doing here, playing at being showroom demonstrators when the entire planet seems on the point of disintegration? Before he'd left home Gawain had had a serious talk with Fiona about the world situation: her leaning against the kitchen worktop, him pacing up and down on the pebble-patterned lino, punching his palm to make his points: the Yanks starting to take casualties in 'Stan – the Israelis pummelling Gaza and the West Bank. That weird little black Hitler in Zimbabwe starving his voter-base into the polls . . . Really, the Cold War had provided a sort of frozen stability – balance of terror and all la-la-la that. But now? Well, he couldn't think of a time when the world had seemed more unstable – or one when the Fighting Rams were more likely to be deployed. And Fiona, who'd recently had her eyes tested and now wore professorial bifocals, had said, That's all very well, Gawain – but think about it: at more or less any point in the past century you could've said the same thing . . . When Miffy started full days at school Fiona had begun an OhYou degree in contemporary history, and so taken to telling him . . . *what was what*, even though she must've understood . . . *it confuses me.* I dunno about that, he'd say, once she'd joined up the dots to create a pattern *of her own devising*, my concerns are largely operational – the men . . . their families and so forth. Fiona had a way of scrunching up her features and tossing her head. In the early days of their marriage Gawain had construed it as an affirmative: *Roger that!* But as the years have passed the gesture has become both more pained – and more emphatic: *Roger out!* He wonders many things, does Gawain – wonders them as *bears of little brain* do:

muzzily – fuzzily . . . Jonathan wears custom-blended aftershave which he has made up for him by a parfumier in the Burlington Arcade. Jonathan fucks Gawain vigorously – and they're long past the point in their relationship where . . . *all the niceties are observed.* Often there are shit and semen stains on the mattress as well as the sheets and pillow slips – sometimes Gawain tries to launder them, and assemble a bed-block as neat and compact as the ones he did during his Academy days. But Jonathan just lies back naked on the exposed mattress-protecter and . . . *laughs.* It's a cliché, he thinks – in films the wronged wife smells the other woman on her husband, but perhaps Fiona can't smell Jonathan at all, sharing as he does *my own male scent?* It's not the constant absences I object to, Gawain, she hisses in the talcum-powdered darkness of their bedroom: I understand perfectly well the pressures of the job – why wouldn't I – Charlie? Charlie One? Repeat: Are you receiving me? The Brigade Adjutant's clipped voice nips his ear again and Gawain jerks upright: Charlie One, receiving you, he rasps into the mic. – That you, Gawain – everything squared away up there? Gawain reviews the situation before replying: The Rams are indeed squared away in their roughly square, Hesco-reinforced compound . . . *penned sheep – spent cartridges – sheep droppings* . . . and have commenced regular patrols: sweating it in full kit down dusty roads and through shadowy bazaars where . . . *there's only dust for sale.* Sip-sip-glugging from their Camelbaks as they scope out the darkened doorways, the full-screw bringing up the rear with his helmet-cam *capturing everything.* Then it's back to the Wimmik – Drives gunning the engine, top cover swinging the geepee-emmgee's barrel loose and easy: capturing an old rag-head in the sights . . . sipping mint tea . . . a wonky-donkey haw-heeing . . . a white plastic garden chair up-ended on a pile of rubble . . . Everywhere Gawain's been in Iraq he's seen them – in the vulgar marble palaces of Saddam's henchmen on the crumbling banks of the Shatt al-Arab, and in the burnt-out shells of government buildings. The very first thing he'd noticed when they deplaned at the aypod was a white plastic garden chair sitting beside the runway – and Tizer had said, Why don't you take a load off, Greeny – things're only gonna get heavier from here on in . . . The company of Kiwis who pitched up a week ago – and who, so far as Gawain can establish, have bugger all to do besides . . . *fuck up my logistics* have taken to mounting bogus little patrols of their own, simply so they can recover more of the flimsy booty from back alleys and shattered patios. Their SeeOh, a limber, dark fellow called Moody who sports a ridiculous sprig of hair on his bottom lip . . . *beard? Goatee? Lip-ee?* had revealed his clever plan to Gawain that morning: A tournament, Greeny – your boys and mine. Fives or sevens, depending on how many're willing – didn'tya say you were a pretty handy loose head yerself? If we can persuade the Jap contractors to join in we could call it the Three Nations . . . If enough of your boys're Jocks and Taffies – or Irish, you could field all the home nations and we'd have six teams! Standing there, looking at Moody, utterly unselfconscious in his ridiculous tit-crowned wideawake hat, Uncle Rodney's oft-uttered words rang in Gawain's ears: *There's a soupçon of the peacock in all army officers à mon avis* . . . So, yes, the Adjutant's figure of speech was about right: if Moody had his way they'd all be squared away – forming a hollow

304

square of spectators in the middle of Camp Val's dusty compound. Literally a sitting target for whichever gang of bandits crept in from the badlands and began chucking over arpeegees and mortar rounds. Not that the Rams had had much contact so far – but the threat-level was rising, and eye-eedees were fast becoming what Jonathan would doubtless call the signature note of the campaign. Each morning Gawain receives emails with video attachments from the EeeOhDee group down in Basra. The videos show devices cunningly concealed in water butts and straw bales. One, rather more macabrely, had been hidden in the head of a putrefying camel . . . *wires worming out of its eyes*: not so much kill- as . . . *rot-teevee*. With each clip he watches, the tension builds up in Gawain's thick neck and broad shoulders – striking lightning pains up into his . . . *loose head*. Yes! he barks into the handset. We're pretty much all squared away up here, David – there're one or two issues, obviously . . . Equally obviously, the Adjutant's no longer listening – he's moved away from Gawain, further into the radiophonic darkness, where he can be heard calling out other call-signs: Charlie Two, Charlie Two, are you reading me? Gawain sits and waits and broods, which is pretty much what . . . *I've been doing my entire professional life!* He wanders back through his hot and sweaty head to New Delhi, and that encounter with the beautiful journalist: I'm not in a position . . . he'd almost certainly said . . . to talk to you as a serving British officer, but what I can say is that the role of the Export Support Team is pretty widely misunderstood . . . while Surinder Sehti had stood there, goggling at his cleavage. There'd been, Gawain thinks, a sort of Line of Control between the two of them – on her side Hindu prudery and womanly rectitude, on his . . . *complete and utter indifference.* Whereas up in Kashmir the real thing snaked over crags and down into ravines, and there were a million men, shoulder to shoulder with their comrades – nose to nose with their foes. What would happen if the balloon went up? A mass Eskimo greeting, p'raps, followed by them all getting down to the . . . *buggery business.* He remembers the encounter at all only because of having said to her, If you hang on a sec' I can give you the contact details for the press people – you're best off talking to them . . . He'd turned away from the door and simultaneously felt . . . *the balloon shoved up between my legs* – a balloon full of *liquid shit!* He'd got rid of Surinder Sehti as quickly as he could, then waddled to bathroom, where he . . . *let fly.* Charlies One-through-Twelve and Bravos Nine-through-Seventeen all present, Boss . . . The stream of pissy shit crackles away into the ether – and Gawain turns his attention to the interplay between the various commanders attached to Battlegroup Main. The weekly orders group conference is his best opportunity to get a grasp on *the wider picture,* an essential task if he's aiming for corps-level command. *And why shouldn't I?* No one knows I'm a shit-pisser – or a shit-stabber for that matter. Oh, Christ! he undermoans, I feel so punctured, so empty – so fucking lonely . . . What's required to make the loneliness of command bearable is, he thinks, the *command of loneliness* . . . And he is alone – profoundly so: only calling home once a week, and, when he does, after listening to a tight-lipped account of the children's doings, waiting in vain for some *basic human warmth* . . . But why should his long-haired General oblige, when for years now it's been Jonathan who's supplied it? To begin with they held their conference calls in phone boxes: Gawain favoured one on the outskirts of Pickering too remote and chilly to be much used. He could loiter there, out of sight behind a hedge – and when the heavy receiver rattled into life . . . *ambush it*. He knew Jonathan called from various boxes in his neighbourhood – shifting randomly from one to another, in case anyone was watching and . . . *established a pattern*. Problem isn't so much your wee wifey . . . he'd said in the happy aftermath of their first full night together, when they lay spooning in the Terylene shadows of a Leeds budget-hotel room . . . it's the mob I'm sort of married to. And so Jonathan had instructed Gawain in rudimentary tradecraft: the dead-letter drops, brush contacts and alpha-numerical codes that're his . . . *standard operating procedure*. It's absolutely essential, he hissed, that you write nothing – and I mean nothing whatsoever – down anywhere: not on paper, not on a computer – nowhere at all. Because ninety-nine times out of a hundred it's what does for people: they write down their lover's name, their controller's or the number of their Swiss bank account, and surprise-surprise, someone else reads it. Then it's all over – finito! But nothing – I repeat no-single-thing you write down will you retain – while all you send me, my love, will be seered into me, and then . . . seared. There's a sort of poetry in this: you need never feel you're betraying anyone, because I don't exist at all. And if I don't exist – well, we don't exist either, now do we? No, they didn't exist: not in the way that ordinary couples do: *Have you met Jonathan and Gawain, they've just moved into the neighbourhood . . . ?* They came into being purely in their fugitive acts of love – summoning up the territories of each other's bodies through kisses and caresses – or in their *midnight special* phone calls, during which they fantasised about all the things . . . *we'd like to do*. But, as the years have passed, so it's become harder to find phone boxes. The Pickering one was decommissioned and its equipment torn out – all that was left was . . . *an empty shelf.* The leather hinges creaked as the wind blew down off the North Yorkshire moors – the heavy, eight-paned door swung open, sucking out the smells of fresh urine and rotten phone books, together with . . . *all our fragrant endearments.* Jonathan bought them both second-hand mobile phones – handsets which had untraceable sim cards installed and were set up so they could only connect to each other. They weren't, Gawain thought, really mobile phones at all – more like the tin-can telephones he and his sisters played with as children – and when he sat in the Volvo, parked up in some forgettable lay-by, he felt reassuringly *tethered* to his lover. But Jonathan was paranoid – he spoke of scanners and interception. He constantly badgered Gawain as to where exactly he was keeping his mobile. No! Locked in an office drawer was insufficiently secure – didn't he have a readily accessible fridge? Or, better still, a deep-freeze to . . . *cool our electro-ardour.* Every time they met in the flesh, Jonathan insisted on changing up – as he termed it – and presented his lover with another Nokia, Ericsson or Motorola, relieving him of the old one, which was – for their purposes at least – already obsolete. To begin with, they'd written to each other as well – both their return addresses being rented boxes in obscure sub-post offices. Jonathan's letters were beautiful things, full of whimsy and lyricism – but they had to be destroyed immediately after having been read. When emailing became more widespread, Jonathan gave Gawain precise instructions on how to create an anonymous account – not on his work or home computer, though, but in an internet café, protected by its anonymity. In Moseley or Moss Side, awkward in his civvies, sat amongst curry-smelling young Asian men who tapped on oblivious, Gawain poked his finer feelings into soiled keyboards. It troubled Gawain – bothered him especially in the days leading up to the deployment – that there was no record of their relationship at all: no photographs of them proudly arm in arm – no love letters scrawled with passionate entreaties, no envelopes stuffed with old tickets – mementoes of the shows they'd attended together, and the journeys they'd undertaken. Nothing. But when he whispered this to Jonathan as they slumbered in the annexe of the Lastingham Grange Country House Hotel – which can be easily accessed unobserved – he'd only chuckled indulgently, Teddy Bear, what matters is that I love you and you love me: we know this to the very core of our being. All those silver-framed photographs gathering dust on unplayed pianos – what're they? Only the residue of exhausted passions – whereas we, dearest, our love remains ever-green and forever young. That there's nothing to prove its existence only makes it realer than the dull and solid world we inhabit . . . Yes, the dull and solid world – what'd made him think of the arms fair and that dreadful bout of diarrhoea? The *dulling* and *solidifying* capsules, probably – two of them, broad-spectrum antibiotics the medic back at Bovington had told him: *will zap just about any Delhi-belly going – granted, you'll trot on for twenty-four hours or so, but after that all the little wrigglers'll be stony and you'll stopper up pronto . . .* There were similar capsules in the medi-packs they'd all been issued with when they deplaned at Shaibah, where, as they awaited their movement order, one or two of the troopers did indeed get the squits – but *touch wood . . .* he massages his own sweaty temples . . . there's been nothing too serious – no epidemic, although the boys still have to be reminded at least five times a day to wash *their mucky little paws.* Really, it isn't Fiona's love he feels the lack of at all – but her *people skills . . .* She keeps her multiple of three in line, does Fiona. And, as the years have passed, and her husband has hauled himself, hand over hand up the chain of command, so Missus Thomas has become more and more . . . *commanding.* In the run-up to the deployment it'd been her quite as much as Gawain who'd . . . *licked the Rams into shape.* As the SeeOh's wife she was expected to head-up that parallel structure of command, the Wives' Club, but Gawain had seen plenty of army marriages founder on this fact alone: *why on earth* should any young mother, raising a family of her own, take on responsibility for this khaki, extended one? The Ruperts and their Lucie Clayton girlfriends were bad enough: time was when they *simply got on with it – we all simply got on with it . . .* He doesn't remember any griping or complaints during his childhood: his own mother had *simply got on with it . . .* Missus Thomas Senior had been loyal to her husband's colours – following them overseas on tours which had anticipated Gawain's own. He remembers running around on the patch in Bielefeld – ringing doorbells and then *running . . . running away.* What'd his mother been up to? A nurse, she was working in the Krankenhaus – and she never spoke of what happened there at all. Except for that one time, mostly Missus Thomas had been a jolly sort of presence – he sees her at the wheel of the family Beetle bombing down the autobahn . . . laying out picnics by the Moselle . . . her with a glass of honey-coloured wine . . . said she was drinking the river – we all laughed, Fay and Jess and me, then she'd sucker-punched us all, started going on about the boy – a squaddie had been brought into the hospital *in bits*, she said: he'd got on the business end of a machine-gun and been *cut near in two*. It was disgusting, Sister Thomas had spat: the whole thing . . . the massed divisions of Brits and Yanks on one side, the Soviet boys on the other – *a children's crusade* had been her precise words – *but there'll be no promised land, only nuclear fire and radioactive brimstone* . . . The Thomas family were all speechless – sat there with slices of pumpernickel mounded with the Heinz Sandwich Spread Granny Myfanwy sent from Swanage. It'd only been years later that this coincidence had struck Gawain: both his parents had been *cut near in two* by similar incidents – his father in Aden, his mother in Germany. Maybe this was why their marriage had also ended up *machine-gunned to death* . . . Although that came years later: of his father during those Deutschland days Gawain remembers little besides the Major crying, Bring out the Bols! to the accompaniment of Barry White's chocolate tones . . . *there's only, only one like you – no way they coulda made . . . two*. The Major had built a plywood bar in the basement – used a job-lot of tinsel for decoration, proffed a mirror ball, too. They threw little parties down there, and Gawain remembers his father slow-dancing . . . *with that bald bloke's wife*, his hand hovering over her big bum *but never touching* . . . The bald bloke was EssAyEss, or so the Major said – why does Gawain remember this? Because it was one of the few occasions in his childhood when he'd been aware of the . . . *wider picture.* He'd never seen so much as a uniform – although the Major took him into the workshop a few times to admire his *whirlybirds,* which is what he'd called them. It was his job to keep these exotic machines aloft – but when Gawain saw them they'd just hunched there, their rotors limp and floppy. Could anyone have anticipated what was to come? True, the Major's brownish hair had also been quite *limp and floppy* . . . while for a serving officer – even in the early seventies – he wore it suspiciously long, but still . . . Gawain knows where his father is now: up there in the Black Mountains, squatting no doubt in some soggy tepee and sucking on a . . . *pipe of peace.* Yet for a moment he sees Derek Thomas plummeting from the aching-blue Iraqi sky . . . *incoming hippy!* — There's a squawk, a flutter – then the twittering starts up again in the radiophonic aviary: Charlie One – Charlie One, are you reading me? Can you give the oh-group the sit' rep' on your Scimitars . . . ? And Gawain hears himself – measured and authoritative – reporting on the progress of the Bowman conversions, secure comms being . . . *pretty much fucking essential,* now the intel' from Brigade is that the Iranians are teaming up with the Shia militias . . . *on our patch – ringing on doorbells . . . running away.* But Ali al-Garbi isn't my patch, Gawain thinks – I'm like any army brat, my patch is . . . *wherever*: Bielefeld, Cyprus, back to Blighty. Derek got himself booted sideways into a desk job and, after a brief Welsh sojourn, in the early eighties the Thomas family had settled for South-coast suburbia . . . *peeveesee trews and Holsten Pils.* Gawain was taking his rugby seriously and considering a military career . . . *he was going one way – I the other.* Derek was probably already having the odd toke . . . *Christ knows where he got the stuff,* while Gawain joined the school cadet corps and acquired a permanently raw knuckle from manipulating the bolt of a Lee Enfield – the rifle he was instructed how to use, in preparedness to fight . . . *the war before the war before this one.* So, Gawain, you'll accompany the vehicles down to Maysan, will you? He hears the GeeOhSee inside his hot head – which is where they all are: all the British forces taking part in Telic Eight – Royal Welch and the Anglians, the King's Royal Hussars and the Coldstreamers. All those battle groups – all those thousands of men, and a few hundred women, concealed in the static fizzing between his ears. Christ! The heat – even at dawn it's hot, then the sun climbs and climbs and . . . *keeps on fucking climbing,* until it reaches a brutally effective position from which to aim and fire its rays – projectiles which can pierce standard-issue body armour . . . *better than a seven-point-six-five round at five hundred metres.* Over the radio net Gawain hears his colleagues being summoned one after another: Steve up in Al-Amarah – Donny down in Dhi Qar – summoned from the blinding light which is itself . . . *another kind of darkness.* And they report on petrol-smugglers apprehended and angry mobs dispersed with warning fire – all the Dixon-of-Dock-Green policing required once you're done with *Tim Collins's bullshit* and are facing an angry mob armed with pitchforks and staves, because you're *asymmetrically bogged down.* He's not asleep, Gawain – not sliding down into the bubbly bath of sleep . . .

Hello, matey! Instead he's daymaring the burning sandy wastes of southern Iraq – the unknowable concrete-and-mud-brick towns and forgotten bazaars where the Rams could well lose themselves . . . *in a wilderness of dust.* All of it – the white plastic garden chairs as well – has been *folded* into the complications of his sun-struck and hurting brain, while Gawain is abandoned . . . *Daddy's not coming.* If he'd been called upon to identify the moment when they'd swung past each other – Derek clambering down the chain of command, while Gawain prepared to inch up its carefully polished links – then it was while his father was posted to Faversham, and the Task Force set off from nearby Southampton for those fly-speck islands in the South Atlantic. They sat together in the airless living room watching it all on a brand-new Trinitron – not that there'd been anything colourful to see in that remote era, when wars were reported using . . . *archive footage,* to the accompaniment of a commentary delivered by . . . *the speaking clock.* Derek lay in his armchair, his growing hair fanned out on its old antimacassar, a Heineken can in one hand, a fag in the other – the very image of indolence, but he sat up straight . . . *when we sank the Belgrano. Yes, we both . . . clocked that.* And Derek had squeezed his Heineken can until it . . . *crumpled – never seen him do that before.* After which he'd huffed and puffed – said it was worse than regrettable – *a fucking crime*: all those Argies – only boys, and conscripts to boot. The Thomas family had had one of those novelty dipping birds on top of the fridge it *dipped and sipped* while Derek Thomas *dipped* towards the telly screen *and sipped* the last bitter dregs of his patriotism down: I'm not pretending to be a great patriot, boyo – but the lady's right, the reputation of the country is on the line . . . It must've been a year or two later, by which time Gawain had been away to camp, where he'd live-fired a Bren . . . *felt its sexy shudder*, that he dared to ask Derek if he regretted it – not having seen proper combat, that is. The Major had thought for a moment. I don't want to piss on your parade, son, he'd said eventually, but combat – in my view – is something very much to be avoided. See, any squaddie worth his salt knows how to keep his head down. Officers? Different cuppa type oh altogether. Got to be seen to be in the thick of it, bullets flying through the peak of your cap, getting a fucking suntan from the falling flares. My expertise consisted in keeping whirlybirds in the air, not putting human beings . . . *in the ground*. But he, too, had had his moment. When Derek finally detached altogether – told Gawain, his mother and sisters he'd *gotta go*, then fluttered up from his telly chair, flittered into an embroidered Victorian nightdress and sailed away into the hills to join Sid Rawle and his tepee hippies – he'd left his son – who by then was wearing the blues of a Sandhurst cadet, and feeling . . . *pretty ally* – wondering if he'd been afflicted with peetee-essdee all those years ago, under the hurting Aden sun. It hadn't been combat exactly – Derek was crewing a Saracen when the lad on top cover panicked as the first Molotov cocktail hit, and unleashed an ill-judged burst. *Seen!* but *not seen*, the lad doing obs' . . . *knobbly knob-head poking out of the front hatch* took it all in the neck and chest . . . *his knobbly knob-head was nearly bloody severed*. After that tour Derek Thomas felt he'd been quite as close to combat as he ever wanted to be, so corkscrewed away into the whirlybirds . . . *We shouldn't've been there at all, boyo. Riot control?*

Bum-sucking on the fag-end of empire we were . . . Charlie One? Charlie One? Even *dripping through* the radio net the GeeOhSee's *chocolate* tones are unmistakable. Everything going well up there in Ali Baba, Gawain? – covering everything in soft, warm sweetness . . . *not a scratch on him – never will be. Relishes the smell of napalm in the morning . . . as he pours it on his cornflakes . . .* For a moment Gawain considers saying something along these lines: *It's Ali al-Garbi, Boss – I know you're only trying to lighten the mood, but really it doesn't help: it's our basic insensitivity to their culture that's making it so fucking hard to connect with these people whose nation WE'RE MEANT TO BE REBUILDING!* But these words only fall to the floor of his own hot head, while he replies: Some bad boys in town the past few days, sir – locals shut up shop, coffee stalls all closed. Our int' cell has a local asset of their own – says they've at least a couple of mortars, arrpeegees . . . etcetera . . . Says they're not all Mucky's boys – if any. Says the Dawa lot're active here now – and we're only twenty-five clicks from the border. I've doubled patrols and put it on standing orders the lads're to be lidded at all times when they're out. – What're you saying, Gawain? – I'm saying it's a bit of a rum do, sir – the atmos' is dodgy, and my lads're fed up with having to fetch and carry for these Kiwis, who've bugger-all to do except Force Protection for this team of Jap construction workers. They're a hell of a liability –. – Who? The Kiwis or the Japs? – Well . . . both, sir. – That doesn't sound like the Fighting Rams' SeeOh talking – chin up, Gawain, I remember you in sparkling form on the rugger pitch – and with your chaps, these Japs and Kiwis you've half the Six Nations. Organise a sevens tournament, old chap, that'll build morale . . . A calendar hangs on the Portakabin wall behind the radio – presumably advertising a local business, although, since the whole thing is in Arabic, it's difficult to tell what kind. The picture page features a young woman in jeans, abaya and headscarf . . . *Filthy Fatima not showing anything she's got! Phwoar! It's hot!* standing in front of what appear to be large refrigeration units. Some culturally sensitive wag in the sig' unit has embellished this with a black Biro . . . *I'll have to have a word – the 'terps come in here* . . . loopy-looping down from the hem of the young woman's robe, the dense, pen-stroked curlicues merging with the pubic-hair type, and making her the smiling possessor of . . . *the biggest fucking bush this side of Saskatchewan.* Saskatchewan – now that was soldiering, that'd been the Fighting Rams at their finest: their squadrons all in beautiful playing-card formation: five Chieftains, three Scimitars, seven aypeesees, laid down in patient rows on the plain, which rolled away in undulating waves of scrub towards a lowering and cloudy horizon. Gawain had at long last been in command: sitting there in the grinding, winking gloom, listening to the servos calibrate the cannon's aim – registering the hushed interplay between gunner and targeter, and seamlessly integrating this with the continual positional updates coming through his cans . . . *I was in the flow, kayaking* down the cataract of action, precisely adjusting the disposition of this mighty force – hundreds of men and officers, scores of fighting vehicles – with mere dabs of . . . *my paddle.* Saskatchewan – there'd been lighter-than-lite beer in the mess, on tap twenty-four-seven . . . *and we all had a thirst.* It'd been a joint show with the YouEssEmm and the

Rams' Canadian hosts. *Inter-operability* was the latest buzz-word, but in practice *they'd lent us poor boys their gear.* Although this wasn't a live-fire exercise, they'd the kit necessary to simulate one – a round on target would hit the kill switch, disabling the vehicle. Nothing for its crew to do but sit there, smelling each other's farts while they waited for it all to be over . . . *but can it ever be over when it's never exactly . . . begun?* Gawain forgot about the brass who'd flown in that morning to observe, and who no doubt were sitting in their stand – a giant sort of bird hide, rising up proud of the scrub and its attendant mosquitoes – snacking on garden salads, cold cuts, asparagus and mayonnaise, slurping up lighter-than-lite beer before taking an idle peek through bipod-mounted bins. He forgot about the miserable months he'd spent with the Export Support Team, posing at arms fairs . . . *a showroom dummy in uniform*, demonstrating state-of-the-art materiel, even as his beloved Rams were suffering . . . *death by a thousand defence cuts.* The talk was all of putting stuff out to private tender, creating profit-centres and public–private partnerships – getting a corporate sponsor and changing the Rams' name to the *the Yorkshire Carphone Warehouse Hussars.* Gawain remembers giving sales spiels to dodgy Middle Eastern buyers – men with furtive, sweaty faces, their eyes quailing behind dark glasses, their fingers nervy with worry beads, their queries matter-of-fact and to the point: the unit prices of shells and the extent of after-sales support. *You're not a fucking salesman*, he'd told his reflection in the mirror above the basins in the gents' at the arms fair *again annagain* – and, it being an Indian convention centre, everything was *conventionally filthy*: shit- and snot-stained tissues strewn in the stalls, and plastic pots soupy with bacilli for those who . . . *manually wiped*. Waiting in the hot darkness for the GeeOhSee to extrude another dollop of wisdom, Gawain sees himself as he'd been four years before: a dinky little Glengarry perched on his blond hair, the breast pocket of his sandy-coloured, belted tunic edged with modest amounts of braid, ribbon and a couple of bits of tinware: *What's that one for, mister? – That one, son? Why, I won that for building a new shower block in an abandoned Bosnian paint factory* . . . But the pathetic accessory which had shamed him the most . . . *wouldn't look out of place in Claire's*, compounding the offence to his amour propre . . . *only took the job 'cause I'd been passed over*, was a little arse-wipe-sized piece of chainmail attached to the right epaulette of his tunic, which dangled down his left shoulder. *Chinka-chink* the chainmail flip-flopped about all day, every day, a constant reminder of his true status . . . *no chaste knight, me – only an impotent one, with a balsawood lance and a foam-rubber-fucking sword*. It's a fool's errand, Uncle Rodney had told him when they dined at his Victoria flat – Gawain bunking off from both regimental and domestic duties . . . *on some pretext or other*. Rodney had been Derek Thomas's best mate when they were stationed in Germany – *a committed bachelor*, is what Derek called him, which had been his way of saying gay – and he didn't have any problem with that, an enlightened man, the Major . . . *I could've told him – could've had a better life, made an honest man of myself*. He and Jenny Thomas had settled on Rodney as their eldest's spiritual mentor . . . *Did they have intimations – had they noticed my enthusiasm for the dressing-up trunk?* It's a fool's errand, Gawain . . . Rodney had said, carefully applying a pat of duck pâté to a beautifully crisp and feather-light slice of toast . . . peacetime soldiering, that is. Derek had dropped out altogether – but his friend had slipped sideways from the Remmy to take a job handling the pyrotechnics for the Royal Tournament. – If you're going to be a chocolate soldier, Gawain, you may as well be in a presentation box . . . Although his godson suspected rather more venal motivations, as Rodney rose up the chain-of-direction, eventually becoming responsible for auditioning . . . *all the principal boys.* Had a bit of money, did Rodney . . . *might be a little something for me*, and did right by himself. That evening there'd been the pâté and the Pomerol – *Château Le Gay, how obvious was that?* – the veal and a vintage Reuilly. All the time they'd been eating, there was a very young naval ensign hard at work in the bedroom – Rodney took him a plate through, but it wasn't until after Medjool dates, some chèvre and a glass of Muscatel that he did *his Big Reveal*: taking Gawain's elbow in his large and fleshy hand, smiling at him enigmatically from behind his bushy-black moustache . . . *must dye it by now*, and guiding him into the gilded gloom where the boy crouched, silk-bristled brush in hand, laboriously painting tiny figures on to the wallpaper. At once Gawain had realised the intent: to create a waist-height frieze, running the entire way around the room. The ensign had looked up from his task . . . *bum-fluffy brunet, a tight grouping of acne on the tip of his nose – yet still perfectly fanciable* and smiled. *Very difficult to get the highlights right on this cuirass, sir,* he'd said – or words to that effect. It had been then Gawain saw exactly what the ensign was minutely rendering: miniature figures in the full-dress uniforms of all the British Army regiments *there'd ever been* – Since Waterloo, his godfather had put in: I mean, going back further than that . . . well, there was no sort of consistency, not even with the New Model Army – officers were always customising their kit. Gawain had gawped at the strange procession: the tiny figures marching in profile around the room, every-man-jack zealously undertaking . . . *a fool's errand* which might well endure . . . *from here to eternity.* The dinner must've been, Gawain thinks, a couple of months before I left for Delhi, *but it stayed with me* . . . such that he couldn't help seeing himself as a brightly painted little figure, rendered in exquisite detail, right down to the highlights on his arse-wipe of chainmail, marching around the arms fair and giving these pathetic demonstrations: running the video loop which showed the negligible impact of shaped-charge projectiles on Chobham armour, directing the tiny team of gunners as they creaked about on the carpeted dais, pretending to unlimber, then fire a mobile artillery piece – and all the while the balloon inside of Gawain was being . . . *filled up with shit.* Once, twice . . . *twenty times* he'd quickstepped back to the gents' and squatted over the hole. Once, twice . . . *twenty times* he'd sworn to himself that this was the end: if he couldn't return to the Rams as their SeeOh, he'd do whatever was necessary . . . *to get the fuck out.* He wasn't, he believed, like Rodney at all – and would never be satisfied by chocolate soldiering. Besides, he didn't think of himself as a homosexual – he was more of a Jonathansexual, or one of those indisputably macho Latin men he'd heard about, who confirmed their hetero status only by *vigorously bumming* pre-op transsexuals.

Gawain felt the web of regimental relationships he was caught up in . . . *intensely* – the sticky storylines of shared experience, the taste of tacky military catchphrases . . . *gumming up the back of my throat.* Demob happy following his decision, he'd stopped at the Eye-DoubleyouEye stand to heft a Dan sniper rifle, and wound up his fellow salesman even as the . . . *balloon began to refill*: What's the effective range? Silencing and night-sight capability? So, suitable for an EssEff solo operation? Say if one wanted to eliminate someone important – someone heavily protected, a head of state, f'rinstance – the head of a rogue state? To all of which the Israeli bobbed his curly head and batted his wiry lashes: Great . . . Gawain went on, squeezing the trigger . . . *Jonathan's fingers inside me, Oh, Lord!* . . . I'll take one and a spare – 'cause he's gone totally insane, have you seen the Hitler moustache? And it's not just his methods that're unsound – my mission is to travel up the Zambezi, infiltrate his governmental structure and . . . *terminate him.* As Gawain recalls, some four years later . . . *up the fucking Tigris*, the Israeli had yelped: Terminate? And Gawain, *chink-a-chinking* his chainmail, had chuckled up: Terminate him . . . with extreme prejudice. Yes, *extreme prejudice* – the extreme prejudice of the homoerotic towards the homosexual wasn't something Gawain could conceive of . . . *as such* – that was Jonathan's department. When they lay together, after sex, his lean face resting between Gawain's plump pecs, his cigarette smoke invisibly *knitting* into the close atmosphere of the Rotheram Days Inn, or the Premier one outside Oswestry . . . *pearl one semen-slide*, he'd say, They hate us because they're more like us than they'd ever dare admit . . . Think of your Rams, Gawain – your precious bloody Rams. Sheeple, they are – sheeple desperate to push their horny heads between each other's woolly, masculine legs. All that martial display? It's a desperate front, put up to deter each other, mostly, from looking inside – inside the pink little bower of their bedrooms, where they lie, their blond tresses in pigtails, glittery pens between their strawberry-balmed lips, keepsake diaries unlocked and lying open wide in their soft laps . . . The first single he'd ever bought – Jonathan told his lover, who'd played loose-head for the British Army fifteen, only two fixtures but they'd been savage ones – was Softly Whispering I Love You by a group called the Congregation, a vast and shaggy chorus draped in chiffon-curtains-for-dresses. It had cost Littler Johnny two-and-six from Woolies – it'd been a woolly era . . . *though they all wore acrylics*: swaying this way and that, softly, statically whispering . . . *I love you*. But Gawain wasn't convinced – unlike his lover he'd never felt his attraction to men sprang from some feminine source. He peered deep inside his troubled chest and discovered . . . *what?* That the part of him most drawn to men was itself – unsurprisingly *when you stop to think about it* – the most . . . *ram-like, butting its way into butts*. Or, rather, longed to do so . . . *find out what I've been missing* – because Gawain had been kept in a purdah as deep as any freezer-unit Fatima: locked down tight in the harem of his lover's jealous affections. *If you ever so much as look at another man, soldier–boy, I'll wipe you off the face of the earth*, Jonathan had said on more than one occasion, in some Holiday Inn or other, backing on to an industrial park – where, below their second-storey window, a corrugated-iron porte côchère, overlaid with damp folds of rubberised carpet underlay, sheltered several large canisters of acidic blue fluid. Oh God! weeds gripping the crumbling edges of concrete hard-standing ... Oh my! the swish from the bypass seeping in through the warped window frames ... Oh no! the ironing board clipped into the cupboard – the hangers clipped on to the rail – the hairdryer clipped to the wall ... *Canderel* ... *Kenco* ... *Sweet 'n' Low* ... *softly whispering* ... *lower-and-lower* ... Don't doubt for a second I could do it, said the man who'd ... *taken my maidenhead.* I have carte blanche – you know that – and Requirements can eliminate an identity just as effectively as they can create one, and a body – even one as beautiful as yours, my darling – can be, um, dissolved in ... *large canisters of acidic blue fluid* ... *weeds gripping the crumbling edges of concrete hard-standing* ... *Assassination as a janitorial duty.* Gawain had ... *on more than one occasion* punched him lightly in the solar plexus: Shut up, you idiot – what about my family, what about the Rams? They aren't going to forget I ever existed. *But they might* ... the stillborn small voice wheedled in the small, still hours ... *they just might.* No, if there was a sinister correspondence here it was between ... *my fidelity to him* and *our rules of engagement*: Check the breech, the block, the safety, the firing pin, the magazine – check *and check again*, but never, ever, what-so-ever *fire the fucking thing.* Apart from his annual small-arms refresher course, Lieutenant-Colonel Gawain Thomas could count the number of times he'd live-fired ... *on the fingers of a Sierra Leonean leper.* Not that the Rams had got that deployment ... *but you catch my drift.* Drifting, they were ... Gawain had seen colleagues grow so bored and frustrated they'd lubricate their penises, then thrust them down the barrels of their guns. They were tethered to reality – not by *big boys' rules*, but solely by these pansy ones of "engagement": *In Bosnia – that grim winter . . . all of 'em at it – just down the road, behind the wire . . . a rack of lamb – picked clean in a ragged blue-check shirt . . . a freezer lorry stopped – blue corpses inside . . . Us trying to look martial in our gay blue berets . . . Ooh, lookit me tam, mam! Children's faces – more blue bricks in a wall of death . . . We did fuck-all but observe a two-can rule – apart from the Boss . . . Out jogging with him . . . boots crunching on hoarfrost . . . thin ice on puddles pistol-cracking . . . Stopped for slugs of slivovitz every twenty paces – eventually he toppled into a ditch and after a while longer. . . slid down the chain of command . . .* The call had come at the arms fair . . . *which is why I'm still there . . .* Fiona had been expecting again . . . *Miffy, our youngest – my favourite . . . to be honest . . .* so Gawain invested in a mobile phone and paid still more to receive calls overseas . . . *it rang while I was actually squatting,* agitating the bunched-up fabric. The voice on the other end hadn't been hers . . . *clenched by pain,* but the Adjutant's: Gawain, izzat you? Bill, here, back at base . . . John, the current SeeOh, had been Colonel Renfrew's own appointment – favouring this piss-artist over his own son-in-law had been him doing his bit for the life-or-death struggle against . . . *nepotism.* John had never had what it took to command the Rams, anyway: he lacked the necessary imagination to look out over a broad plain, upon which his overwhelming firepower had been beautifully arrayed, and . . . *make-believe another exercise was for real.* And so he drank . . . *then slowly sank,* until . . . – Thing is, Gawain, John's taken rather a turn for the worse . . . Well, to get right to the point, he's in one of those rehab' places – not an upmarket one, though, no sign of Daniella Westbrook trumpeting the Last Post out of her hooter . . . When Gawain told his lover . . . *the Butcher laughed like a drain*, then reached for a miniature of Cockspur and chucked it back . . . *How do I know this?* Gawain knows it because *a nice undercoat of over-proof* – as he'd put it – was Jonathan's favoured tipple at the time, and, although Gawain might've considered it . . . *within my remit* to worry about his lover's drinking, he didn't, because let's face it, worrying about people's drinking is *like shaving a dog*: there simply isn't an obvious point . . . *at which you'd stop*. Gawain stopped – he'd voided himself entirely while he received the call. Cleansed, he'd floated back through the antechamber . . . *of hell*. And now, remembering the dirge his lover so often droned in the shower, Gawain concludes: that moment in New Delhi had indeed been it. After knocking and knocking and *hammering* – after standing on the little dais *full of shit* and ordering grown men to unlimber and ready to fire . . . *a toy-fucking-gun*, after suffering the dreadful weight of the chainmail bib . . . *on my shoulder*, he was finally going to be admitted to the inner sanctum, where men commanded men to kill, who were then killed in turn, and the only decisive factors were war-fighting spirit and sheer . . . *force of arms*. The old Lee Enfields the Corps used to monkey about with – the EssAy eighties they trained with at Sandhurst, and the geepee-emmgees they learnt to fire during exercises. The thirty-millimetre cannons armouring the Fighting Rams' steely steeds he'd made it his business to understand right down to the minutiae of their aiming and calibration – while the Sig Sauer he favoured as a sidearm he could indeed disassemble, clean, reassemble and load . . . *in my sleep*. He thought of all the lethal potential latent in these steel tubes and crimped brass canisters – lying dormant, awaiting the deft, unthinking fingers of young men . . . *and a few young women* to awaken them into death-dealing life. Young men . . . *and a few young women* who'd been told and taught and instructed and trained and told again . . . *annagain* how to strip and clean and reassemble and load and aim but never actually *commit to the deadly deed* . . . Had he believed back then, sat up in the small hours in his study-bedroom at Sandhurst . . . *a well-folded bed-block fitted exactly in the desk drawer*, blancoing the epaulettes of his blues with a *fucking la-la-la-toothbrush* – had Gawain *baa-baa-baa-b'lieved* in the army as an instrument that protects those things . . . those values which the country holds dear? *Abso-la-la-lutely!* – Standing in the moonlight – the mocking, flippant moonlight – outside the school disco, watching through the window as the girls bussed in from their sister school pulled up their knee-socks, Gawain had felt no sweaty-palmed nerves, rather he'd agonised at his own lack of enthusiasm . . . *they weren't the partners I wanted*, while being tormented by the perennial question: Will I ever, ever, get to . . . *join this party?* Will you keep the balloon tightly wedged up between your thighs? Will you keep a tight grip on the *handkles* of the human wheelbarrow whose arms-for-wheels buckle beneath you? But most of all: Will you keep everyone's morale up? — Morale is all-important, even as it pisses away from him into the grimly lit toilet of the orders group conference call: the Coldstreamers are steaming, the Anglians want out – the EssEff bods up in Baghdad are *decapitating suspected insurgents with piano wire* . . . or so Gawain's been told . . . *and fucking filming it to boot.* Yet no one, repeat: no-fucking-one is prepared to discuss the . . . *wider picture.* All shop talk is strictly operational . . . *or patriotic piffle.* Which, to be honest, is understandable – justifiable, even. The success of his own marriage is due – or so Gawain jokes *while the guys look at me oddly* – to the same professional focus: Mark in ninety-three, Paul in ninety-five – and their beloved, floppy-eared baby, Miffy, in two thousand. All were the dividends accrued by prioritising operational consider-ations: an outfit like the Thomas family – flexible, responsive, inherently *manoeuvrist* – required a full complement, just like the wider regimental family it was embedded in . . . *the fam' cell.* And if Gawain needed blind-drunkenness as his Viagra, then this was simply one of those wider political issues not within the remit of a serving officer . . . *or his long-haired General.* And if a serving officer's wife chose, in between dutifully squeezing out new recruits, to take a part-time job, off-establishment, as the peeay to a local haulage contractor whose bluff and manly exterior concealed a bluffer and still more manly interior . . . Get the door, love, and get your knickers off – I'm gagging fer it . . . *Her strewn hair and stripped white thighs – his pendulous ball sack swinging as he manoeuvres her around . . . His balls slapping against the backs of those cellulite-crinkled thighs as he takes her from behind – a position her horn-headed husband also prefers . . .* Well – well then! What was this, if not professional-ism, pure and simple? All marriages – Gawain hypothesises, as he'd been taught to at staff college, extrapolating from the small sample he had . . . *us, Mum and Derek – his various weird liaisons since they split* . . . – have this screaming silence surrounding them . . . *a Herc's corkscrew descent into a war zone, cabin negatived by the phos' glow of chaff* . . . out of which speaks the still, small voice . . . *of the loadie*: I think it'd be helpful, Gawain, if you organised some sort of talk or briefing for the Wags – 'course they hear all kinds of stuff from the men, but what do they actually know? Hakuna matata, that's all they should know – Hakuna matata and *I'll protect you*, which was what he'd whispered to Miffy when he found her in the kitchen at some unearthly hour, and, as she sipped the milk he'd warmed for her, she'd wept and wailed: Are you going to die, Daddy? Gawain had snorted at the very idea: Fat chance of that – fat chance of a posthumous VeeSee . . . *not where I'm headed.* But it was small wonder little Myfanwy Thomas had been so upset – those last few weeks before the coaches pulled up outside the sports hall the Rams had been running around *like . . . like . . . headless sheep*, while their boss was on the phone fifty times a day, talking to command at brigade level and at division level – and, on one faintly delirious dial-up, chatting to the remf at the EmmOhDee who was titularly responsible for the entire battle order. To directly lobby for inclusion would be worse than useless – that'd been his father-in-law's mistake in the run-up to Desert Shield. Got too pushy – pushed and pushed 'til he'd a rep' for being pushy – and who wants a pushy git on board? So, no direct lobbying – but to suggest, to imply, to stress the readiness of one's regiment to join the fray – all this was expected of him . . . *and some.* On mess nights, the expectant faces of his fellow officers were illuminated by the silvery radiance of the table ornament – a large silver ram rampant, its woollily metallic neck hung about with talismanic battle honours: little gilded plaques engraved with the names of famous parties the regiment had got to join – Omdurman, Balaclava, Mafeking, Ypres and Lüneburg Heath . . . *He was like me – his beret was some sort of johnny, keeping all that spunk in . . . It fuelled him – made him a martinet. Hung a sign on his tent flap during the desert campaign: I'm ninety-nine per cent fit . . . are you?* At first they were going before Christmas and everyone was in a frenzy . . . *you have to reach a critical mass before you can spread the load*, the mechanics up-armouring the vehicles, troopers jogging back and forth to the Queue-Emm to borrow Allen keys for that irritating counter-sunk bolt – then lying on their bunks, laboriously composing ten-line letters to be read . . . *when they're dead.* Do you believe? he'd once asked Fiona, and she gave him a look . . . *actions speak louder than words.* The only time the question occurred to her sacrilegious husband was when they were at church parade on Sundays, and awash in the gentle surges of orthodox piety . . . *give us this day our daily dead.* Beset by the weeping groan of the organ, Gawain was always visited by these monitory words: *Never tell a military man he doesn't know the cost of war . . .* but could never remember who'd said them. Standing in sweetly sweaty brushed-cotton *fur*, her normally tightly braided hair unloosed . . . *floppy bunny!* He held Miffy in his arms and felt the taut bow of her little spine – held her and thought about all the lethal threats out there. He saw her mashed on a car bonnet, or her eyes exploded into *myxomatosis mush* – and all . . . all . . . because her father was a lying, cheating, perverted . . . *sham – a lady who loves Milk Tray . . . a chocolate soldier who's . . . hollow . . . to . . . the . . . core.* Did he still love Jonathan – had he ever? They'd spent the vast majority of their relationship . . . *elsewhere*, their love . . . *if that's what it is*, was mostly *chaff – electronic interference*. It occurred to Gawain – once . . . twice . . . *a thousand times a month* – that in deceiving everyone around them . . . *we're only fooling ourselves*. Yes, they were fool's errands, their liaisons – a way for them to experience same-sex relations without any fear of exposure: their romantic motto wasn't Amor vincit omnia but . . . *mutually assured destruction*. All it would need was one instance of cack-handed tradecraft and . . . *that'll be it*: he'd come home from a hard day on the phone to find the stunted apple tree in the front yard bowed down still more by its crop of *unseasonable fruit* – while Fiona would be standing in their bedroom window, chucking out more of his clothes while screaming: He's a fucking poof! My husband's a fucking poof! And all these years he's been screwing a spook! So, every scrap of paper shredded – every call record, text message and email deleted. To begin with it'd only heightened the excitement of their affair – evenings, in front of some sedative teevee, Gawain would suddenly clutch at his pocket, terrified he'd forgotten, and that the back-lit lettering I-LOVE-YOU was shining through its material. So he said it *over and over again* throughout the years: I hate the idea – he stroked his lover's saturnine cheek and bestowed several light kisses on it – that if anything were to happen nothing of us would remain. It'd be as if . . . as if . . . none of it'd ever happened . . . Jonathan rolled sideways on to his hip, and, in the sickening radiance of the low-energy bulb affixed to the emmdee-eff headboard of *some executive bed or other*, Gawain saw the smooth pale skin slip-slide over his lover's ribs . . .

so very thin – yet so very strong: Oh, I shouldn't bother about that, Teddy Bear – he'd've groped for Marlboro and lighter . . . *'cause he always does* – it might be fatal for common-or-garden muck-spreaders, but that's not our style. 'Sides, I'm a professional, which is why I've kept everything –. – Everything? Listening to his far-flung colleagues . . . *whistling down the wind*, he recalls taking his lover's neat chin in his fingers, pressing his thumb into its . . . *dear dimple – over!*, so summoning this troubling response: Yep, that's right – everything: every phone call and letter, text message and email, going all the way back to that first note I sent you – you remember, addressed to you in your capacity as Regimental Liaison? Gawain remembered it perfectly well then – and can picture it clearly now: the manila marketing envelope, its *frosted* window on a . . . . *chillily matter-of-fact morning*, then his words – his *hot, hot carnal* words tumbling from the waxen folds: *Touching . . . holding . . . kissing . . . Such joy! Never experienced before – you don't seem to know the poem, but you are my perfect knight, Gawain dearest – I believe utterly in you – your chivalry, your chastity . . . You'll stay here, locked up in the citadel of my heart . . . I'll split myself in two: half of me will go hunting for meat for our table, but half of me will stay here in the castle with you – stay with you and* . . . in the fly-blown Portakabin a ghostly hand lightly brushes the hairs on the inside of Gawain's thigh, glides upwards . . . *tempt you – constantly, insistently . . . tempt you to betray me* . . . – You've kept that? Gawain's had been the indignation of the . . . *patronised*. How could you keep that note when I bloody well destroyed it! – Oh, have you not heard of copies, my only dearest one? Sarcasm always leavened Jonathan's usual flat tones:

332

D'you not know ours is the age of the copy, the version and the simulation? I'm surprised it hasn't occurred to you before, given your status as a . . . *chocolate soldier melting in the high noon of a fool's bloody errand!* So, he'd kept it all – but where? Where the fuck was it, this . . . this . . . *Large Data-set*, because that's what Jonathan termed it: It's all metrics and analysis now, Major Dick – everything we can know is computable. I can analyse the meta-data of our large and loving correspondence – the time and duration of calls, the location of both sender and receiver – or I can examine the content: your gruff little billets doux, with their oh-so-affecting sign-offs: Cheers, Gawain . . . Your Friend, Gawain . . . even – when you forget yourself in the formalities, my sweet spunky sheep – *Major G. Thomas, Acting Adjutant* . . . Then, halfway through December, the Rams were stood down: The fuckers! The dense, stupid, idiotic . . . FUCKERS! It'd been a rare outburst from the Colonel – heard only by his Two-EyeSee, Major Townshend, known to his men as Townie . . . *'cause he goes up there all the time* – but to his fellow officers – and his Sandhurst contemporaries in particular – as *Tizer, Big T, the Orange Drinker, The Frothy Man, the Ring-Pull-meister.* Tizer, who'd been top-dog for so long it was inevitable he'd start . . . *howling on the way down.* Not then, though – all he'd grunted was, You gotta getta grip, Greeny – to which Gawain had snarled: It's just a farce, Tizer, a bloody farce – and the curtain hasn't even gone up yet . . . Christmas came well wrapped and left *in tatters* . . . The Rams, *fighting unfit* wheezed out carols in the camp church, then . . . *headed for the hills.* So did the Thomas fam' cell: there was a hotel lunch in Crickhowell.

Grandad Derek took little Myfanwy on his lap – except that Derek Thomas no longer went by that name, but rather styled himself Uther and wreathed himself further in the Celtic Twilight by wearing a purple velour cloak, with a woman's white silk slip underneath . . . *said it was a kirtle*, and strange hessian leggings . . . *or puttees* he'd cross-gartered to above his . . . *dandling knee.* Your lot at the right point in the rotation? he'd asked – taking, as he still did, a keen interest in his son's deployments: At the right point to join the party, that is? And Gawain gave him the details he required – *'cause it's all da-da-details for military men.* It was strictly against orders – and in direct contravention of the OhEssAy, which Gawain assumes he must've signed somewhere . . . *along the way*, but so what? Who was Uther going to find to utter it to? How would Jonathan have put it . . .? Yes: Saddam's spooks would have to insinuate someone under *the natural hempen cover* of Big Sid's tepee if they wanted to catch Uther, the worse for his potty training and . . . *babbling away*: Charlie Company was down at Caerfin in November. Clawed 'em back – and now we're all ready to go . . . hung out to dry awaiting orders, Dad . . . And awaiting them some more . . . And some more . . . A cartoon spider's web is spun between the pink tip of Gawain's nose and the handle of his spoon, as he sits at the breakfast table reading the report on the Prime Minister's speech: according to Blair the fresh intelligence is . . . *substantive, authoritative and compelling*, while according to Jonathan De'Ath it's . . . *secondary, suspect and almost certainly compromised.* Gawain hopes Blair doesn't let his Christian conscience hobble his messianic belief in his own destiny – he tries to talk about this with Jonathan, but his lover has his limits, his boundaries, his . . . *lines of defence*: No can do, soldier – I could tell you what's going on at the JayEyeSee – or up any number of Whitehall's innumerable and tightly coiled back passages . . . I could tell you, sure – but then . . . He'd throttled Gawain's semi-erect cock and lisped Russian-film-baddy . . . *I vooud haff to keel you!* — Has Trooper Bessemer been to see you, Gawain? Fiona had said at that breakfast . . . *or one very like it*: Cheerios and toast, skimmed milk for the lonely sclerotic heart . . . *home is where the Hostess trolley is*. When they were first together, Gawain hadn't altogether appreciated her unfussy off-the-peg domesticity: job-lots of fixtures and fittings – easy-to-wipe blinds and frumpy soft furnishings. Why would she've had any better taste . . . *than me* – after all, they were both forces brats, accustomed to picking up sticks every few years, so there was no call for any homely tokens that couldn't be portaged to the next campsite. But, as the years had passed, and they'd been to Germany . . . *and back again*, to Cyprus . . . *and bloody back again*, so these never-ending rotations – an infinitely extended run of their fathers' end-of-the-imperialist-pier show – began to torment him: for if you simply went round and around, again *annagain* . . . well, you never actually got *anywhere at all* . . . He fixated on the porridge-grey louvres hanging in the youpeeveecee frames of their married quarters – he fantasised tearing the aluminium rods from the stair treads and hurling them in her . . . *tasteless fucking face*, because his true lover, while minimising his own home decoration, nonetheless . . . *knew how it should be done*. Yes, if there's one attrib-ute Jonathan De'Ath possesses above all others, it's his succulent, juicy, pink-in-the-middle . . . *taste*. Gawain had looked up from the fanatically folded *bed-block* of his Telegraph: she was standing over him, dumpy in a novelty apron printed with a caricature of a neater, slimmer female form: bared breasts and a naked, neutered belly: Why d'you ask, darling? he'd said, entering this endearment in the double-entry account, so magically offsetting . . . *a solid decade of adultery . . . semper-fucking-Fi*. Before she could reply they'd been interrupted by Mark, who propped himself in the kitchen door and said, I'm off now, Mum. Mark, who in the months and weeks leading up to the deployment . . . *needed me the most*. He was at that difficult stage in his development when a growing lad is on the point of bursting into adolescence. Mark had stood then – remains standing now, in the murk of his father's mind, with his soon to be spotty face . . . *and my shifty eyes*, standing, his tie yanked down into . . . *a hangman's knot*, his blazer sleeves rolled up, an Adidas *saddlebag* bulging on his hip, a hand-me-down Nokia in his hand . . . *and what a childish strop he got into about that*. He'd been a figure-eleven target for fatherly criticism: You may be off now, Mark, but I'm also leaving very soon – y'know that, don't you? The boy's sandy lashes *mine, too* fluttered. Yeah, he'd said . . . *or surliness to the same effect*, and his father blazed away: Well, you should also know that were I to enter a combat zone with your degree of personal hygiene and general readiness, I wouldn't last five-bloody-minutes! When Mark had gone, Fiona said, Do you have to talk to him like that? And Gawain came back: I'm simply telling him what's what – he's old enough to know. Yes, indeedy – and old enough as well to hear SeeEssEmm Rowley's

336

parade-ground screech: *Yeeouorribblefuckin'littlepieceofWelshshitThomas Ifuckin'hateyouyoulazyslovenlypansy!* internalised twenty years since, but still howling down the years. Fiona was washing up, so accompanied her remarks with duff percussion: And *tink-tonk* Trooper Bessemer, he's *clink-clank* old enough to know, is he? – Know what? Gawain had been back in the newspaper, which he only ever read on a need-to-know basis, scanning anything which seemed *operationally relevant* . . . His fiancée, girl called *tink-tonk* Carol, came to see me . . . Yes, Gawain had thought: yes, of course she'd gone to see the regiment's . . . *real SeeOh.* Despite this professional rivalry Gawain remained grateful to Fiona – grateful for her mothering of all these lost boys . . . *our own sons included.* So pathetically grateful that every time he'd cause for more gratitude – which in the run-up to the deployment was a daily occurrence – it'd stiffened his resolve: *She will never, ever find out* . . . Her husband would maintain the eternal vigilance of a simple man leading . . . *a sophisticated double life.* Fiona had pressed on: Any-*tink*-way, she's a *tonk* sensitive *clank* soul, this *clink* Carol, and she wants to do right by her trooper. She's fallen pregnant, you see . . . An odd expression – whenever Gawain heard it, he'd see in his mind's eye a tiny Missus Icarus in a Mothercare smock, with melting Fisher-Price wings, tumbling out of . . . *a Clearblue sky* . . . and she doesn't know what to tell him before he heads overseas. Standing, folding his paper, grasping the hem of his tunic and yanking it down . . . *I am the very model of a modern major-gen-er-al!* Gawain had said words to this effect: Really? I'd've thought she'd be keen to let him know – nothing better than impending fatherhood to make a man mind his back in a war zone. – Except he isn't a man, is he, Greeny? . . . Fiona would wheel out the nickname whenever she wanted to make a serious point – why? Because she understands that, while Gawain-the-man may be emotionally absent, Greeny-the-Ram is always . . . *operationally present: They shall not return to us, the resolute, the young* . . . He's a boy, and this Carol knows her boy well enough – knows he isn't likely to cope with the truth. – The truth? What truth? – The truth that *she isn't carrying another little Bessemer* . . . What'd been the upshot of this unscheduled Regimental Parents' Meeting? Sat staring at the Iraqi bint's *preposterous minge*, Gawain reflects: parenting has always been a major component of any SeeOh's job in peacetime – quite possibly the main one. And in time of war, what kind of parent was he becoming? One who sent his much loved children forward to be torn apart by a camel's head exploding through the un-armoured chassis of their Land Rover . . . *abusive – an abusive parent*. And if they knew his truth – that he was queer? Why, to these lads it'd be as bad as their finding out their SeeOh's *a nonce – a kiddy-fiddler . . . a paedo . . . deserving of petrol-soaked rags through the letter-box . . . It was the son wot he done it to . . .* Yes, I'm an abusive parent and a hands-on dad, Gawain reflects, staring at his hands *sunbursting* on the vinyl blotter, which in turn rests on the metal desktop. One of the containers they'd dragged all the way from the aypod turned out to be half full of office furniture. The sign on the tailgate read KEEP BACK! ONE HUNDRED METRES! WARNING! in both English and Arabic – why? 'Cause if you're dumb enough to pull up to my bumper, baby, in your dirty-white Toyota pickup, we'll riddle your stinking knobbly-rag 'ead *with point-seven-six-five rounds* . . . You touch our office equipment and you'll be wrapped in your shroud with a ball of hard-packed earth under your near-severed head, ready for planting before the first call to prayer, *so help me, Allah!* Yes, a hands-on dad who's been keeping an eye on Bessemer: Everything all right, Trooper? Bat ears – burnt face *fatty-greasy bacon* beneath the camo' netting – larking about, he was, 'til being surprised by the SeeOh: Everything all right, Trooper? His playmates, the gooey ends of . . . *lollipops* poking from their chapped lips, *flies in their eyes* . . . stop goosing Bessemer as Gawain comes up. – Sir? Eyes front, expressions *sniggerserious*, eyeing their SeeOh, who stands before them, legs slightly parted, beret at an exact thirty degrees to the . . . *sandy horizon of my own brows*, one thumb tucked in webbing belt, the other precisely aligned with the butt of his nine-millimetre Sig Sauer . . . *ally as I'd be in my Guccis: there's a bit of the dandy in all of us, eh, Rodders.* Making sure you're getting enough fluid down you, lads? Plenty of wets – helps with the heat. Those rehydration salts in your field packs – they're pretty much essential in this heat . . . It's only oh-seven-hundred but under this *water-tight tarp'* of concern, Lieutenant-Colonel Thomas is . . . *melting*, his underpants are *sodden – Let me take those off with my . . . teeth!* is what his lover likes to say . . . *as we're getting our sweds down.* – Such passion! Such raw, unadulterated passion – could it possibly have endured this long if they'd been together, wandering the leafy aisles of some out-of-town garden centre . . . *bickering over begonias?* All good, sir, Bessemer had said – and then: Routine for our multiple is, Sarge won't count us out 'less we've a full Camelbak an' twenty more litres

on board . . . But his SeeOh had seen through Bessemer's readiness
– seen through the reddish fuzz of the trooper's number one, looked
past the streaky-red rinds of his ears. Gawain had eyedeed the weak
chin and the bony wrists of the . . . *committed masturbator* – also registered his bemusement: *Why am I getting all this fatherly attention?*
— The orders group is reaching *inconclusion*: the Adjutant running
rapidly through the list, receiving snappy Rogers and batting back
still-snappier Roger Outs . . . *the first shall be last.* Anything further,
Gawain? – Well . . . speculative stuff, sir, but there're indications of
some sort of link-up between these bad boys coming over the border
and our local, um, Ali Babas. – Response? - Prob'ly a good idea
to do a few hard knocks in town, see what the local notables
have stashed in their knicker-drawers . . . Well . . . the GeeOhSee's
bass-baritone booms over the radio net . . . *eucalyptus and honey –*
keep those airways clear! . . . be seriously careful, Gawain – the sitch
in Baghdad is, as you know, problematic, and the insurgents are,
ah . . . exporting their tactics. *And I wonder who's fucking fault that*
is! – Roger – Roger that – Roger*ing Missus Major-General on a big*
old brass bedstead: Ooh–ooh! Roger . . . *Her finely stitched lacy skin* . . .
crawling . . . *Ooh–ooh! Ro–oger* . . . -out! *But the idle-minded overlings,*
who quibbled while they died . . . *Shall they thrust for high–employment,*
as of old? The noble cadences fade away into the hot and dusty
recesses of Gawain's memory, and for a few moments he follows
them into a past in which . . . *I had a brilliant career ahead of me.*
Then he shakes his . . . *knobbly knob-head*, and before he can be
cut in two yanks off the cans, rises, takes two rocking paces and
yanks open the door: Camp Val, named for General Sir Valentine

Carmichael-Harrington, EmmSee, DeeEssOh and Bar . . . *brilliant tactician . . . unbeatable war record . . . abusive bully*, is spread out before him in all its aggressive simplicity: scabrous and tumbled-down concrete walls on all four sides that've been Hesco-reinforced. There're sangars at each corner and flanking the main gate, while a low jumble of flat-roofed and squalid structures occupies the north-west corner. A helipad is marked out on the dusty maidan, and six or seven Portakabins – of which the comms room is one – in the south-east corner, and scattered just about everywhere else – but mostly concentrated along the eastern wall – are . . . *tents – fucking tents!* It's just as well the local troublemakers haven't taken to lobbing mortars into the camp . . . *'cause there's barely any hard cover.* Camp Val is home to about a thousand men, boys, *and one or two mannish women.* There's no chogee shop for the men, so they've taken to diverting patrols through the bazaar, where they can load up with lollipops, toiletries, knocked-off fags . . . *Marlborough, Pell-Mell* and biscuits of . . . *the Nice type.* Gawain could have put a stop to these shopping expeditions altogether but . . . *flexibility is the essence of command*, especially if you're a . . . *fucking bender.* He could've enforced the two-can rule rigidly as well, rather than turning a myopic eye to its persistent infringement. *Still* . . . on his regular trips down to Basra, what'd struck Gawain wasn't the obvious tension in the streets, the limbless beggars or the red-faced Brits clumping through the vulgar marble halls of their Basra Palace aitchqueue – but the obviousness with which they were . . . *murdering it.* He'd seen squaddies flagrantly filling Camelbaks with cans of Foster's – and when he went to talk to some scaley about glitches with the eye-net, the man'd had the nerve to pull a bottle of Bell's from his desk drawer and ask if Gawain fancied . . . *a wee dram.* There was some tipsiness up at Camp Val – but no outright drunkenness, despite the extra workload of having to support hundreds of Kiwi sheep-shaggers – a considerable force that'd entered the theatre with no defined role . . . *no lines* and no logistical support. Which is what you require to operate effectively any of the following: laser-guided and computer-controlled anti-aircraft systems, squadrons of advanced aypeesees, multiple-launch surface missiles . . . *and so-bloody-on.* Gawain had explained to all the prospects he'd canvassed during his nine months of flogging arms on behalf of AitchEmmGee: Along with your bespoke suit of Chobham armour, gentlemen, comes our dedicated after-sales service . . . *a bunch of dull, uniformed techies on hand to oil your war machine* – plus Jonathan, or some of his pals, pitching up at our embassy to keep an eye on things and apply a little . . . *hands-on parenting*: Hold it like this, aim it like that – this has a range of ex kilometres. Night-sight capability? But of course: simply put on these goggles and at once you'll be plunged into another dimension, where your enemies' heat-signatures worm through the greenish haze of my own . . . *toxic-fucking envy.* That was the deal, wasn't it? The furtive men, with their unshaven sock-puppet faces veiled by cigarette smoke, and their poor taste in . . . *expensive suits.* It was these cowards who'd be the heroes – or at least provide them with logistical support. They who'd take the salute, from the dais, beneath the triumphal arch . . . *they say the detail is impressive – right down to the hairs on the backs of the hands that hold the scimitars.* It's they who'll stand in the hellish light of a burning government building, fending off fuzzy-wuzzies with a fire-flobbing AyKay, while I sit back in this Rolls-Royce of a military machine with my . . . *foot off the bloody accelerator.* In New Delhi, in the toilet stall, all the shitty-Greeny-envy had *pissed out of me* . . . into the filthy hole between the filthy footings. Hovering over his own haunches, *adopting a manoeuvrist approach*, he'd directed the jet and finally . . . *hit the target*: I see . . . I see . . . I see . . . *I'm the new fucking SeeOh!* — Well, he'd said to Bill, I'd better get back as soon as I can, then. He'd touched the button and the most momentous phone call of his career was over. He'd rocked on his haunches as he inserted the Nokia Seven-One-One-Oh back into his bunched-up pocket. Surely, you were never more . . . more . . . what was the word . . . ? *Embodied* – that was it: embodied, than when you were doing a shit. Yet he'd also felt *smeared through space*: a brownish stain, arcing high above the clear waters of the Indian Ocean, across the desert sands, the Mediterranean and the liberal democracies of Western Europe he was . . . *sworn to defend*, before finally falling back to the earth. Soon enough, he'd ruminated, smearing shit around *annaround* his chilli-stung arsehole, he'd be smearing behind it back to Catterick – via Scotch Corner in the rain . . . *and how triumphal is that?* A congratulatory greeting from Fiona – her tacky coral lips . . . *smearing my cheek*, then a speedily scheduled meeting with the full complement of officers in the briefing room. Gawain at the lectern, burping sulphurously – the mega-antibiotic had started working within twenty-four hours, just as the aitchqueue quack said it would . . . *and I burped along with the jetstream.* While I'm awaiting final confirmation of my promotion . . . he told the serried faces . . . e*nvious, envious, envious, indifferent, hung-over, envious – possibly insane* . . . I think the best we can do as a light cavalry unit will be exactly what our Queen and country needs . . . *jut of Patton jaw, shoulders back – chest out*. Gentlemen – and lady – Gawain nodded in the direction of the Rams' new medic, Lieutenant Gail Petersen, whose blonde curls, snub nose, freckles and goo-goo-blue eyes strongly suggested she'd be . . . *another fucking liability* – the geopolitical situation, as I'm sure you're aware, is in a period of rapid transition. In terms of the armed forces' remit, the question is no longer whether we'll see action – but when. Our task is to shear our woolly troopers, for too long now we've been put out to graze – it's time we put the fighting back in the Fighting Rams. A and B squadrons under my command will depart for the Naytoe exercise in Canada at the end of next week. This presents an excellent opportunity for us to begin transforming the regiment overall into a completely manoeuvrist unit. From now on . . . *chest out, eyes front* . . . our entire effort will be focused on the following priorities: physical fitness, mental robustness – and, most important of all, war-fighting spirit! – Afterwards came the sneering: Youngest SeeOh in the Rams' distinguished history is it, Greeny? Later – much, much later – Gawain thought back to Major "Tizer" Townshend's iffy behaviour in the run-up to the deployment. By then, after sitting for hours in an office at Shaibah, waiting for the investigating red hat, he'd had plenty of time to also recall these words from a training manual issued to his int' cell by the green slime who'd instructed them at Chicksands: *Aim to provoke* *humiliation, insecurity and disorientation.* Wearily concluding this must've been Tizer's intention as well – one Gawain had sought to frustrate immediately by putting an arm round his shoulders and guiding him away from his brother officers ... *so much unforced physical contact in the army – it's scrumming down for ... a lifetime*: So, Andy, I realise this is a blow for you ... Tizer's expression was *an exercise in studied indifference*, while his small black eyes, glittering with envy, had tracked back and forth across Gawain's chest ... *leading my fugitive heart.* As the lecturer at Staff College had said ... *Hup! Two, three ... four times: The character of any military unit is intimately connected to the character of its commander –* with Tizer as SeeOh the Rams would've had plenty of war-fighting spirit, certainly, and become *as fit as butcher's dogs*, yet they'd've also been slapdash ... quite possibly aggressive as well – too aggressive. There was the incident when Trooper Sweeney ended up in the infirmary – high jinks that'd got *a little out of hand*, or so all parties concerned ... *agreed to say*, although Gawain wasn't so sure. One thing he was certain of, though, by the time *the balloon finally went up* – the massive, silk and ornately brocaded balloon, with its vast gondola, big enough to house geese, ducks, guinea pigs and plenty of Fighting Rams – the regiment was indeed taking on the character of its commander ... *secretive, divided, insecure* and *humiliated.* The Saskatchewan jaunt had turned out to be the Rams' best exercise ever, and the absolute confirmation of Gawain's skills as a panzer commander – not only providing excellent long-range recon', but also demonstrating how a manoeuvrist doctrine, properly understood and flawlessly executed, could result in the elimination of a far larger *lumpa-lumpa-lumpa* force . . . *Lumpa-lumpa, lumpa-lumpa, lumpa-lumpa* . . . the rows of alien spacecraft sank inexorably down the screen . . . *shitting out bombs: cheeuwww-cheeuwww-cheeuwww!* Gawain, aged *n-n-n-nineteen*, jabbed the button with his thumb while expertly taking a swig of his pint with his other *lumpa-lumpa, lumpa-lumpa, lumpa-lumpa* . . . hand. It'd been that easy – as easy as playing Space Invaders in the student union bar. By the time dusk rolled over the wide expanse of dirt and shrubbery, so many Blue Force outfits had been put out of action it was long after dark before the support crews dragged them all back to base. Handshakes all round – and a YouEssEmm four-star general . . . *Phelps? Phillips?* made a special point of complimenting Gawain within hearing-range of his own GeeOhSee, which was *thoughtful*, and afforded the Rams' new SeeOh with the pretext to come out with some *like shooting fish in a barrel* self-deprecation. P'raps this is what being successful feels like, Gawain had mused . . . *a fucking cliché*. After that there'd been an awful lot more beers, and a night of rising from and falling back to his bed . . . *a human water-feature*. In the morning Gawain rose for good and headed to the deefac, where he drank dreadful Canadian coffee, ate . . . *eggy medals* and blearied over the Rams' shorn heads at a wall-mounted teevee. They'd all seen it live: a new world of possibilities rise up as the second of the towers collapsed in a cloud of toxic speculation. Is this the habit of command? he'd thought, because the news thread running across the bottom of the screen looked uncannily like . . . *baa-baa-baa braid*: a two-up promotion, that's what the deadliest terrorist attack ever on American soil made Gawain

Thomas think about . . . *even as it was happening.* It wasn't a snow globe that'd been shaken up, but a . . . *sand one – bought on a day trip to Ventnor and more or less immediately . . . broken. The pretty colours trickled through my . . . fingers.* There was no possibility of the Rams getting a 'Stan deployment – if anyone were to go, it'd be EssEff bods or the Paras. The months passed, the diplomats shuttled – while Gawain shuffled about the establishment, trying to engender war-fighting spirit. By the time Blix was . . . *buggering about in the desert* he was close to despair. I don't believe I'm speaking out of turn, Jonathan had said, turning Gawain's face to his own, but I can assure you of this much: TeeBee is gonna do everything necessary to get this vote – I've seen the light of destiny in the man's eyes, seen it up close and personal. If he could, he'd have us and the plods grubbing up dirt on every single vacillating EmPee . . . *A fool's errand*, that's what they'd all been on – even as Jonathan's cigarette smoke was warming his neck, Gawain had seen the painted frieze of parliamentarians unroll around the dado of Room Three-Nineteen in the Sudbury Days Inn – which can be easily accessed via the EmmTwentyfive. Brightly painted into their suits, they marched into the division lobbies. A fool's errand, indeed – not that Gawain thinks of it as such until two more years have . . . *bimbled by*, and he finds himself, the orders group conference call fading from his mind, standing with the sun drilling through the camo' netting slung over the Wimmiks. Standing with his Adjutant, the dependable, unflashy, *unflappable* Major Kevin Armstrong, and haggling – *Yes! Haggling!* – over who should go. It's a fool's errand, Boss, Armstrong says, the Kiwis've gone a little off-piste, that's all. Get the Mayor on the blower, Gawain snaps, we need to start damage-limitation right away – what the bloody hell did those sheep-shaggers think they were doing? Anderson touches one tip of his neat moustache with his index finger, the other with his thumb . . . *feel the width*, he swallows the Fox's Glacier Mint he's been sucking, and Gawain watches his Adam's apple rise and fall . . . *time to bite the bullet.* – It's the garden chair thing, Boss – Kiwis' idea is every spectator – all the men, that is – should have one for the Six Nations. They heard about this chap over on the east bank, 'parently he's a big stash of the things . . . Armstrong even wears his aviators studiously – while his desert camos appear, if not pressed, at least . . . *dry-folded.* The Mayor of Ali al-Garbi isn't some marrow-judging worthy, but a wheedling Sheik who wears heavy, gold-plated watches on either wrist and smiles a lot, though . . . *he's fuck-all to smile about.* Gawain has only encountered him twice – once when doing the handover with the Coldstreamers' SeeOh, "Trimmer" Trimmingham. Watch out for that one, he'd said – indicating the third dish-dash along in the room full of . . . *unshaven sock-puppets* who were grubbing up handfuls of peanuts and raisins from tinfoil salvers. The Queue-man had said he could maybe get hold of some Medjool dates, but Gawain nixed this on the grounds of cultural insensitivity, given so many of the date groves – along the Shatt al-Arab and here, on the banks of the Tigris – had been . . . *shot-to-shit.* The sock-puppets coughed up Arabic and the terps spat out English – what was there to communicate anyway, save for infectious distrust? Gawain, picking up from Trimmer's briefing, spoke about provisional reconstruction

348

and military instruction teams, and the sterling work they'd be doing: building schools, hospitals and vital infrastructure – training newly recruited police and army personnel. As his words were chewed over, then regurgitated in the form of nutty burps and fruity throat-clearings, he wondered . . . *who believes this bullshit less – me or them?* Thought this – and watched hands dart out to grab thirty-three see-el bottles of water and magic them under the folds of their . . . *invisibility cloaks – although no boy wizards, they . . .* Gawain wondered at the time if this was really the essence of the current conflict: *hiding things . . .* Hiding mineral water – hiding heavy water, hiding Sarin gas. Had he ever believed the casus belli? That there were fleets of mobile EnnBeeSee units cruising about out there in the sandy sea? True, these men – Shia notables with hidden empires of their own – were hardly likely to've been entrusted with anything by the Ba'athists – nevertheless, they shared the same shattered land, where streetlamps were sawn off at the root, then carted off for scrap, and the way of settling a little neighbourly dispute was to lob a few mortar rounds over on to their rooftop – much as a Surrey householder might plant a fast-growing leylandii. *Who let the dogs out – Bush! Bush!* No! Not dogs at all but *wolvish Rams –* and here we are, *chomping at the bit*, the finest light cavalry in the world, trained to within an inch of our sodding lives, perfectly calibrated pieces of human materiel, upgraded regularly so's to be fully inter-operable with the latest computerised gun-platforms, veritable cybernetic warriors – such as Gawain saw *day in – day out . . .* fighting their way across the monitors of his sons' peesees, but reduced now – just as the army establishment overall was being constantly, politically ... *shrivelled, shrunken, withered* ... to the status of khaki-uniformed menials ordered to *scoop up the human poop* ... So here Gawain finally was, on his way to war, in profile, in a frieze of painted men, doing everything he's not meant to do – but then the guidelines – *and they are only guidelines* – would geld the Rams – leave them bleating, the better to reflect the quibbling of their ... *idle-minded overlings.* Healthy and safe, perhaps, but utterly impotent, wandering about with thick rubber bands around their useless bollocks, waiting for them to ... *drop off.* Gawain was on his way to war – the White Plastic Garden Chair War is how it'll go down in the annals. A commemorative decoration for the Rams' rampant table ornament will need to be obtained from Thos Askew and Sons, Jewellers and Engravers of Pickering, Yorkshire, est nineteen hundred and four, *ting-ting* goes the swinging door: *Difficult job, Colonel Thomas, name's too long for a standard plaquette – now, if it were El Alamein, that'd be another matter* ... Yes, that's how it'll be known – and it'll rightly be judged a conflict of a triviality to rank alongside the Soccer War, the War of the Golden Stool – to which, no doubt, it would be compared by the Staff College instructors – and the Rum Rebellion. Yes, Gawain is at last embarked on his quest – finally he'll have the opportunity to slay the green demon of his own envy. He's looking pretty fucking gleaming ... *if I say so myself* – face bronzed, muscles more toned than they've been in years, Tag Heuer sunglasses dangling around his neck – a corded, lean neck, also encircled by a scrap of khaki cravat. Riding shotgun in the lead Wimmik – again, strictly against established protocols, since that's where you'll get *a camel's head up your arse* . . . but how's a commander to earn his men's respect if he doesn't . . . *lead from the front?* Gawain feels the sweat pooling in his keks, then cooling . . . and cooling. Ice water courses down his face – he's gripped by a frozen exhilaration. The past forty months rewind, *flickering*, and he's back in the deefac on the rolling plains south of Saskatchewan – back watching the mighty tower slump to its knees and keel over into the dust of its own demolition. Then – a commercial break: *Coors Light, the Coldest-Tasting Beer in the World!* Then back to Armageddon: *Poor little Greeny!* suspended on a tightrope between the Twin Towers – out there in the void, all alone, cavorting – dancing in full-dress uniform, celebrating this vertiginously millennial moment – thrilled to the core of his masculine being as he glances to the right, to the left, and into . . . the *void.* Five minutes approx' to our arvee, Boss, the Trooper in the back shouts over the grinding engine, then to the driver: Second left! Through the dirt-filmed crescents of windscreen, Gawain sees the grubby streets strobing past – sees bleached plastic bones . . . rotting concrete organs . . . rusting corrugated-iron flesh – sees this: the very compost heap of civilisation itself, where decay's been under way for . . . *seven-thousand-bloody-years.* It was this the Rams were sworn to defend . . . *with our cocks tucked up between our legs.* Which is harder, Gawain wonders, for a camel's head to penetrate an insufficiently armoured Land Rover, or a rich man to enter the Kingdom of Heaven? *But I'm not a rich man!* His pay is adequate, and, while certainly not enough to cut his lover's dash . . . *at least what I have isn't proffed.* There were grants for the kids' education if the regiment was on a prolonged foreign posting – Fiona had some money from a spinster aunt, while Rodney might . . . *come through eventually.* But there was no long-term job security, for officers and men alike – instead they're bombarded with the management-speak to be expected in any contemporary British organisation obsessed by its own . . . *corporate culture.* The hissing quack of Trooper Hodges's cans is followed by: Man down, Boss – it's Bessemer . . . *Bessemer! Fucking Bessemer* – Bessemer, who Fiona had told him to *keep an eye on.* Bessemer, whose dumb little tart thought the thoroughly decent thing to do was to tell him the truth . . . *and how bloody selfish is that?* Her clean conscience has led directly to this . . . *dirty little incident. Man down . . . No, boy down – child down . . . My child down – the flesh-of-my-flesh . . . Bessemer down! The first casualty of this . . . children's crusade. And they're my children – so how bad is that?* Calling home from Camp Val is a complicated rigmarole – card calls, strictly rationed, can be patched through the radio net, then via an exchange at Shaibah. But some techie-minded trooper in the int' cell has figured out how to piggyback Skype calls on the wonky Iraqi internet. Gawain was unaware of this until two nights ago, when in the hot crotch of darkness he walked into the comms Portakabin and found Tizer with his keks down round his knees, *beating his meat* to the enthusiastic encouragement of an on-screen girl – a very young girl to judge by . . . *the tensility of her tits.* Ever the true and gentle knight, Gawain had simply muttered, Sorry . . . and quietly withdrawn – now, as the Wimmik clanks over a battered metal hoarding *no longer effectively advertising* Freedom Cola, he gets the sit rep' from Hodges he should've had days ago: turns out Bessemer was up for a Midnight Express call with his Carol late on Sunday – but instead of the silky Agent Provocateur lingerie he'd been expecting, he was . . . *sorely provoked*: Gary was meant to be going home in a fortnight, Boss, for the wedding . . . This Gawain already knows, having signed the authorisation himself – nevertheless, banging about in the *hot crotch* of the personnel carrier, he apprehends this fact in all of its very contemporary absurdity: Incredible! Difficult to imagine the Indian Army troops who occupied Basra in nineteen fourteen being allocated such highly compassionate leave – Difficult? Bloody impossible . . . But then, just as the nine-millimetre Sig Sauer holstered at his hip is . . . *so soft – a Dalí gun*, so the impotence of the entire British Army's deployment is confirmed by such . . . *humanitarian considerations. Confound their knavish tricks . . . Confuse their pol-i-tics . . .* Better get aitchqueue on the blower, Hodges, we'll need to have Bessemer casevaced out to the aypod asap. He turns to Ali, the ferret-faced Basrati 'terp who did the same for the Welchers . . . *You can trust him. A bit*, was all Trimmer had said. D'you know what the fuck's happened? is Gawain's blunt enquiry – and he tries to infuse this with great dollops of Jonathan's savoir faire: *I know that you know that I know that you know something I'll never fucking know – which is HOW THINGS ACTUALLY WORK HERE!* It is a difficult situation, Colonel . . . the 'terp says, twisting towards him: his *thin* body hangs down from his *thin* wrist, which is caught in a *thin* hanging strap. Outside, the earth burns in its heavenly crucible, inside the Wimmik a half-eaten packet of Starbursts waggles about in the dash-mounted cup-holder. Ali's smile is . . . *thin*, and from it emerges *slim pickings* . . . Your New Zealander colleagues were looking for these chairs, it's true, but the man who has them is an important Sheik – someone who gives hospitality in the Arab way . . . and he has friends visiting right now . . . Off course there will be upsetting . . . *Off course.* As they roar down streets empty of every living thing besides a *wonky-donkey* tethered to a *pile of shit*, Gawain interrogates the 'terp: Is this man linked to the Jam? To other Iranian-backed militias? What sort of firepower might he be able to muster? Outside, it's pushing fifty in the shade and those shadows are . . . *sharp as scimitars* – inside the Wimmik it's still hotter, and Gawain's *nadgers* . . . are . . . *boiling in their bag.* It's gloomy, too, and the complexity of light and dark passing across Ali's ferrety face expresses all the awful ambiguity of his own position: *What're we doing here? Our enemies' enemies are also our . . . enemies – and we have no real friends at all . . .* This is it, Hodges says, removing the pack of Starbursts from the cup-holder: Al-Afrika Street . . . Yes, *Al Afrika Street*, a soap opera about ordinary Iraqis going about their business in a typical post-conflict situation: cuppas of mint tea, chatting about the weather – *Ooh, it ain't 'alf 'ot, Mum – innanout* of each other's houses with each other's *white plastic garden chairs . . .* Only the central grid of Ali al-Garbi's streets, laid out in the seventies before the Great Patriotic War, are metalled – out here in the 'burbs there are no pavements, while the roadways are dust-fields . . . *irrigated with raw sewage.* Gawain stands, sun-blinded, blinking down at his boots, each surrounded by concentric rings . . . *dust-waves.* He looks up and sees a poster of Muqtada al-Sadr smilingly jollily in black turban and robe. He looks way up: a single off-white cloud is chalked on the slate sky . . . *wool caught on barbed wire.* Quiet! he bellows, although in this highest of noons Al-Afrika Street is a . . . *graveyard*, and besides: If it were incoming, I should've heard its discharge . . . Still, a la-la-la-single cloud in an otherwise empty sky . . . *isn't it rich?* The Kiwis' Samil slumps sideways in the roadway, while beside it is the Wimmik their Force Protection must've arrived in. Gawain admonishes himself to *Stay grounded!* but keeps peeking skywards at the anomalous little cloud . . . *aren't we a pair?* The Venetian-blind-slatted sides of the aypeevee throw shadow-bars that *tiger-stripe my lover's fair skin* . . . Jonathan rolls away from him, up and out of the trench their ardour has dug in the old horsehair mattress . . . *dust-motes – honey-light.* He props his sleek weasel's head in his hand, reaches for the Marlboro smouldering in the ashtray on the bedside table, takes a long, luxuriant drag, and, his lungs . . . *popping and crackling*, exhales a long, luxuriant plume of smoke, over his sternum and belly, igniting *a burning bush!* which dies down to reveal his heavy and serpentine cock . . . *Kaah!* heavy with blood. Swelling, it pushes out from the jungle . . . *hakuna matata* . . . *hakuna ma–* Boss! Boss! *Bosh-bosh!* Fi's brother, Steve, is *bosh-bosh!* downwardly mobile *down the bog* . . . A plumber and a thoroughly decent chap – sticks close. Comes round on a Sunday – and only family do that: Caterpillar boots furry on the tufty mat as he puts his plunger . . . *right down the bog – bosh-bosh!* And I'd only shat in it . . . *minutes before.* He straightens up . . . *'cause he's straight*, smiles, presses the lever and the awful, clotted mass of toilet paper and . . . *the shit of my flesh* disappears in a cleansing swirl. Steve says: Bosh-bosh! All done, mate – no need to worry 'bout that any more. Boss! Boss! Gawain hears – yet doesn't hear. He takes a sip from the *warm plastic tit, mm . . . the milk of Camelbak kindness*, and sends his eye along the upper storey of the *bosh*-bodged buildings, seeing over-wrought iron balustrades, airy bricks, post-conflict satellite dishes, a sky-blue candlewick bedspread flapping on a clothesline, but . . . *no sign of life*. Boss! Boss! There are troopers at all four points, kneeling, gats ready, faces dead-white, lips sealed, eyes wide open . . . *don't bother – they're here*, and so is their SeeOh, who shouts, Drives – stay at the wheel! Hodges, any eeteeay on the 'copter yet? Hodges, involuntarily, looks up . . . *cloud's still there! Fruit-of-the-sky's-loom – particular about his underwear is my boy* . . . Standing in the cold morning light beneath the dormer, one slim, arched foot raised . . . *and questing*, while Gawain implores him to *Stay just another couple of hours – can't you? Won't you?* During the run-up to the invasion, this had become the most frequented of their bivvies: a bed-and-breakfast near Lincoln Jonathan had seen advertised on a web site . . . *Bum-Boys Welcome Here*, and, once they'd sampled its creature comforts, proclaimed satisfactory: These chaps're price-less – utterly otherworldly, so completely trustworthy . . . The chaps in question being Brian and a . . . *my name's John, too*, who, in near-matching cardigans and beards, closely resemble the parish councillors *they in fact are* . . . The parish being Bardney, a village in the middle of *fucking nowhere*, surrounded by a desert of beet fields, which stretch away . . . *at all four points* to where the grey-green outlines of ancient copses . . . *sail along the horizon*. This was a domesticated side to his wild lover Gawain had fantasised about but . . . *never dreamt I'd see*: Jonathan in shirtsleeves, sitting at an awkward little breakfast table set with odd bits of china, steaming toast rack and poxy-little aluminium dishes with blobs of jam and pats of butter on them . . . *don't you love farce?* Yes – yes, he does: he loves the long-running Whitehall one – loves also to *take it on tour*, with his . . . *trousers down round his ankles*. That winter morning, Gawain had showered second, then came downstairs to find Jonathan earnestly discussing with John and Brian the odd – and purely coincidental – fact that his father had worked on some sort of farming co-op in the area during the war . . . *but only briefly.* And you chaps – what brought you out into these homophobic wilds? he was saying as Gawain ducked under beams and brushed past horse brasses on his way across the room. And John – a little older, a little taller, his beard a touch more pointy – *droned on*: We-ell, Brian was working in Doncaster at the time, while I had a two-year contract down in Dunstable, so neither of us was in a position, initially, to quit our jobs . . . Jonathan had been at his most charming, sawing through a thick rasher, separating the *lean from the fat*, while chuckling amiably: Let me get this right – you two decided to run a beeandbee in Bardney purely on the basis of logistics. Sod-all to do with the village or the countryside – presumably the business could've been anything, a takeaway or a . . . I dunno – a seed merchant's . . . I mean, I don't want to be rude, but I don't get the feeling that either of you has long nurtured an ambition to enter the hospitality industry? John had conceded these points without much cavilling. Had Jonathan ever been more endearing as, delicately removing the skin from a slice of black pudding, he'd twitted *mein poofy hosts*: My, ah, friend and I are actually in a similar position – his vitally important work keeps him bolted to the industrious North, while I – a mere dilettante – cannot stop stirring the overheated flesh-pots of the South. My! how they bubble . . . And there'd been more loose talk as he'd worked his way methodically through a very full English: It's strictly hush-hush, he'd said, rustling that morning's Telegraph, in which there'd been the full text of the Prime Minister's statement, but I do have some contacts in the EffOh, and they tell me there's more than a soupçon of casuistry in all this . . . At which the two dull, decent, vaguely left-wing men had tugged their beards sagely and nodded, although Gawain had suspected the precise senses of "soupçon" and "casuistry" eluded them . . . *quite as much as they did me*. Later, back up in their room, under the steeply sloping eaves, he'd been . . . *the very picture of a modern major-gen-er-al!* packing his overnight bag with angry efficiency, while berating this . . . this . . . *Butcher*: It's not clever – and it's not funny! You've no idea who these men really are, or who they may know . . . It's as if . . . I dunno – as if you want us to be found out! And Jonathan, who'd somehow contrived to remove his clothes without his lover noticing, lay back on one of the twin and equally uncomfortable beds and laughed and laughed, 'til Gawain tossed his wash bag to one side and . . . *jumped on top of him!* Then Jonathan's fingers had been softly slipping *spiralling* down the shaft of Gawain's penis, and he'd been giggling, *Have you long nurtured a desire to enter the hospitality industry?* Gawain remembers the *sky-blue candlewick bedspread* slipping from the *wrought-iron balustrade* of his ribs, then he'd flipped *the Butcher* over and . . . *we were fucking*: his firm *hams* gripped in Gawain's sweaty hands – his *onglet* slipping over his bony hips, his *pork chop* hard and heavy. It'd been the first time ever that Gawain had assumed . . . *top cover* – a vantage from which he could both scope out the territory ahead and . . . *perfect my manoeuvrist doctrine* . . . Immediately Jonathan had come, Gawain sensed a profound alteration in their own . . . *rules of engagement: Looking back over twelve years, we have been victims of our own desire to placate the implacable* . . . and he was implacable, Gawain's lover: If you don't believe your outfit'll be able to handle the deployment, you shouldn't be clamouring to go . . . Which was plainly *RIDICULOUS*, Gawain near-shouted in reply, given it's pretty much treason for serving army officers to refuse an executive order – besides, every other SeeOh of just about every other regiment . . . *bar the Corps of Army Music* was feverishly lobbying for inclusion. Don't matter, Jonathan had continued implacably: rot goes all the way to the top – ambitious generals and senior spooks alike, they're all queuing up to tell the Narcissist-in-Chief what he wants to hear. They'd been sitting side-by-side putting on their socks – a moment of shared domesticity Gawain ruined with his own recently won *implacability*: And you, Jonathan – what about you? Are you one of those who're telling the Prime Minister what he wants to hear? He'd stopped *hooding the detainee* with the charcoal-coloured material, his lovely face darkened with the blood-rush of anger . . . *or shame*. It'd seemed to Gawain then – and this is certainly how he recalls it now – that his lover had been arguing with some internal and hectoring voice, because when he finally spoke his own was strange, small . . . *strangulated – and I didn't recognise it*: I think . . . I think you'll . . . just have to have . . . faith –

359

yes . . . faith, Gawain, in my . . . conscience . . . but to paraphrase TeeBee's own aperçu, *It's impossible to persuade towards reason the utterly unreasonable . . .* Then he'd reassumed his *Jonathan mask*, and, speaking through it in the way which made Gawain want to . . . *punch his fucking lights out!* he'd continued: D'you not think it a trifle bizarre, love, that this is a leader who will – I've no doubt – go down in history for simultaneously putting men violently asunder, and playing God yet more by making it possible for us to be legally bound together? Standing at the dormer window, looking out through the thick old pane at the winter *whorld* – the grave-yard wall opposite, its ancient flints frosted – Gawain had dared imagine . . . *let no man put man asunder*: he in his dress uniform, Jonathan in immaculate morning dress, standing to attention before a mumsy-looking Lincolnshire registrar – behind them in the banal function room a small gaggle of their new and accepting rural friends, prominent amongst them . . . *Brian and John – we've pretty much opened up specially for you blokes – wouldn't want to let you down . . . There's not that many, um, gay-friendly establishments in this neck of the woods . . . We're actually off on our own hols the day after tomorrow . . . Marbella – yes . . . Marbella, we've a timeshare there – tiny place . . . just a studio, but we like it.* In full fig and flicking invisible particles from the lapels of his cashmere overcoat, Jonathan had fully recovered: Honestly, Gawain, this pair positively lay waste to just about every gay stereotype in the book – they dress like pensioners, only Jim they've ever clapped eyes on is the old bloke who mows their lawn, while as for interior design . . . He'd indicated the stack of mod cons sat atop a cracked and creaking old chest-of-drawers: electric jug, ancient portable teevee, mini music centre, lamp, and, at the summit of it all, a brand-new wireless broadband router, pinprick lights perpetually winking the message that . . . *we're all bound together with everyone, now* . . . such are the requirements of *inter-operability: Electric jug? Electric jug? Telly, here – are you receiving me, over? All right, Boss* – you . . . all right? — It's Pythian – OhSee of the Force Protection Unit. Bessemer? Gawain asks. He'll make it, Pythian says, but I doubt he'll ever get to make a baby – took the round in his balls. Shitloads of blood, but Wentworth knows his stuff – got one of these flash new compression dressings on it . . . He'll make it back long as the crabs arrive sharpish . . . *Sharpish, eh* . . . Time has, Gawain thinks, been rebooted – clocks and watches resynch'ed: there's a monstrous click – a terrifying hiss, another click, and: Al-l-l-louuuuuuaaakhbaaaaar! the call to mid-morning prayer spurts out over the baking rooftops of Al-Afrika Street, drenching flappy-black abayas and sky-blue bedspreads alike with . . . *fanatical belief – come to my baby shower* . . . Fi had issued the invitation to several of the Wags – and they came, the women – *Queue-men, really* – bearing booties, all-in-ones, sterilising units – pretty much everything required for the . . . *new recruit,* so that *hakuna matata* . . . What the hell happened, man? Gawain asks of Pythian, who, in his dusty desert camos and *Dee-cup* body armour is a . . . *brindled terrier of a man,* sharp-muzzled and snapping at the world's ankles: his deep-set eyes dart up to the rooftops – down to the troopers who're covering the roadway, then back *againannagain* to the dark doorway where Gawain can just about make out a single white plastic garden chair lying motionless on its side . . . *moving – we should always be moving, 'cause* bad shit happens . . . *if you stand still.* Should be moving – stepping over that white plastic garden chair, and moving in through that dark doorway to deliver *a soft knock on hell's darkest chamber.* One carried out by the book: Pythian on point – the SeeOh in the middle – a trooper providing rear cover. But for now Gawain remains . . . *stranded*, the amplified wail reverberating between his ears, together with another of Jonathan's infuriating remarks – or aperçus, as he insists on calling them: *Have you ever considered how ridiculous it is, Teddy Bear, the way our so-called emergency services rush to the scene, sirens screaming, lights flashing – when the crime or the crash, or the cat-up-the-tree has already . . . happened!* Secure is it, Pythian – secure? Pythian nods: For now, Boss – we done it by the book. Pitched up. Fanned out. Covered all the exits. Went in. Gentle as. Asif goes in, talks to the Sheik. He says he's got friends staying – been travelling all night. Sleeping now. But we were that gentle, Boss – we didn't even wake 'em . . . Asif? Gawain queries. – He's our 'terp, Boss, rock-solid bloke. Rock solid. – And bodies, Pythian – how many? – Eight females, Boss. Five kids. Six males, and an as yet unconfirmed number of their, ah . . . friends. Sleeping in this room off the kitchen, Sheik says. Knocked on the door, nice and gentle, like – sec' it opens this fucker slots Bessemer right in the crown jewels. Chivers is there – and they're tight. He loses it – 'fore I know it he's banjoed the bastard . . . *Isn't it rich?* – Where's Chivers now? – He's in the wagon, Boss – bit shaken up an' that . . . Pythian's magicked on some sunglasses and, peering into them, Gawain sees his own . . . *knobbly knob-head* staring back at him, and reflects how at home Jonathan would be in this *looking-glass war. . .* with its frequent opportunities for . . . *narcissism.* It'd taken them ages to warm up the room that morning – the condensation was frozen on the inside of the windows, and, as they lay in each other's arms, it slowly melted, while the fan heater puffed, and puffed some more, but never . . . *huffed.* They lay in each other's arms, and Gawain lightly kissed Jonathan's hair – his eyebrows, and around the coldly beautiful curl of his *shell-like* . . . Jonathan must've switched the electric blanket on surreptitiously – he knows Gawain doesn't like them. Slowly as they'd slipped in and out of sleep . . . *in and out of love,* the sweat had pooled between them. Now someone has *switched it off* – possibly the supernatural being the residents of Al-Afrika Street are being called upon to worship, because the sweat cools, enfolding Gawain in its *chilly embrace. . .* He thinks of the old Vickers machine-guns, their barrels cooled by a . . . *full-metal nightdress* filled with water, and reshivers: *W-Where's Ch-Chivers now?* In hell's darkest chamber, quite possibly – why wouldn't he be? No matter what his basic instincts once were, he's long since been weaned off them and on to a diet of *Quorn and vegetarian sausages. . .* How the fuck's he gonna cope with becoming . . . *a man-eater – hakuna matata . . . are we a pair?* Gawain takes a last look up into the smarting sky . . . *send in the clouds – don't worry. . .* Okay, Steve, he says to Lieutenant Pythian as he pops the popper of his sidearm holster, let's do this thing – and remember: Perry Rat Likes Shooting Arseholes Regularly . . . Pythian grins, and, as he moves towards the doorway, delivers the final and most important part of his sit' rep': Friends're still banged up in this room off the kitchen, Boss – once we knew back-up was on its way I decided to wait it out . . . In the doorway they're joined by Trooper Dennison, who arrives looking *waiterly* . . . a body bag draped over his arm. Adrenalin floods Gawain's system – a still-chillier . . . *shroud* – he sees Trooper Chivers, years hence, wandering the meat aisle of some out-of-town supermarket, one grubby-faced tyke in the trolley's seat, the other grazing, his face smeared with *chocolate goo* . . . and sticky fingers thrust through the wire mesh as he . . . *rides shotgun.* Their father, hunting for Linda McCartney's face in the chiller cabinets, clocks the one of the man he killed – which is no more recognisable as a once-living thing than *the bean burgers it's stacked between* . . . Then they're shuffling along a narrow corridor with doors to either side . . . *making our entrance with our usual . . . flair.* There's a steady tick-tick-*ticking*, keeping the heavy beat of their breathing as they tread on the odd spangles and breast the irregular shafts cast through the transom. Pythian pushes a door open with his boot and swings his gat in the shocked face of a teddy bear propped upright amongst rumpled bedclothes . . . *coulda killed me.* Thought you said this place was secured, Gawain whispers – but there's no reply from Pythian, only the hiss from his radio, which, tuned to the op's open frequency, picks up a final, despairing Alllouuuuarrakkbharrrr! followed by a second monstrous . . . click! Silence – except for the crunch of their boots on the broken things scattered across the white tiles. As they gain the last door, Pythian whispers back: It is, Boss – we've got 'em all in here. Told 'em to be patient – we'd sort it all out when back-up showed up . . . *Looking back over twelve years, our fault has not been impatience.* No, indeed, Gawain admonishes himself as they enter the kitchen, how could I have been impatient when I didn't know *what it was I was missing?* They must've stayed with Brian and John in Bardney more or less monthly in the two years since . . . *the balloon went up.* It made sense logistically – and Jonathan seemed to have developed some sort of attachment, both to the locale and to . . . *mein poofy hosts*: I've told Brian all about my situation, Jonathan confided on their third or fourth visit. Gawain had frozen, shirt half hangered, loose floorboard creaking underfoot, Holly and Jessica in their EmmYouEffSee shirts looking up at him from the yellowed newspaper lining the wardrobe: What the bloody hell d'you mean by that? Jonathan smiled, Only that I've told him I'm married – got a little weepy about it. Said you were pushing me to leave wifey, but there're my kids to consider . . . Right in the middle of their exams – it'd be a terrible trauma for them . . . Gawain had shrugged, hung the shirt in the wardrobe, straightened up and spoken to him . . . *as if he was on a charge*: You're being childish, playing your oh-so-fucking-clever games. You'll endanger what we have – if you haven't already. And for what? *He senses weakness and therefore continues to defy* . . . Jonathan, tucked up under the grubby eaves, had stretched luxuriantly – laughed throatily . . . *prob'ly fuck the Marlboro Man given half a chance.* My, my, Colonel, he'd said, you can be commanding after all . . . *Yes! After all – after all the supine years, the bottom years – the years spent with MY FACE STUCK IN A FUCKING PILLOW!* – Sir . . . Boss . . . Sir . . . Sir . . . Here they all are: in a surprisingly large kitchen lit to operating-theatre-strength by a yard-long, unshaded neon tube bolted obliquely across the unpainted concrete ceiling. Despite their shocked state, their SeeOh is pleased his Rams continue to observe the unspoken rule: full screws and up are privileged to call him Boss, but all other ranks must salute-and-sir. The Iraqis are all cross-legged on a patchwork of linoleum off-cuts – *it's the hunger, must keep 'em . . . limber* – the men facing the wall opposite the door, the women and children the one to the right. The room boasts a sort of parody of a kitchen island: a free-standing central unit *bosh-bosh-boshed* up out of plywood in which an aluminium sink – but no taps – has been implanted. Flex sprouting from hacksawed holes indicates where white goods were meant to go before the sanctions – after all: *cereal cemented to bowls will turn any citizenry against . . . a dictator. No man is a kitchen island – cut off the stale bits . . .* Come upon suddenly, in the heat – *chickpeas? For breakfast?* – the men appear schoolboyish in their awkward helmets and bulky body-armour, standing over their captives *porting their popguns . . .* Trooper Arbroath has a bad crop of acne – *can't find Clearasil in the bazaar.* He squats by a prone figure in the far corner, holding up a bag of saline – a khaki-clad figure, unhelmeted and with a tile-white face: *Bessemer!* At the sight of the boy who's just learnt his baby boy . . . *is another boy's,* Gawain recoils into this sadly typical scene: he'd carpeted Bessemer, along with Trooper Sneddon, two months ago back in the YouKay. The pair of 'em shuffling their boots on the scrap of carpet in front of Gawain's desk: black eyes and split lips had been *equally distributed* – they'd got into a really rather serious scrap over whose turn it was with . . . *the PlayStation*. Gawain had told them: I had to deal with a similar incident on Saturday – but that was between my sons. Actual children – not highly trained professional soldiers behaving like *bloody children!* They'd avoided his paternal eye and *squirmed* to attention. Why? *Because they are bloody children* – the bloody children of parents who'd been dumped on the post-industrial scrapheap: *white goods . . . old fridges and washing machines, piled up . . . one on top of the other – kids get trapped inside them . . . toddlers younger than Miffy – led away from shopping centres by other . . . bloodthirsty children . . .* The Rams always made a lot of their White Rose credentials, but the truth is its petals will be forever stained by the soot which once fell from Redcar chimneys. Most of the regiment is recruited from further north – up the coast, past Scarborough. Not white goods at all, really – let alone Little Englanders, but *Lynndie ones!* Skinny, spotty boys *raised up by hand* on sugar, vinegar and salt – stuck together with glue and *old betting slips . . .* For their fathers and forefathers joining the service had been a way of escaping the *molten steel puddling in their guts* – but for the Bessemers and Sneddons who now made up the ranks? Well, Gawain didn't consider himself remotely cynical – only *clear-sighted*: they'd exchanged under- for unemployment. Instead of hanging round outside the bookie's or sitting at home *fiddling with a controller*, they hung around the canteen or outside the chogee shop – or sat in their barracks *fiddling with a controller*. Yes, yes – they could drill beautifully, and provide the *wetware* for sophisticated modern figting vehicles as well – but none of this would be much use when they ended up *job-seeking* . . . Really, Gawain thinks – looking at the seriously wounded boy . . . *I was meant to keep an eye on*, they're just like me: chocolate soldiers to a man – taken out of our box once in a while to *melt in the mouth – not in the hand*, Jesus! The heat! The heat in Ali al-Garbi this May noontide, which makes the concrete roofscapes *buckle.* The concrete roofscapes pallisaded with their own reinforcing, strung with cabling and clotheslines from which *sky-blue bedspreads flutt*– Pythian! Gawain yelps. The roof! Whatabout the roof – secured, issit? *Perry Rat Likes Shooting Arseholes Regularly* . . . The Rats may well be *Perry*-prepared for battle – but there's no *Rat*-returning of fire to be done as yet – given we haven't even, *Like*-located the fucking enemy! Pythian turns to a Kiwi officer Gawain hadn't so much as noticed, who's propped against the kitchen island: McClintock! Secured the roof, didja? The Kiwi bemusedly levers himself upright – stunned not by Pythian's obvious contempt, but by the dawning awareness of . . . *the massive clusterfuck he's perpetrated.* Yet, if Gawain's honest . . . *if I'm honest*, at this moment in time . . . *at this moment in time*, in the kitchen of Number Twenty-Seven, Al-Afrika Street, Ali al-Garbi, Maysan Governate, *Iraq . . . the Middle East, the World, the Milky Way, the Universe. . . Can I be here . . . now?* No – no, he can't: Double in, Pythian, Gawain says. Check and secure the roof area – take Arbroath and Hodges . . . His radio barks: Hotel, Lima, Foxtrot . . . d'you read me? But no, Gawain only reads the *Power-Points* from a Staff College lecture that appear before him . . . *a heads-up display,* and which're better than a poxy old mnemonic when it comes to remembering the key differences between *AirLand Battle and Full-Spectrum Dominance* . . . Not that either strategic overview alters the fundamental reality that . . . *within the battle-space the effective tank commander maintains multiple perspectives.* Yes! Indeed! Meaning he sees pretty much what all the men under his command see, hears what they hear, feels what they touch and smells what they *sniff at* – or at least tries to, because in practice the Rams have mostly been trained to go mano-a-mano with hordes of . . . *white dots tracking across their monitors . . . now* – Now, Asif . . . *As if?* Be so good as to introduce me to the Sheik of the White Plastic Garden Chairs . . . The 'terp turns to the Iraqi men cross-legged along the wall, all sporting dishdashas, keffiyehs and black polyester trousers which're . . . *flat-fronted for that becoming pot-bellied silhouette – get outta my head, Jonathan!* Mutter-mutter, goes Asif, and then: Gobble-gobble-gobble, cough-cough-cough. The eldest and most venerable-looking of the Iraqis replies: Cough-cough-cough, mutter-gobble-mutter . . . He's a moon-faced man with *pot-bellies* under his hooded eyes, and as he splutters on Lieutenant-Colonel Gawain Thomas recalls some off-the-wall briefing about *cultural sensitivity: Despite having no knowledge of someone's language you can still show – by nodding and making small noises expressing encouragement – that you get their . . . general . . . drift.* Yes, a drift and *a draught* – the Sheik sprays the radio Velcroed to the front of Gawain's body armour with his spittle . . . *stale garlic, recent chickpeas, long-rotting teeth and the . . . blood of innocents . . .* One of the little girls is whimpering – if control of the battle-space is to be maintained, she should really be . . . *put on the naughty step.* – Ask him, please, Asif, who exactly his friends are, where they're from, and what the bloody-hell they're up to – 'cause innabout thirty seconds me and my men're gonna open that door none too gently, and if we don't have a pretty good idea of what's waiting for us on the other side . . . Well, let's just put it this way: whatever grand designs the Sheik may have re' his home improvements will have to be put on hold. Permanently. – *So it goes:* Asif and the Sheik carry on . . . *mutually contaminating,* while Gawain *maintains multiple perspectives* . . . climbing the bare concrete stairs with Pythian – peering through the sights of Abroath's EssAyEighty as it tracks here, *then there,* holding on to a discarded item of clothing or a dropped shoe, *then letting it go.* As Asif does his job, the Sheik stares hungrily at the 'terp's Adam's apple . . . *like to eat it:* He say he don't know – these friends are not his friends, they are the friends of his cousins – but, bismillah, it is the Arab way to welcome guests . . . Had your men not arrived bearing arms, acting insensitively, he would have shown them the same hospitality –. For Christ's sake, Asif, Gawain *baas,* tell the man to get to the bloody point! Up on the roof cross-hairs quarter a satellite dish . . . a white plastic garden chair . . . a pile of breeze-blocks . . . *a sky-blue bedspread flapping* . . . The Sheik *carries on coughing,* while one of the three Kiwis remaining in the kitchen comes up to Gawain, grinning inanely . . . *Bernard-bloody-Bresslaw:* Sir . . . Sir . . . he sirs – but Gawain only snaps: You still here? If I were you, I'd clear right out – we're going in, and need room to manoeuvre. Davis, Patel . . . double in, Rams, and sharpish: get this lot outside – he indicates the Iraqis with the muzzle of a sidearm *I seem to've drawn* – all of 'em. And keep 'em covered – never know what they might have underneath their . . . bedspreads . . . *sure of my lines, eh?* Asif is as well: The Sheik says

370

he believes that they may have AyKays –. – Of course they've got bloody AyKays! The bloody schoolchildren have AyKays in this godforsaken country – what about anything heavier? These are fighters, aren't they, Asif – AREN'T THEY? Gawain's spoken *TOO LOUDLY*, and, despite the shuffling and scraping of the Iraqis getting to their feet and stretching their cramped limbs . . . *EVERYONE HEARD ME*. Hears him – sees him, too: because if the effective tank commander maintains multiple perspectives within the battle-space, so that battle-space maintains *multiple perspectives on . . . me!* They see him – Iraqis, Rams and Kiwis alike – see him standing hunched under the low eaves, peering through the distorting pane at the hooded crows clustered on the church roof – they see him turning towards Jonathan, who stands half naked in the cold light of a winter morning . . . *You've got so bloody thin*, he remembers saying – and further carping: *It's those dreadful little pills, isn't it – they're drugs, aren't they? They're turning you into . . . a . . . scarecrow.* And Jonathan? He'd laughed – he was always laughing nowadays, albeit . . . *edgily*. When he'd stopped laughing, he stretched, thrusting his ribcage into still greater prominence. You've got to enjoy deception, dearest Teddy Bear, he'd said. You must revel in the double life – else there's no point to it. You must experience the sheer exhilaration as you take the short hop over the abyss yawning between one of your identities and the next – 'course, you'd know all about that, since you . . . *do it all the time*. And Gawain, far from being flattered by this, was still more . . . *riled*: I'm not like you, Jonathan – really, there's no comparison. I may be an . . . adulterer, and . . . um, closeted, but I'm not some international-man-of-bloody-mystery! Yes, a world-bestriding enigma, who let fall one exotic destination after another – Caracas, then Cairo – to impress his lover, no doubt – but also to *frustrate any knavish tricks* ... For with no real idea of what Jonathan got up to, Gawain found it impossible to ... *keep my eye on him.* But on that occasion – in Bardney, on the cold winter morning when he'd exposed his hand to Brian and John, Gawain was emboldened, and *apprehended the battle-space*, so for once asked him directly: Where're you going? I don't mean in general – I mean right now: *Where the fuck're you going?* But Jonathan had only deigned to answer obliquely. Downstairs, signing the register with someone else's name, he finally replied, Me? Well, since you ask, Brian, I'm just popping back to my London flat to pack, then it's off to Kuwait – my firm keeps me on the move, sorta circus-dog-trotting-on-a-big-rubber-ball sitch ... Next they were standing out in the lane, scraping the frost from their respective windscreens. The hooded crows had been restive, Gawain recalls: kraarking from the squat flint bell tower of the church ... *hakuna matata.* Jonathan had arrived in what passed for his casual wear – an expensively soft brown-leather jacket, a cashmere crew-necked sweater, cords and leather loafers ... *delicate as Miffy's ballet slippers* – but he was leaving *in full Whitehall fig*: spongebag trousers, black jacket and waistcoat, patent-leather dress shoes, Crombie overcoat with *a velvet collar* ... And of course he'd been driving the silver-grey pillarless coupé, a vehicle which was almost as *absurdly visible!* Gawain had pictured him then – pictures him now: the long ribbon of Lincolnshire tarmac unrolling from the Merc's rear bumper, and from time to time a burst of chaff being fired from concealed barrels – *glow worms* up too late in the Fenland day, draping their smoky tails over drenched fields and dormant hedgerows. So that's it, Gawain had spat. You definitely want us to be found out, don't you? Why – is it the only way you can get your kicks any more? Or perhaps that bullshit about Kuwait was just another lie – or cover story, as you call them . . . *Scccraaape*. Jonathan had rubbed his *hooded* fingertips together – icy shavings fell at his well-shod feet. No, he said, that's not it – I really am going to Kuwait, Teddy Bear, it was just my way of letting you know without having to say it right out – which goes rather profoundly *scccraaape* against the grain. There's no need to get tetchy – after all, it's rather a tricky time at work at the moment for both of us . . . To've shown public affection is, was – would always be: *unthinkable.* That morning, as on all the others, they'd kissed before leaving their room – kissed the famished kiss they always did on parting . . . *Kaaa*, feeding on each other's lips and tongues beyond the point of satiety, 'cause *we never know when we'll make another . . . kill.* So, in the lane, they'd formally shaken cold hands. What did we look like? A to-the-manor-born saying farewell to his man-of-all-work – a deferential type, who, even in this egalitarian age, reaches for an invisible forelock to . . . *tug.* Some of the 'terps go armed – others not. When Speedwell, the Brigade Political Officer, visits from Amarah, he looks askance at Asif and the others loung- ing about Camp Val with the off-duty Rams – their Kalashnikovs locked in the same rack, while they, too . . . *squabble over the Play- Station controller.* Asif's hand *twitches* – and it's notoriously tricky, the safety on an AyKay. The armourer went over it all on Gawain's

373

last Optag: Some fighters'll do a field modification and *fuck it up – see, there's this flange on the dust cover's edge, catches the catch if you aren't . . . careful – rendering it off when it should be on, with predictable results.* Shocked, Asif stutters: I am t-truly not knowing – this Sheik-fellow, he is saying they're friends only –. Okay, that's enough, man. Gawain silences him by raising the muzzle of the Sig Sauer . . . *I'm using my sidearm in a combat situation – never done that before* . . . Patel, you go right – Jenks, you go left . . . He waves the muzzle to indicate where the troopers should take up position so as to have the widest possible field of fire when . . . *I open the door.* Bessemer is being carried out on a stretcher – saline feels chilly *going in*, or so Fi told him after one of her deliveries *when she haemorrhaged.* This much Gawain remembers – but which of their children was it? Troubling, that – makes a bit of a mockery of my claim to be a conscientious *husband and father* . . . Bessemer looks up at his SeeOh, his lips pale and cracked, his top lip sweat-shiny. Sir . . . Sir . . . he *kraark-kraaark* croaks. He may've lost a lot of blood, but he still *glows with pride* – pride at his great and valiant achievement: *wounded in the line of duty when commandeering vital supplies* . . . is what he probably thinks the citation should read – while there's a gaudy Ruritanian medal dangling from the crimson ribbon which unrolls in his mind's eye: cast by Thos Askew and Sons, Jewellers and Engravers of Pickering, Yorkshire, est nineteen hundred and four. *Ting-ting* goes the swinging door: *You again, Colonel Thomas – back from that Eyeracky carry-on, are you?* Sssir, sssir . . . Bessemer hisses – and his SeeOh says: Rest easy, Trooper, you've done your bit . . . then squats down, and before he knows it

Gawain's bestowed a fatherly hand on the poor boy's *burning* fore-head. Straightening up, he cries: Carry him away! Before returning to the . . . *jeweller's: Bit of an unusual one for you, Mister Askew – my boys got mixed up in a little bother, somewhere we, ah, shouldn't've been – if you get my drift . . . Acquitted themselves fine – Rams always do, but non poss any sort of official recognition, and my chaps are understandably aggrieved . . . Together with my senior officers, I thought we'd do a little something for them – if you'd oblige . . . Like a charm-thingie for one of those bracelets – like the one I bought for my daughter but bigger . . . In silver as well – good old sterling silver, like the Rams' table decoration* . . . He passes Mister Askew a colour printout of the photograph he cyber-shot in Al-Afrika Street: it shows the whitest and most pristine of the garden chairs the Kiwis tried to liberate from the Sheik. Askew tips his glasses to the very end of his Wensleydale nose and *examines it. What do I really know about Islam and Muslims? A fragment of their burial service one of the 'terps trans-lated for me: How can you reject Allah, when you were dead and then He gave you life, then He will make you die and then give you life again, then you will be returned to Him?* But sir, Asif insists, you must be careful, I do not know what these friends are . . . Gawain looks critically at the 'terp – he's sporting a red Sunderland EffSee tracksuit top . . . *close to the boys, then*, and with his hawkish profile and tight cap of blue-black curls he's . . . *almost good-looking.* Asif has a pack of Marlboros poking from his back pocket – his shaking hand rests on the edge of the kitchen island. A fly *dashes towards it* . . . so sure of themselves in the air, Gawain thinks, dog-fighting over dog shit – but once grounded they lose their *war-fighting spirit* . . . Everyone in the kitchen hears the clatter of the helicopter passing overhead . . . *Uther's to the rescue!* and Bessemer'll soon be gone. It's time for the rest of them to withdraw as well – Trimmer had been perfectly clear: *Stick around for too long, Greeny, and the mucky lot – the Badr boys . . . well, takes 'em a while to clear their hash heads and sort their shit out, but when they do they'll get on the blower and scare up a mob . . . Cause you plenty of bother – and provide them with plenty of . . . cover.* You, Gawain orders Asif: get over there, duck down for cover . . . *some cover – chipboard versus semi-automatic fire*, and call out to the Sheik's friends. Tell 'em they're to push their weapons out first with their feet, then follow on with their hands high. Asif queries: In Arabic or English – or . . . Farsi? All bloody three, Gawain replies, retreating to the kitchen doorway, from where he believes he'll be able to cover all eventualities . . . *barring explosives.* The troopers give their SeeOh tight smiles and thumbs-ups, and he notes important details: all three have spare magazines duct-taped to the stocks of their rifles for . . . *speedy reloading. On the point of no return* . . . Gawain feels his wife's workmanlike hands on his shoulders: Because that's the way we touch each other nowadays, with cursory efficiency – measuring each other up for a carpet . . . *or a coffin.* What'd Fi said? It'd been when the coaches were arriving – drawing up in front of the mess hall, and the young men were tipping their heavy bergens from their shoulders into the open luggage compartments . . . *what did she say?* There'd been the thin, watery sunlight of a late March afternoon in northern latitudes, and, mounting up behind her the moors all tawny *big cats up there . . . kill sheep so they say – what did she say?* Looked

Gawain in the eye, she did, and said . . . But no, it doesn't return to him . . . While I, he thinks, can never return to her, not with *blood on my hands* . . . *What d'you fancy?* Jonathan sat grinning toothily, across from him in the Royal Oak – an efficient rather than an olde worlde pub, with pool table and jukebox towards the back of the bar, while they were plonked down by the front window, either side of a large fake-wicker basket full of individual sauce sachets . . . *English mustard, vinegar, tartare, brown, gory tomato* . . . *It'll have to be a steak*, is what he always says. Fish'll be frozen – pies'll be processed. Steak'll probably be shit, too, but it's got more in its favour, so, saignant ou à point? Ou entre saignant et à point? Alors . . . peut-être entre à point et bien cuit, 'cause you've always struck me as a well-cooked kinda guy, Gawain . . . And the *well-cooked kinda guy* had replied: Don't be facetious, Jonathan, you're not in some trendy London restaurant now. Worst luck, he'd muttered . . . *the butcher!* And Gawain had an impulse to grab the cutlery, tightly wrapped in a thick red paper serviette, unwrap the steak knife, plunge it in his complacent neck and watch *the fucker bleed out on the carpet* . . . His wife's words at last return to Lieutenant-Colonel Gawain Thomas as he toggles the Sig Sauer's safety, which is just the latest entry on the long list of *everything I'm doing wrong: I don't need to tell you to be careful*, she'd said. Gawain snaps his fingers – Asif coughs out. A pause. He coughs again. A nasty hiatus – then mutterings audible from behind the door. The damned door – the six-panelled *Georgian* door: not dissimilar to the ones Gawain sees every morning back home, when he sets off for work . . . *ranged round the cul-de-sac.* Tell 'em they're surrounded, Gawain calls to the 'terp . . . *'cause there's no butcher here who'll cry cliché!* Do it! And Asif dutifully translates this into . . . *bronchitis.* Another pause, then sc-sc-sccrrrraaaape the door scrapes over the tiled floor . . . He'd driven off down Church Lane without so much as a backward glance. Cruel, really, and unnecessary – could've given me a peck on the cheek . . . *entre à point et bien cuit.* But then we've never been able to talk about the physical side of our relationship much – any more than we've been able to talk . . . *shop!* The men who emerge blinking into the hard light of the kitchen are grey-faced and furtive. There're *one . . . two . . . four* of them *easy-peasy . . . nice and . . .* neat beards, black robes and white clerical-looking turbans. They stand, stranded on the far shore of the kitchen island, and Asif coughs at them: they cough back, and he leaps up swinging the muzzle of his AyKay in an arc which traverses . . . *their bellies.* Sokay . . . click-click sokay, Asif says . . . *his teeth won't obey his jaw*: So-click-click-kay . . . no guns . . . so-click-kay . . . Gawain gestures with the Sig Sauer and the two troopers rise up, move forward and pat the beards down . . . *they'd've enjoyed this in Bardney*, where Gawain had *in point of fact* resisted the impersonal farewell, hung on to Jonathan's gloved hand and asked directly: Why Kuwait, is the balloon about to go up? *Up – we both looked up . . . 'cause I thought that he'd want what I want . . .* Yes, they'd both looked up, and witnessed a similar meterological phenomenon up there in the Lincolnshire sky – an unusual one, certainly, but by no means unprecedented: a single, puffy-white cloud hanging maybe four or five thousand feet . . . *away from the flock.* Jonathan had slowly removed his overcoat, then his jacket, folded each in turn and laid them on the Merc's back seat. When he

378

eventually replied it'd been in the most official of drawls: Ye-es, we-ell, Dicky-dearest has got it into his head there's a viable asset in that neck of the woods. Utter bullshit, I'm sure – prob'ly just some Ba'athist cadre who's weighed up the odds and decided since his life is effectively worthless under the regime he may as well cash it in with us – the Firm's always been a cash-on-demand business, as the epithet would suggest . . . In bed, as they post-coitally slumbered, Gawain's lover was tender and vulnerable, but with each successive layer of expensive material he sheathed his body in, he grew more and more condescending. Only an hour since, Gawain had been revelling in his two-up promotion: *Top cover!* Best possible position for a tank commander – he can scope out the terrain ahead . . . *the clonking mahogany headboard, the striped wallpaper . . . that butcher's bed-head buried in . . . the pillow . . .* Yet there he was, shuffling his *merely serviceable* shoes on the frozen bitumen, racking his brains for the meaning of . . . *epithet.* Kindly escort these, ah, gentlemen outside, Colonel Thomas instructs his men – then to Asif: Tell them we've reason to believe they came over the border in the night, so we're going to take them back to Camp Val for preliminary questioning . . . and . . . if they can't satisfy us as to the legitimacy of their, ah, business . . . well, we'll have to send them down to the DeeDeeEff at Shaibah . . . As he speaks Gawain falls in behind the troopers, the 'terp and the mysterious mullahs – and when he's finished they're all standing, sun-struck, back in the high noon of Al-Afrika Street. Fresh sweat bursts from Gawain's armpits and crotch, soaking through *each successive layer of cheap material . . .* Only the previous week he'd come upon some Rams just back off patrol: they were sitting in the shadow of the compound wall, frying eggs on the ceramic plaques they'd removed from their body armour. The Colonel had stood in silence and watched while the full screw who was doing the frying took the orders: Easy-over, lads, or sunny-side up? Whistling while he worked – until, that is, he became aware of this . . . *deeper shadow* looming over him: Good to see you lads aren't cooking in your Guccis, Gawain had begun easily enough, bantering away. You wouldn't want to have egg on your ties – might put off those well-born Arabian virgins we hear so much about . . . But then the seriousness of their situation had begun to bear down on him. Heavily: Small piece of advice, though. Down in Basra, where things're a fuck of a lot hairier, our comrades are dying for want of adequate armour – you're aware of that, are you? Aware of the wider-bloody-picture? There'd been a surly silence – they looked at the father of the regiment with the sheepy, shame-faced expressions of . . . *the naughty boys they still are.* Naughty boys who took the Duke of Edinburgh's challenge seriously, struggling up the scree of Scafell Pike, wishing, hoping, dreaming all the way . . . *I wanna go to war.* As he'd walked away, the responsibility of command *heavy on my shoulders*, Gawain heard the men burst into excitable chatter – the way schoolboys do when they've been told off by a hated teacher *whose authority is rapidly waning . . . my fault, I fear.* He should've hung on to Jonathan's hand forever, on that frosty March morning – hung on to it and *pressed it to my lips . . .* Then confessed that: all things considered, rather than fight the coming war with the weapons, the tactics and the skill-set designed for another conflict altogether, he'd far prefer it if his own skin were to be sheathed in silk . . . *not sweat.* Should've admitted he couldn't forgive his lover for not shaving off his beards and making his own . . . *public avowal.* And, most sheepily and shame-facedly of all, should've told Jonathan that the only time he'd ever enjoyed a trip to the theatre was when they were at the Academy, and he and Tizer went on a double-date. Tizer nearly lost his nut – 'cause his girl had booked them all tickets to see . . . *some gay-fucking musical!* Okay, everyone? Gawain says, glancing to the end of the street, where the cracked concrete minaret wavers in the super-heated air . . . *admonishing me.* The Rams nod their helmets as their SeeOh does a quick head-count: with the five Iranians added into the mix, there're eighteen suspects – then there're the Kiwis and their Force Protection, and of course the brick he arrived with – *fuck! Ruddy-fucking fuck-fuck! Fuckety-fucking fuck! Fucking Pythian – Arbroath . . . Hodges!* He's lost control of the battle-space, and the confirmation of this comes immediately, in the form of . . . *popcorn being made on a massive scale!* – an automatic rifle firing a burst on the rooftop above. Then, *all hell breaks lose* . . . When it's over – and it's over in seconds – the trooper on top cover in the Wimmik is screaming . . . *more clichés*: None of youse move a muscle! I've got you all covered! Which he does: the evil eye of the geepee-emmgee swings back and forth, from one crumpled *bedspread* to the next. Gawain shouts out, Anyone wounded? And Pythian appears up above, silhouetted against the hurting sky, his arm raised and waving: Man down, Boss! He shouts, It's Hodges . . . *Great! Fucking great* the way he spoke to me – so unbelievably patronising:

Things're ramping up, Gawain – who knows how much time we'll be able to snatch from the jaws of war? Balloon's definitely going up before the summer – of that there seems little doubt: TeeBee's so far up Bush's bum they're using the same toothbrush – and when they run out of toothpaste, either Dicky or John's on hand to oblige. You Rams'll get your precious deployment sooner or later, while as for me? We-ell, let's just put it this way: there're people I care about out there in the sandpit – kiddies, some of 'em, really – and I'd as soon they were all tucked up in beddy-byes before you lot start playing *with your toy tanks* . . . Ye-es, playing with toy tanks, indeed. A month or two later Gawain had been sat at home – their new one, *exclusive to EmmOhDee personnel* – and watching the advance – as he had so many of the critical conflicts of the era – *on fucking telly*. The platforms that'd been Herced into Kuwait headed north in a cloud of dust. How had the brave boys looked on their toy tanks? Not terribly ally – some of them didn't even have desert camos, and were potentially going to their deaths in crappy, standard-issue battledress. A cup of tea balanced on his emerging paunch, Gawain goggled as infanteers moved along the rutted roads into Basra – and how did they look then? Eccentrically overdressed when compared with the Basratis, who trotted past them, lolling across the shafts of their donkey carts, the sleeves of their tartan shirts rolled up, one hand casually supporting a looted air-conditioner unit or a teetering stack of . . . *white plastic garden chairs*. Then there'd been more footage, taken at an intersection where two roads crossed on their way to . . . *nowhere*: a noisy crowd of Basratis doing their best to ignore some skinny-necked boys *from Pwllheli, prob'ly – or* . . .

dunno, Daventry – who were taking a fag-break in a nearby ditch. Stretched out in a Barcalounger Fi *sweetly believed* would help him with his bad back, Gawain had been further transfixed, as all the brand-new fixtures and furnishings vanished from around him: the watercolours of Snowdonia slipped their hooks, the spotlights slid off their tracking, the fitted carpets pulled out their own staples and rolled themselves up – then all of it reappeared, on-screen, piled high on the back of a Toyota pickup which was being driven at speed along . . . *the Via Dolorosa.* In those first few weeks of the conflict Gawain experienced the sort of tense exhilaration Jonathan displays every time . . . *he pops one of those bloody pills.* Walking on Sundays after church parade, with the children up by Fylingdales, he visualised the electro-magnetic waves pulsing from these humongous golf-ball-shaped installations – and thought of those who received them: the spooks and EssEff bods, the *selectively briefed policymakers* . . . This exalted community partook of the wafers, threw back the wine and so were transformed, becoming *completely aware of the wider picture.* But he . . . he'd strode on, Gore-Tex boots slipping and sliding through drenched gorse as the children whooped and skipped beneath a high, wide moorland sky: he strode on, towards a horizon he never reached, all the while muttering this very plain chant: *We have to go . . . We have to go . . . We have to go . . .* Had to go because: *They need us there . . .* Just as the Rams had been needed in Sierra Leone and Kosovo – at Imjin and Inkerman. He strode on, *g-g-grinding* his teeth – and was *g-g-grinding them still!* Was it two hours, or two years later? Sat back in the Portakabin, as he types up his report prior to emailing it down to aitchqueue, his jaw clenched and . . . *aching: Double-youOhTwo Pythian surprised the two suspected fighters, who were hiding on the roof, and in the exchange of fire Trooper Hodges was wounded. Down below, in the street, A Squadron's interpreter, Asif al-Sayyab, assuming his comrades and their detainees were coming under fire, attempted to return fire. Unfortunately, his weapon jammed, and he was shot and killed by one of the detainees who had secreted a weapon . . . Weapon-weapon . . . Under fire – return fire . . .* These clumsy repetitions bother the Colonel – at Sandhurst he'd endless difficulties with his essays, words wouldn't just him obey. *Him just words obey wouldn't . . .* He sits, blinking at the blinking on-screen cursor, fixated by all the sharp edges of the screen architecture – and the virtual shadows they cast. He sits, dirty and sweating . . . *I could murder a beer,* conscious that here, in this little bivouac of light, *I've met my Portaloo . . .* The night-time sounds of Camp Val emanate from the outer darkness: the nearby muttering of troopers on drag-stag, the hubba-hubba of the generators, the distant yelp of the dog pack that gathers outside the walls every evening because once – *and only once!* – some utterly bone trooper on cookhouse duties . . . *tossed out some bones.* Bessemer and Hodges have long since gone – the 'copter bearing them clattering away to the south – yet everything Gawain's sore eyes settle on – pencils, paper clips, a gonk mascot dangling from the computer monitor . . . *by its no-neck –* flinches, *as if the rotors . . . as if the rotors're about to hit it . . . Asif!* His Rams, he thinks, performed well enough – after the intitial shock there'd been no panic: Brit casualties and Iraqi dead were loaded into the vehicles, and the 'copter was waiting for them at Camp Val. There'd been a little confusion – Pythian shouting to the loadie: We've another one here for you! while the paramedics hauled the stretchers out from the aypeesees, squatting down to fiddle with tubes and spigots and dressings. A few minutes later the 'copter *plumped up* its *cushion of dust*, hovered for a moment over the main gate, then swung round, began spitting out chaff and romped away over the rooftops. Watching from one of the main gate sangars, Tizer had bellowed: Contact! Bloody contact! But it'd all been over before Gawain reached him: according to Tizer, a single heat-seeking sam had come scooting up from the east and, locking on to some chaff, swerved hard right and disappeared amongst the tumbledown shacks and vegetable plots along the riverbank without – so far as he could tell – detonating. *But it was a sam, Tizer – you're ABSOLUTELY BLOODY CERTAIN ABOUT THAT?* – For fuck's sake, Greeny, get outta my fucking face! You trying to snog me, or what? It was only then that Gawain had realised: he'd backed Major Townshend right up against the parapet and was *spittling* his cheeks. The mess that evening had been subdued . . . *truculent*: two men down, and the Rams first combat casualties *in decades*. They need us here more than ever, Gawain had said, his hand shaking, tomato soup making *bloody bullet wounds* on the tabletop. Yeah, Tizer grunted, it certainly sounds like it . . . They'd both stopped spooning – soaring eerily above the generators had come this uncanniness: the sound of a sizeable proportion of Ali al-Garbi's female population, who'd gathered outside the main gates, beyond the tee-barrier, and were ululating . . . *all the grief they'd got*. It's as if, Tizer said, they're trying to raise him from the dead with this hocus-pocus . . . *As if – not Asif al-Sayyab* . . . and Gawain had been grim: No one gives a shit about him, Tizer – they're here for the detainees in the TeeDeeEff. No one gives a shit about a lousy traitorous 'terp – a mouthpiece for the hated Crusaders . . . No, and now that mouth-piece was *stopped up* with sand, while a ball of dried earth had been placed beneath his tight and dusty curls, and a carefully folded Sunderland EffSee tracksuit top laid *at his bare feet – how much do I actually know about Islam and the Muslims?* Not much, he'd thought at supper – and reacknowledges now: 'sides the fact they've gotta be planted within twenty-four hours of getting . . . *slotted.* Gawain hits the return key – *I hit the return key*: the grimy and depressed little return key – and the email whooshes into the darkness, a dinky tip-tilting envelope which fades into a faintly oscillating after-presence: a tiny circlet *crowning* the screen, which *spins and spins, again annagain* . . . But it will return – of that much he's certain. Return before tomorrow, when the rugby tournament is due to *kick off* . . . with Japanese and New Zealander teams battling it out with sevens from . . . *all the home nations.* At least, that was the plan until today: when the Wimmik roared back into the compound that afternoon, the first thing Gawain had seen were some of the Japanese contractors practising behind the mean concrete bunker which now housed the detainees: the Temporary Detention Facility, or TeeDeeEff. Small men – hairless men . . . *what would that be like?* who tossed the ball blithely back and forth. A mean concrete bunker – three rooms, one little more than a coal-hole, the others roughly ten metres square, both equipped with roughly oblong openings above head-height . . . *in lieu of windows*, their crumbling edges pierced by the sharp serration of steel reinforcing . . . *up late rubbing Bonjela into Miffy's gums* . . . There was a grim sort of vestibule as well – he'd stood in it with Gareth Trimmingham when they were doing the handover. We're an equal opportunities employer, said the Coldstreamers' SeeOh . . . *thought he was funny*: At least when it comes to entry-level detention – we've 'ad 'em all in here – Badr lot, Mucky's boys, local Ali Babas . . . There'd been a bad atmos' in the dank blockhouse: the wall Trimmer was leaning against had iron hooks hammered into it from which hung lengths of rusty chain: We harsh 'em a bit – by the book, though, nothing too hairy . . . Just getting the message out. Gawain had looked down at the concrete floor, where there was an archipelago of stains which he chose to see as a *sort of diagram or flow-chart* . . . explaining . . . *the work which goes on here.* – Nothing iffy, though, Gareth – you'd tell me if there'd been anything iffy? Trimmer and his Coldstreamers had muscled in on the Sierra Leone deployment – he'd always been a dab hand at *crawling up brass-arse*, had Trimmer. The Thomases had got to know the Trimminghams when their respective regiments were in Germany – Trimmer's wife, Marilyn, had palled up with Fi at an antenatal class. Big girl, Marilyn – very pale, translucent skin . . . *au bleu*, he remembers the pair of them doing their exercises on the floor of the Thomases' three-bed apartment . . . *good deal: five hundred square metres – four hundred a month*, hoiking their heavy bellies about as they shouted Girl Power! at the ceiling. Yes, good mates they'd been, Marilyn and Fi, but as for their other halves . . .

we'd never make a whole. The wives kept in touch, though, and one hot summer morning the Thomases drove down to Mitcham for a barbecue – hauling the old Volvo estate round the Emm-Twentyfive, the kids griddling in the back, Gawain's resentments poisonously drip-drip-dripping down on to the steering wheel. Yeah-yeah – class act, the Guards. Officers got to be city-slickers, commuting into barracks from the outer suburbs every day, just like any other office-bound muppet. Yeah, class-bloody-act – with the emphasis very much on class . . . Then, when they arrived in Mitcham, there'd been instant relief: Trimmer had laid a big bit of plastic tarpaulin over the back lawn, and he played a hose over it as all the younger guests stripped off and ran and jumped and slid and laughed . . . *and screamed.* The other families were all army – couple of bods from Trimmer's outfit, and a smiley, plump and faintly worrying character called Forbes who, Gawain gathered – without needing to be told – was EssEff. Trouble didn't come from Forbes, though, who did a lot of Pimm's . . . *his number one cup runneth over,* then slumped in an armchair in front of the afternoon racing. The wives huddled up gossiping – and Gawain walked in, unannounced, on Trimmer and his bods. They were in Trimmer's den, which boasted shaggy white floor-covering, squashy-black seating – an old Space Invaders arcade cabinet in one corner, and Trimmer's certificates and citations all over the walls. While on the window-sill, various shelves, the mantelpiece . . . *bloody everywhere* had been hundreds of whisky miniatures. One of the bods had been passing Trimmer an open laptop as Gawain entered . . . *a flying-blue-vee,* pointing the way to another world, which, for a moment, they were unwilling to share with him. But then they had, and to begin with Gawain couldn't understand what it was he was looking at – was this some sort of visual trickery? An image flickering into another . . . *and back*: dress on/dress off, old crone/young beauty, shapeless mass/*pile of severed arms* . . . Routine patrol stuff, Greeny, Trimmer had said – and in that moment the *shapeless mass* of his character had resolved into this *bloody atrocity* . . . Trimmer's own words sloshed around in his fruit cup of a mouth. Not a big man, Trimmer Trimmingham – in point of fact, exactly the same stature as his bountiful wife – but with a large and craggy head. A tall-short man, who, when Gawain was looking down on him, somehow contrived to . . . *look down on me.* No, not a tall man – even when he was filmed with a camcorder standing on a pile of severed black arms slathered with crimson blood. No. They'd all stood there in the darkened den – Trimmer, Gawain, Trimmer's bods – the chilly uplight from the laptop bathing their faces, as they took in this . . . *anatomy lesson.* Then Trimmer had hit the *return* and the scene shifted a few hundred yards on. Seeing Gawain's expression, Trimmer had reiterated: Routine patrol stuff – and one of the bods put in: Who was it that day, Boss, the arfs or the rufs? Rather than answer directly, Trimmer deftly manipulated the keys so the images staggered towards them – images of children only a year or two older than the ones who were frolicking outside in the sunny Surrey afternoon. Children wearing cotton shorts and T-shirts printed with the colourful logos of YouEss teevee shows and cartoon characters, who were sitting on the ground in stress positions. Children who'd been deprived of their AyKays –

which were leaning against the exposed chassis of a technical that'd rolled over beside this nameless jungle trail, presumably marking the spot at which Trimmer *and his merrie men* had caught up with them. Armed Forces Revolutionary Council, Trimmer said for Gawain's benefit. Those were the fuckers responsible for most of the limb-severing – though the rufs, the so-called Revolutionary United Front, would get in on the act whenever the oppo' presented itself . . . As he'd spoken, the camera had tracked back and forth, focusing first on one face, then another: a fly strolled along a faintly moustached top lip – sweat polished an ebony forehead. – Our patrols'd come upon this sorta badness – then we'd catch up with the perps easily enough. Why, Greeny? Well, two reasons: first, they'd been running round in that jungle for fucking years with no one on hand to give 'em a slap. Secundo: well, as you can see – arfs, rufs, the other mob as well, all ranks were made up with kiddy-winkies. Take away the stick of sugarcane they were sucking and hand 'em a fucking gat – after you've fucked 'em, course . . . The man filming must have walked backwards at this point, because the view widened out to the entire clearing: the Brit grunts standing about, in their jungle camos with bush-hat brims pushed up, chatting, swigging from their canteens, wiping their mouths and then rubbing their palms together – a universal gesture, intended to convey to anyone watching . . . *actions speak louder than words*. Yes, actions speak louder than words, what with small arms for the eighties still saving . . . *small arms in the noughties*. But that hadn't been the end of it – the camera went on moving: its angle dropping so that the *forest's ferny floor* filled the viewfinder. There'd been,

Gawain thinks, an awful complicity in sharing this jerky and down-cast vision. Outside, all their kids frolicked in perfect safety – inside Gawain's chest his heart hammered. He'd wanted to turn away . . . *go away*, but he'd been trapped in the tiny scrum of Coldstreamers. As they watched, they'd been joined by Forbes, the EssEff cove, who'd wandered into this darkened chamber . . . *without knocking*. Gawain wheezily squeaked, Y-You d-didn't, did you, Trimmer? And Forbes had answered for him: What? Whacked 'em in cold blood? I hardly think so, my horsy friend – we were in country for a bit of lurping first, and I believe Trimmer's mob followed on with our EmmOh . . . See, your child soldier can be as bloodthirsty as anyone – but they're buggers to keep in line, and they've fuck-all in the way of initiative. No: turn left at the cairn of amputated arms and keep right on 'til you run right into the little surgeons. Confession'll be easy enough to extract – if you've a bag of Haribo to hand . . . Which had been Trimmer's cue to say: Fortunately we did, Bill . . . Yes-yes . . . Gawain buries his head in his hands, adopting his own *stress position*. That's what Trimmer'd said to Bill Forbes the EssEff bod: Fortunately we did – got my Queue-man on it before we deployed . . . A top tip, Gawain had thought at the time, which was why he'd had a few when the Rams *were forced to adopt the stress position*: sitting, knees bent and embraced by aching arms, praying for glory or deliverance in the Herc's booming nave, while listening to the men's . . . *boys, really* chorus as they strapped themselves into the webbing: Gorrany scran, Bessie? And the gawky one with the wanker's wristbones chucked the rustling bag in a wide arc . . . *tangtastic!* All the awkward positions – the stressed positions

391

the Rams're *forced to adopt* . . . the pillowslip coldly moulding his face – the lube a chilly dash-then-splodge between his buttocks – the bracken swishing and scratching your thighs, the heather twisting your ankles, the sun cooking through to your . . . *marrow*. Sixteen-mile yomp – fifty-pound pack: sew a couple of Oxo cubes into the hem of your keks – DoubleyouOhs never check there . . . Something to suck on when the going gets . . . stressful. All the awkward positions – the stressed positions *he forced me to adopt* . . . *No more!* It must be thirty-five degrees still in the Portakabin, and the sweat carries on *spurting out of me* . . . a hose played across Gawain's slippery *plastic sheeting*. You'd tell me if there'd been anything iffy, wouldn't you Trimmer? Gawain had asked Colonel Trimmingham in the dirty, dusty, sandy, stained vestibule . . . *were we a pair?* It'd been a repeat of the *stressful position* he'd been forced into in Trimmer's Mitcham den: bent over, compelled to look at the screen and equally unable to make the right noises – the bods' small, appreciative yeahs and deferential coughs. The two young men had been arranged on the grassy slope beside the jungle track – laid on their sides, facing one another . . . *lovers, post-coitally cooing*, with flies buzzing around their eyes – moseying in and out of their nostrils . . . *again annagain.* They wore the same undress uniforms as the children they'd mutilated, but in their case the T-shirt designs were a bit more unconventional: tight groupings of bullet holes . . . *must've fired at fairly close range* still oozing blood. One for the archives, eh, Trimmer? Forbes had said as Trimmer snapped shut the laptop. You wouldn't want some sensitive Guardian-reading soul seeing that, now would you? But what's their solution for evil cunts like that, machetes dripping blood? There'd been a subdued grunt of manly assent *like they'd all come*, Gawain had thought in Trimmer's den – thinks it again now, in the *damp crotch* of the Iraqi night: It was like they'd all come – Trimmer, Forbes, the bods . . . they'd shaken themselves, legs trembling in their chinos and EmmanEss cargo shorts. – Emerging from the jungle, they'd heard the joyous shrieks of the children playing outside in Mitcham. One by one they'd improved their grip on their glasses, bottles and cans, before filing out to join them. It's a dirty and dehumanising job, their expressions had said: killing adolescents who've mutilated, murdered and raped children – but we're the right men for it, precisely because we take no pleasure, *we're merely professionals* . . . And now it's dark o'clock, and outside the main gate of Camp Val *tongues are still wagging* . . . Wagging over the detainees the Rams brought back from Al-Afrika Street – and wagging over Asif, the lousy little 'terp, who – Cambell from the int' cell has reported – just happened to be the son of one of Ali al-Garbi's most prominent Sadrists. Gawain has already put a call in to the Chief of Police and informed him about the incident – although . . . *why?* The man's rumoured to be a pederast who spends his days shuttered up in his vulgar villa on a bank of the Tigris, fiddling about with Yemeni, Baluchi and even . . . Somali boys: the human *flux* and *reflux* of this *indigestible situation* . . . *What do I really know about Islam and Muslims?* He massages his eyelids with finger and thumb, so summoning this vision: a dusty-white maidan under hurting sun – white-robed figures swirling together, then swishing apart to reveal their Saladin: a huge man with a huge black beard who windmills his scimitar's flashing blade. Gawain stands, awkward in Birkenstocks, cargo shorts and a T-shirt bearing the slogan *Play Up and Play the Game* . . . Saladin's scimitar slices through this loose stuff, and it's only then, looking down at his belly . . . *thinly grinning* that Gawain remembers: I'm armed . . . so raises and fires his plastic rifle. The plastic seven-point-six-five round makes its leisurely, specially effected way towards the huge chest of the mighty jihadi – but then, just about everything's plastic nowadays: the case of Trimmer's laptop – the duff spoiler of the Thomas family's crappy old Volvo. The map cases that'd arrived in a job-lot on the day before the Rams deployed . . . *plastic*, and the maps they were issued with at Shaibah . . . *plastic-laminated* that labelled the towns and villages, the saltpans and oil fields, of southern Iraq with the sort of clunky code names beloved of the British military: Cheshire, Westmoreland, *Omagh* . . . *What do I really know about Islam and Muslims?* The plastic bullet hits Saladin's chest and rebounds in still slower motion, end over end, describing a limp parabola that ends, uselessly, on the sand at Gawain's feet . . . *Only this: that the word itself means . . . submission – and I'm through with that* . . . One thing, Greeny, Trimmer had said as he was swinging into one of the Coldstreamers' Wimmiks, I've put it in my report as well, but if you bag anybody coming over the border who seems . . . well, handy, get 'em down to the DeeTeeEff asap. It's not just a matter of finding out what the Iranians're up to – our spooky friends have an asset they're particularly keen to exfiltrate, someone high up . . . Word is he may try to cross over into our – I mean, your sector. Gawain had queried, Our spooky friends? What d'you mean by that? The slime at main? And Trimmer snorted, Hardly – Brigade's intel' wonks are picking up sod-all from the locals. How can they, when they're on lock-down at Shaibah and the aypod twenty-four-seven? No, this is something to do with the big boys – with London . . . *No! This is something to do with the small boys – with Bardney* . . . Before Jonathan had got into the low-slung coupé – before he'd removed his over-coat, neatly folded it and placed it on the car's back seat. Before he'd driven away . . . *without so much as a backward glance*, there'd been *a mouthful of marbles*: suppressed giggles from behind the flinty wall. Jonathan walked along to where it dipped to waist height and looked over – the eavesdroppers had been hiding, shivering, behind a tombstone. Come out! Jonathan cried. Come out, I say! But they hadn't come out – they ran away, their narrow, grey-cloth-clad behinds *shining* in the winter sunlight – or at least this is how Gawain pictured it. When Jonathan returned he'd teased him: I say? I say? What will you bray next, posh boy? But *the Butcher's* face had been leeched . . . bloodless – *bien cuit*: I'm not as blasé as you imagine, Gawain – I care a great deal about the people I work with, who all too often run appalling risks for very little reward – and I resent it, really I do . . . the way these people are caricatured as grubby little opportunists . . . Maybe so, but it'd been the *grubby little opportunists* who'd awaited Gawain in Ali al-Garbi – or at least caricatures of them: Tizer claims the sharkskin suits were all the rage in the Soviet bloc – and are a two-tone legacy of Saddam's ambivalent attempt to cuddle up to the Russians. But the men who wear them . . . *look pretty rough*: sitting in stifling corridors, drenched in cologne, waiting to petition one of the remaining SeePeeAy bureaucrats for a generator or a water-purification plant . . . *for their community.* Any of them, Gawain hypothesises, might be one of Jonathan's precious assets, not waiting to siphon off British and American taxpayers' money, but to piddle out *the Bardney boys' innocent betrayal* . . . He said to her – she said to him, he said to – *others*: *a cat's cradle* of comms, such as he's seen dangling from every post and pylon and rooftop in Ali al-Garbi, the cables of which tighten . . . and tighten, until the grubby little opportunist in the stifling corridor is . . . *garrotted.* Anyway, Jonathan always comes on so fucking strong – like nothing fazes him. But how would he actually cope with this noduf? With Ali al-Garbi, its shabby-shiny sheiks, bullying Badr militia commanders and ineffectual governors, who, so far as Gawain could tell, were all the puppets, either of the sinister black-turbanned clerics or the foreign agents provocateurs who *pull their strings* . . . Yes! Jonathan! What would you make of this? He's spoken aloud and hears his words drop *uselessly* to the Portakabin's floor . . . *Plop! Plop!* followed by the resurgence of the sinister cries at the main gate . . . *fire a few baton rounds over their heads – get rid of 'em.* He stands, picks up his webbing belt and holster, buckles on the assemblage. Picks up his body armour *arms up!* and puts it on. He thinks of his sister, Fay, a yoga instructor and part-time hospital physio' who lives with her long-term partner near Keswick . . . *Geoff's all right*: their rainy, childless Sunday afternoons – visiting the Pencil Museum *again*, followed by a walk on the shores of Derwent Water *hand in hand*, seeing the water dimpled by squalls and *itching for the fells.* Later, there'd be pork scratchings in the snug, followed by a dark night in an overheated room. He wonders if Fay and Geoff's sex is as workmanlike as his and Fiona's . . . *a drubbing really* – more arousal to be had from the *greasy Cumberland sausage on the breakfast plate.* There are, he thinks, these compensations: the small sips of intimacy to be sucked from parched conversations about the weather and current affairs – and, of course, minor ailments, the minute description of which is most long-term marrieds' way of *touching at a distance* . . . Moving towards the Portakabin's door, Gawain becomes aware of a strange sort of pause . . . or . . . gap . . . in . . . every . . . thing, it's . . . *lagging!* One or other of his sons' spoilt whines solders his burning brain to his griddling skull: *It's lagging!* They'd played the game together, the three of them taking turns with the controller: *You're not much cop, Dad, considering you're a tank commander* . . . He'd considered pointing out to the disrespectful brat that there was a world of difference between jabbing buttons and the combination of nimble tactical thinking and heavy psychological lifting required to move armoured vehicles around on a battlefield – but then *my head exploded* . . . even as the truck the Thomas menfolk were riding in continued its mad zigzagging dash across sandy nothingness towards a walled compound. *My head exploded* . . . the screen darkened, and, although the Germans' tracer-fire kept on streaming towards their truck, it was over for him . . . *endex*: he'd never get to assault those Moorish walls. But he did get to see his own hollowed-out and virtual body lying there . . . *such a privilege*, and in the ultra-secure surroundings of Number Seven, Maltby Close, behind the vertical louvres Fi . . . *never bothered to replace*, he'd thought, This must be what it feels like to be a true and valiant Christian knight – or the right arm of the Prophet for that matter, on your way up to heaven, sitting on a half-landing eating sherbet, and . . . *waiting for the virgins.* His sons had kept on sneering at him: You just fire and fire, Dad – you never check your ammo or your health bar on the heads-up display . . . At Camp Val the unloading bay lies immediately to the rear of the SeeOh's own trailer – which is the one nearest to the main gate. When a Rams patrol returns to base they drive their Wimmiks and Scimitars into an external fifty-metre-long sandbagged rat-run, then in through both sets of gates. The troopers get out and stomp over to an unloading bay that's been bodged together with old railway sleepers. Chattering away, they aim their EssAyEighties, Brownings and Sig Sauers nonchalantly – pull the triggers with expressions of mild distaste, then walk off shaking their trouser legs, just as . . . *Trimmer's bods did back in Mitcham . . . It's lagging, Dad, and your head's exploded . . . I owe you three farthings – or the Queen's shilling* . . . Gawain stands on the steps of the trailer, smell-ing the Ali al-Garbi night: faint whiffs of wood- and dung-smoke from the shantytown by the Tigris, the pervasive reek of Camp Val's septic tank – and the fresher, fouler smell coming from the long row of Portaloos which serve as a latrine for Rams, Kiwis and Jap contractors alike. Still, better than the old Roman-style shitters they'd had in the past: *Everyone knew your business – saw you doing it* . . . Back in Yorkshire, the medics had dipped the Rams in all sorts of vaccines – against anthrax, cholera, smallpox . . . *Allah knows what.* The entire regiment underwent exhaustive ennbeesee training as well: out on the parade ground in early-morning drizzle, several hundred men *and a few women* clambering into plastic all-in-ones . . . *Ooh, aren't they cute!* This must be how a baby feels, Gawain had thought at the time, standing zipping himself up, then peeling back the remove-to-stick seal and affixing it to his . . . *bib.* In front of him the Rams crinkled and crackled as they stashed their bottles of decontamination fluid away in their bergens. The entire drill was meant to be completed in three minutes flat, but Gawain seriously doubted if in battlefield conditions they'd manage it . . . *in under forty-five – I've a hundred and one uses for a dead cat . . .* so had said Captain Petersen in her medical briefing for squadron leaders . . . *and a hundred and one ways of treating tummy trouble . . .* She likes that sort of banter, does Gail: jollying the big babies along . . . *so there's absolutely no need for anyone to suffer in silence* – at which *PowerPoint* there was, naturally enough, a raspberry chorus from the boys-will-be-babies along the back row. Yes, indeed: there were a hundred and one ways of treating diarrhoea – trouble was, after a while, *none of 'em fucking work.* So all those ennbeesee suits are being filled up with slurry *from the inside*: a brown tide rising and rising, 'til it submerges *our teary eyes.* Half the Rams had the shits on any given day, despite Petersen's regular top-up briefings on personal hygiene . . . *mucky boys – mucky little puppies . . . always gotta be reminded to wash their paws after playing in . . . the sandpit. Oh the feeling, when you're reeling . . .* Gail's Welsh, too . . . *you step lightly . . .* Gawain steps lightly off the last flimsy tread and . . . *down to the ground.* Trouble is . . . *I'm still lagging* – lagging behind his blond avatar, bulky in its camos and body armour. For a moment he wonders what'd happen if he drew his sidearm and fired . . . *outside*

399

of the screen – would it magically reload? Because that's what hap-pens . . . *at home – I'm lagging* . . . lagging behind the Rams' valiant SeeOh, who moves off confidently across the compound, a deeply superficial zone of intersecting translucent panels, where walls have mouths-instead-of-ears and helpful instructions float . . . *in mid-air.* Gawain barely notices the trooper on stag, whose challenge morphs into a strangulated Ssssir! and a sketchy salute – he's more interested in this effect: *I can see the back of my head!* Out there in the Iraqi night – of course, that's *a far more permissive environment*: Lieutenant-Colonel Thomas's standing orders are that no one leave the camp without their rifle loaded and a round chambered – but that won't stop things going off inside the compound. The Rams, like all soldiers, delight in practical jokes – only last week, Lieutenant Wilton, the TwoEyeSee of B Squadron, introduced one of the oil-dyed sheep he'd somehow managed to trap – then dress in suspender belt, panties and a bra – into the trailer shared by his EnnSeeOhs. Wilton had filmed the scene with night-vision equipment: half-naked men thrashing about, while the *horny devil* was identifiable by its *stronger heat signal* . . . As he follows his virtual self across the compound Gawain considers: These Iraqis need to understand a bit more about us Brits – understand that we value two qualities above all others: a genuine capacity for fair play – and *a good sense of humour* . . . He's reached the main gate and stands peering into the sandbagged rat-run, with its rumble-strips improvised with two-by-fours, and its signs silently screaming STOP! and PREPARE TO BE SEARCHED! in English and Arabic. There're a few discarded Cyalumes on the dirty concrete which still glow . . . *eerily greeny*. Troopers are milling about the grandly named TeeDeeEff, slovenly in off-duty shorts and flip-flops – the vicious hanks of razor wire coiled on the roof of the concrete blockhouse, caught in the sodium glare of the searchlights mounted on the sangars . . . *sparkle*. The troopers are swigging from mineral-water bottles filled with Foster's and *Christ knows what else . . .* Troopers Carr and Compton are arsing about, marching *hup! two, three, four!* up and down in front of the metal door, Cyalumes stuck up under their arms *swagger-stick style . . .* Their sweaty faces are *Sunny-Delightful* in the *grimelight*. Gawain sees Lieutenant-Colonel Thomas approach this parody of keeping watch, and Trooper Carr, sensing his presence, whips round, Cyalume levelled: Halt! Who goes there? COLONEL THOMAS: The only time you aim a weapon at someone, Carr, is because you want to shoot them. You were told that on your first day of basic – and just about every other bloody day since. TROOPER CARR (Cyalume displayed in his outstretched palm): But sir, it's only one of these. COLONEL THOMAS (laughing): Yeah-yeah, I can see that, Carr – I was just winding you up. THE CHOIR (from inside the TeeDeeEff, their dry and cracked lips struggling to form the unfamiliar phonemes): Chhhyour love's gomme chhhlookin' so craazeee ri' now, Chhhyour touch gomme chhhlookin' so craazee ri' now . . . COLONEL THOMAS (with a jerk of his leonine head): What the fuck's occurring in there? TROOPER COMPTON: It's the choir, sir – Captain Cambell sorta . . . put it . . . together. COLONEL THOMAS: A choir? He . . . formed a choir, did he? TROOPER COMPTON: That's right, sir – prisoners' choir, sir . . . Gotta make 'em sing, he said – keep 'em singing . . .

COLONEL THOMAS: But we don't have any prisoners here, Compton (another jerk of his leonine head). All you men: this is the theatre detention facility, got that? You don't imprison prisoners in a detention facility, now do you? You imprison prisoners in a bloody prison – and prisoners-of-war in a prison-of-war camp. THE CHOIR (throats grating, chests wheezing): Ch-chhhyour love gomme ch-chhhlookin' so craazee ri' now, Ch-chhhyour touch gomme lookin' so craazee ri' now . . . COLONEL THOMAS: No, what you do with a temporary detention facility is put detainees in it who've been temporarily . . . detained. And what do you do with those detainees, Trooper? TROOPER CARR (tipsily enthusiastic): Y-You qu-question them, sir – interrogate them to see if they've any operationally significant intel' . . . sir. COLONEL THOMAS: That's right – you question them, which is what Captain Cambell and his colleagues in the int' cell should be doing, not this . . . this . . . bullshit. Now, you men: I know you're all shaken up by what happened today – Bessie's a good lad and one of our own. He's our first casualty – but almost certainly won't be our last. Think of those poor bastards who were brought down in the Herc' by all means, but don't get any ideas about doing a Beharry – tinware only gets handed out once in a blue moon. Okay (he raises his voice), fun's over, lads – off you fuck to beddy-byes. (Gawain stands watching the men's fag-ends as they *firefly* across the compound towards the squadron lines. He turns back and, approaching the metal door of the Tee-DeeEff, knocks on it. It's opened immediately by CAPTAIN CAMBELL, a tall man in his early thirties with a flat pie-dish of a freckled face, split-ends to his red hair and dandruff on his collar.

From behind him come the sounds and smells of a number of distressed humans in a confined space: muttering, sobbing, keening and stinking. Gawain tries to speak, but can't – he just stands there because everything's . . . *lagging*.) CAPTAIN CAMBELL: All right, Boss – everything all right? Any news from Main? COLONEL THOMAS: Ah, yeah – same as, Dave: detainees'll have to be down to Shaibah asap tomorrow – which is a pain, given the rugger's due to kick off. Convoy'll need to be fairly hefty – couple of aypeesees for the detainees, at least four Wimmiks for Force Protection. You can go along if you like – get a decent shower, kip in a proper bed for a night. Those pod-thingies have all mod cons and a hard cover. CAPTAIN CAMBELL: Thanks, Boss – who knows, I might have some stuff to give to the slime at Main as well. COLONEL THOMAS: You did the course at Chicksands, didn't you, Dave? CAPTAIN CAMBELL: Yes, sir, that's right. COLONEL THOMAS: Interrogation – that sorta thing? CAPTAIN CAMBELL: Teaqueue, sir. COLONEL THOMAS: Tea queue? CAPTAIN CAMBELL: Tactical questioning, sir – designed to get them singing, so we can find out who's Jam, who's Badr, who's in it just for the sheer badness. COLONEL THOMAS: So that's why you formed a choir, is it – so they could sing the truth? CAPTAIN CAMBELL (flicking sweat-damp hair from his shadowed eyes): Well, that's really just the warm-up, Boss – the singing. Gotta get them sorta . . . in tune. Then Myerson brings 'em through to me and Marty for the proper do. COLONEL THOMAS: The proper do, eh . . . I hope there's nothing iffy going on here, Dave? CAPTAIN CAMBELL (smiling): By the book, Boss, by the book. COLONEL THOMAS: All right, then – better let me

403

have a butcher's . . . (CAPTAIN CAMBELL swings the door open with more hideous screeching, and admits COLONEL THOMAS to the grim little vestibule. He unlocks a large padlock and opens the cell door. The odour of piss, sweat and fear is palpable – but it's dark, and difficult to make out anything beyond bulbous shapes and lumpy shadows.) COLONEL THOMAS: How many of these blokes are there, Dave? CAPTAIN CAMBELL (reading from a sheet of paper attached to a clipboard he bought for himself at the Ryman's in York): Ibrahim Gattan Hassan al-Ismaeeli, seven-seven-four, Kadhim Abbas Latifah al-Bendali, seven-seven-five, Hussein al-Almari Gibarian, seven-seven-six, Abdul Sayyid al-Lami, seven-seven-seven, Mahdi Ahmed al-Rashid Hameedawi, seven-seven-eight, Amir Ali al-Jabbar, seven-seven-nine, Mahdi Mohammed al-Baghri Noor, seven-eighty. All detainees present and correct, sir. COLONEL THOMAS (wiping his face with the scrap of camouflage netting he uses as a cravat): That's seven, Dave – minus the women and kids we scooped up, eight. Where's the eighth? CAPTAIN CAMBELL: He's in the rap, Boss – touch of heat exhaustion. COLONEL THOMAS: I'm not bloody surprised – it's hot as hell in here. (Having gained his night-sight, he walks the length of the detainees, who sit or kneel on the floor, hands plasti-cuffed behind their backs. They've been hooded with pillow slips, and the loose cloth transforms them into cowering Elephant Men.) Now, Dave, your back-up 'terp . . . CAPTAIN CAMBELL: Marty? COLONEL THOMAS: Up to the job, is he? CAPTAIN CAMBELL (thinking about his girlfriend, who he'd left on a bench outside the Jorvik Centre while he went to buy the clipboard): We-ell, he's all right, Boss – but you know the drill: he's just a stab so I gotta brace him a bit. Keeps saying he'd rather be out with his whippets. COLONEL THOMAS: Whippets? CAPTAIN CAMBELL (he knows his sexual technique isn't that good – she flinches when he touches her): Yeah, he's got a kennel outside Uttoxeter, Boss – but he did six months at Aldershot with some Iraqi exile. One-to-one conversational Arabic. COLONEL THOMAS: So, enough to understand what's going on – and, more importantly: make them understand him? CAPTAIN CAMBELL (who's been bored rigid by MAJOR MCADIE): Yeah, well enough – frankly I sometimes wish I couldn't understand him, he's always banging on about scran. COLONEL THOMAS: Explain, Cambell? CAPTAIN CAMBELL (she was narked when he came back, but he told her: Mad, I know – but I'll get out there and I'll have to proff everything: pillowslips for hoods, Bill Haynes's boom-box so's to give 'em the mega-mega white noise – and a clipboard's fucking essential if you're gonna run an improvised-bloody-torture chamber): Marty went up to Baggers last week, Boss – some 'terp refresher thing the Yanks organised. Anyway, he got to eat in their deefac, came back banging on about the delights therein. COLONEL THOMAS: Enlighten me further, Captain Cambell. CAPTAIN CAMBELL: 'Parently YouEss government makes a pledge to its servicemen and women – not to give them the right equipment for the job, that's a given, but to supply them with surf-and-turf every Friday evening. COLONEL THOMAS: Every Friday evening? CAPTAIN CAMBELL: That's right, fresh-bloody-lobster – not frozen. And fresh-bloody-steak – or crayfish tail at the very least. Had some of that myself once, on hols in Orlando – yabba they call it, and they yabba-dabba-do get their grub in, come what may. You can be plotted up in Falujah, Boss, warming your backside on deeyou ordinance and they'll get it to you – together with a couple of cans of soda –. COLONEL THOMAS: Soda? CAPTAIN CAMBELL: Coke, Pepsi – Doctor Pepper or Tab. You don't get a choice, but it really is the real thing – not some Freedom Cola bullshit – and you always get your two cans, that's their two-can rule, Boss. COLONEL THOMAS: Extraordinary – 'specially when you consider the logistics. CAPTAIN CAMBELL (manipulating the buttons of a cheap calculator he bought at the same time as the clipboard and has clipped to it – she wouldn't give him a blow-job before he went overseas, which was surely the whole point of going to war): I have, Boss – look, it's actually two cans per meal, which makes six every day. They've got what? Somewhere between a hundred and thirty and a hundred and fifty thousand combat troops in theatre – same numbers of support. Round it down to two-fifty kay and that makes one and a half million cans being brought in for the occupying forces every single day. COLONEL THOMAS: It's impressive, certainly – but then you don't get to be the world's only super-power without a certain amount of . . . fizz. (Both men laugh – COLONEL THOMAS stops first: he's looking at the detainees' plasti-cuffed hands, the complicated meshing of their blue and bloodless fingers. He sees the detainees' hands amputated and armoured – sees them fumbling in two long files along the sandy bed of the Shatt al-Arab, trails of bubbles purling from their knuckles up to the silvery surface.) But Marty – he can handle this, can he, Dave? CAPTAIN CAMBELL: No need to worry, Boss – he did the same course as me. Knows the drill: go in clean and act just a little bit . . . dirty. COLONEL THOMAS: Well, he's not one of us, Dave – he's not a Ram, and, frankly, I find him to be a bit of an arrogant buffoon. CAPTAIN CAMBELL: No doubt about it, Boss – but for now he's our arrogant buffoon, and he's well integrated into the hum' int' team –. THE CHOIR: Hum' int', hum' int', hum' int'! THE METAL DOOR: Scrrrreeeaaalllarrrk! MAJOR McADIE (enters carrying a BOOM BOX – he's a paunchy man in his fifties, with male-pattern baldness): Boss – Dave. THE BOOM BOX: Got me lookin' so crazy like now, your touch, Got me lookin' . . . COLONEL THOMAS: Is that Bill's boom box thingie? MAJOR McADIE: That's right, Boss – I see you've met the choir. (He walks along the line of cowering Iraqi detainees, stooping to yank each pair of plasti-cuffed hands in turn.) THE CHOIR: Ooh! Aah! Eek! Arr! Incomprehensible Arabic oath! Fuck you! Aah! MAJOR McADIE: Hear that? If I could just get them to be a bit more bloody consistent, I could sorta . . . play 'em – like an instrument, sorta human synthesiser-type-thing. THE BOOM BOX: . . . Your love's got me lookin' so –. COLONEL THOMAS: That one – he said fuck off, take his hood off, McAdie. MAJOR McADIE: Ooh, no, Boss – no can do. COLONEL THOMAS: Why the fuck not? CAPTAIN CAMBELL: Marty's right, Boss – proper teaqueue requires following exactly the same cycle for all the suspects –. COLONEL THOMAS: Let me stop you right there, Dave – you called these men suspects. Strictly speaking, since we'll be handing them over to their own legitimately elected authorities soon enough, and won't be charging them ourselves, is it right to even think of them as suspects? MAJOR McADIE:

Well, Boss, saving your feeling for the finer points, we definitely suspect one of these rag 'eads of shooting Trooper Bessemer – and either him, or one of his greasy little pals of slotting Asif –. CAPTAIN CAMBELL: And we happened to like Asif – liked him a great fucking deal! (He moves in on the detainees and shouts at their shapeless heads.) A! Great! Fucking! Deal! THE BOOM BOX: Uh-oh, uh-oh, uh-oh, oh no . . . COLONEL THOMAS: Gentlemen, would you mind stepping outside for a moment, please? (The three British officers retreat from the darkened chamber with its hooded occupants stinking of sweat, piss and fear. In the vestibule MAJOR MCADIE knocks on the door opposite, and they're admitted by a dark haired and overweight Lance-Corporal wearing a khaki T-shirt. This chamber isn't as large as the one the detainees are being held in. Extension cables worm in through the crudely barred window-openings, piping juice to orange-blooming light bulbs. A pair of mismatched tables sit in the middle of the concrete floor – one trestle, the other an ancient gate-leg. On them are a digital recorder, an IRON BAR, a hank of electrical cabling, a NOKIA mobile phone, a canvas bag, some mineral-water bottles and a beach-bloated copy of HARRY POTTER AND THE CHAMBER OF SECRETS.) MAJOR MCADIE: Everything all right, Lance? LANCE-CORPORAL MYER-SON: Boss . . . (seeing the SeeOh, and saluting smartly) . . . Sir! COLONEL THOMAS: Were you abbreviating his rank, Marty, or calling him by his Christian name? CAPTAIN CAMBELL: We-ell, it's a bit of a laugh, really, Myerson's Christian name actually being Lance – unusual one for this day and age. What was the deal with your old people? LANCE-CORPORAL MYERSON: Dunno, sir – me da' passed away when I was little, and me mam thinks it might've been a family thing on his side, but she isn't sure. COLONEL THOMAS: I tell you one thing that's for sure, Myerson. LANCE-CORPORAL MYERSON: What's that, sir? COLONEL THOMAS: You haven't got a snowball's chance in hell of further promotion. LANCE-CORPORAL MYERSON (crestfallen): Why's that, sir? COLONEL THOMAS: Because as things stand you're almost certainly the only Lance Lance in the entire bloody army – an army which, thanks to the perfidy of our political masters, is called upon to do more and more with less and less. So, don't imagine I'd dare to degrade such a precious asset as you, Myerson, especially in a conflict situation. THE OFFICERS: Ha, ha, ha, ha! LANCE-CORPORAL MYERSON (his submissive expression a mask behind which his true features are twisted with impotent rage): If you say so, sir. THE BOOM BOX: Hissssssssshhhhhhh . . . COLONEL THOMAS (who was bullied quite badly at all his schools, and especially savagely when he was sent back to the YouKay to board. A variety of epithets were used to denigrate him, although, a lack of imagination being characteristic of tormentors, they all sooner or later settled on John Thomas, Prick Thomas, Cock Thomas, Dick Thomas or abbreviations thereof: Prick, Cock, Dick – *dirty-fucking Dick . . . cummere. Wanna game of slaps? Beat me at slaps like a man, an' I'll stop calling you dirty-fucking Dick, Dick*): Can't you turn that bloody thing off? CAPTAIN CAMBELL (depressing the relevant key): Sorry 'bout that, Boss – loud noise, white noise . . . all part of the conditioning. COLONEL THOMAS: Conditioning, eh – whassat, then? CAPTAIN CAMBELL (leaning back against the table with THE IRON BAR on it, crossing his arms and speaking with added pedantry): All part of maintaining the shock of capture, Boss, which is our best chance of getting these murdering tossers to cough up the goods. See, your Arab feels terrible shame when he's been nabbed – reflects poorly on his manliness, his fitness as a soldier of Allah. Makes him feel sorta useless . . . weak –. COLONEL THOMAS: Impotent. CAPTAIN CAMBELL: That's the whatsit – impotent. Well, we build on that impotence, Boss – that and the detainee's fear, 'cause he hasn't a clue what we're gonna do with him. For all he knows, we're worse than Saddam's goons – take a chainsaw to a bloke's nuts without so much as a by-your-leave. (THE IRON BAR leaps from the table as CAPTAIN CAMBELL speaks, and jigs about in mid-air, giving the comical impression it's conducting him.) THE IRON BAR: Confessiamus! CAPTAIN CAMBELL: Anyway, important thing is to keep 'em confused – disoriented: cuff 'em, hood 'em, crank up the mega-mega white noise, don't let 'em sleep – keep 'em on their toes with a sorta non-stop peetee kinda thing. Lads've been taking it in turns at that end of the cycle – then Marty and me, we make our entrance with our usual flair. MAJOR MCADIE: Go in clean and hard, Boss – give 'em a good old harshing. Sorta spit-shower you'll remember from the Academy. COLONEL THOMAS (who is once more recalling the taste of SeeEssEmm Rowley's spittle at oh-seven-hundred hours on a chilly February morning as the drill inspector boiled over into his open mouth: *You fucking ghastly little bum-boy! You nasty, perverted, wanking Welsh git! You blond-haired nancy – you'll never have what it takes to be an officer in Her Majesty's armed forces! Why? 'Cause you're too busy tossing yerself off and THINKING ABOUT ALL THE*

COCK YOU'D LIKE TO SUCK!): Hmm, I hardly think that's likely to intimidate these men that much, Dave – whoever they may be, they'll all've suffered under Saddam, and most likely lost close relatives to the regime – in the war with Iran, in ninety-one and after. Anyway, the important thing is you're sure of your lines. MCADIE and CAMBELL: Boss? COLONEL THOMAS: I don't want you acting like a couple of clowns in there – the men from Bessemer's squadron were hanging around outside. CAPTAIN CAMBELL: They're understandably upset, Boss, Bessemer was a popular member of the team –. COLONEL THOMAS: Was? He isn't dead, Dave. CAPTAIN CAMBELL: Slip of the tongue, Boss. COLONEL THOMAS: Well, see you don't slip up again, 'specially in front of the men – what's that phone doing here? NOKIA THREE-THREE-ONE-OH (with Wireless Access Protocol): Diddle-ooh-doo, diddle-ooh-doo, diddle-ooh-doo-dooo! MAJOR MCADIE (picking up the phone and rejecting the call): Confiscated, Boss. (He grabs the canvas bag and, opening it wide, displays its contents to COLONEL THOMAS.) Nothing this lot love more than a good natter on the phone – look at all these . . . latest models, some of 'em. THE CONFISCATED PHONES (shifting about in the canvas bag as MCADIE pokes it in a manner reminiscent of a doctor performing a scrotal exam): Clickety-clackety, snickety-snackety . . . COLONEL THOMAS: Bagsie. MAJOR MCADIE (passing the bag): What d'you want 'em for, Boss? COLONEL THOMAS: No biggie, Marty, but I dunno . . . What with that lot freaking out by the gate – and not really knowing exactly who we've scooped up – I think a comms lock-down is best policy. Tizer was meant to've collected up all sat phones on

411

establishment – any cheapo Iraqi ones the men've picked up in the bazaar as well. I'm going to lodge them all with the Provost and he'll issue the chits in the morning. Radio silence 'til rouse-up, understood? MCADIE and CAMBELL (resentful of their own con-ditioned obedience): Boss! COLONEL THOMAS: And make sure the men from Bessemer's multiple don't come sneaking back over here – no funny business, right? MCADIE and CAMBELL: Boss! COLONEL THOMAS: You're on your own time now – and I'd appreciate some concrete intel' at the end of it. I'm going to see what Major Townshend is doing about the sitch on the gate. (Carrying the BAG O' PHONES, COLONEL THOMAS leaves the TeeDeeEff. CAPTAIN CAMBELL watches him go, observing that, while the SeeOh has a martial bearing, he's cursed with round and womanly hips. Remov-ing the Biro from the clipboard he bought at the Ousegate Ryman's, CAPTAIN CAMBELL doodles distractedly at the bottom of the list of Iraqi names . . . *Gawain . . . Hay Wain . . . Haywain . . . Gaywain . . .* The SeeOh has stopped halfway across the compound, and stands swinging the BAG O' PHONES in one hand while he hearkens to the eerie Ullalullalullaalullalulla! coming from beyond the main gate. CAPTAIN CAMBELL, who's done some bugling, appreciates the Iraqi women must be breathing in even as they ululate, so sending this stream of lamentation past their hummingbird tongues . . . *again annagain.* The SeeOh moves on once more, stops, changes direction, moves on again . . . *he's lagging* and CAPTAIN CAMBELL also wonders: Is he rich? A colonel in a line regiment would almost certainly have some private means, but, judging by COLONEL THOMAS's dishevelled appearance when off-duty, and the clapped-out Volvo estate he drives, he must have to survive on his salary. And there's no way he'll promote out of command after this balls-up, whereas he, CAPTAIN CAMBELL, might well be the man of the hour: bracing the rag heads effectively – getting the vital intel' the spooks need, and in the process meting out summary justice on men who've been *perverted by violence* . . . This, along with "private means" being an expression much used by CAPTAIN CAMBELL's mother, a Scots lady of a certain age, who's dressed top to toe by the Edinburgh Woollen Mill. MISSUS CAMBELL (in her son's mind): You've no private means, Davey – you'll be out by the age of forty, and what then? You'll be an oddity – there's no respect any more for those who sacrifice their careers for the sake of public service. Think of Mister Baines . . . (MISTER BAINES being a former Captain in the Paras, who's the Secretary at the links south of Nairn where CAPTAIN CAMBELL and his mother often play a brisk nine holes. Passing by the open door of MISTER BAINES's cubbyhole office, CAPTAIN CAMBELL once saw the Secretary stabbing at his own hand, quite savagely, with a brass golf tee. A glass of neat whisky sat by his jerking elbow – it was ten in the morning.) *You see, Davey, no private means, and perverted by violence* . . . COLONEL THOMAS shakes his head, separating this imagined scene into its component parts: *tweed skirt . . . golf tee . . . whisky . . .* Such flights of fancy *aren't my style* – but he knows where this one took off: *He suspects ME, Cambell – really suspects ME . . .* A slideshow clicks past COLONEL THOMAS's exhausted eyes: all the occasions on which he's dodged the accusatory bullet – or caught it deftly in mid-air, flipped it over and sent it back towards his tormenter. But now . . . What'd

413

Jonathan always said? To maintain an effective cover story you need constantly to rehearse its details – where you live, what you do – the little private endearments you bestow on your "wife". Your interrogators will be looking for the slightest inconsistencies, so it needs to be on the tip of your tongue . . . *Semper Fi.*) COLONEL THOMAS (hefting the BAG O' PHONES): But where're the rest of the phones – there ought to be more phones? (At last he moves decisively towards the squadron lines: the men's tents are ranged in four rows of ten. Between them and the T-wall the Engineers built to shore up the fourth side of the compound sit THE OFFICERS' TRAILERS: streamlined, off-white canisters jacked-up on breeze-blocks.) THE OFFICERS' TRAILERS: We're cold but we're old. We're no kind of hard cover, either – one or two eighty-ones, walked up the path and lobbed over the garden gate – we'd crumple up like tin cans. COLONEL THOMAS: That's quite enough out of you lot. (He moves between the tents, angling for THE TRAILER on the far left.) THE TRAILERS: Bubble-bubble, groan-groan, scccrrrreeeaaal . . . COLONEL THOMAS (musing aloud): Strange the men don't resent us having air con' – then I 'spect they realise those units are pumping out bloody Legionnaire's . . . THE TRAILERS: We're diseased death traps – you'd best believe it. (COLONEL THOMAS approaches THE TRAILER at the end of the row, mounts its flimsy steps, knocks on its flimsy door – which swings open. He enters, feeling the surface shift beneath his boots in an unsettling way. It's gloomy and chilly in THE TRAILER, and as he advances the sweat on his chest, back and arms cools unpleasantly.) COLONEL THOMAS: Tizer? Tizer? You in here, mate? (A laptop computer, cracked open on the worktop, catches COLONEL THOMAS's eye. He picks it up and prises screen and keyboard apart. A slideshow is under way: Tizer on exercise in the Brecon Beacons, Tizer in the mess back at the Rams' aitchqueue, Tizer on holiday in some tropical paradise – in all of these photos the six-foot, fourteen-stone cavalry major is cradling either a cute puppy or an adorable kitten, his expression guardedly winsome.) COLONEL THOMAS (sensing THE TRAILER is occupied): Wonder who he got to take them ... MAJOR TOWNSHEND (who sits on the floor between a storage unit and the foot of the folded-down bed): Hnnn ... Hnnn ... COLONEL THOMAS (crouching down): For Christ's sake, Tizer, you all right? MAJOR TOWNSHEND (his voice gruff, muffled by his hands): If they're that bloody f-fat, how c-can they wipe their arses? COLONEL THOMAS: What's that? What did you say, Tizer? MAJOR TOWNSHEND: I said, if they're so f-fat, how can they WIPE THEIR ARSES! COLONEL THOMAS: How can who, Tizer? How can who wipe their arses? MAJOR TOWNSHEND: Fat bastards, Greeny – those fat bastards with big bellies and big buttocks, and those little chicken-wing arms stuck way up on their fat shoulders – how can they reach to ... wipe ... their ... arses? How, Greeny? (He grasps the foot of the bunk and hauls himself semi-upright, releasing a foul stench.) COLONEL THOMAS: Oh, Jesus, Tizer – have you been drinking? (This isn't a query, although COLONEL THOMAS senses there are more power-fully deranging forces at work here besides alcohol: MAJOR TOWNSHEND has shat himself.) MAJOR TOWNSHEND: How could I possibly be fucking pissed, when the SeeOh's imposed a FUCK-ING TWO-CAN RULE! COLONEL THOMAS (persisting with the logic of the exchange, although he's now realised his TwoEye-See has suffered a catastrophic mental breakdown): C'mon, Tizer, old chap – y'know it's only a guideline – I've certainly never enforced it rigidly in the officers' mess: you and that Kiwi captain did for the best part of a bottle of Jay an' Bee the other night –. MAJOR TOWN-SHEND: Not talking 'bout booze, Greeny – talking 'bout shit . . . two cans of shit. Got two cans of shit . . . (He lets go of the bunk and topples sideways on to the floor, where he lies, curled up and sobbing.) I've shat myself, Greeny . . . I've shat myself . . . COLONEL THOMAS: What's got into you, Tizer – did something happen? Was it the incoming when you were up on the gate? (He hears CAPTAIN PETERSEN's touchy-feely voice even as he speaks – she tried her therapeutic banter on him during the pre-deployment flap: *It's not a case of musts or shoulds, Colonel – we can feel very oppressed by such inflexible commands . . .*) MAJOR TOWNSHEND: I'm just fed up with it, Greeny . . . wiping your arse – it's too far to reach, mate . . . Can't get up there any more, 'sides, I was meant to . . . THE TRAILER (rocking on its worn-out suspension): Crrreeeaaak-crrreeeaaak, crrreeeaaak-crrreeeaaak! He was meant to be SeeOh – you only got promoted 'cause of your father-in-law: you crawled up his daughter's cunt to get into his back passage –. MAJOR TOWN-SHEND: . . . command the regiment – I was. Passed out from the Academy above you – I was only just pipped for the Queen's Medal, wasn't I . . . Did a sight better than you at Staff College as well . . . COLONEL THOMAS (laying a hand on his shoulder and speaking kindly): Listen, Tizer, I dunno about all that – what I do know is we've an evolving situation here – I daresay the Jam and the

Badr bunch are equally pissed off about what went down today –
can't you hear the women outside the gate? IRAQI WOMEN:
Ullalullaullalullaullalullullalulla! MAJOR TOWNSHEND: Yeah, I can
hear 'em, Greeny – what d'you want me to do about it? (He struggles to rise, releasing more shitty gusts.) D'you seriously think
they're gonna attack? COLONEL THOMAS: Shouldn't think so – they
know the catfish air boys are within a few minutes' fly-time. Have a
gunship overhead popping off perfectly targeted cannon fire be –.
(He stops short, overcome by the absurdity of discussing operational
matters with a big man who's curled up *like a baby*, and who's shat
himself . . . *like a baby*.) Listen, old man, we've gotta get you to the
rap – get you cleaned up. See what Gail reckons to it. MAJOR
TOWNSHEND: She wanted me – y'know that, don't you? COLONEL
THOMAS: Who? Not Gail, surely? MAJOR TOWNSHEND (rolling
over on to his back and addressing his SeeOh formally): No,
not Captain Petersen, sir – Princess Di. COLONEL THOMAS: The
Princess of Wales? What're you on about, Tizer? MAJOR TOWN-
SHEND: When we were still at Catterick and she came up on an
official visit and stopped by the Wives' Club – long before she palled
up with that grease-ball . . . Not that I'm bothered, 'cause she never
done it with him – wouldn't do that . . . Wouldn't muss up her . . .
hair. PRINCESS DIANA'S HAIR (which hangs in the gloom midway
between the two officers, a disembodied nineteen eighties do, the
tips of which curl into whispering lips): I never let him touch
me with his oily Muslim hands – never let him run his soiled fingers
through me. MAJOR TOWNSHEND: You see it, Greeny, you see
her hair? COLONEL THOMAS (rising unsteadily to his feet): I . . .

417

feel . . . dizzy. THE LAPTOP: You spin me right round, baby, right round –. MAJOR TOWNSHEND (singing): Like a record, baby, round-round –. (He stops and speaks.) And you're a poof, Greeny, so you are. COLONEL THOMAS: You – you what? MAJOR TOWNSHEND: You heard me: you're a fucking woolly-woofter! You . . . you . . . (laughs) . . . thinking no one in the regiment knows – that's gotta be the funniest thing ever, 'cause everyone knows, Colonel GAYwain. THE LAPTOP: Uh-oh, uh-oh, uh-oh, oh no . . . COLONEL THOMAS (bending down and wedging his hand in MAJOR TOWNSHEND's armpit): C'mon now, Tizer, that's enough – I want the Doc to take a look at you. THE LAPTOP: Yeah, you borrowed me last night – claimed you were gonna watch some utterly bone film, but really you spent hours looking at Calvin-fucking-Klein male underwear models – don't you know anything, you plank: when you surf anywhere on the web you leave a big fucking spunky trail. COLONEL THOMAS (grabbing THE LAPTOP, squinting at the screen and frenziedly manipulating its keys): I'm gonna fetch Gail in a sec', Tizer – get her orderly, too. Get them to calm you down! MAJOR TOWNSHEND (sinisterly calm): I'm perfectly calm, GAYwain – it's you who're in a poofy-fucking-tizzy. COLONEL THOMAS (jabbing repeatedly at the backspace key and watching the cursor eat a long string of letters, numerals and symbols): I'm not in a tizzy . . . I'm not – I've got the sitch . . . under . . . control . . . THE RAINBOW WHEEL (spinning on the screen): You spin me right round, baby, right round . . . THE LAPTOP (joining in): Like a record, baby, right round like a –. COLONEL THOMAS (slamming shut THE LAPTOP): Okay, that's enough – you've shat yourself, Tizer, that's how calm you are! (He strides the two paces to THE TRAILER's door.) THE TRAILER: Creeeaaak-creeeaaak! Creeeaaak-creeeaaak! A single eighty-one round on top of me and you'd both be brown bread – I'm not a military vehicle at all, I'm a holiday home – same model as that buck-toothed twat who used to be foreign secretary drags behind her on her creeeaaak-creeeaaak hols! COLONEL THOMAS: I'm gonna lock this door from the out-side, Tizer – but you'll only be alone here for a few minutes . . . MAJOR TOWNSHEND: Yeah-yeah . . . Whatever – what do I care, GAYwain. You done me now, boyo – you've unpacked my . . . fudge. THE KEY: Screutch-eutch. THE LOCK: Ickle-snickle-snikk. (COLONEL THOMAS stands on the steps staring distractedly into the mid-distance, to where the ceaselessly revolving RAINBOW WHEEL slips in and out of the searchlights' beams.) THE RAINBOW WHEEL: Establishing network connection . . . Establishing network connection . . . Establishing network connection . . . COLONEL THOMAS (massaging his stinging eyes with thumb and forefinger as he muses aloud): Well, this could well be it – could be all over . . . Truth out – marriage over, career too . . . Prob'ly best for all con-cerned if it were . . . Jonathan and I – we could go to Bardney . . . buy the business off of Brian and John – make a proper go of it . . . they haven't even thought of getting a web site built yet . . . THE RAINBOW WHEEL (still spinning in the maroon nowhere): Don't you looooove faaaarce . . . ? THE LOUDSPEAKER (bolted to the minaret of a mosque three hundred metres south-west of the compound): Myyyyy faaauuult IIIIIIII feeeeeaaaaar . . . ! COLONEL THOMAS: Kids can visit at weekends – plenty of room for them . . .

Be a bit peculiar to begin with, but they'll enjoy the old place – it's quaint . . . Make beds up for them in those little attic rooms . . . Have to be a bit circum– well, Miffy still comes into our bed sometimes . . . in the night. Fi'll prob'ly be a bit angry to begin with . . . THE LOUDSPEAKER: IIIIII thooouuught thaaat yooouuu'd waaant whaaat IIIIII waaant . . . COLONEL THOMAS: Odd for Jonathan as well – quite a change of scene . . . and pace. Still, he grew up in a bit of a backwater, he'll readjust – and we'll have our love. THE LOUDSPEAKER: Where are the clow-ow-ow –. SERGEANT LANDON (arriving at speed, in helmet and body armour, and carrying his rifle): Sir! (He salutes smartly.) COLONEL THOMAS: What's occurring, Landon? SERGEANT LANDON: Just been on the radio net, sir . . . it . . . it doesn't look like Bessie's gonna . . . gonna . . . COLONEL THOMAS: Pull yourself together, Landon. SERGEANT LANDON: Sorry, sir. They got Bessie down to Main all right, but he'd lost a lot of blood and they've been operating for hours . . . They aren't very ho-ho-ho –. COLONEL THOMAS: Don't worry . . . THE RAINBOW WHEEL (very faint but still spinning): . . . I'm heeeeeere! SERGEANT LANDON: Thing is, Boss, men've somehow got wind and they're up and about again – in a pretty aggy state, too. COLONEL THOMAS: I'll deal with that, Landon – I want you back at comms. Base is on full lock-down now . . . (he hefts the BAG O' PHONES) . . . if any of the men still has a mobile phone, I want it impounded, and no one's to enter or leave the base before rouse. Swing by Captain Petersen's quarters on your way – give her a knock and tell her she needs to go see Major Townshend sharpish, he's had a bit of an . . . accident. (He salutes SERGEANT LANDON smartly, and moves away, leaving the squadron lines. He passes by the vehicle park: rows of aypeesees and up-armoured Land Rovers still releasing the fierce heat of the day into the hardly less hot night.) THE STEELY STEEDS: Tick! Tick! Tick! Tick! COLONEL THOMAS (seeing the whirring gimbals of the carriage clock on the mantelpiece in the dining room of the Bardney beeandbee): Jonathan'd probably hate it, though – sabotage things . . . insult our guests while I was working hard at trying to get us accepted in the community . . . (Nearing the squat outline of the TeeDeeEff, he sees several troopers loitering about, smoking.) COLONEL THOMAS: What's going on here, men? What're you doing up and about again? I've already had to disperse you once . . . TROOPER PHIL-POTT: We heard Bessie ain't gonna make it, sir. TROOPER WESLEY (stepping forward from the shadows – a lowering and truculent figure): Slotted by those rag 'ead cunts! TROOPERS HIRST and SUTCLIFFE (appearing beside him): Yeah, those rag 'ead cunts, sir – they gotta be corrected . . . innit – straightened out, an' that. COLONEL THOMAS: I realise you're upset, men . . . TROOPER WEST (a big, open-faced lad who's now the Rams' finest goal-kicker): Upset, sir . . . fucking upset! COLONEL THOMAS: Yes, upset after today's incident – but there's absolutely no justification for this behaviour. Rouse is at oh-five-hundred as per – I suggest you get your sweds down NOW, and that suggestion is a BLOODY ORDER! (He stands watching the men as they sullenly bestir themselves and head back towards the squadron lines. From the cunts, fucks and rag 'eads that float back towards him, COLONEL THOMAS realises all the hard work he's put in over the past three years has been instantly and catastrophically annulled. The BLOODY ORDER! screeched so shrilly and camply, has cost him what little respect he ever had. A wave of disaffection radiates out from the group of troopers in the form of a dark shadow rushing before them towards the squadron lines. When it arrives, it lifts the slack canvas of their highly vulnerable accommodation, so meeting and merging with the still fouler revelations plopping from MAJOR TOWNSHEND's mouth. As COLONEL THOMAS looks on, transfixed, he sees his three children sprint from between THE OFFICERS' TRAILERS – this great tsunami of contempt and revulsion rearing up behind them. Their mother stands beside the point-fifty-cal' on top of the main gate sangar, a camcorder in hand, getting live-action footage of the moment an exemplary twenty-two-year-long military career was swept away.) FIONA THOMAS (shouting through a ram-cum-bullhorn): Okay, okay! Great stuff, people – but I'd like to do the whole wave-of-disaffection scene again. Positions, please, everyone! DEREK THOMAS (appearing beside her dressed in full Utherian clobber: sheepskin cloak, conical wizard's hat and leather buckler, holding a shepherd's crook, with his long beard hanging down to his velveteen codpiece): No need for a second take, Fi . . . (he gently pushes down the ram-cum-bullhorn) . . . I think we all got the point: my son's a homosexual. Frankly, if any of you lot're at all surprised, it can only be because you're kneeling, hooded and handcuffed in a dark cell, while a man torments you with a boom box. THE BOOM BOX (rising up through the roof of the Tee-DeeEff, all lit up by disco strobes): Uh-oh, uh-oh, uh-oh, oh no . . . DEREK THOMAS: Not my problem – I knew he was that way inclined when he was a little boy. That's why I asked Rodney to be his godfather . . . to look out for him . . . Thought Rod – being an iron himself – might be a positive influence on Gawain, get him to realise what a fool's-bloody-errand peacetime soldiering really is. THE RAINBOW WHEEL (which throughout has been scooting about the compound, snitch-style – shooting through tents and trailers, bouncing off walls and the sides of vehicles, spinning the while – and now rises up to hover above the main gate): Maaaaaaybeeeeeee neeeeeext yeeeaaarrr! COLONEL THOMAS (muttering as he paces in a tight figure-eight, again and again): There isn't going to be any next year – not now. Besides, Dad, this isn't bloody peacetime soldiering, is it – and it isn't my fault the Rams've ended up policing Ali al-Garbi rather than racing to cut off thousands of Soviet TeeSeventyTwos at the Fulda Gap. DEREK THOMAS (mockingly): The Fulda Gap, eh – talk about fighting the last existential con-flict rather than the current ethically dubious one. THE RAINBOW WHEEL: Stop lagging, Gawain, and come with me – come with meeeee to Bardneeeeey! I can download this image at high speed: You getting the old Volvo out of the garage . . . Murder to start on cold mornings, isn't it – needs plenty of choke. Got your shopping bag, have you? Bag-for-life, isn't it – eco-friendly and all that. You've already told Jonathan you're off to Market Rasen to do the shop, and there he is, freshly showered and shaved, wearing clean jeans and a pressed white shirt, all lithe and graceful in the oaken parlour. JONATHAN DE'ATH: (who appears beside THE RAINBOW WHEEL, floating in a bubble of Bardney beeandbee, its translucent surface eerily lit from within by the wan light of a winter's morning in rural

Lincolnshire): I'll just fill these individual dishes with what's left in the catering tins. COLONEL THOMAS (calling all the way from southern Iraq): Make sure the jam and marmalade at the bottom isn't manky! JONATHAN DE'ATH: Wilco, Boss. (He slips an apron over his adorable head and ties the tapes behind his back.) THE RAINBOW WHEEL (scooting over from the main gate to hang beside the bubble of Bardney): Got him where you want him now, haven't you? COLONEL THOMAS: Dunno what you're talking about . . . THE RAINBOW WHEEL: C'mon – enter our competition for a twenty-pound turkey, simply leave your business card in the goldfish bowl on the bar . . . Really, Gawain, is your imagination this simplistic? Your fantasy of being out and proud is merely to replace one gay couple with another – it's not being on top cover at all, it's clambering right underneath it. JONATHAN DE'ATH (who stands, blobs of jam dripping from spoon to dish): Don't forget the meat order from Lancaster's. COLONEL THOMAS: I phoned it through yesterday, love, they'll have it all ready for me. JONATHAN DE'ATH: Make sure they've put in the sausages and bacon –. COLONEL THOMAS: Don't worry. JONATHAN DE'ATH: And the chicken and duck breasts – remember, we've eight for dinner tonight. COLONEL THOMAS: Please . . . Jonathan, I've got it all in hand. JONATHAN DE'ATH (calling louder as the bubble rises): Steaks, too – fillet and rump! Then those ham-hock pies Lancaster's do so well – mm-mm, love that jelly! And there should be both white and black pudding – some veal, too . . . COLONEL THOMAS: I promise! THE BUTCHER (shouting now, as the bubble rises still higher): Most important: the beef – we've got to have the beef, Gawain, if you don't bring home

424

the beef we've both had it . . . THE RAINBOW WHEEL (which orbits the bubble of Bardney with increasing speed as they both lift off into the Iraqi night): Your love got me lookin' so cra-azy right now . . . COLONEL THOMAS: Don't go, Jonathan! Don't go rainbow wheel! THE BUTCHER: You had your chance – should've finessed me years ago . . . COLONEL THOMAS: Finessed you? THE BUTCHER: Y'know, the pack of cards . . . COLONEL THOMAS: What do you mean, Jonathan? THE BUTCHER (setting down the catering tin and grabbing a low beam to steady himself as the bubble rises yet higher): The packs of cards the Yanks had made – ones depicting Saddam's top fifty-two bad guys, with him as the ace-of-spades . . . COLONEL THOMAS (shouting now): What about them, Jonathan? THE BUTCHER: If you'd come out you could've forced me out as well – that's what the Yanks've been doing: scooping up the low-value cards, bracing 'em hard . . . then the faces start popping outta the woodwork – pushed or shoved. COLONEL THOMAS: I couldn't've done that, Jonathan – what about your career? What about the OhEssAy? THE BUTCHER: Fuck my bloody career, Gawain – fuck it. It's all bullshit – same as your career. A fool's errand – isn't that what your faggy old Uncle Rodney calls it? You and your precious Rams, rooting about in that shit-hole – me and my exiguous colleagues, floating around the world, haunting remote storage facilities while the Company boys get out their car batteries and uncoil their hoses. It's all the same bullshit: an entire-bloody-civilisation embarked on a colossal – no, a cosmic – fool's errand! COLONEL THOMAS (running around in circles, clutching his bag of CONFISCATED MOBILE PHONES to his armoured breast): Please,

Jonathan, dooooon't goooooo! (But it's too late: the RAINBOW WHEEL and the dancing bubble, circling one another, rise higher and higher, dip down over the main gate sangars in salute, then disappear into the darkness.) THE LOUDSPEAKER: Maaaaybeeee neeeext yeeeaaarrr! (COLONEL THOMAS stops short, shaking his woolly head – then moves off purposefully towards the concrete blockhouse allocated to the Provost. Piled up beside it, glowing weirdly in the searchlights, is a huge stack of plastic chairs – the white garden variety, with arms that are injection-moulded into a parody of Sheraton. He fishes a bunch of keys from his trouser pocket, unlocks the door, gets out a torch and uses its beam to locate a safe, which he unlocks with a second key. He deposits the BAG O' PHONES, locks safe and door. Striding back across the compound, he pauses beside a signpost the Kiwis have erected with pointers indicating the many thousands of clicks to Auckland, Christchurch and other of the Southern Hemisphere's suburbs. Looking up, he sees one inscribed BARDNEY, THREE THOUSAND, THREE HUN-DRED AND THIRTY-FOUR. He walks on, shaking his woolly head some more, and, reaching the TeeDeeEff, stands, head cocked, listening.) CAPTAIN CAMBELL (muffled but still audible): Come on . . . C'mon – for fuck's sake, you've been pissing in your pants all fucking night. Pissing in your pants and moaning you gotta go to the toilet. Right! Fine! Now you're in the fucking toilet and you can't fucking piss! IRAQI DETAINEE (more muffled and scarcely audible): Pliss, I no unnerstan' . . . pliss . . . CAPTAIN CAMBELL: You'll unnerstan' well enough when we cut your fucking cock off and make you suck the piss out of it! IRAQI DETAINEE: I no

unnerstan' –. CAPTAIN CAMBELL (shouting): Marty! For fuck's
sake! Will you get your sorry arse in here and translate! MAJOR
McADIE (also muffled): What did you say, Dave? CAPTAIN CAM-
BELL: I said I was gonna cut off his fucking cock and make him
suck the piss outta it. MAJOR McADIE: That's, um, pretty difficult
to get across in Arabic, Dave – their expressions for these things are
fairly . . . well . . . metaphoric. CAPTAIN CAMBELL: I don't care
how fucking metaphoric you are, Marty, as long as you make it clear
to this piece of low conniving rag-head shit what I'm literally gonna
do to him. Got it? MAJOR McADIE (in Arabic): My comrade wishes
it to be known that he will remove your noble, thrice-blessed manhood while you sit in our tents and drink coffee. IRAQI DETAINEE
(in Arabic): These Crusaders are simply deranged . . . (in English)
I no unnerstan' . . . pliss, I no unnerstan' –. (Sound of metal door
being torn angrily open.) CAPTAIN CAMBELL: Get the fuck outta
here, you piece of shit! Oh, fuck, you stink . . . (COLONEL THOMAS
knocks heavily on the outer door, which is at once opened a crack by
MAJOR McADIE.) COLONEL THOMAS: Open up, Marty. MAJOR
McADIE (swinging the door wide): Certainly, Boss, just observing
the formalities. (He slams it shut once the SeeOh has entered.)
Where've you been, Boss? COLONEL THOMAS (entering the interrogation room): Where haven't I bloody been, Marty – the men are
all acting up, and I'm afraid Tizer's had some sorta . . . turn. (He
sits down heavily on a white plastic garden chair that's to hand.)
Something must've . . . (he massages his eyes with thumb and
forefinger – it's fast becoming the signature gesture of the Yorkshire
Hussars' Commanding Officer, his equivalent of Patton's hands-on-

hips or Schwarzkopf's decisive karate chop) . . . pushed him to the limit. (As the dark chamber comes into focus, he notices the IRAQI DETAINEE.) Jesus, Marty, who's this when he's at home? MAJOR MCADIE (checking the label affixed to the detainee's plasti-cuffs): This one's Amir, Boss – cute little Amir . . . Ain'tcha a cute one, Amir . . . Ain'tcha a cutie . . . (He chucks the wild-eyed DETAINEE under his chin, and, as the man rears back, his face catches the light and COLONEL THOMAS sees bruises and a cut below one eye.) COLONEL THOMAS: He doesn't look too cute to me, Dave – he looks like someone's been knocking him about. CAPTAIN CAMBELL: Straightforward conditioning, Boss – nothing hairy, but we've had this one solo a couple of times now – we think he may be the one. COLONEL THOMAS: The one? CAPTAIN CAMBELL: The one Colonel Trimmingham mentioned, Boss – the one the slime in London said might be coming over the border. COLONEL THOMAS (angry, but feebly, homosexually, so): For Christ's sake, Dave! Boss-boss-boss – bosh-bosh-bloody-bosh! If he's their asset, they'll want him at Shaibah in one bloody piece – how's it gonna look if we pitch up with damaged goods? MAJOR MCADIE (pulling the pillowcase back over the DETAINEE's tousled head): Unexpected item in the bagging area . . . Unexpected item in the bagging area . . . Please remove . . . (He yanks the DETAINEE upright, steers him by his thumbs back into the cell where the others are and forces him to kneel. COLONEL THOMAS and CAPTAIN CAMBELL follow on behind. SERGEANT HAYNES, a skinny, nervy young man, whose hair has bleached highlights, is standing over the IRAQI DETAINEES with THE IRON BAR in his hand.) COLONEL THOMAS:

428

Ha-bloody-ha – didn't you hear what I said? CAPTAIN CAMBELL: Thing is, Boss, we gotta keep the pressure up if we want any decent product – we reckon this is the fucker who slotted Asif as well, so we gotta . . . sorta . . . dilemma, Boss . . . COLONEL THOMAS: I'm not seeing your dilemma, Dave – I repeat: we have no jurisdiction over Iraqi citizens who've committed criminal offences, you know that. CAPTAIN CAMBELL: But, Boss, if this man represents a threat to Coalition forces we're entirely within our rights –. MAJOR MCADIE: If it is him. COLONEL THOMAS: Well, now you've rebagged the item, Marty, I dunno what to . . . expect! (All three British officers crack up and, crouched over, palms on thighs, wait out the incoming hilarity.) So . . . so . . . s'pose you better . . . keep the pressure . . . up. But one thing, Dave. CAPTAIN CAMBELL: Boss? COLONEL THOMAS: We are still allowed to keep detainees hooded and cuffed, are we? CAPTAIN CAMBELL: Boss? COLONEL THOMAS: Thing is, wasn't it this sort of carry-on landed us in hot water during the Troubles? CAPTAIN CAMBELL: Troubles, sir? COLONEL THOMAS (looking at his intelligence officer with frank disbelief): Oh, forget it, Dave – you carry on. CAPTAIN CAMBELL: You carry on, Haynes. (HAYNES bangs THE IRON BAR on the concrete floor.) THE IRON BAR: Zoingggg! Zoingggg! COLONEL THOMAS: But I don't want any of that Majar or Abu-bloody-Ghraib badness – we're Fighting Rams, Dave, not banjo-picking hillbillies. We have our . . . honour. CAPTAIN CAMBELL: Absolutely, Boss. COLONEL THOMAS: As soon as Gail's seen to Tizer, she'll be over here to give these men an exam – should've been done hours ago. So, clean 'em up a bit, will you – it stinks in here. I know it isn't politically correct, but besides being a damn fine medic, Captain Petersen happens to be a lady. MAJOR McADIE (simpering repulsively and making a mincing gesture): Ooh, I'm a la-ady … COLONEL THOMAS: Marty … CAPTAIN CAMBELL: Don't you worry, Boss, we're recording all the teaqueue sessions anyway – couldn't step out of line if we wanted to –. MAJOR McADIE: And we don't want to. COLONEL THOMAS: Want to what? MAJOR McADIE: Step out of the line, Boss – me and the missus have got very keen on the line dancing, we have. She had to drag me along to begin with – thought it'd just be a bunch of old fossils Zimmering about, turns out lots of younger people're doing it nowadays as well … COLONEL THOMAS (staring hard into McADIE's pouchy red guileless face): I'll bear that in mind, Major McAdie. CAPTAIN CAMBELL (conducting COLONEL THOMAS from the cell, then swinging open the door to the third and darkest of the TeeDeeEff's chambers): See, Boss, we've set up a monitoring post in here – our equivalent of the old one-way glass. THEWLIS here keeps an eye on everything – makes sure it's all recorded. CORPORAL THEWLIS (rising from the collapsible picnic table he's sitting at so abruptly his white plastic garden chair topples backwards): Sir! COLONEL THOMAS: Carry on, Thewlis. CAPTAIN CAMBELL (pointing to THE LAPTOP on the picnic table): See? Feel free to join Thewlis, Boss. You can watch us take one of the detainees through a cycle. Reassure yourself everything's … kosher. (CORPORAL THEWLIS retrieves a second white plastic garden chair from the gloomy recesses of the cell and COLONEL THOMAS slumps down in it. CAPTAIN CAMBELL leaves, and can be heard talking to MAJOR McADIE next door in undertones.

COLONEL THOMAS tries to concentrate, but he's been awake for over twenty-two hours – he looks up blearily at the hole hacked in the concrete wall which serves as a window, and thinks he sees there a huge and tufty caricature of a face . . . *Miffy can't go upstairs to the loo in the new house by herself – not if it's dark. Says Laura will be up there – but grown all giant. Giant clown doll Fi knitted for her – red button eyes, thin black-threaded lips . . . Staring at the back of poor Miffy's head as she . . . lifts her nightie –.* COLONEL THOMAS is jerked awake by:) CAPTAIN CAMBELL (shouting but muffled): You're beginning to seriously piss me off! You low piece of shit – you utter fucking knob-head. Don't look away – don't look away from me! Look me in the eye, you disgusting man. You disgust me. Is that how your fucking burqa of a mother brought you up? Is it? To sit around in your own piss and shit! For fuck's sake! (The live-feed from the camera set up in the interrogation room is lagging so that everything CAMBELL shouts in the adjoining cell is repeated a split-second later by THE LAPTOP's crappy speaker.) THE LAPTOP (tinnily): You're beginning to seriously piss me off! You low piece of shit . . . (and so on). MAJOR MCADIE (in Arabic and muffled): My colleague is very angry with you – very angry! He says you have a head that resembles a door handle and that you are improperly toilet trained. He commands you to face him . . . in the eye looking . . . THE LAPTOP (tinnily and in Arabic): My colleague is very angry with you – very angry! (and so on). IRAQI DETAINEE (in Arabic, scarcely audible): I do not understand why you are doing this to me – I'm an honest man. Honest and peace-loving. When you British arrived in Ali al-Garbi, I went out into the street to welcome you –

431

I threw flowers! THE LAPTOP: I do not understand why you are doing this to me – I'm an honest man ... (and so on). MAJOR MCADIE: He says he doesn't understand British, Dave – that's a good one. It's like he thinks we really speak something called British. CAPTAIN CAMBELL: Spare me the fucking commentary will you, Marty – just tell me exactly what this bastard is saying. (Fully awake once more, COLONEL THOMAS blearies at THE LAP-TOP's screen, and sees looming there the IRAQI DETAINEE's bruised and bloody caricature of a face, while to either side of it hang the red and sweaty ones belonging to CAPTAIN CAMBELL and MAJOR MCADIE.) MAJOR MCADIE: As I said, Dave, a literal translation from Arabic's always tricky: it's a flowery sorta language, doesn't lend itself to matter-of-fact statements – unlike Parseltongue! (Both men laugh.) IRAQI DETAINEE (wonderingly, and in Arabic): Who are you idiots? You call this interrogation – this isn't interrogation. I was interrogated by the Mukhabarat after the ninety-one rising – the one you and your allies, the Great Satan, said you would sup-port. I was taken at dawn, together with six of my fellow fighters, to the EssEssOh's aitchqueue in Kut. The first question they asked me – which is the first question any Iraqi asks another he wishes to obtain information from – was: Who's your Sheik? You people really are the most consummately, comprehensively ignorant occu-piers it's possible to imagine – this remains, at root, a tribal society, and over this have been imposed still more divisions – religious, ideological, ethnic – such that any given individual will have an immensely complex and ever changing network of friends, enemies and potential allies. So, in ninety-one, Saddam's torturers first asked who my Sheik was – and then, when I'd told them, they got out the car battery and the jump leads. A little later on a chainsaw was brought into play – if you clowns had bothered to physically examine me you'd know this already. So, I ask again: who are you idiots? Clearly you're not cut from the same cloth as the British officers who came here in the nineteen twenties – men my own grandfather remembers from his childhood. They were racists, pure and simple – yet they took the trouble to study our culture and language systematically, whereas you – you! You're a pathetic joke! CAPTAIN CAMBELL: Voluble fucker, ain't he, Mart. What was all that carry-on, then? IRAQI DETAINEE (continuing in Arabic purely for his own grim amusement): Nor can you be the descendants of the men who were stationed here – because they were mostly Indian sepoys. Traditional behaviour on the part of the Little Satan – get one subject race to oppress another. But now the Great Satan's in on the act, too – those pictures of the abuse at Abu Ghraib, the prisoners all piled up on top of each other – Kurds on top of Sunnis, Sunnis on top of Shias – same martial-races policy, really – and that Munchkin standing alongside, looking like some public-school educated British subaltern of the imperial era, tormented by his homosexuality and his inability to grow a bear –. CAPTAIN CAMBELL: All right, all right – shut the fuck up with your jabbering. Anything in that lot, Marty? MAJOR MCADIE: Difficult to make out, Dave – seemed mostly . . . background info'. CAPTAIN CAMBELL: Not interested in that, we want hard intel' – and preferably a confession. C'mon, Marty, put your fucking back into it – either this muppet or one of his mates mowed down Bessemer. Slotted

Asif as well – a 'terp like you, albeit rather better at his job. His relatives – his peeps, they're still out there, prob'ly with bombs under their burqas –. IRAQI WOMEN: Ullalullaullalullaullalullaullalulla! IRAQI DETAINEE (musing to himself in Arabic): Could be the dawn prayer – these jokers wouldn't know even know the difference. It's the Fifteenth Night of Shabaan – and they certainly don't know the signif –. CAPTAIN CAMBELL: Will you shut the ruddy-fuck up! It's like you're . . . you're . . . under the misguided impression you're the important person in this room – that you're holding the fucking conch shell and have the right to speak. Well, you're not holding the FUCKING CONCH SHELL! Can you see a conch shell in this dumb rag head's greasy-fucking-hands, Marty? MAJOR MCADIE: Can't say as I do, Dave . . . CAPTAIN CAMBELL (screaming into the IRAQI DETAINEE's ear): No! No! No fucking conch shell! You're not the main man here – I'm the fucking main man here! If you don't start cooperating with us, you're fucking set, you are – fucking set: we'll go round your miserable stinking hovel, we'll rape your mother and your sisters . . . IRAQI DETAINEE (to himself, in Arabic): Always with the raping! I've no sister, only one much older half-brother – probably not to your taste when it comes to sexual violation. And my mother is currently dying of ovarian cancer in the hospital the SeePeeAy claims – in a report I've seen – to've rebuilt, but which is in fact a burnt-out shell to this day. MAJOR MCADIE: Um . . . he said 'ukht, Dave . . . CAPTAIN CAMBELL: What? He said yuck-ten? MAJOR MCADIE: No, he said 'ukht, Dave – it means sister. He said sister – I reckon this one understands a sight more British than he's letting on. CAPTAIN CAMBELL (shouting into the IRAQI DETAINEE's ear): So, you're holding out on us, are you, you fucking fuck! Turns out you're the only gay in the village, does it? (He disappears abruptly from the laptop's screen and can be heard shouting still louder:) Haynes! Haynes! Get your sorry arse in here – and bring that crowbar with you . . . COLONEL THOMAS (bleary from his nap, and speaking of inconsequential things, *as you do*): What's the book, Thewlis? CORPORAL THEWLIS: It's an old Harry Potter one, sir – Harry Potter and the Chamber of Secrets. COLONEL THOMAS: Oh . . . yes . . . I remember reading that aloud to my kids – it's jolly good, isn't it? CORPORAL THEW- LIS: Yes, jolly good, sir – and sorta 'propriate reading material, given the circs . . . But I can't wait for the new one – my mum's gonna go into Gateshead, queue up and buy it for me, like. COLONEL THOMAS: It's such a phenomenon, Thewlis – that'll be a jolly long wait. CORPORAL THEWLIS: Jolly long, sir – but she's a real trooper, my mum. She'll take along a fart sack and some scran – plot up just like a Ram on stag –. SERGEANT HAYNES (his voice issuing from both tinny speaker and from the vestibule): Ollie-ollie-ollie! THE IRON BAR: Zoing! Zoing! Zoing! SERGEANT HAYNES: Ollie-ollie- ollie! THE IRON BAR: Zoing! Zoing! Zoing! CAPTAIN CAMBELL (speaking through the laptop): You hear that, do you? That's my main man, Billy Haynes, that is – and he isn't a commissioned officer in Her Majesty's army, you fucking fuck, he's come up the hard way, has Billy. You hear that iron bar? He's gonna shove it right up your homosexual arse if you don't start giving us some answers: What were you doing in Sheik al-Abhadi's house? Why did you have percussion grenades on you and five hundred YouEss

435

dollars in cash? Are you a spook? You look like a fucking spook – a fucking gay spook! IRAQI DETAINEE (in Farsi): Did my beloved only touch me with his lips, I, too, like the flute, would burst into melody . . . But he who is parted from them that speak his tongue, though he possess a hundred voices, is perforce . . . dumb. CAPTAIN CAMBELL: Marty? MAJOR MCADIE: Haven't a bloody clue, Dave – it's not Arabic, must be one of the Persian lingos. CAPTAIN CAMBELL: I know you understand English, you piece of shit in human form – and if you understand it, you can fucking well speak it, eh? So speak to the iron bar! THE IRON BAR: Zoing! Zoing! Zoing! COLONEL THOMAS: We mostly read comics in my day – English ones were difficult to get when we were overseas, but I'd an aunt in Caernarfon who'd send me a bundle every month or so . . . Hotspur . . . Victor . . . the Eagle. It was pretty unsophisticated stuff by today's standards, all about square-jawed Brit bulldogs taking the fight to the beastly Hun, but I pored over them, sopping it all up. CORPORAL THEWLIS: Sir . . . COLONEL THOMAS (rising un-steadily from his white plastic garden chair and looking bemusedly at the darkened chamber ill lit by THE LAPTOP's screen): Oh . . . Oh, well – better be getting on, then . . . You – you carry on, Thew-lis . . . Carry on with your . . . reading. HARRY POTTER AND THE CHAMBER OF SECRETS: Try and stop him – 'cause I'm a real page-turner, so I am – and that's how I've got hundreds of thousands of boys like this one into reading, making them capable in due course of absorbing the entire Western canon, and along with it the values of liberality and tolerance which have underpinned our civilisation for millennia. THE IRON BAR: Zoing! Zoing! Zoing!

Confessiamus! COLONEL THOMAS (distracted): Yes . . . carry on, Thewlis . . . (He leaves the cell and meets SERGEANT HAYNES in the vestibule.) SERGEANT HAYNES: Everything all right? COLONEL THOMAS (glancing into the large cell where the IRAQI DETAINEES are kneeling, hooded): It's just like a game of slaps, really . . . SERGEANT HAYNES: Slaps? COLONEL THOMAS: Y'know – like boys play at school: you touch your fingertips together and then try to slap the other chap before he . . . slaps you. SERGEANT HAYNES: Oh, yeah, slaps. (He strides into the cell and walks along the row of IRAQI DETAINEES, yanking down each pair of plasti-cuffed hands.) Slap! Slap! Slap! Slap! Slap! Fucking slap! IRAQI DETAINEES' CHOIR (in yanking order): Ooh! Aah! Eek! Arr! Incomprehensible Arabic oath! Fuck you! Aah! SERGEANT HAYNES: That's it, sir, isn't it – that's the go of it. COLONEL THOMAS: Yes . . . well . . . carry on, Haynes. (He takes one last look round at: the stained concrete walls and floors, which now and forever are the set-dressing of suffering, then leaves the TeeDeeEff. THE AFTER-IMAGE of THE LAPTOP's screen goes with him: a mystically glowing portal into another world, beckoning him on across the compound towards the Regimental Aid Post. He follows it, oblivious to the restive troopers, who've crept back once more from the squadron lines and stand in loose knots, smoking and swearing.) THE AFTER-IMAGE: I'll never leave you, GAYwain, I'll always be with you – I'll always be right at hand to show you smooth young stomachs with CALVIN KLEIN stretched across them . . . And show you down below, as well! Mm! Such loveliness once the male shape-wear is removed . . . COLONEL THOMAS (to himself): I never so much as laid a finger on

437

any of the men under my command. THE AFTER-IMAGE: Under being the operative word –. COLONEL THOMAS: What're you talking about, you evil sprite! I'm not a bloody paedo! CAPTAIN PETERSEN (arriving at a brisk trot and saluting sketchily, her handsome face uglified by anxiety): Boss? Boss? Are you okay? COLONEL THOMAS: Perfectly all right, Gail – just tired, but then we're all tired, aren't we? How's Major Townshend getting on? CAPTAIN PETERSEN: Not at all well, I'm afraid –. COLONEL THOMAS: Has h-he b-been s-saying things? CAPTAIN PETERSEN: Dreadful things, Boss . . . THE AFTER-IMAGE: If you've forgotten what the instructor tried to din into you as you drowsed in Lecture Room Nineteen after lunch, let me, with my connection to the world wide web, reacquaint you with the exact wording: According to the United Nations Convention against Torture and Other Cruel, Inhuman or Degrading Treatment or Punishment, any act is outlawed by which severe pain or suffering, whether physical or mental, is intentionally inflicted on a person for such purposes as obtaining from him information or a confession . . . COLONEL THOMAS: I'm well aware of that, Gail – he said some pretty dreadful things to me. THE AFTER-IMAGE: . . . When such suffering is inflicted by, or at the instigation of, a public official or person acting in an official capacity, this will constitute under the terms of the Convention a . . . war crime. CAPTAIN PETERSEN: He was really raving, Boss – I had to give him a heavy sedative, he'll be out for hours now. COLONEL THOMAS (more focused): Time enough to get him down to Shaibah before he starts up again? CAPTAIN PETERSEN (bemused): We-ell . . . I s'pose so, Boss. COLONEL THOMAS: That's

438

the ticket – you carry on, then, Gail, they're expecting you over at the TeeDeeEff. High time those detainees were given their medical exam – and a full cavity search, I'm afraid. CAPTAIN PETERSEN: But, Boss . . . COLONEL THOMAS: Gail? CAPTAIN PETERSEN: It's Trooper Bessemer, I've just got off the radio net, he's . . . he's dead, Boss. THE AFTER-IMAGE (portentously): Their lives cannot repay us – their death could not undo – the shame they have laid upon our race –. COLONEL THOMAS: Oh, my God – this changes everything. The poor boy . . . the poor bloody boy . . . Oh, Gail . . . (He looks about for a white plastic garden chair to collapse into, but there's none.) I'm sorry, I seem to be . . . lagging. CAPTAIN PETERSEN: Lagging, Boss? COLONEL THOMAS: Oh . . . Gail – what d'you think . . . I mean . . . I mean . . . (summoning himself) . . . c'mon, yes . . . You – you'd better tell Dave Cambell and McCadie, Gail, but other than that . . . for now, best the men don't know. CAPTAIN PETERSEN: But, Boss – there's the detainee in the rap –. COLONEL THOMAS: In the rap? CAPTAIN PETERSEN: The one who collapsed from heat exhaustion, sir, he's in a very bad way. COLONEL THOMAS: Gail, I shouldn't have to remind you of our obligations under the Geneva Convention – those men should've been seen to hours ago, it's important it be established what sort of condition they were in when we scooped them up, we don't want any comeback on this. CAPTAIN PETERSEN: I'm not sure I understand what you're driving at, sir – as for the men, I'm afraid they already know about Bessemer. COLONEL THOMAS: Know? Know about Bessemer? Oh, fuck – oh, God! I ordered a comms lock-down on this base . . . CAPTAIN PETERSEN: Y'know how the army is for gossip, Boss. COLONEL THOMAS: Yeah, I know . . . I know . . . *You know nothing, GAYwain – you've lost your grip on it all. Think of your wife and the tedious mystery her body is to you: a skin bag stuffed full of giblets and charged with an unearthly power – think of the Rams: passed to you hard and clean – but you've fumbled them both, GAYwain. You've failed to keep possession and knocked them on – kids and Jonathan, too* . . . CAPTAIN PETERSEN: You all right, Boss? COLONEL THOMAS: Whaddya mean? CAPTAIN PETERSEN: Are you feeling all right . . . physically . . . You're white as a –. COLONEL THOMAS: I'm perfectly fine, Gail – prob'ly just low blood sugar. CAPTAIN PETERSEN: Here . . . look . . . Boss . . . (she reaches in the breast pocket of her battledress) . . . just got it out of the fridge. COLONEL THOMAS (receiving the chilly thing): Thanks . . . really . . . thanks. (He walks away from her without saluting and wanders towards the squadron lines, the slogan *Work, Rest and Play* . . . *Work, Rest and Play* . . . spooling behind his glass-paper eyelids. Nearing MAJOR TOWNSHEND's trailer, COLONEL THOMAS sees two figures loitering in its shadows, and hears the low thwock-thwock of ball bouncing on boot. TROOPER BESSEMER (contemptuously): Oh, it's you, is it . . . (he neatly volleys the ball into his companion's open hands) . . . what's your game? COLONEL THOMAS: Who is that? Who are you men? What're you doing up and about when I expressly ordered everyone under cover? TROOPER BESSEMER: S'me innit – s'me 'n' Asif, innit. ASIF (lightly volleying the ball back): You're definitely you, Bessie – and I'm definitely me. COLONEL THOMAS: Wh-What're you doing here? ASIF: Good question, Colonel – I should be on my way to Najaf, to be buried within sight of the Imam's shrine, as were my forefathers and their forefathers before them. But Bessie here didn't want to miss the rugby Sevens. TROOPER BESSEMER: Yeah, Rams' Ingerland Seven'll be mashed without my goal kicking. (COLONEL THOMAS tries to hold his eyes on BESSEMER's eager, guileless, goofy, *betrayed* face – but they keep rolling down to the *steak tartare* between the boy's legs.) ASIF: Yes, lost without his goal-kicking, just as your government's entire programme of introducing representative democracy to Iraq while simultaneously installing a government capable of upholding the law and enforcing international standards of human rights will begin to seem pretty threadbare if you don't get a grip on your men. COLONEL THOMAS (looking at the Mars Bar in the palm of his hand): I . . . I'm trying to do my best – by you, Asif – by the Rams . . . by your people as well. And I'm trying to protect those back at home – Fi, Miffy, my kids and everyone else's. LAURA (MYFANWY THOMAS's knitted clown doll, grown monstrously large – perhaps fourteen feet high. She comes on long red woolly legs out from behind MAJOR TOWNSHEND's trailer, her white-wool face looming uncannily in the orangey gloom): The kids don't need you, GAYwain – you can't help them. Look at yourself, man! (COLONEL THOMAS peers down at his softening torso: the ceramic plates of his body armour are bending and buckling – his battledress is melting into gloopy globs.) ASIF: In the nineteen twenties a young man called Harris came here – he was a flyer with your ArrAyEff. Harris pioneered a strategy which became known as area bombing: systematically destroying civilian housing using a combination of high-explosive to blow their roofs off, followed by incendiaries to create a conflagration. The effects were predictably devastating – and twenty years later Harris employed the same method to lay waste to German cities. Now you come here, armed with a fucking Mars Bar, and expect us to bow down before you . . . (he steps forward and casually snaps off COLONEL THOMAS's forearm, removes its khaki wrapper and begins chomping on chocolate flesh, nougat sinews and toffee bone) . . . Mm, buttery fingers – thing is, there's so very little of you to bow down before. (Gawain's Flakey knees bend, buckle, then Kit-Kat-snap! as he Twixes forward – straight on to his Caramac face. His chin, together with a third of his cranium, comes away, and he has the queerest experience of seeing from within the mould of himself . . . *chinless, that's me*, while witnessing a still-stranger dissolution, as scores of milk-chocolate-coated balls of honeycombed malt tumble through his eye sockets and roll away across the hard-packed sandy ground . . . *I'm losing my Maltesers*.) COLONEL THOMAS: Help me, lads! Help me! I'm melting! TROOPER BESSEMER: Yeah, well . . . (he steps forward and plants his boot in the sticky-brown puddle which was once his SeeOh) . . . best thing, really – for a chocolate soldier who's standing in front of the odd little carpeted ledge beside the flat's front door, picking up the sweat-stained bush hat which tops off his costume . . . *sigh!* Oldster togs his youngsters affect to despise, but *the zoetrope revolves*: soon enough they'll be *slippering about* themselves – 'though prob'ly not in grey nylon tracksuit bottoms and a sweatshirt bearing the slogan SANTE FE EXPERIMENTAL PSYCHOLOGY CONFERENCE NINETEEN NINETY-SEVEN on its saggy-blue breast. Reaching deep in the pocket of his

Donegal tweed jacket, Busner's fingernails find twists and twirls of tin foil . . . *why?* Prowling from room to room of the flat, his eyes sweeping more surfaces for keys, wallet and mobile phone, he thinks more *on't*. Where'd he been when he bit into the chocolate soldier? He'd painstakingly picked the gold foil from the soft brown face – this much he remembers . . . *never forget foil on filling*. Also, he'd been slumped down in a white plastic garden chair, on the cracked concrete apron Camilla calls "my patio". Yes! That was it: at Milla's, last Sunday. She'd called up and invited him to: *Come and sit on my patio, Gramps – it's been ages . . . Ben so wants to see you . . . I'll do a roast for lunch . . .* She had – and Zack had brought the box he picked up in Tesco's on the Kentish Town Road: they'd laid there, two layers of sturdy troopers with red foil trews and blue foil jackets – and when Ben lifted the lid on them, Zack'd made some feeble joke about fighting the next war with the chocolate soldiers of the last. Oscar had been in attendance, bullshitting the way lay-therapists so frequently do – making references whenever possible to "the work", under the illusion this would ingratiate him with his old man. So, it'd been "the work" on "my patio" on the first sunny Sunday of spring. Hungry pigeons waddled along the thin *tendencies* of branches – Camilla waddled in and out of the kitchen. Zack hadn't seen her or Ben since Christmas, and he'd been struck by her weight gain, or was it . . . *water retention? The poor thing.* Worse still, mother and son are coming to resemble each other more than is healthy: Ben, a hulking fellow of twenty-one, affects an Abstract Expressionist hairstyle, his brown locks statically charged into thick brushstrokes. His grandfather supposes this an attempt to be fashionable on the young man's part, but if so it hardly comes off, since he had indeed been wearing the same sort of charity-shop clobber . . . *as me.* No elegant arras supporting an ebullient jacaranda – and no wittily urbane conversation either: instead, two or three spider plants in cracked pots, the pigeons – and Ben hunched in another white plastic garden chair, twirling the frayed end of a toothpick in front of his hooded eyes *'cause he still self-stimulates* . . . Ben-the-burden . . . *who'll always need to be supported.* Ben, who has no more social skills than he ever did, and so had either answered his grandfather's questions with adolescent grunts, or else sat surlily silent for the few minutes his mother could compel his attendance, before he'd rifled the chocolate-soldier box and beat a retreat to his stuffy room, leaving behind a single melting one, and a more solid, choicer remark, muttered then remuttered, which reverberated in his grandfather's mind . . . *We've been put on earth for a reason* . . . *We've been put on earth for a reason* . . . Busner spots the mobile phone, tethered by its white flex to a plug socket . . . *charging.* Why was he bothering with it at all? *But it won't cost you a penny* . . . Milla had chided him when he tried to refuse her gift . . . *infuriating! As if money's the issue.* I've prepaid for a hundred minutes, but really it's for us to call you – check you're all right, and stuff . . . Ben, hearkening at least to this tech-talk, had unleashed his own *data-stream*: the phone was nothing special . . . *nothing special* . . . You can only send text messages with it and make voice calls . . . *and make voice calls* . . . The new three-gee network was already overwhelmed with data-streaming . . . *overwhelmed with data-streaming* . . . The new network eliminates circuit switching –

it's all eyepee now: packet switching using elayenn and doubley-ouayenn networks . . . *using elayenn and doubleyouayenn networks . . .* 'Course, this is pitifully inadequate, too . . . *'Course, this is pitifully inadequate, too . . .* Simply to interrupt him, Zack had asked: Pitifully inadequate for what? Which silenced Ben for a moment – then he'd looked into his grandfather's eyes. Looked directly into them in . . . *a manly and forthright manner,* something so unexpected Zack had almost called to Milla and Oscar, who were in the kitchen to . . . *come quick and see!* But, thinking better of it, he held his grandson's fierce gaze and had been gifted with: *Pitifully inadequate for the Singularity . . .* another queer phrase which returns to him now as he untethers the phone and slips it into his jacket pocket. We've been put on earth for a reason/Pitifully inadequate for the Singularity – the two snatches of dialogue revolve around each other in his cloistered mind as he locks the flat's front door, pockets his keys and heads down the stairs. There're hairy dags caught in the thick pile of the runner and all along the hallway's . . . *dusty ravine* – to where *there's nothing new . . .* under the transom's rectangular sun: a mess of junk mail on the mat, and the letter-box's flap bearded with leaflets and flyers. Then, in the street . . . *all is flux!* A great envelopment of traffic noise and traffic stink which threatens to *drag me down.* He staggers, grabs the concrete stan-chion of the bus stop and manages to stay upright. Luvverly day fer April, 'ow long you bin waitin'? Busner oils his rusty jaw with saliva – prepares to speak for the first time in hours, then realises the street drinker . . . *same tracksuit bottoms as me,* isn't addressing him, but an old lady . . . *old? prob'ly same age as you,* who stands clutching a Yorkshire terrier to her sunken chest, one of the little dog's stiff hind-legs scratching frantically . . . *at nothing*. The street drinker, who holds a can of Polish lager, carries on *crazily*: 'E's a cute wee doggie, can I 'old 'im? Once upon a time Busner would've felt it incumbent on him to intervene – and by this act alone to . . . *diagnose*? But not any more – the man may be a schizophrenic self-sedating with alcohol, or an alcoholic suppressing the first psychotic withdrawal symptoms . . . *it's the same diff*. No, a personality dis-order is only hysteria or melancholia *by another name* . . . The dosser, whose smelly neck is now within the terrier's biting range, might even be on the autistic spectrum . . . *whatever that means nowadays.* One thing, however, Busner knows for certain: there's no need for more epithetic psychiatry – and nor is there for . . . *a pathetic superannuated psychiatrist.* Wossiss name, then? the dosser asks, and Busner thinks: he's the true mendicant – a real Sannyasi. Snug in his seedy Kentish Town flat, the former paterfamilias has been reading up on Eastern religions – he fancies himself as a white-haired old Brahmin, who, after many years of uncomplaining service to family and society, removes his sleeve protectors and green eyeshade, picks up his staff and begging bowl and then . . . *hits the road.* But this ragged travesty of his aspiration – this *fool*, staggering about on the *blasted pavement*, has . . . *upstaged me!* Busner lurches again – grabs the bus stop . . . *again* – then, through his woozy vulnerability, sees *the shield I seek!* held by a squire who steps forward from . . . *the dust cloud of an Icelandic volcano*, the grey matter lying thick in the creases of his . . . *cotton surcoat*. For a stretched and gummy moment, Busner struggles to grasp what it is he's seeing, as the young man's fingers flick *ping!* and dabble *pong!* against the glassy surface . . . *what is this odd manipulation?* If he abstracts the shield-of-light with which the young man fends off Kentish Town's flaking stucco, Busner sees only this: one arm rigidly extended, the other crooked, its hand fidgeting . . . *he's stimming – like Ben!* And the young man's fixation on the tablet computer? Well, back in the day Busner might well've diagnosed this as an *oculogyric crisis* . . . but now? Isn't this precisely the sort of affectless fixation a contemporary clinician would expect . . . *from an autist?* He's aware . . . *they can't be avoided* of the panicky reaction there is to these new digital technologies – the guilty unease of those who once touched and smelt and tasted, but who now sit stock-still, seeing the world for the most part *through a glass far too brightly.* His old colleague Harold Sikorski is just one amongst a host of psy-professionals and neuroscientists who've taken to the airwaves to warn the watchers that, because they've allowed the über-autists of Silicon Valley to feed them their thoughts, visions and reveries, and to calibrate their very movements, their brains have been rewired. *Utter poppycock!* of course – and quite extra-ordinary that someone such as Harold should jettison everything he knows about genetics and human evolution to begin bruiting it about that the gross anatomy of the brain – unaltered for nigh on a quarter of a million years – has suddenly begun to mutate because . . . *we spend too much time on the phone!* And yet . . . and yet . . . this much Busner would concede: there is something chang-ing – not with the brain . . . *but the mind*, with the way human consciousness, taken collectively, is starting to experience its own reality. It's an experience Busner's compelled to join in: his eyes gripped by the young man's tablet computer – by this *palimpsest of panels* which slide and shuffle and force upon him such incontrovertible facts: *A crucial component of any incoming government's policy will be to avert the industrial action that's widely expected, should public-sector cuts be as deep as anticipated . . .* which are ousted in an eye-blink by a . . . *smirking Osborne.* What, Busner wonders, does Ben see when he looks at a face on-screen? For an autist it must be a liberation of sorts: freed from the requirement to guess at their interlocutor's mental states on the basis of the infinitely subtle interplay between gestures, words and glances, they can simply . . . *communicate.* Busner remembers speaking to Frankie via Skype when she was on sabbatical in Iowa – or, rather, he has before him right now the ghastly wallpaper on the walls of her study-bedroom, a *geometric spew* he spent some time contemplating, because, although they chatted away intimately enough . . . *neither of us looked into the other's eyes.* They hadn't felt the need to do so – there seemed no requirement for windows into each other's souls, because these inner worlds were *sutured together* by the long threads of machine code . . . . Osborne has been supplanted by the *pom-pom* of a single diagrammatic virion which floats in space, at once endless and measurable in microns. *Despite the falling away from universal inoculation, the measles virus has proved less infectious than feared. A study by the National Centre for Virology has established that transmission rates be–* gone, ousted in turn by the door's bullying concertina. The *parfit gentle knight* sheathes his shield and mounts ahead of him . . . *riding that old emmemmarr sawhorse – but why?*

And the street drinker, as anticipated, bunks on by the back door –
while *my contemporary* brings up the rear with her flea-bitten dog.
Busner touches his Freedom Pass to the worn patch and is rewarded
with a tiny tweet from a . . . *cybernetic forest filled with pines and
electronics*, and the indifference of the driver-operator, who keeps his
eyes fixed on *the distant horizon of the terminus* . . . On the top deck
there're no passengers, only rows of seats covered in snazzy, electric-
blue moquette. The bus moans for re-entry – then lunges back into
the traffic stream. The young man touches down in one seat, and
the retired psychiatrist collapses, Oof! into the one behind – and by
the time he's recovered the shield is once again . . . *fending off the
world* – although, Busner concedes, this might not be the right way
to think about it at all. Maybe every child who received the triple
vaccine – and this young man had to be a near-contemporary of
Ben – was similarly affected, and now found the real furniture
of the world rather more insubstantial than the screen architecture
they fixated on. *Pitifully inadequate for the Singularity*, was it? This
despite the fact that good ol' Gramps picked up the bill for the
highest-speed internet connection available – *good ol' Gramps, eh* . . .
Once Oscar had sloped off, so had Ben and Camilla – their exits as
sudden, momentous and *slight* as the substitution of one screen for
another. After a while, marooned on the deserted patio, waiting
for the pigeons to *shit on me* . . . he'd followed his grandson inside
and found him in his tunnel of a bedroom, wedged between the
Dexion shelving units, which were now warped and buckled, such
was their load of books, magazines, papers, seedees, deeveedees,
veeaitchess tapes, obsolete computer equipment, and – so far as his

grandfather could see – just about every toy the monarchical and only child had ever owned . . . *what I have I hold on to*. Listening to Ben playing the monotonous keyboard – looking about at chunky beige boxes which seemed, even to him, the sarcophagi of an earlier machine age, Zack had remembered lobbying for time on the huge old EyeBeeEmm mainframe at Heath Hospital . . . *I was an early adopter* – at least of the expression "early adopter". He and Ford had fed the data in laboriously, by hand – they'd also written the program which helped establish . . . *so far as we were concerned* that, at any given time, any given social group only had a fixed amount of sanity . . . *to go round*. Had he imagined then that within thirty years a machine the size of a small room would be conjured into a box he could hold in the palm of his hand? No – emphatically not: the sixties and seventies had been all per ardua ad astra: Zack and his fellow psychonauts, while affecting to despise the militarists' techno-trip, nonetheless *saw ourselves as strangers in a strange land* . . . It wasn't until the space programme peaked, then splashed down in *the idiopathic ocean*, that the world turned in on itself. Before, there'd been a few politicians who banged on about computers and automation – the horse-lipped one with the *liquid lithp* had been a particular enthusiast – *wossiss name?* Bit of a cunt, really – him and Wilson both. *All pipe smokers're cunts!* he barks – and *Johnny Astro's fringe* yanks his lashless eyes around. For a few moments they stare at one another, as the young man tries to establish if he's being ridiculed – but then: *he sees my sweat-ringed headgear*, so allocates Busner to the social group of street people, amongst whom there's . . . *hardly any sanity to go round!* Then:

eyes-front! Shield up! and the emblematic virion is back, questing for somewhere . . . *anywhere to bind.* The young man flickety-tics the virion into a Mercator projection *with measles*: a rash of differently sized spots, some INFECTED, others FATALITIES – they are further labelled ACTUAL and PREDICTED. Busner shakes his battered old bonce and ruefully considers: I never fancied myself as much of an epidemiologist anyway – the Quantity Theory couldn't predict how insanity was spread, only how much of it there was . . . *to go round annaround.* All mass panics – he'd hypothesised at the time – could provide this adaptive advantage: by concentrating insanity in one portion of society, they'd afforded their fellow Britons greater mental well-being – because what were the emmemmarr refuseniks if not . . . *crazy?* He remembers the miserable and semi-drunken nights when Camilla had ranted and raved, blaming the triple-vaccination for her son's tangled neurological wiring – cursing the entire smoothly incomprehensible edifice of . . . *so-called medical science – what's got into everyone?* What's got into all the ape-men and ape-women, grovelling by the waterhole and chucking rocks at each other? Advancing, then retreating, then advancing again . . . *willing to wound, and yet afraid to strike?* Do they really conceive of natural selection operating in this way – as a millennia-long game of *grandmother's footsteps?* Tiring of the young man's fixation, Busner slips away – back to that windless tunnel full of plastic crates crammed with obsolete microcircuitry. His own grandson sat for hour upon hour, throughout the Kilburn nights, his eyes glued to not one but . . . *three screens!* Years later it'd come out: Wilson didn't smoke a pipe at all – it was a peearr stunt he'd dreamt up himself.

Thought it made him look more like a man of the people – truth was, once the heavy door of Number Ten had swung shut, he pulled out a fat Havana and Marcia *clipped its sweet-smelling prepuce for him* . . . then held its bared tip out to his mealy mouth so he might suck on *the white heat of technology* . . . That'd been the temper of the times – a very feverishness about *time itself* . . . It was accelerating – oscillating at forty-five revolutions per minute, 'cause there was something going on, although no one really knew what it was – neither Mister Wilson, nor Mister Jones – *let alone Ronnie!* Who'd fallen victim to the most salient delusion of the prophet, which is the certainty . . . *his time has come.* The bus's time has come as well: it wrangles some cyclists across the junction by Tufnell Park tube, then buckets on along Junction Road. To either side are estate agents, convenience stores and more estate agents: the city feeding on its own bricky substance, and in so doing adding more *excremental value* to what once must've been solid middle-class homes with front gardens full of hollyhocks *tended by Pooters* . . . Now those nodding blooms had all been lopped off, and replaced by cubic hutches stuffed with electronic goods. Camilla had called yesterday – called the mobile phone she'd given him. She'd been in a state – which was why he'd brought the bloody thing out with him today. She'd been following up on her twin, current obsessions, both of which are *computer-based*: the new equipment she wants him to get for Ben – and the relationship she believes her own machine has gifted her . . . *stupid Cupid.* I'm not so out of touch I don't know what an ExBox is, he'd said as they'd sat in the front room of the Kilburn flat, where, on the trestle table which served Milla as a desk, sat her own . . . *window on the world*: her laptop – always open, always on, always *importuning*. But no, it hadn't been a games console that was required – she called Ben in to make his pitch. He came and sat opposite his grandfather, still twirling the splintering toothpick before his absent eyes, and droned on about screen definition, processing power and – most importantly – bandwidth: *It's lagging, Gramps – lagging . . . s'like . . . s'like . . . I'm not really there . . . I'm not really there – and then I get killed again . . . and then I get killed again . . . and again . . . and again . . .* His benefactor had responded with Victorian rectitude: *Well . . . we wouldn't want that to happen . . .* Then, to confirm Ben's assessment of the lethal – if virtual – situation, Zack accompanied him to his room and perched behind him as he sent his avatar scrambling across a landscape of mesas, cactuses and freeway underpasses jumbled up with the burnt-out shells of vehicles. Facing the triplet of screens, his own mind securely lodged in the pixelated brain pan of the rangy figure ever loping ahead, ammunition bandoliers crossed on its sweat-slick, bulgy back, the *lummox* was liberated into . . . *loquaciousness*: Have you read the Report from Iron Mountain, Gramps? he'd asked, and when Gramps hesitated because . . . *it sounded like the sort of thing I ought to've*, Ben ran on: It's a top-secret YouEss Government report . . . *Government report* . . . Proves they've never had any real intention of pursuing peaceful policies . . . *pursuing peaceful policies* . . .War's essential for the economies of the superpowers . . . *for the economies of the superpowers* . . . so war must be permanently maintained . . . *be permanently maintained* . . . Strange . . . Zack had thought then –

and Busner thinks now, as the bus reaches the Archway and heels over to round the sentinel tower – a recently recladded smoky-black pipe which sucks up *the drunk, the deranged, the poor . . . the autistic.* Yes, strange – strange the way these conspiracy theories had mounted up throughout his own lifetime . . . *the Zinoviev Letter brought the news of my birth*, only to break, over and over, on the wilder shores of collective credulity. What did they want? Only certainty – any certainty: better the Elders of Zion or the Comintern – or even the autistic SeeEeOhs of Silicon Valley tech giants pulling the strings than . . . *nobody*. You should read it, Gramps . . . *You should read it, Gramps . . .* I'll print you off a copy . . . *I'll print you off a copy . . .* There's a small group I belong to . . . sorta online forum . . . people interested in these sorts of things . . . *in these sorts of things* . . . Busner spots the street drinker – he's quit the bus and, can of beer still in hand, waltzes across the road through a squall of leaves and plastic bags down-draughted by the tower. Prob'ly headed for the Whittington . . . Busner thinks of all the hospitals where he's *plyed the hypo* . . . over the years, or otherwise restrained those who *can't restrain themselves*, so tear the little Yorkies from the pensioners' arms and . . . *cuddle them to death!* What was the bullshit Milla had bought into when Ben was little? *Holding therapy!* that was it: hanging on for dear life to the little bouncing ball of Benness, trying at all costs to prevent him stimming . . . *but we couldn't stop him being palilaliac . . . stop him being palilaliac* . . . Well, it's holding therapy I've been engaged in my entire professional life – and not just me, all my colleagues as well. Yes, psychiatrists, psychiatric nurses – medical doctors generally. Then there were the upright lawyers, the honest coppers and the staunch soldiers – all the capable arms the anxious and *over-stimmed* citizenry longed to be encircled by. But Milla had held on to Ben for so long *he's rooted to the spot!* Held on to him too long – *and fed him too much! Might he have an eating disorder?* If he did, would it help him to know? Prob'ly not – such diagnoses were useful only for triage on the battlefield of life. They were tourniquets to be tied round the forearms of chocolate soldiers to stop them melting when they step on an *improvised neurotic device* . . . As the bus groans up the steep acclivity of the Archway Road, the radio news, idly heard over breakfast, repeats: *The Ministry of Defence have confirmed that Sergeant Brian Culcross of the Second Battalion Royal Marines has been killed in action by an improvised explosive device* . . . Poor young man, he thinks – then looking round he sees the cyber-warrior has gone, taking his light-shield with him, and he's alone on the top deck *lager and limeade – whatever happened to that?* He feels fairly certain it was still on sale in newsagents when his children were small – granted, this proto-alcopop had been less than four per cent proof, but nevertheless it'd been freely available to minors, evidence – if any were needed – of a more *innocent era* . . . In this respect at least: Busner and his fellow parents had insufficient data – there'd been, as yet, no effective prevalence studies, so the dirty old men, the flashers and the paedophiles . . . *carried on in plain sight.* Staring at the flower-frothy front gardens of the houses leading up to the single concrete span of . . . *Le pont des Suicidés,* the old soul doctor seeks to *shrive myself* – For surely it was understandable that those who'd taken the Hippocratic Oath in the pinched and pallid fifties would feel themselves always to be, sensually speaking . . . *on the ration: I've a couple of luvverly bits of throbbing gristle kept back for you, Missus Fitz – the ones Mister Maurice likes* . . . Yes, another ingredient to be *added into the mix* . . . his uncle's homosexuality. There was nothing much in the literature, so far as Busner could recall – no long-term studies of the effect on children of having a homosexual parent in societies where it's illegal. Idly, he begins forming the parameters of such a study – oilcloth examples stretched over balsawood methodology . . . *but will it fly?* Moodily, he considers his own sexual orientation . . . *no – no he was never my north or south,* which would seem to scotch any case for nurture – as long as, that is, a sample can be considered statistically significant when it consists solely of . . . *moi, a horny little devil* . . . who, even in his teens, while Johnnie sobbed his heart out at the Palladium, was fixated on rather more sublunary things – throbbing things – my heart skipped a *boop-boop-shee-boop!* beat whenever I saw a gastrocnemius *swelling above a white ankle sock* . . . Throb*throb* . . . Throb*throb* . . . Throb*throb* . . . Slowly, sadly, Busner becomes aware that the throbbing in his crotch, far from being the return of priapism . . . *it was like a pogo-stick – so rigid I could've bounced around town* . . . is an incoming call. He gropes in the pocket of his tracksuit bottoms, caught up in the same sick anticipation as when, having paid two bob plus a further sixpence for postage and packaging, he tore the latter off, put the exray specs on and dashed out into Redington Road, certain he was finally going to glimpse . . . *the heavenly convexities beneath a Maidenform brassiere.* CAMILLA! the phone's tiny screen cries – and for an instant he thinks the phone is

Camilla, throbbing with unfulfilled desire in the palm of his hand. If he touches her *rubberised nipple* and presses her lips to his ear, he'll hear: *Gramps? Is that you? Are you there?* We're both, he thinks, lost to the world, even as the signals volleying back and forth between our handheld communication devices, and a perfectly calibrated network of orbiting satellites . . . *enable us to find one another.* He hesitates, knowing once he speaks their psyches will be squeezed together – squeezed and *squeezed – but the pips'll never come!* A chilly, sodden-cardboard-smelling wave of nostalgia for old phone boxes passes over him – and along with it a more uncomfortable memory: during the awful hours he and Miriam had spent flinging each other's infidelities in their faces, she'd laid claim to all the maturity, all the interpersonal skills – effectively *all the sanity* . . . there was to go round. What clinched it so far as she'd been concerned was this: If I've any worries about the kids, d'you know who I talk to, Zack? Not you, obviously – it's never you. You're far too busy – and your time is far too precious. No: I talk to Maurice – talk to him on the phone. Sometimes I rattle on for ages – just letting it all out. And you know what, he never – and I mean never – gives the slightest indication he's bored, or that he's *anything better to do* . . . Wearily, Busner shoves the mobile phone back in his pocket – if it's urgent she'll call again. If it isn't *she will as well.* The bus plunges past a playing field. An old man with lank white hair wearing an unseasonal donkey jacket pushes a white-lining machine towards some rugby posts, seagulls *scrumming down* behind him. Besides, what if he does answer the insistent phone, what'll he get? Much, much more, in the same vein, of the saccharine injection she'd administered every day since she forced the phone on him. For, Camilla Whitehouse-Busner has compounded the ridiculous conjunction of her name by falling passionately, improbably . . . *in love.* And a woman in love is desirous above all, not for reciprocation or consummation – let alone Wagnerian supersession – but simply someone with whom she can . . . *yak about it on the phone. You don't blame me, do you, Gramps?* was how she'd told him about her own notional infidelity the previous Sunday. Guileless, she'd been, in a flouncy old apron, her cheeks flushed and two chopsticks shoved through the rather greasy and disordered *chop suey* of her hair. Zack hadn't seen either her or Ben since a Busner family gathering just after Christmas at Redington Road: Dan and Pat handing round readymade EmmandEss nibbles . . . *the little pricks!* They'd just moved in, and the house had seemed echoey and musty with old-man-smell – at once empty and cram-packed with . . . *ghosts.* Since then she'd gained weight – or at least he'd thought so as she ducked down to fetch a saucepan, or reached up to get some ingredients, because her belly was *preggily* prominent. Zack'd wanted to ask then – Busner still does, now – about her endometriosis, but couldn't find the right tone, *being effectively retired* . . . until hours later, when, after his strange talk with Ben, he'd come upon her in the kitchen again, leaning back against the grotty old units, her face in her hands. It'd been Zack rather than Doctor Busner who'd gently touched her shoulder, softly enquired if everything was *all right?* Although he knew perfectly well that it never had been and never could be. But when she'd unveiled her face and her features emerged . . . *they were luminous – Peek-a-boo, Gramps* . . . she'd said. *Peek-a-fucking-boo!* After which she'd said something like, Ben loathed it when we tried to play peek-a-boo with him – d'you remember, Gramps? He'd scream and scream and lash out at me . . . It did me terrible damage, Gramps, honestly . . . Tore me up inside – deep inside . . . the sheer intensity of his rejection . . . But she wasn't feeling rejected any more, oh no: *You don't blame me, Gramps, do you?* Blame her! Blame her for what, precisely? Mark's father had seen plenty of his patients over the years who, having been diagnosed in early adulthood as chronic schizophrenics . . . *though not usually by me*, had nonetheless, with the onset of middle age, experienced some sort of remission. The hectoring internal voices fell silent – to be replaced by the dreary chit-chat of those actually *eyearrdoubleyou* . . . But with Mark things hadn't gone that way – as his autistic son had grown, so his conviction that he was an alien spymaster, and Ben – using the work name, Mandinkulus – the agent he was running, grew stronger. Mark's stays in the safe houses earthlings call mental hospitals became longer and more frequent. During the brief periods he was at the Kilburn flat he was often so disruptive poor Milla had had to call the police. Watching his eldest son's once handsome features gradually coarsened as he suffered blow after blow from the liquid cosh, Zack often reflected on this grim truth: if Mark was engaged in a war against humanity – and, in particular, a war against its profligate expenditure of time, a dimension he believed to be in cripplingly short supply supply – then for him to prevail would require . . . *sich zu Tode siegen.* So, in advance of his last attempt at being cared for in the community, Miriam had organised a bedsit for Mark in Stanmore, and they'd take it in turns to drop by, feed him his meds and brush up the Digestive crumbs and shreds of hand-rolling tobacco which are his principal contribution . . . *to the gross domestic product.* It's horribly claustrophobic and airless in the smoke-stunk bedsit – yet paradoxically exposed and vacuous: the surface of a distant world, frozen beneath the diamond-studded black velvet . . . *of the void.* To sit on the mean little sofa for half an hour was . . . *an eternity* – to listen to Mandinkulus's controller, as he detailed the vital intelligence which was being gathered . . . *a torment.* So, to Camilla, Zack had said again: Blame you? Blame you for what, precisely? Bloody hell, Milla, far from blaming you, I'm cheering you on from the terraces. Who is he? How's it going? At the time he'd congratulated himself for not adding: Have you told Ben? And now he feels still better about this omission, because back in her Kilburn kitchen the inconvenient truths had tumbled from Milla's chapped lips: the object of her desire wasn't in the least bit obscure, but a writer of sufficient notoriety that even Zack had heard of him. This, despite the fact that Zack had long since waved goodbye to the gleaming ghost-ship of contemporary mediatised culture, as, with its snazzy paintwork and crew of soon-to-be-cashiered celebrities, and its hack band playing on *andon*, it set course for the day-after-tomorrow. D'you actually know him, personally? he'd blurted out in the kitchen – hardly a tasteful question to fling in the face of a woman hungry for love . . . *but it was the right one.* Camilla had blushed furiously, applied *holding therapy* to her large breasts, and said: D'you remember that creative writing course I went on? Ah, yes, Milla's creative writing. Oscar placed a soft hand on his softer heart, threw back his head and out came long and liquid lines of John Dowland – his brother Daniel, when he wasn't dozily doctoring, painted canvases which were large and so painfully Fauvist that, on viewing one, his father couldn't help muttering: *an unholy bloody mess* . . . a critical truth to which Daniel had angrily assented: Of course it's an unholy bloody mess, Dad, because that's what I'm trying to express, the unholy bloody mess which was my childhood! Lottie kept on with her singing – and Frankie used to dance, while the twins, pushed by Mummy, pursued a panoply of cultural and artistic goals, none of which, in their father's opinion . . . *they're ever likely to reach*. It was perhaps unjust of him, but Busner suspected that Milla's literary ambitions had more to do with fitting in with her adopted family than any overwhelming desire on her part to render this world – or any other – in prose. He'd seen her efforts: folded sheets of narrow feint torn from blocky jotters, which, when unfolded, released tentative observations . . . hesitant descriptions . . . duff dialogue. Exposing to ridicule a style so staccato adjectives were *st-st-st*-stuck to nouns. But was it any good? He felt quite unable to judge . . . *because I don't actually care?* Quite possibly – which was where the cold *slapactually* had come from. Camilla, reddening still more, stood her ground and explained that the writer-he'd-heard-of hadn't been one of the tutors on the week-long course – which was held in a whitewashed former farmhouse deeply immersed in creamy Devon – but, rather, being something of a celebrity, had arrived on the last evening, when the group had pretty much *curdled – gone rancid, Gramps – there were that many female hormones flying about* . . . But Camilla had prevailed, so been seated beside him at supper – Zack could imagine the scene: a refectory table, warm bread torn on worn boards, the chilly looks of the wannabe women writers, and the two of them chatting together . . . *warmly*. Warmly enough for her to ask for his email address and for him to give it. She'd written on her return to London – and he'd replied, and she'd replied to his reply, sending the fragment of her own work he'd agreed to read – to which he'd replied in turn, saying it *showed promise*. These had been his exact and dismissive words – and Camilla conveyed them to her father-in-law all *amber* . . . with such praise. Aglow – and in love. The bus has stopped by the lights at the junction of Southwood Lane, its engine gasping against the window of a fried-chicken takeaway. Busner's forehead *is tenderised* by the toughened glass – his face swells up at him: *My old face . . . my old mottled face . . . I wear the motley of my . . . face – a tatterdemalion of experience . . . moles . . . antediluvian acne scars . . .* He sees diamonds of mirror set in mirrored batons – he sees the *Mandelbrot set* of the Formica they reflect. On a modular, back-lit menu holder he reads: One Piece Chicken and Chips . . . Ninety-nine pence. Two Piece Chicken and Chips . . . One pound and nineteen pence. Three Piece Chicken and Chips . . . One pound and forty-nine pence. These are, he thinks, exact words, but do they . . . *show promise?* Appalled, he'd stared at Milla as she'd burbled on: *I'm not saying he's in love with me, Gramps – I'm not delusional . . .* Poor Milla! Sitting in Kilburn, night after night, pouring it all out into her laptop, deluding herself that its poorly insulated circuitry can cope with . . . *such gush*: I'm not delusional – I know it isn't going to be a normal relationship.

For a start, we can't be together – not physically, 'cause we're both married – 'though I don't think Mark would . . . mind. Once more Zack had had to bite down on bitter merriment: Mind? Mandin-kulus's controller? The first inter-specific double-agent known to humankind, mind? He scarcely has a mind – but then nor did Milla, or so it seemed: He lets me write him one long email every week – that's all the contact we're gonna have . . . I did go to some of his readings and lectures and stuff, but he told me he isn't com-fortable with that, and it would be better – sorta purer – if we just corresponded . . . 'cept . . . well . . . Out came more desperate dribs and disillusioning drabs: the writer-Zack'd-heard-of wouldn't reply to the missives Milla sent whooshing through the ether – some of which, she admitted, ran to several thousand words – but he assured her he'd remain hooked on the very end of the very last line. Zack would've said something sharp enough to . . . *nip it in the bud*, had Milla not at this point uncrossed her arms and arched her back, so that her heavy breasts lifted and her chopsticks clacked against the spice rack. She'd shuddered deliciously – and it'd occurred to Zack that this was some weird climax, brought about by her own onanistic literary activities: her ceaseless jabbing . . . *at the slick little buttons.* Why? Zack had asked of her then. Why? Busner asks aloud now – or, rather, lows pitifully as the bus surges up East Finchley High Road past the Bald Faced Stag: *Why? Why? Why?* Penitent, he applies the lash: *She was raped . . . inna rape field . . .* and, while he knows he wasn't her rapist . . . *I am her sorta therapist.* And what manner of therapist – even when relatively young – knowing as he does *no means no*, nonetheless wilfully *misunderstands . . .* The

463

well-worn liberal cri de cœur . . . *We're all to blame!* echoes through his hurting head, for if you added up those misunderstandings they'd certainly be sufficient to make a single, devastating *violation* . . . He remembers all manner of pushing, pulling and tugging – and, on one occasion, *tearing* – appalled, he sees it, mounting up *massily* in the direction of Muswell Hill: the *stopped* dandelion *clock* of her petticoats and her shocked-white *face*. And now . . . and now . . . the entire world had long since pushed into and pulled out of Milla – pushed and pulled *againannagain*, until her generative parts had begun to . . . *bleed, poor Milla!* and gone on flowing into all the internet's multitudinous tubes. Busner sits miserably arraigned before a jury of *white-faced Columbines* in the court of tragicomedy, their beautiful lips smeared . . . *with the greasepaint of our lust – It's my fault!* His fault her insides haemorrhage – his fault she's no thought of a happily uncomplicated and cuddly liaison. Delusional, she emphatically is – and he's always known *and made use of it.* For who else but a delusional person would care so delusionally for Mandinkulus – and not just during childhood, but once he'd reached his majority as well. She still accompanies him on weekly trips to the nutritionist – to the occupational therapist, to the fraudulent cranial osteopath. She maintains the great go-round of impersonal encounters constituting Ben's asocial life. Associative mating – that was the explanation du jour for the massive increase in autism diagnoses. Might Mandinkulus's controller be an autist as well as schizophrenic? He'd certainly been a systematiser as a child – a sorter-out, a colour-coder and a liner-uper. Busner searches the basement of his own memory, where nothing any longer seems to be to hand. Had Mark looked into his eyes when a child? He cannot remember – and this summons a tear . . . *light, fresh and . . . coolly* rolling down his cheek. It's Camilla, he knows, who keeps Ben's own museum-of-everything in order, adding in plastic-bag-loads of more plastic to the dry-stone walling of seedees, deeveedees, records, cassette tapes, books, magazines, toys and obsolete computer equipment that fills the Dexion shelving units, which in turn fill the Kilburn flat. Was this evidence of her own Aspie tendencies? Tendencies that've now come to full and frenzied fruition in the weekly email she sends to the man Ben calls the orfer? Ach! Busner cries aloud to the empty top deck, such meshugas! The bus is accelerating along Queens Avenue towards Muswell Hill – soon it'll reach sufficient velocity to escape the poisonous atmosphere of central London. Sensing the outer space beyond the asteroid belt of suburbia, Busner pulls hairy lapels up to stubbly cheeks . . . *Mm, scratchy.* Which is the name of Ben's cat, a more than averagely dumb moggy which occupies the sofa in the front room, where it fulfils its nominative destiny by rendering both upholstery and its own coat more and more threadbare. But then: a balding narcissist . . . *could there be anything more human?* He'd boarded the bus unthinkingly – committed to the rubric of the random, but now he sees where it's all been headed, for his own head is strapped into some sort of *brace . . . or restraint!* And he cannot prevent himself from staring down all one thousand, eight hundred and eighty-four rigidly straight feet of its mind-bending central corridor . . . *the longest in Europe!* And cannot stop himself, try as he might, from seeing this unearthly vision: his post-encephalitic patients at

Friern ... *my enkies!* performing a wildly intricate ballet in one of the old airing courts – *There they are!* in their twenties togs, tripping and dipping to some seventies jig ... *I'm an ape-man, I'm an ape-ape man* ... Apish they are – as nimble-footed as chimpanzees, what with their compulsive ticcing, their wildly unpredictable movements and their jazzy fulgurations, which fling their brittle bodies up into the air, only for them to fall back to the desolate ground. This much Busner readily recalls: That brilliant summer, during the era of the moon landings, when he'd awakened the post-encephalitics from their marmoreal half-century-long slumbers – and begun to see symptoms of their malady *everywhere* ... In the festination of football players flocking round goal mouths – in the echolalia of politicians interviewed on the radio ... *now the problem is happening now, problematically,* and in the city itself, taken in toto, which even forty-odd years ago seemed to be on the point of either catatonic dissolution or speeding up and up until it all *flew apart* ... But what'd been her name, the old and eloquent enkie who he'd awakened with some of his precious ounce of L-dihydroxyphenylalanine? This much he definitely does remember: *It cost a thousand pounds!* While ... for the life of me, I can't ... it's on the tip of my ... Anyway, one minute she'd been wholly trapped – a sparrow-like woman enmeshed by the bizarre neural net of her malady – the next she'd *spread her wings* ... Compos mentis, she'd regarded the craven new world with a certain Edwardian pomp and detachment. She'd been, he thinks, really rather remarkably trenchant – a scientific socialist in her distant youth, she'd been delighted by humankind's apparent progress. She wasn't in the least discomfited by the wholesale transformation which had taken place while she Rip-Van-Winkled. The voices of her youth – whether meek and mild or admonitory and hectoring – torn from pulpit, lectern and platform while she slept, had been transformed into this great *scritch-itch-itch* . . . He peers down at the mobile phone lying in his hand: Milla will try again soon enough – and next time he knows he'll feel compelled to answer . . . *something might be wrong . . . with Ben.* . . If only she could be more like the old enkie: stoical, and quite unable to . . . *get any reception.* I'm a coward, Busner thinks, and I ought to confront her but it's *awfully ticklish!* He snorts – merriment provoked by this anachronism, accessed from his memory banks by another: All change, please! Muswell Hill – the Broadway! All change, please! The driver-operator has acquired, he realises, a third role, that of the master-of-ceremonies in *the Good Old Days*, whose announcements, Busner recalls, had a stagy, cockneyfied feel: *Leddies an' gennlemen, I gives you . . . Muzzerwell 'ill!* So strong is this impression that, descending the stairs and stepping off the bus, he half expects to see arrayed before him the top hats and ostrich-feathered toques of a music-hall audience . . . When the vision fades, he's standing on the two thousand and ten pavement in front of an internet café. Plastic decals stuck inside its windows advertise LEBARA with African faces wreathed in smiles – joy occasioned, Busner assumes, by the coming of modern electronic communications systems, for this is, he gathers, a service which allows far-flung Swazis, Rwandans and Gabonese to call home for . . . *mere pennies a minute.* He sees their uncles in jungle clearings, lifting the receivers of coin phones bolted to baobab trees. He hears the shhhk-shhk as they fumble in their pockets, then come up with cowrie shells, which they feed into a specially adapted slot: *Poosh de Button A! Poosh de Button, man . . . Poosh it!* What, he wonders, can these happy exiles be saying as they yak away for hour upon hour, their wordstream coursing around the world? The old world . . . the old cold world . . . the *grey sunken cunt* of the world, full up with cold-old women, their flea-bitten terriers and their cold-old calcium-whitened turds . . . *give-a dog-a* . . . Full up, most especially, with Africans – one of whom exits the café at this point. He's wearing a spiffy, maroon-leather jacket, and, as he reaches into its unzippered side pocket, Busner's groin throbs *sympathetically* – goes on *throbbing*, as the African answers his phone and without any formalities launches straight into vous n'avez pas l'autorisation pour gagner . . . a blatant soliloquy he si vous souhaitez poursuivre, while old women keep trundling by with their wheeled wicker . . . *tumbrels.* And still Busner's crotch throbs – and still the African *francophones*: un projet de loi pro-forma connaissement peut être téléchargé notre *site of special schizophrenic interest* – because it's next to impossible nowadays, Busner thinks, to distinguish between neglected psychotics who hurl their voices to the carping winds – and those, such as this import-export merchant, who only wish de vous informer, cher monsieur, que nos conditions sont tout-à-fait standard et entièrement concurrentielles –. The African turns away abruptly – and, bereft, Busner reaches into his tracksuit bottoms to release his own diddle-oooh-doo-doo! Hello . . . Hello . . . Gramps? Issat you . . . ? Standing in the bees-wax-smelling hall of his own mind, with Milla calling to him,

Busner feels no anxiety: there're no buttons for his daughter-in-law to push . . . *besides le mien.* So, he identifies himself – and, as he begins walking towards the Quadrant, it all comes squeaking out. Much of it the same as he'd heard the previous Sunday, but with *new and improved* anxiety: I'm worried, Gramps . . . *you've always been worried.* Ben's been behaving pretty strangely . . . *he's always behaved pretty strangely* . . . I didn't want to say anything last Sunday . . . *you couldn't stop talking last Sunday* . . . but he's barely been out of his room in weeks, now . . . *he's barely been out of his room in twenty-one years, now* . . . I can cope with that, Gramps, but what I can't cope with is the stress of not knowing what he's getting up to . . . *none of us know what he's getting up to* . . . I think he may be mixed up with that computer-hacking collective, Anonymous. He's got hold of one of their masks – the one with the moustache and goatee . . . *he's got scores of masks – his own face is a . . . mask . . .* I'm worried to death, Gramps – what if he's hacking into government computer systems and stuff like that – what if he's doing stuff like that other autistic man – *Gary McKinnon – I've read all about him in doctors' waiting rooms.* On she talks, *onanon,* the pulsion of her plosives pushing him *onanon,* until he finds himself in the Quadrant, blankly observing the buses *butt and bore,* and only semi-aware Milla has shuffled between the objects of her affection, and it's now the orfer whom she wishes him to talk to: He's heard of you, Gramps, he admires your work – he's giving a reading next Thursday in Camden Town. If you went along you might be able to grab a few seconds with him, explain to him that I'm not some sort of cyber-stalker . . . *but you are!* and then things would . . . *les choses*

469

seraient quoi, exactement? Proceeding up Duke's Avenue towards the brown pile slumped atop the hill, Busner, only paying the slightest of attention to this *museum audio-guide*, marvels at the contemporary world: cloudy castles rise up above Alexandra Palace, the same impossibilist battlements and vaporous curtain walls he remembers from earliest childhood – yet at ground level he observes this: an old man clutching the side of his head, passing a young woman clutching hers. In the near-distance there are two or three others, all, so far as he can tell, similarly afflicted by the toothache of conversation . . . *it's good to talk*. But listening to Camilla is tooth-grinding as well as tooth-aching: He writes a lot about psychiatry, and stuff – that's how I got involved, I read this story he wrote about an autistic kid, and I think he really sorta gets it . . . Maybe he does, Busner thinks, maybe the orfer does get it, which is why he's so very determined keep the poor soul at arm's length: That's what I'm trying to do with my emails, Gramps, tell him all about me . . . and Ben, every last detail of our lives – 'cause he gets it, he really does, and one day . . . he'll realise I'm sincere, and we'll be together – not that I've any thought of it happening in this lifetime! she yelps – the self-deprecatory bark of an old sheepdog, too doddery now to *round 'em up*, and he says: Don't say that, Milla – you mustn't talk like that . . . which is the soured milk of human kindness – although she *laps it up* . . . I mean it, Gramps – I know you don't believe in kismet, but I do – I really believe we'll be together eventually . . . not in our human bodies – and not in heaven, that's just silliness, but somewhere . . . On she goes – *onanon*. She must realise, surely, that he isn't listening? Busner has reached Ally-Pally, and stands looking up at its gaunt super-structure, barnacled with satellite dishes and weedy with antennae. The Bhagavad-Gita has little to say on such matters – but from a magazine he's read recently in a dental surgery Busner gleaned this much: *a sightline to a communications mast enormously improves mobile phone reception* . . . which must aid the penetration of those carcinogenic waves into the delicate tissue of the brain, such that if the two of them keep on like this, soon enough *tumour will speak unto tumour* . . . Nevertheless, there may be a more providential way of regarding his tethered predicament – walking round the other side of the building, Busner gains a peak perspective, and can descry the entire north-east quadrant of the city, from the *Parnassus* of Totteridge right round to the *Elysian Fields* of Epping Forest. Meanwhile the surrealistic commentary continues: If only I could know what he really thinks, Gramps – what he really thinks about . . . me . . . Which is indeed the very nub of it, Busner concedes, making his way towards a bench. Is it, he wonders, the mobile phone that's brought him here by some occult means? Busner reflects with some irritation on his first attempt at the aimless wandering of a Hindu holy man: he'd left Kentish Town with no preconceived plan or route, yet wherever the way had divided he'd received a *techno-nudge* . . . He thinks of Ben's thumbs, nudging at the controller – thinks of Ben's avatar, its burly, burnished torso and brassiere of bandoliers. For Ben's still gaming – still toggling his way along the *virtual road to nowhere*. Sitting behind him, in the frigid light of his serried monitors, Zack had watched as this buffo figure explored the cavernous interior of a ruined building *not unlike*

Ally-Pally . . . Bounding over acres of rotten flooring, kinking to avoid the fire-resistant tiles crumbling from its lofty ceilings. It's like there was a nuclear war sometime in the mid nineteen fifties and this is what the world's like years later . . . *and this is what the world's like years later.* True enough, Busner ruminates, but if the entire wandering world had received such a techno-nudge, it wasn't then but a few years later, during the Missile Crisis. What'd been the name of the Soviet submarine commander? Ah, yes! Arkhipov – he refused Khrushchev's order to fire his nuclear missiles, so preventing almost certain Armageddon. Well . . . the world's still here, and Milla's still here, and my swollen feet are still here . . . He collapses on to the bench and begins unlacing his training shoes, ruminating the while: Preventing an apocalypse, why . . . that's tantamount to creating a world – this world. Yes, this Arkhipov was a god – or, more likely, a demiurge, and yes, this is indeed what the world was like after his act of special creation . . . *AyAy Forty-Eight to be precise*: a dystopia of discontinuous technologies populated by mutants created in a selective breeding programme presided over by *the blind-bloody watchmaker!* Y'know about Wikileaks, don't you, Gramps? Ben had asked and asked again: *Y'know about Wikileaks, don't you, Gramps?* the words chucked over his shoulder had fallen heavily in his grandfather's lap. Then he'd hit a key, and the computer's alternative world had been replaced by a jerky view of flat-roofed concrete buildings and mud-brick hutments. Tiny figures were dish-dashing about . . . *running scared from the eye-in-the-sky.* Then the whole scene shivered, shook and disappeared into *buff puffs* . . . Gunsight footage from a YouEssEmm Apache, Gramps,

Ben had said, and said again: from a YouEssEmm Apache, Gramps
– it was an airstrike in Baghdad three years ago . . . *three years
ago* . . . Whole load've civilians – including some journalists – were
killed . . . *were killed* . . . The Pentagon've consistently denied it – but
here's the evidence . . . *here's the evidence* . . . There indeed had been
the evidence – and apparently there was a lot more: These Wikileaks people, Gramps, they've hacked into some secret sites – but
that isn't how they get most of their stuff, they get most of their
stuff from leaks . . . *they get most of their stuff from leaks* . . . Hence,
Zack had drily observed, their name – but Ben, as ever, had failed
to register any irony, and simply kept on scrolling down . . . *and
down.* Zack may've been a little disconcerted by the political turn
his grandson's enthusiasms were taking – but he'd thought nothing
of it until . . . now: I can't explain what it is about him, Gramps –
I s'pose with someone you meet socially, you get to see them in
all sorts of . . . social situations when they're . . . socialising . . . *The
fingers leeched . . . lifeless . . . bone-white catkins on the unfunny bone . . .*
Busner thinks of Pierson Minor, a fellow pupil at Marples'
Independent Academy, who'd been struck down by polio and disappeared glamorously into an iron lung. When he returned his arm
was strapped to his head – which worked well to straighten out the
rigours of the disease. Agony for the kid, though – unable day or
night to lower his arm. Zack thought he'd been sympathetic at the
time – *I'm far more so now*: I can sorta socialise with him, though,
Gramps – I check his Facebook account and stuff . . . look at clips of
him on YouTube . . . then there's his writing – you can tell an awful
lot about someone from their writing, can't you, Gramps? Innaway

it's even more revealing than the stuff they reveal in real life . . . Busner thinks the two phenomena are undoubtedly related: Milla's new love and her newborn anxieties for her . . . *big baby* and his virtual activities *eyearrdoubleyou* . . . Because that's Ben's version of Milla's real life: the real world he enters only to eat or take a shit, before returning to his alternative realities. You ought to ask yourself, Gramps, why it is they want so much data, Ben had said, and then he'd shown his grandfather the stark outlines of this ulterior realm. Flow charts, block and Venn diagrams, standard deviations, and all sorts of other graphical-statistical representations came flying back towards them from the prow of Ben's inner-space-ship. Being *of an age*, Zack'd thought of nine-out-of-ten, and ninety-nine, and nine per cent compounded on gilts – but this data wasn't selling anything. Ben had said: I'm not going anywhere near any government systems, Gramps, I'm not a total mong . . . *I'm not a total mong* . . . Zack had sensed then – and Busner feels certain now – that his grandson hadn't meant to imply he was a partial mong, but that *he isn't a mong at all – it's us who're the mongs* . . . An entire society of amiable Downs folk, wandering about hugging each other and responding beautifully to music, while the others – the cooler, more calculating others, such as Ben – got on with reaping these digital whirlwinds: You 'n' Mum, Gramps – you think all the gaming I do is a waste of time . . . *a waste of time* . . . But it's taught me loads . . . *taught me loads* . . . taught me that one person – a person others call disabled – can not only beat the system . . . *can not only beat the system* . . . he can capture its commanding heights . . . *its commanding heights* . . . You got troll feet, says a child who's arrived beside Busner's lofty bench and stands sneering down at them. Busner smells salty breath . . . *like Ben's* and registers chewing that, despite its only having claimed his attention this very moment, still seems to've been *incessant* . . . The child, whose sex is non-determinable *at least by me* . . . wears a T-shirt with a cartoon face on it, and *Bennishly* won't allow his bright-blue button eyes . . . *to meet mine.* I am . . . Busner begins – and as he speaks his fancy hardens into conviction: . . . a troll. The child's eyes widen pleasingly . . . *I'm not a troll*, is what Ben had protested: I'm not a troll, Gramps, or a hacker like that stupid mong, McKinnon . . . *like that stupid mong, McKinnon* . . . Before Busner can say anything else to the child, Milla squawks in his ear: A troll, Gramps? What're you talking about? – I'm just saying, Ben told me he's not a troll . . . To which she replies: Well, I'm not a troll either! I don't post any comments or anything like that – I just keep an eye on his Facebook page . . . While this mother talks, the child has arrived at Busner's bench. She stands a few yards away, her face twisted by paranoia: Who's this dirty old man? What's he been saying – or, worse, doing, to her little boy? She pushes the pushchair back and forth on the gravel path *crunch-munch* . . . *am I hungry?* and would undoubtedly *beard me* . . . were it not that . . . *I'm on the pho-one!* Delighted by this stand-off, Busner watches as the mother – predictably, she's *anorexic – common enough sequel to untreated post-partum depression –* wrenches the child away and buckles it into the pushchair. Next they're on the terrace below, the pushchair's wheels *skitterolving*, while Milla goes on *andon*, because, however monumental the orfer's indifference . . . *we're meant to be together.* It's this fervent belief that their love will be requited on some higher plane which elevates her, Busner thinks, to the ranks of the Tzadikim Nistarim: the thirty-six individuals alive at any given time whose purpose – hidden from the world and themselves – is to justify humankind in the eyes of God. Not that he's studied the relevant parts of the Talmud . . . *read my own bar mitzvah portion pho-pho-phonetically*, but in a secular age you'd expect the love of an absent man to substitute for the love of *an absent God* . . . She runs on – Busner senses tendrils on his nape questing towards the cavernous interior of Alexandra Palace, and places his grandson in the great and gloomy hall he remembers from his last foray inside . . . *ten years ago?* Ben Whitehouse-Busner *bulky by name – bulky by nature* . . . stumbling past these botched pantographs of municipality: a bamboo arras, freestanding screens of neon-indigo nylon ill concealing gilded stacking chairs piled up to thrice-head-height. Ben has *hybridised* with his gaming avatar: he's stripped to the waist, his breasts . . . *gynecomastia?* are sweat-oiled, *lifted and supported* . . . by those bullet-filled bandoliers. He points the nostrils of his pump-action shotgun towards the mouth of some grim stairwell, then pivots round to aim at the back of *Gramps's head!* and . . . *fires!* He's every reason to turn his nose up at me, Busner thinks: after all, when he was little I saw him all the time – far more than I did his father, or any of my other children. But then Ben just sort of . . . stopped *and so did I*. The whispering and repetitious lummox had attended an ordinary secondary school in Cricklewood with a specialist unit. The teachers were well-meaning and Camilla was happy enough – Ben was under no pressure to attend classes, or

476

indeed, so far as his grandfather could ascertain, do anything much at all. *So he didn't.* Simply went there each day and sat around reading in the woefully understocked library – or fiddled with the school's near-obsolete computers. *Oh, the pathos!* One time, must've been in the boy's teens, Zack had gone with Milla to meet with his teachers, and they'd chanced upon Ben, as amorphous and beige as the sag-bag he was sat on. Just sitting there – only sitting there, his stimming reduced to the compass of a single finger, metronomically waggling in front of his starting eyes. But it was Zack who'd admonished himself: *Such a waste . . .* although of what he wasn't entirely sure. There was something there, though – even when little Ben was a blur of repetitions, verbal and physical, at the very core of him his grandfather had sensed a profound and watchful *stillness . . .* One which, as the years have passed . . . *and the screens have proliferated,* he's seen mimicked by more and more people – in the streets, on buses and trains, and no doubt in the privacy of their own *qramped quarters . . .* An epochal signal had once been beamed from the roof of the People's Palace – this much Busner knows: a wooden puppet splintered into its myriad constituent waveforms, then reassembled a mile or two away by *clever Scotsmen . . .* He's seen, he thinks, an image of that image of the puppet's white face, *stimmed* into being by cathode rays. Only the first of a horde of such of such electro-revenants . . . *ghosts of ghosts,* wafting around the world, walking through walls, and welling up from the illuminated missals they hold *ever open before their beseeching eyes . . .* Busner hunches forward to tie his laces, while Milla supplies the commentary: Yeah, all right, I'll admit it – I do post comments as well – I can't help myself – but I use a made-up name – else he might be angry . . . Which is so like someone who's part of a couple. It's sorta like I'm with him already – you don't think I'm crazy, do you, Gramps? Busner's toenails are mildly fungally infected, giving them a wood-grained appearance: I'm not a troll, he thinks, I'm a puppet . . . And as Milla *bores on* . . . he sees shavings of himself swirl up into the suburban skies. What was it Ben had said to him, *and said again?* That a vast amount – though not the entirety – of the world's internet traffic passes through the YouEss's communications infrastructure . . . *through the YouEss's communications infrastructure* . . . which is where it's *grabbed* . . . Busner sees a fake gold watch, poised for long and painful moments above a slag heap of miniature teddy bears and silvery trinkets, then slowly jerking *towards the slot* . . . You have to ask yourself, Gramps, why exactly it is they want so much data . . . *why exactly it is they want so much data* . . . The systems they have at GeeSeeAitchQueue are capable of logging in excess of fifty billion events a day . . . *in excess of fifty billion events a day* . . . No, no! Busner expostulates, of course I don't think you're crazy, Milla! So off she goes again. Such a waste, he thinks, a life grabbed, winched up, inched towards the slot, then . . . dropped . . . in a rape field, she told me . . . poor Milla. Such a waste . . . all those sixpences I fed into the machine – where would it've been? Torquay! Yes, Torquay! They'd always put up at the same seafront hotel, and Zack spent so much time fiddling with the buttons *the grabber became my hand* – not that this helped when it came to getting hold of a fake-gold watch. Rather, he thinks, this was the origin of my own cack-handedness, this cybernetic assimilation of the rigged arcade game. He remembers sitting in the hotel dining room while a deaf waiter unloaded steaming soup bowls from . . . *a dumb one*, which was Henry and Zack's little joke. When? Late forties he supposes – Maurice's companion at the time had been . . . Joy! Yes, Joy – Joy came in between a *brace of Barbaras* . . . A brittle woman – and fanciful. One brisk day, watching the palm trees shiver along the esplanade, she'd said to little Zachary, Oh, look, darling, they're all listening in to the same gossip *on their party line* . . . A decent woman, though – and Zack had liked her. The Brown Windsor *dyspepsia* lay *dumbly waiting* in the shallow bowls. The clock ticked on the mantel – then several seconds later . . . *tocked.* Into this bell jar Zack had insinuated the following remark: Why don't you and Joy share a room, Uncle Maurice? The silence had intensified – then solidified so much . . . *a pin would've floated in mid-air.* Maurice took his time dabbing his dab of a brown moustache with his napkin, and eventually said, Not everyone is obsessed by the sexual relation, Zachary. What you said is extremely rude . . . and embarrassing for Joy. You'd better go up to your room now . . . Lying on candlewick *rubbing my little prick* . . . Gulls squawked outside – I imagined them to be *ecstatic cries* . . . Not everyone is obsessed by the sexual relation, Zachary *but he was* . . . After he'd gone I found his weird account books – double-ledger entries: the totting up of all the arseholes he'd penetrated and the pricks that'd penetrated him. I was able to find one for that very day. A hypocrite? Not at all – simple self-preservation. Came upon him a few years later – very moist in the morning room at Redington Road, crumpled up his copy of the

479

Times and exited left . . . *pursued by his demons*, and leaving a Du Maurier smouldering in the onyx ashtray. I smoothed out the page: BLETCHLEY BOFFIN CONVICTED OF GROSS INDECENCY, and read it intently: *He has absolutely no sense of shame, one of the arresting officers told the court. He was a real convert who truly believed he was doing the right thing* . . . Zack wouldn't have known who the boffin was if he and Henry hadn't heard him on the Third Programme a few weeks earlier, speaking about building a mechanical brain and whether, if it could be done, the machine would *think like we do* . . . Fake-gold watches grabbed and homosexual code-breakers nabbed, then annihilated in front of the Knutsford Quarter Sessions. Where'd the poor fellow lived . . . Winslow? No, that's the play . . . *Wilmslow!* And the furtive fumble had been with an Arthur Murray – but he was a namesake – not related, so no possibility of *dancing away the heartache* . . . As for the mechanical brain known as Ben – he resembles no relation of mine: it's Whitehouse features that're buried *currants* in all that . . . *spotted dick*. He's sexless as well, Ben, for a young man in his early twenties – not a whiff of it. Hardly his great-great-uncle's great-great nephew . . . *not everyone's obsessed by the sexual relation, Zachary*. No, indeed – obsessed, rather, by quite different forms of command and control . . . *From computers just like this one, Gramps – computers they have all over the world . . . computers they have all over the world . . . anyone who has the right security clearance can task the system . . . can task the system* . . . Which is really, when Busner stops to think about it, what Milla's doing to him right now! Enough, Milla! he barks: That's enough now! You can't be serious about this business with your writer-chap – wasting

480

your life like this. You're still young . . . comparatively. Camilla doesn't want to hear this – she's tasked his system, and now she *owns me* . . . So off she goes – but Gramps *fucking Gramps!* isn't listening to her, but to Ben-from-the-recent-past: D'you know what Skype is, Gramps? he'd asked Zack as they'd sat peering into the faraway nearby of his three angled screens . . . Next year Microsoft is going to buy Skype, Gramps, and this'll give them direct access to the computers of six hundred million registered users . . . *six hundred million registered users* . . . Thing is, the encryption they use to keep these users' communications secure . . . *to keep these users' communications secure* . . . Well, it was Microsoft which devised the very techniques the EnnEssAy uses to get around them . . . *to get around them* . . . Ben's pudgy fingers pressing the keyboard, shaping the curious flow charts and garish little logos which *blipped from screen to screen* . . . Ben's salted, infertile breathiness: See, Gramps . . . Boundless Informant . . . Project Bullrun – and this one is my favourite, it's called Egotistical Giraffe . . . *it's called Egotistical Giraffe* . . . They use it to target something called the Tor browser . . . There'd been more palping, and the hectic four-dimensional data-juggling was infected by *septic streaks* as Ben scrolled down: These're all web sites, Gramps, but not normal ones – these're hidden sites . . . it's called the Dark Web . . . *it's called the Dark Web* . . . But the spooks're figuring out how to crack it . . . *how to crack it* . . . They can already invade private networks on Google and Facebook – GeeSeeAitchQueue has a program called Tarmac which allows them to intercept satellite communications . . . *to intercept satellite communications* . . . The product is shared between the YouEss and the YouKay agencies and their allies, the Five Eyes . . . *and their allies, the Five Eyes* . . . A few of us have realised what their real objective is . . . *what their real objective is . . . Oh, and what's that?* Ben's Gramps had asked him ingenuously – and now, sitting on the bench, looking over towards the Shangri-La of Epping Forest, he apprehends the city's ancient and *glacial flow* . . . as Milla's inexhaustible longing . . . *trickles coldly . . . chemically . . . into my ear.* There'd been an odd glint in his grandson's usually lustreless eyes when he answered: They want to make it so nobody nowhere can ever communicate electronically without their being able to collect that data, store it and analyse it whenever they want . . . *and analyse it whenever they want* . . . But why? Zack'd asked Ben. Why do they want all that data – the vast amount of which has to be *utterly bloody inconsequential!* . . . The woman in the bookshop at Belsize Park told me he's actually separated from his wife . . . There's nothing on his Facebook account . . . Anyway, it'd be ridiculous – someone like him updating his status . . . On Camilla runs, her data-stream purling as it joins with the great cataract of telephony meta-data which courses round this watery world . . . *what's their objective?* Ben may reverence the factual, but there's one truth no one wants to crack their molar on: history is a cock-up from which *we're all trying to escape* . . . Safely sat in his smelly cave, Ben had simply said, I'm not entirely sure yet, Gramps – but when I find out I'll let you know, I'll let you know . . . *but when I find out I'll let you know* . . . Worrying words which summoned this admonition: There're a lot of young men – boys, really – like you, Ben, who get odd ideas into their heads. The coming of these computer technologies has made fantasists of us all – we stare at these screens for so long we cannot help sliding into *machine dreams* . . . He had, he thinks, put his arm round his grandson's shoulders at this point – but the mannish boy's eyes remained locked in *oculogyric crisis* . . . However, underlying it all, Ben, are the same old political realities: states are inherently secretive, this means they can be very nasty indeed if they think anyone's encroaching – whether it be a terrorist organisation, another state, or *a young man in his bedroom armed with a keyboard* . . . Yes! Zack had spoken straight into that moon-face, and for a couple of seconds he'd compelled those limpid brown eyes to look into his own. Yet, with Ben's mother's still banging on in his ear, Busner wonders if he shouldn't've been *rather more forceful* – certainly not agreeing to pay for yet more computing power to be installed in Ben's cave, the floor of which already *writhes with rubberised creepers* . . . Because, while he'd actually held his grandson's empty gaze, Zack had had this odd intimation: *The egotistical giraffes are already among us!* craning up to tear the freshest, juiciest data from the top of . . . *the decision tree.* Yes, the egotistical giraffes had arrived, and were well on their way to capturing *the commanding heights!* Milla! Busner at last shouts her down: I can't talk to you any more *not that I have*, I've got to go . . . Camilla's voice rises towards hysteria: Just say you'll go along to the reading and speak to him – that's all I'm asking . . . please . . . And, terrified that if he doesn't accede she'll keep him hanging on the phone forever, he agrees . . . *and she's gone.* So gone – the electromagnetic squall of her dying down *as if it'd never happened* . . . leaving him staring out over suburban London to where, in the mid-distance, he can just about make out the long, low, *spurious* structure of Friern Hospital, closed down now for, what? at least a decade. From this vantage, Busner thinks, I can see all the way back to the early seventies – and if I'd the right equipment, I could film that past as well. It's swimming up to him now, from the emulsification of memory: the silvery summer when he and Enoch Mboya awakened the post-encephalitic patients – Mboya had a sort of photographic memory, but it'd been empathy, Busner thinks, rather than some neurological quirk which made the charge nurse able to recognise all of the poor passengers on that *ship of fools* . . . Enoch had seen those ticcing, spasming, festinating human machines for what they truly were: unique individuals, with hopes, dreams and emotions all deformed by the decades they'd spent buried deep in the system. Deep in there, first drenched in paraldehyde, then slopping with Largactil. Deep in there – far, far down that long, long lens of a corridor, the bare fact of their existence transposed on to the buff cardboard of the state and *filed away* . . . While as for their bodily reality. . . *Ach!* They'd stunk – stunk of the drugs, the disinfectant, and all the shit and filth the disinfectant was meant to mask. Busner remembers changing one woman-mountain's nappy – scraping the impacted excrement from the crannies of her obese thighs, then *filming her with a thirty-five-millimetre Bolex – a lot of camera for an amateur at the time* . . . But he'd always had a thing about photography – and sees now . . . again . . . Maurice, Henry and whichever Barbara was in harness at the time – sees their dead faces floating in his viewfinder. Those mass-produced Box Brownies and Kodak Instamatics – they'd been

484

the beginning of this massive privileging of the eye over the other sense organs ... *the gateway drugs to the palace of retinal delights.* Before that – both at Kingsley Hall and his own Concept House in Willesden – Zack had also made films of his distressed housemates: presenting these objective images to them in the hope they'd abandon their own distorted ones. But the Bolex – and the enkies, that'd been different: it wasn't they who'd required photographic evidence of their condition's objective reality ... *but me.* Required it, because, notwithstanding his own clinical experience, he'd been unable to believe the testimony *of my own senses* ... He remembers setting up the *egotistical giraffe* of the Bolex's tripod, then focusing tightly on the woman-mountain's waste of a face – remembers squinting through the viewfinder at her frigid cheeks and cracked eyes, then waiting for something – anything! – to happen. Eventually, he'd gone to the recalcitrant nursing staff and got hold of thick rubber bands and bulldog clips so he could rig the Bolex up to film entire reels of this morbid catatonia in one continuous take. And then, when the films had been developed and played back? Busner writhes on his lofty bench: because these are discreditable memories that *slash at me*: razor blades, attached with rubber bands and bull-dog clips to ... *the windmills of my mind.* Lesley – *that shit, Lesley!* He'd developed the films, then shown them to Zack on a Steenbeck editing machine at the film cooperative in Camden Town. Sitting in hash-honking semi-darkness, fixated by the pimples on the hateful fellow's bare and sweaty shoulders ... Do you break a butterfly on the wheel – *or a psychiatrist for that matter?* Lesley belongs, Busner concedes, to a fairly discreditable period of his life:

when he was racketing around in Willesden wasting Maurice's money – and taking ill-advised acid trips with *really rather doolally people* . . . Lesley – that *man of the people* – had styled himself the Concept House's multimedia coordinator, but where would he be now? Up some Welsh valley, prob'ly – coughing his perished lungs out in a wonkily pitched wigwam and walking a ten-mile round-trip to pick up his Assistance, while continuing to extol the self-sufficient philosophy of the *Whole Earth-bloody-Catalog* . . . There'd been something to those films, though – if they were speeded right up, it could be observed that, amazingly, the catatonic post-encephalitics demonstrated the normal repertoire of human responses – smiling, frowning, grimacing – but much, much slower. A tiny flirtatious moue took, Busner recalls, about forty minutes to pass across the north face of the woman-mountain. By contrast, when he and Mboya made films of those patients caught up in an akathistic whirr – ticcing, chewing, perseverating, jerking, jigging, marching back and forth – then viewed the results slowed right down . . . *we saw still stranger things*. He'd never written up his notes – never completed his projected research paper on the Friern post-encephalitics. In part, of course, because the trial he'd organised to justify the purchase of the wonder drug had been *nothing of the sort*: there'd been no control group, while Zack was quite simply *out of control* . . . To begin with, these elderly men and women, benighted for decades, had experienced a period of astonishing remission – and were released from their fleshly imprisonment to dance, sing, cavort . . . *and love*. But after a delirious few weeks they'd all begun to fall apart again, and then it'd been worse – far worse – for them: *because Enoch and I had made them self-aware.* They'd tried adjusting the post-encephalitic patients' dosage of L-Dopa but to no avail: the ticcers grew more frenzied, while the catatonics, acquiring a saturnine gravity . . . *sank back into the black hole of their own malady.* All Zack had been left with were the cine films – and another blot on *my already maculate career . . . Apeneck.* Busner caresses it, seeking to ease all the tension that's built up since he sat down. Yes, he'd kept the cine films – in particular the ones of that indomitable old lady, *whose name was?* Busner lets his *arms hang down* – not *to laugh,* though: for a sob escapes him at the thought of that *Archaeopteryx,* fossilised since the early twenties, whom they'd disinterred and brought blinking into the era of disco lights *and dolly birds . . .* Yes, he'd kept the films of her, and on stoned seventies evenings he'd set up the projector in the main room at Redington Road and screen them for the psychological carpet-baggers who came in search of the *latest marvels . . .* Busner stands, and begins the descent from the People's Palace, lying on one of the big leathery pouffes *I brought back from Morocco that summer – Tangier was full of Yanks, mostly poofs themselves . . .* He's lying on a pouffe puffing a joint of Moroccan hash, watching those hollow-boned and featherweight hands rotate invisible cranks and yank immaterial levers – for the sad fact of the matter is *I remember the films rather better than their subjects . . .* He'd tell his dopey doctoral audience: This is a sequence I shot at Friern Mental Hospital a few years ago. The subject is one of the long-term post-encephalitic patients there – remarkable woman for her pathology alone! There'd be general laughter at this point – *yes! Laughter!* while the silent

487

songbird, pinned to the screen by the projector's smoking beam . . . *went through her motions.* Busner has reached the foot of the hill and begins plodding through a new-old development of Queen Anne-style houses built from honeyed brick, each equipped with its own, *triply-anachronistic* Regency garage. Yet who, when all's said and done, is really temporally out-of-joint? For the forty-year-old commentary continues: We found out she'd been a munitions worker during the First War, and so realised what she's doing in this sequence is operating a piece of equipment called a . . . *turret lathe.* Yes! A turret lathe! Busner stands, peering at a bright yellow sign bolted to the dark and oily wood of a telegraph pole. On it there's an electric-red triangle – and inside this there's the outline of a man flung back, arms outstretched and *spasming* as the energy streams into him from a large and stylised . . . *lightning bolt!* Yes, a turret lathe! They'd lain puffing on their pouffes and watched the old woman's hands twisting and turning at incredible speed – then he'd rewind the spool and play it again, only this time much, much . . . *slower.* A wondrous vision emerged from the blur: her movements were no mindless reflex, but a precisely calibrated sequence of willed actions. He'd wanted to film the enkies in the first place, to separate out all these individual motions which constituted their *incontinent spraying* . . . There'd also, Busner recalls, been a duplicated negative of the sequence in which the old woman operated the turret lathe – and when Lesley had developed it and screened the film, Zack witnessed a still-stranger phenomenon. The stoned social scientists and psy-professionals saw it as well: a vision so startling it hauled them up from their floor cushions to stand and stare. Busner stands, *out of sync'*, looking up at another *egotistical giraffe* – a seeseeteevee camera which sneers over the precincts of Alexandra Park Station from the top of its pole. If he were to somehow acquire an athleticism . . . *I've never had*, shin up, remove the memory card from the camera and take it to his grandson in Kilburn, what might Ben discover? With the film of the old enkie the frames had been out of sync': in one her right hand pulled an invisible lever, while her left turned a transparent flywheel – but in the next it'd been the reverse: right hand on the wheel, left on the lever. When viewed slowed down, the effect was uncanny – the stoned disciples of Marcuse and Foucault would scratch their hairy heads and exclaim wonderingly, Didja see that – iss like . . . like . . . *time's been rearranged* . . . Really, Busner thinks, likeness didn't enter into this bizarre representation – at a neuronal level, it was believable, p'raps, that the elderly former munitions worker had simply jumped from one fixed ticcing sequence to another, but at a cerebral one? At a mental one? It was the stuff of science fiction: this old woman's brain, locked up in its bony cell for decades, had been fanatically *working out* . . . building up the head-speed necessary to leap the rails of causality and move *outside of time* . . . I will, Busner thinks, go back to Friern and see what's what with the miserable old gulag. As for the films – what'd happened to them? Doubtless disappeared into the attic at Redington Road – together with all the rest of his experimental psychology detritus, the strange fruits of his half-century spent combing the wilder shores of human experience. Such as the clumsy prototypes for the Riddle – the enquire-within-game-cum-diagnostic-tool he'd developed in the late seventies, and which was such a commercial success . . . *I was able to keep a roof over the rest of the tat.* Including his collection of outsider canvases, which Charlie strenuously objected to having hung on the walls she'd had repainted *at great expense* . . . After Maurice died, Zack went up into the attic to have a grand clear-out — but the atmosphere had stymied him: he'd slumped down on a perished steamer trunk and shuffled through stacks of old scallop-edged photos . . . *the Porter Twins, Ramsgate, July, nineteen thirty-seven* . . . but found himself unable to discard . . . *any.* Then the outsider paintings had caught his eye — they were under the eaves in the furthest corner of the attic, a stack of unframed canvases: raw slices of mental distress, the outermost of which was ill lit by a scummy skylight. He'd hunched his way over and worked his way through them — so far as he remembers, all the paintings . . . *aspired to the condition of a Géricault,* although when Busner thinks of a *portrait of a lunatic with delusions of military command,* it isn't any of these which comes to mind, but rather . . . *my grandson.* Slumping uncomfortably on a ridged bench which has been *designed against crime* . . . Busner considers the security cameras whose visual fields he's been walking into and out of all morning: there's one bolted to the wall of the motor insurance broker's next to his flat — a second above the entrance to the bookie's on the other side of Fortress Road. There must've been one on the bus as well — there was certainly a sign to that effect. He stares at his old-man hands — which shake. He sees all these clips of his day unrolled across the angled prow of Ben's three computer monitors. It's an *Edweirdian* procession, given his sweat-banded hat has been multiplied many times to form the peaks and troughs of *a sinuous wave* . . . Back in the early seventies, he'd drawn a distinction between the photographs the post-encephalitic patients would themselves have taken before their headlong plunge into the abyss of their affliction and the films he made of them a half-century later. All photography was – when you sat stock-still to consider it . . . *chronophotography*: the Victorians' box-cameras sopped up time as much as space – and then, when the plates were developed, they showed the endurance of lifeless, material things – between which wormed the trails left by merely ephemeral life-forms. The films he'd made with the Bolex did something different: capturing all the innumerable moments the enkies had lost and imprisoning them in an enduring . . . *now*. It was the same, surely, with the innumerable seeseeteevee cameras that *in the years of my dotage* have sprouted from perished brickwork throughout the city *buddleia sightings* . . . and drunk deep of its populace's watery doings: millions of images of comings and goings, of stopping and starting – all gulped down into a great slopping reservoir of . . . *simultaneity*. A train comes snaking into the station . . . *a train came snaking into the station*. It's one of the new ones . . . *it was one of the old ones*. He sees long carriages, snazzily painted – behind their wide windows are yellow staves from which hang the dark musical notation of . . . *people*. He sees green and gold paint and tarnished brass – the Turneresque explosion when the engine clears the canopy and lets off steam. He swipes his Freedom Pass on another sensor and mounts confidently . . . *You must take the ay train to go to bee*, there's a seeseeteevee camera in the corner of this carriage as well. Imagine . . . *he imagines* . . . not just today but your entire life has been subject to this level of surveillance – that you were secretly filmed on the slow stoppers bringing you back from your schools. Ancient rolling stock without connecting corridors – stuck in compartments with impenitent bullies who pulled up your shirt and punched you to the accompaniment of jolly ditties . . . *Hymie Kikey's gotta get on his bikey!* Then . . . later, when you were studying medicine at Heriot-Watt, the long journey north – sometimes travelling on Mallard, lulled by the sound of its wheels on the rails . . . *Hurry up and get on Hurry up and get on Hurry I couldn't care less I couldn't care less I couldn't care less* . . . Imagine there'd been a lens concealed behind the sepia-tinted scene inset above the Brylcreemed antimacassars opposite: bluebells and bucolical sheep a good cover for the *egotistical giraffes* of another era. But what would they've browsed on? Only little me, passing perfectly well in my Dave-Wax-tailored suit – passing so well I'm insouciantly puffing on a . . . *Passing Cloud*, and passing my finger into my big Jewish nostril so I can remove smutty snot, 'cause everything was shat on in those days by . . . *the Flying Duck*. And imagine there'd been a camera in Fergus's hairy belly, whirring silently while your fingers wandered into the nylon jaws of Isobel McKechnie's . . . *mantrap*. Then, still later, more cine-surveillance on the slow train to Carstairs Junction: recently qualified doctor and soon-to-be-retired steam engine both still . . . *puffing away*. What would a camera lens have captured as you gazed out across rumpled fields *o'er bog and quagmire*, and the unholy mess of opencast mine workings? P'raps the guilty shadow of the previous night's self-abuse, conducted under clammy and none-too-clean sheets in a cheap hotel near Waverley – 'cause it was a two-day commute in the early sixties. Queuing in the porridgey corridor with hungover travelling salesmen in their striped pyjamas and blanket-material dressing gowns. Peering out through a lancet window at Edinburgh Castle, floating on a mound of yellow smog, as you waited your turn to lie in the enamelled horse trough of a bath, where candid shots could've been obtained of you *washing away the dried fish paste.* Then, changing at Motherwell, and waiting by a huge old wall – anthracite-black and rain-dank – puffing on yet another gasper, would a camera have captured your innermost thoughts – your hopes and precious reveries? Doubtful – but it might well've seen you eating the fish-paste sandwich a weepy Missus Fitz had made for you back in Hampstead, and which had spent the night on the sill outside your grim room. She was a highly emotional woman, really – while it was simply extraordinary *the things we used to put in our mouths* . . . Cameras at Wishaw and Carluke as well, set up to snatch snippets of young Doctor Zachary Busner en route to his first psychiatric residency – cameras appropriate to the era: of cream Bakelite, Meccano and black vulcanised rubber. Cameras that sopped up all your most moist mercurial moments — see them flow-fuse together, quicksilver streams of images coalescing in an enormous *oddwobbling* instant — a *tear* welling up in the *eye of God* . . . C'mon – Pete-the-Podium-Restaurant-Manager manoeuvres Busner so expertly through the press of suits and wheelie-bags by the reception desk that his cup-of-elbow . . . *doth not runneth over.* All is as it was, Busner thinks: and when at last I get back to where I started from? Well, I'll've risen because I rose – which is why I've risen again: risen into my

493

rancid T-shirt and ruinous tweed suit. He improves his grip on staff and bowl, enters the *smoglock* of the revolving door – round *annaround* it goes. Captured from above by seeseeteevee what might be seen? The akathistic whirr of its glass blades *never ending or beginning on an ever spinning reel* . . . and caught up in it . . . *lagging*, the amnesiac ancient, who at last staggers into the open air, totters from beneath the glassy portico of the Bethan Tower and, responding to some dirty-dowsing intuition, turns left down Deansgate in the direction of the Castlefield Canal. He tastes the alco-crud in his rusted old throat – feels the *mortar* crumbling between the courses of his own . . . *perished brickwork.* The paving beneath his sandalled feet is hard – unyielding. He longs for bed again *annagain* – any bed: a cardboard paillasse and mattress of soiled nylon sleeping bag would do so long as it afforded repose. As for his covering, why, that could be a rug sewn together out of knitted squares *sky-blue* . . . *fraying green* . . . and a pinkish, oldish nylon quilt . . . *spotted by saliva.* As to where *I'd lay my head* . . . a charity shop sweatshirt stuffed with more of the same will be *just dandy* – especially if set beside it are a half-full can of Special Brew and a box of Biscuit Bob's Dog Treats for early-morning . . . *snacking.* He looks up at the advertising hoarding bolted to the archway above the dossers' bivouac – a new model car whooshing along an open Highland road, apparently . . . *the Lion Goes from Strength to Strength* – then back down to find . . . *someone's been sleeping in my bed!* Two someones, in point of fact, whose heads he hadn't noticed, so surrounded are they by discarded puffa-jackets and plastic bags full of rubbish. One of the heads is narrow and *electrocuted* by a shock of ginger hair – the other is . . . *brachycephalic – Christ! Will it be these Latinisms which survive my decline and fall!* and has a disturbing divot of black hair. This is no coincidence, for now Busner spots, wedged between biscuits and beer, the flap torn off a cardboard box, on which has been scrawled: EX-ARMY SOLDIER ON THE RD WAS 25138694 I HAVE PTSD CAN YOU HELP ME TO FIND A BED FOOD SHELTER THANK YOU'S SO MUCH COMPLEX SIMON . . . Busner's kicking the prone form none too gently and shouting loudly enough for passers-by to stop and stare: What the bloody hell're you doing here, man? Are you stalking me? Are you? Answer me! However, it isn't Complex Simon who answers him – he awakes with the instant alertness of a well-trained military man, rolls over and sits up, blinking – but Ann. Ann, who opens her lashless lids and simply says, And? – And . . . And . . . ? Busner splutters, dancing on the spot, striking the pavement with his staff: And *zoingggg-zoingggg!* what!? To which Complex Simon calmly observes: And we're reporting for duty, Doctor Zebadius Obadius Anthraxobadus, all present and . . . sorta . . . correct. – It takes Simon and Ann only a couple of minutes to bundle up their stuff, and then all three of them are down on the towpath, looking out across the confluence of canals to a patch of waste ground on the far side, where other ladies and gentlemen of the road have pitched their hump-backed and DayGlo tents. It's a peaceful scene, Busner says, could be a campsite in some area of outstanding natural beauty. To which Ann predictably conjoins: And? – And nothing, Busner replies, striking out tents, viaducts and the looming wasp-waisted Bethan Tower with a stroke of his staff. Lissen, he continues testily, what're you two

495

doing here, and what're your intentions . . . ? Simon's about to answer when this old man, he played one *he played knick-knack on my thumb, With a knick-knack paddy-whack, give a* – I'm sorry, Busner says, groping through his many pockets . . . *I am Kali, answerer of phones – why, why won't he stop? Stupid bloody boy–*. Ben's been trying to call you, Doc . . . Busner's warder, his PeeOh, *my ruddy-fucking screw*, spits out: Trying to tell you he'd given Ann 'n' me some squids, fortyish – nothing stupid. Put us on the coach up here to –. To do what precisely? Busner counters – but the fight's gone out with the proud ships and a used condom *short-circuited eel* floats on *the scuzzle . . . the scummle . . . the scuds* . . . And? Ann *ands*, puffacuff in lips *all cold sore NO, NO! BEEN HERE DONE THIS!* To which a small but prissily officious voice – repellent yet so familiar as to be *mine all mine* – pipes up: *Yes, but you've never really seen it from the mentally ills' point of view – not fully. You've flirted with madness, made a fetish of it, used it for your own ends – but even the psychosis Freud accorded everyman eluded you. Fond of 'em, aren't you? A whimsical wee thing your precious fondness can be* . . . then the voice further modulates – becoming shriller and more convinced of itself, its timbre that of stone . . . *and tablet. Which, I'll grant ye, may well be a sweet little meat – but when it's tucked under an idle wagging tongue, confectionery is a crutch, just as alcohol is a crutch, and the carnal relation is . . . a crutch. Why, religion itself may be abused by being used as a crutch – but the worst crutch of all* . . . the voice descends into weaselly quibbling . . . *the one thass truly an abomination in the eye of Almighty God, is pride!* Busner, shaking shaggy his wispy locks, seeing satisfaction in the morning midge cloud dancing on the duck-shit-dappled canal, is so relieved the sermon's object is collective rather than only *me . . . personal, like,* that he salutes with his staff the heads which thrust through the glistening surface tension of the present, hatted and capped against the chapel's notorious chill, and unable to remove them since their shoulders, arms and hands – all remain trapped in the past. *It's the chapel . . .* is as far as Busner's prepared to go – and when Simon and Ann take him under either arm and begin walking, willy-nilly, he doesn't mind. Yes, Simon resumes, Ben's worried about you – Camilla, too. They'll feel better if we, like, sorta –. Escort me? Busner objects: Take me to a bloody Buddhist retreat like a prisoner in chains? You know what you are, Simon, you're a ruddy-fucking screw, and all screws are nonces – it's a well-attested fact *no innocence, never was – and after chapel in his tuck-shop cubbyhole, what did he say to you then?* Said: Every boy wants to be of good report. *And what did you say?* Said: What d'you mean by that, Bobby? *'cause that was me name, auld man, wasnae it?* It was. *Say it.* Say what? *SAY IT!* Your name was Bobby – and Simon, walking ahead of Busner along the towpath, turns back, his *hydro-* . . . *hydro-* . . . *hy-* . . . round head so . . . so . . . incredibly . . . round: You all right, then, Doc? – Oh, yes. Busner's right at home now, surrounded by derelict old warehouses and the solidified grime of inner-city dereliction . . . *You wannin' the cludgie? Clock this: big man here too sissy to come out wi' it* . . . He remembers the alleyways scored between the tenements down Leith way – alimentary canals, carrying everything even this thriftiest of cities couldn't choke down . . . *D'ye wanna tap, s'only five bob?* For a knee-trembler – a ruddy fuck up against the cludgie or

497

some other shit-hole, his balls puckered-up . . . *sloes* . . . the cold wind blows on *hawthorny* little pricks, and the rub of the . . . bricks . . . *Aye, coming back to you now, is it? With you now, is it?* As much to silence the voice – and *obnubilate* the visions of the chapel at State Hospital, Carstairs, Lanarkshire, on that fateful October Sunday in nineteen *whenever*, Busner, although he plods on, staff marking each dyad of paces with a sure double thwock on the hard-pocked mud-path, answers, Yes, I'm good enough, Simon – and happy to have you along. Yes – and you, too, Ann, you, too – happy to have you both along for the journey. But I'm jiggered if I know what you'll do once we get to Holy Island, beyond turning round and heading right back – and that wasn't what we agreed for you . . . Simon, who's pacing ahead, with Ann trailing from one capable arm, while his sleeping bag's a stole draped *all ladylike* over the other, throws back: Well, we'll worry about that as and when, shall we, Doc – as and fucking when . . . Upon which Bobby, sitting in his nineteen *whenever* cubbyhole, comments: *Every mental defective wishes to be of good report* . . . And Busner whispers, Not Simon, I'd fixed it all up for him – and Ann. Mukti at Saint Mungo's said he'd take them on . . . group therapy and meds for his peetee-essdee . . . Sort out some sheltered accommodation for them both as well – yet here they are. *Every mental defective wishes to be of good report* . . . Bobby whispers . . . *dinnae fash yersel' – you're no daftie, Doctor B, but you're still trying to be the big compassionate man, eh*. Bobby, a homunculus really – wizened, a child-man born of the system, with the squeaky voice and painted-on features of a ventriloquist's dummy. Utterly institutionalised, taken away from his family in Perthshire when he was a troublesome wean . . . *at the Perth Special school they hadnae objection if parents wanted to remove their children, but no one ever came for me, Doctor Busner. Me mammy wrote – monthly at first: news of her new husband, my half-brother and sisters – but then she musta got fed up, aye* . . . For a couple of years there were bags of sweets at Christmas – but these had to be shared – then nothing. Bobby had absconded – absconded again. Ran away to Glasgow, met a man at coffee stall near George Square. Went back with him to a cold old tall house on the edge of the Gorbals. Up five flights the man put him to bed on an iron bedstead in an attic room beneath an uncurtained dormer. Strip of lino on the splintering floorboards. Piss-pot under the bedstead. His hot hard prick between Bobby's buttocks in the middle of the night *served me right.* Sitting with him after chapel in his Aladdin's cave – the prisoners' tuck shop he's made his domain – young Doctor Busner is prepared to listen. Listening, he already understands, is the best he can do for any of the patients, who for the most part are deeply submerged in the Chartreuse pool of Largactil which fills the harled and white-painted detached villas of State Hospital. He has ideas, though, does the freshly minted psychiatrist – and he's on his own: the Chief Psychiatrist, appointed by the Scottish Office, comes at best weekly, and they administer electro-shock treatments together – a perverse ceremony, conducted wearing nylon robes and rubber aprons: False teeth out, rubber stick between rubber gums. No pre-med – and the rubber earplugs for doctors McClintock and Busner rather than the patient, who, as the current lances between his temples, is at first galvanised into a series of hideous spasms, then goes *all rubbery* . . .

sweaty. Doctors McClintock and Busner suck on bulls-eyes, lemon sherbets . . . toffee bonbons – sometimes tablet: in short, any crutch they can find to take away the taste of *that rubber.* In winter, the lights dim – not just in the room where the treatment's administered, but in the entire unit, which goes dark as the patient's screams echo along its distempered corridors. Busner thought it was all wrong at the time – but knew better than to question McClintock's methods: he was too busy *passing* . . . Passing at his digs, where he did nothing to disabuse his landlady, Missus Kane, of her peculiar notion that his origins were Belgian – passing at State Hospital, where he made it his mission to . . . *understand – not judge.* Since judgement might well be seen as . . . *the mark of the Hebrew.* Understand the scene in the day-room, where the patients sat, volleying invisible balls . . . *the Largactil kick, they called it.* Passing in the meetings – which were entirely pro forma: the rubber stamp *for the rubber stick* – and all the while reading voraciously: Sartre and Freud . . . Camus and Jung – Ronnie's paper on his rumpus room at Gartnavel, which gave the young intern his big idea to do something similar for Bobby and the other lost boy-men: treat them as individuals, not pathologies. To be mad is an affliction, says Doctor McClintock – and to be bad is a curse, but to be both mad and bad is to suffer *the torments of the damned* . . . Dunno why you say that Doc, Simon chimes up, it's the way of it nowadays . . . Somehow they must've swum through the mercurial morning to Piccadilly – Busner has a wan recollection of waving his staff at the memorial for Aids victims beside the canal, and delivering an extempore lesson – words to the effect that: progress in human conduct – while intermittent and piecemeal – nonetheless does occur, and here was the evidence: an acceptance of same-sex love all the more profound for being *prosaic – we're out and we're . . . dully municipal.* To which Ann had remarked: And? Then they'd presumably been on the station concourse, faffing out tickets from the machine – and now, as in epic films hymning the long samba of trains through the twentieth century . . . *'Stamboul, Vladivostok – all points East . . .* Busner stares out of the window at the grey-and-red carriages swaying their way between the piebald flanks of the bare hillsides. He's hooked on this worn-out line: I'm on the train and we're past Lockerbie so the . . . I said WE'RE PAST LOCKERBIE AND THE RECEP–. It's the torment of the damned, Busner remarks to the carriage at large: having to listen to one side of a conversation, because, unlike listening to two people talking, with a mobile phone call you're compelled to supply THE OTHER SIDE OF THE CONVERSATION! Eyes swivel round and lock-on – earphones are squelched from waxy ears. The carriage lights *dim* as the shock passes through them all. It's a Bateman cartoon, Busner thinks, observing round mouths and ink-spot eyes: *The Man Who Objected to the Mobile Phone Call . . .* And Simon whispers: Shut the fuck up, Doc, you'll get us put on report . . . *And every mental defective wishes to be of good report . . .* Just as every psychiatric intern looks forward to his day off: a Saturday on which he's arranged to borrow the Superintendent's Javelin. He'll meet Isobel off the train at Lanark – he'd rather she didn't come anywhere near Carstairs Junction. She quietly regards his chosen career path as that of a failure, on course as she is to become Scotland's first woman thoracic surgeon . . . *unum contra Edina.* It's late in the year for fine weather in the central belt, but after a dreek week – throughout which the State Hospital's buildings have been bombarded by hale and rain – the day promises to be sunny. He has it in mind to drive her to Tinto Hill – Isobel's expressed a wish to ascend this conical eminence, the highest prospect for miles around. She's a red-cheeked, high-hipped, long-striding young woman with cornflower-blue eyes, spun-gold hair and decided views on the benefits of fresh air and vigorous exercise – but it's Bobby who's planted this notion in Zack's hot head: *that the carnal relation he seeks may be more easily achieved en plein air* – up on the brae which rises from the rushing Clyde, where sheep safely graze and a daughter of the manse might very well feel *away from the flock.* At Baldovan Institution for Defective Children the inmates had in fact been old men, most of them diagnosed decades before with dementia praecox. The wards were high ceilinged, their narrow sash windows bare of curtains – the floors highly polished. In between the government green walls and below the government green ceilings, Izal disinfectant fought a never-ending war against the odours of human dereliction. The morning bell went at seven, and it was everyone out of bed and to attention: *Praise God from whom all blessings flow, Praise Him, all creatures here below, Praise Him above, ye heavenly host, Praise Father, Son and* . . . the holy ghost of the nurses' kindness, which had long gone, to be replaced by the Incontinence Parade: *We'd t'wear white moleskins, so everyone could see if ye'd pissed or shat yersel'* – then *the older boys'd hold ye down and they'd gi' ye a hammering wi' a sand shoe* . . . The defective children would form up in two lines to march into breakfast – old Mister McDougall, who'd been gassed at Ypres, leapt about looking for cover from invisible shot and non-existent shells, but the nurses in their starched white uniforms ignored him . . . *'cause he'd been a hero*. Bobby, rendered iconic by shelves stacked with catering packs of Jacobs Cream Crackers, boxes of Angel Delight, one-pound tins of jam, and many wax-paper-wrapped loaves, dispensed wisdom along with his life story – and, as he'd talked, young Doctor Busner, his woolly head full of Raskol-nikov, Roquentin, *Ravachol* . . . had thought: At last . . . I'm getting somewhere – getting closer to understanding the mind of the Out-sider. Homosexuality had been, Bobby told him, rife – his exact words, and later, after the dreadful incident, when they returned to Zack, he cursed his own naivety . . . *a mental defective always wishes to be of good report*. Give a good report as well – a report carefully tailored to fit his listener's requirements: the evidence of long-term abuse in the system *was just what I needed*. Bobby was kissed and fondled by one of the older boys at Baldovan – Baldovan, where they went out to work on a local farm, the boys in their blue-grey parish tweeds riding the trailer behind the tractor, then, when they reached the open fields: *we were harnessed up, ye ken six ti' the plough, ye ken – like draught animals. Braw wee ponies, we were* . . . ones that needed a proper rub-down at the end of a hard day's work. Thursdays was tripe – Sundays pie – at Christmas there was a feast of tatties and mince. The bogey-roll of pipe tobacco twisted around his sinewy arm in a figure-eight, the charge nurse made his way along the row of men and boys, who were bent over and gobbling. The porridge fell – a disgusting grey slurry – from the old madmen's slobbering mouths. Bobby had been the youngest inmate, but the nurse still tore off a plug for his pipe . . . *if yi' were canny yi' got yersel' a protector who'd gi' you his sweet ration in return fer a rub-a-dub-dub* . . . three men in a tub, and who do you think they were? He's spoken aloud, he realises, because Ann looks up from her copy of Escapes, the Virgin Trains magazine. And? she queries. And? – And what? Busner counters testily. And what's the rest of the rhyme? Is that what you're asking – 'cause SURELY YOU KNOW? He's spoken too loudly, he realises, once more attracting the attention of their fellow travellers, who, oblivious to the drama unfolding outside the train's windows – the long slopes of the Lowther Hills, their heathery covering flaring blue-green in the summer sun, the sudden flashes of tumbling burns – are determined to *get in on the act*: The butcher, Ann, the baker, and the bloody candlestick-maker! Satisfied, are you? She gives her narrow head an Indian waggle of offended assent – and Simon, roused from uneasy sleep . . . *what does he watch in the cramped cinema of his mind – what dusty, sweaty atrocities? What anguished transformation must he endure each time he . . . wakes?* reproves him as severely as any charge nurse: Keep a lid on it, Doc – you'll get us thrown off the fuckin' train! a telling-off itself interrupted by: This old man, he played two, he played knick-knack on my shoe, with a knick-knack paddy-whack, give a dog a . . . Busner, having fumbled the phone out of his pocket, stares uncomprehendingly at NO CALLER ID, a phrase . . . *or slogan* which has, he realises, been bothering him for a while, implying as it does that whoever's trying to reach him is the coldest of creatures – some *billion-dollar brain* lacking the *idiopathic substratum from which all instincts – murderous, sexual – arise* . . . Stares and stares, while the ringtone reels in more and more opprobrium: Give a dog a bone, This old man came rolling home, This old man, he played three . . . Busner sees it on the faces of his fellow travellers, their outraged expressions as they swivel away from . . . *these ancient yet manmade landscapes,* to glower at this poor aged man struggling to find REJECT CALL . . . He does, and, in the after-tone of the ringtone, Complex Simon . . . *it's a soft diagnosis, really – either he's traumatised or he ain't,* says, Some other fucker's trying to get hold of you, Doc, and they aren't giving up – have you got any idea who it is? And Busner, speaking through the fog which blanketed the chainlink fences of State Hospital on that Saturday morning in October, *nineteen hundred and black and white,* says, Really, Simon, I haven't the foggiest. – Well, why don't you answer it, then – put us all out of this knick-knack misery? To which Busner rejoins, The phone's really only an aide memoire, Simon – you know that. Ben set it up as a sort of auxiliary memory, because, I must confess, I'm finding it a little difficult to remember things . . . *aye, ye havenae been rememberin' yer auld pal Bobby at all these past, ooh . . . how long's it been, Doc?* My past, Simon, nowadays it seems increasingly tangled up in the present – and it's the present that's the loser. All I need now in order for me to lose the plot entirely is for the future to begin impinging . . . Simon, round head rolling as the train heels into a curve . . . *have they always done this, like . . . like . . . motorcycles?* says, I don't suppose you can remember, then, why the fuck you picked on that knick-knack shit for your ringtone? Busner ponders this: I'm too long in the toenails to be startled by any coincidence – after all, they keep growing when you're dead, and if you go round a second time everything's bound to recur . . . and yet . . . and yet . . . The decision to head for the mindfulness retreat had, he thought, been Milla's – it would, she'd implied, be a sort of soft entry to the hard business of being a Sannyasa: *I've volunteered there a couple of times, Gramps, they've got a fantastic vegan cook, and the island itself is really lovely* – if you find the meditation practice a drag you can chill out in the peace garden, get your strength together before you strike out on your own. Have a look here on their web site – see . . . lovely setting. I've printed off some sheets which'll tell you what happens on a retreat, why don't you have a read of them . . . It had looked for a while as if Daniel and Pat were going to try to put a restraining order on him – have Zack declared mentally unfit in some way . . . *maybe even put me on a section – such larks!* Milla's plan had mollified them – so once spring had uncoiled, the cherry blossom leaping from hilltop Hampstead brighter and gayer than . . . *any previous year,* and Simon and Ann had been, he thought, *halfway housed* . . . he'd set off for Scotland, with an overnight in Manchester, because Ben seemed to feel two days' travel would be *rather too much for me* . . . and since Ben, in the weeks before his grandfather's departure, had stepped forward from the shadows of his own affliction to . . . *take matters in hand – most surprising, that* . . . Zack hadn't demurred, although it'd seemed an . . . *awful fag – I'm fagged right out* . . . *hung over, too* . . . *Christ knows what happened last night* . . . Night was the best time to abscond from Baldovan as well – or so Bobby said. Moreover, given the M'Naghten rules, once a mental defective had turned sixteen, if he could survive on his own outside the institution for a month, he'd be considered discharged. The rub-a-dub-dub didnae gi' the boak to Bobby . . . *I realised I were homosexual me sel', Doc – are ye shocked? An' honestly, if it weren't fer those activities I'd've had no human contact at all, year in, year-bloody-out* . . . But the incontinence parades remained a daily ordeal . . . *ah couldnae control me sel'* . . . which made the nurses' sanction doubly binding: . . . *croton oil, Doc – oh, jeezo, thass filthy pap, so it is* . . . three long-stemmed, tulip-shaped glasses filled with the vicious purgative, then drunk down under the watchful eye of the Sadist-in-Chief – and this on top of the tin mugs of liquorice water she doled out to everyone each evening . . . *ye'd be on ti' cludgie fer the best part of a day, no kiddin'* . . . No kidding, because he'd had no childhood – and no education beyond a general cert' in institutionalisation. Bobby went further and further each time – the flight from Perth to Glasgow had been a failure, he'd ended up turning himself in to the police at the station on Saint Vincent's Road, but the next time he was determined to win his freedom. He assembled his supplies in the gardener's shed . . . *Pa Broon was a good sort – gave him me baccy ration* . . . spare keks, a doorstop ham sandwich wrapped in waxed paper, and an old Winchester bottle full of water . . . *which still honked of paraldehyde.* But the best-laid plans of men reduced to the status of mice are always crummy: a couple of miles away from Baldovan, he'd met a man on a country lane – a simple man, Bobby said, simpler than he himself, who was walking along all alone, blond hair all wispy, eyes full of sweet-smelling hay, the wide legs of his shiny-kneed black suit flapping in the breeze: *We lay down on the grassy brae and took sexual satisfaction from each other – juss rubbin', but jeezo, I shot aff fast. Then I set about attackin' him – and there wass an old branch lying there to hand, so I let him have it wi' tha' an' his heid began bleeding profusely. Aye, we musta been a strange sight, right enough: me holding up this person who's still bleedin' and tryin' t' flag down a car . . . No wonder no one stopped . . . .* Bobby's account has, young Doctor Busner thinks, the surrealistically inverted logic of a dream rewound: Why yes – of course: no wonder nobody stopped, given his victim was bleeding profusely, which in turn implies it'd been perfectly logical for Bobby to've hit him with the branch – which in turn exposes the necessity of their taking sexual satisfaction from one another. And really, isn't this what everyone – mentally defective or not – wishes for: to be of *good report* – and that good report to be of a life well lived, which means with hindsight: the clotted blood liquefies – flows back into the Perthshire simpleton's veins, he walks backwards up the lane – Bobby trots backwards to Baldovan . . . His Mammy arrives to take him home . . . *My own umbilicus retracts . . . a tape-measure*, pulling *Baby Busner bouncy-bouncy* back into Mama Busner's sheltering womb. This, he thinks, is the Samsara we really seek – not eternal recurrence, but a very provisional revision of our own lives: the spin-cycle spun the other way until it . . . *all comes back out of the ging-gang goolie-goolie wash-wash!* There's a moment of silent contemplation on the eleven twenty-four Virgin Pendolino service from Manchester Piccadilly to Glasgow Central – the long carriage rocking back and forth, the passengers seated in modular pews telling their plastic beads – a mobile prayer session: he sees rising from their bowed heads a plume of ones and noughts – their digital being, refracting through the train's tinted windows, scattering into the sky, rising up and up into diaphanous curtains of data . . . *our Fata Morgana – our delusional . . . event-horizon.* Yes, a moment of silent contemplation, as the Virgin steward makes his way along the carriage, dispensing Styrofoam beakers full of *hottish* water with individual sachets containing single tea bags – a moment in which to appreciate that this *is happening to me – and me alone* . . . Yes, Busner thinks, it's pretty much high-noon but I'm sundowning – the sun is going down on my tired old mind. What was it Bobby said they sang at Baldovan? *Now I lay me down to sleep, I pray the Lord my soul to keep* . . . Yes, and I pray to die as well, because this mental disintegration isn't funny any more: the past showing through into the present . . . *a ghostly image*, which remains on the screen . . . *long after it's been switched off!* Off they go, bowling along the lanes. He can tell she's impressed by how well he handles the Javelin – impressed also by the very fact he's been able to borrow it: This chap Hillier – he must think very highly of you, this is a fancy motor. Zack explains: in the two months since arriving at State Hospital he believes he's begun to make great strides. There's a willingness, he tells her, to consider new approaches – after all, State has been established to deal with all of Scotland's criminal lunatics – and what should you do with such patients when you have them concentrated? Why, euthanise them! She laughs merrily – and he grips the Javelin's steering wheel a little tighter. He knows she's twitting him – knows she's subtle enough to make this complex allusion to his own origins, the matter of which is otherwise, obviously, beyond the pale . . . *wish I was.* She's clearly attracted to him, and, while they aren't exactly walking out together, they've been *mucking about* now since their final year at Herriot-Watt – mucking about in fleapit cinemas and train compartments. Mucking about – his fingers advancing and retreating, circling, then advancing some more. From his close readings of Sexual Behavior in the Human Female, Zack believes Isobel may've achieved climax on more than one occasion – he doesn't trust his own inexperienced senses to tell him. She won't touch him in return, though – not, that is, until it becomes necessary to restrain him. Tush-tush, she says, and, Now-now . . . Och, no! she's exclaimed on several occasions, while *Will you mind yourself!* is a phrase he now uses to remonstrate internally: *Will you mind yourself!* is what he thinks when Mister Hillier or Doctor McClintock say something so crassly insensitive – *no! vicious!* Zack worries he'll . . . *blow*, 'cause, after all, *We're all Jock Tamson's bairns* . . . even the mental defectives amongst us . . . *even the Jews*. Isobel, sitting in the Javelin's passenger seat, the hedgerow galloping past her downy cheek, is as remote from him as when she's in his arms: he caresses her – and she responds ever so slightly, her lissom body gently quivering, so that he thinks of fledglings lying dying by shattered shells. She screws her eyes tight-shut when he kisses her . . . *and if I should die before I wake*, and her perfect pipette of a tongue takes samples of his . . . *I pray to God my soul to take*. Some evenings, after they've been out together in Edinburgh, and he's on the last train back, he squirms in his seat, agonised by his *great balls of fire!* His erection won't've subsided by the time he reaches Carstairs Junction, and he'll quit the station *doing a duck walk* . . . but Groucho's rather than . . . *'cause my Uncle took the message and he wrote it on the wall.* Yes, something's stirring deep in the damp flannel crotch of the nation – and not just the English nation. Phil McTavish, who's the only one of the charge nurses Zack gets on with, jokes that everything – and everything, mind – takes ten years longer to reach Scotland: *See, Zacky-boy, the war only ended here in fifty-five, right enough – while as for rock 'n' roll, we can reasonably expect Scots instruments to be electronically amplified sometime in the nineteen seventies* . . . One mod con that definitely hasn't reached South Lanarkshire – or Edinburgh for that matter – is the contraceptive pill. Young Doctor Busner tries to imagine the young lady he's mucking about with standing at the counter at Montrose's on Princes Street, with the pharmacist – a tall, balding coot Zack's had his own run-ins with – calling down Free Presbyterian brimstone on her lovely virginal *heid*. From old masters and the Nouvelle Vague, Zack has gained a vision of post-coital bliss – man and woman together, entwined drowsily naked and unashamed. After the shock treatments, the patients are taken back to their wards for a resting period: bleached faces on starched pillowslips – graven hands . . . *crucified feet*. Their cells are heated by electric coils set into the concrete ceilings – so it is they switch from *one current to another*: first galvanised, then grilled – and all in their modesty gowns. The treatments come in groups of three or four, depending on McClintock's expert assessment of just how psychotic they are. Looking down at the whey-faced creatures on the table, their eyelids the only moving things in a world shocked to its core, Zack has thought, *Rien ne distingue les souvenirs des autres moments: ce n'est que plus tard qu'ils se font reconnaître, à leurs cicatrices* . . . Or possibly that was . . . *much later.* When the current sparks they convulse, and the patient orderly . . . *a tricoteuse indeed*, points at their bare and pitiful feet: D'ye see, Doctor B – d'ye see his toes curling up like that? That means it was a good one – a beauty, you'll see . . . But all he sees are the patients' big toes, twisted into savage and bony little parentheses – so ironising the bunions and corns of their fellows – and all he thinks is they say toenails keep growing after someone has died, and that this so-called treatment – sending an electric current stabbing into an animal's brain – is a kind of death. – Will it be soft-going? she asks, one elegant and stockinged foot up on the Javelin's bumper. Y'know, Isobel, Zack says, this is a pretty old banger, really, the Super just keeps it in mint condition – my pal Bobby and a couple of the other trusties have to clean it every Saturday morning, which is why it's gleaming . . . Yes, the gleaming Javelin is parked up at the base of Tinto Hill, and, as they trudge up past indifferent sheep, he glances back from time to time, to see the car . . . *a flashing chevron* sewn on to the buff material of the autumn heather. Isobel walks ahead of him – and the going is indeed . . . *soft*: he was treated to a suspender clip as she'd matter-of-factly pulled thick woollen socks on over her stockings, and replaced patent-leather heels with heavy walking shoes. Now the hem of her pleated skirt swings wildly with each of her high-hipped strides, and he sees . . . *all that softness*, and the white flash of *saucy briefs from the Pompadour range.* Yes, she flings back, your pal, Bobby – what's that carry-on about, Zachary? Y'know, I can't think it'll be good for your career to be seen to be too friendly with the inmates . . . Blowing hard, Zack hardly knows where to begin with this – and now, dipping the tea bag in and out of his waxed-paper cup . . . *small ball of tepidness*, he says aloud: That was the very moment at which I should've realised the thing didn't have legs . . . Ann looks up from her perfectly bound Escape and says, And? And, Busner responds, chuckling, it was because of Isobel McKechnie's own legs that I didn't . . . He carries on dunking the tea bag, because the water isn't sufficiently hot for it to properly infuse – carries on, reasonably certain his reply will have wrong-footed her, but Ann won't take an answer for an answer – she goads him: And why didn't the thing have legs? Busner ponders this, and Simon – who's been slumped, mostly inert, since the train left Lockerbie – chimes up: Giss your phone, Doc, and if I can connect to the wifi I'll find out about the train for Ardrossan. Busner summons the enigmatic black slab and passes it across the table: Pass code, Doc? and Busner says, It's got recognition-thingie . . . Ben made me set it up – I just have to place my thumb on the button-thingie . . . Simon looks at him *like I'm an idiot*: You've still gotta 'ave a pass code, Doc – your own pass code. Iss four digits – you'll've chosen something memorable, like . . . an important year of your life, something like: *Knick-knack paddy-whack, give a dog a bone* . . . or a crumb at the very least. He'd caught up with her at the first of the hill's false summits – *I've caught up with her at the first of the hill's false summits* . . . and Isobel does indeed . . . *give me a bone*: Zack opens his arms and she nestles chastely in them, while he strokes the hair ruffing up from the confinement of her woolly bobble hat. Feeling the slim stalk of her, wrapped in her bark of tweed and gabardine, Zack looks past her shoulder, out over soft and successive hills. Clouds are *ruffing up* above the valley of the Clyde – while the sun is already sinking to the west, thrusting its rays up their *vaporous skirts* . . . P'raps he should've taken her down to New Lanark, and they could've walked up to the Falls – a famously romantic spot. All that water pounding down on the ragged rocks . . . *it might've stirred something in her flinty soul.* It's Isobel's *to be seen to be* which niggles at him, because, he realises, this is the very nub of who she is: a young woman who will, no doubt, grow older, wiser – become a brilliant doctor, keep a straight back – heal and nurture, but, throughout it all never, ever lose sight of what it means *to be seen to be.* Each morning at Missus Kane's, Zack sits at the breakfast table, glaring at the back of her fat neck as she patrols the tiny parlour, sniffing suspiciously: *Was that you in past eleven last night, Doctor Busner . . . ?* and slicing his iron-hard fried bread into a semblance of a dagger, while imagining what it might be like to commit an acte gratuit. This much he already understands: *to be seen to be seen* is the kiss of death – the cold lips of conformity sealing your own . . . *forever* – and, Jew or not, capable of passing *or not, I refuse to live my life like that!* Yet still he strokes her hair – still she leans into him, and, amazed, he senses her capable surgeon's fingers twisting the leathern buttons of his tweed jacket. An old canvas army knapsack hangs from his shoulder – in it the escape-from-virginity kit he'd put together for her that morning: two thick rugs liberated from Missus Kane's bailiwick, a thermos flask full of coffee, one of Maurice's hip flasks charged with a quarter-bottle of Bell's, and a blueberry muffin he ate in the cab on the way to Heathrow. It's a fresh morning for June, and, standing at the dropping-off point, sucking on a final *gasper,* the Butcher feels goosebumps on his recently showered skin, and the crepitation of his *kippered* lungs. It's always been a problem: dressing for these sorts of trips – ones in which he'll traverse twenty or thirty degrees Celsius in less than twenty-four hours. Squinting towards the low rise of the Chilterns through his Marlboro smoke, he smiles wryly (You really ought to consider giving it up, y'know . . .), remembering the reversible jackets and other Sapperesque stratagems he'd adopted as a young EyeBee officer – no need for that malarkey nowadays (. . . and drugs? Even if they're on prescription, old boy, you can still develop a crushing dependency). Besides, there're some occasions on which it's best to *be yourself* . . . *be spontaneous!* He remembers, years ago, coming from the essbahn at the Hackescher Markt – the Wall had only been down a couple of years, and the middle of town was full of all sorts of riff-raff – watchers, too. Close to his hotel, a street whore stopped him – some poor *double-denim* refugee, fleeing the fashion disaster which had been the old Soviet bloc: Be yourself! she'd cried to the cold night air – her corpse breath sullying *life itself,* while her hand, clutching his overcoat sleeve, had been *tendoned* with track marks – precocious of her to've acquired a bad habit *so well*: Be yourself! Be spontaneous! she'd urged him (Did you? Did you . . . go with her?), and he'd laughed in her face: Eff-off, Christiane Eff – which'd been *most unfair,* for how could she possibly have realised the careful planning it required each and every day to be *this self – that self . . . any bloody self at all.* At Security in Terminal Four the plastic tray bumps to a halt, leaving the rollers spinning, and the Butcher thinks of bluestones hauled all the way from the Preseli Hills, for this

515

situation is *pretty fucking stone age* . . . The rollers're still spinning as the woman in front of him expertly hefts the baby through the metal detector's arch, and, spying her little Dior clutch bag rocking to a halt, snatches it up. But the security staff are having none of this: Excuse me, madam! has the force of a command, from the one with severely pinned brown hair who's no doubt . . . *childless*. Standing on the other side of the arch, watching the playlet unfold, the Butcher admires the fluidity of their union: woman-and-accessory – then thinks of Sally, who doesn't realise he's well aware of her little subterfuges – the pill long since neglected, the diaphragm no longer inserted. It's greediness, he thinks: her hands on his meagre buttocks *yanking* him into her. His sperm is an ingredient she needs to *make her own baby*. His climax is of no moment at all – why would you care if the fridge experiences pleasure when you get the milk out? The security guard wears elbow-length, *Preseli-blue* rubber gloves – the fashionable woman holds *the EffAy cup* aloft, offering it to be frisked with perfect equanimity: she understands there's no statute of limitations – *radicalisation might happen in the womb* . . . Although nothing as radical as what Sally hopes for: the demographic bouleversement of . . . *a spinster birth*. Over brunch at the Wolseley, she's broached the question, dipping brioche – her own increasingly doughy features . . . *yellowy, envious*. Dipping brioche, she's broached the question over brunch at the Wolseley – increasingly yellowy and envious, *her own doughy features* . . . She's spoken of cycles, treatments, what might be available on the EnnAitchEss – and he's batted such things aside . . . *she'll have to go*. He sees her quite happy in the provinces. True, there'll have to be numerous

cycles: around and around they'll go, hormones cranking her repro-
ductive machinery *againannagain* – but at long last there'll be the
dividend: a beautiful pink and burbling *trophy* . . . Sally holds out
to be taken by her sweetly boring husband. The Butcher has had
such a fate in mind for this *let's face it: greybeard* . . . pushing
three years now. The pattern is well established: the Butcher will
introduce her to some sheepily good-natured fellow, who, feeling
forever sexually in thrall to her – he's not that attractive, and, what
with the work-out her former lover put her through, much less
erotically sophisticated – will remain dutiful, faithful and – most
importantly – utterly incurious. Would you step through the
detector now, please, sir? says the other one, who's equally lardy-
arsed, but with hair tied up in a turban. And suddenly tiring of the
charade the Butcher flashes his diplomatic passport and steps
around the arch. There's a brief flurry of concern – a supervisor
comes scampering along the *production lines of fear* . . . then the
Butcher's gone, striding past other transiting souls, who, unbelted
and unlaced, are doing the perp' walk of late capitalism – past glassy
walls of whisky bottles and wire baskets full of stuffed animals and
neck cushions. (So much stuff – most of it complete tat. Really, air-
ports are basically shopping centres accessible by air.) The Butcher's
Ferragamos are tightly laced – the Butcher's trousers are precisely
cinched. The Butcher wears a midnight-blue medium-weight suit,
plain white shirt and a stab's regimental tie – which is a dull green
shade, patterned with silver crowns espaliered by crossed swords
ding-dong, the witch is dead . . . He could've flown from Northolt
with the crabs – Herc would've taken him straight into the aypod.

Requirements had false-flag stuff for him – desert kit, too. You've gotta be fucking joking, he'd said to Barrington Waring, with whom he goes *way back*... I'm going in and out, not trying to make the bitch come ... And Barry, feeling perhaps that such locker-room banter is a little de trop, *now we're senior management*, smiled tightly and pushed one of the new laptops across the table. See this, he'd said, chaps at the Doughnut have managed to slim the gubbins right down. Looks like a bog-standard Toshiba – and if you pulverised it and analysed every last fragment you'd find nothing to the contrary ... The Butcher, laughing, pushed it back: In and out, Barry – y'know me, anything I need to bring back will be in here. He'd tapped his own head with his own *heavily encrypted finger*. But I'll take a phunky phone if you've got one to spare ... Barry did: Looks like one of the new Samsungs – push-to-talk, wireless link-up so you've email access, all that business. But if you do this ... and then ... this, it's a completely secure satellite phone – here're all the numbers you'll need. Connect direct to the Chief or ... whoever ... The phone lightly clonks against the Butcher's bony hip as he bounds along the travelator towards the departure gate, passing *camel trains* of Kuwaitis, the womenfolk *humped up* in their abayas, dragging giant wheelie-suitcases, while their menfolk stride ahead, flicking prayer beads with one hand, the other swinging free, as they talk to the mobile phones they've tucked up under their headdresses. Clonking lightly against his hip, the Samsung Barry gave him is his only luggage as the Butcher bounds along the travelator towards the departure gate, *buzzing* – buzzing with the buzz which ever buzzes through his up-ended shoebox of a house: the buzz the black Venetian blinds cast on the white walls in the form of ruled-straight shadow-lines, and which, in his mind at least, are the visible expression of the (You don't have to do this y'know) electro-magnetic waveforms constituting *life . . . the universe . . . Sally's never-to-be-born baby – ev-ery-thing . . .* His only luggage the Samsung given him by Barry, which against his hip lightly clonks: his cheeks *buzz* as molecules of Roja Parfum de la Nuit lift off from pore after pore – Buzzing, the Butcher is, from his breakfast pill and the two double espressos he *milked* from his counter-top Gaggia, buzzing with the matter at hand: not that this is the first time his actions will've diverted the destiny of humankind, so creating . . . *a world of my own*, but, nonetheless, even an operator as experienced as the Butcher can feel a little trepidation when he's plying the scalpel on *my own flesh . . .* Is it Amir, is it? This question has tormented him ever since Dicky asked him to do this *little favour* – other colleagues have been out in the field, desperately trying to tie up any loose ends. Clearly, now fuck-all's been found in the way of ennbeesee, the official enquiries are going to go from now until the Last Trump: the Butcher sees a committee room in Portcullis House, its bland slab of conference table and modular multimedia carousel – sees a harrumphing Chairman and dozing EmPees and scratching hacks. Sees the Angel of the Lord slice off all their foggily bureaucratic heads with his *Samsung scythe . . .* Yes, it'll go on forever, with the pols grilling their barely civil servants, even as their own disingenuous noses *grow and grow . . .* But, while the source known as Curveball has bounced out into the open, and the Iraqi provocateurs who claimed to've had sources in the

Mukhabarat are too flaky to be a threat, there's this other fellow . . .
is it, Amir – is it? whom Dicky, John – maybe even TeeBee's filthy
little fucker of a flack – were dumb enough to trust, and possibly
even meet with, although *they couldn't be that stupid – could
they?* And if it is Amir? Well, he wouldn't scruple to dump them all
in it *since he's no fucking scruples at all.* No scruples – and no hesita-
tion in going to the highest bidder, because if you're a half-Iraqi,
half-Iranian Shia, with smarts enough to've worked your way up
from nowhere to become a senior officer in the Islamic Republic's
intelligence services, then defected during the great patriotic war,
then *played both ends against the middle,* well: loose ends are your
stock-in-trade. But is it Amir . . . *is it?* The intel' had come through
via the slime's aitchqueue – then to the Doughnut, and finally to
VeeBeeArr: the asset they were interested in had successfully
crossed the border near a town called Ali al-Garbi, but before he'd
had the opportunity to identify himself to Coalition forces he'd
been scooped up in a hard knock and taken to the local base . . .
hard edge – and the light touch of . . . fate. The Butcher is buzzing: he
hasn't spoken to Gawain in over a month – they risked one call
shortly after the Rams arrived in theatre, and Lieutenant-Colonel
Thomas had waxed unexpectedly lyrical about the black sheep:
You're not gonna b'lieve it, Jonathan . . . when the Republican
Guard pulled out of here they set fire to the wellheads, whole town
was blanketed in the smoke for days – turned all the sheep black!
It's pretty bloody funny, really – when we arrived at the camp
gates there was a flock of the poor silly things waiting for us . . .
Prophetic – or what? Deplaning in Kuwait, the Samsung Barry gave

520

him clonks lightly against his hip – the Butcher's cresting the great wave of his own humanised electro-being. He popped a couple more pills on the flight . . . *it'll be a long day*, and watched a film in which a young couple both get it together . . . *and don't* – a fairly tedious counterfactual, he thinks, compared to the one he's trying to engineer. Close protection are waiting for the Butcher ground side, and he can tell they're impressed by how insouciantly Savile Row-suited he is – and how unencumbered: No luggage, sir – not even carry on? says the burly, shaven-headed Green Jackets Sergeant commanding the detail – and the Butcher says nothing, only shoots *my cuffs* . . . a silent rebuke to the Sergeant's own exposed forearms, with their childhood Biro doodles *called tattoos* . . . At his request they drive him to the Shuwaikh district, where the general provisioning shops are. The Bangladeshi has purple lips and a boil on his forehead – he disappears between stacks of jerry-cans and coils of tow-rope to search for the items he's been asked for, and, when he's assembled the pile on the counter, the Butcher points out a canvas holdall and asks him to, Put it all in there, will you? He slings the bag in the back of the Wimmik and, getting in beside the driver, turns to the Sergeant: I've business at the Hilton before we can get going . . . They take him along Arabian Gulf Street, past the kebab joints. Kuwaiti girls sit at the pavement tables smoking shisha-pipes – the Butcher smells the fruity fumes as the car barrels by, and thinks of Sally lying tiger-striped by shadows while he rubs lip balm around her anus. The driver pulls up by the Hilton sign, and the Sergeant says: Off limits to uniformed personnel, sir – we'll park up and wait. The Butcher walks along the curving concrete esplanade between the white reef of the hotel and the white sand of the machine-made beach. There are parboiled Brits on sun loungers – the families of EffOh staff stationed in-country. He hears them talking about Sven-Göran Eriksson's love life – someone sing-songs in an undertone, You're beautiful . . . it's true. He enters an air-conditioned shopping mall through soundlessly sliding doors, and, passing by racks festooned with pashminas, lifts one to his discerning nose so he can savour the faintest odour of . . . *Kaaaashmir.* In the lobby area he speaks with an Indian dressed in the chain's natty-green uniform, and then he's conducted to a back office. The sign on the door reads: MISTER MARSHALSEA, HEAD OF SECURITY. — Less than an hour later their convoy is under way: three Wimmiks, no less – the one carrying the Butcher in the middle. The desert, the Butcher thinks, should be clean and stark and ecstatically eternal – but the environs of Kuwait City are grubby, cluttered and painfully . . . *provisional.* A breeze has got up and grit spatters the windscreen. They drive out along Highway Six, passing old Mercs and newer Toyota pickups coming the other way, plus the occasional British military truck painted the colour of *old custard* . . . with young squaddies lolling on top, keffiyehs round their necks, goggles masking their exhausted eyes. They take the road for Umm Qasr, which curves around the city, and the Butcher watches the sun set into a golden haze of dust behind the gleaming towers of . . . *El Dorado,* while a perfect crescent moon rises in the west, its low rays lighting the scrublands along the coast and glimmering on the waters of the Gulf. The border is, the Butcher thinks, similarly allegorical: a Portaloo in lieu of a guardhouse, which is manned by someone who does indeed have *shit-for-brains*. They wait while he phones here, then there, to check their authorisation – then wait some more for the aypeesee to arrive from Shaibah. The Butcher wants to get out and stretch his legs, then sit in the cool of the desert night on a conveniently located white plastic garden chair – but the jobsworth Sergeant won't let him unless he puts on a helmet and twelve kilogrammes of body armour. Clearly, this is a man who knows nothing of what it takes to preserve . . . *fine tailoring*. When the vehicle finally arrives, he insists the Butcher cross-deck into it, which he does purely in order to *keep the peace*. They continue north. The Sergeant says, In-and-out job, is it, sir? And the Butcher, his hips painfully grating in the poorly upholstered bucket seat, gives a small, tight smile. Looking through the tinted side window at the moonlight glazing the dune crests, the Butcher ponders the revolution that's taken place inside his head. It began, he thinks, years ago – although he failed to notice it, so slight, to begin with, was the modulation in the tone adopted by *my malignant deceiver*. But then he stopped lisping! Stopped lisping – and stopped teasing and back-biting as well. His voice became deeper, his accent more public school – and he began delivering little homilies rather than snide asides (Such a bore, that – there's a limit, isn't there, to such badinage, don'tcha think?). When, with the darkened desert streaming into his gaping pupils, the Butcher considers his relation-ship with Squilly . . . *a hundred and one nights of jittery fabulation*, it occurs to him that at some point in the past decade or so . . . *I passed him by*. Squilly, who, for as long as the Butcher could remember, had been dominant, always yanking his chain, forever threatening him with the lash of his lisping tongue, had failed to move with the times – failed, specifically, to get older. What was it Kins used to sing after his second drink of the evening . . . *Put your head on my shoulder, You need someone who's older* . . . his saggy red face suffused with sentiment. The Butcher, who's now been up for twenty hours and is strung out *taut as Tamsin's gee-string*, wouldn't mind resting his head on the shoulder of the man sitting next to him – a private contractor who's customised his rifle with childish decals . . . *Eat Lead . . . Die Another Day . . . Pudsey Bear . . . Shits, Shits – I See No Shits* . . . He must've slept (With his head on my shoulder), the sweat pooling in the bucket seat, because next he's waking up, and *drenched . . . shivering – have to run a caucus-race* . . . They're under searchlights in the rat-run. The Sergeant swivels round and delivers this snide critique: Bit of a late arrival, sir, I hope whatever you've brought in that holdall justifies the risk you've exposed me and my men to . . . But the Butcher only grunts, and, sitting up, begins groping under the seat. You'll need to sit tight 'til they've check– the Sergeant begins, but stops because there's a small group of very obvious brass coming towards them along the sandbagged gulley, and next the door of the Fuchs is being opened: I'm Major-General Fitzhugh, says a tall, stooping, donnish man, and this is my Two-EyeSee, Gerry Fox – and you are? Jonathan, says the Butcher, getting out of the aypeesee and stretching luxuriously. Reaching back in, he pulls out the holdall, and, turning to the Sergeant, says, loudly enough for the rest of his men to hear: You're not a fucking nanny, man – and this is no nursery. If I ever run across you again, I'll thank you to do as you're told and keep your fucking trap shut . . . A little abrupt, Fitzhugh says as they weave through walls of sandbags and chainlink fences draped with hessian cloth – did he do something to nettle you? And the Butcher, stepping lightly, says, I'm here on a matter of state security, General – something profoundly important to AitchEmmGee. That chap seemed to feel the safety of a handful of 'roided-up ex-nightclub bouncers was more important – I didn't . . . There's silence for a while, except for the crunch of their shoes on sand, then their cold slap on cooling concrete. Met you once before, the General says, as they come round the end of a T-wall and see the base spreading out before them, row upon row of low concrete buildings, set out *with something of hell's lack of imagination* . . . You were lunching with your Chief at the Cavalry and Guards . . . Pulling up short, the Butcher reins in Fitzhugh, Fox and the other unnamed bods, and, giving the General a *full scan*, matches him: Ah, yes – Charles, isn't it? You were taking your wife to see the History Boys, and wondered whether either Dick or I had been . . . Fitzhugh's face *is an allegorical painting* in the moonlight: Unease and Relief *fighting each other to a standstill*, he says, Yes . . . yes . . . that's right – astonishing memory you have . . . I s'pose that rather goes with the territory. Now, er, Jonathan, this matter in hand – this man you're interested in . . . Well, thing is, our people up in Ali al-Garbi may've braced him a little hard . . . I don't know – could be he had some pre-existing condition . . . Anyway, when they arrived here at eleven hundred he was –. Really? the Butcher interrupts. That's splendid news – now I won't have to do the business myself, chop him up, bung the pieces in this holdall I picked up in Kuwait City and bury

525

it in the bloody desert . . . A suitably shocked silence meets this lethal insouciance: the professors of violence stand staring at him, waiting no doubt for the rider: *only joking* . . . which doesn't come. Instead, the Butcher says: In which case you might tell me where I can get my head down, General – I can identify the body in the morning. They walk on, passing guard posts manned by . . . *heavy smokers* (Wouldn't mind bumming a fag myself). From reports he's read, the Butcher knows the Shaibah base is the size of a small town – a home to tens of thousands of mainly British troops, their support staff and civilian contractors. By night it's . . . *a faubourg of shadows*, out of which, from time to time, a helicopter lifts . . . *spitting out feux d'artifice*, and dances away over the perimeter wall. They pass by the tinted windows of a bar established circa two thousand and three in a reinforced concrete bunker – looking in, the Butcher sees all the gamesmanship to be expected: big men – and a few big women – taking time out from *punching well below their* weight to play pool and darts by *little boys' rules* . . . On a wall-mounted screen there's the former Royals and Blues officer reassuring them they're . . . *beautiful*, although, in his parka, in the purity of his love, awaiting his angel, he most certainly . . . *isn't*. They trudge on – and the Butcher knows Fitzhugh is silent only because he's struggling to find the appropriate words. In the Butcher's experience, which is rich, varied and includes being *roundly buggered by them* . . . military men are usually pretty inarticulate. But at last, as they near what are clearly accommodation units of some sort, the General chimes up: Thing is . . . ah, Jonathan . . . Thing is, our man from Ali al-Garbi's still here – in a bit of a state actually . . . Sound chap, so far as I can gather – played loose head for the army in his day . . . Anyway, Provost Marshal's sort of got . . . involved – inevitable, really, after the kerfuffle up at Majar al-Kabir . . . The General keeps tailing off, clearly expecting the Butcher to interject – but he doesn't, so eventually Fitzhugh is compelled to: Thing is . . . he'd rather like a word with you. Of course – the General now rushes on – I realise this is pretty unorthodox, but, given the highly unusual circs, we rather thought you might be able to put his mind at rest . . . smooth things . . . over . . . as it were. In the silence which follows this *ridiculously big breach*, the Butcher hearkens to his own inner-counsel (In my not especially humble opinion, Johnny, you've no need to remain loyal to any of 'em – politicians, the military and especially your own doubly duplicitous colleagues. I always counselled you against this career – and now look where it's taken you.) To which he soundlessly replies, What's it to you, anyway, you bigoted old fool – this is my lover you're talking about, my noon, my midnight – my talk, my song? Everything you refused to acknowledge about me – everything you could never accept. (Well, not to be too pat, or too pi: times change – I do accept that. Y'know, I, more than most, am able to concede that my prejudices were formed by my background. Views which were once wildly heterodox have become really rather mainstream – you take my own field, local government finance . . . Why, when I published my first book in . . .) On it drones *onanon*, but, whereas when it issued from living lips, the Butcher experienced each and every phoneme as . . . *a lash across already opened wounds*, he now finds these familiar words nothing but comforting, so, as Kins pontificates, he says to Major-General Fitzhugh: All right, then, I'll see if I can calm the silly fucker down – then I'll have a word with the Provost Marshal, find out exactly how far things have got. You can dump your bag in here, sir, says one of the General's bods, unlocking a metal door and swinging it open. The Butcher walks in and Fitzhugh follows: We call 'em pods – for obvious reasons. None too comfy, but you're under hard cover, which is more than can be said for the majority of our men – certainly those in the outlying bases – but I'm sure you people in London are perfectly well aware of that. The Butcher looks at the landlord-magnolia walls of the pod. He looks out through the thick Perspex window at the distorted view of the pod opposite. He drops the holdall on the single bed and looks at Fitzhugh, who must've escaped being retired by one of his own greying whiskers. The General takes off his wire-rimmed spectacles and massages his saggy eyes. His face is dead in the mortuary light. The Butcher takes an interest in a tray with tea bags, coffee, sugar sachets and miniature youaitchtee milk pots – then hitches his silk-weave trousers at the knee, so he may bend and open the dinky fridge. Inside there's a green apple and a Mars Bar on a small plate. The Butcher picks the chocolate bar up, his fingers absorbing the chill and *savouring it*. Fitzhugh says abruptly, We're launching this sort of media strategy here – EffOh initiative, but thing is to sort of normalise relations. The Butcher queries: With the Basratis? And Fitzhugh laughs shortly, Heh-heh, no-no, 'fraid we're rather out of the running there – no, normalise relations with the media. One of the bods steps forward – he has a Coldstreamer's Captain's badges, longish dark hair and a slightly sloppy, dew-picked expression. He wears his camos . . . *as if they were fucking chinos* and hands the Butcher a press pack blazoned with the slogan A BETTER BASRA, in what some press officer presumably imagines is a sexy typeface. The Butcher looks into the bod's eagerly exhausted face and says, You're beautiful. Fitzhugh laughs his little laugh: Heh-heh – the bod blushes – and the Butcher says, Just thinking of your chap with the hit single – hear it everywhere I bloody go. He chucks the folder on to the bed beside the holdall and says, Shall we, gentlemen? Fitzhugh says, Don't you want to have a wash and brush-up? And the Butcher says, I'm not going on a fucking date. Then they're walking through a narrow defile between yet more hessian-swathed fences and Fitzhugh's maundering on about incoming rockets and arrpeegees: Since things've hotted up every-thing has to come in by night, air-wise – even then the Merlins can touch down only for a few seconds, unload, and they're away again . . . The Butcher sees Portakabins and Hesco walls, sangars and breeze-block-built blockhouses jumbled up in the moonlight – thinks of how it is that any large military camp represents the sum total of – (A lot of grown-up children playing with building blocks, wouldn't you say, Johnny . . .). They pass through a wicket gate manned by a Gurkha sentry who punctiliously examines all their eyedees. One of Fitzhugh's bods indicates the locked rack of side-arms beside the gate: No weapons inside the Divisional Detention Centre, sir, so if you've . . . ? The Butcher gives him a cold, old look: Don't be silly, young man . . . And to Fitzhugh he says, Y'know what the military historians will call this phase of the conflict when they come to write it up, General? Fitzhugh, who's chaining his

529

automatic to the rack, grunts interrogatively, so the Butcher tells him: Losing – that's what they'll call it. Fitzhugh doesn't respond to this provocation, only gestures to the low concrete blockhouses and says, This is where all those detained in our sector are brought for processing – Rams brought eight down from Maysan this morning, unfortunately two of them were dead on arrival . . . They turn into another narrow defile between fences *all dressed up – but with nowhere to go* . . . at the end of which something whitely insubstantial looms, which, as they draw nearer, turns into a translucent white plastic tent, lit from within so its occupants appear in the form of two clearly defined black shadows writ large on the canopy: one the bulky outline of a man seated upright in a chair, the other long, low and rectangular. Moths and other night insects are crawling over the translucent fabric . . . *bamboozled muons and positrons*, their antennae twitching, their tattered wings fluttering. A vast sheet, the Butcher thinks, has been thrown over the camp, one patterned with towers, domes and cupolas – all the superfluous ornamentation you'd expect to see if you were *arriving by camel for Belshazzar's feast*. There're two red caps standing at ease beside the tent flap. They're wearing full body armour and snap to attention as Fitzhugh's party strides towards them. At ease . . . at ease . . . he says – and to the Butcher: I could, ah, dismiss these men . . . Jonathan, but I'd rather not. The Butcher takes the ArrEmmPee Corporal to one side and shows him his EssEyeEss eyedee and diplomatic passport: I'll be speaking to your boss shortly, he says in an undertone, but in the meantime I want you and your colleague to skedaddle, roger that? The red cap, who must be *a deal smarter than your average plod*, simply gestures to the private to fall in, and the two of them evaporate into the Iraqi night. A dog starts barking somewhere out beyond the perimeter. Barks and barks and *screams* some more. Y'know, Fitzhugh says, they don't treat the poor mutts as pets at all – never allow 'em in the house, it's against their religion. Haram, the Butcher says, and Fitzhugh says, Bless you, and the Butcher says, No, it's haram – it means forbidden. It's forbidden to have a working animal in the home – now . . . if you'll excuse me? The *beautiful* Coldstreamer Captain salutes the Butcher, and Gerry Fox says, Thirty minutes enough for you? And the Butcher replies, More than . . . and the defeated brass and their bods *tactically withdraw*. The Butcher stands for a moment, sniffing the night air: burning dung and cooling piss – the after-reeks of cordite and phosphorous from the chaff fired by ascending Merlins. Soon, he thinks, I'll be standing in Sloane Street, looking in the window of an Italian suit retailer, and wondering whether I can face the ignominy of buying off-the-peg *never allow them in the house – it's against their religion* . . . The Butcher remembers a reception at the Embassy in Vienna twenty years past – the usual suspects: EffOh wonks and their wives . . . the Anglican vicar . . . the British Council representative – who had indeed borne an uncanny resemblance to Wilfrid Hyde-White – and the opera singer or ballet dancer he'd brought over from Blighty to be preyed upon by sharp-beaked, flabby-faced and chiffon-winged Austrian lady culture-vultures. Bored to distraction by the speechifying, the Butcher had wandered away *towards pastures old*: wood-panelled reception rooms and salons with pale striped wallpaper in which the dust motes rose from over-stuffed armchairs to hover below lead-crystal chandeliers. He'd touched up the old ivories of an ancient Bösendorfer baby grand – he'd sipped his not-so-Qualitätswein, and admired a sub-Sargent: a jut-jawed lass, her face at the epicentre of an explosion of silks and satins. He'd peered at another painting: *Henry de Worms, First Baron Pirbright, Politician, Writer and Historian of Austrian Descent* . . . and marvelled at the timelessness of such *solecisms* . . . A servant came soundlessly across the Persian rug towards him, bearing a silver salver on which there was a small pyramid of gold-foil-wrapped bonbons . . . *exquisitely* . . . *captivatingly* . . . *clichéd*, and the Butcher took one and slowly unwrapped it. Why does he remember this episode so distinctly? Not only because of the chocolate *testicle* which melted on the palm of his hand . . . *not in my mouth* – but also because of the message the servant dutifully delivered, verbatim: *Mister Amir is outside the embassy building, sir. He's in a metallic-green Volkswagen parked at the junction of Salesianergasse and Strohgasse – he says he's only half an hour, sir* . . . The Mars Bar is melting in the Butcher's hand (You'll mess up that suit of yours . . .), and the cracked actor's words, penned for him by his filthy little flack, have also been retrieved from his database: *Looking back over twelve years, we have been victims of our own desire to placate the implacable* . . . He pulls open the tent flap and hunches inside. Gawain sits on a white plastic garden chair. He's wearing full body armour and holds his helmet in his lap. His face is drawn, bloodless – its expression is utterly vacant. The corpse of a man lies on a table in the exact centre of the tent, naked except for threadbare boxer shorts in a faded blue-and-green Paisley pattern, and irradiated by the harsh white light of an unshaded bulb clipped to the tent's ridgepole. It's this *clash of patterns* that troubles the Butcher initially: the Formica tabletop the corpse lies on has exactly the same multicoloured speckles as the ones in the canteen at Saint Alban's Grammar . . . *these eggshell fragments shored against my ruin.* The corpse is that of a man in his early fifties, of Middle Eastern origin, with a thin ascetic face . . . *you've waited twelve years, why not wait a little longer?* Its skin is less picturesque than General Fitzhugh's face: a sickly beige canvas daubed with purple and maroon patches where the contusions inflicted before death have subsequently *clotted* . . . One eye is so bruised it's swollen completely shut, the other's wide open and staring dully at the dull roof of the dull tent – whoever worked the man over did so systematically, *dully*, over many hours. The Butcher takes two strides and is beside the table, looking down into that face – a face he matches against scores of potentially relevant images he retrieves from his vast data-bank of all those he's ever had business with. One time at Thames House, Ventris, a senior plod, thought he'd belittle the Butcher by introducing him to one of the so-called super-recognisers they retained – in this case to try to match the walk-ups who'd streamed in after the Twin Towers attacks against thousands of indistinct mug-shots the Pakistanis had reluctantly ponied up. While the super-recogniser was actually doing his bit, the Butcher scanned the screen over his shoulder for a few seconds, then tapped here, ping! and there, ping! Those're your matches, he'd said curtly – now go and give 'em a pull and stop piddling to the press about how under-fucking-resourced you are . . . But this face – this thin, intellectual face, with a nose which would've been pretty, had it not long since been broken *twice* – once by the Iraqi Mukhabarat, once by the Iranian Vaja – this face the Butcher matches against younger, live versions of itself, met initially in Vienna in ninety-one . . . next seen across a café table in Aman in ninety-three . . . through a plate-glass window in Cairo in ninety-five . . . reflected in the wing mirror of an old Peugeot in Tehran in ninety-nine. Not that he needs any comparison: he knew who the man was that morning, standing in the blankly buzzing clarity of his own house . . . *pulling up my pants.* He stares down into the corpse's open eye, seeing there, caught in the already fraying net of its retina, a single silvery image, *frail as Victorian découpage . . . I also want to pay tribute to our Intelligence and Security Services for the often extraordinary work that they do.* He looks closer, and can just about make out the faint reflection of *ram's horns* . . . Goodbye, Amir, the Butcher says, teasing down the dead Iraqi's eyelid with the very tip of his beautifully manicured finger-nail . . . *they say they grow when you're dead – like all horny things* . . . At last, he turns his attention to his lover: Are you in shock? are his first words – his next: You should eat this – I can see you've low blood sugar . . . Gawain's eyes swim, then weep as he brings . . . *the Butcher* into focus. I've had enough chocolate to last me a lifetime, he says blankly, tears running down his cheeks. Jonathan turns away slightly, stripping the wrapping from the softening Mars Bar: Well, his tone is brusque, in that case I'll have it myself – nothing's passed my lips since London. Gawain stirs *dully*, says, *still more dully*, What was that titbit, then, Sally's clit? And the Butcher darts a sharp look at him: This isn't a fucking film, Gawain – and we don't have time for histrionics of any sort. You need to buck up and tell me exactly what happened if you and your men're to avoid a court martial. Gawain stirs in the white plastic garden chair, his hands tightly gripping its white plastic arms. He blinks furiously, trying to turn it all – the corpse, the tent and the Butcher – off and on again . . . a factory reset. I thought . . . he says at length . . . I thought you and your people rather wanted rid of this man anyway – that was the impression I got from the intel'. The Butcher's mouth is gummed up with chocolate, toffee and nougat – which is just as well, because by the time he's able to, he speaks rather than shouts: What my people want is of no fucking account, Gawain – this man had a name, and his name was Amir Ali al-Jabbar, and he happened – strange to relate – to be a fucking friend of mine! The Butcher drops the crumpled-up Mars Bars wrapper to the gravelly ground and kicks it under the corpse's table. He balls his fists and thrusts them deep into his trouser pockets. He can't look at Gawain, yet senses this emanation coming from him: a steady pulsing, as from a *bright light* . . . He thinks of the press pack lying on the pancake-thin mattress under the hard cover of the pod: it isn't the sort of thing the EffOh wonks would want publicised, but it appears that Lieutenant-Colonel Thomas, commanding officer of the Yorkshire Hussars, has finally become *who he's truly meant to be* . . . Did you murder my friend Amir, Gawain? The Butcher at last *pops the question* . . . the answer to which will in all probability terminate, rather than commence . . . *our civil partnership.* Gawain shifts awkwardly from buttock to buttock. Murder's a bit much, he mutters. Killed, then, the Butcher snaps back – and Gawain shakes his head. Killed's also an overstatement – this man was detained by me and my men during a routine hard knock. A brief firefight ensued and he shot and wounded one of the Rams – Trooper Bessemer, who subsequently died. It might be that my men were a little over-enthusiastic when it came to interro–. You what? the Butcher cries, at last turning to look at the *lost sheep* . . . You what? You had strict instructions to get anyone who came over the border down here and turn them over to the slime. What the fuck, Gawain . . . what the fucking fuck . . . Silence falls heavily on the lovers, and the Butcher remembers the blond's woolly leg thrown across his own, under the duvet, beneath the eaves of the old cottage in Bardney where *we spent so many happy hours* . . . He shivers disgustedly – the object of his repulsion is fixated on his own *cloven hooves*. Suddenly the Butcher is all business: Okay, you need to start talking now – and you need to start talking well. I want the names of every one of your miserable little troopers who had any contact with these detainees, either on the op' or subsequently. Fitzhugh says the Provost Marshal knows about Amir's death – and there's another, isn't there, Gawain? Gawain stirs in his absurd chair – a garden party guest who's had rather too much of the Pimm's – and says, One of the detainees just upped and died on us – must've had a heart condition or something . . . It unsettled the men, Jonathan – what with their comrades getting banjoed, they just . . . sorta . . . lost it. The Butcher is on him in two strides: his hands on the arms of the white plastic garden chair, *he stoops to vanquish* . . . And you – you, Gawain, you just sorta let them lose it, did you? Then it all vomits forth: the thick, stinging, sweet-sickness of it – the smelly-melting dissolution of this *chocolate soldier*. Gawain hunches forward – the helmet drops from his lap and rolls under the dead man's table. Gawain puts his balled fists in his swollen eyes – and smites his armoured breast as he tells his lover of Tizer's breakdown: I dunno why he hasn't said anything before . . . He's clearly been thinking it for years – since I bested him for SeeOh . . . Surprised he hasn't used it against me before – then again, I personally led the detachment which went to clear up after the Kiwis . . . strictly against – but I was in all sorts of difficulties already, Jonathan – you must understand . . . What the Butcher understands (I do so wish you wouldn't harp on that – it's just a silly nursery rhyme) is that it's over. He lets Gawain run on *and on* . . . hears him out on the matter of his terrible deployment – the impossibility of being pro-moted out of command . . . His isolation – his sense from the very beginning of being embarked on a *fool's errand* – doesn't Jonathan remember? All those slightly alcoholic afternoons, when they'd sat in hotel rooms, and Gawain had *moaned on about his fool's errand of a career* . . . The Butcher hears him out (If you'd only think of yourself differently, perhaps you'd do different things – power of positive thinking and all that jazz . . .), fixated on the beaten and broken face . . . *of my brother-in-arms*. When at last his once beautiful cavalryman *whinnies* to a halt, the Butcher (an unpleasant epithet – so suggestive of bloodthirstiness) says this: Swift writes of the King of Lilliput that his vision was so acute he could detect the movement of a clock's hour hand. Well, we'd need a sovereign of that stamp in order to register the minute gradations in rank and preferment which have animated your entire fucking life! Or at least starts to say this – but ends up SHOUTING IT! Dry white balls of his spit sticking *dagtails* to the unshaven and sweaty face of the . . . *Fighting Ram*, as more of the cracked actor's nauseating lines, declaimed on the world stage of the Commons, repeat on him: *To suffer the humility of failing courage in the face of pitiless terror . . . That is how the Iraqi people live . . .* and how, he thinks, Amir Ali al-Jabbar died. Never has Jonathan De'Ath felt quite so cursed by his prodigious memory as now – because it's with the thistledown from that summer morning, twelve years since, on the banks of the Bridgewater Canal *tickling my nostrils . . .* that he bids farewell to . . . *my one true love.* A farewell which consists of Lieutenant-Colonel Thomas – in direct contravention of every order he's received, most notably the ones setting out the implementation of the Universal Declaration of Human Rights in combat zones – racking his woolly brain for the names of every one of his men who came into contact with the detainees. When Gawain's done, Jonathan – who the entire time has been bracing himself half upright on the arms of the white plastic garden chair – finally *straightens up . . .* The Provost Marshal will cease any investigation of these deaths immediately, he says in the dull tones of an *efficiently negligent civil servant.* Your men will forget about the incident soon enough – or, rather, they'll forget their own lethally irresponsible behaviour, because it's very much in their interests to do so. You will return to Ali al-Garbi today, Gawain – as soon as possible. A movement order will come in from Brigade by oh-nine-hundred tomorrow: you will escort Major Townshend back to the YouKay personally. I suggest you use the time you have together to impress upon this mentally unstable man the consequences of any more loose talk. It's up to you to find the appropriate leverage – don't let yourself down, Gawain . . . He's standing at the entrance to the tent, its white plastic flap . . . *in my white plastic hand.* He's looking at that dear and guileless face, appreciating – even if disgustedly – the new lines which have appeared on it *since we last lay together.* Deep and suffering lines, which will give the Gawain of the future – the civilian Gawain, who his former lover already sees *sporting a ghostly name badge* – that attribute which *au fond* he's always most conspicuously lacked, to whit: *character* . . . A fool's errand, Gawain – that's what your poofy Uncle Rodney called peacetime soldiering, and that's what you've harped on about for years as well. Well, you may think the significance of the expression lies in its ostensible meaning, but I don't think so: it's a cliché, Gawain, a fucking cliché. I used to find it endearing – your propensity for these hoary old idioms – your getting-back-to-the-drawing-board at-the-drop-of-a-hat and your eyes-in-the-back-of-your-head, which – or so you assured me – allowed you to see if your troopers weren't cutting-the-mustard. But let me tell you, I see your idiolect for what it is now: the language of a man who thinks in clichés – who, to all intents and purposes, is a fucking cliché . . . Outside, it takes Jonathan a few moments to gain his night-sight – then he looks up to a sky that's a dark violet field scattered with periwinkle stars in which a single grey cloud floats. It might, he thinks, be the smoke from ordinance that he didn't hear explode, or some altogether more *pathetic fallacy* . . . He finds the red cap easily enough, skulking by the rack of sidearms, and the man escorts him to the Provost Marshal's office, which is a Portakabin on top of two other Portakabins accessed by a metal stairway. You're up rather late . . . are Jonathan's first words, as, hand outstretched, he advances towards the man's metal desk. They're spoken with all the charm of which he's capable, while he simultaneously thinks, How shit a plod have you got to be to end up here? The Provost Marshal, a full and corpulent Colonel, looks up from the laptop he's been fiddling with: Ah, yes, he says, you must be the EssEyeEss bod Gerry said was coming in – have you caught up with this twerp from Ali al-Garbi, yet? They shake hands and Jonathan sees what the Provost Marshal has been doing, sitting in the Iraqi night, wearing a helmet and full body armour *'cause Portakabin versus mortar isn't good odds . . .* He's been playing Minesweeper, that's what the Provost Marshal has been doing – using his forensic skills and carefully honed powers of deduction . . . *to avoid tiny squares appearing to go up in smoke.* They sit and chat for a while, Jonathan and the Provost Marshal – whose name is Ted. Jonathan feels they hit it off rather well. Ted gets one of his staff to make Jonathan a cup of tea. When Jonathan's ready to leave, they shake hands rather more warmly than they did initially. The Provost Marshal says, Do you need a burn box for those? And Jonathan, who's borrowed a white plastic bag to put the paperwork in, replies, No, I think I can manage, thanks, Ted. They stand chatting on the external stairs for a few minutes – Ted up above, Jonathan down below. It's still dark, and the Divisional Detention Facility – its blockhouses, wire-fenced compounds and walkways – is lit up by sodium lights. From this angle the effect is as of a circuitry diagram, and Jonathan thinks this just, because if the entire rationale for the Shaibah Logistics Base is to exercise power over the inhabitants of south-eastern Iraq, then this place – where men are hooded, shouted at, subjected to white noise, forced to maintain stress positions and deprived of sleep – is *where you put the batteries in* . . . the only problem being that *they're not included.* That man Thomas, Jonathan says lightly: the Yorkshire Hussars' SeeOh – I've told him he can return to Ali al-Garbi in the morning? And Ted, equally lightly, replies: Not a prob' – Adjutant General's lot are all over the shop anyway, and when they do get their act together there're umpteen similar snafus to deal with . . . Ted hitches up his webbing belt and accepts the Marlboro Jonathan offers him with a Ta, don't mind if I do, before continuing: Thing is . . . our political masters are on a hiding to nothing: they've instructed us to incorporate Human Rights legislation into the rules of war, but, let's face it, war's about depriving humans of any rights they may have. Bit loopy, if you ask me – loopy for the grunts bracing the Ali Babas and trying to contain the militias, loopy for my lot when they end up having to brace the grunts over their, ah . . . bracing. Ted stoops to take a light from Jonathan's vintage Dupont: Mark my words, seven thousand different sorts of bullshit are going to be generated by this . . . um, conflict – your man's particular bullshit will be easy enough to lose track of. Even when we do try to investigate something thoroughly – and are given the resources to do it – the enquiry's one embuggeration after another: suspects redeployed – posted here there and everywhere – while civilian witnesses are getting the frighteners put on them, and military ones? Well, we both know the story, the last thing anyone associated with the regiment will want is to cast a shadow on their deployment – as for the Iraqis, after the shit they've been through they're pretty bloody realistic: they'll take the compo and keep it . . . zipped. Five grand YouEss'll buy you a lot of white plastic garden chairs . . . Standing in front of the open fridge door, listening to its low buzz, Jonathan thinks of his house. (You think of your house, not your home – which saddens me, Johnny.) He sniffs the musty and over-conditioned air of the pod, then glances round to check the holdall he bought in Kuwait City is still there. A small shock – a slight prickling of the nape hairs. He popped his last thirty-six-milligram tablet of methyphenidate hours ago, just before cross-decking into the aypeesee, but most of the dosage is time-release . . . *and should still be powering me.* But . . . But . . . he can't remember having said goodbye to the Provost Marshal – has no memory of leaving the DeeDeeEff, can't recall if he was escorted to the pod –. (Or if you made your own way here – d'you know, I think you might be lagging . . .) How d'you know about lagging? Jonathan addresses his father's death mask, which hangs from a metal hook screwed into the pod's metal wall: You never had anything to do with computers in your life – let alone computer games. (Don't you remember that driving range we used to go to?) The one in Staines? (No, Sunbury – anyway, there was always a lag – albeit a small one – between the physical ball striking the net, and the filmic one appearing on the screen. What's that, Johnny, if not . . . lagging?) Jonathan stoops to open the fridge, the Samsung phone Barry gave him knocking softly against his prominent hip bone. Stooping to open the fridge, the phone Barry gave him – a

Samsung – softly knocks against his hip bone, which is prominent. Jonathan's prominent hip bone knocks against the phone Barry gave him, *Sam . . . sung* as he stoops to open the fridge. The Mars Bar he remembers being in it is gone. (Of course it is, you ate it in that vile tent – chewed it up while standing right beside a corpse. Really, Johnny! I mean . . . really!) He remembers there being a Mars Bar in there – but it's gone. It's gone: the Mars Bar he remembers being in there, and in its place, on a small plate, there're polythene-wrapped cheese sandwiches which they eat at the summit, their backs against the cold concrete of a freshly poured trigonometric marker. As they swig the whisky-laced coffee, Zack explains what it's for, and the basic principles of the Ordnance Survey – information he would've assumed was at the tips of her capable fingers – after all, what the hell is there to do in Fife, besides go for bracing country walks? But no: there are these charming lacunae in Isobel's understanding of the world – ones which he, her soon-to-be lover, the *thief of her maidenhead*, can impart with a mature capability he hopes she finds . . . *reassuring*. And if he were to take that maidenhead here, on top of Tinto Hill on a blowy-bright October afternoon? Take it in a charmingly casual way – no fuss *nae bother . . .* The two of them at first sitting on Missus Kane's paired and folded rugs, their backs against the trig' point, passing the cup of whisky-laced coffee back and forth, wolfing down the cheese sandwiches, before falling on each other's mouths and necks. If he were to – and she weren't to demur. *She weren't to demur . . .* he thinks, the whole thing rests on her *demurral*, if only she weren't so *demure*. It is, he thinks, a form of *the linguistic turn*, something he's read about, and understands intermittently, as the Javelin's anti-quated indicator stalk lifts *intermittently* from its housing to signal left: Zack could, he thinks, throw his life away on any woman to whom the word demure could be applied *unreservedly*. He sees them shuffle along this timeline – it's an Astonishing Tale *right enough, Doc*: doctors Zachary and Isobel Busner, escalating into the future up a spiralling ribbon of genetic coding, their two handsome six-footer *Scots* sons at their side, while enlarged molecular models float overhead, symbolising sagacity and the virtues of an enquiring mind. All this, and the very heaven of lying promiscuously entangled with a completely naked and bewitching Isobel – the two of them bundled snugly in the rugs, their clothes having been slipped off without let, hindrance or embarrassment and stuffed themselves into his vest. Or would it quite possibly have gone dreadfully wrong? *Ooh, yes – I'm liking this more, Doc* . . . A mistimed attempt at a kiss – because, let's face it, you don't grab at a young lady when she's trying to talk seriously about Aldermaston. Teeth clash harder, more jarringly than civilisations. She wouldn't like that – and in a trice he'd abandon all hope. The day would grow instantly higher and colder – the hills would feel alive with storm troopers. He'd suggest they walk back down to the car – they might catch the matinee at the cinema in Biggar? A two-prong strategy: it's con-ceivable she'll unbend a little in cramped, warm darkness – or he can cut his losses, enjoy the flick: *It'll probably be some old weepy, it's a tiny circuit – they don't get the new releases for months* . . . is the sort of thing he might well say. Then, having divvied up, and been escorted past hunched-up crones, chittering weans, cap-crammed old fellows in from the kale yard – all of them supporting their invalid teeth with *sugary crutches* – the plan would very likely go wrong in this way: his stupid dumb cock – his unabashed penis. All the rest of him is flabby – he knows that – and would remain so . . . *in any conceivable future*, but his prick, his dick, his John Thomas? Donald Campbell, skipping across the glassy surface of Lake Windermere in Bluebird, spots an object unidentifiable for crucial seconds, closing in on his port bow – collision is unavoidable, and the last thing he sees before his attempt to beat his own water-speed record ends in tragedy is that his nemesis is a rigid, streamlined and emphatically Jewish penis, the obscenely domed tip of which plunges through the jet-powered speedboat's hull with all the intellectual power of *Moses Maimonides* . . . But that lies in the near-future *possibly* . . . If the film showing at the Biggar Rialto pleased Isobel, she'd soften – say it was something like The Inn of the Sixth Happiness, a nineteen fifty-eight vehicle for Ingrid Bergman, in which, faintly preposterously, she plays Gladys Aylward, a humble Englishwoman gripped with missionary zeal. Isobel McKechnie, upright daughter of the manse, would like that – she'd sit watching Bergman make her way through a London fabricated out of well-known landmarks, and edited together with two-second bus rides and four-second walks. She'd smile faintly as Bergman – a mere cleaner in the Chelsea home of Sir Francis, the patron of the Missionary Society – agitated meekly to go to China. And Zack? He'd sit there in the darkness, listening to Scots teeth being ground down all around him, and dealing with the ache of his engorged genitals by focusing so intently on every last line of dialogue, were he to find himself, over half a century later, on a train heading north – a train which passes within a few miles of the cinema where he'd likely sat on that October Saturday afternoon – he'd recall them better . . . *than my own name, which is?* Sundowning, they call it – this much he knows: an ugly verbal coinage, he thinks – but then that's the modern idiom all over, with its reckless propensity for dangerously weaponising nouns. In this case taking a lovely natural scene and making of it a sun lounge full of screaming and mindless Strul . . . Struld . . . Struldbr – oldies. What's my name? he asks the young man who sits opposite him, his skin greasy . . . *pimpled*, his black hair hacked about on his haunted temples, and the young man replies, Doctor Zebadius Obadius Anthraxobadus, but we just call you Doc B for short . . . *yes, Doc B, that's it – you can push Doc B, but not too far* . . . *It's a hard life for a young woman, but it doesn't seem hard when I look back on it, just . . . beautiful* . . . is the sort of dialogue to be expected, being spoken by Bergman's white-haired and plump predecessor, after her fatal fall from the rotten old balcony of the Inn, but before her final expiration. Bergman, who's already impressed the local Confucian Mandarin – a surprisingly convincing portrayal by the ailing Robert Donat, his jaundiced skin playing its typecast part – with her combination of piety and obstinacy, won't be deflected from her evangelical course, any more than Zack's hand would be deflected from the smooth nylon runnel of Isobel McKechnie's hosed thighs. *Not here* . . . and, *not now!* are the sort of lines he'd expect her to come out with, as Bergman carries on trying *to pass* . . . her Swedish accent further informing the otherworldliness of an interwar China re-created by bussing

546

laundrymen from Toxteth and Limehouse to Borehamwood, and thence to Snowdonia for the location shooting. Yes, Isobel would fight him off in the Biggar Rialto – and Zack would persist, even as romance blossoms between the Swedish film star impersonating an English missionary, and Curt Jürgens, an Austrian actor mumming it up in heavy makeup as Captain – later Colonel – Lin Nan, a military intelligence officer, charged with readying the remote province of Yang Cheng for the onslaught of the Japanese. His mixed Chinese-Dutch blood accounts for his stature, his appearance and his lowering self-hatred, *My heart and my mind are Chinese – only my blood is mixed* . . . Each time his fingertips reached a certain indefinable point, Isobel's thighs would close on his hand, and Zack would bite his tongue, willing himself not to *shoot aff* . . . The foot-binding is curtailed, Bible stories are recited to muleteers – Gladys ends a prison riot by putting a stop to the abusive practices of the guards . . . *Sounds right stirring, Doc – might gi' ye ideas* . . . Might – would, very possibly, were it not that with each scene he'd see that garden of earthly delights, Isobel McKechnie's body, retreating from him. The Zeroes come winging in over Glyder Fawr and up the valley towards Capel Curig – the dying Donat in his silk dressing gown witnesses the bombing of his set, and Gladys and Curt lead the orphans of the Inn of the Sixth Happiness to safety, singing a jolly rhyme from her Edmonton childhood. It would go with them, Isobel and Zack, as they left the Rialto and got into the Javelin – which would be parked immediately outside, this being the way of things back then. It would go with them to Lanark Station, the children's *Knick-knack paddy-whack, give a dog a bone . . .* a jaunty and nonsensical accompaniment to his terrible frustration: Yes! Give a dog a bone – even a Jewish dog with a furiously twingeing circumcised boner deserves one. But no: *this old man would come rolling home,* his frustration intact, and on this occasion would very likely have to bathe the black-balled member under cold water in the cold bathroom, along the cold corridor from his cold room at Missus Kane's . . . *aren't ye forgettin' something, Doc?* The following day he'd probably write her a letter – which was what you did back then – apologising for being gallus, and hoping the incorporation of dialect demonstrated quite how serious he was about *fitting in. You're forgetting something, Doc . . . forgetting what any red-blooded man who wass tha' frustrated might do – ye ken: she'd been leading ye on all day. Flashin' her legs at ye all the way up the hill – kissing ye, lettin' ye touch her down there, it's no surprise if ye'd've lost patience and woulda –.* What? Behaved like you, Bobby, with the mental defective you met on the Perth country lane? I don't think so . . . *But when ye drapped her aff at Lanark, and she wass goin' awn an' awn about some play she'd seen at the Edinburgh Festival – and how the new American President was a handsome enough chap, but as a Papist not to be trusted – lots else besides, well . . .* Well, what? *You could be forgiven for losin' your temper, Doc . . .* Forgiven for all manner of pushing, pulling and tugging? Forgiven for tearing? Forgiven for the stopped dandelion *clock* of her petticoats and her shocked-white *face?* Forgiven for ruining a pair of saucy briefs from the Pompadour range? No, if he'd've assaulted her like that, Zack wouldn't have been forgiven, ever – either by Isobel McKechnie or, more importantly, by himself. He would've seen her off almost as if nothing had happened – because that was the way of it in those days: hot-headed marital rape followed by a frigidly polite breakfast. He would've seen her off, standing on the darkened platform, his lungs full of smoke and sick at heart – he'd have understood he'd grievously misjudged her – or, more importantly, himself: his was not the divine hand, outstretched to *create a woman . . .* He'd know at last who his father was, because Maurice's gentle reproof would resound in his head louder than any angry patriarch's. Sat in the Superintendent's Javelin for half an hour, maybe more, smoking and banging his head on the steering wheel, he would've felt an unutterable shame – the immemorial shame of his lost tribe. Would've felt as well the utter uselessness of his work at State Hospital: the pathetic little concessions he might've managed to wring from the Superintendent and Doctor McClintock, what would they amount to? Allowing the prisoner-patients to associate for a half-hour longer a day, getting permission for them to mount a dismal little Christmas show – a review Zack would direct himself, called something like You, Too, and featuring topical sketches about spy planes getting shot down over the Soviet Union, interspersed with the patient-performers . . . *doing little turns – Donald, where's your trousers . . .* This was hardly the sort of therapy likely to reverse the abuse Bobby and the others had suffered in the system . . . *you've no knick-knack idea, Doc . . . every time I absconded from Baldovan it wass the same routine on recapture: bath filled to overflowing wi' ice-cold water, then a towel wrapped round yer heid, an' they'd say, Aye, thass what ye get for bein' crabbit – an' they'd put ye under for . . . I dunno – minutes at a time. I thought I'd died . . .* Driving back to Carstairs along deserted roads, the shame would continue to build up in young Doctor Busner's head – a dreadful pressure, and he'd take this hydrocephalus to bed with him, tuck it up between Missus Kane's clammy sheets, after he'd covered them with the blankets he'd removed that morning – the blankets which had never *shamefully* been used . . . *shamefully. Shamefully, they'd ask us criminal lunatics: would ye be happy taking tea wi' the Queen? That was before they moved us from the Criminal Lunatic Department at Perth Gaol – I'd absconded again, this time from Gartloch, where I was bein' held on a section . . . Gi' me sulphanol, they did – two tablets three times a day . . . crushed in wi' water. . . I went gaga, Doc – completely gaga. Couldnae walk – they'd t'lift me on to the commode. They stopped gi'ing t'me – but others died, Doc, nae kiddin'. . . Sent me to a speech therapist: Say three bags of coal, Robert . . . Three bags of coal . . . Very good, Robert, well done . . .* And in the morning? He'd eat his rubber egg and his celluloid bacon while listening to The First Day of the Week on the Home Service. It'd probably be something like The Essential Elements in a Vital Christian Experience, a reading from the Riverside Sermons by Harry Emerson Fosdick. He'd sip his strong tea, and quail beneath the judgemental glare of Missus Kane, a keen Sabbatarian, who, while she'd probably object to his going to State Hospital on a Sunday, would certainly censure him very stiffly if she knew about what had possibly happened in the Javelin the preceding evening – a long, low, streamlined car, which he'd drive back to the hospital, crouched beneath the thunderhead of his black shame: *confectionery is a crutch, alcohol is a crutch, the carnal relation is . . . a crutch – why, religion itself may be abused by being used as a crutch – but the worst crutch of all . . . the one that is truly an abomination in the eye of Almighty God, is pride . . .* which would make sexual pride doubly anathema, *Would ye no agree, Doc?* After chapel most of the patients would shuffle off to their cells, to spend the rest of the day in sedated seclusion – but the cast of You, Too might well assemble in the workshop for an afternoon's scenery building and painting. Young Doctor Busner would, no doubt, be very proud of the set for the revue – which might well be something like the spread wings of an advanced, high-altitude surveillance aircraft, which in turn could require some of the more trusted inmates to do the *knick-knack-nailing* – being careful not to *knick-knack* on their thumbs . . . Which implies they'd have the use of hammers, nails and also a saw. Sore-headed, young Doctor Busner would be, what with the whisky he drank the afternoon before – sore-headed, and that head also sunk now in a stygian remorse-hole: he should indeed write that letter to Isobel – write her the sincerest and most heartfelt apology imaginable. And, as the elements of the set were bashed and bished into being, he'd most likely sit at the charge nurse's table in the corner of the room, speaking when asked for his opinion or advice, but mostly ignoring the patients – a criminal *some might say lunatic* neglect, especially given these are all dangerously insane men. Men who've to fill out a chit for each tool they're issued with from the locked cabinet – a chit which must be signed for by Doctor Busner in a ledger at the time, then counter-signed when the tool is returned. Yes, he'd sit there all afternoon, probably, and, it being the way of things then, he'd likely smoke a number of cigarettes while composing a letter of such heartfelt eloquence Isobel would not only be completely mollified, she'd be mortified as well and return post-haste – arriving at Carstairs Junction the following evening, and quite possibly going straight from Missus Kane's to find him in the Wee Bush, a single-storey, corrugated-iron-roofed hostelry of humble antiquity named by Burns himself. Looking up from his mournful pint of eighty bob to see the radiant slip of a girl slipping in through the door, Zack might well be forgiven for quoting the ploughman poet: *Better a wee bush than nae beild at a'*... No, no – a ridiculous counterfactual: the letter would never reach her in time. He'd sit there alone in all likelihood, trying not to think about the vapid and sexually frustrated days stretching ahead of him, with no leave before Christmas. It wouldn't be until he heard the siren rising and falling – its hand-cranked moan an unwelcome reminder of his parents' wartime deaths – that young Doctor Busner would come out of his dwam and fully regain his senses: *This old man, he played nine, he played knick-knack on my ... spine.* Yes, it would very likely be in the unsettling waves of the siren that young Doctor Busner would locate the frail barque of his career and see it foundering. Of course, nothing could ever be definitively established – the signatures were in the ledger for the police and all subsequent official enquirers to examine, so no one could prove he hadn't seen the chisel, the screwdriver and the saw that Robert Inchin and Kevin MacDougall used to kill the charge nurse, the warder and the motorist whose car they'd hijacked on the White-loch Road. *A grisly tale – right enough, Doc* ... A tale so grisly it'd become the stuff of local legend: How the two escaped inmates had flagged down the car, a Morris Minor driven by the Secretary of

Carnwath Golf Club, who was returning young Ethel Smith home from an evening reception. How they'd dragged Mister Morton out, stabbing him in a frenzy with the chisel and screwdriver – the forensic pathologist identified no fewer that seventy-eight wounds – before severing his head with the saw *stay in the car, girly – dinna fash yersel', thass all ye got t'do: stay in the car . . .* Soft tops, some Morris Minors – and Mister Morton's would have to be one of those. *It wass a good idea, Doc, your rumpus room, where we could sorta . . . express ourselves. A good idea as well to let a mental defective wear his ain clothes rather than the parish tweeds – makes him keener t'be of good report.* All this would crowd incoherently into young Doctor Busner's head – because, of course, he wouldn't know exactly what'd happened yet – only that the siren was rising and falling, while Missus Kane stood in the corner of the parlour she grandly designated her peegees' dining room, hands on hips, and the set expression of a woman who'd cheerfully track an escapee from State Hospital down and sever his head with the breadknife she'd just used to slice the malt loaf . . . *he played knick-knack once again.* The police would strenuously and quite reasonably object to their patrol-man – who would've had the misfortune to've driven past, then, recognising Mister Morton's motor, turned back – being so savagely attacked. All parties would assume MacDougall was responsible: he'd been detained indefinitely at Her Majesty's pleasure for the murder and rape of young Ayrshire girl – whereas Inchin was a mere mental defective, caught up in the system . . . *he put the Golf man's heid up in a fork of the tree, Doc – it wass a dark night, an' she couldnae see what'd happened, only hear the drip-drip-drip of his blood*

on the soft top o' the Morris. I didnae know who was more terrified, Doc:
her or me . . . so the police would probably return him to State rather
than taking him directly into custody. Which was why later that
morning young Doctor Busner would be allowed to see him . . .
Fentazin makes ye walk around all day wi' your heid on one side,
Doc . . . when I wass at the Criminal Lunatic Department in Perth, the
warders hated it when we called them nurse. Nurse! Nurse! we'd cry –
needlin' 'em, like, 'til they got completely fed up – then they'd take uz
to the back end an' gi' uz a proper beating. Then they'd t'fill out a harsh
sheet – which is what they called their report, setting out how we'd
attacked them . . . The drip-drip-dripping of blood from the Golf
Club Secretary's severed head down on to the soft top of his own
homely little Morris Minor would become the stuff of local, national
and then global legend. Twenty-two years later, attending a conference on affective disorders in Caracas, Doctor Busner would hear
two young Venezuelan girls telling the story on a bus in Spanish!
How *La hermosa niña* sat there, petrified, and when the police
patrolman opened the car door, he told her on no account to look
back – but she had looked back, and she'd seen the wide-open dead
eyes of *La cabeza cortada* staring straight back at her. Bobby would
stare straight back at Doctor Busner, his expression utterly guileless,
and he might even have the strange boldness – born of *wanting to be*
of good report, which would lead him to discuss the whole matter the
way he might any other institutional trivia – the cludgie blocking
up, so-and-so getting his radio confiscated, somebody kicking off in
the kitchen, then being packed off to Medwin Ward for a few days.
Bobby, a grinning homunculus, his brown hair too thick on his

forehead – the dense pile of a rug *or an animal*. Bobby, too stupid to understand that this was it: there'd be no beating with a sand shoe or an extra jolt of emulsified paraldehyde – yet cunning enough to grasp that young Doctor Busner would be sick with anxiety, lest his liberality in the wood-working room be blamed for their escape and the killings. Bobby would start out on some mad inconsequence, such as, Ain't it true, Doc – that you're more likely to suffer from mental illness if you're working class than middle class? To which Zack might well angrily object: Professionals! Psychiatrists in particular, Bobby – we've a higher risk of the major psychopathologies than anyone else! But that's because diagnosis is itself an opportunistic … And then he'd flounder, not wanting to say "crime", although when they'd brought Bobby into the room he would've appeared not cowed but relieved – and Doctor Busner, still being really rather young and utterly inexperienced, might have had another shot at sympathising with the benighted creature – but it'd prob'ly be no use, because looking deep into Bobby's eyes he'd be forced to acknowledge: this was not the relief of a merely craven man, who, terrified by the wider world, has fought his way back into the system – but the relief of a butchering animal, who, having made his kill, slinks back to the wilds beyond the perimeter fence. Jonathan eats the sandwich moodily. Was there more to be said? Yes, there's always more to be said – and no matter how effective his own intervention, there will be further phone calls and meetings. He may well have to see Gawain again in a quasi-official capacity. It would be too easy for it to end here, definitively – yet it should, because it's Gawain who's turned out to be the butcher after all …

not me. (P'raps I was wrong to call you that . . .) You were right about the other two, though (. . . it prejudiced your idea of yourself – made you rather moody. You never actually did anything that bad so far as I'm aware – not personally . . . Once or twice there was some rough stuff . . . in Manchester, I believe . . .) Jonathan lets Kins *bang on* as he eats the sandwich: he needs to consider the probabilities – has to figure out what the future might hold. The Butcher is perfectly accustomed to applying his superior powers of induction to the future courses of others – this is the very essence of an intelligence officer's expertise, but somehow Jonathan De'Ath has never tried to get a firmer grasp on his own. He stands eating the cheese sandwich, seeing not the perimeter fence through the Perspex window, nor the magnolia-painted wall of the pod, but the cassette tapes, compact and digitally versatile disks, external computer hard disks, photographs and photocopies which constitute his large data-set: an electroencephalogram of his and Gawain's entire relationship, registering the rise and fall of their passion for one another. He's kept it all sealed up in a clunky-old attaché case. He moves it every few months or so – the case will spend a while on the topmost shelf of a cash-and-carry in Southall, then get deposited in a safe belonging to, say, a solicitor in Nantwich. If you were to put him on the spot, Jonathan would probably justify this wild irresponsibility in the following way: Living, as I've done, a life in the shadows, with no emotional security whatsoever, I've cleaved to this relationship above all others – so I needed a record of it, had to be able to hear his voice, read his words, even look at wonky seeseeteevee footage of him entering and leaving some of our rendezvous. It's been my touchstone. But now? Now the large data-set is too hot to handle – it will need to be extracted from the storage cupboard of a corner shop in south Lambeth and . . . destroyed. Yes, destroyed. Jonathan sees himself, a serial killer manqué, his victims obsolete three-and-a-half-inch compact floppy disks which would require an equally obsolete computer to read the files they contain, each of which consists of cut-and-pasted gruff and cliché-ridden sentiments: *I thought love would last forever, I was wrong . . .* Jonathan suspects his violent feelings towards Gawain may well moderate, but for now he cannot picture the Fighting Ram's woolly head without just-swallowed processed cheese *repeating on me . . . pour away the ocean and sweep up the wood*. He turns his attention to the holdall he bought in Kuwait City. At the time he was simply playing for it. (Playing for what?) For time, idiot! He hadn't wanted to arrive at Shaibah in full daylight and face sliminess of all sorts – possibly some political interference. There was this ulterior objective – and also winding up his close protection detail, who, no doubt, are very handy when it comes to dishing it out, but, as he'd suspected, were *quite unable to take it.* Jonathan dishes out the items he requested from the spotty Bangladeshi in his sisal-smelling shop on to the shiny bed cover: a khaki boiler suit, a heavy-duty rubberised torch, a canvas water bag, a pair of workman's steel-toe-cap boots and a folding entrenching tool. True, this is the sort of stuff he might've smuggled across a land border in the glory days – there'd been a certain erotic frisson to be gained from helping a petrified Czech cipher clerk into a boiler suit . . . *fingers fiddling at the belt, straying . . .* The pod's atmosphere is at once foetid and astringent . . . *a locker-room ambience*. He'd known Amir was dead before he left London – so the exfiltration kit had been nothing but wishful thinking . . . *reverse all the clocks*: let the poor man acquire yet more strength and vitality from every blow he was dealt, and so rise up from the concrete floor of whichever dark chamber in which the Rams had penned him. To die like this! Jonathan sobs aloud, at the hands of sheepily ignorant dole-queue-dodgers! Oh, Amir! Slowly, and with infinite weariness, Jonathan begins to undress: first the immaculately tailored midnight-blue, mixed silk-and-linen suit – next the Territorials' tie, then the handmade Charvet shirt with the three-button barrel cuffs. He stands naked for a moment, in his Zimmerli briefs and purple handmade cotton socks. Wo Regenten wohl regieren, he sings in a light, clear baritone – and is answered from within by (Kann man Ruh und Frieden spüren), sung in deeper, muddier tones. His hand strays down over his prominent ribs and flat belly, Und was Länder glücklich macht, he breathes as his hand cups the liquid heaviness of his genitals – only to be answered by (Wo Regenten wohl regieren). But there's nothing stirring in this mixed merino and long-stemmed cotton pouch, no quivering *erlang-lang-langet*. The methyphenidate and the military fuck-up have joined forces *and rendered me impotent . . .* (Not surprised, old fellow – booze alone'll do it to you, and there're those pep pills you're always popping . . .) It's true, Jonathan speaks aloud, that our relationship is at long last getting on to a better hippety-hoppety footing, but that doesn't mean I have to TAKE ANY SHIT FROM YOU! The remainder of his preparations are carried out in silence, apart from the wheezing of the air con', and the buzzing of a single insomniac fly . . . *or should it be . . . spy. Stay Safe Always Drive Defensively* reads the sign beside the rat-run which leads to the base's main gate. Jonathan stands in the shadow of the sandbagged walls, hidden by the camouflage netting draped from one of the flanking sangars. He's considered all the possibilities that lie in wait . . . *for history is a pattern of timeless moments*, the vast majority of which can tell you nothing, *being dead . . .* Now he settles on this, the most probable timeline: he'll walk, quite casually, up to the Paras who're on drag-stag, flash his diplomatic passport and EssEyeEss eyedee, wait for them to scare up Gerry Fox, speak to him on the phone, then pass it back to the quite-likely *jug-eared* grunt. Would they be amazed by this sight: a middle-aged British man wearing a khaki boiler suit and workman's boots, and carrying a holdall, ducking casually under the first barrier, the second – and the third, sketchily saluting the lads in the last sangar, then wandering off into the greying Iraqi dawn? Yes, yes – they would. Just as the upstanding men – and a few women – of the armed forces community would probably be amazed when, in a few months' time, the Prime Minister pays them a surprise visit and stands – the smile on his face off-centre, since it's been pinned on him . . . *by the invisible hand of the market.* Yes, yes – the military would pose alongside him for public consumption, and their own uneven smiles might perhaps remain for a while after TeeBee's had gone, but soon enough *they, too, will fade . . .* Just as Jonathan would've faded into the grey dawn six months earlier. And where would he go, this antisocial ghost? Why, to the airport of course – that's where he'd go: to Basra International Airport – designated by his military brethren as an air point of disembarkation – where he'd wangle his way on to the next transport out of Iraq. (And how would he get there?) He'd walk there, old man – walk there because you'll be with him, and, dutiful son that he is, he knows there's nothing his father would like more than to stretch your legs and your lips simultaneously. (But, I say, Johnny, won't it be terribly dangerous out there – and moreover quite a slog?) P'raps, but Jonathan would need the slog – need as well the detoxifying sweat which would, soon after he strode off into the slate-grey sands, burst from his every pore, because even in late spring the daily temperature never falls *much below thirty degrees* . . . He'd stride past the hulks of burnt-out technicals, left there pour encourager les autres, and at the point where the bumpy and tank-tracked tarmac divides – one way leading to Basra, the other to the aypod – he'd take the left fork. But then, after perhaps half an hour of footing along the roadway, the crepuscular light *negativing* the isolated buildings and shaggy palms, he'd almost certainly walk off into the desert – after all, risk is one thing, foolhardiness quite another. When Jonathan was far enough away from the road to be indistinguishable from . . . *a wonky-donkey*, he'd get out the phone, which all this time would've been *Sam-sunging softly against my hip* . . . Barry might've expected him to use any one of its enhanced functions to report the serendipitous (For him and his fellow-conspirators, maybe!) debacle to the Chief – but all Jonathan would require of this expensively and cleverly modified piece of technology is that it give him a compass bearing. At his own home, in Vauxhall, he would've already sat at his computer: a blade of anodised-black aluminium which is

implanted *quivering* in the black-metal surface of his bare desk.
Sat there, the buzz fizzing through him as he laboriously examined
the off-road route between Shaibah Logistics Base and the aypod,
using a combination of satellite photography obtained by the Firm,
and rather more homely Google Earth images . . . *see the little boys,
caught on the pedal-operated irrigator, and flattened across a ditch by the
eye-in-the-sky? People who search for Saddam Hussein also search for
Osama bin Laden* . . . (Why, why would you've done that, Johnny?)
Oh, Jonathan might well say, I'd a hunch we'd need to exfiltrate
ourselves with some subtlety . . . Then he'd strike out towards a
horizon against which would be outlined just a few of the thousands
of defunct oil derricks scattered across the Iraqi oil fields. And Kins,
observing these anodised-black hammer-shapes, quivering in the
convection waves which would already be rising, might well make
some allusion to Mjölnir, and how an analogy might be drawn
between the thunder and lightning of the Wagnerian cosmos and
the shock and awe of the Coalition's assault on Saddam's regime.
And, as his son made for the horizon, in all likelihood Kins would
continue in the same vein, speaking gently but insistently about the
nature of good and evil, and how he'd known things were seriously
awry from *pretty early on* . . . never personally lending any credence
at all to the government's claims. (Forty-five minutes!) he'd expos-
tulate in Jonathan's heating head (I couldn't drive into Hemel and
buy a few groceries in forty-five minutes), and, although his son
would try to explain that readying long-range artillery shells with
biological or chemical warheads to be fired might well take considerably less time, Kins's dander would be up by then: he'd seize

the opportunity afforded by this unprecedented situation to *speak his mind*. (It might help you, Johnny, to really understand the true consequences of all these epochal events if you just tried sympathising with the fate of a single man.) And, although Jonathan would very likely try coming back at him, dragging up Kins's homophobia, his adultery and his failure to protect his sons from their mother's abuses, this would be a mistake – for when it comes to the logical nit-picking humans term "ethics", who's more likely to be a past master: a middle-aged homosexual spy with a dependency on prescription drugs or a dead sociology lecturer? (Hypocrisy is what you're accusing me of, Johnny) would be a familiar enough line of argument from Peter De'Ath (But you ain't comparing like with like, old boy. There's a distinction to be drawn here between cultural values – which do indeed change with time and place – and core morality, which, while perhaps not reducible to some fundamental aspect either of people or of the world, nonetheless remains remarkably consistent over time – think of the Golden Rule and the Categorical Imperative . . .). And because this is *the beginning of a beautiful friendship*, with the two of them stumbling over low and gritty dunes, the sun coming up behind casting their shadows far out *into the future* . . . Jonathan De'Ath wouldn't lose his temper, not even if Kins strayed *beyond his remit* and began chiding him over Kelly. (You can easily imagine the sort of man he was, Jonathan – dutiful, compassionate. He belonged to that odd religion, didn't he?) Baha'i. (That's the one – and what do they believe in?) The One True God and the spiritual unity of humankind (Sounds jolly familiar to me, Johnny . . .). By now – an hour or so after waving goodbye to the grunts in their sangar, Jonathan could well be tiring (I do wish you'd see a doctor about this pep pill thing of yours . . .), and so would likely take another pill . . . or two. The multicoloured and ever mutating vortices into which human movement can be transformed by the application of motion-capture might make of these minuscule actions – the popping out of pills from blisters of plastic-and-foil – a thrilling arabesque, but Jonathan would think of Kelly, propped up against his tree on Harrowdown Hill, his trusty penknife open beside him, his fingers busily and efficiently at work . . . *poppety-pop goes the weasel*. Think of Kelly and his lonely trudge into an unredeemable future – one Jonathan might be seen as having assisted in summoning. Yes, he'd think of this, and, hearkening to the wild dogs barking at the rising sun, he'd pick up the holdall and press on. (I don't think I ever told you much about my experiences during the war . . .) Is the sort of sally to be expected from Kins, who'd be carried along as well – while his son would very likely think back to the baby, held aloft at Terminal Four security, speculating that *everyone deserves his own particular mind-child* . . . Barking dogs and mounting heat – the maddening split-second substitutions of flies for grit: one moment here, the next . . . *not*, and then the pathetic realisation, old leg-man that he is, that Jonathan has forgotten the canvas water bag, in which case all at once the scarred desert will be at one with his *sore throat* . . . His resignation would be in John's inbox before the Herc landed at Brize Norton – he'd've at least made this much use of Barry's Samsung, surely? And then what? Sitting in the transport's booming fuselage, listening to the squaddies clustered round a laptop, who'd be watching one of the video montages it's become de rigueur for your comrades to compile when you finish your tour: footage of the grunt footing it down dusty alleys, bracing a few rag heads, rattling around in an aypeesee and playing videogames – all to the accompaniment of the tinny-synthy chorusing *you're outta touch – you're outta time . . .* Kins might well want to discuss this unprecedented phenomenon – the mediatised twisting of reality implied by this: young men returning from a war zone, where they mostly pretended to be in another war zone, watching video footage of themselves simulating combat. In his clumsy, slightly crass but for all that *well-meaning* way, Kins would quite possibly use the opportunity to begin speaking a little about his time in Lincoln-shire, at Collow Abbey Farm (Not far from Bardney, where I believe you've taken to putting up with your, ah . . . friend). Jonathan, however, while not wishing to offend his father, would nonetheless ignore him and instead ponder this new future on which he's embarked: True, superannuated spooks who've specialised in hum' int' aren't exactly at a premium in today's highly sophisticated, computerised workplace, but *the show must go on . . .* (You could do worse than think about a move into academia) is the sort of thing his father might well suggest (after all, you were a full scholar . . .), but all bets would, *pretty bloody obviously*, be off, the second Sally put her cards on the table. At the Wolseley, almost certainly – a favoured haunt of the old Butcher, who'd be greeted fawningly by the maître d' and led straight to it. The old Butcher believed, not unreasonably, that Wolseley's Art Nouveau decor and lacquered-red-and-gold colour scheme complemented his own soigné appearance: the heavy gold signet ring on his crooked pinky *Brandy Alexanders, I think today, Rafael* . . . the hint of crimson silk in the lining of his jacket, the whiff of brimstone *on his breath* . . . However, that was the Butcher that was – Jonathan would fidget with the menu, order something bland . . . *and eggy*, sit there sickened to the core of his fastidious being by Sally's *break-out!* A line of pimples across her pretty forehead – at least seven or ten, of which four have bilious-yellow heads: the insignia, he'd realise soon enough, of *a long-haired general, who's just received her two-up promotion* . . . Jonathan would've seen the Chief and Personnel already. In fact, the procedures associated with the retirement of a senior EssEyeEss intelligence officer are, you'd probably be right in assuming, blandly routine. You'd probably be right in assuming the blandly routine procedures the retirement of a senior EssEyeEss intelligence officer are associated with. Routine procedures – bland ones – are in fact associated with senior intelligence officers' retirement from the EssEyeEss. (A full-salary pension, I believe – there remains at least some value attached to public service . . .) Although not, in your case, to the most public service of all. (I was a very young man – just twenty. My call-up papers came the week I went up to the varsity. You can have no idea of the agonies I went through that week before applying to go before the tribunal.) But surely it's as Maeve has always said: you can't've been unaware of the existential threat Nazi Germany represented . . . (There's knowing and not knowing, Johnny – you more than anyone should be aware of that.) There's also passing the egg-test, and failing it: when – in an onrush of tears and nervous hilarity – Jonathan learnt from Sally he was to

become a father, how might he react to this blow, so long anticipated it was effectively preceded by its own impact? Put one hand
on the next rung of the cold climbing-frame *p'raps . . . and smell
old dried blood . . .* Sally would smile at him through her tears of
contentment – and Jonathan would wonder if he'd ever be able to
touch her again, while inside he'd be falling, tumbling down
through the open framework of his now exposed life: Bong! Bong!
Bong! Even as the far from exemplary sentences were, quite possibly,
being handed down on Cooley, Kenyon and Larkin for the prisoner
abuse they perpetrated at Camp Bread Basket in two thousand and
three. What could Gary Bartlam have been thinking of when he
left the films to be developed at his local branch of Snappy Snaps?
Presumably, he'd a vague notion the process was fully automated,
and no human operative would see the pictures of Iraqi detainees
lying in pools of their own urine, or being shifted about the place on
the prongs of a forklift truck – *so much discounted stock.* The Butcher
was the sort of amoral cynic who'd've very likely arraigned Bartlam
for the crime of computer illiteracy, rather than being an accessory
to prisoner-abuse. For, if you wanted to capture and conceal such
fugitive images, the digital realm is where you would logically go.
Remember the seven pees – Jonathan does. He learnt them during
his youthful days as a yomping stab – and, although by the time we
could theoretically place him in the Wolseley, hearing the news
of his impending paternity, he'd've long since stopped attending
regular refresher courses and training weekends, he'd remain, nonetheless . . . *on the reserve.* That prior planning and preparation
prevents piss-poor performance is a given for the ageing roué – quite

as much as the juvenescent soldier – who must *go equipped* with Tadalafil or Sildenafil in jelly or pill form. The irony that the tumescence which led to this procreative act had been artificially induced wouldn't be lost on him – nor would the fact that he'd become heavily dependent on fluoxetine, initially prescribed for him by the medic at VeeBeeArr, with a view to ameliorating the depression many active men face upon retirement. Why ironic? Because Jonathan De'Ath, being the man he might've been, would know that selective serotonin reuptake inhibitors are – according to the meta-analyses of trials big pharmaceutical companies would rather didn't receive too much media attention – little more than nocebos: drugs which convince you of their organic efficacy by psychically bamboozling you with their side-effects: *Mmm . . . I feel shit – therefore I must also be feeling . . . happy.* The eggs Florentine Jonathan would've ordered could lie there in their little dish – so much expensive vomit, quite likely anticipating the smelly mess of coldly coping Lincolnshire mornings. Because if you're already prepared to subject yourself to this counter-intuition: *Mmm . . . I feel shit – therefore I must also be feeling . . . happy,* running a bed-and-breakfast might well seem a good idea, especially one in a fairly remote village, the owners of which – having rather failed to make a go of it, but being a bit older, and with pensions of their own – might be considering a move to . . . Marbella. Jonathan wouldn't regret leaving the Firm too much – couldn't conceivably miss the mandatory Friday-evening drinks, when the officers and their auxiliaries gathered on the terrace of VeeBeeArr to congratulate themselves on the control they surreptitiously exercised over the world's events, even as they lost control of their own minds – and eventually, in the case of some older and younger officers alike, their bladders. No, he wouldn't miss this – any more than he'd miss the innumerable intrigues and the ceaseless undertones of secret conversations, which, towards the end of his career, were being entirely digitised – such that loyalty became a function of the impossibility of factoring prime numbers rather than a chap's inner decency and manifest stiff upper lip. We might picture the Butcher, as was, transforming in these latter years into *mein poofy host* . . . since it'd be perfectly obvious to these Lincolnshire hicks . . . *who wears the trousers*. We might see him on any given day, spooning the jam and marmalade from kilo-size catering tins into the small aluminium dishes they place on the guests' tables. We can conceive of him taking orders: so many eggs – so much bacon. He might well lick the stub of a pencil before bending his shell-like attentively to these decent-looking men and their equally decent-looking wives, for, coming from where they do, with their vague air of being ex-forces or something of that ilk, the De'Aths would attract a certain sort of clientele to Wagon Wheels: couples in their late fifties and early sixties – on the verge of retirement but still active, the sort of folk for whom sensible is a positive virtue, *in shoes and people alike*. Yes, the ageing couples would clear out for the day – garlanded with binoculars, to tramp the sodden fields and perhaps visit the little church of Goltho, all that's left of the medieval village which struggled to survive here for centuries, farming the marginally productive land, before succumbing to economic forces *beyond their control*. If you were to go to Bardney, and stay there, you might – in the decade, say, between two thousand and five and two thousand and fifteen – be able to raise a child relatively unaffected by developments in the outside world. A task that'd be rendered easier because this remote area of northern Lincolnshire could well remain throughout these years under-penetrated by the burgeoning network of high-speed fibre-optic broadband – and something of a desert for mobile-phone reception as well. Of course, it'd be pretty rough on poor little Gawain De'Ath – which is what, conceivably, Jonathan would insist on for the child's name: his quid pro quo for *having to have the fucking sprog in the first place!* (Now, now, old boy – there's no call for such histrionics. Such a bore.) It'd be pretty rough at the village school, where Gawain would be the only real bumpkin – since all the rest would have eyePads and eyePhones, and computers at home. But then, at least as Gawain got older, he might be able to explain to such little friends as he did have that his dad hates the news and won't have so much as the *local rag* in the house. This despite the fact that – as he'd undoubtedly tell young Gawain – Jonathan had worked in regional journalism himself before taking early retirement. Yes, Bardney would be good place to raise a child – and to shelter from the fallout of the successive government enquiries which would, one assumes, necessarily follow the debacle of Britain's involvement in the occupation of Iraq. (I still think it's pretty iffy – calling your son after your boyfriend. A boyfriend you seem to've pretty comprehensively rejected.) I can understand that, Dad – but I am pretty iffy. And I think, were I to have a child under such circumstances, giving him the name Gawain would be an aide-memoire. (Explain?) It'd help me to remember to protect both him – and his namesake. The Iraqis could be bought off – Amir's people as well. No one on the Brit side would wish to look too deeply into the murky business of prisoner and detainee abuse – as Lieutenant-Colonel Thomas would likely put it: they'd be keen to *kick it into the long grass* . . . (Well, I think they should investigate all the allegations properly – it's an absolute scandal, yet another way in which this entire illegal conflict has perverted the British people's moral natures, so they've accepted – quite uncritically – such atrocities as torture and arbitrary detention. Your colleagues were responsible for sending dissidents back to oppressive regimes we wished to kowtow to – which makes them both accessories to torture and . . . murder.) For my colleagues I've some sympathy, Dad – the Great Game is always difficult to play: the pieces either animated or unwieldly – scampering away across the chequerboard or suckered fanatically to their squares. For Gawain and his troopers I've more sympathy still (But yet he disgusts you?). Now, yes, he disgusts me – by the way, what d'you think that thing is over there, behind the concrete structure with the sort of pylon on top of it? (Looks like just another one of those oil derricks our brave boys managed to destroy while helping these benighted people reconstruct their nation.) C'mon, Dad, you're being, hic! facetious. (What's that you're swigging from, Johnny – have you got a bottle?) It's whisky, Dad – your preferred tipple, I believe . . . You always loved the heat of a shot gouging down your sad and scraggy red neck, now didn't you . . . (There's no need to be insulting, Johnny – where the devil did you get hold of it?) In Kuwait City, at the Hilton. I popped in to see an old colleague . . . (Well, you might offer a fellow a wee dram, since he's along for the ride.) Don't fret, old man – you'll get yours in good time: it'll just sort of seep into you – you wait. (And justice for the abused Iraqis and their families – that'll just seep into them, will it?) Jonathan De'Ath, would, one assumes, keep plodding on as the sun rose in the shocked sky. Every few hundred metres he'd either find or create sufficient shadow to check the *erlang-lang-langet* on the Samsung to ensure he was maintaining the right bearing for the aypod – then he'd plod on, bickering with his father's imago: The more flagrant malefactors – those whose crimes were, say, exposed at Snappy Snaps – they will, of course, be punished – but war is, Dad, by definition a brutal business. What can you expect of nineteen-year-old boys, mostly from disadvantaged backgrounds, called upon to police a failed state in which every adult male goes equipped with an automatic rifle? (Go on! Give us a top-up, there's a good chap – anyone would think you were enforcing a two-can-bloody-rule!) It was just another of the Narcissist-in-Chief's fantasies that the Universal Declaration of Human Rights could somehow be applied on the battlefield and to its aftermath – utterly delusional: there can be no rights where there's no authority capable of enforcing them. But, hic! anyway, given the way their political masters dumped them in it, I think they acquitted themselves well enough – and certainly behaved with far less brutality than almost any other army would in similar circumstances. (But there were abuses, you can't deny that?) I can't – and I don't seek to: I wish only to protect the reputation of a man I loved for nigh on thirteen years – a decent if weak man. A man who would, I wager, when he realises his lover has managed to cover

571

up his and his men's, ah . . . indiscretions, quietly resign his commission and slip sideways into civilian life. (I can't imagine it'll be easy for him to find a job that'll both satisfy him and allow him to exercise his skills as a tank commander.) Ye-es . . . that would be a tall order, but really Gawain's abilities have always been more pastoral than martial, don't you think? (So . . . what, the priesthood?) Don't be bloody ridiculous, Kins – not everyone longs to decay away in Little Piddling-in-the-Marsh with your beloved cleresy. No, I see him doing something people-centred, which also allows him to maintain his splendid physique. (He could set up a keep-fit business of some sort – there's quite a premium placed on an ex-military man. At Lancing all our peetee instructors were old soldiers . . .) No, no . . . No, no . . . Muttering away to himself, Jonathan would carry on north-north-west . . . That's not it at all – can't see him in his combat keks and khaki T-shirt, pacing up and down in front of a lot of dismounted desk jockeys, bellowing at 'em to give him at least one, if not twenty . . . Jonathan would see instead: Colonel Thomas installed as the manager of a leisure centre on the outskirts of a small Welsh town – although he hopes Gawain would never be so crass as to style himself so in civilian life. No, but the Rams' regimental blazer probably would be worn, with a plastic name-badge reading MANAGER on its lapel – he'd look the very picture of a modern major-general, having received this two-down demotion: picture him inserting the letters into the peg-board: FTNESS CLASS FOR MUMS AND TODDLERS IN THE SMALL POOL – then clap his hand to his forehead, having spotted the typo: he'd have to un-peg them all and *start again* . . . And Jonathan De'Ath, over in Bardney, how'd he be getting on at around this time? He and Sally would've taken on a couple of local school-leavers to help with things around their own establishment – which might be doing well enough, if, that is, Jonathan were to stabilise his prescription drug habit, acquire a small appetite and the skills required to satisfy larger ones. Don't forget the meat order from Lancaster's! is the sort of thing Sally De'Ath might shout down from their bedroom on a cold winter morning. To which Jonathan almost certainly would reply, I phoned it through yesterday, love, they'll have it ready for me . . . If they were dependent on the business for income, it'd be a parlous state of affairs, but they aren't – and being the sort of people they are – with the invitation to the Lord Lieutenant's Christmas Eve drinks party quite likely prominently displayed on the mantelpiece in their snug little sitting room – they'd prob'ly have *a bit of money behind them.* Make sure they've put in the sausages and bacon, dear! Sally De'Ath could conceivably call down. And it seems fair to assume, given her age and class proclivities, that, despite having had just the one, she'd've put on rather a lot of weight. She wouldn't exactly be fat, though – the riding would keep her firm, if solid. Because she'd definitely ride, Sally – and encourage little Gawain to do so as well. That the unwanted son he'd named for his discarded cavalryman lover would turn out to be a natural horseman might just be one of the consummate ironies which sustained Jonathan above the thick and oily sump of depression which would – after nigh on a decade pretending to be a heterosexual in the provinces – be ever threatening to engulf him. Be that as it may, kindness would remain his watchword – kindness could be the much needed catholicon, a balm to all the moral queasiness which would affect him at times, such that looking out of the window of the attic bedroom, where he might well keep some mementoes from his Service days in an old suitcase, he'd see the sodden acres of mud rising and falling, and would stagger a little on the tipping deck of social convention. And it might well be then – Sally and Gawain having set out for the stables – as he struggled to remember how many guests there'd be for dinner that evening, and how many had requested duck breasts and how many chicken, that the phone would ring in the vestibule. He'd probably take his time going to answer it – why hurry, when it's probably only going to be the Vicar, asking him if he'd consider reading a passage from Luke at the carol service . . . *And it came to pass in those days, that a decree went out from Caesar Augustus that all the world should be taxed* . . . The voice on the end of the line would possibly be disguised in some way – either with one of the distorting scramblers available commercially or with some more clandestine equipment – but probably not: in any case, if the caller were to have a verbal tic of some sort – such as palilalia – whereby a phrase is repeated immediately, either in its entirety or partially . . . *either in its entirety or partially*, then Jonathan could be forgiven for thinking there was something wrong with the phone. I have your large data-set, is a plausibly threatening entrée – especially when immediately followed by: I have your large data-set . . . we need to agree the terms under which I'm prepared to return it to you in its entirety . . . we need to agree the terms under which I'm prepared to return it to you in its entirety . . . Given how much Jonathan De'Ath has harped on the brilliance of his memory, it might be far-fetched to suppose that during all the kerfuffle of the move from Lambeth to Bardney, not only had the retrieval of this cache of love tokens and its relocation been . . . *fluffed*, but that he'd also *forgotten all about it*. But he had. (I've always rather thought you made too much of your photographic memory, Johnny – it seemed to me more of a parlour trick than anything else. Granted, Sirbert was formidable at mental arithmetic – and I daresay you inherited a little of his facility – but the almost mystical construction you've placed on all this . . . Well, it's the sort of nonsense you'd expect from a drug-addled hippy . . .) Memory loss can indeed be a side-effect of prolonged use – both of methyphenidate and selective serotonin reuptake inhibitors such as Fluoxetine. If that use is combined with steady – albeit not excessive – alcohol consumption, the effects could be considerably worse. Sitting in the vestibule of *Dunbuggerin'* with the *dog-and-bone* pressed against his *shell-like*, Jonathan could well experience a dreadful little turn. All the horse brasses and brass bed warmers they acquired from John and Brian along with the business – and which Sally prevails upon the school-leavers she pays five quid an hour to polish – could well begin to spin round his weary head. He might think back to the last trip he'd made to Mohandra Patel's corner shop on the South Lambeth Road, where he'd picked up the heavy old nineteen eighties attaché case, with its two hasp combination locks. If there were such a man as Mohandra Patel – a mustachioed, morose and paradoxically smiley-faced refugee from Kenyatta's Kenya, who'd been prepared for trifling sums to do a number of small jobs over the years for the man he knows as Dave Kendrick – then, Well, I hope you're enjoying it out there in the sticks, Dave, is the sort of thing he could be expected to say as he took "Dave's" twenty-pound note and slipped it into the back pocket of his jeans, followed by: You going next door for some tapas? Sitting in Rebato's, a rustically themed Spanish restaurant next door to South Lambeth News, Jonathan De'Ath could surely be forgiven for having a large glass of Rioja, followed by several more. This would, after all, be his swansong (Kann man Ruh und Frieden spüren, eh, Johnny), and, while his father had in point of fact had appalling taste in music – preferring to hum numbers from Showboat rather than attempt the sublimities of Bach – at this decisive juncture in his life, he might well hear Kins's familiar tones fluting in his inner-ear (Wo ein guter Hirte wacht!), and so reflect on his twenty years of herding sheeple for the secret state. He might meditate on the increasingly febrile nature of that state, which, as he sits beneath the darkly varnished decorative wagon wheel bolted to the artisan-roughened white plaster, revolves around his clotting head, making of Rebato's . . . *a home from what'll never be my home.* The unavowed special EssEyeEss electronic surveillance unit inside British Telecom's aluminium-faced office block, Keybridge House – the secret tunnels which do indeed vermiculate the entire subsurface of Vauxhall Cross, and which EssEyeEss employees use to transit between VeeBeeArr and Tintagel House, the nondescript adjoining office block. The back passages and dirty alleyways linking together the Hoist, the Vauxhall Tavern and Chariots Roman Spa – amongst a number of other local, gay-friendly businesses – these had been his stomping ground, and now he'd be *stomping away* . . . If only he'd visualised this: a dark-haired man in his mid forties, running a little to fat, but still upstanding – elegant, even – walking purposefully towards Stockwell tube station, a chunky outdated attaché case firmly gripped in his right hand. But after the full bottle of wine he'd probably've drunk, Jonathan – in common with his former colleagues – wouldn't be capable of visualising anything, so might well simply abandon the case on the quarry-tiled floor and wander off in the other direction. Back towards the river for a valedictory look at the deceptive bend, before tottering to King's Cross in time to catch the two-forty-eight to Lincoln. (If it's running – the engineering works on the East Coast line are a national disgrace. But anyway, Johnny, I find your scenario pretty implausible: tipsy or not, you'd hardly be likely to forget this cache of love letters and associated material – a secret trove you'd been assiduously concealing for years.) He'd be demob unhappy, Jonathan would – freed from secret service and secret affair alike. *Hakuna matata* . . . is reassurance easily offered when all that bothers your life-partner, and the mother of your son and heir, is that you remember: *We've eight for dinner tonight* . . . He would've remembered that – remembered the steaks – fillet and rump, too. Ensured the presence in the cardboard box of the ham-hock pies Lancaster's do so well – not forgotten white and black pudding, some veal, too. Most important: he'd never neglect the beef – because they'd have to have the beef. If Jonathan didn't bring home the beef *we've both had it* . . . He'd realise he'd lost the large data-set on the train, as it was shuttling across the fenlands. Quite possibly he'd be staring blankly out of the window at the blank sky and the bare ground, and the very many piggeries, when he'd recall, say, that Javier had offered him a complimentary portion of pigs' livers wrapped in bacon. A titbit he'd enjoyed so much, he'd quite forgotten about the attaché case. No panic. He'd get on the blower as soon as he reached Bardney – but no, Javier had less memory of Mister Kendrick's case than Mister Kendrick did. As lunchtime had gone on, the restaurant might've got busier – there could've been a party in from a nearby office, celebrating some hysterical compliance clerk's engagement, or health-and-safety officer's charity freefall. It'd be a falling sensation Jonathan De'Ath would experience listening to the breathy voice of *my blackmailer* . . . He'd think back to the first few days after the loss of the large data-set, when – being analytic to a fault – with each successive hour that passed the tension would in all likelihood have eased out of him. Scrawled postcards and notes, unlabelled Dictaphone cassettes and compact floppy disks which would be entirely obsolete, unless you happened to be the sort of hoarder who also hung on to contemporaneous computer equipment – none of it could've appeared particularly interesting to an opportunistic thief, who'd quite likely dump it all in the nearest skip, take the attaché case over to Electric Avenue and flog it to one of the bric-à-brac stall-holders . . . *might've got a fiver for it.* Yes, after a week or so, Jonathan De'Ath could well have begun to relax a little. With each subsequent month he'd likely relax a great deal more. Years could well go by during which the whole immense and ulterior realm of cyber-surveillance would come, kicking and screaming into the light – yet with each one, Jonathan De'Ath would think himself and Gawain more secure. Bradley Manning and Wikileaks – Snowden, and his revelations – the slow welling up of oily calumny from the gutter press concerning Camp Breadbasket – the ongoing enquiries into Baha Mousa's death and the fallout from the Battle of Danny Boy: all were the result of agents in the field not observing a basic protocol and *writing things down . . . Careless whispers* cost lives: Yes, he'd kept the things his son's namesake had written down and spoken – but their love hadn't lasted forever, and by now that post-card of the Pontcysyllte Aqueduct – together with scores of other scenic views – would've entirely rotted away in the Essex landfill site the contents of the notional skip had, almost certainly, been added to. The important thing is that the bulk of this data had been in analogue forms. Yes, yes, of course there were a few digital traces, cirrus scratches on the surface of the ever swelling cloud, but there was no conceivable way that any entity – biological, machine or cybernetic – could have gathered together the call logs from North Yorkshire public phone booths in the mid-to-late nineteen nineties, or the records of Bradford internet cafés during a similar period, let alone correlated them with the movements of two given individuals – no matter that those individuals were themselves instruments of the state. *I have your large data-set . . . we need to agree the terms under which I'm prepared to return it to you in its entirety . . . we need to agree the terms under which I'm prepared to return it to you in its entirety . . .* To which a reasonable response might be: How the fuck d'you know I called it my large data-set? To which the breathy blow-back could well be: You wrote it on a file card, Mister De'Ath, that you sellotaped to one of the folders full of letters, postcards and photographs – some of which are quite candid, naked shots of a largish, blondish man who I've obviously been able to identify as Gawain Thomas, formerly a Lieutenant-Colonel in the British Army, now the manager of a leisure centre in Crickhowell . . . *now the manager of a leisure centre in Crickhowell* . . . Others of which are of nothing more significant than white plastic garden chairs . . . *nothing more significant than white plastic garden chairs* . . . Are you working for a state or non-state entity? could well be the sort of question his former lover would've described as bone – but, sensing this was no ordinary contact, Jonathan might nonetheless ask it, and be rewarded with: I assure you, Mister De'Ath, I am entirely freelance – what I do, if you'll forgive a little spiritual pride, is for the benefit of all humanity, and I do it entirely on my own cognisance . . . *and I do it entirely on my own cognisance* . . . Given the aspiration – both breathiness and blackmailing-wise – Jonathan might be forgiven at this point for picturing his interlocutor as a man wearing a Nehru jacket with a white Persian cat in his lap, who sits in the splendid reclusion of his futuristic secret lair: a great cavern full of helmeted men in uniform jumpsuits, carved out of a solid block of Polystyrene and sunk deep beneath the ocean. Forgiven, because in all likelihood his interlocutor would be a man wearing a Nehru jacket – albeit one he picked up for three quid in the Mind charity shop on the Kilburn High Road – and sitting with a cat on his lap, albeit a moulting, tabby one with an unimaginative name such as . . . Scratchy. How might Ben White-house-Busner – bulky by name, bulky by nature – have acquired Jonathan De'Ath's large data-set? (Well . . . in any number of ways, I s'pose. I mean, it does strike me – although I'm no expert on the matter – that the computerised retrieval of data, the use of global positioning satellites for navigation and even the integration of utilities and retail distribution systems into the internet, has rather bamboozled us all, such that we regard the persistence of material objects in the real world as really rather, um . . . well . . . spooky.) Yes, indeed – spooky. The world is big – humans and objects are, for the most part, small. But both humans and objects persist in time, and the stereotyped and repetitive behaviour of the former – who will persist in doing the same things over and over, again *annagain* – means that the coincidence of the two can quite often be statistically correlated so as to produce at least rule-of-thumb predictions – how else do you imagine economists make a living? (I really don't see what you're driving at here, Johnny – and, by-the-by, how d'you know about Wikileaks and Bradley Manning and Edward Snowden, if it's two thousand and five and we're walking the fifteen sad, scraggy red-faced miles from Shaibah Logistics Base to the British Army's air point of disembarkation?) Shut the fuck-up, old man! How do you know anything at all – given you're dead! Jonathan bellows, words plucked from his mouth by hot zephyrs and . . . *shredded.* Yet he'd also scarcely believe he was walking through the sad, scraggy red-faced desert of southern Iraq, if it weren't for the creak and bang of tumbledown corrugated-iron pens, and the baaing of oblong-eyed goats and oil-blackened sheep – weren't for all this, and also for the breathy voice which speaks to him from out of a possible future, and straight into his inner-ear: My objective isn't pecuniary, Mister De'Ath – and nor do I have any connection with the world of espionage . . . *and nor do I have any connection with the world of espionage* . . . Really? he speaks aloud, just as he imagines he'd speak if it were ten years in the future, and the ship of state was – titularly at least – helmed by an ex-political researcher with a face as smoothly pink as a baby's just-smacked bottom. Plus ça change, plus c'est la même chose isn't the sort of hackneyed phrase we'd expect a man of Jonathan De'Ath's stripe to come up with, but he might well come out with it, sat in the Bardney bed and breakfast he's been penned up in this past decade, watching the world turn only at a remove. – Really? – Yes, really, Mister De'Ath, although you'll've realised my cyber-capabilities must be considerable simply to have located you in your retirement . . . *simply to have located you in your retirement* . . . Yes, he'd've been sitting there this past decade, hope-lessly strung out and mired deep in the stasis horrors he always feared more than any possible violence or exposure. Sat there, shrunken, watching his son grow. Would he love little Gawain? Might the perverse choice of name engender or hinder his affections? And could the fact that Gawain took after his mother result in this sort of freakishness: that as Sally takes him to the Lincoln Equestrian Centre for larger and larger jodhpurs, little Gawain comes uncannily to resemble his namesake rather than his father: blond-haired, round-hipped – his expression, when caught in repose, sweetly baffled? On his infrequent trips up to town – which he'd undertake to see his accountant or solicitor, one imagines, rather than his tailor, the mundanities associated with his entail preoccupying Jonathan rather more now than the profundities of his shirt-tails – he'd walk through town from King's Cross. He can be pictured, can he not, stopping by the railings of a park on a misty October evening, and hearkening to the sound of a former Sergeant in the Green Jackets – a man he'd probably fail to recognise – shout at twenty or so podgy office workers, Orlright! C'mon, you lot – drop and give me twenty, and keep your backs straight! Seeing the slogan printed on the T-shirts that cover those arched backs might give the man formerly known as the Butcher pause for thought: British Military Fitness, mm, *I've skinned that hump* . . . Yes, skinned it – which is why, years after the event, he's having to dig deep and provide plenty of *help for cowards* . . . We can hypothesise that in the decade following the death of Amir Ali al-Jabbar at Camp Val in Ali al-Garbi, Maysan Governorate, southern Iraq, a number of similar cases might come to light – it's not a matter of allocating blame or a human rights-induced hissy-fit, simply a statistical likelihood that . . . *shit happens*. A case might be brought in two thousand and five concerning the shootings of five Iraqi civilians by British soldiers in Basra in two thousand and three, and the death of a sixth in detention. By two thousand and ten the number of allegations of unlawful killing and other abuses made against the British Army might well have ballooned. A turn of phrase Jonathan De'Ath – ruefully recalling the unkind words he spoke in the mortuary tent in the Divisional Detention Facility at Shaibah Logistics Base – might well find a touch ironic, recalling how eager the *dear silly old sausage* . . . had been to see . . . *the balloon go up*. With pushing one hundred and fifty cases of unlawful killing and serious abuse registered with the British courts, lawyers involved in taking depositions and examining evidence might be expected to find that the various techniques used in the so-called harshing of Iraqi detainees – techniques which, in one case at least, would've been proven to've led directly to the man's death – had also been applied across no fewer than, say, fourteen British military facilities – leading to the fairly plausible claim that this represented systemic abuse rather than *a few bad apples* . . . an idiom much hated, it can be predicted, by a man who'd previously delighted in a rather less fructuous sobriquet: And the steaks – don't forget the steaks, Jonathan! Listening to the distance sough down the line – looking at the small print of Caistor Sheep Fair circa nineteen hundred, which Sally might well have hung above the telephone table, Jonathan could be forgiven, surely, for despairing of this provisional reality he's stumbled into. What the fuck d'you have on me, or him – you can say right now, or simply get off the line and leave me in peace! is what any normal person would say, and, inasmuch as Jonathan De'Ath would by then be a householder, a parent and *mein poofy host*, it seems reasonable to accord him this prospective normality. To which Ben Whitehouse-Busner – sat in his Kilburn bedroom, with its impressive computing power and large quantities of stuff – would, no doubt, respond accordingly: The audio- and videotapes of the tactical questioning sessions at Camp Val that took place in May two thousand and five while your ex-lover was in command have, following my acquisition of your large data-set, also come into my hands . . . also come into my hands . . . Oh, yes. They have. *Then fa-ancies flee a-way . . . I'll care not what men sa-ay . . . I'll labour night and day, To be a . . .* Walking is what a man might well do under such circumstances – especially if he'd a golden retriever called something like . . . dunno – is Bonnie plausible? Yes, Bonnie: a silkily supple dog, always smarming round legs and fence posts, then dashing across the flooded furrows of winter fields. *Come along, now, Bonnie! Heel, girl . . . Morning, Jonathan . . . Morning, Margaret . . . Dreadful weather, I'm glad to see you're wrapped up well . . . Oh, I'm only going for a short walk, Margaret – over to Collow Abbey Farm . . .* He'd think often – one assumes – of his father (Hard not to, really, if he's somehow completely internalised his notion of my psyche), think especially of the long walk Kins had taken during the late summer of nineteen forty, down through the Lincolnshire fens, then the woodlands and fields of Hertfordshire and Cambridgeshire before eventually reaching London – travelling by night, and arriving on September the seventh, just in time to witness the onset of the second mass raid. He'd told Jonathan that as he gained the summit of Pole Hill, the Luftwaffe's bombers were circling over the East End, round and round, again *annagain – like a chair-o-plane.* This image of his father, as a latter-day John Wesley, undertaking a strange un-evangelical progress – avoiding the towns, preaching not the Good News, but keeping to himself the shameful truth of his conscientious cowardice – would quite possibly strike deep with eldest son. Out there in the fields, where a crow lies dead in a cattle trough – and the seepage from a silage hopper stains a stony path a toxic green. Or so they say. *Bonnie! Bon-nie! Bonnie!!* Look at her run – you've that good a visual imagination, surely? If not, you could feed the words golden retriever running into the search bar and soon enough be seeing those gambolling legs and the fur . . . fly. Out there in the beet fields, stopping by a five-bar gate and leaning over it to examine the lumps of old masonry sunken in the turf – evidence of long-gone sanctity. Then undoing, quite possibly, your leather belt and slipping your corduroy trousers down off your hips. You wouldn't be wearing expensive Swiss underwear any more – Sally'd buy you sensible boxer shorts in packs of five from EmmandEss. You'd tuck your tiny nubbin of a Ritalin-shrunk penis back between your legs and scream out to the dead crow – and the live pigeons which in all likelihood would wheel about the winter field – I'm Chelsea Manning! Holding the pose for as long as you dared: shirt, pullover and jacket hoiked up – pants and trousers down, as a small child does when . . . *pissing in public*: I'm Chelsea Manning! screamed with all the well-paid conviction of Issur Danielovitch playing Kirk Douglas screaming, I am Spartacus! Back at Church Lane, at the bed and breakfast known as Wagon Wheels, Jonathan might give Bonnie a rubdown, since she'd quite likely be drenched – both from the dew and because she probably leapt into duck pond. That's retrievers for you. The old, thatched house would be called Wagon Wheels not because of the ancient association with the land, and the high farm carts they used to bring the harvest in with thereabouts – but because these were the premises of a garden-ornament business that limped along for a few seasons in the late nineteen eighties, before succumbing to the harsh economic reality. It's conceivable. Just as the soil in this part of north Lincs was too infertile for profitable agriculture in the era before artificially synthesised fertilisers, so it might've been unable to sustain much garden ornamentation in the days before . . . *teak decking*, a phrase that conceivably could've stayed with Jonathan

De'Ath for a decade and a half now – and might well be echoing in his head, back in the vestibule, sitting once more beneath the print of Caistor Sheep Market as he waits to be rung again by the man who's acquired his large data-set – a man with a breathy voice, who repeats the last few words of every phrase . . . *the last few words of every phrase* – a quirk, which in the few minutes Jonathan has already spoken to him, would've struck him, n'est-ce pas, as having an uncanny resonance with his own (internal voice? I hardly think so, Johnny – what I have to say may often seem like old hat to you, but I hardly think it's a mere echo of your own thoughts), which fall away to the carpet, to the skirting board, to the phone line pinned to that skirting board, to the Dulux Timeless silk emulsion with which that phone line has been coated – and to the small blobs and flecks of that Dulux Timeless silk emulsion, which, if you were to peer very closely, you'd find trapped in the carpet's pile . . . *you just can't get the staff nowadays.* Yes, his thoughts might well fall away, but his awareness would remain – his awareness of his former lover's baffled expression as he removes the soiled towels from the hopper in the men's changing room. Strictly speaking, a menial task far outside his remit as Facilities Manager, but Bryn is off sick. Possibly. This awareness is a faint, violet-coloured luminescence – you'd never spot it, unless you knew what to look for – and where to look. When the phone – an ugly contemporary appliance, the receiver of which could well be propped up in a sort of socket or cradle – eventually trilled into life, he'd answer it with this query – or one very like it – already prepared: What do you want? To which Ben Whitehouse-Busner's reply not could, or might, or possibly, or likely, or probably, but very definitely would be: I'd like to add you to my professional network . . . *I'd like to add you to my professional network* . . . If there were any other way of doing this, without being quite so manipulative, I'd privilege it . . . *I'd privilege it* . . . a way of putting this Ben knows will pique the curiosity of the spook he's managed to hook . . . *on the end of my line.* Have you met Ben Whitehouse-Busner? No, really, have you made his acquaintance? The question needs to be posed, because he doesn't, as such, have any social life. We could go further: he doesn't, as such, have any social existence, preferring to tread water a little bit abaft as the ship of time sails on . . . *as the ship of time sails on* . . . You may've seen a film about an autistic savant calculating betting odds in fractions of a second – or read in some fiction or other descriptions of a lummox of an autist: pen-portraits of him at different ages, and viewed from different perspectives – his mother's, his grandfather's – and wondered at the egregiousness of their stereotyping . . . *and wondered at the egregiousness of their stereotyping* . . . No, no! Don't worry – I'm not going to repeat everything: on the contrary, I'm going to explain about the, frankly, wilful palilalia and much else besides – including the reason my much loved father refers to me as Mandinkulus, and believes me to be his deep-penetration agent. But first: some toast. Some prefer nettles . . . the title in Japanese can be phonetically transcribed as, tade kuu mushi mo sukizuki, and written in Japanese characters as 蓼食う虫も好き好き – pretty, aren't they? And a logo-syllabary points the way, does it not, to our own emergent universal grammar of sounds, images and text? A language that, when piped through fibre-optic cabling and hosed on to the inside of the screen, bears a strong resemblance to this, arguably the most complex writing system ever evolved by human-kind. Young Westerners who become obsessed by Japanese culture – usually as a result of their absorption into the comical milieus of anime and manga – are called weeaboos, which sounds as derisorily silly to the Japanese ear as it does to the occidental one. Each to their own – which is the English equivalent of the Japanese idiom Tanizaki used for his novel's title. One that's translated literally as Water-pepper-eating Bugs Will Eat It Willingly, but was rendered by the eminent Japanologist Edward Seidensticker as Some Prefer Nettles – and what I prefer is the heel of a standard Hovis loaf. Always have preferred it – always will. Each to their own. A style of life is determined, I feel, as much by these sorts of decisions as by any major aesthetic – let alone ethical – ones. The choice of food-stuffs and their preparation: the application of the butter, smoothing it out to the edges of the bread as an expert plasterer plies his hawk. The great advantage of the heel is that it has a sort of inbuilt rim, such that, once the jam or marmalade has been added to the butter, the by now semi-liquid morass can be sufficiently contained to enable me to raise the heel to my mouth and take a large bite without its disintegrating into crumbs, buttery blobs and spatters of confiture – which would upset Milla. Here she is, leaning into me for a brief hug as she squeezes past to half fill from the kitchen tap an old mug which came to us, two Easters ago, with a Cadbury's Milk Tray egg laid in it . . . Aaaah! Your mother's smell, they say, you never forget – on your death bed it'll return to you, performa-tively: odours of breast milk, lipstick and Avon Skin So Soft each playing their unfaithful role, betraying your high, loving purpose with this low and fatal blow. Getting angry ain't my style – nor am I the empathy-free zone beloved of dualistic psychologists, who autists believe incapable of realising the inner worlds of others. What inner world? What others? Pah! I embrace Milla – she snuffles into the hollow of my shoulder – I hear the faint spatter of water drops on the lino at our feet. I know she's sublimated her love for me into her romantic obsession with the orfer these past five years, and, being Marshall's child quite as much as I am Mandinkulus, I understand the message: her sexual feelings are now so much digital scrim, leaving her nestling in my arms . . . *Mm-hm, just having a bit of toast – dunno, round five, maybe?* She frees herself, turns, heads back out of the kitchen and along the corridor to the front room. Freed, she turns – along the corridor she heads, from the kitchen to the front room. To the front room she heads, freed from the kitchen along the corridor. Chiasmus mirrors semantically the rubric of public key encryption used for secure internet communication: consider each clause as a prime number, multiply them together and not even the most powerful quantum computer conceivable could factor out *what it really means* . . . The actions of humans – wildly unpredictable despite their instinctual basis – are like this. Milla and Gramps have always seen me as stimming – whereas from my vantage it's them who're ever attempting to manage chaos by doing the same senseless things over and over *again annagain* . . . It's dusty throughout the flat – and greasy in the food-preparation areas. In the bathroom the war-without-end between sepsis and antisepsis has long since been fought to a standstill in trenches of congealed soap topped off by the barbed wire of our shed hair. Yet for me it's still being fought. I once heard a woman on the radio – a theoretical physicist, I assume – explain how we might perceive Einstein's relativistic universe by analogy with the way a picture plane of only two dimensions can nonetheless represent three. I've no idea whether this is a good analogy, having been able to see four dimensions in two, three or however many – or few – others, for . . . well, predictably *for as long as I can recall* . . . I love Camilla aged twenty-two, holding the little ball of balling Benness to her heavy, milk-filled breasts – I can still taste the brassiness of the buttons on her bib-and-braces, which I suck upon frenziedly as she struggles to unbutton. I love Camilla aged twenty-six, clasping a bigger ball of threshing Benness in her aching arms – and I love Camilla aged thirty-four, driving our clapped-out old Vauxhall along Kilburn High Road, while I hunker down in the back seat, counting up the raindrops speckling the car windows and multiplying the total by the number of times the bald old tyres revolve between the junction with Cricklewood Road and the turn-off for home – because that's what the flat is: home. Profoundly so. I mention the prodigious calculating only in passing – I've no wish to contribute to egregious stereotyping. Not that it matters much, but . . . well, I can admit it: I've allocated a name to every prime number up to and beyond the largest currently identified by human computing – which, if you're not exactly au courant with such matters, I can tell you has seventeen million, four hundred and twenty-five thousand, one hundred and seventy digits. I call it Meat Blanket. I can factor this prime as easily as a teenage girl does French knitting. I see them in the afternoon – I'm seeing them in the afternoon, standing at Camilla's window . . . *Oh, whatever you fancy – I had a pizza earlier* . . . the curtains bunched in one of my hands. See them coming down the road on their way home from Saint Augustine's Church-of-England High School. Funny a craze like that should come back again: weaving plastic thongs into multicoloured plaits . . . Camilla says they did it when she was a girl – I'd like to've done it with her, but, while the capacity of humans to slide along their own timelines is far greater than they realise, it's not possible to slide along just anyone else's. For that to be possible you need the forensics: the notes on torn scraps of spiral-bound pads, and the letters beautifully calligraphed on Smythson's bordered writing paper – the emails composed on the tedious certainty of the Outlook Express grid, then cut and pasted into standard word-processing files and saved on compact floppy disks. I'm seeing the French knitters on the brilliant winter afternoon, standing at Camilla's window – seeing them float along the road in a succession of billowy after-images – their beautiful youth frozen in space and time, À l'ombre des jeunes filles en fleurs . . . Everything was tightly and chronologically packed into Secret Sam's attaché case when I picked it up at the stall on Brixton Station Road. *Jesus! That's heavy, mate . . . I know, young man – couldn't get the bleedin' thing open – you'd think those old combination locks'd be easy-peasy to crack . . . We-ell, some of 'em are, but these are proper Manifoils – same kind as spooks use . . . You seem to know your stuff – anyway, there it is: a locked-up-tight attaché case – sorta lucky dip, really. Yours for twenty shitters . . . I'll give you a tenner – if I break the locks opening it, it'll be worthless ... Oh, for fuck's sake! I can't make enough at the moment to buy a fucking bog roll – now you're gouging me! Maybe – maybe not, like you say: it's a lucky dip ... C'mon, young feller – be reasonable. I can see you're innerested – giss fifteen ...* At the bottom were passwords for anonymous email and cloud accounts, all written out in a mock-crocodile-skin-covered notebook, also from Smythson's. The upper middle classes are as restricted in their shopping for luxury brands as the underclass are in our lucky dip of discounted stock at Lidl: *Oh, no, Mum – not Black Forest-fucking gateau again! Sorry, Ben – but that's what was on offer ... again.* It would, of course, be ridiculous to imagine I'd been search-ing for something of this sort ever since I began collecting stuff in earnest – because, of course, I already knew it was there, lying beside a pair of red, polka-dotted Doc Martens and ... a pink oboe. The human distinction between events which are determined and those adjudged contingent evaporates from this perspective – while the minute variation between the official Pikachu figurine and a knock-off one manufactured in Hong Kong remains as acute as it was, is and always will be. I admit it: I am a little bit of a chameleon – what does Gawain's Uncle Rodney say? There's a soupçon of the peacock in all army officers à mon avis – while Jonathan would concede there's a soupçon of the sociopath in all good intelligence officers. Carefully rearchiving his large data-set, I've come, if not exactly to admire him, at any rate to feel at home with him – his waspishness, his snobbery and his exaggerated sense of his own pantomimic ... *Milla – you've a bit of cottage cheese on your chin ... here ... let me – I have a hanky ...* derring-do. Inevitably,

I've found myself incorporating elements of his persona into mine, since, having no social existence of my own beyond interactions with eBay vendors and flea-marketers, I tend to use whichever mask is lying to hand. In this respect, the rise in autism diagnoses during my lifetime has played to my advantage, providing me with an off-the-peg set of characteristics – the stimming, the food-pickiness, the eye-avoidance, the palilalia – with which to play, in turn, to the gallery of my family. Not to Milla, though – oh, Milla! From this angle your dear face looms: a Mount Rushmore of a woman you are to me, in all your maternal splendour. I grab for your breast – you grab for my hand . . . *Oh, Ben! C'mon – Be-en* . . . and place your own behind my head, cupping it, drawing it closer . . . and closer . . . *Oh* . . . until my mouth suckers on . . . *Ben!* to your nipple . . . *chupp-chupp-chupp-chupp* . . . a steady, rhythmic siphoning off of these: a casein homologous to bovine beta-casein, alpha-lactalbumin, lactoferrin, immunoglobulin, lysozyme and serum albumin – the essential amino-acid pattern which is optimal for human infants . . . *chupp-chupp-chupp-chupp* . . . She manages somehow – bless her – to read a few lines of the newspaper folded on the table next to the ashtray in which my father's hand-rolled cigarette smoulders, and, saint though Milla undoubtedly is, she cannot help experiencing relief – bordering on Schadenfreude – that we're in Camberwell rather than Khorramabad, where dead children, plastic-wrapped, are the subjects of the grainy black-and-white photograph which accompanies the article. They're being laid out in an improvised mortuary, bodged up from breeze-blocks. The Zagora Mountains have always been an earthquake zone – always will be, but Missus Thatcher will only resign as PeeEmm once, and Milla, who has a little badge on her bib 'n' braces with the familiar tight-bouffant hairdo silhouetted on it, and the slogan, DITCH THE BITCH, is happy enough today, only to be mildly revolted when . . . *chupp-chupp-chupp-chupp-mmmm-hn'!* I let her nipple flubber from my sharp-edged little gums, rise bow-legged – the way toddlers do – and, looking back down into the plastic arena, call her attention to . . . *that great big poo what I done, Mummy . . . Oh, Ben, darling . . . Oh, where're the Wet Ones . . .* One thing you can say for the realm of the senses is that there's no irony in them whatsoever – no saying what is not in order to call others' attention to what manifestly is: which is that we're not in on the cosmic joke forever being whispered behind humanity's back concerning the terms of our own existence. We know each other for who we really are – Milla and I. We were raped in a rape field – has she told you? And a traumatic experience like that will force some together – while others fly apart. Gramps, bless him, has never been able to remove his pathologising spectacles and see me for who I truly am – and at least that, I can concede, is truly ironic – given he's spent his entire career critiquing the validity of just these diagnostic criteria, together with the aetiologies and outcomes they wilfully predict. Anosognosia is the sort of word old Zack likes to drop into conversations – he understands his colleagues have it, just not he himself . . . *there's still half that pizza in the fridge, Milla – I'll have that . . .* He certainly doesn't get that almost all of humanity is afflicted with a chronic form of anosognosia – he, Milla, my many and variously fucked-up uncles and aunts and cousins are all labouring under the same overarching

595

delusion. Not Mark, though . . . *think I'll go and see Dad tomorrow, Mum . . . I'll give you a tenner to get him some tobacco . . .* A patient diagnosed as schizophrenic by the celebrated psychoanalyst Winnicott once said to him – or so he reports: We schizophrenics say and do a lot of stuff that's unimportant and then we mix important things in with it to see if the doctor cares enough to see and feel them . . . Extraordinary to think Mark's been mixing all this important stuff into what he says for decades now, but his own father – his own father! – an eminent psychiatrist with thousands of hours of exposure – hasn't understood a word of it. We should be charitable to dear old Gramps, though – especially now he's sundowning. It won't be long before the neurofibrillary tangles and the amyloid plaques completely choke his cerebrum. The French idiom is revenons à nos moutons – and we can see Zack trying desperately to revenir to his, but the one he most needs to pen is out there on the hillside, baaing pitifully, caught up in a neurofibrillary tangle – caught the way a poor little lambkin might be in the tangle of barbed wire atop a tumbledown drystone wall somewhere in the Ettrick Forest. Click-click . . . Baa-baaa . . . click-click . . . the stonechat dips its head, flicks its wings, clicks out its nominative destiny and flies away, but Zack's little lambkin of a thought remains hopelessly trapped – will I be able to free him in time? It's late January and I phone Jonathan again: *I'd like to add you to my professional network . . . – Either you're insane, Ben, or you're a very misguided young man . . . – I'm twenty-seven, Jonathan – as you presumably already know – because you've contacted your former colleagues, and with their assistance put a trace on this line . . . – You're asking me? – No,*

Jonathan – it's a statement of fact . . . – Aren't you at all worried, Ben?
This is a matter of state security: you're asking me to give you back-door
access to the entire EssEyeEss and GeeSeeAitchQueue internet – and
through that to the YouEss systems as well. By comparison, hacking into
the Pentagon would be a mere misdemeanour. I've only to put one call in
and there'd be a Swat team landing a bloody helicopter in Mowbray
Road in minutes . . . – I'm well aware of that, Jonathan – but what
we really have here is a Mexican stand-off, isn't it? It'll take time –
I realise that. I'll need to talk him round – convince him of the
case intellectually, to a degree – but also establish an emotional
relationship with him. Despite the inversion of our ages, I need him
to feel that I'm a wiser, older brother. His father used to sing: Put
your head on my shoulder, you need someone who's older . . . But he
was no Billy Eckstine – mine's the shoulder Jonathan needs to put
his head on, so I can give him a little rub with my velvet glove.
Really, my evolving relationship with him is exactly the same as the
ones he used to cultivate with his various assets and field agents.
Jonathan's no fool – he gets it. It's a Tuesday afternoon in February
and Dad and I are in the chain coffee outlet at Heath Hospital.
Dad hasn't been on a section for a while – but if he gets a
little wiggy they'll let him come and stay on the acute ward at Heath
for a few days, really out of respect for Gramps, who, whatever his
other failings, was always a supportive colleague. Dad's going
on . . . *positional ataraxy – take it up, then drop it much harder so*
it crackimup twice – once in the fons, once down the box part . . . about
the repositioning of the transuranic galvinator, which needs to be
brought into Mercury's orbit so that its beam will connect to all

human consciousnesses simultaneously, drawing every single individual on the planet into a vast neural net . . . *interleaved with
plates of burlap and grease tied to the back of a milk floating on my
bread, Benny dearest* . . . Winnicott's patient was right – but it'd be a
profound mistake to think the important things Mark says are
metaphors of some kind: there's nothing less analogic than the
world of the schizophrenic, in which everything is entirely and
absolutely like . . . itself. You try living with captious voices bickering
in your brain, which get louder and louder throughout the day, until
their very howls are the fact of your own dissolution streaming,
screaming through the cosmos. Oh, I'm forgetting – you already do:
for that's the fundamental insight afforded by schizophrenese –
that's the thing my father and all the other street soliloquisers are
ever attempting to tell us anosognosics: we share their malaise – we,
too, labour under the compelling delusion there's a voice being
piped into our brain which orders us to do this, go there, feel that
and think whatever it pleases us to think. You call it your self – the
hectoring voice which calls you. Wouldn't you like to be rid of it –
to take a pill or recite a prayer, spin the wheel again and again, and
have the silence descend on you, fine as silica, silky as sand – or
Bonnie's coat . . . *Bonnie! Bo-nnie!* Gramps used to think – when he
could still think clearly about such things – that Mark's transuranic
galvinator bore some resemblance to James Tilly Matthews's Air
Loom – the celebrated subject of the first known case study of a
paranoid schizophrenic. Confined to Bedlam in the first decades
of the nineteenth century, Matthews wrote painstaking technical
descriptions of this strange contrivance, which, when operated by

malevolent agents, skilled in the science of pneumatic chemistry, emitted the rays that tangled up his mind: inducing the magnetic fields which paralysed his circulatory system and concentrated the blood in his brain. Matthews thought there were numerous agents scattered throughout London, all of them equipped with air looms – all under the control of a mysterious figure known as Bill, or the King, who identified their targets. And, as I say: there's nothing in the least bit metaphoric about schizophrenese – unlike, say, classical Persian ... *Out beyond ideas of wrongdoing and right-doing there is a field. I'll meet you there. When the soul lies down in that grass, the world is too full to talk about* ... It's perhaps difficult for us to understand quite how central the poetry of Jelal al-Din Mohammed Rumi was to Iranians of Amir Ali al-Jabbar's genera-tion – he once told Jonathan he couldn't remember ever visiting the mosque as a child, whereas classical Persian was taught daily, and mostly through the medium of the works of Shams Tabrizi. Shams, the Sufi mystic, threw Rumi's scholarly works into a pool of water ... *Bonnie! Bon-nie! Oh, you ridiculous hound!* but when the poet retrieved them they were still dry. I bet you wish the same would be true of your mobile phone, once you fished it out of the Virgin Trains toilet you'd dropped it in. In the nineteen sixties the Iranian economy was growing, and, while left-wing intellectuals and the religiously orthodox might have resented the Pahlavi dynasty, for Amir: It was a beautiful childhood, Jonathan – a beautiful childhood. We had so much freedom in Khorramabad – we could go where we pleased ... Any adult would look out for any child, so our parents never worried about us. It was, truly, as if we were one big family. Going to the bakery in the morning for my own family's bread, I'd use my pocket money to buy two or three extra of the flat sangak loaves. Shater Ali was a very imposing figure and a well-educated man – to be a baker was considered a high-status occupation. He'd flip the loaves from the paddle on to the counter and I'd stand there picking out the pebbles and bits of gravel. For you see, the sangak was baked in this way so as to – as we say in Farsi – take the sweat off it. I remember Shater Ali, if we ever were cheeky enough to say the sangak was too sweaty, would either quote the anecdote about Rumi and Shams, or else blame the English – because in Khorramabad, in the Zagora Mountains of Iran, in the nineteen sixties, the English – and in particular the English spies – were responsible for everything that was bad or went wrong. It rains on your birthday? Blame the English. A fox got into the hen house? Blame the English. You have a pimple on the end of your nose? The English have somehow managed to interfere with your skin . . . And here I am, Jonathan, sitting in a car in a Viennese back street, *telling it all to an English spy* . . . Oh, yes, Amir, telling it all to an English spy equipped with an air loom in the form of a short-burst veeaitcheff transceiver, one which – when he's transmitting – he often hides inside a stuffed Garfield the Cat, suckered to the rear window of whichever work car he's driving. As for little Amir: Walking back to the family home with the sangak loaves piled up on a sheet of newspaper, my friends would swoop on me from all directions – hungry little birds. And they'd peck-peck-chat-chat away at the warm flatbread with their fingers – that's why I'd usually try to buy a couple extra, because otherwise I'd reach home empty-handed . . . It's April, and Milla's going out to see her old friend Mona, which makes her happy: *You seem happy, Mum . . .* is the sort of thing I might say to her, as I peck-peck-chat-chat at her cheek. But I don't want to blow my cover. I'm not too worried about her coming into my room when I'm phoning Jonathan – but she might . . . *there's some of the leftover chilli-stuff in the back of the fridge, or I've left a fiver on the kitchen table if you want to get a take-away . . .* Audio take is what Jonathan's colleagues used to call it – but audio takeaway would be better: *I can see that you're serious, Ben . . .* – *You left enough material in the attaché case, Jonathan, for me to begin building a fairly convincing picture of your activities over the years – and I'm an imaginative person . . .* – *So let me get this perfectly clear, Ben: you want me to give you access to these secret networks, so you can effect some sort of . . .* But no – don't say it yet, Jonathan. You're being premature, not the sort of démarche someone as diplomatic as you should ever attempt. One thing the agent known as Mandinkulus has never suffered from is being premature: I know how to bide my time, since time is what I'm in full and vacant possession of – what does it matter if I spend an hour or five, seeing if I can pile these seven knock-off wind-up Pikachu figurines up on top of each other over and over, again *annagain* . . . The repetition can be aggravating – anguishing, too. The important thing is it's only the first reiteration that truly matters: the reflection, the double, the go-round of the frayed, saliva-damp end of one of the tooth-picks Milla buys for me in boxes of five thousand from a catering supplies wholesaler in Dollis Hill. I thought you should know: after Colossus, the wartime computer built by the boffins at Bletchley

Park was broken up, its spare parts were cannibalised to build the new trunk-call phone exchange – also in Dollis Hill, and not far from my grandfather's old therapeutic community. I think you should also know about the Sage system, which went online in the year that Gramps lost his virginity. Tush, now – he's had few secrets from me for years now, whatever he believes. Sage was a great leap forward for human connectivity: since its inception in the counting houses of Sumer, the unicameral mind has held sway, with its psychotic delusions of personhood and autonomy. The hive mind has been activated only by religious enthusiasm or pathological hysteria. Or both. But with Sage humankind began its return to the cybernetic Eden where traditional peoples reside – a dappled, forested and lush place, where the mind that directs the arm which holds the axe that strikes the tree that's rooted in the earth which is nourished by the rain that's Mother Earth's own circulatory system knows full well they're all one and the same thinking, feeling thing, world without end. Oh, poor Milla! Poor Mother Earth has suffered the torment of those bloody scars – the endometriotic lesions left by opencast mining, nuclear-testing and all the rest of the slashing and burning those unmindful and self-harming axes have done. Oh, poor Mother Milla, whose very sensitivity and self-awareness are themselves the new nerves grown by these lesions. A tool, a technology – what it's called hardly matters: the Sage system, with its network of early-warning radar stations, could render incoming Soviet ballistic missiles as so many swarming white dots, which appeared on the screens of bunker-bound technicians. Equipped with light guns, they'd shoot these white dots to fix the eyeseebeeemms' positions for the computers calculating their trajectories. Sound familiar? Sage represented the most ambitious attempt yet to create a working model of the world manipulable from and by the seat of my pants – which wear out, believe me, what with the industrial levels of sitting down I do. It's May, and the general election has come and gone. There's an atmosphere of nothing much throughout the land and I phone Jonathan again. Milla's out shopping and I've just showered, so I speak to him while I'm walking up and down the hall, towelling myself – winding the towel into a thick cord with which I strop my moobs . . . *You've contacted some of your friends, then? – You know I have . . . – But strictly on the quiet – just as a favour to you? – You know that as well . . . – There's a stilted, Pinteresque quality to these exchanges, I feel . . . – I thought you never went out . . . – I can read . . .* He wants to get it straight – a ridiculous expression, since what he desires is to understand the whole compass of my ceaselessly stimming delusion. And I reach out to him in his fastness of beet fields: Yes, it's true, I believe a sort of wormhole could be opened up by connecting an ordinary, internet-enabled phone to the secure secret internet of the five eyes. The Sage system has burgeoned and extended over the past six decades to the point where the content of the world wide web, and the covert intelligence gathering programmes of the major Western powers, taken in sum, constitute a map of the entire collective human being, which is itself the same size as that human being. If Jonathan will only provide me with the codes necessary to open that wormhole . . . Why, the entire system can be turned off and turned on again – resetting human consciousness, so that henceforth we will always be together. Never alone. Of course, I explain to him, as I rub the tightly wound towel around my genitals, releasing small puffs of skin particles from my pubic hair . . . *fine as silica – Bonnie! Bo-nnie! Disturbing the dust on a bowl of rose leaves* . . . This is where it's all been leading: the myriad iterations of human mediatisation – the faces staring at the screens, the fingers pressing the keys, pushing the buttons and toggling the levers: the boldly going extension of cyber-space by autists and their avatars, who've no need to look into another's eyes to know what they're thinking, because in this new-old realm space and thought are entirely coextensive. Yes, I tell Jonathan . . . *Yes, I tell Jonathan* . . . the palilalia is indeed a spell, summoning through ceaseless stimming repetition this new-old reality. Yes, I tell Jonathan – if you're a computer-gamer as skilled as I, equipped with an internet connection of sufficient speed to avoid any lag at all, then you can perceive the transition between individual frames . . . *the transition between individual frames* . . . And since human visual perception consists in comparing the twenty-two stills our retinas register each second so as to extrapolate the trajectories of moving objects – what is the individual subject, save for a Sage system with ideas above its workstation? *with ideas above its workstation?* Okay – I know I promised there'd be no repetitions, but they do provide . . . emphasis. The confirmation of our camera-like status, and our ability to make our own chronophotographs, comes with the so-called wagon-wheel illusion, whereby the spokes of a wagon wheel seem to travel backwards while it travels forward – you're familiar with that, Jona-than? Your own house is called Wagon Wheels, while you were sitting beneath one on the fateful Friday lunchtime when you lost control of your large data-set. Sufferers from some neurological conditions also experience what's called cinematic vision, whereby they retain one of the twenty-two stills for several seconds in their visual field, such that subsequent frames show through, much in the way that successive computer screens show through one another when the system is . . . lagging. Encephalitis lethargica is one of those conditions, and my own grandfather – my dear old Gramps – who tried awakening survivors of the encephalitis lethargica epidemic when he was working at Friern Mental Hospital in the nineteen seventies – managed to capture on film the physical correlate of cinematic vision, which is, of course, the reordering of time itself. Yes! I exult to Jonathan, no longer attempting to hide what's gripped my unfeeling psyche: Yes! I do indeed believe in a binary rapture to come, as the entire system is switched on again and the Meat Blanket bites of all humanity's minds are uploaded to the cloud – the cloud born of war, dark and monsoonal, which, as it absorbs and reconfigures the human being, rises, growing lighter and more radiant. We will have at last attained our home on high – and in so doing will realise it was always right to hand, while down below on the surface, Mother Earth's endometriotic lesions will begin to heal. And yes! I exult to my phoney friend, I am indeed the nerd messiah of this great awakening of human mind, brought on unwittingly by the high-functioning autist-nabobs of the tech industry and the military-industrial complex! It is, I think, the provisional character of this torment that would strike Jonathan most, sitting in the vestibule, under the print of Caistor Sheep

Market. Spring has sprung in north Lincolnshire as well – but, while the jingling of Sally and Gawain as they trot along Church Lane might be as rhythmic as the prose describing it, there'd be no outdoor activities for Jonathan beyond the meat-run to Lancaster's and the daily dog-walk . . . *Bonnie – Bo-nnie!* Not that Ben White-house-Busner would've given him an ultimatum, but for now Jonathan – with the tinny receiver grinding his shell-like, as this psychic turbulence twangs into him – would probably resolve to . . . *string him along.* After all, he's very likely already spoken to Stephen Marshalsea, who of all those on his new-entrant course he's remained closest to – quite possibly because Marshalsea decided fairly early on he wasn't cut out for the lifelong night shift of espionage, so left to take up a job with Hilton Hotels, which, with its world-girdling chain, has often provided the EssEyeEss with convenient cover for agents and informants alike. June comes running down the road with dandelion clocks lifting off from its silky-soft hair into the warm air of suburbia, and the French knitters follow on behind . . . *will you heel, girl! Come here, I say – Bonnie! Bonnie! Oh, confound the animal* . . . I stand behind Milla, who's typing her weekly email to the orfer – a different blend of psychic turbulence, one stirred not shaken: *Y'know, Benny, Gramps is really beginning to lose it, I think Dan and Pat are going to put him in a home . . . – That's a shame, Mum – I thought he wanted to become a sorta Hindu holy man . . . – Obviously that's out of the question, Ben – he can scarcely remember his name . . . – Maybe if there were a place he could go, just for a few days, somewhere he could do a bit of meditation and stuff. It'd calm him down – maybe convince him the whole thing's a bad idea . . . – Yes, but where? – What about Holy Island, Mum – you enjoyed that retreat you went on up there . . . – Funny you should mention it – I was just writing to the orfer about Holy Island. About how being there really helped me to dump a lot of negative thinking . . .* It's a measure, I feel, of my ascendancy in such relationships I do have that both Milla and Gramps refer to the orfer as the orfer – and it's a further indication of my status as a sort of parhelion, or sun dog, lighting up their glassy heavens, that neither of them seems to notice the oddity of what follows. It's late June, and Gramps comes over to Kilburn to pick up the smartphone I've obtained for him. I coax him into learning to use it with a simple stratagem – one of the most useful human motivators there is: narcissism. Look here, Gramps – if we feed your name into this search bar, see what comes up . . . *see what comes up . . .* Who would've thought the old man to have had so much digital presence in him? Me for one – there they all are: videos of him giving keynotes at conferences, academic papers he's written which others have uploaded, third-party accounts of his career and notable figures in his field with whom he's been associated: *People who search for Doctor Zack Busner also search for R D Laing, B F Skinner, Thomas Szasz, Gregory Bateson, etcetera . . . etcetera . . .* It galvanises the sorry old duffer, such that soon enough he's tapping, wiping and tweezering with the best of them. Shortly before he arrived I replaced the phone's sim card with the one from the phone I've been using to call Jonathan. In our last conversation I was a little terse: *I don't think you're taking this business seriously enough – I think you think I'm simply delusional, and that the whole problem is going to go away . . . – I can't do what you ask of me, Ben – if it's money you need I'm happy to provide it. Can't we just meet up and do the handover? I've found what you have to say absolutely fascinating, but I'm pretty much at the end of my tether now . . . – I'm going to take you on tour, Jonathan – I'm going to take you back to where it all began . . .* I wave Gramps off and watch him weave between the French knitters as he makes his way, staff and begging bowl in hand, along the road. Begging bowl and staff in hand, weaving between the French knitters, my avatar makes his way along the road while I wave him off. His schedule is in the phone – and I've made all the arrangements: he'll stay tomorrow night at the Hilton Deansgate in Manchester. I know Jonathan's put an illegal trace on me through a private detective – now he'll be carried along with my avatar: a grinning helium balloon with a clown's face on it, which will bob-bob-bob-along behind Gramps as he zeroes in on the Castlefield Canal. That Jonathan's old colleague Marshalsea is in post as Head of Security at the Hilton brings the whole delicate matrix of this circuit tantalisingly close to completion: it'll only take Marshalsea to realise that what's bothering Jonathan is indeed something which threatens his precious nation's security for him to put the call in to VeeBeeArr. If they then call him back while he thinks he's calling me? Well, I can't be one hundred per cent certain, but I believe this may be sufficient for all the wires to finally connect and the upload to begin. The alternative scenario – which I've already painfully experienced again *annagain* – is for VeeBeeArr to obtain the number of Gramps's smartphone, put a call in – and for him to answer it. In which case I can feel the barrels of the Met's armed response unit already boring into me – so many pump-action shotguns, their side-by-side muzzles . . . *dead eights*, pointing the way to eternity. I can see a tactical response unit pitching up at Wagon Wheels as well – Jonathan fancies himself, I think, as something of a philosophucker, who once saw in the strobe lights of a gay disco the way human mind and vision are interleaved: he turns his aquiline nose one way, I think, and the rabbit's inside the cage – he turns it the other, and hippety-hoppety . . . *the rabbit's free*. As for Gramps, I consider him to be the unwitting discoverer of this epochal capability for transcendence which humanity stands on the brink of acquiring – so it only seems fair it should be his own guilt-ridden and unravelling old psyche that's the first to be absorbed into the great cloud of digi-being. It's quite impossible to imagine what this physical revelation of a psychic truth that's ever been present to him will feel like – quite possibly he'll think he's achieved some sort of enlightenment. If Gramps had've assaulted Isobel McKechnie on the summit of Tinto Hill, then Bobby would've escaped – and upon recapture he might've said those awful things to the young Doctor Busner, terrible and enduring judgements concerning his character, which he'd very likely have repressed for all these years. Obviously not completely repressed – only Fan-Dabi-Dozi-Freudians believe such a nonsense is possible. No, they'd've bumped up to the surface of his consciousness from time to time, informing and reinforming his spurious commitment to an existential approach to mental illness – lurking in his buffo performances, which began when he was a young barefoot doctor at Kingsley Hall, and went down to the basement to help Mary Barnes with her shit-painting – continued at his short-lived therapeutic community in Willesden, and indeed manifested throughout his career in his crouching, so as to look his psychotic patients directly in the eye and tell them *I understand – and I sympathise: believe me, I really do – I understand about* . . . the air loom, or the transuranic generator, or the mobile phone – whatever it is THEY have cunningly adapted so as to enable THEM to mess with your head. He would've sat with Bobby in the cell set aside for the patient-prisoners who weren't allowed open visits, and under the bored yet viciously judgemental eyes of *a ruddy-fucking screw* received this damning estimation: *You're a coward, Doc – a coward to your very marrer, so you are. Ye couldnae help me, and ye'll never be able t'help anyone – your heid's full of nonsense an' blether* . . . *Och, an' pride as well – a fearful pride* . . . and it would go on like that for some time – a pitiless character assassination, delivered in Bobby's reedy, importuning tones. At the end of it, young Doctor Busner wouldn't be simply demoralised – he'd know his life had jumped the rails, such that henceforth everything would have this dreadful air of the conditional, the provisional – and the not quite real. And a few years later, after the Cuban Missile Crisis, when it became known that a Soviet submarine commander had refused Khrushchev's order to fire his nuclear missiles, Zack would, quite likely, have understood this might be what'd happened to him at State Hospital on that October Sunday in nineteen hundred and sixty-two: his entire life had been pushed into the realm of the possible and the probable – such that nothing about it would ever be definite. Which is why he might find himself floating back up into consciousness on the three-eighteen service to Ardrossan Harbour from Glasgow

Central with little clear memory of how he got there – not just proximately, but unable to clearly identify the pattern of moments that, linked together, could've produced any such eventuality. The vigorous but elderly Scotswoman sitting opposite him could well appear completely bald to begin with. Then, as Busner gains more awareness, he might think – because people do think such things, critiquing their own visual epiphenomena: the sun dogs which howl in the corners of their brilliant vision – that this image of her pinched and pious face is being downloaded on to his mind-screen, which is why there's a certain amount of show-through – in this case of the antimacassar behind her head, with its logo's enjambment of Scot and Rail. But, becoming more alert, Busner could very well be forced to recognise that yes, he's sitting with Simon and Ann in a group of four seats, and that opposite them is indeed an elderly Scots Buddhist nun, in full dark robes, her head completely shaven, wearing bifocals and telling the beads of her rosary, as a ScotRail steward comes along the rocking carriage pushing a tea trolley. Simon'd prob'ly say something like, Are you going to Holy Island, your Reverence . . .? 'cause he's no fool, really – and, while almost certainly mentally defective now, for years he's understood perfectly well how to be *of good report* . . . The Buddhist nun would be, one imagines, stern but not dismissive – despite the fact that Simon, having slept rough last night, would certainly smell. After all, it ill behoves any mendicant to look down on another. She'd tell their little group she would indeed be taking the ferry over to Brodick on Arran with them – and that from there, there'd be a bus connection to the little village of Lamlash, where the boat would arrive to take them over to Holy Island. But that, no, she wouldn't be part of the three-day course on mindfulness the three of them had been enrolled on by Doctor Busner's daughter-in-law – because, in all likelihood, she'd have garnered the name and status of the wild-looking, white-haired man wearing the bilious tweed suit, who looks to be in his late seventies, still hale, if a little bit confused – rather, she'd be decamping pretty rapidly to the far side of the island, where there are a number of secluded meditation huts, in one of which she's intending to spend several months of reclusion, listening to the gulls' screeching, the hawks' piping and the fighting of the feral Shetland ponies – whose battles for masculine supremacy quite often result in fatalities on the rocks below. A great shame – especially given that, since Holy Island was acquired in the nineteen nineties by the Buddhists of the Samye Ling Monastery in Dumfriesshire, there's been a concerted programme to make this a haven of biodiversity, teeming with native species, rather than a *killing field* . . . No doubt, the elderly Scots Buddhist nun wouldn't be averse to continuing on this theme – averse, neither, to conversation itself, of which she would very soon have a complete and utter dearth. However, the contemporary world being the way it is, the strong likelihood is that her interlocutor's mobile phone would at that very moment begin to ring insistently – although ringing, she'd surely testily remark, is hardly the right word for the tinny tunefulness it'd exhibit as it knick-knacks into life, and plays right through the numerical rondo for a full minute before Doctor Busner manages to locate the device and hit REJECT CALL. In the slightly stunned atmosphere which always follows a forgettable incident of this sort – the inversion of public space, such that the entire world is reduced to eight feet by three feet, the precise dimensions of the old Kay-eight and Kay-six telephone boxes designed by Giles Gilbert Scott, whose own father was responsible for the rather more expansive and luxurious appointments of the Foreign and Commonwealth Office – the nun, wishing to extend an olive branch to this humiliated and confused elderly man, could well recall Pete Seeger's version of the nursery rhyme, which was released as a single in the late nineteen fifties. She might also remember seeing a film of him playing it on television – his long neck angled strangely, the expression on his eternally boyish face strained as he knick-knacked his way through the tediously ordinal nonsense verses . . . *Aye, but ye ken wha' a paddywhack is, now don't ye, Doc? Ye ken it's the cord wa' holds the poor wee sheep's heid up – if ye cut it, the animal cannae raise his heid again.* To which the elderly Doctor Busner – who, like many afflicted with dementia, finds the distant past readily to hand, while the present forever eludes his grasp – might reply that the version he had in mind when he chose the ringtone was in point of fact being sung by a hundred or more Chinese orphans as they were led to safety, during the Japanese advance into Manchuria, which was the precursor to the war before the war before the war before the war before the war before the current one. To which the elderly Buddhist nun would possibly respond by asking if Doctor Busner had himself grown up in China? To which Doctor Busner – not being even seventy per cent gaga yet – would certainly respond that no, he'd heard the nursery rhyme sung by the orphans in a film he'd seen in the early nineteen sixties

called The Inn of the Sixth Happiness, about a Christian missionary in China. To which the elderly Scots nun – showing that
irritation common to occidental Buddhists, who're driven to this
self-annihilating practice by their own screeching egos – could very
well reply with a choice remark about the lazy inferences afforded
by sight. But Doctor Busner would likely not respond to this, sunk
in these self-same lazy inferences as he might well be – and seeing
there Doctor Robinson, played by the veteran character actor
Moultrie Kelsall, who stands on the steps of the Chinese Missionary Society's residence in the town behind the Nationalists' lines
and cries out, I've been praying night and day – we're not leaving
without those children! To which Curt Jürgens playing Colonel Lin
replies, I'm sorry, Doctor– breaking off because they both hear it:
the children's reedy voices lifted in happy song – and both then see,
coming through the ancient gates with their flanking rampant
dragons, Isobel McKechnie playing Ingrid Bergman playing Gladys
Aylward at the head of the fugitives. And when the rondo's done –
at least for now – the four mendicants would have passed through
the purgatory of the ferry terminal, and might well be sitting up on
deck with the dogs and their owners, listening to the triply guttural
sound of Glaswegian being gobbed through a public address system.
Sitting – one suspects – on red plastic chairs bolted to the buckled
green-painted plates of the softly heaving deck, and either idly
scanning a notice stuck to a bulkhead advertising a bus tour of
Arran which goes round and around all day, such that you simply
have to hop on and hop off to see the principal attractions – or looking beyond the ferry's bows, to where in the mid-distance Holy

Island is being calved by Arran, in a great and milky mist cloud. This being a phenomenon fairly often to be observed in the Inner Hebrides late on a sultry day in early July when the midges descend to skitter about on your Oh So Soft skin. Skin that would, so to speak, come into its own that very evening, when, after what one assumes would be an excellent choice of vegan dishes prepared by spiritually seeking volunteers from pulses, polenta and the like, those enrolled for the three-day mindfulness course would gather in the Peace Hall, a modern building across the courtyard from the old, harled and whitewashed farmhouse, which one imagines would be the main centre of the Holy Island community. Here, under wide, wooden, Scandinavian eaves, the fledgling psychonauts would unroll their mats, gather their cushions and do their best to assume a half-lotus, or at least a cross-legged position in front of a young Sinhalese Theravada Buddhist monk called something like Bante, or Banghe, or Bhante – frankly, my Pali ain't what it used to be – before he, one hopes, shows them his own copy of the Diamond Sutra, inscribed on the leaves of an ancient codex bound in dark wooden covers, then lays it on the polished pine floor, and sets beside it the two mobile phones he uses to time the session overall and the three periods of meditation. Sitting there on a chair – because Bhande, whom we can picture as a smiley-faced, Nescafé-skinned fellow, his firm breasts visible in the décolletage of his orange robes – would've said he didn't expect the older participants to cross their legs. Doctor Busner might well set to one side any lingering cynicism, provoked by the advertisements he's seen about the place for Dharma Handicrafts, and throw himself wholeheartedly into the practice. Feeling the air whistle into his crusty old lungs – hearing it clarinet down through his aged and hairy nostrils, while concentrating hard on the little Hitler-moustache-shaped patch of skin on his top lip that his expelled breath brings to life as he breathes in and out, over and over, again *annagain*, Doctor Busner could well feel he was reaching the point where he'd be released from Samsara. And when Bhande struck a bell three times and commanded them all to bring their awareness back to the sounds in the room, Busner would almost certainly hear the little groans and oofs made by those who were rising and stretching to either side of him: an ex-soldier with post-traumatic stress disorder, and a young woman with an electrified shock of hair on her narrow skull, who might now turn to Busner and say: And? To which Busner could well reply: And now I think I feel refreshed enough to speak to my grandson. There wouldn't be much mobile phone reception in a place like Holy Island, one suspects – but if you walk through the peace garden, past the statues of the Buddha half hidden by the luxuriant flowers, then head out of the gate and down to the foreshore, and make your way along, clambering over stiles and swishing through bracken already drenched with dew, I believe you might reach a point where, with the dusk fast falling, and the peregrine falcons looping double loops high over-head, and the seals snuffling in the shallows, one of the little dots which indicate signal strength in the top-right-hand corner of your phone's screen would turn from white to black, whereupon the phone would instantly thrum into life. At that hypothetical moment, no seventy-eight-year-old retired psychiatrist, tired and confused, could reasonably be expected to check the name of the caller before he touched his finger to the representation of a red button. No, he'd be more likely to be thinking – as he had been that morning – of his dear, long-departed uncle, and of how Maurice always used to bellow into the phone when he answered it: Push Button A! Push it, I say! He certainly wouldn't imagine for a second that if he answered the person – or entity – who'd been trying to reach him all day, and who goes by the teasing but minatory ascription NO CALLER ID, he'd bring down the full weight of the security state on his beloved grandson. Nor would he suspect that if it was BEN CALLING when he touched the definitive red spot, he might at that instant find himself absorbed into a computerised collective consciousness – but he certainly would be aware of the man who at that very moment is striding along the pathway, through the wheat field, towards the isolated copse which hides the old church of Goltho. There's a golden retriever running out ahead of the man, smashing its way through the ripening wheat . . . *Bonnie . . . Bonn-ie!* The dog runs back towards him, then runs away again, circling him over and over. In the man's pocket there could well be blister packs of pills and a trusty old penknife. Yes, although he's never met this man, Busner is aware of him at the moment he touches the bloody button, because although he's forgotten the name of the man's great-aunt, he's aware as we all are, all the time, of death.